CEPHRAEL'S HAND

A Pattern of Shadow & Light
Book One

MELISSA McPHAIL

Outskirts Press, Inc.
Denver, Colorado

Cephrael's Hand
A Pattern of Shadow & Light Book One

v3.0 r1.1

Cover art by Shane Zundel & Brandon Lidgard

Outskirts Press, Inc.
http://www.outskirtspress.com

Paperback ISBN: 978-1-4327-5967-4
Hardback ISBN: 978-1-4327-5969-8

PRINTED IN THE UNITED STATES OF AMERICA

In acknowledgement to the hordes of loyal friends and family who read multiple editions of this voluminous tome, you have my enduring gratitude and appreciation. To Sarah, Juliet, and Shon, thank you for being so patient with mommy while she spent so many evenings and weekends writing.

Part One
Awakening

Sea of Agasan
The Empire of Agasan
Hallovia
Valden
Rivaldi
Jhva (Jungle)
Mahrkit
Sluring Isles
Calgaryn
Aracine
The Gandrel (forest)
Acacia
Towermount
Eidenglass Range
Rogue Valley
Jeune
Veneisea
Xanthe
Tregarion
Cair Xerses
Cair Rethynnea
Bay of Jewels
Jamaii
Cair Thessalonia
Kroth
N
Map of Alorin

Eastwatch
Morwyk
Saldaria
Kandori
Tambarre
FIRE SEA
MYACENE
AVATAR
Doane
SAND SEA
Taj al' Jaharah
TAL'SHIRA by the SEA
M'NADOR
Raku
ASSIFIYAHS
Haden GORGE
KUTSAMAK RANGE
Sakkalaah
AKKAD EMIRATES
DUAN 'BAI
VEST
LORNAK
Shixa
The TALONS
FORSAKEN LANDS
Malchiarr
DHEANAINN

GLOSSARY OF TERMS

Underlining within definitions denotes words that may be found in this glossary.

Adept (a´-dept) n. [Old Alæic] **1** One born with the instinctive ability to sense and compel one of the five strands of *elae* **2** a race of such persons, each with attributes intrinsic to the strand of *elae* that modified them *[an adept of the third strand]* **3** A Healer, Nodefinder, Truthreader, or Wildling.

Angiel (ahn g´eel) [Via Veneisean < Cyrenaic *aggelos*, messenger] Cephrael and Epiphany, the Maker's two blessed children "who were created in the genesis to watch over the realm of Alorin and all of its peoples" [sic] - *Sobra I'ternin*.

Awaken (ə w´aykən) v. [Old Alæic *wæcnan*] Adepts who have Returned awaken to their inherent abilities usually during the transition of puberty but sometimes as early as two years of age.

Balance (ba´lləns) n. [Veneisean *bilanx*, scales with two pans] The term used to describe the highest force of cause and effect in the realm of Alorin; the natural laws of the realm which define how far the currents may be twisted out of their natural paths by wielders of *elae* before manifest retribution is incurred by the wielder. These laws are of much consideration among the various Adept Guilds and a topic of intense speculation and theorization.

Cephrael (seph ray´ el) n. The Maker's blessed son, made in the Genesis to watch over His worlds. Cephrael is often considered the Hand of Fate, doling out the Maker's ultimate justice. See also angiel.

Drachwyr (dra ´k wīr) n. [Old Alæic] An Adept of the fifth strand of *elae*: the drachwyr were banished to the icy edges of the realm in the year 597aV.

Elae (e-lā´) n. [Old Alæic *elanion*, life, force; the power of life] **1** The itinerant (roaming) energy that, in its accumulation and formation, creates the pattern that becomes the foundation of a world **2** pertaining to any of the five codified strands of this energy, each with distinctly separate attributes.

Epiphany (ee pif´ any) n. The Maker's blessed daughter. Epiphany is the speaker of the Maker's benevolent will. See also angiel.

Espial (espy´-al) n. [Cyrenaic *espyen* <*es-* + *spähen,* to spy] The term used to describe a nodefinder of the highest degree who has completed all levels of training and gained license from the Espial's Guild to travel between the realms.

Healer (hēl´ər) n. [Old Alæic *hælan* <*häl,* whole] An Adept of the first strand of *elae* who has the ability to see the life patterns of living things and compel the creative forces of the first strand to alter them.

Leis (ley) n. [Old Alæic *leis*] The shortest pathway available to a Nodefinder when using the pattern of the world to travel, often connecting spaces within a small geographic area or even the same structure.

Merdanti (mer-dán tē) n. [Agasi] **1** A hard black stone named for the region of Agasan in which it is found **2** a weapon forged using the fifth strand of *elae* and usually made from this stone.

Na'turna (nah toór- nah) n. [Old Alæic < *nare turre*, of the earth] a non-Adept; mortal.

Node (nōd) n. [Old Alæic *nodus,* knot] The points where the pattern of the world conjoins. Nodes connect places in vastly different geographic regions and allow a Nodefinder to travel great distances within a few steps. Nodes also connect to the neighboring realm of T'khendar due to the nature of the latter's formation.

Nodefinder (nōd-fin´dər) n. [Old Alæic *nodus*, knot + *findan*, find] Adept of the second strand of *elae* who sees the points where the pattern of the world conjoins (called nodes) and can use these points to travel vast distances; see also *Espial*.

Patterning (pat´ərn·ŋ) v. [Veneisean *patrun*, patron, hence something to be imitated, pattern] The technology comprising the use of patterns to compel the strands of *elae* to move against their natural course, an action (also called *wielding*) which is often erroneously referred to as magic.

Raedan (ray´-dan]) n. [Old Alæic *rædan,* to guess, read, counsel] **1** One trained to read the currents of *elae* and thereby able to discern the workings of patterns and their effects throughout the realm.

Realm (relm´) n. [Veneisean *realme* (altered by assoc. with *reiel*, royal) < Cyrenaic, *regere*, to rule] **1** A kingdom **2** One of the thousand linked worlds, each represented by an elected Seat and four Vestals in the governing cityworld of Illume Belliel **3** The realm of Alorin.

Return (Returned, Returning) (ri tu´rn) n. [Veneisean *retourner,* turn again < Cyrenaic, *tornare*] An Adept who has died and been reborn. See also Awakening.

Sobra I'ternin [origin unknown] The ancient text most often attributed to the *angiel* Cephrael, which details the natural laws of patterns in thaumaturgic application. The book is itself written in patterns and has yet to be fully translated, though many Orders are dedicated to its study, translation and adaptation for use in the magical arts.

Strand (strand´) n. [Agasi *strônd*] **1** Any of the parts that are bound together to form a whole *[the strands of one's life]* **2** Referring to any of the five composite aspects of elae and its attributive fields of magic (respectively: creation, motion, form, energy, elements).

Thread (thred) n. [Old Alæic *thræd,* to bind] A colloquial term used when speaking of a group of four men of a specific race, as opposed to a String, which is a grouping of six.

Tiern'aval (Teer na-va´hl) n. An island city, one of the Free Cities of Xanthe, which vanished at the end of the Adept wars circa 597aV. The city's fate remains a mystery.

T'khendar (tuh kén dar) The realm created by the Adept wielder Malachai ap'Kalien, which creation precipitated his defamation and subsequent madness.

Truthreader (trooth - reed´ər) n. [Old Alæic *treowe,* true + *rædan*] An Adept of the fourth strand of *elae* who is able to hear (and sometimes see) the thoughts of others and is thereby able to discern the time, place and form of any occurrence in their memory, i.e. its truth.

Vestal (vest´ al) n. [Cyrenaic *vestir,* to endow] **1** An Adept elevated and empowered with the responsibility of enforcing the laws, regulations, activities and codes of his respective strand of *elae,* and of overseeing all Adepts subject to it **2** one of five highly-trained and advanced Adepts elected as voting members of the Council of Realms, ranking just below the Seat of the realm in authority.

Weld (weld) n. [Cyrenaic, *welden,* to be strong] The most major joints in the pattern of the world. All leis and nodes connect through a weld, thus a weld allows travel to any location. Welds also form the joints between the realms and facilitate travel from realm to realm.

Whisper Lord n. [Collq.] One of the Wildling races of the Tyriolicci clan, known for their frenzied fighting style and ability to skip through time.

Wielder (wēld´ər) n. [Cyrenaic *welden*, to be strong < Old Alæic, *valere*, a show of strength] A person of any race who uses patterns to compel one or more strands of *elae*, thereby influencing the strand's properties to create the effect he has postulated; a sorcerer in the realm of Alorin. Adepts and men become wielders through training and study.

Wildling (wahyld´-ling]) n. [Old Alæic *wilde*] **1** An Adept of the third strand **2** Any of the twenty-seven non-human races whose native abilities are attributed to the third strand of *elae* but who may or may not be possessed of paranormal abilities.

Zanthyr (zan´ thər) n. [Old Alæic] An elusive Adept of the fifth strand of *elae*; zanthyrs can shapeshift between two forms: one human, one animal. Some have been known to work *elae* as wielders, but the extent of their abilities is unknown.

DRAMATIS PERSONAE

The Five Vestals

Alshiba Torinin—the First Vestal, an Adept Healer
Dagmar Ranneskjöld—the Second Vestal, an Espial
Seth nach Davvies—the Third Vestal, an avieth of the Wildling races
Raine D'Lacourte—the Fourth Vestal, a truthreader and *raedan*
Björn van Gelderan—the Fifth Vestal, branded a traitor

Members of the Royal Family of Dannym

Gydryn val Lorian—King of Dannym
Errodan Renwyr n'Owain val Lorian—Queen of Dannym
Ysolde Remalkhen—the Queen's Companion; a Fire Princess from Avatar
Ean val Lorian—Crown Prince of Dannym
Creighton Khelspath—ward of Gydryn, blood-brother to Ean
The Queen's two sons (*deceased*)
Ryan val Lorian—brother to Gydryn, posted as Ambassador to Agasan
Fynnlar val Lorian—son of Ryan, a prince of Dannym
Brody the Bull—Fynnlar's bodyguard

In the King's Cabinet & Guard

Morin d'Hain—Spymaster
Donnal val Amrein—Minister of the Interior
Mandor val Kess—Minister of Culture
Vitriam O'reith—Truthreader to the King
Kjieran van Stone—Truthreader to the King(*missing*)

Rhys val Kincaide—Lord Captain of the King's Own Guard
Bastian val Renly—a lieutenant of the King's Own Guard

Of the Peerage & Their Households

Gareth val Mallonwey—Duke of Towermount and General of the West
Tad val Mallonwey—Heir to Towermount
Katerine val Mallonwey—daughter of Gareth
Lisandre val Mallonwey—daughter of Gareth
Loran val Whitney—Duke of Marion and General of the East
Killian val Whitney—Heir to Marion
Melisande d'Giverny—mother to Alyneri (*deceased*)
Prince Jair bin Kandorin—Prince of Kandori, father of Alyneri (*deceased*)
Alyneri d'Giverny—Duchess of Aracine, an Adept Healer in the service of the king

Tanis—an Adept truthreader, Melisande's ward
Farshideh—a Nadori midwife, assistant to Melisande, Seneschal of Fersthaven

Stefan val Tryst—Duke of Morwyk
Wilamina—Dowager Countess of Astor
Ianthe d'Jesune val Rothschen—Marchioness of Wynne
The Contessa di Remy—wife of the Agasi Ambassador's Aide

In the Akkad

Emir Zafir bin Safwan al Abdul-Basir—Akkadian Emir, Unifier of the Seventeen Tribes
Rajiid bin Yemen al Basreh—Prime Minister of the Akkad
Ware—an Agasi expatriate, one of the Converted
Istalar—a holy man

At the First Lord's Sa'reyth

Dhábu'balaji'şridanaí (Da-boo balah gee shree da nye) called Balaji
whose name means He Who Walks The Edge Of The World

Şrivas'rhakárakek (Shreevas rah kara keck) called Rhakar
whose name means The Shadow Of The Light

Jayachándranáptra (Jai ah shandra naptra) called Jaya
whose name means Rival Of The Sun

Ramuhárikhamáth (Rah moo hareek amath) called Ramu
whose name means Lord of the Heavens

Amithaiya'geshwen (Am myth aya gesh win) called Mithaiya
whose name means The Bosom of God's Nectar

Náeb'nabdurin'náiir (Ni eb nabdoor en ni ear) called Náiir
whose name means Chaser Of The Dawn

Vaile—a zanthyr
Leyd—a zanthyr
Loghain—a Tyriolicci (of the Wildling races, called Whisper Lord by the races of men)

On Trell's Travels

Fhionna—a Wildling
Aishlinn—Fhionna's sister
Lily—a girl of M'Nador
Korin—Lily's betrothed
Sayid—a Khurd guard
Kamil—a Khurd guard
Radiq—a Khurd guard
Ammar—a Khurd guard

Krystos—an Agasi nobleman, owner of the Inn of the Four Faces in Sakkalaah
Carian vran Lea—a pirate of Jamaii, an Adept Nodefinder
Sister Marie-Clarisse—a Sister of Chastity of Veneisea
Sister Marguerite—a Sister of Chastity of Veneisea
Jean-Pierre Marçon—Lord Commander of the Tivaricum Guard of Veneisea
Kardashian—a thief
Yara—an old Kandori woman

On Ean's travels

Cayal—a soldier of the King's Own Guard
Dorin—a soldier of the King's Own Guard
Thane val Torlen—Duke of Stradtford
Lord Brantley—Earl of Pent

Comte D'Ornay—a Count of Veneisea
Claire—Comtesse D'Ornay, a Countess of Veneisea
Sandrine du Préc—an Adept Healer in the service of Queen Indora of Veneisea
Alain—an Adept truthreader, nephew of the Comte D'Ornay
Matthieu—an officer in the Comte D'Ornay's household guard

The Gods of the Akkad

Jai'Gar—the Prime God
Azerjaiman—the Wind God
Sons of the wind god—North son, Shamal; South son, Asfal; East son, Sherq
Daughter of the wind god—West daughter, Qharp
Naiadithine—Goddess of Water
Inithiya—Goddess of Restoration
Angharad—Goddess of Fortune
Thalma—Goddess of Luck

FOREWORD

"In the fifth century of the Fifth Age in the realm of Alorin, the Adept Malachai ay'Kalien wielded the itinerant power widely referred to as elae to create—nay, not a mere dimension as is so widely professed—but an entirely new world, whole cloth, out of Alorin's own ether.

News of his accomplishment resounded throughout the thousand realms of Light, for it was a feat unheard-of and unimaginable. Many were horrified by the working, naming it the penultimate blasphemy.

Seeking understanding, Malachai appealed to the great Adept leaders who gathered in the revered Hall of a Thousand Thrones on the cityworld of Illume Belliel. He beseeched their mercy—if not for him, then for his fledgling world—but he met strong opposition. Aldaeon H'rathigian, Seat of Markhengar, was most outspoken in his outrage, and succeeded in a brief campaign to sway other Seats to his views. Thus was Malachai's infant realm ruled an abomination, and its maker condemned an outcast. Even the Alorin Seat, Malachai's own representative, turned his head in shame.

Destitute, Malachai appealed to the darker gods.

And they did not refuse him."

The Adept Race: Its Tragedies & Triumphs, Chapter 19,
The Legend of T'khendar – as complied by Agasi Imperial Historian,
Neralo DiRomini, in the year 607aV

PROLOGUE

The dark-haired man leaned back in his armchair and exhaled a sigh. He was troubled, and his dark-blue eyes narrowed as his mind raced through the possibilities still available, each branching with a hundredfold new and varied paths. It was impossible to try to predict one's future—what a lot of nonsense and wasted time was spent on divination and augury!—when so many paths were in motion.

Much better to mold the future to one's own desires.

Shifting his gaze back to that which troubled him, he reached long fingers to retrieve an invitation from his desk. The missive was scribed in a male hand upon expensive parchment embossed with the image of an eagle. It was the royal standard of a mortal king, but this concerned him not at all; what troubled him so deeply was the signet pressed within the invitation's wax seal.

A rising breeze fluttered the heavy draperies of his ornate bronze-hued tent, whose peaked roof provided coppery illumination beneath the strong afternoon sun. He glanced over at an ebony four-poster bed and the exquisite woman lying naked behind its veils of gossamer silk. They fluttered in the breeze along with her raven hair where it spilled over the edge, one supple breast left visible for his pleasure. He knew she wasn't sleeping, though she pretended it so to give him time with his thoughts.

He looked back to the seal on the parchment in his hand. It was a strange sort of signet for a prince. He wondered if the man had any idea of its significance?

Surely not. None of them ever remember, in the beginning. Yet if the seal was true—and how could it be otherwise when none but the pattern's true owner could fashion it?—then he had very little time to act. Twice before he'd come upon a man who could fashion this particular pattern, and each time his enemies had reached the man first. This time would be different.

The drapes fluttered across the room, and a shadow entered between their parting. Not a shadow, no. *Some*thing. The air rippled into waves as heat rising from the flames, and a cloaked figure materialized, already in a reverent bow. "First Lord," he murmured.

"Ah, Dämen." The dark-haired man waved the invitation gently. "This is quite a find."

Dämen straightened and pushed back the hood of his pale blue cloak, revealing a face like a mask of polished steel; metal yet living flesh. "I knew you would be pleased."

The First Lord returned his gaze to the pattern. As he studied its twisting, sculpted lines, which formed a complicated endless knot, he glanced up beneath his brow and inquired, "These invitations were sent broadly?"

"To nigh on four corners of the globe, *ma dieul,*" replied the Shade. "Four-hundred invitations, maybe more."

The First Lord frowned. "Unfortunate, that. This pattern cannot help but garner notice. The others will certainly recognize its substance. It will draw their eye to him."

"That could be fortuitous for us if it lures them into the open," Dämen offered.

"No, this Thread is too intelligent. They will send others to do their bidding." He lapsed into thoughtful silence.

After a moment, the Shade prodded gently, "What is your will, *ma dieul*? Shall I retrieve him to safety?"

"No—*assuredly* no," and he enforced this order with a steady gaze from eyes so deeply blue as to be ground from the purest cobalt. "Balance plays heavily in the life of any man who claims this pattern, and we cannot take the chance of losing him again."

"The others will not hold to such restrictions, *ma dieul*," the Shade cautioned.

"More to their error," the First Lord returned. "If I've learned anything from past losses, Dämen, it's what not to do." He tapped a long finger thoughtfully against his lips. "We must bring him in carefully, slowly, for the revelation will not be an easy one."

The Shade frowned, his chrome-polished features perfectly mimicking flesh. "Your pardon, First Lord, but if he did not Return with the onset of adolescence, what chance remains?"

"A slim one," the dark-haired man agreed, knowing the chance was so minute that it would take a great tragedy to draw out his Return. He regretted the future in the making. Often times of late, he regretted the future more than he did his long and tragic past. The First Lord pursed his lips and shook his head, his eyes determined, though still he hesitated. There was no question of the need, but life was a precious, tenuous thing. He regretted every one over the countless years which he'd been forced to end. Still, he'd waited too long, planned too carefully…sacrificed too much. Mercy was a virtue he could ill afford. "I fear steps will have to be taken."

"Well and so, *ma dieul*," the Shade replied, and there was much not said in his tone. His gaze conveyed his unease.

The First Lord needed no reminding; he would have to be so precise in this planning. Every detail, every possible ramification must be considered, for the moment the man crossed that ephemeral threshold they called the Return, he would become like a beacon for their enemies' vehemence. And that was something no mortal could survive. His mind spinning as he conceived of his plan, he settled his cobalt-blue eyes upon his Lord of Shades and detailed his orders.

The Shade bowed when his master was finished. He did not relish the tasks ahead, but his obedience was beyond question. "Your will be done, *ma dieul*," he murmured. Then, straightening, he faded—there was no other means of describing the way his form shifted, dissolving like dawn shadows until nothing remained where something had been only moments before.

His most pressing matter thus decided, the First Lord tossed the invitation aside and turned his gaze to the glorious creature awaiting his pleasure on the bed.

The woman stretched like a cat and then settled her vibrant green eyes upon the First Lord. "Come back to bed, *ma dieul*," she murmured in a silken voice akin to a purr but echoic of a growl, "for I have need of you."

He returned her a lustful look. She was a feast for his senses in every possible way. "And I have need of you," he replied in a rough whisper, his desire filling him.

Lifting his own naked body from his chair, he returned to her.

Leilah n'abin Hadorin, youngest daughter of Radov abin Hadorin, ruling prince of M'Nador, stood trembling on the balcony that overlooked the vast gardens of her father's palace in Tal'Shira. She lifted a shaking hand and touched her cheek where an angry red handprint flamed. *He's never hit me before,* she thought as tears leaked from her dark brown eyes.

But he's never caught you eavesdropping while he plotted with the enemy, either.

Considering the circumstances and her father's ill humor of late, a single slap in the face was a mercy.

'Fool girl!' she heard her father's acid hiss, his dark eyes flamed with fury. *'You're lucky I caught you spying instead of one of Bethamin's Ascendants or their Marquiin! Get you gone from my sight while I consider how to deal with you.'*

Leilah wiped her cheeks, wet with tears, and choked back a sob. She hadn't been spying, in truth—though to be certain she'd overheard far too much of the conversation to deny the accusation with any conviction—nor could she tell her father why she'd been hiding in his study. Radov had never been known for his compassion, but since the Ascendants of the Prophet Bethamin arrived in Tal'Shira by the Sea, he seemed to have lost all taste for it.

What does it mean that he considers an alliance with Bethamin?

Nothing good, of that she was certain.

The Prophet's teachings had been banned by M'Nador's neighboring kingdom of Dannym, and the Queen of Veneisia had issued an official censor, which was practically the same thing. M'Nador had long been allied with Dannym and Veneisia; that her father spoke of an alliance with Bethamin could only mean he intended to betray his other allies.

The thought chilled her. Even now, both kingdoms supported M'Nador in their war against the Akkad, sending troops and supplies, even precious Adept Healers who were few enough in number that releasing even one from the service of their own kingdom was a noble sacrifice.

And now my father allies with Bethamin.

Leilah didn't like the Prophet; every time she listened to his teachings, she came away feeling cold inside. Since Bethamin's Ascendants and their gauze-shrouded Marquiin had come to Tal'Shira, the sun hadn't once appeared from behind the overcast that had arrived as if part of the Prophet's entourage. The palace staff had grown edgy and fretful and talked in whispers now, and her father's Guard had become increasingly sharp-tempered, just like their monarch. Leilah saw how everyone was falling prey to the mantle of gloom that surrounded Bethamin's minions, yet apparently she was the only one who did.

She thought of the Marquiin again and shuddered.

They were Adept truthreaders—or had been, once; for they weren't like any of the other truthreaders she'd met. There was a darkness about the Marquiin, a sense of cold malice. Everyone said that truthreaders—*real* truthreaders—couldn't lie, but Leilah wouldn't trust a Marquiin for the whole Kandori fortune. She couldn't bear to even approach the mind-readers, for they all exuded a sour stench that made her wonder what foulness was hidden beneath the grey gauze that covered them from head to toe.

Even before she learned of her father's planned alliance, she'd tried to speak to her older sisters about her fears—that is, the two not as yet married off to sheiks or Avataren lords—but they'd complained she was hurting their heads with talk of politics and sent her from their solar. Her brothers were all long gone, seeking their fortunes in foreign lands or leading her father's armies into battle against the Akkad, but she doubted they'd believe her anyway; they all thought of her as 'little Lily,' as if she was still running around half-naked splashing in the palace fountains and not a girl of sixteen, of birthing age.

That was the other problem, the reason she'd been in her father's study without his knowledge: to use his personal seal. Her own letters were meticulously read by her father's spies, but his seal was never disturbed. It was imperative that her letters left the palace under this guise, else... Even as a shuddering sigh escaped her, she smiled through her tears at the memory of her true love Korin's handsome face, of his sultry dark eyes and his amazing lips, of the feel of his hands on her bare skin...

It had been almost a year since she'd seen Korin, for as soon as her father learned of her interest in him he'd banished the boy from the kingdom. The moment still felt as devastating in memory as it had upon its experience. Then had come Fhionna and her dangerous plan, the secret letters ferried back and forth, the promise of rescue...

Soon none of this will matter, she tried to reassure herself. *Soon he will come and whisk me away, and we'll sail as far east as the seas will take us. There, we'll raise children and goats and live happily in solitude, needing nothing but each other.*

Smiling, sighing at the thought, Leilah dropped her hand to the little purse at her side where she kept his secret letters and—

Oh no!

She spun around looking for the handbag. It was gone! Abruptly she remembered falling in her father's study after he'd struck her. She'd felt something catch and tug, but the moment had been too shocking to notice much else. The little chain must've caught on the edge of the table.

With a sick feeling of dread, Leilah realized her purse was still in her father's study. It wasn't only her and Korin who would face her father's wrath if he discovered those letters; Radov would stop at nothing to unearth her accomplices. Fhionna and Aishlinn would eventually be hunted down and given fifty lashings just for ferrying the letters back and forth, and that's if they survived their own capture.

Shaking for a different reason now, Leilah knew she was doomed if her father found those letters. Coupled with her act of 'spying,' the letters would brand her a traitor in her father's eyes.

She caught her lower lip between her teeth in a horrible moment of indecision. She'd been sent away in no uncertain terms so her father could receive Bethamin's Ascendant and his Marquiin in his chambers, but perhaps if she was very quiet...if they'd moved to speak in the adjacent gallery instead of her father's personal study as was Radov's usual wont, if she didn't so much as make a peep...perhaps they wouldn't even notice her returning for her purse.

Leilah rushed back inside the palace and headed down the long, wide passage toward her father's chambers. In truth, she would rather face the lash for disobedience than feel the force of her father's wrath should he learn of her illicit love affair. If Leilah was discovered in that act of defiance, being sold to Avataren slavers would be a mercy.

The two guards on duty outside her father's chambers eyed her dubiously as she entered, but they didn't stop her. *They'd probably enjoy watching the lashing,* she thought resentfully, though what she would've done if they'd prevented her from entering she didn't know.

She slipped on tiptoes close to the wall of the large anteroom toward one of two doors that opened into her father's study. Pressing an ear to the door, she heard nothing, so she slowly turned the handle. Hope welled in pulse with her anxiety. She might just be able to slip in unnoticed…

Even as she made it inside, she saw her little purse across the way, half-concealed beneath the armchair, exactly as she'd imagined. The room was empty, but the doors to the gallery were open. She would have to pass them to reach her purse. Heart pounding loudly in her ears, Leilah rushed across the room, but just as she reached the open doors, something made her pause.

She stood transfixed an inch from the portal's edge, her heart beating so loudly it was deafening. Waves of chill air seeped from the gallery, heavy and dense, laden with malevolence. Leilah shrank from its touch. That was when she heard the moaning. It seemed a wail not of mortal death but of a dying soul; even more frightening was the sure certainty that the horrible moan came from her father.

As if caught in a dream, Leilah felt herself drawn inexorably forward. She felt powerless to stop herself from looking. Slowly, she inched her head around the edge and saw… she saw…

She saw.

And then she ran.

ONE

'Failure is the province of the craven and the dead.'

– The Vestal Björn van Gelderan to one of his generals during the Sunset Battle of Gimlalai, circa 597aV

Trell's horse snorted and shifted beneath him as a gust of hot wind surged up from the desert valley, flattening the sparse grass that grew like wisps of hair between jagged, sun-scorched rocks. The wind brought with it the smell of heat, baked earth and sand, and a gnawing apprehension that was as unwelcome as it was strange.

Trell turned in the saddle and focused grey eyes on the ridge at his back. The view was not unlike that of another ridge, this one lording over the rushing, charcoal waters of the River Cry; a lonesome ridge where he and his best friend had held off the entire Veneisean army with little more than fifty men. That was near two moons ago, however. Now his friend Graeme was dead, the Emir's forces occupied Raku Oasis, and Trell was a celebrated hero.

Gentling his stallion with a pat on the neck, Trell looked back to the view of the desert valley and the creatures flying above its vast sea of dunes—sleek, golden creatures with hides like molten bronze. He squinted at them beneath the duck-billed brim of a dun cap, which was making a valiant attempt to shade his eyes from the sun. But this was the M'Nador desert; the sands were as bright as the day, the blue sky was as parched as the land, and there was an ever-present glare that made a man's eyes tired before their time.

If only you were here to see this, Graeme… Trell thought as he gazed, captivated, at the gilded beasts soaring high above the sands. They flew with sublime grace, their enormous shadows floating across the dunes in unworldly silence. Trell was amazed at the breadth of their wingspan, at the golden-fire hue of their hides and the way their scales glinted in the long rays of the afternoon, sparkling so brightly as to leave spots before his eyes. *And are Nadori soldiers standing upon the walls of Taj al'Jahana on the far side of the Sand Sea watching you also?* he wondered. *Surely my enemies are no less entranced than I.* Though no doubt the Nadoriin would be working feverishly to find a means of destroying the creatures rather than appreciating them for their mystique and purity.

Sundragons.

They'd been summoned back from the cold, dark corners of the realm by the Emir's Mage, summoned to do his bidding and eager to please—if the stories were true—in exchange for their reprieve.

"Ghastly things, aren't they?" a familiar voice commented from behind.

Trell glanced over his shoulder to find his friend Ware reining in his stallion. Ware was a tall Agasi who lost no height sitting the saddle of his lean desert horse. He was darkly bearded and generally hairy, but his blue eyes displayed an intelligence Trell had found common in men of the Empire; the Agasi were an educated people, be them prince, blacksmith or sellsword.

Looking past Ware, Trell noted that the rest of his men had descended the ridge and were dismounting now, a dozen Converted in all. Soon it would be time.

"They're beautiful," Trell answered, turning back to the distant dragons with a look of appreciation on his sharp-featured face. "I wish Graeme could have seen them."

Ware grunted skeptically and flicked at a horsefly with his reins. "I don't know. They're fierce creatures. Sheik Am'aal was nearly bitten by one of the things when he got too close to its tail. The creature snapped its head around with the speed of a striking viper, and if it weren't for the Sheik's agility at ducking—no doubt from all those arrows he's made a habit of avoiding—he'd have made the beast a tasty snack."

"Reasons not to get too curious, I suppose," Trell commented. He'd never cared for Sheik Am'aal. The man was a consummate philanderer; all those arrows he'd avoided tended to be from well and rightly-offended husbands. "A fierce beauty then," Trell conceded, "but beauty nonetheless."

Wearing a look of curiosity mixed with amusement, Ware broke into a crooked grin. "What are you doing among us lowbreeds, Trell of the Tides? You ought to be composing poetry in a white tower somewhere, you and your 'beauty' this and 'glorious' that and general high-minded musings—oh, don't think I'm criticizing you," Ware added, noting Trell's faintly indignant look. "Not a one of us would challenge your tactical brains, but you seem to me a learned man, a man of philosophy, not one of blunt violence and greed like so many of these Converted," and he jerked his head toward the company of mercenaries chatting rakishly behind him.

Hearing this, said men offered scatological culinary recommendations, to which Ware returned his ideas of what they could do with their suggestions. It was a friendly exchange.

Ignoring the banter, Trell allowed a slight smile. *I do, do I?* It was no secret that he remembered nothing of his past prior to awaking in the Emir's palace five years ago, and friends and acquaintances alike were often sharing their opinions of his origins—sometimes in jest, sometimes in sincerity. Trell didn't mind either way. On a rare occasion, someone made a comment that almost triggered a memory, and he lived for those almost moments—yearned for them every waking minute, in fact.

Ware was watching him with a keen look in his blue eyes, as if Trell was far more intriguing than Sundragons. "You could've been a nobleman's son sent from Tregarion or Calgaryn to study abroad, but there was tragedy, and you wound up here."

Trell smiled ruefully. "Triad cities, those two. But am I from a Triad kingdom, do you think?" He turned to Ware with a hint of torment in his grey eyes, a look he sported often when pondering his mysterious past. "The Emir likes to say I floated in from the Fire Sea, a gift from the Wind God," and he threw up his hands with a flourish in imitation of their supreme leader. "Even if it is true, the Fire Sea borders many kingdoms, Ware. I've the same dark hair and coloring as that Barian Stormborn of the Forsaken Lands, and the height and features like those merchants you and I dealt with in Kroth. Some say I even have the look of your own blood, Agasi—a moonchild."

"Just so," Ware admitted with his eyes pinned on his younger friend. "You could be any of these, Trell of the Tides."

No one knew exactly where Trell's nickname had originated. 'Man of the Tides' was what the Emir's men had called Trell until he woke from the fever that had nearly claimed his life, remembering little more than his given name. After that, they'd tacked on 'Trell' to humor him.

"But I think you're right—about the Triad that is," Trell concluded. "I do as the Emir asks of me, but while I've never lost sleep over battling Nadori infidels, some part of me cringes at fighting the men of Dannym or Veneisea, as if I know I'm slaughtering my own blood." Unthinking, Trell's hand found its way to the sword at his hip, a sleek blade with an eagle-carved silver hilt and a sapphire pommelstone, a brilliant cut gem whose clarity and vibrant color made even the Bemothi traders envious. The sword was his only possession, his only connection to the life he'd once led, and though it was merely another mystery, Trell considered himself blessed to have it.

High above the Sand Sea, the six dragons had completed their midair rendezvous—or whatever the purpose of their gathering—and were breaking away into pairs again. They flew north, west, south, but not east. East was where the Nadori army was camped at Taj al'Jahana, on the far side of the vast sea of dunes.

The war had gotten bloodier in the past fortnight, though the enemy dared not try to retake Raku again—not after the slaughter on the Khalim Plains. Trell had ridden through that wasteland of death, and he shuddered at the memory. Now the Emir's forces were deployed along the Sand Sea escarpment, from Heziz in the north to the Qar'imali in the south, and so long as the Veneisean army remained trapped across the River Cry—which duty had been assigned to Trell's company of Converted until their unexpected reprieve two days past—then the Emir's troops had only to concern themselves with their northern flank. "Do you think we'll win?" he asked Ware without removing his eyes from the dispersing dragons.

The Agasi shrugged and wiped an arm across his sweaty brow. "Who can say? I'm not even certain what you'd call a victory. There has always been war in the Kutsamak Mountains." He glanced to the dirt beneath his boots and kicked at it with one toe. "Tis more apt to call them the haunted mountains—Raine's truth we're like to be walking on the dust of the dead even now."

A whistle of alert from one of the men called their attention back to the ridge. A turbaned Basi was scampering down the steep incline and doing a much faster job of it than the horses had. He was the holy man Istalar, and he would be their guide through the shrine. "The time comes," someone commented, referencing Istalar's return from watching the position of the sun.

Well knowing what was to follow, Trell and Ware exchanged a look and then dismounted too. Trell grabbed his satchel with his few possessions and slung the strap diagonally across his chest. Then he turned toward the jutting cliff in front of them wearing an uneasy frown.

More unsettling than the scent of magic that permeated the air those days, raising the hackles of any self-respecting soldier, was the feel of the place they were about to go. Trell had sworn no oaths to the Emir's desert gods—he wasn't Converted—but he was the first to admit that something sentient resided in the shrines of the

Kutsamak, and he had no desire to question its nature any further. The Emir often sermonized on the sacred shrines, admonishing respect from his Converted, but it was the obvious divine residence that had convinced Trell to revere them. Whether this was in homage or aversion was no one's business but his own.

The holy man came to a dusty halt in front of them. He was the only Basi among their party, an elder member of the Emir's own tribe, and he wore a white and grey-striped turban, one fold of which was pulled across his nose and mouth. This he removed to speak, revealing a heavy grey beard. "It is time, *A'dal*," he reported to Trell, using the desert word for leader. "We are allowed to enter now to receive your blessing."

Trell nodded wordlessly, and the holy man led them away, skirting the ridge toward the sheering cliff at its end. Trell glanced to left and right and then followed, but he couldn't help feeling exposed on the open mountainside, even dressed in his earth-hued tunic and britches that blended so well with the sand…even with the Mage's dragons patrolling the sky.

A shadow befell them as they walked, and Ware looked up as a pair of Sundragons flew between them and the sun, casting them into blessed shadow. "Never thought I'd be grateful for those beasts," the Agasi muttered.

Trell matched his gaze, peering in his intense way. "I still wish Graeme could see them."

"Graeme was a good lad, true enough," Ware remarked, "and I know he was your brother-in-blood, but he wouldn't have appreciated these creatures as you do." The dragons moved on and the sun returned, and Ware settled Trell a discerning look. "Graeme was not your equal, my friend. Few men are."

Trell barked a laugh. "Save your honeyed words for the ladies," he chastised, aiming a punch at Ware's arm. But in truth, he was startled by the compliment.

Ware made to respond but seemed to change his mind, perhaps when he noticed that Trell's expression had quickly sobered. Everyone thought Trell spent more time in his head than was likely prudent, and most were quick to tell him so; even in battle he maintained a sort of pensive composure, an attribute all of his men had commented upon. Ware peered at him curiously. "What's going on in that head of yours today? You're even more aloof than usual."

Trell shot him a sideways look. "I am never aloof."

Ware arched a dubious brow. "You know what I mean."

Trell turned profile again and frowned, because he did know what the other man meant. *Dare I tell him? Raine's truth, I'm desperate to talk to someone.* But could a man like Ware understand the constant torment of not knowing one's own memory? Could he understand the fear Trell harbored over his unknown past, or the feelings of frustration and duty that drove him to embark on his current course? To his own shame, Trell didn't trust that he could. He said instead, "I heard you might be going on mission for the Emir's Mage."

"Aye, that's so," Ware admitted. His eyes upon Trell spoke plain enough of his wish to know in turn what Trell would be doing now that their company had been pulled from the lines—it would take a dimwit indeed not to wonder what sort of fell assignment Trell had been given that it required a god's blessing. But Ware would ask nothing of his *A'dal*, even if the question was likely burning his tongue.

"I think everyone's grateful to be away from the Cry," Ware answered, turning in profile to Trell to frown at Istalar's back, "though it may seem hard for some of these younger fools to believe anyone could tire of battle and glory. But since the Khalim Plains, I..." and Trell saw Ware glance out across the Sand Sea, his gaze darkening with the memory of what had transpired among the maze of dunes. "Well, I've seen enough of death for awhile, and the Mage is rumored to have many errands he needs run—chancy quests, they say, ripe with danger." Winking, he added, "Sounds like my kind of entertainment."

"No doubt," Trell agreed, but his smile wasn't quite reflected in his eyes.

"I dunno..." Ware continued as if compelled to explain himself to his once-captain. "After what the Emir's Mage did for us on the Khalim Plains, well...men are lining up to serve him. I guess I'm one of them."

Trell arched brows. "Lining up? I hadn't heard that."

Ware scratched at his close-cropped beard and regarded Trell shrewdly. "They say when the Mage speaks, even the Emir listens."

Trell pulled off his cap and pushed a hand through his dark hair, dislodging wavy locks that seemed perpetually tousled despite having been beneath a hat all day. *The Emir's Mage*...he thought with narrowed gaze.

The man had arrived at the front six moons ago seeming little more than the Emir's shadow at the time, a quiet stranger with a genteel manner and a compelling gaze. Six moons...and now the Emir fell silent at his command? Trell had other reasons to feel unsettled by the Mage. Since the man's arrival, Trell had found the Emir too often cloistered away behind locked doors—and himself excluded from his usual confidence. Clenching his cap in his fist, Trell turned to look full at Ware. "Have you ever met the Mage?"

"Not yet. You?"

Trell frowned. "Briefly, once."

"And you're suspicious," Ware declared. Then he goaded, "You're sure he means to take over the world and is using the Emir to achieve his own nefarious ends."

Trell opened his mouth to protest, but when he caught the teasing glint in Ware's gaze, he managed a sheepish look instead. "You know I'm suspicious of everyone."

"That's just about the only thing you have in common with the rest of these degenerates, Trell of the Tides," Ware consoled with an amused grin, clapping Trell on the shoulder. "No one has to teach a soldier to be suspicious of magic, or of those that work it."

They were coming to the end of the trail where a bare rock face edged a deep ravine. Even as Trell was assessing the high mountain cliff, there came a raucous cry, and then a second in answer. The men were buffeted by searing wind as the same pair of Sundragons that had passed earlier swooped down from the sky and alighted atop the cliff before them. Sitting forty paces tall, the beasts folded their massive wings, wrapped serpentine tails possessively around the rocks, and peered down with predatory stares.

"Look, Trell," Ware noted dryly as he squinted at the creatures, "even the Sundragons have come to honor you. You truly are the hero."

Trell gave him a withering look.

But it did seem as though the dragons had come to say their farewells.

Farewell. It seemed a wondrous word. He was still trying to absorb the truth himself:

that he was leaving the Emir's service after so many years; leaving at the Emir's own insistence and with his blessing; leaving to live a future that might help him uncover his past. And leaving in the *middle* of a war…that was the most unbelievable part of all.

Trell hadn't been able to bring himself to tell his men, though he knew they would support him, even congratulate him; yet he felt a deserter for abandoning them. That his doing so was at the Emir's command lessened nothing of his guilt—war was war, and every capable hand was needed.

But he has the Mage now to help him, Trell thought more bitterly than he would've liked, his own memory of that night on the Khalim Plains springing to mind. *What need has he of an orphan with a few new tactics when the Mage can turn entire armies to dust?*

Yet for all his resentment at being excluded of late, Trell wanted to believe what the Emir had explained to him, wanted to trust that the war was nearing an end.

Ware was meanwhile peering at the Sundragons, oblivious to Trell's inner turmoil. "Wonder who's commanding those beasts now?"

"I thought you said the Mage controlled them," Trell muttered.

"Well yeah, when he's around."

"What do you mean?"

"Just that he hasn't set foot in Raku since we gained the walls. Word is, that's why he summoned those Sundragons you so admire, to watch over the army in his absence."

The dragons in question looked to be staring at them even as Ware spoke their name. They made Trell uncomfortable with their sinewy necks and those spiked crests along their heads and spines like deadly, gilded manes. "That's a good question then," he murmured while fervently hoping he didn't look a tasty treat to the creatures. "Who else could control them?"

"No one, I hear," said Faloin, a Veneisean expatriate who was walking close behind them. Trell glanced over his shoulder. All of the Converted had their eyes pinned on the dragons, and everyone seemed to share in the same unease. "They're not like horses to be ridden or cattle to be corralled," Faloin continued in a tone of wary distrust. "They say they're thinking beasts, and the Mage just tells them what to do, no different than issuing commands to you or I."

"Look out boys," Ware observed, raising his voice to include everyone. "One day we might be taking orders from them."

"But they don't condescend to speak to none but the Mage, the way I hear it," another of the Converted commented, a heavily bearded Krothian whose dark eyes were fastened on the dragons. "Even the Emir can't control them—it's 'please' and 'thank-you' if he wants so much as to gain their sainted audience."

"Do they actually talk?" someone else asked.

"What need?" came a reply from back of the line. "I heard they can read our very minds!"

Faloin snorted. "Ain't that just an ill wind."

All the men fell silent then, perhaps guarding their thoughts.

They were walking beneath the dragons' shadows with the beasts veritably towering over them, golden eyes staring down with fierce intensity, when the holy man Istalar passed a rocky outcropping, turned abruptly, and disappeared into the mountainside.

Only when one was right on top of the cave entrance could it be seen, a jagged grey-black parting just wide enough for a man to pass between. Trell was next to follow, then Ware, and then the rest, save two who held the watch outside.

Violet glass globes set in carved niches in the walls illuminated the cave with reddish-plum light. How the candles stayed perpetually lit was quite beyond Trell, but such held true for all the sacred shrines. As he stood there letting his eyes adjust to the dim light, it occurred to him that this might be the last time he entered one of the sacred places, and the idea held both relief and unexpected sadness for him.

Following globe to globe marked the way deep into the mountainside, and Istalar led with quiet resolve. Already Trell noticed a difference in the air—the feeling was akin to walking into a den where a beast lay in wait. Something *dwelled* there, some…entity. Trell didn't know what gods he believed in, but he didn't doubt the existence of a force larger than himself, and it was just such a force that inhabited those hallowed hills—it was this very force to which the Emir had sent Trell in order to gain divine favor on his journey.

In silence then, Trell followed Istalar into the bowels of the mountain, set upon a task that he both dreaded and desired. He was accompanied by a contingent of men he had grown to respect, yet this very fact troubled him, knowing he might never see them again. So he hid this truth from them as surely as his own truths were naught but distant dreams as yet unformed.

Trell's eyes were well adjusted to the light by the time the passage opened onto a boundless cavern. Trell stopped short, for he'd never seen a shrine the likes of this. A roaring waterfall fell from the shadowed ceiling, and its spray of chill mist formed a shimmering veil of color and light. An iridescent spirit seemed to dance within the pale shaft, shifting hues with every movement. The water lit the cavern, yet its light did not pass without the hallowed walls, for Trell had not seen the light until he entered the cavern itself. The effect was beautiful, and yet so obviously arcane that Trell shook off the ghost of a shudder.

Istalar walked to the water to kneel and make an opening offering and prayer, while Trell waited apart from the rest of his men. Mist collected on his clothes, his hat, his cheeks. He pulled out a kerchief and wiped his eyes as he scanned the faces of the others. They were not so bothered as he—mostly they looked bored—but Trell knew they would not be making an offering to the god of this place, as he would, and they would not be hoping to receive a divine blessing.

As he watched Istalar bowed at the water's edge, Trell felt a surge of apprehension knowing he would soon be kneeling there in his place. He wondered what sort of response he was likely to get from the god of the shrine—him, who wasn't even Converted. Trell would have been all too happy to go on his way without visiting the shrine at all, but the Emir was having none of that. He was a religious man, Emir Zafir bin Safwan al'Abdul-Basir, and while he might have a foreign Mage working for him, he certainly didn't want his kingdom's gods working against him. Ritual offerings were necessary any time one wanted a blessing, and the Emir wanted a blessing for Trell, his near-adopted son.

Istalar finished his prayer and beckoned to Trell. Feeling as nervous as he had that day five years ago when he was first presented to the Emir, Trell walked to the water's edge and knelt on the wet stone beside Istalar. "Now," said the holy man, "you must make your offering and your prayer." Trell must've looked miserable, for Istalar encouraged, "Fear thee not, Trell of the Tides; the god of the shrine is benevolent toward you."

Trell turned to him wanting more than anything to know how he could be so certain, but all he managed was a humble, "I don't know the right words to say."

The holy man's steady gaze seemed the embodiment of faith. "The gods know our *hearts*, Trell of the Tides. Words mean nothing to them. Open your heart in prayer. They will answer you." With that, he rose and took seventeen steps away from the water—one in honor of each of the desert gods—before straightening.

Trell whetted his lips and looked at the water, a luminous pool of liquid light. He reached into his satchel and retrieved a dagger that had once belonged to Graeme and was thereby special to him. His only other possession of value was his sword, and it was too precious to part with, even for a god's pleasure. He hoped the dagger would suffice.

Catching his bottom lip between his teeth and feeling ridiculous, Trell let the dagger slide from his fingers into the water. It was swallowed by the light.

Now what? he thought. He had no idea how to pray.

'Open your heart' Istalar had said.

Trell drew in a deep breath and closed his eyes.

His heart held painful things: feelings of loss and the frustration of years of not even knowing his own heritage. His heart held mixed emotions: it seemed a lifetime's dream of discovering the truth of his past, and yet that same dream stirred such fear in him. What if he discovered that he wasn't the man he thought he was? What if in his prior life he'd been an outcast, a bastard, a thief...a coward?

His heart held grief...and guilt.

Trell was trying to think of what else his heart held when he heard someone whisper. He wiped the accumulated mist from his eyes and turned a glance over his shoulder, but no one was near; indeed, the men were clustered far away from him involved in their own affairs. Feeling faintly unsettled, Trell turned back to the water and closed his eyes again. At once he heard the voice again. Trell strained to understand it, but the harder he tried, the more the words eluded him.

Frustrated, he dutifully recalled the torments of his heart instead, though it pained him to dwell on them so. Only then, as he surrendered to the powerful pain of his deepest feelings, did the ethereal voice speak and his heart receive its message. Thusly do the gods impart their blessings: spirit to spirit, like the faintest breath of wind...

Follow the water, Trell of the Tides.

Trell sprouted gooseflesh from head to toe.

His chest ached, his throat constricted—it was as if his whole body was trying to keep his soul from escaping—and he knew; *knew* with certainty that not only a god had spoken to him, but also that his soul had resonated with its blessing.

Follow the water, Trell of the Tides.

For the space of that moment, Trell thought there was no sound on earth except that soul-capturing, melodic whisper.

Then there was only the roar of the waterfall and the low hum of male voices engaged in their usual vulgar commentary.

Overcome by the experience, Trell rose and backed away from the water in the same manner he'd seen Istalar follow. The holy man was waiting for him seventeen steps away. Trell straightened and turned to face him, looking troubled but feeling both fulfilled and strangely hollow, his soul still yearning after a touch—a presence—that had vanished beyond its reach.

Istalar smiled crookedly through broken teeth, yet his was a genuine smile. Trell had always liked him. "What did Naiadithine tell you?" he asked.

"Naiadithine?" Trell hadn't known this was her shrine, but once he thought of it, he realized that he should've guessed from the outset. Naiadithine, Lady of the Rivers, had claimed Graeme for her own when he fell into the Cry, never to resurface. It only followed that the Emir would send Trell to her for a blessing. "I think…I think She told me…" he pulled off his cap again and pushed a wet hand through his hair. "She told me to…follow the water."

Istalar nodded sagely. "Follow the water, Trell of the Tides," the holy man echoed.

Trell gave him an uneasy look, and another chill scurried down his spine. "Yes," he whispered, feeling far too close to arcane dealings for any sort of comfort. "*That* exactly."

Istalar took Trell by the arm and pulled him further away from the water and the men. "The Emir looks upon you as a son," he said then, "and he would be bereaved should harm befall you. Before you journey into the West, there is something he wants you to understand."

Trell didn't quite like the sound of that. "Which is?"

"You leave a place of safety for one of danger."

Trell arched a brow. "A war is a place of safety?"

"No, Trell of the Tides," the holy man replied, his gaze deadly serious, "the Mage's shadow is a place of safety, and you are soon to leave it. You must learn to use your three eyes."

"Three eyes?" Trell repeated.

"The eye of your mind—your intelligence; the eye of your heart—your conscience; and the eye of your soul—your instinct. These are your three eyes. You must use them all, and *trust* them all. This *above* all."

Trell nodded. "Very well. My three eyes. Is that all I must know?"

"No." Istalar pulled on his greying beard, smearing the mist that had accumulated in glittering droplets. His brown eyes looked troubled. "You must know that the realm is not at rest. Far beyond this war that plagues our people, darkness lurks where light once resided, and there are unexplained—"

A terrible rumbling erupted, drowning out his following words.

Trell exchanged an uneasy look with the holy man, and then the earth shook with a jarring force. It pitched Trell off-balance and sent water careening out of the pool. Trell and Istalar both reached for each other. "*Daw*, what was that?" Trell hissed, casting a fast glance around.

Shouts echoed from the higher cave, and another spasm shuddered through the cavern. Trell stumbled into the wet wall with another curse.

"We're under attack!" a man shouted—Trell never knew who, though it sounded like one of the men he'd left guarding the cave entrance. The Converted's voice was still echoing a thousand-fold *ack-ack-ack's* when another clap of grating thunder assaulted their ears, and a veritable wall of sharp stones tumbled down, forcing those below to dodge and roll. "What's happened?" someone called to the sentry above.

"Radov's wielders are attacking the Sundragons. Run my fellows! The cavern is collapsing upon us!"

As if to prove his point, the floor seemed to tip and then crash into place with an angry, jarring shudder. Trell's feet were simply no longer beneath him, and the next thing he knew, he was blinded by a searing pain as his skull met the unyielding rock. He heard it inside when he hit, a hard clap that was both a blunt thud and fiery pain, but he was only vaguely aware of the cry that left his lips, or of the chill water that soaked his garments in short bursts as waves careened out of the pool. Some small part of his mind recognized moans and shouted prayers amid the shattering of stone. Then he felt himself being roughly shaken, and he strained to focus.

Istalar crouched beside him. The holy man's face was smeared with blood streaming from a nasty gash above one eye. He was speaking, but Trell couldn't hear him.

"What?" Trell managed through the ringing in his ears. "What?"

The rumble in the cavern was deafening, but somehow Istalar pitched his voice above it. "You must hurry!"

Trell fought to sit up, but no sooner had he done so than he vomited. His head pounded with a vengeance, and he couldn't tell if it was blood or water that soaked his hair—probably both. Istalar helped him to stand, but Trell had hardly gained his feet before dizziness overcame him and his knees buckled. The holy man caught him around his chest and pushed him up against the wall. "Go!" he urged. "Go now. Before it is too late for you!"

What was the man saying? He couldn't tell who was talking, couldn't remember talking, was anyone talking? *Gods and devils* his head was a pulsating agony, and red fog clouded his vision.

Men were scrambling to escape. Water poured across the floor, sloshed around Trell's ankles, and then rushed along into the darkness to find its own way out. There were bodies unmoving on the floor, dark forms half-covered in luminous water. Did the god live in the water? Was the water the god? What was wrong with him? Why couldn't he think clearly? And what was the holy man doing?

Istalar had undone his turban and was wrapping the cloth around Trell's head. Trell pushed feebly at the holy man's hand, mumbling, "No—not…Converted."

This can't be right, he thought somewhere among the fog of pain. Not now, not when he was so close to… Clarity returned in a lucid moment. *Please, Dear Naiadithine, I daren't die before I know who I am! Where do the lost souls go?*

Istalar tied off Trell's makeshift bandage and ripped away the remaining cloth. He took Trell by both shoulders and captured his dizzied eyes with his own. "Follow the water, Trell of the Tides!"

Trell wiped his eyes again. "Follow the water…" he mumbled.

The holy man pointed toward the deeper cavern. "Follow the water!"

Trell blinked and gazed in the direction Istalar was pointing. Then he shook his head and lifted a hand the other way. "No—there," he protested even as the holy man was pushing him in the opposite direction.

"There is no escape that way!" Istalar insisted, half-dragging Trell toward the deeper caves. "The cave is gone!"

Trell looked over his shoulder and saw that indeed, the entrance had all but collapsed. They were trapped.

This isn't right!

Istalar half-pushed, half-dragged him out of the main cavern and into one of the caves. It was illuminated by the sacred water, its low ceiling just barely out of Trell's reach.

The mountain growled again, petulant and fierce. Tiny stones pelted Trell's head and shoulders. Istalar looked up with a sharp intake of breath, and then he pushed Trell forcefully and yelled something Trell couldn't make out because of the roaring in the cavern—or perhaps it was the roaring in his ears; it was hard to separate the two. Trell splashed face-down in the water, just barely escaping the tumble of rock that sealed off any retreat.

Dripping and shaken, he got slowly to his feet and stood for a moment staring at the fall of rock while he battled a surge of fury that pierced through his disorientation. Had the jumble of stones claimed Istalar? He felt a choking pressure in his chest at the thought.

Trell said a soldier's prayer for Istalar—for it was the only one he knew—and then stood frozen by a terrible thought: *is this happening because of me? Because I angered Naiadithine with that pathetic excuse for an offering?* But the narrow escape had imparted a surge of clarity, and Trell soon realized he was wasting precious time. The rock had sealed off his escape but had done nothing to stop the water, which poured through the cracks between the stones as if running a last flight from death.

Follow the water, Trell of the Tides.

Had Naiadithine known this was going to happen? Trell looked down at the water swirling around his ankles, luminous and pale. There *was* something about it, something that tugged at his memory even as the icy current tugged at his heels.

*Come...follow...*it seemed to say.

Trell went.

He chased the current, head pounding painfully with every splash. He could see by the water's luminous light, which cast reflective shadows on the near walls but was never bright enough to reveal the cavern ceilings. Trell let the water be his guide, and though its fingers were icy and swift, and darkness pressed as heavily upon his shoulders as it did upon his consciousness, Trell was determined not to be afraid. Fear was the worst evil ever to plague a man, for with it came hesitation and with that, inaction, failure, death.

Follow the water, Trell of the Tides.

Perhaps it was the clap to his head that had conjured such blind trust, or perhaps it was the recognition that he had little to lose save his life, and what had that been to him until now? Existence, perhaps, but a parched one. He remembered neither parents nor siblings, if he had any. He could share no childhood memories, nor boast of that one doe-eyed girl who'd stolen his heart even as he stole her virginity.

He couldn't remember his mother's smile, or his father's wisdom—assuming he was even a legitimate son.

And yet his was a life Istalar had sacrificed his own to save. This he also recognized.

So as he raced along, wet and shivering in the strange cavern of water-light, Trell knew he owed Istalar—and the Emir, and Graeme above all—at least a brave attempt to live, to escape if he possibly could. All the while, the divine water communed with his spirit.

Follow the water, Trell of the Tides.

He wandered in the chill caverns for two long hours before he reached the end, time enough for his feet to grow numb, to trade sweat for shivering. All thought was reduced to sheer determination. His teeth were chattering loud enough to echo by the time he found himself wading deeper and deeper into a stream that eventually pooled to his waist, the current strong as it tugged him toward the dark, wet rock that was the cave's—and his, he knew—certain end. He could see by the water's light that the ceiling was perhaps five paces above, close enough to know there was no escape above and none behind.

He tried not to despair, but couldn't help thinking, *Has it truly come to this?*

Yet as he stared at the swirling water, reason prevailed. *All this water, but it doesn't rise to claim me.*

There had to be an opening somewhere beneath.

Trell ripped off Istalar's bandage and labored out of his boots. He checked to ensure his sword was secure in its scabbard and the scabbard firmly around his waist—for life without his precious sword would be worse than nothing. Then he took three quick deep breaths and dove beneath the pool of liquid light.

Icy fingers stabbed him, vindictive in their insistence that he gasp from the cold, but he held his breath with steadfast defiance, opened his eyes, and let the current carry him, only trusting that Naiadithine would not betray him in his leap of faith. He was quickly pulled into a narrow opening, a funnel for the water, barely wide enough to swim through.

Daw! he thought, agonizing as he forced himself to hold his breath, forced his arms to stroke and his legs to kick despite the icy water. If the passage thinned any more, he would be caught there, trapped deep inside the mountain's guts, left to drown.

Breathe! his body shouted.

Breathe! his lungs protested, burning in his chest.

Trell felt the fingers of desperation grip him.

Then, in a moment of surprising clarity, he realized he'd experienced this before, this dreadful panic that threatened to overpower all mental control. Somewhere, sometime…he'd almost drowned!

Trell was so elated that a sudden peace flooded him. He found a renewed determination to keep swimming.

He knew the moment the current yanked him in a new, more forceful direction that he was free of the tunnel, and he prayed as he swam upwards that he would find air at the top. It was a harrowing few seconds, but then he surged into the open with a choking gasp that echoed off a low ceiling.

The current carried him swiftly along. Slowly, the blackness cleared from his vision and the fire left his lungs, and he knew he was in an underground river. There was water-light enough to see the wide stream and the smooth, wet stone of the low ceiling, but it was a faint light, moon-pale, as though Naiadithine had done her part and was leaving him now.

His muscles cramped beneath the water; his teeth chattered, his head throbbed, and his body was numb and heavy; yet for the first time in nearly half a decade, he was grateful to be alive. He grinned stupidly as the river carried him, using his pack and its empty canteens to help him stay afloat, oblivious for the moment of any pain or danger—for *he had remembered!* Not a dreamed memory, but his own true recollection of life before the Emir's palace.

A roaring began that quickly grew in volume, and suddenly Trell was plummeting downward in darkness, falling...falling...as he felt himself rushing through air and took in one last breath. Then followed a harsh plunge into depths unknown, being caught by the current again and pulled along, only to strike against something—caught painfully on his arm, what was it?

He held on.

The greedy current tried to pull him further downstream, but he hooked his arm around the line—was it a line? He felt along it with numb fingers. *No. A chain.* Trell wrapped both arms around the chain and swam up along its length. He clenched his teeth, fought the blackness piercing his thoughts, and kicked as hard as he could.

Don't stop.

Finally the current died and he was heading upward through still water that gradually grew warmer. He let go of the chain and swam with hands of ice and lungs of fire until he burst free into darkness and saw the barest glimpse of a circle of starry sky. He drew in his breath with a shuddering gasp that echoed back at him.

He knew at once the cause. *I'm in a well.*

There was the chain attached to its post. No doubt he'd unwound it all trying to pull himself up. He reached for it again, hoping to use it for a rope out of the well, but his body was trembling so violently that he couldn't even make his fingers close around the metal. The well's edge was too high for him to reach, and the walls were too slick to climb.

With the fall of adrenaline, fatigue and hours in the cold set in to claim their share of him. Trell cried for help, but he heard only the echo of his voice, meek and trembling like an ewe's pitiful bleat. He called out several more times nonetheless, and then splashed his arms in the water until they were too heavy to lift.

But no one came.

Because he couldn't hold the chain, Trell looped one forearm within it as best he could, and then he rested his wet head against the cold metal while his teeth chattered and his body trembled. He knew it was important to stay awake, but it was only heartbeats before his eyelids won their battle to close.

As he sank into darkness, his last memory was Naiadithine's whisper...

Follow the water, Trell of the Tides.

TWO

'Trust, but do not be deceived. Be prudent, but do not delay. Azerjaiman waits for no man.'

– An old desert proverb

Trell regained consciousness like the slow pouring of honey, swimming up through a mind-fog of darkness and the near memory of chill water to the unexpected sensation of comfort. Opening his eyes, he found himself in a massive ebony bed, three sides of which were draped in diaphanous silk, the fourth layer drawn back with a black satin cord. And beyond the bed? The dim walls of a tent, but it could have been the tent of a sultan or the Emir himself, so opulent were its trappings.

Sunlight brightened the tent roof to a pale copper, and the room was luxuriously furnished with ornate chests and tables upon which rested a number of beaded lamps, a deluge of books, and several odd-looking statues. Plush Akkadian carpets covered the raw earth, and the ebony bed itself was a work of art. Where had he come to find such luxuries in a desert camp?

Voices floated to him from a nearby room, but their words were muffled. He sat up and immediately regretted it. The onset of dizziness and a dull throbbing in his skull reminded him of the very real nature of his ordeal. Lying down again to wait for the world to stop spinning, he reviewed what he remembered:

Someone must've found him and pulled him from the well.

Someone had brought him here—wherever *here* was.

Someone had healed him.

Then there was that memory of drowning once before, a brief image intense with desperation and panic and even the choked recollection of gulping water—*salt*water; *yes, sea water*—into his mouth and lungs. Trell analyzed this memory with great care. It was the first recollection he had from a time before waking in the Emir's palace. Though it was the mere flash of a picture, yet it contained all the things a memory should have: emotion, associated perceptions, and even his own thoughts at the time.

It was fantastic.

My very own memory.

Trell broke into a smile as he lay staring at the copper-hued ceiling. Having just that small bit of memory gave him great hope that he could remember more of his former life. Maybe the Emir was right to send him away, yet the idea still pained him more than he cared to admit. Trell remembered that day as if it had just happened…

When the Converted Commander Raegus n'Harnalt had arrived with a hundred men to relieve Trell and his company at the Cry, Trell's men had cheered.

"Ho, Trell of the Tides!" the other commander greeted Trell as he'd dismounted in the middle of Trell's camp with his men filing in around and behind him as best they could in the confined space. There was little enough flat ground along the Cry, so the steep walls of the surrounding canyon were mushroomed with brownish tents. The rock ledges were hot enough to cook on by midday—which was fortuitous really, for wood was scarce—and canvas tarps, secured haphazardly between rocks, provided the only shade. The sun was just coming up when Raegus arrived, but Trell's company had been active for hours—only those who'd held the night's watch were sleeping beneath the shade of their desert tarps.

"The Emir is most pleased with your service," Raegus told Trell as he approached holding out both hands in greeting. "You are to be given a hero's welcome in Raku."

Trell clasped shoulders with the other commander and then pressed a fist to his heart in the desert fashion. The formal greeting thus concluded, Trell pulled off his cap and ran a hand through his unruly dark hair. It was barely dawn, but already the heat was rising, sweeping in on the tide of sunlight as if surfing its outermost reaches, a broad band of sweltering air that withered everything it touched. "Then you are here to relieve me?" Trell asked, squinting at the man as he replaced his cap.

Raegus broke into a broad grin. Bemothi by birth, he had the long, rounded nose and almond-shaped eyes of his countrymen, but his tanned face was disfigured from numerous battles: a long scar marked a ragged line along his jaw while another ran from temple to cheekbone, pinching the corner of one eye; an old burn puckered the skin of his neck with its purplish hue, and his nose had been broken in two places. Still, his smile was genuine as he opened his arms and raised his voice to include all within earshot, "Nay, Trell of the Tides, we are here to relieve everyone!"

His declaration was met with a cheer that soon echoed from ridge to ridge, the good news spreading fast among the men. No doubt the Veneiseans heard the outburst on the other side of the Cry. Trell privately hoped they wondered if yet another victory had been gained while they baked in the sweltering heat, stalemated and outsmarted by a nameless commander of a band of renegade expatriates.

Trell admitted the men's reward was overdue, yet he couldn't share in their joy. For him, it had been a bitter victory, and every day spent overlooking the Cry was a reminder of how much he'd lost to gain it.

As celebration broke out around them, Raegus noted Trell's somber expression and clapped a hand to his shoulder. "Graeme Caufeld was a fine soldier and a good friend to all of the Converted," he said in confidence. "The Emir wishes to honor Graeme's memory as much as he plans to honor you and your men. We could not have gained Raku if not for your efforts, Trell of the Tides, and the Emir was the first to recognize you for this."

Trell knew the man was sincere, but mere words could not relieve his guilt, nor honors replace his friend. "Come, Raegus," Trell said in his quiet way, turning his eyes away from the other man lest he read too much in his gaze. "I will show you the camp."

Trell led the way up the ridge, pointing out supply tents and strategic positions, until eventually they arrived at the Overlook—a carefully concealed bunker with an expansive view of the Cry as well as the Veneisean camp on the opposite riverbank. Safely ensconced beneath the overhanging rock, Trell informed Raegus of the lay of things. "Archers are there, there, and there," Trell told the other commander, who was Converted and wore his characteristic white turban wound through with stripes of tan. Trell pointed to small mounds on the far side of the gorge as he indicated the lairs of the Veneisean archers, who lay in wait like sand snakes, hoping to spy an incautious and unprotected head.

"I see the bulk of the army has retreated," Raegus observed.

"Yes, they've pulled back about two clicks downriver to a valley with its own water supply."

Raegus turned him a grin full of dark amusement. "I take it the river has claimed a few Veneiseans, some perhaps who strayed too deeply?"

"More than a few," Trell remarked without removing his eyes from the gorge and the archers. Knowledge of where an enemy was supposed to be didn't mean he stayed there, and Trell had kept his men alive by teaching habits of constant vigilance, which he was the first to live by.

Raegus turned to lean against the rock wall, his back to the river, crossing arms before his chest. Trell noted his nonchalance and wondered how long he'd last there at the farthest edge of Akkad-held lands; the river and its enveloping gorge had a way of claiming men who lacked the appropriate respect.

As it happened, so did Veneisean archers.

Raegus meanwhile settled Trell a curious, and perhaps slightly challenging, look. "The Emir told me the Veneiseans are rebuilding the bridges at Orlan and Fayle, but I noticed that your entire company remains here. Are you not concerned?"

Trell was gazing down at the frothing, ashen waters of the Cry wondering how many lives they'd claimed, though only one truly mattered to him. He exhaled wearily, his mind only half-engaged with the conversation. "This war will be over before the Veneiseans succeed in crossing the Cry, Commander, much less in building a bridge to aid them in the endeavor. It took Akkadian engineers a decade to successfully span those waters—learning as they did through trial and error—and rest you assured, the Veneiseans haven't the trick of it."

Trell turned away from the rushing river then and the body of his friend lost in its depths. He motioned Raegus back toward camp. "No, Commander, this gorge is the only place the Veneiseans stand a chance of crossing the Cry, and we—*you*," he corrected absently, "...you and your men have that duty now."

Respect colored the Commander's gaze as he watched Trell descend from the shaded protection of the overlook, zipping down a rough-hewn ladder with spry agility. He said nothing as they headed single-file down the hazardous escarpment, but before they regained the camp, he took Trell's arm in a sudden firm grip. "The Emir says you were a gift from the gods, Trell of the Tides," he observed as if a gruff confession, holding Trell's grey-eyed gaze with his own darkly serious one, their faces inches apart. "I think I understand why."

Trell shook his head and looked away, wanting no more undue praise for a battle he considered, ultimately, a failure. "Good luck, Commander," he said, pressing fist to heart one last time. And with a final glance, he added, "We are all depending on you now."

They'd set off that afternoon, with the men in an enduring cheerful humor. All the way to Raku Oasis, they boasted and bragged, reminisced and jested; what had once been painful memories were quickly fading, transitioning from a place of close discomfort into a distant one laced with nostalgia. Such was the mind's capacity for change, for adaptation and reconciliation, and even for forgiveness; to alter a man's memories such that what was once overwhelming became later subject to rejection, to laughter.

Trell thought it an amazing thing to witness; though he couldn't help but wonder if this was the same mechanism—this altering factor of the mind—that kept him from remembering his own past. Yet if the mind was capable of healing emotion such that the common man may eventually recall a few battles fondly, what could've so wounded him that he was unable to remember anything at all of his former life even now, five years later?

Catching himself at his own thoughts, Trell admitted that this was his philosophic side, the one his men jested about, the one Ware so often commented upon...and the one Graeme had always held up as proof he was noble-born. This was the side of him that took over after a battle, when even death itself lay bleeding at his feet and the gods offered no answers.

This was the side that asked endlessly, *Who are you?*

Trell knew he sought shelter in his thoughts when no shelter was to be found elsewhere. He could vanish into them so completely that the outside world seemed insubstantial in comparison, and hours might pass before he returned to it. Such was the rare luxury he allowed himself during the ride back to Raku; indeed, his company was riding beneath the thick walls of the oasis before he woke from his thoughts, woke to the cheering of a thronging crowd.

From the battlements on high, ranks of Converted threw raucous kisses and olive twigs in good-natured mockery of the traditional rose, while the soldiers inside the city spread sand before their path, bowing and taunting as much as they applauded or cheered. Men that Trell had never met shouted his name as he rode.

The Converted were a motley band of renegades. They hailed from places as dissimilar as Dheanainn and Kjvngherad, yet a common element bound them, one that transcended background or heritage, crime or treason, and this same element in turn bound them to the Emir.

For the Emir had given them back their honor.

This and more. He'd placed them on equal footing, to advance not according to birthright but to ability, to gain in reward of strength and agility proven on the field of battle.

Trell wasn't one of them, for he'd sworn no oaths to the pantheon of desert gods, yet the Converted considered him a brother in war. His past was lost, even as theirs was lost—if one was by design and the other through tragedy, it mattered little to these men, and Trell had proven himself time and again, gaining the loyalty and admiration even of those who'd heard only his name.

Knowing all of this, Trell gazed around him and tried to smile, to at least acknowledge the gratitude and fellowship they offered.

The hero's celebration lasted all the way to the palace of the former Sultan of Raku, who'd found his death at the hand of the Emir's personal guard. The Emir's chief minister was waiting upon the steps of the palace to greet them, an unusual honor, for Prime Minister Rajiid bin Yemen al Basreh was rarely seen in public. Trell knew him to be a mysterious sort of man who spent most of his time in the Akkadian capital of Duan'Bai, where he headed up not only the Emir's governing cabinet, but also a deadly network of spies and assassins.

Unsurprisingly, al Basreh remained beneath the light of torches and a waning moon only long enough to greet Trell and his men and deliver an astonishing message.

"The Emir is most approving of your service," he told Trell's company in the desert tongue as they collected before the massive steps leading up to the outer palace gates. "You men have been relieved of duty on the Cry. What is next for you, you are no doubt wondering?"

Indeed, they all were, and replied as much.

"So I shall tell you," al Basreh returned, nodding sagaciously, his dark eyes peering out from the shadow of a gray and black-striped silk turban. "We are at war, my fellows, and much is expected from the Converted; toil and sacrifice, even unto your very lives, but for you..." and here he flashed the shadow of a smile. "For you, heroes all, the *choice* is yours. You may serve our *Su'a'dal* wherever you so desire, for such is a hero's right, to decide where next he shall shed the blood of his enemies."

They were astonished, and then they cheered.

"Go then," al Basreh raised his voice to be heard above the din. "Be the master of your fates, and write the next chapter of your lives with fidelity and honor." He pressed a fist to his heart, and the men, sobered only slightly by his poignant words, did the same.

As the band dispersed then, still humming with surprise, al Basreh descended the steps to greet Trell. If they were not exactly friends—and Trell wondered if the older man trusted anyone enough to name them a friend—still, there was a familiarity and respect between them. "The Emir wants to see you, Trell of the Tides," al Basreh said in low greeting. "He could not be more proud of a son of his own blood."

Trell thanked him for relaying the Emir's appreciation, and asked as they headed up the stairs and through the gates, "What news from the front?"

"A missive from Taj al'Jahana," al Basreh replied, his tone revealing no small measure of his own amazement, "and most unanticipated."

As they entered the palace grounds, there was vigorous cleaning and mending being done to repair the ravages of the initial invasion: carpenters and artisans aplenty were hard at work well into the night. Al Basreh kept his voice low as they walked beneath scaffolding and ladders and around clay pots of plaster and paint, while turbaned men rushed to and fro and spoke in hushed tones so as not to disturb their betters. "Radov requests parley," al Basreh confided once they were away from the industrious workers.

Trell nearly missed a step. "If I didn't know you better, I'd be certain to think you jesting!" he replied in a fierce whisper. No wonder al Basreh had sounded surprised—it seemed an impossibility. "Does the Emir think he seeks peace? Surrender?" Prince Radov of M'Nador was an obstinate ox of a man, with a mulish demeanor and generally disagreeable nature. To think he would consider a surrender after eight years of war—of which Trell had known only five—was to imagine the Emir suddenly denouncing all his gods and taking up the Blood Art alongside Dheanainn Fhorgs.

"The Emir has a letter from him," al Basreh replied. "The truth of it is, we have beaten Radov, and he knows it in his bones."

The news was truly shocking. Trell couldn't have been more amazed to see cows flying across the Sand Sea—which reminded him, strangely enough, of the Mage and his dragons. Surely they played no small role in bringing Radov to his knees. "I suppose the Emir's Mage will attend the negotiations?" he murmured. "Does the Emir mean for me to attend as well?" *Is that why the Emir pulled us from the Cry?* For Trell did not believe it was merely to reward them. Awards were given after the war was won, not during its fiercest fighting.

"No," al Basreh answered. "The Mage is attending to other matters, and as for you..." Here he almost smiled again. Twice in one night, it was a record-breaking evening. "For you, Trell of the Tides, the Emir has special plans."

His Imminence Emir Zafir bin Safwan al Abdul-Basir, Prince of Princes, Unifier of the Seventeen Tribes, rose from behind an ornate desk laden with battle maps as Trell entered his study. Zafir's bald head was shining from the heat, which lingered like a disease within the room, making the air heavy and thick though the sun had long fallen to slumber. He opened arms to Trell and embraced him as his guards were closing the massive mahogany doors, but he pulled away again just as quickly and gave Trell a frown of consternation. "You are no longer whole," he observed, shaking his bald pate sympathetically. "I sense a cavern of loss within you."

Standing there before the only father figure he could remember, Trell felt a new fissure of pain slice through his heart. "Holding the Cry has taken its due toll," he admitted. His every exhalation carried the taint of guilt and the ache of loss.

"Naiadithine's waters are greedy," the Emir agreed, naming the mother-spirit of the rivers, "and I know that you and Graeme Caufeld were close friends."

Trell turned his head away to hide the surge of grief and fury that threatened his composure—damn the injustice of Fate! "It should have been me," he confessed, staring angrily at nothing. "That arrow was Death's hand reaching for me, *Su'a'dal*."

Zafir placed a strong hand upon Trell's shoulder. "But Jai'Gar knew it was not your time," he consoled softly, naming the Prime God, Father of All Fathers. He captured Trell's gaze with his own dark one. "We will honor Graeme, you have my word."

Trell simply held his gaze and nodded, for to say anything more would have been too painful.

"Now then." The Emir banished the subject as he turned to walk back to his desk. "If I know you, you are wondering why I pulled you from the Cry. I suppose al Basreh told you of the parley."

Trell forced away numbing thoughts of Graeme and gave the Emir his full attention. "A letter from Radov?" he replied. "It's unbelievable."

Zafir grunted as he sat down in his red leather chair—the Sultan of Raku's once, now restyled with painted gold filigree. He spun a piece of parchment toward Trell that he might see the red wax seal upon the bottom. "There it is, imprinted with the infidel's own signet," he said, waving Trell be seated also, "lest I would have named it a foul hoax."

Trell took the proffered seat across the desk while frowning thoughtfully at the letter. He could not say if the seal was genuine, having never seen Radov's personal signet, but he knew who could. "I suppose al Basreh—"

"Oh, indeed," Zafir interrupted with an offhanded flick of bejeweled fingers. "Al

Basreh assigned his spies to investigate, but they uncovered no deception, and the seal is genuine. It seems this parley is legitimate."

"Then the war could truly end." Trell said the words like an exhalation, but his tone was rife with disbelief. It seemed an impossibility—there had always been war in the Kutsamak. While trying to imagine what a world without this war would be like, his gaze strayed out the open windows, across the city of Raku and beyond, toward the endless expanse of the Sand Sea.

"Which brings us to you, Trell."

The Emir's words brought Trell's attention gaze back to his leader.

Zafir was watching him steadily, his dark eyes unreadable, but Trell got the distinct impression that something of grave import was transpiring, something beyond a mere assignment of duty. And knowing this with such certainty made him immensely uncomfortable.

Zafir nodded as if to confirm Trell's suspicions. "The time has come, Trell of the Tides."

Trell felt a sudden hollowness open in his chest, such apprehension as he'd never experienced, even when facing the field of battle. "Time for what, *Su'a'dal?*"

Zafir's round face grew at once solemn. "It is time for you to leave us, my son-of-the-seas."

It took a moment for Trell to fully comprehend the words, coming as they did on top of such surprises as he had already faced that day. "I…I don't understand."

"Trell…" the Emir smiled upon him, but there was a sadness in his dark eyes. "I know you are plagued by the mystery of your past. I cannot think of a better means of rewarding you than to set you on your way. Your heritage is your birthright. Seek it now with my blessing."

"But *Su'a'dal…*" Trell protested, every part of him railing against his leader's pronouncement, "we're…we're at *war*." Surely this was a cruel jest, to send him away when he was most needed.

"You have served me with the fidelity of my own blood-sons," the Emir proclaimed, and truly, his voice became choked with unexpected emotion. "You have made gains for our cause of which even the gods have taken notice. Though it pains me greatly to see you go, the Wind God Azerjaiman has spoken to me in this, Trell of the Tides. This is the desire of Jai'Gar, his wish for you, and I dare not defy His will."

So it had transpired, the ending of Trell's life as he'd known it, the beginning of a new life that would lead him beyond the sands of the Akkad. He'd kept a sleepless vigil that night upon the walls of Raku, gazing distantly into the starry heavens trying to make sense of events, to find any sort of justification for Graeme's death and his own good fortune.

Yet was it truly fortune that he was being sent away upon the eve of what could be their final victory? To be denied the moment of looking upon the Triad generals knowing that he had beaten them, outmaneuvered them, bested them on the tactical field—*him*, a nameless one, with no title, no heritage at all to speak of. Was it fortune to be denied the triumph of seeing Radov on his knees? Trell harbored no true hatred for the Nadori prince, but neither could he respect a man who'd denounced his gods in favor of greed. Trell had made the Emir's cause his own, and he wanted to see the conflict through to the end. He would've stood his ground and argued his case with the Emir, but…

Azerjaiman had spoken…

To his utter chagrin, there was no arguing with a god.

Thus did the dawn find Trell setting off with supplies and silver and a small contingent of Converted, leaving with the Emir's blessing under the guidance of Istalar, who would take him to the shrine to gain divine favor on his journey…

Trell exhaled a sigh that touched the silk drapes of the bed. He tried once more to sit up, and this time the dizziness was a minor discomfort. As soon as he felt stable on his feet, Trell walked to an obsidian basin, poured water from its matching pitcher, and washed his face. Raising his head to the mirror poised above, he regarded himself as if studying a stranger. His hair looked no different after cave-in and river and hours of sleep than it did any other time: a short, tousled jumble of raven waves with the occasional curl thrown in for good measure. The unruly mass had always seemed a strange contrast to his angular face, and the hard months of battle had only increased this disparity.

Staring at his grey eyes, at the shadowed lines connecting cheek to jaw, Trell didn't see the scholar that his friends Ware and Graeme claimed. He just saw a face, a face that answered to a name but had no history; a face that might resemble someone else's or might not; a face that had two makers somewhere that had contributed eyes and nose and chin…but which came from his father and which came from his mother?

Letting out a heavy sigh, Trell frowned at himself and pushed wet hands through his hair. "Who *are* you?" he asked the face in the mirror.

Silence followed, only the mystery declaring its rule over his life. He shook his head and turned to find something to wear.

To his surprise, his clothes had been washed and new boots laid out for him. Everything was there—his sword, even his satchel. Trell stared blankly down at all of his belongings. How had he made it through a river and swum up a well with all of that weighing him down? It was a fair miracle. Perhaps it had indeed been Naiadithine's blessing that bade him to follow the water.

He dressed slowly, all the while straining to catch something of the muted conversation continuing beyond the heavy drapes, but no words ever floated clearly through to him.

When he was ready, Trell inhaled a deep breath to the fullness of his lungs, and exhaled as he walked to the heavy drapes, found the parting, and pushed through. The quiet conversation stopped abruptly as he stepped from bedroom into parlor and found himself in the company of three others.

The young man seated in the wingback armchair was lean and boyish, with glossy black hair smoothed back from a noble's peak, flawless caramel skin, and pale amber eyes. He wore a long tunic over loose britches in the desert fashion, the fine linen dyed a cerulean blue that seemed especially vibrant against his tanned skin, and he greeted Trell with a smile of pleasant surprise.

The woman sitting sideways on the divan with long legs crossed at the ankles could have been a statue for her perfection. To say she was lovely would be an insult to her beauty, though her sculpted features were not soft. High cheekbones, full lips of graceful line, a strong nose flowing smoothly into arched ebony brows, and intense green eyes that studied Trell with obvious candor. She wore a fitted gown of heavy emerald silk, and slim suede knee-boots dyed to match, and her long raven hair was sleek as it draped around her shoulders like a shawl.

The third man, who stood behind the woman with arms crossed, was not a man at all; this Trell knew at once, for he had met his like before. The man's skin was leathery and as black as pitch, and his long, hooked nose and furious scowl seemed the caricature of a mummer's mask. His golden eyes were fixed on Trell with undisguised malice—though Trell rather suspected this was a result of the man's ill-disposed features more than any personal disregard. Utterly hairless, and dressed in loose black garments bound at the joints by leather straps, he was called a Wildling at best, a Whisper Lord by race, and though he was not wearing any daggered gloves, he was no less frightening—nor, as Trell suspected, less deadly.

"Be welcome," the youth greeted in the desert tongue, drawing Trell's eye back to him. "Please…" he motioned Trell approach their circle.

Trell noticed other things about the room then: the plush carpets, the tall glass lamps fringed with strands of gemstones that gleamed alluringly in the room's muted light, and a mysterious breeze that stirred his hair and cooled his neck yet had no obvious source. "Where am I?" he asked, also in the desert tongue, which he spoke fluently—not that this was any measure of his past either, for he'd learned through the years that he also spoke Agasi, Veneisean, and the Triad common tongue with equal ease.

The young man leaned sideways in his armchair, propped ankle over knee, and twined fingers in his lap. He was barefoot, and his toenails were painted with black enamel. So were his fingernails, Trell then noted. "Why you're…" the youth began, but then he seemed to reconsider his answer. "You're in the mountains west of Jar'iman Point. Three days by horse to Raku."

Trell lifted brows. Amazing to think he'd traveled that far on an underground river, but then the river set its own course, while a horse did not. "I'm…very grateful to be here," Trell said, feeling unusually awkward among these strangers. He glanced from the glaring Whisper Lord, to the unreadable woman, to the youth. "You—did *you…?" Devil's wind…where do I begin?* "I was in a well," he managed.

The youth smiled and nodded, though there was something about the gesture that made it seem more than a simple response. It was a generous smile, bright and… sharp, if such a word could be used to describe the way the youth's wide mouth ended in crisp corners. "You were in a well," the young man confirmed, seeming amused by this. Then he spread his arms. "And now you are here. Feel welcome. We are all guests in this marvelous place."

Trell approached tentatively. "Did *you* find me?" he asked. "Do I have you to thank?" He glanced at the room's other two occupants, but instinct told him they'd had nothing to do with his rescue.

The youth broke into another of his wide smiles, though this time Trell was sure there was something secretive about it. "No doubt you are quite curious how you came to be here," the youth observed agreeably, and he glanced at his two companions.

The woman stood with slow grace, all the while focusing her catlike green eyes on Trell. Then, saying nothing, she turned and left the room.

The Whisper Lord cast Trell another malignant glare—or it could have just been a noncommittal look; it was hard to say with Whisper Lords—and followed the woman through the parting of drapes. He pulled them closed behind him, shutting Trell in the room alone with the youth. "Please join me," said the latter. He indicated an armchair near his own. "I am called Balaji."

Trell nodded as he sat. "I am Trell."

"A strong name," Balaji noted with approval. "Trell of the Wash was one of the great swordsmen of old. You likely know him as Trell of the Longshore. Trell d'Bouvalais was the famed sorcerer who established the first Ring of Mages in the Citadel on Tiern'aval, and then there was Nach Trell dan'Eliar, called Trell the Terrible by the western Kings, who conquered all of far eastern Avatar beyond the Fire Sea in the time known as The Before, in the uncharted years preceding the Fourth Age of Fable." He paused and eyed Trell with his head tilted slightly to the side as if assessing him. "But you are likely named for Trell Tavenstorm," he decided, "the wielder who helped forge the pact that formed the three allied kingdoms known as the Triad. A great man—all of them great in their own right."

Trell had never heard of any of these people—at least not that he could remember. His name was fairly common; he hadn't realized it had noble roots. "And who are you named for?" he asked conversationally.

Balaji broke into that same secretive smile. "Me?" he asked, looking amused again. "My full name is Dhábu'balaji'şridanaí, which means 'He Who Walks The Edge Of The World.' "

"That's a bold naming," Trell observed.

Balaji barked a laugh. "So it is!" he agreed, as if the notion had only just occurred to him. "So it is!"

Balaji's gaze was drawn to the drapes then, and Trell leaned around in his chair to find the Whisper Lord returning. He carried a silver tray set with two crystal goblets and a full decanter of clear fluid, all of which he set on a table nearest to Balaji.

"How kind of you, Loghain," Balaji said.

The Whisper Lord Loghain handed a goblet to each of them, replying, "I thought you might be thirsty." Then he withdrew, all the while wearing that furious scowl.

Trell followed the man with his eyes until the Wildling had disappeared through the curtains again. Then he leaned back in his chair and frowned.

Balaji just looked amused. "Often things are not as they seem, my new friend Trell," he observed, "and especially in this place." He held up his goblet and offered, "To Freedom, however she grace thee."

Trell joined him in the toast, though he found the tribute unusual, in keeping with the rest of his experience thus far. The drink was made from the fermented juice of white grapes, known locally as *siri*. It was cold enough to make the goblet sweat, and Trell thought the drink had never tasted better.

"Now," said Balaji as he lowered his goblet with a satisfied smack of wet lips, "to your questions."

"I was in a well," Trell repeated. "It's the last thing I remember."

Balaji nodded. "Yes, yes. You were near death when you arrived. Had not the

Mage worked his power, you'd be having conversation with your gods right now."

"The Mage?" Trell found the revelation both startling and curious. "You do mean the Emir's Mage, do you not?"

"Indeed."

"But why would he have gone to such lengths for me?"

Balaji shrugged. "Who knows the inner working of a Mage's mind?"

Trell frowned. "But how did the Mage find me in a well?"

Balaji took another sip of his *siri*, eyeing Trell over the rim with his strange eyes that seemed to reflect the fields of wheat whose color they'd claimed. "He has eyes and ears in these mountains, my new friend Trell. Surely you did not think your Emir would hire the Mage simply to strut around like a preening peacock, as if to strike fear into the hearts of your enemies by his presence alone?" Trell managed a sheepish smile. "No," he agreed.

"Ah, there's hope for you yet," Balaji teased, raising his goblet to Trell. "The Mage then. He brought you in on the back of his horse three nights ago. Those who pulled you from the well knew the Mage had the power to resurrect you should he so desire. Near death you were when you arrived with him, all blue and stiff with shock. I'd never seen a man turn such a color. After the Mage worked his healing upon you, he sat by your side all the night and through the next day, until you were out of harm's reach."

It seemed a strange fortune, this chance rescue. There were some who claimed it was never lucky to gain a magician's eye. Trell wondered what interest the Mage could have in saving his life? "Is the Mage here now?" he asked Balaji.

"Alas, his duties called him elsewhere."

"Am I..." Trell wasn't sure how to phrase the question. "Am I being...held here?"

"Assuredly not!" Balaji declared. "Though the Mage has recommended that you partake of our hospitality until the moon is full."

"Why?" Trell tried not to sound suspicious, but his first instinct was distrust. Did the Mage want something from him in return for his life? One of Ware's mentioned quests, perhaps?

"Having healed you, I suppose," Balaji meanwhile offered, "the Mage has some insight into your true condition. He knows how deeply your injury was felt, and how long before your stamina is truly restored."

Trell admitted this could be true; he knew that healers had to create a deep rapport with those they were healing.

"Then again," Balaji added with a grin and a shrug, "who knows the inner workings of a Mage's mind?"

"Yes, you said that once already," Trell remarked sourly.

Balaji regarded him with good-humor. "Enjoy your time of relaxation, my new friend Trell," he offered in his agreeable way. "We are each of us guests here, and you have the best of the rooms—the Mage's own. Read his books, explore our lovely valley, join us for dinner—tonight will be a banquet in honor of Loghain's departure—and introduce yourself to the others who come and go; you never know when friends made here will come in handy," and there was a twinkle in his strange golden gaze as he said this last. "Then be on your way in a few days when the moon is full," Balaji finished. "That is always the best time to begin a journey."

"How do—" Trell began to ask, but Balaji stood and smiled down at him. The youth seemed amiable enough, but there was something about that sharp smile that set Trell's teeth on edge. "Perhaps we can converse more at a later time," Balaji suggested, and there didn't seem to be much in his tone inviting question on the matter. "Alas, the day grows on, and I have duties. If you will permit me…" he motioned to be away, and Trell could do little beyond nod—Balaji was nothing if not polite, and Trell had never found it in himself to respond with outright rudeness. He did scowl after the youth as he left, however. Then he downed the rest of the *siri*, pushed out of his chair rather heatedly, and returned to his rooms.

Trell spent some time looking over the furnishings of the Mage's quarters, examining the many books lying around, peering through the glass lamp shades, plucking at the dangling gemstones…and wondering why the Mage left so many priceless and personal things lying about for Trell to see. *He puts a lot of faith in a man he doesn't even know*, Trell thought. By midday, he was overcome with restlessness. Launching off the bed, he belted on his sword, slung his satchel diagonally across his chest, and headed out.

The tent complex was immense, and the way out somewhat confusing, but at last he emerged into daylight and pushed a hand over his eyes to shade them from the brilliant day. He stood midway on the hill of a forested valley. Long grass softened the gentle slope that descended toward a wide stream studded with large, bleached rocks, while evergreens and hardwoods adorned the higher hills. There was a fragrance, too, that Trell remembered, and now he could place it: it was the sweet smell of grass, an entire *valley* of it.

Trell knew immediately that he was not in Akkad-held lands. *And more than a three-day ride back to Raku, that's for certain.* The Kutsamak Mountains were arid and bleak from Raku westward to the Haden Gorge, the lands not becoming fertile with vegetation until one neared the mountain city of Sakkalaah. All this greenery placed him far from Raku.

So. Had Balaji lied to him? Or could the youth have erred in estimating how long the ride would take?

All Trell could decide was that either he'd come a lot further in that underground river than seemed possible, or the Mage's horse could fly.

So where have I seen a view such as this? Trell wondered as he turned his gaze back out across the valley. For he knew that he had; it just felt too familiar. He'd spent the past five years in the Akkad, with only an occasional jaunt through the jungles of Bemoth or eastward to the Fire Sea, but he recalled all of those landscapes with perfect clarity. No, this one resonated against a much deeper memory, one of rolling hills and white-capped mountains.

Perhaps it really is time for me to get out into the world, he reasoned, still trying to justify away his pangs of guilt. *The Emir was right to send me away. Nothing about the Akkad stirs memories for me, but here, beyond the desert…these trees, these mountains…something awakens.*

He was quite absorbed with these musings when a frenetic click and clattering sufficiently jarring to his ears pulled him from his thoughts.

Trell looked to the west, where a quiet stream disappeared into a copse of hardwoods, itself nestled in the bosom of two hills. The sound was coming from that direction, so he set off across the open field and into the wood. He wasn't long among the trees before he came upon the source of the noise: two of his fellow guests practiced swordplay in an open grove—that is, if you could call such a battle practice.

The Whisper Lord Loghain was stripped to his waist and wearing only his baggy pants, which were secured with black leather straps at thigh, calf, and ankle. His leathery pate gleamed with the sheen of sweat, and the skin of his muscled chest, though pitch-black, was streaked with tiny cuts that bled as true as any human's. He now wore the Whisper Lords' characteristic fitted gloves, and the long daggers extending from each finger of his gloves flashed with deadly precision as he fought his opponent.

She was equally impressive, wearing only a bodice of sheer green silk that covered her torso but left her long legs bare, at least as far down as the slim green suede boots, which hugged her calves at the knee. Her long raven hair was caught up in a heavy bun, but many strands had come loose during their sparring. She was also perspiring, and in places that revealed aspects of her femininity which other ladies would have deemed mortifying.

Trell, of course, was quite appreciative.

He settled onto a fallen tree to watch them—though mainly he watched her. She had legs like a fine-bred mare, long and lean-muscled and spectacular. She was slender yet curvaceous, but more impressive than her physique was that she fought as fast and as furiously as the Wildling. Instead of deadly gloves, she sparred with two short swords, each of them with hilt and blade as black as her opponent's skin.

The Whisper Lord dodged, darted, lunged and spun. She snaked between knives, blocked his advances, made a few of her own, and escaped like the wind. Their blades moved too quickly to follow with the eye, and the sound of their meeting was the rapid scraping of a master chef sharpening his knives.

Their dance continued a little longer, and then the woman darted between the Wildling's crisscrossing blades and scored a long, thin gash across his chest before dodging away in a backward flip to land with her booted feet at an angle of attack. Trell blinked, trying to remember what she'd done—trying to reason out *how* she'd done it.

The action stilled.

The Whisper Lord backed away, still wearing that furious scowl. And yet, now that Trell had a moment to study him, he noticed a subtle difference in the Wildling's eyes as he looked upon the woman. Trell thought he saw approval in Loghain's gaze, and certainly appreciation. "*Caalaen'callai*, Vaile," he said in a voice that was the whisper of sand across glass. He bowed to her.

She smiled and bowed in return. Then they both turned heads and looked at Trell.

Who felt immediately the intruder, though surely they'd known he was there for quite some time. He got to his feet. "Your pardons," he was quick to say in the desert tongue, "I hope I'm not—"

"We were finished," interrupted the Whisper Lord quietly in the common tongue. "She has beaten me again."

The woman chuckled. Her voice was low, sultry. Exotic. "You have let me win again is more the truth," she corrected. "Come here, Loghain." She tossed both her dark blades into the grass and motioned him over. He went like an obedient child. She laid her hands upon his chest in an intimate manner, long fingers splayed, and closed her eyes. Trell drew in his breath, guessing at once that the woman was an Adept—that much at least, if not more. *A Healer? And a warrior too?* Trell decided he would have to be very careful in this woman's company.

A good rule all around, actually.

The pair separated. "*Dama,* Vaile," Loghain thanked her. Trell saw no difference in the cuts on his chest, but he knew that an Adept's healing worked on a deeper level, encouraging the body to heal itself. No doubt by tomorrow the welts would be gone.

Vaile touched Loghain's cheek endearingly. "*Quor ito a'dama,* Loghain," she replied in a purring sort of way.

The Wildling turned, nodded to Trell, and walked back toward camp, vanishing within the forest.

The woman came toward Trell. She stood taller than him in her heeled boots. "I am Vaile," she said in the Triad common tongue, extending her hand in a northern, and curiously masculine, fashion.

Trell clasped wrists with her. "Trell," he replied in her chosen language, trying very hard not to look directly at her breasts, or more specifically at the protrusion of her hearty nipples as they pressed wetly against the sheer silk of her bodice. *She fights like a warrior, speaks like a Northman, and dresses like a sultan's mistress…*

Vaile gave him a sly half-smile full of quiet amusement. Her eyes were unbelievably green, greener than the grass of the hillside, or the fir trees, or any green he'd ever encountered. She walked over to a boulder half covered in moss and picked up a bundle of cloth. As she let it unfold, Trell saw it was the bottom half of her dress. Re-affixing the skirt around her waist, she then retrieved her blades from the grass. Straightening with both in hand, she offered, "Walk with me?"

Trell was happy to oblige.

What strange company I'm keeping, he mused as they headed off together through the trees. *Strange company the Mage keeps, too.* There was something about these new acquaintances that made Trell very aware of his humanity—or at least of his mortality, which was an odd sort of thing.

So, he decided, trusting his instincts more than he trusted his eyes, *neither Balaji nor Vaile are human. What then? More Wildlings like the Whisper Lord?* He began a running list of possibilities in his mind.

One seemed to fit right away, and Trell turned to Vaile—only to find her watching him with an almost predatory look in her emerald eyes. Trell instinctively drew back a little. "My lady? Have I offended you?"

The look vanished as Vaile laughed. Her voice was haunting in mirth, almost like a purr. "You take me for a *lady,*" she murmured. "How delightful!" She shifted her swords into one hand, then reached behind her head with the other and began unworking the knot at the nape of her neck. Soon her mass of raven hair tumbled down her back. "It seems the Mage has taken a liking to you, Trell," she observed then. "You have the gods' own luck it would seem."

Or at least the blessing of a god, Trell thought. He adjusted the strap of his pack across his shoulder and asked, "Why do you say that?"

"Surviving cave-in and river and cold," she answered, giving him a strange look. "Isn't that enough?"

Trell broke into a crooked grin. "Oh…yes, of course. I just thought for a moment you meant because—"

"And now the Mage has taken a liking to you," she repeated, grinning as she finished his sentence for him, "and that is lucky too."

They reached a running brook whose water seemed the color of the wet river stones that lined its basin. Vaile knelt at the creek's edge and splashed some water on her face and neck, then cupped her hands and drank.

Trell asked as he waited, "You are a Healer?"

Between sips, she replied into her hands, "You saw me heal, Trell." Lifting her eyes to him, she inquired with a knowing smile, "Why do you ask a question that has already been answered?"

Trell regarded her with a pensive frown. "Perhaps I am not so quick-witted when I find myself in such…unusual company."

She stood and pinned him with a challenging gaze. "Do you mean to say *I* am unusual?" Her bodice was now fully soaked down the front, rendering it nearly translucent.

Trell didn't attempt to hide his eyes as they admired her, nor his approving smile. "I think you are most unusual, my lady."

She laughed. "And you are charming—for a Northman."

Her statement unexpectedly pinned him fast. "A Northman," he repeated, his surprise all too evident in his tone. "What makes you say that?"

She settled him an assessing look, a very feline gaze through half-lidded eyes. Instead of answering his question, she offered her hand…and a smile. "Come."

Her very touch tingled his skin. Images of the two of them entwined in the Mage's massive ebony bed flashed to mind. Fast reigning in his desires, Trell reminded himself of the things he'd already seen this Vaile do; if she was a wielder, she might be spell-casting him, which made him twice as wary as he held her hand.

As soon as they were walking again, following the cool stream back toward the camp, Vaile pulled his hand in front of her and turned it to study his palm.

"And what future do you read there, my lady?"

She glanced over at him beneath a fall of her silken hair, a pair of intense green eyes staring among the strands. In fact, the image reminded Trell so strongly of a panther whose path he'd crossed in the jungles of Bemoth that he snatched his hand from her grip and reached for his sword all in the same reflexive instant.

Vaile stopped at his side and cast him a quizzical look. "What do you fear?" she asked in that low voice so echoic of a purr. "Not me, surely."

Trell considered her. This was no mere woman to treat like a lady of the court. This woman was *dangerous*. She exuded threat with every graceful motion. "I think you are much to be feared," he answered.

"You are a guest here, Trell," Vaile said, "just as I am, just as are Balaji and Loghain and the others you have yet to meet. Why would you think I intend you harm?"

Trell kept his distance, his fingers wrapped firmly around the hilt of his sword. "Do you?"

At first her eyes widened, but then she fell into quiet laughter. The sound was honey to his ears, making him want to taste the mouth that made such a sound, to press his mouth against the throat that produced it. Oh, she was bewitching all right.

Vaile settled him a shadowy smile and tossed a silken strand of hair from her cheek. "Not at the moment."

Perhaps it was her candor that relaxed him, but Trell managed a slight smile and released his sword. "For some reason," he observed as he fell back into step beside her, "that doesn't reassure me."

"It would mean my life if I harmed you," she told him quite seriously then. As they headed out of the trees back into the open field, she went on to explain, "Every guest is safe under the Mage's roof. His rules are sacrosanct. None dare cross them."

"Rules? What do you mean?"

She held her hand toward the campsite that was just in view, an amalgam of conjoined coppery tents. "This place is a sa'reyth. A sanctuary. Three hundred years ago, before Malachai's terrible war, there were many such places where..." and here she paused, considered her words, "where those who were not welcome among human society could dwell in peace and safety. The sa'reyths were safe havens where enemies could meet on neutral ground, where the feuding races of Alorin could shelter together. The sanctuary rules were inviolate. This is the first of the sa'reyths to be restored, and we...we outcasts are grateful for its return."

They reached the stream and Vaile jumped its banks on light feet. Trell followed, asking then, "How long has this sanctuary been here?"

She glanced over at him. "Since the Mage's return."

"Since his return? From where?"

"I have not followed him in all of his travels," she replied with amusement.

"I didn't mean to pry. It's just..."

She gave him a tolerant sort of look. "It is understandable for you to be curious. But what of your history?" she asked then. "Where do you hail from—besides, most recently, a well?"

Trell chuckled and shook his head. "That is a loaded question, my lady. And one I can't answer to even my own satisfaction. Five years ago I awoke in the Emir's palace in Duan'Bai with no memory of my former life or even my name. They called me Ama-Kai'alil or 'man of the tides.'"

"Man of the tides," she mused as if tasting of the words. "Why this name?"

"I'm not sure. There is a city named 'The Tides' on the Akkad's southeast coast—called Kai'alil in the desert tongue—but..." and here he shrugged.

She gazed at him with unexpected compassion. "And how did you come by your name today?"

Trell held a low branch aside for her, then followed behind, answering, "I dreamed of it upon waking in the palace. It was an...odd dream. Now they call me 'Trell of the Tides.' I guess once a name has stuck..."

She nodded, looking sympathetic. Vaile took her blades in two hands again and began twirling them absently. Trell watched with appreciation for her skill. He added as an afterthought, "It's funny, but I don't even know how old I am."

She turned and looked him up and down with one raised eyebrow. "Twenty and one, I would say," she decided. "I have an eye for the passing of years."

"You cannot have passed much more than that yourself, milady," Trell noted, somewhat unconvinced by her pronouncement.

She laughed uproariously over this. "You do not have an eye, Trell of the Tides!" She gave him a friendly clap on the shoulder so he would know she was not offended. Then she shook her head, repeating through another bout of laughter, "No eye at all!"

Trell gazed at her, at her unlined face, her smooth complexion, the line of her hip, the lift of her breasts. *Impossible!* he thought. *She cannot be more than a few years older than me.* At the same time, he decided she could be correct about his own age, give or take a year or so. He had been a youth like Balaji when he awoke in Duan'Bai—ten and five, perhaps, or ten and six? The desert aged a man beyond his days, though Trell had spent most of his time attending the Emir instead of riding the patrols like Ware and Gray. He'd watched his friends lose their fair skin and their city-bred softness to the hardened lines of hard labor and battle.

Trell was smiling at dear memories when he felt eyes upon him and turned to find Vaile watching him again. "Do you regard everyone with such candor?" he asked by way of mild complaint.

"You are a handsome man, Trell of the Tides," Vaile replied as they walked up the grassy hillside. She shifted her blades into her left hand and placed a finger at the corner of his eye. "You have the brooding gaze of a poet." She took his hand and held it up for him to view. "You have the hands of a priest but the shoulders of a soldier, and you speak with the wisdom of a scholar—when you are not acting the fool in front of beauty." She dropped his hand, adding, "But this is hardly a fault. A man who can appreciate beauty has a soft heart, unjaded as yet by life and loss."

"You flatter me, my lady."

"I speak things as I see them," she disagreed. Then she flashed a devious look. "Were I not already paired, I might take you for a pet—a paramour to please my desires."

"I doubt I'd enjoy being your pet," Trell returned in amusement, and he added suggestively, "but *pleasing* you wouldn't be too terrible at all."

She reached and cupped his cheek. "Careful what words you speak to a woman who never forgets, Trell of the Tides," she whispered. "Men come and go, but I..." and here she dropped her hand and turned her gaze away. "I endure."

It was the first hint Trell had of the woman beneath; her intimations of heartache weren't lost on him.

"Come," she said then, glancing his way with that elusive smile back in her eyes. The wall around her true emotions had returned, as impenetrable as ever. "Tonight is Loghain's last evening with us, and Balaji has prepared a feast in celebration of his departure. We must see what the little one with the bold name has conjured up for dinner." Catching Trell's curious look, Vaile was quick to add, "Figuratively speaking, of course."

THREE

'To know love is to know fear.'

– Attributed to the *angiel* Epiphany

The skiff bobbed on icy waves as two sailors rowed in tandem, oars dipping cleanly in and out of a choppy sea. A waxing crescent moon looked down upon the little boat and limned a silvery trail back to the hulking shadow that was the royal schooner *Sea Eagle*. The air was damp and pungent with the scent of brine, but the sky was uncommonly clear, and the wind carried an exhilarating sense of promise.

Or at least Ean thought so as he stood with boots braced in the prow of the skiff watching the dark expanse that was the Calgaryn cliffs growing taller, broader, vaster, until they towered over the little boat. There were no lights upon the great crags to tell the rowing sailors where beach ended and deadly rocks began, neither lighthouse nor lantern to serve as a beacon across the blanket of ebony ocean, only Ean's ears, keen to the roar of the waves upon the distant shore.

"There," he said, pointing with arm outstretched. "Two degrees to port."

"Aye, your highness," said one of the sailors as he and his partner adjusted their rowing to shift course.

"Tis strange," said the skiff's fourth occupant, who was seated on a bench behind Ean wrapped in an ermine cloak. Ean's blood-brother since childhood, Creighton Khelspath had sealed his destiny to Ean's, to go where the prince went; to serve, and to protect. Now he and Ean had both gained their eighteenth name day, the age of manhood that brought new titles and new responsibilities, yet neither felt quite ready to face the world beneath the mantle that accompanied their new status.

"What's strange?" Ean asked without turning. He shifted his head slightly as if to maintain his focus on the minute sounds of the sea. The blustery wind whipped his longish hair, lifting and tossing it in wild designs while his cloak flapped behind him, so that he seemed a figurehead as he stood in the prow, a sculpture of some undersea godling.

"Strange to be coming back here after so long," Creighton responded, a simple answer that yet shouted his anxiety. His eyes were also fastened on the smudge of darkness towering before them, but it wasn't the treacherous shoreline that troubled him. "Strange to think of ourselves as the King's men again, instead of just the Queen's."

"Would that there was no need for such distinction," Ean muttered, scratching absently at the growth of beard he'd gained over the past six months at sea. He'd spent five long years arguing with his Queen mother about her relationship with his King father—the entire time he'd been sequestered on his mother's home island of Edenmar, in fact—and the disagreement had created a flood of bitterness.

Now all that had changed—at least, that was the expectation. Two moons ago Queen Errodan and her entourage had returned to Calgaryn to make peace with

King Gydryn in the name of their only surviving son. Ean hoped his name would be enough to bridge the canyon between his estranged parents; a great part of him feared nothing could span so immense a distance.

Suddenly the little boat surged upwards, and the crashing sound of waves gained in volume. "We're here!" Ean blurted with sudden excitement. Moments later, he leapt from the boat and sloshed through hip-deep surf to stand, dripping, upon the shore. To left and right, jutting cliffs sliced into the bay, but between them lay a swath of sand that sparkled faintly in the moonlight. Looking buoyant, Ean opened his arms and spun around as if to embrace the air of his homeland, breathing deeply of its fragrance.

The sailors took the skiff all the way in, surfing the last wave until the flat-bottomed boat scraped the shore. Creighton swept up his ermine cloak into the safety of one arm, then stepped across the bow onto the beach, turning to face the waves as his boots sank into the soft sand.

Above them spread another sea, this one a starry splay of jewels surrounding the moon at its zenith. Just east of the satellite, high within the arch of sky, flamed a seven-pointed constellation. Creighton swallowed. "Ean," he murmured, pointing with his free arm. "Look."

Ean lifted his gaze to follow along Cray's line of sight. His ebullient expression faded when he saw the grouping of stars. "Cephrael's Hand."

At this utterance, both sailors turned faces to the sky.

"Tis an inauspicious omen for your return," Creighton observed, unable to hide his sudden unease.

One of the sailors grunted at this, and the other spat into the sand and then ground his boot over the mark.

Ean cast him a withering look. "Ward for luck if you wish, helmsman, but *we* make our destiny, not superstition."

"Epiphany's Grace you're right, Highness," replied the sailor. "But you won't begrudge me if I keep my knife close tonight, I hope?"

Ean caught sight of Creighton loosening his own blade in its sheath and stared at his blood-brother in wonderment. "Creighton, you and I both have studied the science of the stars. How can you believe—"

Creighton turned him a troubled look and cut him off, hissing under his breath, "How can you not, Ean?"

Ean pushed a chin-length strand of cinnamon hair behind one ear and crossed arms over his chest. He couldn't discount the terrible events that had happened beneath the taint of Cephrael's Hand—*two brothers lost*—even if he chose not to believe in the abounding superstitions surrounding the constellation. The memories evoked a sigh that felt painful as it left his chest. "We blame the gods too often for things no one controls," he answered his friend.

"That's your father talking," Creighton argued.

Ean shot him an aggravated look. "Sometimes he's right."

A gusting breeze brought the stench of seaweed and wet rock, and something else, some proprietary scent seemingly owned by that beach alone. Ean remembered it well; it and all of the memories it harbored, memories carried like autumn leaves spinning in funnels across the sand. "I said goodbye to both brothers upon this very spot," he observed, recalling a much younger self who watched as first one brother and then the next was carried away toward an awaiting royal ship at anchor, much as the *Sea Eagle* was now. Neither brother had returned from their journey south, one lost to treachery, the other claimed by the Fire Sea. Now Ean stood upon this shore not as a boy but as a man, and it was never more apparent how different his life had become, how much the fingers of tragedy and obligation had molded and changed him.

"The Maker willing, we shall meet them again someday in the Returning," Creighton said respectfully, repeating a litany they'd both recited too many times already in their young lives, "and know them by Epiphany's Grace."

"Aye," Ean agreed with a hollow sigh.

"Aye," intoned the sailors, who couldn't help overhearing.

Ean grimaced as he gazed out at the *Sea Eagle* and the tiny flame of a lantern bobbing gently from its mainmast. Once, a royal schooner could always be seen at anchor just off these cliffs, awaiting the King's command for his pleasure, but after the loss of the *Dawn Chaser* five years ago, King Gydryn sailed no more.

"Come," the prince said then, shaking off the somber memory of his lost brothers. "Let's see how far we can get before they spot us."

Together they waved the sailors goodbye and turned to begin the long trudge up the beach. Creighton muttered as he followed, "I only hope they're not inclined to shoot first and ask questions later. There's nothing quite like a bolt in the shoulder to sour one's homecoming."

"No one could mistake you for a brigand in that outfit," Ean noted with a grin.

Casting him a defiant look, Creighton adjusted his ermine cloak and straightened his shoulders. "You never get a second opportunity to make a first impression," he replied stubbornly. He smoothed his velvet jacket, whose violet sleeves were slashed with silver, and pressed out the long line of ornate silver buttons that glittered down the front—indeed, he'd spent many an hour polishing said buttons in preparation for their homecoming. "And Katerine's favor is worth any effort."

The prince chuckled. "A first impression? Correct me if I'm mistaken, my friend, but wasn't it Katerine val Mallonwey who looked raptly on as you tried to escape that seaskunk on this very beach?"

Creighton cast him an aggravated look. "How was I to know it was mating season?" He shook his head and scowled at Ean's back. "I had to burn that cloak. The smell never would come out of it." Ean laughed again, and Creighton lifted his head and glared sootily at him. "I do believe you take perverse pleasure in my misfortunes."

"Creighton, the entertainment value alone is priceless."

They navigated around and between two hulking rocks that muffled somewhat the crash of the sea, and it was there that the prince reached for his blood-brother's arm. "Now then," Ean said, leveling Creighton a look full of amusement, "you swore you would explain once we were ashore. Why all the pomp? The cloak, the endless polishing of buttons? I notice you've even cut your hair, though Raine's truth a blind monkey could've made a straighter job of it."

Creighton grinned foolishly, like a boy in love is wont to do. "Tonight, upon our return," he confessed, barely able to contain his ebullience, "I'm to see Katerine."

Ean's grin vanished. "You told her of our landing?"

"Of course not."

"Cray, this landing is for our safety—you know the threats upon our lives and the precarious situation of my father's throne. If you told Katerine or anyone—"

"Ean, I swear, I did not."

Ean gave him odd look. "Surely you don't expect to wake her in the wee of the night then. So how…?"

A faraway, love-struck look beset his friend, and it was a long moment before he managed to put his thoughts to words. "It's like I can feel her, Ean," he at last confessed. "Even now, she lies abed thinking of me. I can't explain it, but I know that when next I set foot within Calgaryn Palace, Katerine will be there to meet me. Somehow." The distant look faded, replaced with Creighton's boyish smile. "So," he concluded with a glance down at his finery, "I've come prepared."

"I see," Ean said, even though he didn't. He started them walking again. "I take it then that you mean to propose tonight."

Creighton grinned. "Am I so transparent?"

"T'was the ermine betrayed you," Ean said with a wink. "It begged me save it from a torturous hour of maudlin rhetoric. *Ode to Katerine,*" he began, placing a hand dramatically upon his heart, "*t'were I but able to describe thy beauty, shall I compare thee to a thistle—*"

Creighton looked injured. "It wasn't to be that kind of thing at all. I wrote her an epic poem…"

But any hopes he might've had of sharing said poem with Ean were quickly dashed by the prince's laughter, which nearly rivaled the roar of the waves.

Creighton's long face split with a sheepish grin. He reached inside his vest and withdrew a velvet pouch. Emptying its contents onto his palm, he held it out to Ean. "I was going to give her this."

Still smiling, Ean took the ring and looked it over, arching brows. A single ruby was set in delicate silver filigree fashioned in the shape of a rose "It's beautiful," Ean said, admiring the workmanship. "It must be very old." He handed it back to Creighton.

"It belonged to an Avataren Fire Princess," Creighton murmured while returning it carefully inside his vest.

"Ahh…" Ean winked in understanding, for he knew now who had given Creighton the ring. "So my mother and her Companion are in on this farce. I'm hurt that I wasn't also entrusted with the secret."

"Only for your own protection, Highness," Creighton said with a lopsided grin. "We wouldn't want any rumors going about that *you* were planning to propose."

Ean chuckled. The truth was there were so many rumors about him that he couldn't keep them all straight.

Turning his attention back to the climb, Ean exhaled a pensive sigh. His blood-brother's earlier confession spoke truth; it was strange to be returning here as men to these places where they'd played as children. It was upon that very beach that he and Cray had so often sought refuge from Ean's eldest brother Sebastian, who'd had a penchant for throwing pie tins full of mud and rocks when he was in a temper; where all the boys had come to devise new ways to torment their tutors, secretly and momentarily united against a common foe. Strange to find comfort on a chill and treacherous shore; yet it was here he'd fled when first one brother and then the next was taken, snatched away by the pitiless snares of Fate.

And stranger still to find comfort lingering here, like an old friend waiting by the wayside.

At the rocky edge of a wide sea cave, their way angled up, climbing the cliff along the cave's edge. It was an arduous trek on steep steps that had fallen into disrepair, but after a year spent aboard the *Sea Eagle*, scampering up masts and hauling rigging under the watchful eye of Ean's maternal grandfather, the Queen's Admiral Cameron L'Owain, both boys were primed for the climb. Their last few years of study spent in Queen Errodan's home of Edenmar, northernmost of the Shoring Isles, had been more strenuous than all the years before. They'd interned as blacksmiths, longshoremen, stonemasons, and sailors, all at the insistence of Ean's mother, who would have her son understand the labors of the men he meant one day to rule.

'I cannot protect you forever,' Queen Errodan liked to admonish, *'but I can educate you in the ways of the world, and teach you to protect yourself.'*

At times during the last five years, Ean had despised his mother, the way boys called to task often will, but now he was grateful for the skills she'd made him master. He only hoped his father would count them as merits in his favor.

Not that he wished for the formal acknowledgement as crown prince—he'd have willingly traded places with his cousin Fynnlar, who traveled the globe on a whim and a fancy—but Ean knew the past could not be unmade any more than one's imminent death could be delayed by spitting into the sand.

Creighton was hopeful of his future and eager to marry, but Ean wasn't looking forward to kinghood—*Raine's truth*, how could he want a crown when it only fell to him though tragedy and betrayal? And how could he look forward to his calling to claim the crown knowing it meant his father's death? Never had Ean felt the loss of his brothers more than in the sure knowledge that he was taking their place in line for the throne. Yet the cold fact remained: there were no other eligible val Lorian heirs. Ean was the family's last hope of retaining the Eagle Throne, and he shouldered that responsibility as any good son should, though he wept in the knowledge of what had passed to lay the promise at his feet.

The boys climbed in silence after that, both the intensity of the path and their own deep thoughts quelling further talk. They were far above the sea when someone called from the darkness. "My prince, is that you?"

The boys paused and looked ahead as footsteps approached from the path above, and soon a soldier's mailed form solidified in the moonlight. "Why 'tis you," he said as he neared. "And you also, Lord Khelspath, Fortune bless you're both safe. Her majesty is most aggrieved about these circumstances, but your highness's safety necessitated—"

"Eammond, it's also good to see you," Ean cut in, placing a friendly hand on the soldier's shoulder. Queen Errodan's silver coat of arms glimmered on his breast in the moonlight, a barely discernable trident on Eammond's dark green surcoat.

Eammond nodded once. "Aye. Let's be off then. This way, if you will, my lords."

The rest of the climb was taken in silence, so it was that as they neared the crest, the unwelcome sound of a battle floated down to them. Eammond held up his hand to halt them, fist closed. "Stay here!" he hissed, and then he was sprinting up the last switchback in the trail.

The boys exchanged a worried look. "Ean, we can't just—" Creighton began.

The prince cut him off. "Of course not."

They raced after Eammond.

It was a battle indeed that greeted them at the crest, and in that first shocking moment when he came upon the scene, Ean was stunned to inaction.

The moonlight revealed a writhing mass of soldiers.

This is madness! he thought, staring open-mouthed as he tried to make sense of the scene.

Creighton drew up short behind him, and his gaze also betrayed his confusion. "Is it your parents?" Creighton asked in a breathless rush as the green-coated Queen's Guard fought red-coated palace soldiers. "Could they…could they be fighting again?"

"No," Ean whispered, suspecting it was treachery that turned soldier against soldier, not their monarchs' whims. He motioned to Creighton to follow, and they ducked through the tall sea grass looking for an opening in the fray. As yet they hadn't been spotted, and the prince hoped he might find an opportunity to intervene—

Suddenly he felt the cold press of steel against his neck. "I have him!" shouted a voice next to his ear.

Ean stilled beneath the blade, but not before he felt its sting against his throat.

In the clearing, the fighting slowed. Eammond was among those who looked down the wrong side of a deadly blade, and Ean suspected with failing hopes that his allies were on the losing side.

"Good work," said a burly soldier dressed in the king's livery who pushed his way through to where Ean stood. The prince couldn't turn his head to look, but he suspected Creighton was nearby, held in much the same fashion. "Let's see his weapon," the leader said as he reached for Ean's sword. He looked only at the hilt and the deep sapphire set as a pommelstone.

"That's a Kingdom blade all right," confirmed the man holding Ean.

"Aye, but the other has one too," said someone else.

The leader frowned over at Creighton, who stood at sword-point a half-step behind Ean, and then back again. He grabbed Ean's chin roughly and turned his bearded face from side to side, the knife at his throat barely loosening in time to avoid garroting him in the doing. "Can't tell with the beard, but he could be the right one."

"You'd think the other'd be him," grumbled another of the men, also in the uniform of the palace guard, "look how he's all gussied up."

"Just so," the leader noted. He narrowed his gaze at Ean. "Well then, which are you? The prince or his dog?"

"I am Prince Ean!" Creighton inserted before Ean could respond.

"*I* am Ean val Lorian," the prince said evenly, holding the man's gaze with angry eyes. "And you're a corpse when my father learns of this."

The leader laughed and spun his arm to the others. "Aren't we all soiling ourselves now, men?"

Eammond spoke up to be heard over the round of raucous jesting that followed this remark. "You may have fooled us," he declared while disdainfully eyeing the blade aimed at his heart, "but the King's Own Guard is coming even as we speak. Be certain they will know you for the knaves you are. Release us now, and I will beseech their majesties for mercy, though tis undeserved."

"I just can't be certain which one you are," the leader remarked, ignoring Eammond completely. He lifted his gaze to the man holding Ean. "Best to kill them both."

"Agreed," said the man, and the prince felt the blade's deadly sting against his throat even as Eammond and Creighton both shouted, *"No!"*

Ean reacted as he'd been taught—seven years of sword training took charge of the moment. The prince slammed his heel onto the bridge of his captor's foot, hearing the crunch of bone, and spun into his embrace. The blade bled his neck, but then he had his hands on the weapon and was forcing his captor backwards into the long grass. Fighting broke out behind him as others joined the struggle, but Ean's only thought was how to gain control of the dagger. The man's black eyes bored into his with ruthless menace as they wrestled, and Ean realized that he couldn't overpower the older man. But he was spry and agile and very determined not to lose his life that night. When the man stumbled over a jutting rock, Ean used the momentum to force him backwards—just four quick steps and they were at the cliff's edge. Ean wrenched free as the man fell with a howl of rage.

Heart racing but too furious to be afraid now, Ean drew his sword and turned to dive back into the melee.

It was the first time the prince had ever swung a blade with mortal intent, and he felt powerful and righteous in the doing. His years of training held him true, and only moments later, he took a man through the chest. The latter sputtered blood as he fell to his knees, and Ean backed away, covered in the other's blood, his own chest heaving, both repulsed and exhilarated in the same terrible moment. He was the first man Ean had ever killed, but he was not the last that night.

Ean had just dispatched his third enemy when strong arms grabbed him from behind. They wrapped around his chest and squeezed inward and upward, choking the breath out of him while pinning his arms against his sides. The pressure was so great that Ean was forced to drop his weapon, feeling needles pricking his hands and arms and seeing spots before his eyes. The man dragged him, kicking and grunting, into the long grass, where he threw him down. Ean rolled at once, but the man was quickly on top of him again, knees pinning his shoulders and legs pressing his arms into the ground, his heavy weight crushing the prince's chest, one hand hard over his mouth. "Now then," he whispered, pulling a bundle from within his surcoat. "We'll do this the right way."

Dark eyes watched the prince with hungry anticipation as their owner unwrapped his dagger. "This is Jeshuelle," he said, showing the blade to the prince as Ean struggled to be free of him. "She's named after the first slut I slew. She was a fighter, she was, nearly bit my ear off while I was bedding her. I dug out her heart when I was finished and filled the dead hole with my seed." He scraped the point of the blade against Ean's jacket, making an X across his heart. "That's the only way to be sure, you know," he added with a grim smile. "Take out the heart and they as sure can't bring you back."

Ean fought against desperation. If only...if only...

Laughing, the man raised his dagger—

It was the keening that stopped him—froze him in place with a wild look of recognition. The sound stopped everyone in fact; soldiers on both sides of the conflict simply froze, their senses immediately numbed, ears cringing against the terrible cry. It grew in volume, a horrid, uncanny wail that nothing in nature could ever hope to approximate. It was a cry from beyond the grave.

"What in Tiern'aval *is* that?" someone was heard to ask, but none other found voice to marry with words.

"*Shite*," hissed the man atop Ean. While all others stood transfixed, he leapt off the prince and scuttled low through the long grass on hands and knees like all the daemons of Hell were chasing him.

Benumbed by the strange turn of events as much as by the terrifying howling, which only grew stronger and louder with every passing moment, Ean rolled to his feet. He was lightheaded, his chest ached, and his neck was still bleeding. He pushed one hand over the gash along his neck, retrieved his sword from the grass, and stumbled back toward the clearing. It was a strange scene. The men stood immobile but with their blades still leveled at one another, as if in silent agreement to first discover the source of the wail.

Had Ean been wiser, had he not just been nearly suffocated, garroted and stabbed, he might've thought to follow the one man who seemed to know what approached and himself run far and fast. But like so many of the others, Ean was morbidly curious to learn the source of that dreadful, ear-splitting cry.

An errant cloud moved off the moon, and in that moment, they came.

Moonlight bathed the clearing in silence, its arrival shepherded by a cloaked man who walked toward them through the meadow. Even as Ean watched—and had he not been watching from the very start he never would've believed his eyes—deep shadows began rising up from the low blanket of night; solidifying, congealing darkness unto themselves until they at last coalesced into creatures of legend and myth.

It cannot be!

Ean denied the image his eyes so clearly witnessed. Half as tall as horses, entirely black with eyes like darkly golden fire, they lifted their paws out of the night-shadows that made them and gathered around their master, red tongues lolling.

Darkhounds.

Had it been daylight and sunny, still they would have cast no shadow, for darkhounds were shadows—made real.

And then the stranger reached the clearing, and they became intimate with a new kind of terror.

"You men," he said, pointing to Eammon and the other of the Queen's soldiers, "bind yourselves."

Several hounds trotted forward on soundless paws, and Ean saw that they carried ropes in their mouths. Ean wondered why no one protested, why no one turned to fight, why no one moved in challenge. That is, until he tried to speak out himself and found he could not.

The stranger turned toward Ean then as if feeling his questioning thought. Pushing back the cowl of his hood, he locked gazes across the distance with the prince, and Ean knew he was dreaming. "Look at me but once, Prince of Dannym," said the stranger with the silver face that gleamed like polished steel, metal yet living flesh, "and I have the power to bind you to my will."

Even as he spoke the words, Eammon and the others wordlessly took the ropes and began tying each other's hands. They moved as if of their own accord, yet their eyes were wild. Ean tried to find his voice, pushing against the confines of his throat, but though he screamed inside, not even a squeak emitted. He tried to lift just one finger, and the effort left his heart pounding and the sound of blood throbbing in his ears. Only his eyes were free to move, and he searched the darkness for a sign of Creighton, but either his blood-brother had fallen, or he was out of Ean's line of sight.

The heavy thunder of horses brought meager hope, but all too soon Ean saw it was not the foretold King's Own Guard that approached. Two dozen men reined to a halt in a scramble of hooves, and the stranger spun his head to fix them with his deadly stare. "You're late."

"We had to elude the King's Guard," the man in the lead said breathlessly. "We led them for a chase, but they'll be here soon."

"Get the prince on his horse and be off then." The stranger looked back to Ean. "Go with them, Highness."

Ean found his legs suddenly moving quite without his willingness. It was a feeling so foreign and so frightening that had he been able to do anything other than the stranger's bidding, he might have collapsed with the shock. He couldn't even affect a jerking motion in the pretense of fighting against the stranger's will; his legs simply no longer belonged to him.

As Ean neared the horses, a man came forward with a moon-pale stallion in tow. The prince's fine destrier had made the crossing with the Queen two moons ago, and the horse Caldar seemed so out of place amid this strange night that Ean almost didn't recognize him.

Before he knew it, however, he'd sheathed his sword and had one foot in his stirrup and the other slung across Caldar's back. Only as he settled into the saddle did he realize that he could now move his arms freely. His legs were so leaden, however, that he marveled they were still attached to his body and actually caught himself looking down just to be certain.

In all, the entire night seemed far too incredible to be believed. Struggling to make sense of the overwhelming situation, Ean looked to the heavens, to Cephrael's Hand gleaming brightly above him. *A Shade and his darkhounds? Is this some kind of twisted jest?*

It was so impossible that Ean held onto a desperate hope that this must be an elaborate deception, that a court magician had been solicited to create the illusion, or that they were all somehow made to hallucinate the same appalling vision. Everything had happened so unexpectedly—one unlikely moment opening onto the next such that one part of Ean wondered if he merely watched a disjointed farce populated by actors who missed their cues and whose improvisation led the entire scene into unpredictable directions.

Another part of him, however—the larger part—knew that there would come a time of reckoning where the truth of this night would have to be faced, and he dreaded that moment with every fiber of his being.

The Queen's men had just finished binding each other when the hounds began their unnatural keening again. This time there was unmistakable hunger in the whine.

Ean shuddered reflexively.

The stranger's expression grew steely as his gaze flitted across the assembled soldiers, statues made of flesh and bone. To his hounds he said, "Spare none."

The darkhounds attacked with predation and men screamed like terrified children. Horribly, it was the Queen's men alone who were allowed their voices as the hounds rushed around them, sating their deep hunger on those who'd meant Ean ill, leaving Eammond and his men untouched save by the blood that soon washed the clearing. Ean found something so unbearable in that knowledge—to die such a death without being allowed even the grace of voice to give vent to the fear and pain in one's last moments…

The prince shuddered and looked away. Wicked they might be, and with malicious intent, but they were men. No man deserved such a fate.

"Creighton Khelspath!" commanded the stranger then, his clear voice rising above the ravening din. "Attend!"

Ean swung his head to look for his blood-brother, for he had still not seen him among the group.

At first he saw no one but the dying, but then a form rose up from among the long grass bordering the scene. Creighton wore a horrified look upon his face, as if death had already claimed him, and he walked with a staggering gait, clearly in pain. Ean wanted desperately to call out, to give words of encouragement and hope even if they were meaningless, but he found that his voice was still denied him. So he watched helplessly as his blood-brother crossed the distance, miraculously passing untouched amid the feasting darkhounds and their flailing prey.

Tears came unbidden to Ean's eyes, and he reached for his sword with sudden desperation that he might do *anything* to stop this, but his fingers couldn't close upon the leathered steel. The sword was there at his side, yet it might've been aboard the *Sea Eagle* for all he could use it.

Creighton halted in front of the Shade. His face was ashen, his expression now void of emotion, as if already defeated. The Shade stared at him for a long moment, and then he shook his head. He slowly drew forth a sword from beneath his dark cloak. "Kneel," he commanded.

Creighton dropped to his knees.

The Shade walked to stand behind Creighton, and Ean saw that his sword gleamed with a silver-violet sheen. He placed the tip against the back of Creighton's neck, and Ean thought he might loose his mind. *No! No! Noooooooo!*

"It was not meant to be this way with you," said the Shade. Then he spoke for a long moment in a language Ean didn't understand. Creighton never looked up, never turned to Ean though he was clearly within sight, yet Ean heard his voice as clear as day in his mind.

Ean, tell Kat that I love her. Tell her I will always love her. Tell her I'm sor—

The voice ended with the Shade's two-handed thrust.

And Ean found he could scream after all.

"*Reyd!*" the leader of the horsemen urged the Shade's attention. He looked anxiously toward the road and the thunder of soldiers who would soon be upon them.

"Yes, *go*," replied the Shade, still holding the sword that impaled Creighton so horribly, his body slumped and twisted like a broken marionette. "Go!"

The men pealed away, and Caldar leaped into a canter, following the other horses without Ean's prodding. Indeed, the prince was tumbling amid crushing waves of pain and loss and was barely conscious of anything else.

Three brothers, was all he could think as his world spun and his gut twisted and his chest heaved with silent heart-wrenching sobs. *Three brothers lost.*

FOUR

'The eyes do not see what the mind does not want.'

– origin unknown

To Ean in retrospect, that wild night's ride east seemed no more real than had the knife to his neck or the keening of the darkhounds; what memory remained with him was only the immense, crushing sense of loss.

"*There is no afterlife*," Ean whispered the Rite for the Departed as Caldar cantered among the other horses, the prince's knuckles white where they gripped his reins, staring through grey eyes that burned with tears. "*There is no afterlife*," he whispered in prayer, "*there is only the Returning; And there is the path of those who elevate to Knowledge, to immortality in bodies and immortality in essence. Of gods in the known, there remain only Cephrael and Epiphany, themselves immortal, the only true immortals, who were made in the Genesis to watch over this world. All who pass, pass into the Now, for the Now is eternal. The Maker willing, we shall meet them again someday in the Returning and know them by Epiphany's grace.*"

Ean found himself saying this benediction over and over; it was to become his prayer for many days to follow. He took some solace in the familiar words, only wishing he'd had fewer occasions for their use in his brief years of life.

They stopped at dawn to eat and rest the horses. By that time the Shade had joined them. Ean glared hatefully at the man as he moved among his band of renegades, a tall figure dressed all in black, with dark hair smoothed back from a widow's peak, his chrome-like countenance mirroring his surroundings. The Shade's mask of silver skin was so reflective, in fact, that at times he seemed almost faceless, his features simply a reflection of the flora around him.

The prince was allowed off his horse to rest and relieve himself. Afterwards, he slouched against a tree trunk casting hateful glares at the Shade. Beneath the anger that warmed him despite the chill autumn air, he admitted a perverse fascination with the man—though he told himself that only in knowing his enemy could he hope to overcome him. The Shade's silver face unmistakably named his nature, and his fell magic of the night before left no choice but belief, yet Ean still recoiled against the truth.

Dear Epiphany…what has happened that Shades return to our realm?

He knew only a little of what had occurred during the Adept Wars, wherein the mad wielder Malachai ap'Kalien had nearly exterminated the Adept race, but he'd heard enough stories of Shades to make them a fearful enemy. Yet every tale spoke of Shades and their master being banished from the realm altogether.

But if Shades have returned…? Ean wondered how many of the tales about them were even true. More puzzling still was what interest a Shade could have in him?

Before the creature appeared, Ean had been certain that one of Dannym's powerful families was behind the attack, perhaps the same group who'd tried to claim the Eagle Throne seven years ago with his oldest brother's death…but what interest would a Shade take in gaining a simple throne?

Ean grunted and shook his head at the thought.

It made little sense. The more he thought about it, actually, the more disjointed the facts became. Taking several deep breaths, Ean pushed aside his anger and hatred that he might better focus on the facts.

First the fighting soldiers—clearly someone with powerful allies had infiltrated the palace guard sent to welcome him; that much he followed, for it fit with his first hypothesis of a powerful noble family.

Then there was the capture by the madman with the dagger named Jeshuelle. He'd been dressed as a soldier, but he seemed quite too enthusiastic about killing Ean. Was he part of the same group, or did he have a different agenda?

Then came the Shade, who'd spared the Queen's men but let his hounds devour the others...

Ean shuddered at the memory and tried to push the images from mind, but the more he tried not to think about the grisly scene, the more he saw the vision of Creighton with the Shade's sword impaled through the back of his neck. The feeling of desperation and loss that accompanied this memory scoured his insides raw; it was a heartache too near to him, and too-oft known in the last five years. *Three brothers! Three brothers lost!*

Fighting a sudden sense of panic that was so full of protest and fury that it threatened to choke him, Ean closed his eyes, leaned his head against the tree where the Shade's power had pinned him, and did breathing exercises to calm his racing heart. Never before had be been so grateful for the painstaking hours he'd spent in tutelage with his mother's Master at Arms learning to calm his mind and control his thoughts ever before picking up a sword. Mastering the art of distancing himself from his thoughts had seemed an eternity in the coming, but now he found it so easily...

It seemed only moments later that someone kicked at his boot, yet when Ean opened his eyes, the sun was midway to its zenith. The prince looked up to find the Shade staring down at him.

"Time to ride, Prince of Dannym."

Ean felt such an immediate and visceral hatred for the man that it threatened to choke him. He spat his anger in the Shade's face without thinking, the damning oath coming out in a hiss.

The phlegm stopped a hair's breadth from the Shade's nose and hung in space yellowly, as if caught out of time.

The Shade stared down at him with obsidian eyes—they were truly and fully black to the core, but like obsidian, there was a golden glint from within their depths. "Tis a foolish man who makes a liege lord of pride," he told Ean evenly, and as he did, the phlegm evaporated with a hiss, leaving only a puff of mist. "I give you this warning once, as a courtesy: Do not think to challenge me. Do not plot escape. Dare not hope for rescue. You live or die by my grace now, Prince of Dannym." The Shade's polished silver features reflected the clouds and the grass, but his obsidian-black gaze revealed nothing. Ean felt the first caress of dread as he looked into those depthless eyes, as if staring into the very heart of despair.

The Shade spun on his heel, cloak billowing out behind him. "Move out!"

They traveled all through the next day beneath an overcast sky, stopping here and there for a few hours' rest in the blustery wind, but mostly moving rapidly southeast. They were well into the foothills of the snowcapped Eidenglass range when they finally broke ranks and set up what seemed a more permanent camp, erecting tents, carving out clearings for cooking fires, and picketing the horses.

Ean was given full use of his body for the first time when a shovel was thrust into his hands. He spent most of the afternoon and well into the night digging a pit deeper than he was tall, and when he was done, he handed up the shovel, expecting them to pull him out, only to learn that he'd been digging his own bed.

"You can't keep me like this!" Ean shouted after the retreating guards, whose jeering laughter burned like salt in the wound. He kicked the earthen wall and spun angrily around, wishing he'd done a lesser job of the task, or that he'd even half wondered *why* they wanted the damnable hole, so that he might've made provisions for his own escape! He shouted obscenities at them until his throat was raw, knowing they only laughed at his impotence, but it made him feel a bit better to be doing something.

When he'd exhausted his anger, Ean finally threw himself down on the ground, smoldering. This latest mistake taught him the truth of something his grandfather, the Queen's Admiral, had been telling him for years: anger, fear, grief—these emotions dulled the senses, weakened the warrior, turned a thinking man into a frenzied man, and ultimately, into a dead man. He knew that his bitterness and loss over Creighton's death had immobilized him as effectively as the Shade's mysterious power.

I am not powerless, he admitted, *but I have been stupid!* Had he been thinking clearly—had he been *thinking* at all, instead of trading ill thoughts with the host of lesser emotions who'd been keeping him company—he might've been able to leave some mark of his passing to help lead those who surely searched to his location. He cursed his own stupidity. And then he let go of it.

Ean saw his plight clearly now. If he meant to escape, he would have to master his feelings—not in brief stretches, but completely and forever. A part of him railed against the idea, for Creighton deserved to be mourned. Yet the prince knew that if he played the mourning brother, he might not live to seek justice for the wrong; and the pursuit of justice—rightful vengeance, even—was far more conducive to escape.

Exhaling a ragged sigh, the prince rested his head against the earthen wall and looked to the heavens...and there, as if to mock him, seven stars glowed brightly between a break in the overcast.

Cephrael's Hand.

"Are you following me?" Ean snarled. "Have you some plan for me?"

But if Cephrael was listening, He deigned no response.

It happened in the early morning, several hours before daybreak. Ean lay shivering beneath a cold drizzle at the end of a sleepless night, when he sensed more than heard someone nearby. He started fully alert and sat up, turning, but not fast enough. The man was atop him like a leopard with knees pressing into his shoulders, muscular legs pinning Ean's arms at his sides—*not again!* The prince kicked and struggled against the man, but he was pinned just as solidly as before.

Ean could barely make out the assassin's face in the darkness, but he recognized the voice that spoke as he pulled out a bundle of cloth. "This is Jeshuelle," the man whispered.

Seven bloody hells!

Ean never knew what made him yell for the Shade, and especially why he used his given name to do so. "Reyd! *He—*"

It was all he managed before the assassin stuffed a foul-smelling cloth into his mouth and covered it with his free hand. "Now, now," he chided, clicking his tongue. All Ean could see of him was that he had that same hungry look in his dark eyes. "No one's nearby to hear you scream, princeling. I took care of that."

Ean kicked and bucked, moving what parts of him he could to try to dislodge the assassin. He had no doubt that this lunatic meant to kill him, but he'd be damned if he gave him an easy go of it.

Smiling sublimely, the assassin raised Jeshuelle and brought it down into Ean's chest, the blade hitting a rib even as it severed muscle and flesh.

Ean screamed. The pain was a fire that shot down the entire left side of his body.

The assassin pulled Jeshuelle free, yet another agony. The prince thrashed and yelled at the top of his lungs, yet never making more than a muffled whine around the foul gag. The man raised his dagger for another go of it, and Ean thought desperately, *No!*

The assassin laughed and struck—

But his knife…stuck. Hissing an oath, he struck at Ean again, but again the dagger stuck in the air just inches above Ean's bleeding wound. Now the assassin cursed in a language Ean had never heard and took two hands to the hilt. With teeth bared, he grunted and hacked toward the prince's chest, but no matter how he thrust, he could not make the blade move a hair closer to Ean's wound.

Ean was just as astonished as the assassin.

"You there!" a man shouted from above, and his voice was music to the prince's ears. The wavering glow of torchlight grew in strength. "What's going on down there?"

"*Shite!*" snarled the assassin. He scrambled off Ean, and the prince rolled onto his side and spat out the foul gag. "He stabbed me!" Ean gasped. "I'm…" but he was unexpectedly weak, and the world spun. It was suddenly all he could do to lay there drawing labored breath, letting pain run its course.

He heard the sounds of men climbing down into the pit, but the pain and the sudden vertigo had everything spinning too violently to follow what was happening.

A man's form appeared over him. "Bloody hells," he growled. "Hurry! Find the Shade!"

"No," said a second voice with authority. "The other, who arrived tonight."

Strong hands lifted Ean then. Soon he felt wind and mist on his face, but it was all he could do to hold onto consciousness. Already the maelstrom threatened to suck him down, down…

He remembered the flames of a torch sensed through closed eyes. He recalled being placed on a pallet and lifted, carried. Pain kept him company while events of the world came and went; the throbbing ache in his chest somehow became mingled with the beating of Ean's heart, the fiery threads of pain and life interminably intertwined. Ean opened his eyes once to a sea of swimming faces…and then he knew only darkness.

Some time later, Ean swam back toward wakefulness, ascending through twilit waves of disorientation until he hovered just below the surface. He tread water there, just shy of awareness, unable to open his eyes to the light beyond; but listening, hearing the conversation taking place nearby.

"…then it's done," said a man. It might've been the Shade.

"So it would seem," replied another whose voice was like the deep sea, melodious and fluid, akin to a purr but echoic of a growl. While Ean understood their words, something about them sounded strange. Strange, yet…familiar. "He is now present on the currents."

"And so the danger to him grows," said the first, almost sadly.

"As your master knew was inevitable. But tell me of the assassin."

"Beheaded."

"Unfortunate. I would've liked to question him."

"It would've proven futile. He was Geshaiwyn."

"Geshaiwyn," repeated that deep voice, sounding somewhat mollified. "That would explain how he fled you before."

"Yes, but another will come. They always contract in pairs."

"Geshaiwyn bleed like any other. What of the crew? The Wildling may have compromised your security. I hope you didn't spare—"

"Decidedly not! Do you think me a fool?" The Shade added in a hardened tone, "The time for mercy has long passed."

"Death is a mercy if your master fails," replied the second voice.

Silence followed, lingered. Ean began to wonder if the conversation was over and thought of swimming back into the beckoning depths. The dark waters were inviting of oblivion, and he was beginning to feel the pain again remaining this close to wakefulness. Then he heard them speaking once more and told the deep waters, *Not yet…*

"Who will teach him now?" asked the first.

"He must teach himself. There is no one left to do it."

The first grunted. "There is *you*. There is Markal—"

"His Calling has not yet come."

There came a stubborn silence, as if in protest. Finally: "Then you are right. There is no one." The sounds of motion followed, and what might've been the sweeping aside of a flap of heavy canvas, as if a man now stood in the portal. "When will—?" began the first.

"In three days." The tent flap fell closed.

This time the silence was enduring. Ean willingly lifted his arms and sank back down into oblivion's embrace.

"Wakey, wakey." Someone shook Ean roughly by the shoulder, and he blinked open his eyes to meet those of a stranger peering down at him. Ean didn't recognize the man, nor the unfamiliar tent, and he looked around feeling disoriented. "Shade says you're well and healed, princey. Time to up an' at it. Help break camp."

Ean shook off the fog of his recovering sleep and slowly sat up on his pallet. A stiffness in his shoulder reminded him at last of the events that brought him there. He found the wound bandaged, but an itch beneath the cloth demanded his attention. When he pulled off the wrappings, he was shocked at what he saw.

It can't be!

There was hardly a scar where the blade had struck, only a circle of new pink flesh. He knew Adept Healers had the talent to speed a man's body in its efforts to repair itself, but how long had he been asleep for such a wound to be so far advanced toward wellness? And who had healed him?

"Hurry now. Got to move on." The man tossed Ean a dirty tunic and then ducked out of the tent.

Ean donned the shirt at first with a heightened awareness of his left shoulder, but he soon realized that it was truly healed, if slightly stiff. It was a relief to move of his own accord, however, and knowing the Shade had taken steps to heal him meant he didn't want him dead—at least, not yet. If they were letting him move freely, and if they really didn't mean to kill him, perhaps he still stood a chance of escape.

His hopes notwithstanding, it was a curious few hours. The location of the campsite was as unfamiliar as the men who now watched him. It wasn't just that he didn't recognize their faces. They spoke in broken sentences, as if missing a knowledge of all the words that made the language flow easily off the tongue.

He stayed alert however, looking for any opening, gauging his surroundings. It wasn't until he came upon his sword strapped among his saddlebags that he began forming a plan. Being careful that no one was watching, he slid the weapon free of its concealment and hid it instead behind a fallen tree at the edge of the campsite.

Not much later, he saw the opening he'd been hoping for. It was as if Fortune favored him that day. Most of the men were on the far side of the camp. Only two remained nearby, and they were disassembling the tent used by the Shade. The creature himself came out and headed past where Ean sat on the fallen tree. Ean let his arm stray behind him, taking hold of his sword. The feeling of the weapon in his hand, of its warm, leather-wrapped hilt and familiar heft, gave Ean a renewed sense of purpose. This was the man who had murdered his best friend in cold blood. He deserved to die. The prince let the Shade walk past him, and then with his eyes fastened on the man's back, Ean followed.

Perhaps it was dishonorable, what he intended. Perhaps he would've lived with regret over such an ignoble deed. Indeed, later he would only wonder if the Shade hadn't done him a service.

Advancing silently, Ean raised his sword, fully intent on spearing the man through his spine even as he had done to Creighton, when suddenly the Shade was facing him. He'd seemed to simply reform himself in the opposite direction.

Ean drew back in alarm.

The Shade grabbed the sword by the blade and snatched Ean close.

"*Foolish*," he hissed, nose to nose with the prince.

Ean felt a chill spreading through his fingers, and he looked to his sword to find a silver-violet flame licking its surface. He released the blade and backed away, instinctively recoiling from the ill-conceived power.

The Shade flipped the weapon and snatched the hilt out of the air. In the same instant, he lunged at the prince.

Ean shouted in alarm, skipping back to avoid the man's advance, but he wasn't nearly fast enough. In a terrifying moment where time seemed to slow, the blade came spearing toward his chest, right above his heart—

And exploded in a cloud of ash.

Ean coughed and gagged to the sound of the Shade's dark laughter. Feeling both furious and ashamed, the prince wiped soot from his eyes and spat ash from his mouth. "Damn you to hell," he whispered, only then truly understanding the futility of his position—and hating the man all the more for it.

But his words brought the Shade to ire. He snatched an unresistive Ean by the shirt and pulled him close. "What know you of hell, Prince of Dannym?" he said, his breath cold and strangely odorless, a dry arctic wind. Obsidian eyes bored into val Lorian grey, and Ean felt fear—the *Shade's* fear—seeping into him through their contact. The moment was both startling and uncomfortably intimate. "I know Hell, for I have died there," the Shade confessed in a tone so dreadful that Ean felt the hair rising on the back of his neck. "Hell is a blessing compared to what awaits us all if he fails. Remember you that, Prince of Dannym."

He shoved Ean away, and then, inexplicably, punched him.

The prince spun with the impact and hit the earth with a hard expulsion of breath, silver stars marking his blackening vision. The warm taste of blood filled his mouth, a fitting complement to the bitter ash that still tainted it.

As if in answer to the angry query in Ean's glare, the Shade replied coolly, "For respecting so little, those who saved you." He pitched Ean's useless sword hilt at his feet, turned his back on the prince and left him there.

FIVE

'All good men are cleaved by the struggle between duty and desire.'

– Gydryn val Lorian, King of Dannym

"This is it."

Franco Rohre looked up beneath his brown hair at a sign swinging over the door of the tavern. The establishment was easily the seediest of dives in the small harbor town, a truly forgotten sort of place where naught but shadows came to die. The guttering flame of a single lantern illuminated the stoop and its sign. "The Gilded Boar." Franco read the faded lettering beneath a peeling image of its namesake and wondered why anyone even bothered giving name to such a place.

The man beside him made a derisive grunt. "Fitting."

Franco frowned. "I don't see how it fits at all, my Lord Raine. Why would he take rooms here? Surely he is not without means."

"Scion of the royal house of Agasan and uncle to the Empress?" Franco's lord returned derisively. "He has all the coin in the world." Raine pushed back the hood of his cloak and exhaled a sigh that seemed to convey the enormity of their task. "But I didn't mean the inn's condition befitted him, Franco," Raine corrected. "Rather that the name is consistent with all the others. Didn't you notice?"

Franco pushed the hair from his eyes. He was bone tired. They'd traveled to seven cities in five days pursuing a trail that was already cold, and he couldn't have been less interested in the names of the damned taverns. "I confess my attentions have been focused elsewhere, my lord," he murmured.

"I see." Raine gazed upon the dilapidated inn as if to penetrate its soiled walls with his eyes alone, as if to pull forth the man they hunted with the force of his will. "Then permit me to recall some of them for you. The hostel in Dheanainn was called the Blood and Boar; in Kroth it was the Black Boar. In Cair Thessalonia it was the Boar's Return. In Tregarion it was *Le Sanglier Bleu de Rivière,*" he finished in his native Veneisean tongue.

"The Blue River Boar," Franco translated.

"You see the theme now, no doubt?"

Franco did, though it shed no light for him. *And really, do I care about his whim and fancies? Isn't it more pertinent to wonder if I shall still be alive to draw breath the moment we catch him? If* they caught him, mind, which was a very big *if*. Still, Raine seemed to want to mull over the subject, and Franco was loathe to deny the realm's most famous truthreader what conversation he could muster, especially when so many topics were taboo between them. So he asked, "What is the significance of the boar, my lord?"

"An excellent question. I have been putting some thought to it. Perhaps it has some personal significance from his time before he took the Vestal oath. Perhaps in Agasan it has some meaning?" and he cast a look of inquiry at Franco for confirmation of this last. Franco forced himself to hold Raine's gaze, the latter's eyes so colorless as to be cast from diamonds. But their lack of color was not what disturbed Franco.

The Empire of Agasan was Franco's homeland—the province of Ma'hrkit, to be specific—and he'd been well educated in both its mythology and its Houses; indeed, it was his experience that in Agasan, the two were inextricable. "The van Gelderan crest is the Imperial Diamond Crown on a field of white," he answered with admirable composure despite the gaze that held him fast, "and the animal isn't used by any of the Great Houses, though several of the Lesser Forty contain it. Could it be a part of his personal seal?"

"No. His signet is one of his patterns." Raine exhaled a sigh and turned back to the inn.

Franco suppressed a shudder of relief to be released from his gaze; it was like the truthreader had no awareness of how compelling his questions were upon others, or of how powerless a man was when held in the thrall of his gaze.

But he has to know, Franco thought. He was *Raine D'Lacourte!*

Franco studied his lord as the name rang repeatedly in his head, an echo of the chant from Raine's hoards of loyal followers. His was a well-known profile—he was one of the most recognized of any of the Five Vestals—which had been captured in many forms across the realm; a profile that was shared by relations of equal fame. Raine was, after all, himself the cousin of queens.

"Perhaps the boar holds no significance at all and is simply a whim," the truthreader noted, seemingly heedless of Franco's study of him, so embroiled he was in his own musings. "He is prone to whimsy…of a fashion."

So it would seem. Though from everything Franco knew of the man they hunted, what seemed like whimsy was probably planned and counter-planned to the ninth hand of chance.

No doubt Raine knew this, also.

They looked at the inn together then. Not that Franco believed the man was here. Not really. Not after visiting so many cities in pursuit of him and finding only the dust of his passing. Yet for all his assuredness in this conclusion, with each tavern or inn they approached, Franco feared…. feared that this time he *would* be there, that he would come face to face with him. Above all else, he feared what that might mean to his own future.

Franco worked the muscles of his jaw, clenching and unclenching, and wondered if Raine felt the same hesitation, the same wary anticipation of confronting the man. *Well, the feelings might be shared perhaps,* he decided, *if not our reasons for them.* That much seemed true, for they'd been standing on the opposite street corner now for some time, neither of them entering.

As if hearing the thought, Raine turned Franco an apologetic smile that didn't quite touch his eyes. "Yes," he agreed. "I am stalling. But no longer."

He set off across the street, a regal form in modest garments and a suede-trimmed chestnut cloak. Franco forced himself to follow.

They were not unlike each other in coloring and build, and Franco's long legs matched Raine's pace for pace. Both were tall and on the slender side of muscular, and both hailed from a noble Adept house, but where Raine held his head high and stared down any foe with an untarnished soul, Franco hung his head in shame.

They reached the tavern stoop, and Raine opened the door and swept inside without breaking stride. A grizzled old man looked up from his tankard long enough to expectorate on the floor at his feet. Then he went back to nursing his ale with both hands as if a Healer's medicinal tea. The tavern's only other occupant was the portly tavernmaster who was clearing tin dishes from a beer-blackened table.

Franco paused just inside the doorway while Raine walked across the room. "Evening, Goodman. You are the proprietor here?"

The man continued about his work and answered in a despondent voice, empty save for its weariness, "Who wants to know?"

"I do."

It was in his tone this time, Franco noted. The special inflection. All truthreaders learned it in due course, but the Vestal Raine D'Lacourte's was honed to the finest point, sharper than Vaalden steel and as compelling as a zanthyr's blade pressed to one's throat. The tavernmaster looked up sharply, and his eyes widened as he recognized Raine's countenance. He dropped his tray of dishes with a resounding clatter. "You!" he gasped, taking a reflexive step backward. It was the first sign of life in him.

"Aye," Raine agreed solemnly.

Franco reflected that it must be a strange thing to be recognized in any tavern the realm over, to have stories told about you for the entertainment of kings...to tell kings your own stories in the privacy of their chambers. Yet Franco also knew that for every tale told of the Fourth Vestal, Raine D'Lacourte, there were four times as many told about the man they were hunting.

Having now recognized Raine, the innkeeper gaped at him. "L-Lord D'Lacourte," he stammered. "I—I didn't do it! Whatever they told you, it wasn't me!"

Franco knew Raine was used to this sort of thing. He received the most amazing confessions as soon as someone realized he was a truthreader—*that* truthreader, the legendary Vestal.

"I'm not here to question you," Raine reassured the proprietor, not that it helped a great deal. He took the man by the shoulder and pressed him down into the closest chair, which was fortuitous because the innkeeper was shaking like a luffing sail. Franco thought it a fair miracle the man's bones weren't rattling in his skin. "I'm looking for a man who may have stayed here," Raine said.

"Ain't r-rented a room in t-two score, m'lord," the man stammered with the gaze of a caged rabbit. He continued with a solid stream of denials that ended back at the beginning. "Ain't rented no rooms to no criminals, I swear."

"You may have merely seen him then," Raine offered—truly, he had the patience of a saint. "If you would but take a moment to recall—"

"Nobody important's been in here, m'lord. I swear it." The man had broken into a cold sweat, and his eyes were getting rounder with every breath. Franco wondered what crime he was so afraid Raine would uncover. When faced with the conversation of a truthreader, many a good man nearly shattered his sanity over the silliest of things. *Actually, that's the more common case. The true criminals know no remorse. They stare his lordship in the eye and lie through their gnashing teeth.*

Franco clenched his jaw tightly with the thought, as if to hold back his own confession.

Tis what you attempt with nearly every breath!

More and more of late he'd been having conversations with some part of himself—the part that used to be sufficiently drowned in wine but which had begun sobering up when he'd embarked upon this quest with Raine. The voice had since become an insufferable nuisance.

It's time you faced the truth, it chastised, *cowardly inebriate that you are.*

Shut up!

"If you will just—" Raine was trying meanwhile to get the proprietor to calm down, but it was clear there was nothing to be done for it. He exhaled with sudden impatience and in one motion caught the tavernmaster's shoulder with one hand while he pressed his other across the man's face in a particular manner useful only to truthreaders. The tavernmaster jerked once, his body stiffened, and he exhaled a low groan that was the moan of wind through the rafters.

Franco looked at the rigid man with his eyes rolled back in his head and suddenly couldn't stomach the sight. He rushed outside, heart pounding, and leaned against the wall as the door slammed, resting his head against the rough wood.

What in Epiphany's name are you doing? he asked himself to no avail. What would happen when they found the man they hunted? What would he say when he saw Franco serving Raine?

Not that Franco could've refused the truthreader—*the Fourth Vestal, by Cephrael's Great Book!*—not without facing a host of disconcerting questions he wouldn't have been able to answer. Not without risking everything! As it was, he barely had the man's trust, and who could blame him? There was a canyon of betrayal between them.

Franco pushed palm to forehead. *Gods above, I am doomed.* Had he really spent the last three-hundred years in his cups?

Three-hundred and eighteen you cowardly sot!

All that time spent avoiding the Vestals, only to run squarely into the most fearsome of them—

Fearsome? Raine? balked that irksome voice. *He's got the manners of a courtier and the build of a scholar. He'd be lucky to best a squire in battle.*

Franco gritted his teeth. *Raine D'Lacourte fought the Sundragon Srívas'rhakarakéck at the Sunset Battle of Gimlalai!*

He lost didn't he?

Yes, but not his life. He is fearsome, Franco insisted as the voice of his conscience subsided to inane name-calling, *more so than any Shade and his pack of darkhounds could ever be.* Indeed, the Fourth Vestal was ferocious when running down a truth, and unlike darkhounds, the sunlight didn't banish him back to shadows.

Franco knew that sooner or later Raine was going to ask him some very uncomfortable questions, and he just didn't know what he was going to say when he did.

You should end it now—put us both out of our misery.

Franco dropped his hand and closed his eyes. Gods, he really was going mad, talking to himself like this. How obliviously happy he'd been in his world of wine.

Sobriety, in comparison, was hell.

Letting out his breath heavily, Franco pushed a hand through his hair and lamented that he couldn't escape his current situation at least—if not his ultimate fate.

In point of fact, as he looked sorrowfully around, he saw any number of places he could go, a host of escapes. T'would take naught but a walk down the street to vanish once again into obscurity—*and dissipation*—for Franco's brown eyes saw things that most men's could not.

Franco Rohre was an Espial—called a Nodefinder by most, a Delver by some—and he saw the aetheric places where the pattern of the world conjoined, bringing together lands as distant as Agasan and Avatar in the space of a single step.

Of course there were no welds such as the latter near the shabby inn. These major links in the pattern of the realm were scarce and difficult to find without a weldmap. But the minor ones, called nodes, were common, and the smallest leis even more so. These last were like tributaries leading to rivers, the rivers leading to the sea, seas opening to oceans. So was the pattern of the world evidenced in creation.

'All things are formed of patterns, from a single blade of grass to the most majestic of mountains: air and water, fire and earth; Life itself.'

It was the first axiom of the *Sobra I'ternin,* one of the Adept race's most treasured texts. Everything they knew of Patterning, of the physical laws that bound the Adept race—a literal mountain of knowledge—came from the merest fraction of the *Sobra I'ternin,* of which only the first third had been translated. There were countless fraternal orders devoted to the translation and study of the work. Raine D'Lacourte counted himself a member of several of them, in fact.

Franco knew he could travel upon any one of the nearby leis, which seemed softly glowing stars to his eyes alone. As Franco mentally explored the leis in a manner which his innate talent allowed, letting his awareness pass through their ethereal portals into what lay beyond, he saw one that opened onto a moonlit field, another leading to an empty room, yet a third seeming a forest path...yea, by the time Raine emerged from the Gilded Boar, Franco could be half a world away.

But honor kept him rooted.

Honor, pshaw! You're too much of a coward to abandon even that loathsome oath.

My *oath.* Franco quailed at the memory of its making, the vision of himself kneeling before—*no!* He would not bring the image to bear. It was the last thing he wanted fresh on his mind for Raine D'Lacourte to pluck.

Not that the Fourth Vestal was likely to be eavesdropping on his thoughts. Franco knew that for all of Raine's formidable reputation, he was the most polite of truthreaders and would never covertly pry into a man's head, but he also knew that thoughts had force. Think them too loudly, and a truthreader like Raine couldn't help but overhear, even from across the room. Franco accordingly banished the very hint of oaths from his mind. Some thoughts could travel far enough to be heard on the other side of the world.

A cloud moved off the moon at last, and Franco gratefully lifted his eyes to the heavens—and froze.

It was there, *right* there, as if hanging above his very head...as if tolling for him. Seven stars as unmistakable as Raine's countenance, and even more historically significant.

"Cephrael's Hand!" Franco whispered. He'd seen the constellation before, but never like this—burning bright as a beacon fire and seeming large enough to touch.

The door opened and closed, and Raine came to stand at his side. He lifted his gaze to follow Franco's upturned stare. "Ahh..." Raine murmured, and there was much said in his simple exhalation. He pointed to the lowest corner of the grouping of seven stars. "It's rising, see? You can tell from the position of Nibis in relation to Canis," and he indicated the single stars in question. Then he dropped his hand and narrowed his gaze as he watched the sky. "The superstitions are not entirely misfounded, you know. Someone inevitably dies beneath the inauspicious light of those stars." Then he turned his head and cast Franco a droll smile. "But so do others die beneath the full moon, and the Evenstar, and the daylight." He pulled up his hood then. "Come, Franco. Let us leave this cheerless corner of the kingdom and find a coach for hire."

Franco looked to him in surprise. "A coach? Does this mean...did you find him?" A flurry of explanations for their change of plans crossed Franco's mind, and a fleeting hope that they might find rest instead of relentless pursuit.

"Sorry, no," Raine replied as they walked. "He was here, as we thought, but has since moved on. The proprietor had but the slightest memory of him, nearly faded into obscurity."

"Then why are we—"

"There was something else." Raine turned him a serious and somewhat disquieting look. "Something...unexpected. I must study the currents from a node."

Of course, thought Franco. They were within a night's ride of Calgaryn, after all, one of the oldest of cities, and its crowning palace was older still, though newer walls had long been constructed over the original structure. Most of the ancient strongholds were built upon *nodes* or *welds*, though the primitive cultures that built them knew only that such places harbored an inexplicable pulse of power.

"I am sorry to press on when rest is such a needed commodity, Franco," Raine offered unexpectedly. "I know you are tired, even as I am, but we can find some respite at least in the coach tonight while on our way. That, I hope, is some relief to you."

While motion across a node was almost instantaneous, every passage required Franco's energy and intense concentration, and they'd traveled over such a long, disjointed path that Franco had often spent each free moment in study of the nodes that he might get them to their next destination without traveling to the far side of the globe and back to do it. Six nights without sleep, traveling every day—seven days running on this, their latest trip, but they'd been at it together for over a month. Yes, he was exhausted.

Franco nodded soberly. "I appreciate that, my lord."

Raine considered him as they walked. "You have served me well in this endeavor, Franco. I think perhaps we have wronged you by not calling upon you sooner. In the Second Vestal's absence—"

Franco cut him off lest he say more. "My lord, you and the other Vestals have done me no wrong. It is I who have betrayed you—a wrong that no amount of service shall ever right. When I should've fought, I...cowered."

And when you should've died, the First Lord spared you, but oh, at what cost!

Shut up!

Raine regarded him quietly. "The Adept Wars have faded into lore, and the dead have moved on or Returned—may Epiphany guide them. You and the others were... well, many of you were but children when the Citadel fell and the mages were slain. You've paid your penance in the intervening years, Franco. I don't believe you should continue to abase yourselves, and neither does the Alorin Seat."

Franco clenched his teeth and swallowed. *Gods,* he really was doomed. To cover his disconcertion, he said, "You found something, you said?"

Raine cast him a narrow look at his clumsy change of topic, but he was too polite to press the matter. "I shall study the currents," the Fourth Vestal confirmed, "and then we will better understand the nature of this development."

As they rounded a corner beneath a bright lamp, leaving the sad street and its lonely inn, Franco gave the place one last look and then turned forward again, frowning. "I just don't understand," he murmured as he shoved hands into his pockets and hunched his shoulders against the evening's chill as much as his own fears. "What business could a Vestal have in such a place as that?"

Raine shook his head, and an old frustration resurfaced in his expression. "A Vestal could have no business there whatsoever," he answered. "Our task is to oversee our strand of *elae* and monitor its use, and to protect and defend its Adepts. I can find no reason for my oath-brother to go to any of the places he's gone." As he spoke, he fingered a heavy silver ring on the third finger of his right hand, the aquamarine stone cut deep and square. Each of Alorin's five Vestals wore such an oath-ring, including the man they followed.

And you've seen that ring up close, have you not? Become intimate with it even?

Franco gritted his teeth. Maybe he was being haunted. Perhaps this voice was a doppelganger come to hound him for his crimes.

The ghost of your murdered conscience, you twit!

Raine meanwhile exhaled with vexation and continued in a quiet voice no less fierce for its restraint, "Why take the trouble to occlude each innkeeper's memory when he knows I can truthread them? Why stay at seven inns named after the same animal? Why vanish for centuries, return in utter secrecy, and then traipse across the continent leaving a trail on the currents that even a novice *raedan* could follow?"

Franco had wondered that much himself. Though he was no *raedan* to decipher the workings of the world by a careful study of *elae's* currents, he knew enough to understand how the power that surged through the pattern of the realm formed currents of energy as it flowed along its channels, energy that carried upon its tides a record of every manipulation of a Lesser Pattern—events the uninformed called magic. The Vestal Raine D'Lacourte was the foremost *raedan* in the realm, and his fame in reading the currents was legendary.

Raine remarked with a tinge of bitterness, "Why does my oath-brother do *anything* he does?"

Franco was immeasurably glad that this question was obviously rhetorical.

"I think what troubles me most," Raine continued, more to himself than to Franco, "is wondering how long he was here before he deigned to alert me. Was he truly in T'khendar these long centuries, or has he been here among us all the time, working in secret, in silence, incognito...watching us—laughing at us—as our magic dies. Malachai's legacy." He let the words hang in the air so Franco might better absorb their meaning, so that the fears they revealed grew longer, stronger, in the way the afternoon shadows lengthened until they merged into night.

Franco tried not to look at him. *Too much. I understand too much. No man should bear such burdens of truth.*

The First Lord does, his conscience reminded mercilessly. *He faces truth in every waking moment. With every step, he presses forward staring boldly into the sun, even knowing the blindness that inevitably follows.*

Misinterpreting Franco's silence, Raine placed a hand upon his shoulder. "I don't mean to unnerve you with all my talk, Franco, and in truth I shouldn't burden you so with my thoughts. I hoped to find clarity in the orderly discussion, but I fear I have only become more ensnared."

Franco drew in a deep breath as if to summon his resolve. "We will find him my lord, and then he will tell us what we need to know. He will understand what's happening, and why so many haven't Returned."

Yes indeed, the First Lord knows why the Adept race is dying. So do you.

Shut up! Shutupshutupshutup!

Raine was gazing curiously at him. "I hope you are right. My oath-brother was the first to take the Vestal oath, the first to decipher the *Sobra I'ternin* and work the Pattern of Life…the first to do a great many things." He shifted his gaze in front of them again, but he did not seem heartened. "There are some who believe he has deciphered Cephrael's great work in full," and he added under his breath, "and as many again who blame him for what has happened as if because of it."

Franco gave him an uneasy look. He never liked repeating what people said of the Fifth Vestal—it felt like defaming his sworn liege to even repeat the words, yet the subject bore mentioning now. "My lord, they say…they say the Fifth Vestal, he's—"

"Our enemy now," Raine finished soberly. "Yes, I know what they say."

Franco pressed, "But if he's truly deciphered the *Sobra I'ternin*, then he would know High Law in all its fullness."

Raine turned him a telling look. "Which is why, Franco," he replied in a tone of resigned acceptance, "we must all pray that Björn van Gelderan is *not* our enemy."

The mad voice of Franco's conscience laughed bitterly.

SIX

'A change of work is as good as rest.'

– The Adept Healer Alyneri d'Giverny, Duchess of Aracine

The boy Tanis swore under his breath as he stumbled down a path through the Queen's Garden, tripping every few steps on a root or hopping with pain as a particularly sharp stone pricked through the thin soles of his court shoes. He should've changed into more appropriate footwear, he knew, but the truth was he'd forgotten to harvest the coneflowers that day, remembering nothing of the promised task until he was leaving the dining hall with a belly full of meat pies and his head humming with news—none of which would be worth his salt when his lady was expecting a cleaned batch of coneflower roots on her worktable in the morning.

His lady, the Adept Healer Alyneri d'Giverny, Duchess of Aracine, was not a patient young woman, patience being an attribute which, in her view, was only needed when faced with the ineptitude of others and 'really shouldn't be considered one of the cardinal virtues,' as she often lectured. Tanis normally wasn't so neglectful of his duties, especially when assigned him by his lady—who, though she was only four years older than him, became a formidable demon when her desires were thwarted—but the Harvest Festival was set to begin tomorrow, commenced by a parade celebrating Prince Ean's long-awaited return, and Tanis could barely think of anything else. His excitement filled him completely.

At dinner, all of the boys had been talking about Prince Ean—indeed the entire dining hall was abuzz with discussion of him, nearly obscuring any mention of Festival, which was the usual highlight this time of year. Queen Errodan herself had returned to court two moons past to make the arrangements for her son's return, spawning heady talk of herself and the king and their infamous arguments—and more recently of a secret paramour rumored to share her bed at night—but Prince Ean alone dominated discussion at table on the eve of his homecoming.

At Tanis's table, Tad val Mallonwey had the most to tell, for his eldest sister, Katerine, was being courted by the prince's blood-brother, Creighton. Katerine routinely read Creighton's letters to Tad, all of them ripe with details of Creighton and Ean's adventures, and in Tad's retelling to the other boys, he'd made the crown prince into both hero and warrior. Tanis wondered if his highness could possibly live up to the image Tad's stories boasted of him.

Tanis had little to add to the dinner hum himself, for he knew but one story of the royalty, and it was trite now, dusty and irrelevant with age: long ago, his own lady, her Grace, was betrothed to one of the val Lorian princes, and the connection had once made Tanis a star among the noble boys. But Prince Ean's middle brother had found his death at sea—coincidentally upon the same ship as her Grace's own mother. All hands were lost when the *Dawn Chaser* faltered in an early winter storm. T'was a tragic tale now, and not one for so festive an affair as Prince Ean's homecoming.

Was it any surprise, really, that the lad had forgotten his duties in light of such rich anticipation? *Not surprising, no,* Tanis thought, though he also knew that his lady would grant him no leniency for forgetfulness.

Thus did he find himself shuffling through the gardens in the moonlight searching for the plot of prickly purple flowers.

The Queen's Garden was a swath of vibrant nature nestled within the sprawling palace complex, the latter nigh on a city unto itself. While Queen Errodan had resided at court, her garden had been a grand and lovely place with orchards and fountains and expansive lawns, with hedge mazes and quiet groves and even a tree swing or two. A complement of thirty groundskeepers had tended to it with loving care. In her Majesty's absence, however, much of the garden had gone to seed, for the King would spare only a single elderly gardener to its upkeep, and the latter managed little more than to keep the weeds from overtaking the gate.

Tanis loved the garden, even in its wild state, but it was not so friendly a place at night. Large as it was, an entire army could be hiding among the long grasses—cavalry, pikemen and archers at the ready—and no one be the wiser. The ivy-choked walls became a threatening harbor for bats by night, and the old moss-covered oaks along the east corridor creaked and rustled with every passing breeze. As he moved beneath them, Tanis couldn't help but fear that they were discussing how best to consume him.

Trying not to think too much on the disposition of the oaks, Tanis crossed a path that lead away west toward the orchards and a far door that opened directly into the royal wing of the palace, one that was always manned with a host of steely-eyed guards who would just as soon shoot you as hear an explanation as to why you were anywhere within bowshot.

Tanis turned north, however, moving down a well-trodden path lined in slate quarter stones nearly overgrown with wooly thyme. He reached a circular court dominated by a fountain whose marble archer seemed a pale ghost in the moonlight. Taking a break to empty a stone out of his shoe, the lad's gaze followed along the line of the archer's ever-drawn arrow, upward to the heavens. He absently pushed a lock of ash-blonde hair from his face, and his eyes widened.

Cephrael's Hand, by all that's unholy!

The ill-omened constellation burned so brightly, Tanis thought he might reach up and pluck the very stars from the sky. Straightening again, he was reminded of a poem.

'A man may rule his household,
And a King govern his land,
But Death walks in the thrall of Cephrael's Hand.'

So the saying went. Tanis wasn't sure what he believed when it came to such things—he wasn't sure what he believed about most things, these days. Since gaining his fourteenth name day, what was now eight moons ago, Tanis had begun his Adept training from the King's truthreader, Vitriam O'reith. Though he'd long known he would train as a truthreader, it still seemed something out of fantasy—something from someone else's life; the kind of person who did interesting things, who traveled to fabulous places far and wide, like the Fire Kingdom of Avatar or the Akkad.

Tanis wouldn't have chosen Master O'reith for his instruction, however, not if he'd had his way about it, for the truthreader was exceedingly old and made for a tiresome teacher. Tanis thought it would've been so much more exciting to learn from the king's other truthreader, Kjieran van Stone, who hailed from the Empire of Agasan and had studied Patterning at their famous Sormitáge, but Kjieran had been missing from the palace for some time—at least three moons—and Master O'reith refused to say where he'd gone.

On a secret mission for his majesty, no doubt, Tanis had decided.

For all his excitement at finally studying the Art—and he *was* excited, even though it meant enduring Master O'reith's tedious lectures—the lad was learning that being a truthreader wasn't as thrilling as the stories made it seem. There were a god-awful lot of rules to remember, and why did he have to learn so many names of people who'd died hundreds of years ago? *'Tis not that they died, but that they lived, Tanis youth,'* Master O'reith always lectured. Tanis felt that entirely too many people were lecturing him these days.

He scowled up at the constellation. Somehow, he suspected, it was lecturing him too.

The 'educated races' were apparently supposed to know better than to let their heads be filled with 'peasant superstitions,' at least according to Master O'reith, but Tanis couldn't deny that bad things seemed to happen when that constellation showed up…wherever it showed up.

Tanis was so absorbed by these thoughts that he failed to notice a shadow approaching from the adjoining path to the north until it quite unexpectedly bumped into him. The lad started like a hare spooked by a fox, jumping half out of his skin, while the approaching shadow very nearly shrieked. Both lost their balance and reached for the other.

Tanis inhaled the scent of jasmine and felt soft hair beneath his hands before the woman composed herself and took a tidy step backwards. In the moonlight, he knew her face as well as his own. "Your Grace," he murmured as he quickly stepped a proper distance away.

"Tanis, what in Tiern'aval are you doing out here in the middle of the night?" Alyneri didn't have to put her hands on her hips, for her tone spoke volumes.

Tanis gave her a tense look and rubbed at one eye.

She arched a brow at him. It was a sure sign of warning. "Well?"

As the lad tried desperately but vainly to come up with some acceptable truth that would spare him a scolding, he saw a swath of shadows approaching from behind his lady, and soon a host of soldiers had joined them.

Leading the pack was a bear of a man whose face Tanis knew well but whose company he usually went out of his way to avoid. The soldier had stormy grey eyes sighted down a thin, flaring nose, and his reddish beard was in contrast to the mane of brown, shoulder-length hair that was held in place by an earl's bronze circlet. As ever, he sported his chain of office, a heavy necklace of linked gold disks that was worn only by the captain of the King's Own Guard.

"Oh good," the captain said, noting Tanis with the suspicious indifference of a grizzly toward a nosy chipmunk, as if knowing he could squash Tanis easily. "You found him."

"I did no such thing," Alyneri remarked without turning. She was pinning Tanis with a steady stare. "I'm waiting, Tanis."

Tanis glanced from her Grace to the burly captain, who was backed by a score of stone-faced soldiers, and decided her Grace was definitely the more amiable ear. "I forgot to harvest the coneflowers, milady," he confessed, "and I knew you were expecting them in the morning, so I—"

"Oh, is that all?" Alyneri waved off the rest of his explanation and started down the path again, her moon-pale braid swishing along her back like a wildcat's tail.

Tanis gazed after her looking baffled.

"Well? What are you waiting for, lad?" the captain complained, giving him a shove to start him moving. "We'll lose sight of her at this pace, and I've no interest in spending the night hacking my way out of this thorn-infested mire of overgrown cabbages."

Thus prodded, Tanis stumbled into motion, doing his best to catch up with her Grace. As he nursed his wounded pride, he thought of informing the captain that they certainly didn't grow cabbages in the Queen's Garden, but he suspected the man wouldn't find the information at all useful, and he knew enough of the Lord Captain Rhys val Kincaide to know that he did not appreciate information which he didn't find useful. Tanis had, in fact, heard the captain say to his men more than a few times that what he dubbed 'useless' information did nothing but tangle a soldier's clear thinking. Oftentimes these admonitions were emphasized by way of a gauntleted hand smacking the back of their head—just one of many reasons Tanis usually avoided the Lord Captain like the plague.

He did, however, ask him, "Sir, where are we going?"

"Shadow take me if I know," the captain grumbled. "The Duchess says she knows a shorter route to the tunnels, and I'm thinking she means to go by way of the infirmary, but the next thing I know she's leading us through this forest of weeds."

"But why are we going to the tunnels?"

Rhys gave him an annoyed look. "You sure talk a lot for a truthreader. That O'rieth character hardly ever says a word."

"Master O'reith has long passed his eightieth name day and often falls asleep with his eyes open," Tanis returned matter-of-factly. "He only speaks when directly addressed."

"Seems to me you could learn from him," Rhys observed.

Tanis scowled at the captain and decided to ask the same question of his lady instead. A brief sprint and he'd caught up with her. Alyneri was nearly a head shorter than him since his last growth spurt, but for all of that she rivaled the wind for speed when she was on a mission. "Your Grace," Tanis said as he tried to fall into step beside her, though he quickly discovered it was impossible for his longer legs to match her pace and managed instead only a clumsy sort of skipping gait. "Why are we going into the tunnels at this hour?"

"Because the Lord Captain demanded it," she returned with no small measure of irritation. "What he thinks I can do, I vow I don't know. The man is dead. I told the captain this, of course, but like all soldiers, his ears hear only the orders of his superior, which become instantly etched in that stone he calls a brain. Don't ask the man to think for himself—Epiphany help us if he should ever have to solve a problem not related to his given task!"

Tanis gathered much more from this diatribe than one might imagine, being used to gleaning important facts from among his lady's vitriolic outpourings. "Why would he wake you to attend a man if he's already dead?" Tanis asked. "That's much more the vein of a truthreader's talent."

"That is entirely the point I tried to impress upon him, Tanis." Alyneri sniffed with annoyance. "Apparently Vitriam is closeted with his Majesty in his war council, and I suppose that van Stone character had nothing to offer either. Had his Majesty found the resolve to acquire the services of more than two truthreaders in the last ten years, perhaps the captain would've had someone else knowledgeable on hand to advise him. As it is, the King's Guard are desperate to identify the dead man. Perhaps you will be of some assistance to them, Tanis, for I vow this entire episode will result in nothing on my part but several hours of sleep that I shall never recover."

There wasn't time for any more questioning, for just then they reached the Rose Door. It was mostly hidden behind a sway of cabbage roses hanging from a trellis that sagged dispiritedly away from the stone wall.

Alyneri stopped before the heavy iron door wrought with the image of its namesake and allowed the captain and his men to catch up. "There you are, my Lord Captain," she said with upraised hand. "Instant access to the tunnels and the specific room of which you mentioned."

Rhys gave her a reproachful look, which Tanis was hard-pressed to decipher save that the captain had found something displeasing in what she'd just said.

Her Grace evidently understood it, however, for she cast him in return an affronted look that might've splintered granite if aimed carefully enough. "Well, are we going to stand here all night, Captain, or did you want me to have a look at your dead body?"

Rhys grunted his disgust with her and barged past, yanking the door open on rusted hinges that shrieked in protest. Tanis cringed, Alyneri glared, and Rhys hunched his shoulders as if in grave effort to control his temper before ducking beneath the portal.

Inside, a stairwell was lit by sconces at intervals along the walls, strange lamps that gave off a golden gleam very unlike oil or tallow or wax or anything at all that Tanis had ever seen burning. He also noticed several of the captain's men making the sign to ward against the evil eye and wondered what they knew about this place that he obviously didn't. The sight gave him an odd but familiar feeling, one that always seemed to herald ill things to come, much like the feeling he got about that constellation in the sky.

The stairwell wound interminably down, but eventually they reached the end, and Rhys headed off down a long tunnel that was also lit by the odd lamps. Had he been alone, Tanis would've stopped to discover what fueled them; as it was, he barely kept apace with her Grace, who easily walked as fast as the towering captain and looked several times as if she meant to overtake him—and would have, had the captain not stretched his long legs to new lengths that he might retain his lead.

At last they came in view of a pair of iron doors not unlike the Rose Door in craft, though they were wrought with the val Lorian eagle and were of a far more intricate design. Rhys turned a corner past the doors, and there he stopped. The dead man lay sprawled upon the floor, but more immediately baffling to Tanis was the gaping hole in the tunnel ceiling above him.

The hole spanned nearly the width of the corridor, a circular expanse that had seared cleanly through stone and earth, vanishing upwards into darkness.

"What could make a hole like that?" one of the soldiers murmured behind Tanis, while another asked, "How far up does it go?"

Within the hole, what should've been rough was as smooth as glass, and the deep earth held an unusual, iridescent cast.

"It wasn't cut, that's for certain," yet a third soldier observed, a man Tanis knew and liked. The Lieutenant Bastian val Renly was a fair-haired, good-natured man whom Tanis had spoken to on occasion and who always had something encouraging to say. "It's like the stone just…melted."

"Magic," the first soldier whispered, and upon Bastian's sharp glance, he pressed, "What else could have made such a hole, Lieutenant?"

Bastian turned a troubled gaze upward. "Yes," he mused, "but *what* magic?"

"All right, enough of that," Rhys barked. He looked to Alyneri and directed her attention to the dead man lying before them.

Tanis scrunched his face up trying to imagine what could've happened to the man to make him so…*grey*.

"Well? What do you think, Duchess?" Rhys asked Alyneri.

Alyneri pushed her pale braid off her shoulder and crossed arms beneath her breasts. "I think he's dead."

Now that they were well in the light, Tanis noticed that she was wearing her least-favorite dress, one that she only wore on visits to the country. His lady was usually quite discerning about her appearance, for hers was an unusual sort of beauty, one often commented upon and not always favorably. There were of course some ladies of the nobility who called her looks 'odd,' and others less discreet that named them 'disturbing,' but Tanis thought her exotic and lovely. It was the contrast in her coloring that drew stares, he knew—her large amber eyes alone would not be cause for talk, but pair them with that caramel skin and pale flaxen hair, and she did stand out in a crowd.

Rhys meanwhile seemed to be harboring ill wishes toward her Grace, if told from the vein that bulged and pulsed along his neck. "Yes, but *how* did he die?"

"It would seem," Alyneri began, placing a finger to her lips in thoughtful fashion, "that the air left his lungs and did not return. That, I believe, is a defining aspect of death."

Rhys glared so hard Tanis feared the strain upon his bulging eyes. "Can't you work some Adept hocus-pocus and figure out what killed him? I mean—*look* at him! What turns a man such a color?"

"He is quite grey," Alyneri agreed. "But as I told you back in my rooms, Captain, I am a healer, not an auger. I deal with the living, not the dead. I cannot tell you how this man expired any more than I can tell you who he is, for I have never before laid eyes upon him."

Rhys looked as if he needed something to punch. He wasn't ready to give up, though, no matter Alyneri's defiance. "You didn't even touch him," he insisted, "how do you know that you can't learn—"

"*Because*, my Lord Captain," Alyneri cut in coolly, "I am a trained healer. Being that you are not, you will have to trust me when I declare I have nothing to offer you in this matter."

"Your Grace," Bastian inquired then, "have you any idea as to how the man came to be lying here? Did he fall down that hole? Can you tell us anything of his condition in that regard?"

"I can. He clearly did not fall to his death, for his bones lie unbroken."

Rhys rested a hand on his sword hilt and paced a small square. Suddenly he spun and looked at Tanis. "You, lad. You're training to be a 'reader. Do your truthhold thing and see what you can discover of him."

"Touch him not, Tanis," Alyneri advised. She was staring at the dead man with a calculating look. Tanis was relieved, for the last thing he wanted to do was get closer to the man. He looked like something the savage Shi'ma had got a hold of with their potions and herbs, only they'd shriveled his whole body instead of merely his head. "And what of Kjieran van Stone?" Alyneri posed. "Have you not asked him, my Lord Captain?"

The captain glowered even harder. "That bloody man's been missing for months."

"Missing?"

"Fully vanished, your Grace," Bastain val Renly added, "to put it bluntly."

"How does one of the king's only two truthreaders simply vanish? Someone saw him leave through one of the gates, surely."

Rhys glared belligerently at her, but the lieutenant answered, "Kjieran could've thrown himself from the walls into the surf for all we can explain his absence, your Grace."

Alyneri waved a hand dismissively. "Fine, I'll leave such matters to your capable hands. In the mean, let me recommend that no one touch this body until someone else *qualified* has a chance to study him," and she added under her breath, "not that I know who that could be." She looked to Rhys then. "One thing I can tell you of a certain, Captain, is that nothing—no natural force, be it physical or chemical—could have so destroyed a body."

"Magic," that self-same soldier repeated his earlier pronouncement, wherein Bastian echoed grimly, "But *what* magic?"

All eyes lifted then, gazing upward into the dark hole that seemed to have bored through stone and earth like a smelting iron through butter. If the man had not fallen down it, had someone—or some *thing*—gone up? How had the hole come to be there? And where did it lead?

The sound of boots fast striking the stone floor drew everyone's gaze, and the men in the rear cleared way as a blue-cloaked palace guard rushed up. "My Lord Captain!" The man managed a breathless greeting as Rhys turned to receive him. "My lord, two sentries just returned from the—" he looked around at present company and licked his lips, lowering his voice. "From off the moors, sir. You'll want to hear their report."

Rhys arched brows. "Indeed." He turned to Bastian. "Lieutenant, see that no one gets within bowshot of this passageway." He left promptly with the Palace Guard and two of his own men.

Bastian turned to Alyneri. "Your Grace, if I may prevail upon you to linger one moment longer that I might have a word..."

Alyneri had been frowning at the dead man, but she turned to Bastian and gave him a polite nod. "Certainly, Lieutenant." It was always clear when her Grace candidly approved of someone, like the lieutenant, in stark comparison to her opinion of the Lord Captain Rhys val Kincaide.

Tanis was contemplating his chances of staying below to talk with the lieutenant as well—for he was more than a little curious about those iron doors and what lay behind them, and he still wondered why the men had made the sign against the evil eye, and what was burning in the lamps—but Alyneri was having none of that. "Tanis, why are you loitering around?" She crossed her arms and arched a pale brow at him, drumming the fingers of one hand upon her arm. "The night's not getting any younger."

His curious aspirations thus thwarted, Tanis made haste to collect the forgotten coneflowers.

SEVEN

'The mysteries of a woman's heart cannot be measured; they are as the expanse of time and space, endless and unknowable.'

– The Espial Franco Rohre, to the Queen of Veneisea, while posing as a minstrel in the Veneisean court

"What do you mean their trail vanished?" his Royal Majesty, Grydryn val Lorian, King of Dannym, demanded of the soldier before him. The latter cringed under the scrupulous gaze of his monarch, looking harried and uncertain.

Errodan Renwyr n'Owain val Lorian, Queen of Dannym and the Shoring Isles, stood watching the exchange with her back pressed stiffly against the velvet-paneled wall, arms crossed, fingers thrumming steadily, as if this tiniest of gestures could disperse the intense emotions that roiled within. She saw the limning of the horizon through the long wall of glass-paned doors, saw the paling of the leaden sky. Ean was meant to be with her when dawn came. Instead, she stood alone.

Alone in a roomful of strangers, she thought. Yet she knew each man who sat in the chambers of the king by more than mere name and ranking. She knew their families, their histories; once she would've known their private pleasures and their secret crimes, so trusted she was with her husband's confidences—and so adept were her own spies at gathering information about the king's Privy Council. But now Errodan was the outsider, allowed in this room on this evening by the king's grace alone.

Errodan drew in a slow breath to still her nerves, to calm the fearful thoughts that beat at her like frightened bats. They'd called her after midnight with the news, and she'd arrived in Gydryn's private chambers just as the first of what was to become a succession of soldiers was making his report. Each report had been attended by as small a number of ears as possible, necessarily including those of the king's truthreader, Vitriam O'reith, who'd pronounced each man's report the honest truth. Yet Errodan wondered if the old man still had his wits about him. Most of the time he sat in silence with his colorless eyes glazed over, as if spending his off moments in another dimension altogether, and he seemed less and less connected as the night drew on into morning.

Besides the truthreader, only three men had been called to Gydryn's private chambers: Rhys val Kincaide, Captain of the King's Own Guard and his First Lieutenant Bastian val Renly; and Morin d'Hain, head of Dannym's intelligence network.

Morin was the only unknown to Errodan. He was the youngest man ever appointed to Gydryn's Privy Council, by far the youngest to hold the position of Master of Spies. He'd been appointed in Errodan's absence, but so far she was pleased with what she saw in him.

Which was well and good, because secrecy was vital. Gydryn had many enemies who hungered for the crown, and if it was known that Ean had been taken…rumors were as destructive as battering rams when adroitly wielded.

"Get up, get up," the king grumbled, waving irritably at the soldier before him, who had nearly prostrated himself with his remorse—not that he'd had a hand in losing the prince himself, but most of the king's men felt this loss as if personal to them. Too, Gydryn was a formidable presence in the room, with his mane of raven hair and beard barely etched with silver, his grey eyes piercing.

The soldier got back to his feet and stood there looking contrite. He was one of two who'd followed a trail away from the battle site, but they'd also traveled the furthest from the scene and were therefore the last to arrive back at the palace and present their findings to the king. "We've been waiting all night for your report, man," Gydryn said. "Just explain yourself."

"Yes, your majesty," the solider managed. "Kalyn and myself," and he looked behind him to the closed double doors beyond which, ostensibly, the other soldier waited, "we were among the first on the scene, assigned to Lieutenant Posten's company. We'd been riding to the rendezvous at the cliffs where his Highness put ashore—"

"His Majesty knows all of this, solider," Morin cut in. "He was asking you about his Highness's trail."

The soldier glanced at Morin d'Hain looking unnerved by his presence. "Um, yes, milord. Well, the uh, lieutenant, he assigned us—"

"Soldier, we've already heard from the lieutenant," Morin interrupted again. "Please tell his Majesty about the prince's trail."

"Oh, yes, that. Well, Kalyn and myself, we headed east after helping release her Majesty's men," and he cast a tentative look toward Errodan. "We, uh, we found the trail not too far beyond the clearing where the battle took place. We followed the trail for about three clicks, and then it just…ended."

"Ended how?" Morin asked.

The soldier gave him an apprehensive look. "I mean, milord, the uh…hoof prints just ended as if they up and rode into the air."

"A clean line of dirt, as if brushed away?" Rhys asked.

"No, my Lord Captain. It was grasslands, and til that point the meadow had been rightly trampled. Wasn't no way to take two dozen horses across it with the rains we had yesterday and not leave a goodly path of mud. No, this was grass all stamped on like and then grass that wasn't touched. It was like they just up and road into the clouds—"

"Yes, so you mentioned," Morin pointed out.

"Sorry, milord. I do tend to repeat myself."

Grydryn shifted in his chair while Errodan tried once again to calm her racing heart and fend off the thoughts of doom and disaster that badgered her. "What is your explanation for the vanished trail?" asked the king.

The soldier's eyes widened considerably. "Your Majesty, I don't…well I mean, *I* thought—"

"*Yes*, you thought…" demanded the king impatiently.

The soldier visibly swallowed. He looked nervously around at the others in the room. "Well, don't we all think the same thing?" he whispered. "I mean…I dunno what the others said, milords, but I saw it with my own eyes and if it wasn't…" He mustered his courage and braved, "if it wasn't magic as obscured their trail, Sire, I don't know what could have done it." The statement thus made, he cringed as if expecting a rebuke but was met only with silence.

Indeed, Errodan reflected, what could any of them say? Every solider who'd reported that night spoke of arcane events—darkhounds feasting on traitors dressed in the livery of the palace guard, a man with a silver face, magic that bound them to another's will—yet there was so little evidence to corroborate their stories. For all she knew, the soldiers mightn't have met Ean and Creighton at all and simply tied each other up—the latter of which, in fact, *had* actually occurred if any of them were to be believed.

After a tense silence, Morin asked, "Soldier, when you were at the scene of the battle, did you see any bodies?"

"Bodies, milord?"

"As in dead people," Rhys muttered.

"Uh, no. But there was a lot of blood."

"Blood," repeated Morin. "You're certain it was blood?"

"Well, uh…no, now that you mention it, I didn't exactly taste it, milord. We found her Majesty's men in a big clearing that was pretty well torn up from the battle. They were all tied up with nobody near." He scratched his head. "Right strange, you know, finding them there like that."

"And the blood?" prodded Morin.

"Well, like I said, it was dark and the field was muddy and wet. Whatever it was, if it wasn't blood, it was right sticky and the air sure smelled like blood—all acrid like." He looked uncertainly at the others. "Was there no blood?"

"We're less interested in the presence of blood than we are in the astonishing lack of bodies to account for it," Morin noted.

"Oh. Well, I didn't see no bodies, milord, and that's Raine's truth, but I swear something had happened there. It was just strange. The whole place felt…well, Raine's truth, milords, it felt *wrong*. All wrong. And those men—her Majesty's men—they were rightly spooked. They talked a lot about dogs, but I never saw no dogs, but I'm sure they weren't faking being scared to Shadow of them."

"One more question," Morin said. "Did you see Creighton Khelspath anywhere?"

The soldier looked baffled. "No, milord. Wasn't he taken with the prince?"

"Thank you, soldier," the king murmured. "You may return to your post."

"Actually, I'm off duty now, Sire—"

"Get out, man!" Rhys barked.

The soldier fled.

When the doors were closed again behind him, Morin leaned back in his armchair and rested his head against the cushion, closing his eyes and pressing steepled fingers against his lips. Errodan regarded him thoughtfully. He was not a bad looking young man, with blonde hair, brown eyes and a cleft chin kept cleanly shaven, though he was nowhere as handsome as her three sons and hardly older than her oldest would be now—*may Epiphany bless and keep him*—had he not been murdered in cold blood by Basi assassins. Morin was clearly sharp-witted, however, and didn't cringe from the truth. Errodan had heard his name frequently while still in Edenmar, and it was always spoken with a certain mixture of awe and fear; a good indicator that any Master of Spies was doing his job well.

"Too strange," Rhys noted while Morin deliberated. "Her Majesty's men are certain the traitors were eaten and Creighton was slain, but none of them can tell us what happened to the bodies of the men that supposedly died just inches away from them."

Bastian val Renly cleared his throat. "Milords," he offered tentatively, "is it possible...did the—the darkhounds, if it was darkhounds did this thing—did they eat the men, bones and all?"

"We haven't ascertained it was darkhounds did the deed, Lieutenant," Rhys snapped.

"I think we can be certain it wasn't her majesty's terriers, captain," Morin said with closed eyes.

"And what of poor Creighton?" Bastian went on. "Epiphany preserve us—we're honor-bound to send word to the boy's father if he is truly dead, but we'd be fools to tell one of the most powerful nobles in Agasan that his son was slain by a *Shade*, of all bloody things, and then have no body to account for it!"

Gydryn knuckled his forehead looking pained. "Where is Creighton's body?" he looked to his men with hardened resolve. "I will not believe the boy dead without seeing him lying before me."

Errodan was immensely grateful to hear those words. Teams of soldiers were already scouring the kingdom for Ean—*my dear, dear boy!*—and Gydryn's determination meant more would leave in search of Creighton as well.

"We must proceed very carefully," Morin advised, finally rejoining the conversation with a statement that spoke volumes. "There is the slimmest of chances, found in the inexplicable involvement of a man named as a Shade, that the prince's capture did not go off as planned. If that is true, then there might still be a way to turn this catastrophe into a coup of our own."

Errodan feared the result if they couldn't turn events to their favor. They'd invited dignitaries from seven kingdoms—Ean had personally pressed his seal to four hundred invitations—to attend a fete for a prince, but now they'd no prince to present. Few of the nobility knew just how unstable the Eagle Throne was. Beyond the people in that room, in fact, only one other might have some inkling...

Morwyk, Errodan thought scathingly at the same time that Morin said, "This has Morwyk written all over it."

"*Morwyk*," Rhys growled. He spat on the floor and ground his boot over the mark.

"I would be thrilled to lay this at the Duke of Morwyk's feet, Morin," Gydryn said, sounding dubious while casting Rhys an annoyed look, "but I don't see Morwyk orchestrating such an appalling scene—really, a *Shade*, Morin?"

"Not the Shade—by Epiphany's Grace, we'll find the actor who performed that stunt, I assure you, Sire. And a dozen well trained hounds 'half the size of horses' can't be easily concealed. We'll find them too, as well as the man who trained them." He tapped a finger on the arm of his chair. "No, I mean the earlier half of this plot, before the inexplicable arrival of a man pretending to be a Shade. That's when Morwyk's heretofore well-orchestrated plan fell to pieces."

Errodan was the first to concede there were few men in the kingdom with the necessary support to both learn of Ean's arrival as well as to infiltrate the Palace Guard with so many traitors. It was no secret that the Duke of Morwyk had his talons set on the Eagle Throne. He was an outspoken critic of the war in M'Nador and Dannym's support of it, and he preyed on his king's patience with seditious talk behind the thick walls of his castle in the south.

The king was well aware of Morwyk's plotting. He was rumored to be raising an army 'for defense of his own eastern holdings,' but every day they caught another of his spies in court. Gydryn had many enemies, yes, but few were as powerful as the Duke of Morwyk. It would've taken someone with Morwyk's connections—and riches—to pry information on Ean's secret landing from otherwise loyal men.

As if hearing Errodan's thoughts, Morin said, "The names of the king's men who rode to retrieve the prince, those unlucky bastards who were apparently consumed by hounds…they weren't impostors to the Guard. They were commissioned men sworn to serve you, Sire."

"What's your point, Morin?"

"My point is that this trap wasn't just thought up overnight and scraped haphazardly together. We know Morwyk has hundreds in Calgaryn—even within the palace—who are loyal to him—"

"And gains more every day this damnable war continues," Rhys grumbled.

"Rhys," murmured the king.

The captain looked belligerent but held his tongue.

"So in your estimation there were two plots to harm my son?" Errodan asked. "One that failed and one that…didn't?"

Lieutenant Bastian val Renly cleared his throat again and broached hesitantly, "Is no one willing to believe that the Shade and his darkhounds were real?"

The men in the room exchanged looks. Even Errodan found the idea implausible.

"I only ask because this isn't the first inexplicable thing that's happened recently."

"That body in the catacombs, you mean," offered the king.

Bastian nodded. "And the hole, Sire, melted through stone and earth."

The king frowned as he considered these facts in a new light. Finally he looked to Vitriam. "What say you, truthreader?"

Errodan had rather forgotten he was there. She frowned at the man—he looked for all intents and purposes as if he'd fallen asleep with his eyes open. *No doubt it takes him a minute or more just to draw breath*, she thought irritably. *The man is so ancient!*

After a long silence in which it seemed as if the man was inhaling one spoonful of air at a time, the elderly truthreader straightened in his chair and looked to the king. "I can only say, Sire," he announced at last, "that those of her majesty's men to whom we spoke believed wholeheartedly that the man they saw was a Shade, that his power to bind them was real, and that the dogs were darkhounds raised from the shadows of the night."

"So he was convincing," Morin said. "That only makes him a gifted illusionist."

"Indeed, Spymaster. Indeed."

They retreated to their own thoughts, and Errodan began to think the matter had been abandoned when Vitriam chimed in again with, "But would it not also be imprudent, Spymaster, to dismiss the possibility out of hand? Shades did once walk the realm, and darkhounds seem mythical now only because none living have ever faced them. One may go many years without seeing a redbird, or live all his life without meeting the Olyphaunt. These are not reasons to believe a thing does not exist."

Morin still looked skeptical. "Björn van Gelderan and his Shades were banished three centuries ago to T'khendar, truthreader."

"Yes, so we are all told," Vitriam agreed. "Yet it has been occasioned that the banished return, some having never known or even cared that they were banished to begin with."

Errodan frowned at him. She was convinced that sometimes the truthreader just talked utter nonsense.

Morin still seemed unconvinced, but he let the matter rest. "His highness's situation notwithstanding," he said, nodding to Vitriam, "the problem we face most immediately is one of perception. Until the prince is found, or until we receive word of him, no one can know of the true events of this night. Things must proceed as usual."

Errodan shook her head in frustration. "We cannot have a parade without a guest of honor, Morin."

"Indeed, your Majesty. We shall explain the circumstances as the tardy arrival of the *Sea Eagle*, and not call off the parade until it is obvious the ship isn't going to arrive. The captain should have received the bird with his new orders by now. He will head out to sea and not return until we send word again. With any luck, no one will have seen the *Sea Eagle* in near waters at all."

"The Festival and fair should begin as usual then," Errodan offered. "It will distract our noble guests from Ean's absence and give them other matters to gossip about."

"My men are accompanying the palace guard in their searches for the prince," Morin said. "We shall spread a number of false rumors to keep Morwyk's spies guessing. I've already dispatched a team to investigate the battleground more closely and follow up on these many disparate and confusing leads."

"We will speak of this to no one," Errodan ordered. "As far as any of us know, the Prince's ship is merely late."

Thus agreed, everyone looked to the king.

"One week," Gydryn told Morin d'Hain. "You have one week to find my son." He had no need of finishing the sentence, for they all knew the conclusion that followed.

Or the val Lorian reign may soon be at an end.

EIGHT

'Our faults are etched in stone for the ages, our qualities writ in water.'

– The Immortal Bard, Drake DiMatteo

Alyneri placed the teacup of brewing herbs into the older woman's hands with a concerned look. "Are you certain this is all I can do to help you, Lady Astor?"

"What ails me, my dear, isn't anything you can fix with herbs and tea," the dowager Countess of Astor returned, calmly shaking her grey-streaked coiffure. She settled the teacup in her lap alongside a napping Shinti-Hansa, whose black nose barely peeped from its mane of golden fur. The dog sneezed in its sleep, and Lady Astor spared a hand to scratch its head, adding, "Nor would I wish it. Sixty turns of the seasons is long enough life for any woman. I have given my lord husband four sons and seen them all reared. What more can I hope to do?"

To travel! To see the world! Alyneri thought as she straightened, but she dared not speak such, not in current company. Ten sets of feminine eyes looked on as she tended to the Countess that morning, and though their gazes seemed placid enough, she knew ill thoughts lurked beneath quiet waters.

"I must disagree, Wilamina," said Ianthe val Rothschen d'Jesune, better known as the Marchioness of Wynne. She was Veneisean by birth, *and has the high horse to prove it,* Alyneri thought resentfully.

"If a Healer such as our Alyneri offered to cure me of the ravages of age," Ianthe proclaimed, "I should take her ministrations as good medicine."

"That is because you are young, Ianthe," Wilamina returned sweetly, "and know no better."

"Not so young as our fair Alyneri," Ianthe said, turning cool blue eyes on the healer. The Marchioness was golden-haired and lovely and married to one of the wealthiest men in the kingdom; what power she lacked in title, she made up for in riches. "I have heard all the girls abuzz with Prince Ean's expected return this afternoon. Will you be attending the parade also, Duchess, to put your favor in with the rest of the hopefuls?"

It was a slight, and everyone knew it. Lady Astor dropped her gaze to her tea, but the Marchioness's eyes bored into Alyneri like blue coals ablaze with spite.

"I do not think so, Lady Wynne," Alyneri replied, wishing she had the same sort of ill-disposed humor that she might come up with comments as artfully hurtful as the Marchioness. "I was betrothed to one prince already, after all. Whoever could wish for such a thing twice?"

"But was not Ean val Lorian your childhood sweetheart?" Ianthe pressed. "I would think you excited to welcome him home now that you are free of your other… obligations."

"That is a difference between us, Lady Wynne," Alyneri returned evenly, though it took a great force of will not to leap at the shrewish woman and claw out her eyes. She turned back to Lady Astor. "If you will allow me to do nothing else to help you,

Lady Astor, I will have more tea sent to your apartments. It will assist with the pain in your knees, at least."

"That would be most kind of you, Duchess," Lady Astor murmured without looking at her.

"Can you really cure old age, your Grace?" This came from the young Lisandre val Mallonwey, who could not herself be older than Tanis. Alyneri knew her to be a gentle soul among these serpents, and feared she would not remain long untainted by their poisoned tongues. She wondered why Lisandre wasn't with her elder sister Katerine, who was being courted by the prince's blood-brother and knew better than to break her fast with this crowd.

"No, Lisandre," Alyneri answered with a smile. "A Healer's craft limits her to what the body itself can accomplish. I merely help it to help itself, to speed the process, if you will."

"But there are those who do not age, are there not, Duchess?" This from the Contessa di Remy, herself a citizen of the Agasi Empire and whose husband was aide to the Agasi Ambassador.

Alyneri nodded. "There is something known as the Pattern of Life, which is said to slow the aging process, but I am told that its working is quite painful and not to be undertaken by the faint of heart."

"Only the young wish for immortality," Lady Astor pointed out. "The old know better."

"The old don't like being old, so they hope to die quickly and get it over with," Ianthe observed imperially. "I would work the Pattern of Life and live forever."

"That's because you are young and stupid, Ianthe," Lady Astor snapped, "and know no better."

"It seems so complicated," Lisandre said with a sigh.

"Surely you understate your talents, Alyneri," Ianthe remarked, boldly calling her by name though they were neither peers nor friends, and Alyneri clearly outranked her as a duchess of the Court. "I myself have seen Veneisean Healers do miraculous things."

"Oh, pray tell me, Marchioness," Lisandre said happily. "I do so enjoy hearing of miracles."

Ianthe smoothed her swirling coiffure of golden curls, not a hair of which was out of place, and answered Lisandre as her pale blue eyes regarded Alyneri with barely veiled malignity, "My cousin, the famed Healer Sandrine du Préc, while traveling the jungles of Bemoth, once healed a man of the bite of the Valdére viper. The doomed man was perilously close to death when he arrived at my cousin's tent, but she laid hands upon him and commanded his soul back from the clutches of Shadow. He walked away, wholly healed."

"Your cousin must surely be Maker-blessed to work such miracles," Lisandre murmured, awestruck.

Alyneri was unimpressed. "I have heard of your cousin," she said. "She is an ingenious wielder."

Ianthe sucked in her breath with an affronted hiss.

Indeed, at this mention, the eyes of every lady and lady-in-waiting lifted from their own affairs and settled upon Alyneri instead. Well what of it? They despised her anyway. "It is no secret that Sandrine du Préc studied at Agasan's Sormitáge," Alyneri pointed out. "To many, being a wielder is not a crime."

Ianthe didn't miss a beat in retaliating. "If the name be such a blessing, Duchess pray tell us why you haven't gone to study at the famous Adept university? Oh, now I do recall: His Majesty needs you *here* to personally attend the royal family. It must be then that no other healer in the kingdom has your skill."

Lisandre chittered uncomfortably, "Surely her Grace just makes a jest, Marchioness. The Prophet says it's the Maker's divine breath that infuses his devoted Healers with the ability to mend the sick and injured, and that wielders work the Shadow-light, a dark and deadly power that poisons them against the Maker's brightness."

Alyneri turned to her in wonder, so startled to hear the words from her mouth that the Marchioness was momentarily forgotten. "Why are you quoting the Book of Bethamin, Lisandre? How did you come to read banned literature?"

An uncomfortable silence followed, with the young girl looking frightened and the others uncharacteristically holding their tongues. Finally, Ianthe replied, "The truth is, my dear Duchess, there are some in our kingdom who see beyond the decrepit religion of a bygone era and have embraced the Prophet's revolutionary teachings." She gave Alyneri a poisonous smile. "Morwyk is a visionary."

"Morwyk," Alyneri repeated darkly, the name sounding a curse on her lips.

"Take care, your Grace," murmured the Contessa di Remy. "Your tone is somewhat lacking for respect and belies your thoughts."

"No, no, Contessa," Ianthe murmured while glaring daggers at Alyneri. "It is no crime to speak one's mind in our society—we are not the Empire, thank Epiphany. Do go on, my dear," she said. "Tell us all about what you think of our kingdom's most powerful duke. No doubt you have little fear of repercussion, being such a *close, personal* friend of his Majesty."

That time Ianthe had really crossed the line—even her gaggle of hens dropped their eyes to their own affairs rather than seem complicit in a slight against their king. Alyneri's expression darkened, and she opened her mouth to respond in defense of the king's honor as much as her own, when aid came from a surprising source. "Alyneri d'Giverny," said a voice from a sunlit corner near the windows, "Duchess of Aracine, is a peer of the Court, and as such her opinions are of value to their Majesties."

All eyes turned to behold the strikingly exotic form of Ysolde Remalkhen, the Queen's Companion, herself an Avataren Fire Princess from the Fourth Line of Kings, and royal to the core.

Alyneri gave her an immensely grateful look.

Ysolde stood. She was tall, lithe and graceful, and her dark eyes revealed barely a line though all knew her to be nearing fifty name days. She wore a slim desert gown of tangerine silk that veritably glowed against her amber skin, and her long raven hair was captured in a net of firestones at the crown. She spoke with the unmistakable accent of Avatar. The other ladies dropped their eyes and wisely kept their peace. "It is well known that her Majesty is also quite interested in the study of Patterning," Ysolde informed the room, knowing ears were attuned to her every word.

Lisandre, innocent that she was, braved, "But my lady, the Prophet Bethamin teaches that Patterning defies the Maker's will. It seeks to escape the binding laws of our world, sacrosanct rules that should be obeyed, not evaded or…or defiled with foul magical workings."

Ysolde turned her calm gaze upon the girl. "You have learned well of the Prophet's teachings. No doubt you will make a devoted follower." As Lisandre beamed from the compliment, Ysolde walked toward Alyneri with the silent grace of wind flowing across the desert sands, saying as she went, "I go now to break my fast with the Queen."

All the women rose and curtsied, and Alyneri escaped behind Ysolde.

In the hall, Ysolde stopped Alyneri with a finger to her lips. Conversation drifted out from within the room.

"…make an enemy of the girl, Ianthe," Lady Astor was saying. "She is young, but she has the King's favor—"

"And apparently the Queen's as well," added the Contessa di Remy.

"I cannot abide her posturing!" Ianthe snapped. "She mopes about like a widow, Wilamina, but she was only *betrothed* to the val Lorian boy. There was certainly no marriage."

"Still, you needn't have insulted her so."

"She is far above herself if she thinks us equals," Ianthe returned in a spiteful hiss. "She has a title only in respect for her family's service as Healers to the crown. It's not as if she's in line for the throne. Besides, *look* at her, Wilamina. Have you ever seen such a mongrel of an offspring? That pale hair and those strange eyes and her skin as tanned as a camp whore's?"

"She did have on a truly drab sort of dress," Lisandre observed, sounding puzzled by the matter.

The Contessa di Remy could be heard to say then, "I am told her father was a Nadori prince—a cousin to Radov, and very powerful before his death."

"Nadori blood," Ianthe veritably snarled, "is inferior in the extreme."

"I vow, she does act queer," the Contessa admitted. "Has she no ladies-in-waiting at all?"

"She has palace staff assigned to her," Lady Astor reported, "but you're right, Fiona," she told the Contessa. "Tis high time the *Lady* Alyneri started acting the part if she intends to think herself one of us. She is no longer a girl of thirteen to run about with her skirts above her ankles."

"It is utterly disgraceful the way she tromps off wherever she pleases," Ianthe agreed, "neither with ladies nor a suitable chaperone. I've seen her riding alone into the city—even in the countryside!"

"Or just taking the truthreader boy along with her," Lady Astor noted. "Tis unseemly. People will think them lovers, and him just a youth of ten and four."

"Shameful, *shameful*!" the Contessa clucked. "In the Empire, such activities would never be condoned."

"She should've been married off long ago," Ianthe muttered, "preferably to a man who knows how to take a strong hand to a woman who doesn't follow the Cardinal Virtues and worship properly in the Five Temples. A swift paddling or two in Tregarion's Temple of Propriety would no doubt teach the *Duchess* Alyneri d'Giverny of her place."

Conversation drifted to Prince Ean then, and discussion of how soon it would be appropriate to congregate upon the Promenade for his arrival parade.

Outside the room, Alyneri dropped her eyes, unable even to look at Ysolde. "I want to thank you, my lady," she whispered. "My true feelings betray me when I am least prepared for them."

Ysolde placed a finger beneath Alyneri's chin to lift and capture her eyes with her own. "Daughters of the Sand must help one another."

Alyneri was startled by the compliment. "But, your Highness—"

Ysolde pressed a finger across her mouth. "Your father was a Nadori prince and a friend to Avatar—heed not the opinions voiced by the jealous, for their minds are poisoned against you. You are descended from royalty, Alyneri d'Giverny. Why else would her Majesty have allowed the betrothal to her treasured middle son?"

Alyneri was speechless.

The Queen's Companion hooked her arm through Alyneri's and walked them down the hall. "Too long have you been alone in this unfriendly court. You have neither companion nor mentor here to aid in your upbringing, am I right?" Alyneri nodded. "Yet you have survived as best you were able. Daughters of the Sand are strong. Dare not be shamed by your heritage." She paused and ran a hand gently across Alyneri's hair, touching a finger to her cheek, and two beneath her chin. "Wear it proudly."

With those words of admonishment, the Queen's Companion kissed her upon the forehead. Then she departed.

Alyneri leaned back against the wall and watched Ysolde retreating down the marble-sheathed hallway. There was something truly exotic in her movement, something elemental; she walked as rising flames, as a breeze caresses the fields of wheat. Alyneri never imagined finding a champion among the Queen's entourage, and especially not one so powerful as the Princess Ysolde Remalkhen.

She took a deep breath and pushed off the wall with her shoulders, steeling herself against their hurtful tongues. Ianthe's yowl was barbed, but she had no claws to speak of. No, she was only angry that she'd allowed Ianthe to see that her barbs actually stung. And yet...

Then what do you fear?

Captivity, she knew at once, remembering the repulsion she'd felt at Lady Astor's words. *The captivity of a Lady's life, tied to a man or a bit of land, with no future or purpose save the breeding of fine sons.* It seemed a cruel fate for anyone, but especially for a young woman with a sense of adventure and a burning desire to see the world. Her own mother had traveled widely in her youth and studied with some of the realm's most accomplished Healers. It was on one such expedition that the Lady Melisande met Alyneri's father, Prince Jair, and had fallen madly in love. Alyneri adored the story, and as a girl she'd hoped to live a similar romance.

Strangely, as if knowing her to be a receptive soul, Fortune's daughter Love found Alyneri at a young age; but Alyneri's hopes for love each time had ended in tragedy and heartbreak. Now she prayed never to be stricken with the malady of love again.

Putting on her most serene of faces and leaving all thoughts of spiteful women and lost loves behind, Alyneri marched down the hall with a purposeful stride. She couldn't travel to Agasan to study, perhaps, but she could at least take a carriage to her country villa, and the day wasn't getting any younger. She meant to be away long before Prince Ean's parade began, and not just because of the delays it would cause at the gates. *No*, she admitted, she would rather spend a week enduring Ianthe's vicious lashings than come face to face with Prince Ean val Lorian.

NINE

'True friends are a sure refuge.'

– Aristotle of Cyrene, circa 101aF

Tanis yawned prodigiously as he walked down the Promenade, wishing he'd gotten a little more sleep and a lot more breakfast. The plum and apple turnovers he'd snared from the bakery, although yummy and hot from the ovens, had barely stayed with him to the First Circle—that inner wall separating palace from outbuildings—and now his stomach was growling again.

The Promenade was crowded with workers finishing last preparations for Prince Ean's parade. Some were raising banners on high poles, while others hung silk streamers or mounted torches that Tanis knew would flare with vividly colored powders as Prince Ean passed. Already there was a growing congregation of doe-eyed females arriving and milling about, although never straying far from their typically stern-faced matrons.

Rather than fight the rising throngs, Tanis detoured off the main and followed a cobbled road through the back lots, past the barracks and storehouses and grain silos. It was there that he happened upon his best friend Tad among a gathering of Duke val Mallonwey's men.

Tanis found the young heir to Towermount outside one of the storage silos overseeing the packing of grain, flour, and other staples for the trip back home. Tad was a handsome youth, with a shock of light brown hair falling over brown eyes, a pointed nose, and a toothy sort of grin. Only this morning he seemed less than his ebullient self.

"Oh, hullo, Tanis," Tad said when the lad tapped him upon the shoulder. Tad was slouched upon a barrel watching the lines of men passing sack after sack out of the storage cellar, hand to hand down the line, until they piled them into a wagon. Tad held out a hand to the line of men. "As if they can't manage this themselves," he grumbled. "I could be doing something useful like sitting in on father's strategy meetings with the King—or at least watching Prince Ean's parade with Killian and the others! But no, my Da has to send me off to count sacks of flour."

Tanis slipped onto the barrel beside Tad. "The soldiers have to eat," he pointed out.

"It's demeaning, Tanis," Tad complained. "I'm sixteen, for Epiphany's sake. Whenever will I have the chance again to study real war tactics? This is the opportunity of a lifetime!"

Tanis knew his friend hoped to emulate his father and become a great war commander. "There's always the Akkad," he suggested helpfully.

Tad scowled at him. "You can't run off to serve in the Akkad and hope to come back to the kingdom in good standing, Tanis," he grumbled. "Not that I haven't thought of it before—Raine's truth, we all have, I expect. I might win fame and fortune fighting for one of the Sheiks, or even might be lucky enough to serve the

Emir himself, but then what? My da would never accept me again, having gone to fight for the enemy. Besides," he added glumly, "who'd want to convert and worship their desert gods? *Azerjaiman*. What kind of a name is that? Can you hear yourself praying, 'Azerjaiman preserve us!'" Tad broke into a contemplative smile as he pried at a broken shard on the barrel. "Will you be going to the parade, at least?"

Tanis sighed. "No. Her Grace scheduled a trip to the country."

"Today of all days, why?"

Tanis shrugged. "I didn't ask. It's better not to ask, really. Infinitely better. Anyway, this morning she just left me a note."

"Shade and darkness, Tanis," Tad grumbled. "I'd have thought at least *one* of us would be there to see Prince Ean come home. Epiphany's Grace you'll be emancipated soon. Then his Majesty can take you on as a commissioned Adept, and you'll be able to watch the parades whenever you want."

Tanis didn't think being an emancipated truthreader was quite so liberating as Tad imagined, for rarely did a commission to the royal court give one *more* free time. "The King employs two truthreaders already," he responded. "He may have no need of me." The funny thing was, Tanis really hoped he wouldn't. He knew very well of her Grace's upset with not being allowed to travel or study abroad, and Tanis also hoped to one day study at the Sormitáge.

Not that it was entirely fair to blame the king. Fewer Adepts seemed to be born every year, and those few discovered among the populace were immediately considered the property of their monarch. Tanis, like many others, worried the Adept race was dying. Malachai ap'Kalien's genocidal war had wiped out a huge portion of the population, and in three centuries it still hadn't recovered—*at least not in Dannym, anyway*, Tanis mused.

The kingdom still had a fair number of Adept Healers in the service of the crown, but his Majesty had sent most of them to the war as a show of support for his ally, Prince Radov. A lot of people were angry about that—Raine's truth, they were angry about sending sons and husbands to fight at all, especially in someone else's battle—and there was a lot of discontented talk in court on the subject.

The upside of all this—and Tanis always looked for the upside—was that a trained Adept had a lot of options open to him. That is, if he could escape the service of his king.

While he was pondering where he might want to serve instead, Tanis watched a host of soldiers emerge ahorse from the stable yard and canter off toward the gate. *Must be headed to meet Prince Ean*, he decided, though there was nothing jovial in their expressions as they rushed past.

"Commission or no, I hear you're doing well for yourself already," Tad noted after a moment, casting Tanis a grin.

Tanis turned him a puzzled look. "What do you mean?"

"Called into the counsel of the King's Own Guard is what," Tad said, shifting on the barrel with sudden interest. "What did the dead man really look like, Tanis? Was he as ashen as they say?"

Tanis grimaced. "Fairly." He didn't bother asking how Tad found out about the dead man, whose very existence was supposed to be a state secret; Tad always seemed at the forefront of the latest gossip.

"I wonder who he was? A spy most likely, but on whom was he spying?" and he shot Tanis a conspiratorial look.

"He didn't seem a spy," Tanis muttered. His mind was only half on the conversation now, for he'd spotted two men just then exiting a coach that had pulled into the yard, ostensibly to avoid the traffic on the Promenade, and there was something about one of them...

"I'll bet it was that Anke van den Berg," Tad said. He turned to Tanis and inquired juicily, "You don't think they were having an affair, do you? The dead spy and the Ambassador to Agasan?" Tad's eyes glittered as he whispered, "Word is Anke killed her last husband by drowning him in his own bathtub. They say she just stood there smiling as he struggled. I wonder what she did to this poor chap?" Tad's imagination was already off and running. "Must've been poison, I would think. Those Agasi are famous for their poison—and their wild magic. Could it have been magic, Tanis?"

"Magic?" Tanis murmured, preoccupied. "Oh, yes. Her Grace said it was certainly magic."

"That proves it then!" Tad sounded triumphant. "It must've been Anke. Who else around here knows anything at all of Patterning?"

Had Tanis been paying attention, he would've told Tad that Anke van den Berg wasn't a wielder and likely knew very little of Patterning. Instead, he watched as the two men passed in front of them. Tanis wondered what it was about the second nobleman that snared his attention. It wasn't the manner of his walk, or his slim build; nor was it his brown hair or his chestnut cloak, which was trimmed in suede and stitched along the hem with an intricate design of golden boxes. No, there was something else about him that Tanis couldn't quite put his finger on...an odd feeling of recollection. As if Tanis should recognize the man, though he was certain they'd never met.

The lad watched as the two men halted long enough for the slightly broader of the two to tend to his bootlace, which had come undone. In that brief moment, the second man's gaze came to rest on Tanis, and the lad started with an intake of breath.

Then the moment was gone. The broader man made a cheerful comment about poorly made boots not holding up to the challenge and they headed off again toward the First Circle.

"That's funny," Tad commented. He, too, had noticed the pair.

"What's funny?"

"That man looked awfully familiar—the slim one. Did you see him?"

Tanis was tingling from head to toe. "Yeah," he murmured, startled and excited and deeply thrilled all at once. "Did you?"

Tad frowned at him and turned away in mild disgust. He began gazing longingly toward the Promenade, which was demarked by a long line of towering elms.

Tanis watched the endless stream of sacks being passed along and tried to calm his fluttering heart, for he knew the man now.

The Vestal Raine D'Lacourte! It was a thrill beyond measure to think of meeting so famous a personage. "Tad," Tanis muttered. He elbowed his friend to get his attention. "*Tad.*"

"What?" Tad grumbled.

"Tad, did you see who that man was?"

Tad gave him a strange look. "I said he looked familiar is all."

"He looks familiar because he's one of the most famous men to ever walk the realm!" Tanis could barely contain his excitement.

Tad seemed taken aback. "Really? Who was he then? A bard?"

Tanis drew himself up, as if proud to announce the name. "The Fourth Vestal, Raine D'Lacourte."

Tad barked a laugh so loud he drew looks from his father's men. More quietly, he said, "Tanis, be serious!"

"I am! Didn't you see his eyes? They were colorless, just like mine."

"So he's a truthreader. So what? That doesn't make him the Fourth Vestal."

Tanis gripped his arm. "I'm telling you, he *is*."

"Don't be absurd, Tanis," Tad scoffed, pushing Tanis's hand off his arm while casting him an odd look. "Why in Tiern'aval would any of the Vestals be coming to Calgaryn Palace?"

Tanis retreated to his thoughts, but he wasn't convinced. *He is the Vestal. He must be!*

Tad was meanwhile gazing curiously at him. Abruptly he grabbed Tanis's head and began prying at his right eyelid. "Did you take one of your lady's powders?" he accused while peering intently into one colorless eye. "What's wrong with you today?"

Tanis shoved him off and sat there feeling disgruntled. He didn't care what Tad said. He had that feeling again, the one that always heralded things to come.

In the case of that morning, however, it was his lady who came, and she looked none too thrilled as she marched up with long skirts in hand. "Tanis, why in Tiern'aval weren't you waiting for me at the South Gate?"

Tad and Tanis quickly jumped to their feet, and Tad bowed slightly with a cheerful, 'Morning, your Grace,' while Tanis gazed fretfully at her and rubbed absently at one eye.

"You're not staying for the parade then, your Grace?" Tad asked with a cheeky sort of grin.

Alyneri settled him a suspicious look. Tanis often wondered if she didn't have a little truthreader's talent in addition to her own, for she certainly seemed to know when a boy was up to no good. "Why no, Lord Towermount."

"You mean you don't want to see Prince Ean?" Tad inquired innocently.

"Sadly, the sick do not choose the days in which they need my ministrations," she answered, which of course was not an answer at all.

"So you're excited to see Prince Ean then?" Tad pressed.

Tanis knew Tad's mind, but he didn't think it would work, this trying to catch her Grace in a question she didn't want to answer truthfully so that Tanis could tell she was lying. Even so, there were plenty of ways to avoid telling a lie, and no one knew that better than a truthreader.

"Excited is not the word I would've chosen," Alyneri replied impatiently.

"Really? What word would you've chosen, your Grace?"

"Impertinent," Alyneri replied tartly, "in description of you, Tad val Mallonwey. Now, if you will excuse us, our carriage is waiting."

Tad bowed a grinning surrender. "And a good day to you also, Duchess."

Alyneri cast him a withering look as she retreated with Tanis in tow.

When they were well away, Alyneri said, "What was that all about, Tanis?"

"What do you mean, your Grace?" the lad asked with his most innocent of looks.

She gave him a chiding glare. "What prevailed upon your friend to inquire so doggedly about my interest in Ean val Lorian?"

"I really couldn't say," Tanis answered. He turned to her directly and held her gaze, a particular truthreader's skill he'd been practicing. "I didn't know you had an interest in Prince Ean."

"I…well, I—" Alyneri was no more immune to a truthreader's compelling voice than anyone else, but she was quite impervious to Tanis. She overcame the slight compulsion in his tone, tossed her chin high and replied indignantly, "I have no undue interest in Ean val Lorian whatsoever."

"Well then," Tanis said equitably.

Alyneri shot him a fiery look. For all she was four years his senior, he was quickly learning his craft, and it was evident that she'd noticed it and found the situation displeasing.

"Have you heard anything more on the man we found last night, your Grace?" Tanis asked, steering the conversation away from a discordant head.

"No. The evening was an entire waste. Would that I could bill the Lord Captain for my hours of lost sleep."

Tanis noticed then that she wore the same plain dress she'd had on the night before, and he finally connected its meaning. "Are we going to see Farshideh then?"

She nodded. "I would've left last night if the captain had not detoured me."

Tanis gave her an injured look. "You would've gone without me?"

"Don't take it so personally, Tanis. I couldn't find you anywhere."

Because I was in the gardens doing your business! Tanis thought with teeth clenched, but he knew better than to lay blame upon her Grace for what was really his own failing.

"Anyway, there is little I can do for Farshideh, I fear." She exhaled a sorrowful sigh and shook her head. "Only Patterning might save her life—my mother could no doubt have done the working—but I…" and here she bit back vengeful words and finished instead, "Well, you know I have not trained in the Art."

She didn't need to say that King Gydryn had forbidden her to attend the Sormitáge, for Tanis knew it as well as anyone. He said he couldn't spare her, but Tanis knew that her Grace thought the king was scared of losing her, too. So much had changed since Alyneri's mother, Lady Melisande, died; since the Queen stormed off to the Shoring Isles spouting vitriolic threats with her youngest son in tow.

So much had changed.

The carriage was waiting for them at the South Gate. Tanis climbed in behind his lady silently longing to remain, Farshideh notwithstanding; what with Prince Ean's imminent arrival, the beginning of Festival, and the mysterious but exciting appearance of the Vestal Raine D'Lacourte, Calgaryn Palace seemed an utterly thrilling place to be just then.

Their leave-taking was delayed only moments more by the exodus of another great number of mounted soldiers storming through the gates. Tanis stuck his head out of the coach's window to watch them pass. *That's twice now I've seen soldiers leaving under a dark cloud of fury.* "Where do you think they're going, all those men?" he murmured.

"Probably to the harbor to receive Prince Ean," Alyneri muttered. She was rummaging through her traveling bag and not paying attention.

Tanis frowned after them. "If they're going to the harbor," he said, "they're sure headed the wrong way."

"I've heard enough of Ean val Lorian for one morning, Tanis," Alyneri complained. "Do come back inside."

Tanis pulled his head in and closed the window, but he couldn't help wondering why he felt so certain that something was wrong.

The drive to his lady's country estate was long, and Tanis napped while Alyneri made notes in one of her little suede-bound books. It was well past midday when they turned into the drive, wherein Tanis's stomach started growling fiercely enough to wake him. He was therefore pleasantly surprised when they exited before the steps to find the staff in line and the cook—a mostly pleasant woman who pinched his cheeks but always let him steal from her kitchen—handed him a warm bundle with a wink and a pinch.

Alyneri's Seneschal, Farshideh, stood atop the steps wearing her warm, dark-eyed smile, but even Tanis could see that her health was failing. Her iron-grey hair was obviously thinning, and her dark complexion looked pallid. She walked with support of a staff, and her back was alarmingly stooped such that she could no longer straighten to her full height.

Alyneri was shocked at her deterioration. "Farshideh!" she exclaimed and rushed up the steps. "What are you doing walking about in this condition!"

"Is that any way to greet your old nursemaid?" Farshideh chided.

Looking duly contrite, Alyneri dutifully embraced her with a kiss on both cheeks, followed by Tanis in the same manner. Then, pressing hands together before their hearts, all three bowed to one another.

"Much better," Farshideh said, smiling then. "*Khosh Amadid!*"

Thus welcomed, Farshideh dismissed the staff back to their posts and turned inside, with Alyneri holding her arm. "I see you wore my favorite dress," she remarked in her deeply resonant voice that Tanis so loved, her words drenched by the heavy accent of the desert province of Kandori where she was from. Tanis had thought to learn that accent once, to pretend himself a Sheik, but Farshideh had only laughed and explained that to effectively learn the accent, one must learn the language, and the complicated tongue had been well beyond Tanis's skill. Her Grace spoke the language well, however, having learned from her father in her youth.

"Farshideh, please, will you let me escort you to bed now?" Alyneri pleaded.

"Lying around in bed all day won't straighten my back, *soraya*," she returned, using her name for Alyneri, which meant princess. "I spent enough years assisting your mother to know that much, and tea is no more a cure for what ails me than wine will mend a broken heart."

Alyneri sighed. "I know, but—"

"But nothing. We have an understanding, you and I, do we not?" and her voice was firm.

Alyneri heaved another regretful sigh. "Yes, Farshideh."

"*Khoob*, that is well for the sun."

Tanis found himself smiling at the familiar expression, which made no sense whatsoever translated into the Common Tongue. Farshideh was full of such phrases. Another one he liked was, 'Only the wind knows the truth in the water.' He had no idea what it meant, but it sounded wise. He'd tried using it with Tad once, but his friend had only insisted he was taking his lady's powders. Maybe if he'd spoken it in the desert tongue instead…

"Tanis, *khortdad*," Farshideh said, using her pet name for him, which he knew meant 'perfection' and which always embarrassed him in the knowing, "run along to see Grettel Hibbert in the kitchen. She has something prepared for your stomach."

"*Mamnoon*, Farshideh," Tanis thanked her, pressing hands together and bowing.

"*Khahesh mikonam, khortdad*," she replied with an approving smile.

Tanis darted off, for he'd already consumed the two mulberry tarts Mistress Hibbert had given him upon arrival, and they'd barely taken the edge off his hunger.

Alyneri and Farshideh settled into chairs beside the fire in the Seneschal's office. The autumn day was unseasonably warm, but Farshideh too often was touched with chill lately, so Alyneri stoically endured the fire's stifling heat.

It pained her no end to see her friend in such a state. Farshideh had served her mother and her grandmother before, and she'd been as much a mother to Alyneri growing up as the Lady Melisande. Alyneri knew the pestilence which ate away at her dear friend, making her weaker every day, and she knew also that while she herself hadn't the knowledge to heal Farshideh, others might. But Farshideh wouldn't hear of it.

'Azerjaiman draws our breath to him when he wills,' she always told Alyneri whenever she brought up the matter, *'and Naiadithine claims our waters. Huhktu takes our bones, and Baharan our bodies, and our spirits soar free with Inithiya. Death is a necessary part of life, soraya.'*

Well settled into her armchair with a blanket across her legs, Farshideh reached for a heavy ledger which she opened on her lap. "Now then," she said, one finger following a line of figures that was the income for Alyneri's estate, "we shall talk the beans and the donkeys."

Alyneri sighed and nodded, but as Farshideh went over Alyneri's financial incomes and expenditures, reciting with uncanny detail every transaction with farmer, fisherman or hedge lord, Alyneri could think of nothing except her fears. Even more than she feared the loss of her friend—which she feared greatly—Alyneri also feared that with Farshideh gone, there would be no one—*no one*—left alive who loved her.

TEN

'Be wary of deep water and dogs that do not bark.'

– An old pirate saying

E**rrodan stood** with her back pressed stiffly against the plastered walls of the king's Privy Chamber, arms crossed, fingers thrumming steadily. She awaited news—any news of her son—from the many patrols Gydryn had dispatched earlier that morning, but thus far none had returned. The pacing had helped calm her nerves somewhat, but after the fifth or so annoyed glance from Gydryn, she'd forced herself to stand in one place.

Across the room, thirteen powerful men sat around a long rowan table carved in the image of an eagle. Gydryn slouched in a throne-sized armchair at the head of this table, fingers clasped across his broad chest, raven hair swept regally back from his high brow. He had more silver in his hair than when she left him five years ago, and deeper lines etching his eyes, but he'd lost not a shade of his imposing demeanor.

She had no place being there, a mere woman among such a council of war, but this was where the king's men would come with their report, and she'd be damned if she waited anywhere else. She marveled her husband had the mind for politics with his last living son kidnapped, but as Gydryn had chided her when she mentioned as much, the Emir wasn't likely to cease hostilities against M'Nador simply because a prince went missing.

Round the table from the king, Dannym's leadership was debating a pressing conflict, the essence of which was contained in the statement uttered just then by Gareth val Mallonwey, Duke of Towermount and General of the West: "If the damnable letter isn't a hoax, then we must act!"

"Again, I must demur, your Grace." This from Morin d'Hain, who seemed naught but a fair-haired youth amid this gathering of weathered men. "The very idea that Emir Abdul-Basir would write such a letter is unthinkable. Abdul-Basir is a pious man. This war is his god's missive—his mission. He would not surrender any sooner than he would denounce the Wind God Azerjaiman."

Gareth rounded on him like a bear to an offending coyote. "Wind gods, desert gods, Azerjai-*whatever* in Epiphany's name their damnable deities are called—it's all we've heard out of you, man! Have you *nothing* of consequence to offer this table?"

"Something concrete would be helpful," Loran val Whitney, Duke of Marion and General of the East, also muttered in his unmistakable Highland lilt.

"My lords," d'Hain returned, unflustered by their criticism, "the world of shadows rarely offers anything of substance, though much is of *consequence*, if only one is of a mind to assemble the pieces in their proper order."

"How dare you insinuate I am lack-witted, d'Hain!" Gareth snarled. He was a big man, completely bald and generally fierce, with a warrior's build and all the patience of a grizzly roused early from hibernation.

"It was no slight against you, Gareth," Donnal val Amrein muttered. Donnal's sad, dark eyes and sense of grave conscience could calm even Gareth's volatile temper. "Let us take a step back and summarize what we know from the reports heard today," he said to the group. "Morin admits that his people uncovered no plot of assassination—"

"Which is not to say *assuredly* that one doesn't exist," Morin qualified, earning another black glare from the Duke of Towermount.

"—and that indeed the seal upon the parchment is genuine."

"It *is* Abdul-Basir's," Morin confirmed.

"We know that our ally, Prince Radov, also received a letter requesting parley, and that his, too, was proclaimed genuine by its seal."

"Quite so," Morin admitted. "The seals were not forged—though I submit the signet could've been stolen."

"*Raine's truth,*" Gareth grumbled with his eyes pinned on the fair-haired younger man, "you're as duplicitous as that damned Basi, Abdul-Basir. 'The seal is his, but the letter's a fake,'" Gareth mimicked. "The letter's real but it's probably forged. There is no plot but there's surely a plot—what *use* are you to us, man?"

"Gareth." The king's deep contralto seemed the rumble of distant thunder alerting to a coming storm.

Errodan's pulse quickened just hearing his voice. Countless times over the past five years, her loneliness had prodded her to lament—even curse—her love for her king, yet knowing with a pale certainty that she could no more empty her heart of Gydryn val Lorian than she could recall her dead sons from the grave. Betimes she wished she might tear the offending organ from her chest rather than feel such mixed passions toward her king husband.

"Morin has provided us with the information we sought of him," the king told his general. "It is not the province of the Intelligences to solve, merely to watch, to investigate, and to report. It is then, as Morin has accurately said, upon our shoulders what to make of the facts with which we are presented."

"Few enough, those are," Gareth grumbled.

"So it may be," said the king, "yet it is what we have to work with." He looked to Morin, "Even a pious man may have motives beyond those of his god, Morin; that is, should his god's needs be fortuitously aligned with his own desires. More importantly, however, let us not affix our discussion so permanently upon the authenticity of the letter, but rather upon inspecting the peculiarity if its arrival." At this, he looked expectantly to his General of the East, Loran val Whitney, who had only just returned from the front in M'Nador. It was Loran who'd delivered the fateful letter from Emir Abdul-Basir.

Errodan drew in her breath and let it out with measured patience. *Raine's truth, it all comes in waves—Ean and Creighton missing, this damnable war, the unexpected arrival of the letter, the strange man in the tunnels…*

Loran's blue eyes scanned those assembled. Of the few who had not spoken were two of his own men, both of them unknowns to Errodan other than they looked battle-weary; two of Gydryn's lesser ministers; Morin's undersecretary; and Gareth's favorite captain. None of them would speak unless spoken to. The only who hadn't yet spoken—unsurprisingly—was Vitriam O'reith.

"He would like us to think otherwise, but Radov is stalemated," Loran advised the group. He'd changed from his customary mail and armor to attend this gathering, but as he shifted in his chair, Errodan thought he moved as if still encumbered by it. "As you've no doubt heard, Abdul-Basir has a new Mage whose demonstrated power on the Khalim Plains sent Radov's wielders scurryin' for cover. Rumor has it that this Mage is the man responsible for the beasts that now patrol the skies over the mountain passes and the Sand Sea alike."

Gareth harrumphed irritably at this, and Morin muttered as he shook his head, "Sundragons. Most unfortunate."

Loran cast him a rueful look as he continued in his highland lilt, "Sending men into any of those venues now is sendin' them to their deaths, and with nothin' gained to show for it save well-fed dragons. The loss of Raku Oasis was devastating—the stronghold was Radov's claim upon the Kutsamak. When the Basi took it, they castrated Radov's forces. Battle remains pitched between Heziz and the Qar'imali, but to what end, I'm nae sure. It's more for show and attrition than for any strategic victory."

"Radov must retake Raku!" Gareth declared.

"An' so he intends," Loran assured him, "but at what cost? While dragons rule the skies, he dares not risk an assault upon the oasis."

"Then order an archer to put an arrow into the beasts," Gareth remarked with due impatience, as if the solution was far too simple to have taken so long to implement.

Morin grunted dubiously, earning a smoldering glare from the Duke of Towermount. "Forgive my outburst, your Grace," Morin apologized. "But you must understand. Sundragons are fifth-strand creatures."

"What of it? Wildlings bleed the same as men."

"Wildlings, yes. Avieths, Fhorgs, Whisper Lords, these and many other *third*-strand races. But Sundragons are not Wildlings, Duke. They are fifth-strand—"

Gareth waved impatiently at him. "*Third*-strand, *fifth*-strand, what in the Maker's name are you talking about, man?"

Gydryn regarded his Master of Spies thoughtfully. "You speak of *elae*," he said. "The Adept power, what fuels their unusual talents."

"Indeed," Morin confirmed, and his gaze strayed to the only Adept among them, the truthreader sitting beside his king.

Vitriam met Morin's gaze with his own colorless one. "*Elae*," the Adept offered, "has five strands." He raised a wrinkled hand to the group with his open palm facing them. "You understand, this five-stranded approach is merely a means of codifying, for our own purposes, a power which in many ways we Adepts still struggle to understand." He placed palms together then and interlaced his fingers. "Each Adept is intricately, inherently, and inextricably bound to one particular aspect of *elae*, what aspect we call a strand. Each strand has its own properties and is governed by its own correlated patterns; and each Adept's talent is derived from the patterns inherent in these respective strands.

"Truthreaders, such as I, are bound to the fourth strand, Wildlings to the third, Espials to the second, and Healers to the first—that is, the patterns we work through our native talents are patterns specific to each of those aspects of *elae*. No strand is so powerful, nor so little understood, however, as the fifth." He settled hands into his lap then and fell into silence, looking for all the world as if he'd fallen asleep with this eyes open.

Errodan frowned at him. The man was like a wind-up toy, doing his dance and then petering out. If you wound him up again, he would only repeat what he'd said the first time, clarifying nothing.

Gareth looked equally irritated. "Does *any* of this have a point?"

Morin advised, "Tis a peculiar characteristic of fifth-strand creatures, like the Sundragons that have caused us such strife, that they cannot be injured save by weapons of their own devising."

Now the light of understanding dawned on Gareth. "You mean like those damnable zanthyrs."

"Just so."

Gareth's expression turned pinched. "I hate zanthyrs."

Morin continued, "We know so little about the fifth strand's characteristics because, to date, only zanthyrs are of its aspect, and as everyone knows, no one knows much at all about zanthyrs."

"But you just said Sundragons were fifth-strand," Gareth reminded him.

To which Vitriam intoned in his methodical voice, "The Sundragons were banished to the fringes of the realm centuries ago by the Vestal Alshiba Torinin."

"If we could move this discussion back from the fringes of legend and myth…" Gydryn remarked at the same time that Gareth demanded, "Then who is this Mage to recall the damnable creatures?"

After a moment's pause and a hesitant glance at his king, Loran took up his report again. "Tis obvious that to remove the Sundragons, we must eliminate the man who controls them," he said wearily. "As one can surmise, however, this endeavor poses its own set of…challenges."

"What of Veneisea?" Gareth pressed. "Where in bloody Tiern'aval is General D'Lacourte and his Maker-forsaken army?"

"Trapped on the far side of the River Cry," Loran answered. "Still."

Morin leaned back in his chair and folded hands in his lap. "There are rumors that Abdul-Basir has a Converted among his elite staff, a brilliant tactician who thinks like a Northman."

Loran shrugged. "So t'would seem."

Donnal val Amrein inquired then, "Loran, is it accurate in any way to say that our forces have the upper hand?"

Loran exhaled heavily as he shook his head. "No—assuredly not."

"Am I wrong in thinking that under current circumstances, the Akkad could hold Raku—and thereby the Kutsamak—indefinitely?"

"No. Tis Raine's truth." This time Loran sounded bitter.

Donnal glanced at his king before slowly remarking, "I believe I understand his majesty's mind, then, in asking: if for all intents and purposes the Akkad has the upper hand in this war, why is Emir Abdul-Basir requesting parley instead of demanding Radov's surrender?"

Gydryn lifted his gaze to Errodan upon this utterance, as if putting the question to her directly, and the look in his eyes made her grow cold. Her firstborn son had been murdered at just such a parley, some seven years ago now. At the time, Dannym wasn't even involved in Radov's war. The mystery of her oldest son's death still haunted her, plaguing her dreams as frequently as his loss consumed her heart.

Whyever indeed? she wondered, knowing they had good cause to suspect anything that came from Abdul-Basir.

The door opened to admit Gydryn's secretary Quinn, who walked quickly to the king's side, bent and delivered a message. Gydryn rose as Quinn withdrew and pressed palms flat upon the table. "Whatever the letter's intent, we must decide today how to respond to it. I leave that task to you, gentlemen." With that he followed Niall out of the room.

Errodan watched him go, wondering what could've pulled him from this task, only knowing it was not news of Ean. The men at the table resumed their circular debate, and Errodan, in the quiet of her turbulent thoughts, resumed her own chant, fueled by fear.

Three sons! Three sons lost!

ELEVEN

'Cephrael knows no mercy. His will is absolute.'

– D'Nofrio of Rogue, Sormitáge Scholar, circa 323aV

Balaji's banquet for Loghain was a feast suited for the Emir's palace. It took place on the highest point of the hill in a tent open on three sides to let in the cool evening breeze as much as the view. It was attended by many, but Trell met few of the others, for he was seated between Vaile and Balaji, and the youth kept him occupied with questions of his time in Duan'Bai. Throughout the meal, there were a number of toasts to Loghain, which Trell participated in by way of an upraised goblet, but otherwise, he was kept quite unaware of the conversation beyond his circle of candlelight. He couldn't help but wonder if this was Balaji's intent.

The banquet seemed to end without warning, as if the result of some clandestine signal that Trell missed, and everyone dispersed like nocturnal crawlers fleeing the light of day. Vaile was the last to leave, leaning around Trell's chair to give him a chaste kiss on the cheek and bid him goodnight, and then Trell found himself alone, still seated at the table and wondering how so many people had vanished so completely in such a short span of time.

Because he wasn't tired, and because the hills and the starry sky and the sweet-smelling breeze called to him, he decided to take a walk, naturally gravitating to the highest point in order to gain the best view.

It was there, much to his surprise, that he found Loghain. Indeed, the man startled the wits out of him when he moved suddenly, for Trell had rather thought him a misshapen rock, what with his black skin and dark clothes and his golden eyes turned in the opposite direction.

"Nice view, isn't it," Loghain observed after first apologizing for startling Trell. He bade Trell take a seat on the boulder beside him and offered him a sip from his flagon.

Trell sat and accepted the proffered drink with his thanks, thinking it odd to find such gentility in this deadly Wildling. Trell had seen the man fight—he'd no doubt that Loghain could disarm and disembowel him faster than he could envision it—yet here he was inviting Trell to sit and drink with him on his last night in sanctuary.

"It's beautiful," Trell agreed as the liquor flamed his throat.

He joined the Whisper Lord in gazing at the starry sky, leaning forward to rest elbows on knees. Even in the desert, Trell had never seen so many stars at once or a vista so broad and endless. He spotted the constellations of Cavval's Ladle and Gorion the Archer with ease, and he couldn't be sure, but he thought he could detect the first few stars that were Adrennai's Harp, the rest of her constellation still hidden beyond the hills. The five stars of Nefdini's crown were high in the north, and he found Sepheune's Trident glittering low in the southern sky.

"Sometimes," Loghain said softly, "...sometimes, I come here to the First Lord's sa'reyth just to see the world like this. You can almost forget the troubles of these times when you're here...for a little while anyway."

Trell turned to watch Loghain, who was staring distantly out across the hills, his fierce, hooked nose and prominent chin in profile against the stars. "Do you follow the constellations?"

"Some of them. Once I could name them all. Once...long ago. They've been renamed since, and I haven't bothered to relearn them—all, that is, save one."

"Which one?"

Loghain pointed. "That one. There." Then he added darkly, "The only one that matters."

He was pointing to Cephrael's Hand. It was resting low in the northeastern sky, just above the hills.

"I'll be damned," Trell remarked, scratching his head. "The bloody thing seems to move in leaps and bounds, doesn't it? I could swear it was midlevel to the western horizon when I last saw it from the ramparts of Raku."

Loghain turned his golden eyes to Trell, and there was a look of approval there. "It does seem to move," he agreed.

Trell was frowning at the constellation. "A bevy of trouble, that one," he muttered. "Is there a race on Alorin that doesn't have a superstition or a prophecy surrounding it? But when all is said and done, it's just a bunch of stars."

"Prophecy is rarely worth its weight in coin," Loghain agreed in his quiet way. "There is an old saying that a fake fortuneteller can be tolerated, but an authentic soothsayer should be shot on sight."

Trell smiled. "Strange isn't it? People want answers from the gods, but when they get ones they don't like, they blame the messenger."

Still gazing at the constellation, Loghain sighed. "Would that Cephrael's Hand was simple superstition," he remarked.

Trell arched a brow. "Surely you don't put faith in it?"

Loghain gave him a wry look. "Tis wise not to blindly follow the blind sheep," he agreed, quoting the common adage, "...but wiser yet to see where the sheep go before dismissing them out of hand. Sometimes the blind have no need of their eyes and know better where they are going than those of us who are deceived by what is plainly in sight." All humor faded from his golden gaze. "You understand....what *everyone* sees may have been put there to be seen for a reason."

"To mislead, you mean."

"Indeed," Loghain confirmed with a heavy sigh. "In these times, 'tis wiser to trust your soul's perception, Trell of the Tides, before you trust your eyes."

The phrasing seemed all too familiar. *'You must learn to see with your three eyes,'* Istalar had told him. *'The eyes of your mind...the eyes of your heart...the eyes of your spirit...'* It was the first time Trell had remembered the holy man's admonishment since that fateful eve. Hearing the words echoed from a Wildling's mouth gave them an altogether unnatural and resounding truth.

Loghain reached into his belt pouch and removed a bit of something, a piece of which he bit off and began to chew thoughtfully.

Trell gave him a curious look.

"I have a...tempestuous stomach," the Whisper Lord confessed. "Chewing ginger root soothes it. Do you need some?" he held out the cleaned root.

Trell raised a hand. "No, thank you."

He shrugged. "Sometimes Balaji's cooking comes back to bite you in the night. He keeps ginger root in a jar on the dining table, should you have need of it later." With that, Loghain stood. "Well, I'd best be off while the night is young."

Trell got hastily to his feet. He noted then that Loghain had changed into traveling leathers as black as his skin, and he had a pack at his feet. "What, you're leaving tonight—now?"

"I prefer to travel in the dark," the Whisper Lord said, flashing the shadow of a grin, "and I have a long road to travel in a short span of time." He held out his hand to Trell in parting, and Trell took it at once. "Fare thee well, Trell of the Tides," Loghain said as he released Trell's hand. "As the First Lord bade you, take care to leave when the moon is full and not before. These are ill times, and dark workings are afoot; 'tis best that you embark upon your journey beneath the good will of Fortune's eye."

Trell broke into a rueful grin. "Somehow, I don't think I shall be allowed to leave any sooner."

Loghain laughed. He had a rich, buoyant laugh, the sort of laugh you'd expect to hear from a man with a warm heart and a generous spirit. "I hope that should we meet again, we will find each other on the same side of this great battle. You strike me as a good man, Trell of the Tides. It would grieve me to have to kill you."

Trell grinned. "Not nearly so much as it would grieve me to die."

Loghain barked another laugh, his golden eyes glittering as they regarded Trell. Then he leaned to retrieve his pack, tossed it over his shoulder, nodded a last farewell, and headed off along the crest of the hill.

As Trell watched him go, it occurred to him that he was among people who harbored great wisdom. Balaji, Vaile, Loghain…these Wildlings—if that's what they all were—did not view life in the same way as the rest of mankind. As he made his way back to the Mage's tent, Trell wondered what Loghain meant by 'this great battle.' Somehow he did not think the Wildling referred to a war between nations.

The next morning, Trell took his pack and headed off into the hills—with Balaji's blessing—to explore the surrounding mountains. He needed to know if he was well and truly recovered, and there was nothing better than a long uphill hike for determining one's level of health. Trell spent that night atop the highest ridge making long entries in his journal and watching the sun set behind distant, snow-capped peaks that could not be any part of the Kutsamak range.

Stranger and stranger…

He returned the following afternoon, reaching the complex of tents as the sun was setting again behind the valley's green hills. Trell ducked inside the tent and discovered that the sa'reyth had once again gained some new tenants. To his left, in a plush sitting room viewed through beaded curtains, two women dressed in diaphanous desert gowns sat upon a settee with knees pressed together, talking in whispers. Trell only glanced at them long enough to note that Vaile was not among them and then moved on through the curtained partition.

The next room also hosted new arrivals. In a near corner, two dark-haired men were engrossed in a game of Kings. Judging from the placement of the carved marble pieces, which were scattered across the black and white chequered game table positioned between their armchairs, they'd likely been there for a while. The slighter of the two men, who was facing Trell, could have been Balaji's older brother with his sleek, dark hair and pale golden eyes.

In the opposite corner, yet another of Balaji's raven-haired cousins sat reading a book upside down—at least it seemed upside down to Trell, who could make no sense of the strange, scrawling script on the pages open across the man's lap. The stranger's black-nailed fingertip followed vertical lines from the bottom of the right-hand corner, up a line of incomprehensible symbols until it reached the top of the page, then crossed to the bottom of the next earlier line, and so on.

Trell didn't realize he was staring until the stranger glanced up. He broke into a welcoming smile. "Ah, you must be the man Rhakar and Ramu found in the well," he said.

Rhakar and Ramu—names at last! Trell committed the names to memory. He wondered if they would be there tonight, his faceless rescuers.

"Glad to see you well and recovered," the man added in his friendly way.

They are all quite amiable, Balaji and his brothers, Trell thought, and for some reason, he was made wary by this very fact. People who could afford to be friendly to strangers usually had reason not to fear them. "I'm Trell," he said, approaching.

"Trell," repeated the stranger with an approving eye. "That is a sound naming. I am Náeb'nabdurin'náiir, but you may call me Náiir." He indicated the chair across from him with a smile of perfect teeth and leaned to remove some large books that had been resting there so Trell could be seated.

"You are related to Balaji?" Trell inquired as he moved toward the chair, noting that Náiir wore the same loose desert robes in the deepest black. He dropped his pack beside the chair and sat down. It was heavenly to sink into soft, over-stuffed leather after sleeping on hard-packed earth.

"You might say that," replied Náiir as he carefully set the books down beside his chair, one at a time.

Trell remarked, "I cannot hope to repeat Balaji's name, but I assume yours has a meaning as well?"

"Indeed," Náiir confirmed with a smile. "In our language, my name means Chaser Of The Dawn."

"And what language is that?" Trell asked. The curiosity in his tone was more than mere idle interest by then. He'd been trying to guess Balaji's race since his arrival, though it was only instinct that told him the youth and his brethren were other than human.

Náiir leaned sideways to rest an elbow upon one chair arm. "Ours is an ancient language. You would likely not have heard of it."

"Is that it written there?" Trell nodded to the book in Náiir's lap.

Náiir frowned down at the book, closed the cover on his finger to mark his page, and held up the cover for Trell to see. "This book?" he inquired.

Trell blinked and leaned closer. The cover read, *Codex & Inscriptus of the Fallen Races.* "But…" he said, taken aback, "but inside…"

Náiir opened it to the page he'd been reading and turned the pages to Trell. He could clearly make out the words in the written style of the Common tongue. Trell sat back in his chair, perplexed. "That's not the language I saw scribed there when I walked in," he insisted.

Náiir regarded him with veiled amusement. "This is one of the Mage's books," he offered helpfully, "which is another way of saying it is a magic book, and that is why it may have shown itself differently to you both times you've looked upon it." He closed the book and set it down in his lap again. Folding black-nailed fingers upon it, he noted, "It is my experience that people of magic like to own things of magic, just as they prefer to associate with other races of magic."

"Why do you think that is?"

Náiir shrugged. "It is a natural instinct, is it not, to associate with those that look the same and think the same?" He waved a hand absently as he continued, "Common realities—even common ostracism—result in common understanding and thereby a sense of community. These sa'reyths are a perfect example." He opened his hands, palms up, to the room at large. "Everyone here has no place of their own in this world. *Everyone* here has made loneliness an ally, and isolation a retreat." He settled Trell an arch look. "But surely I am not telling you anything you didn't know."

Indeed, Trell knew exactly what Náiir meant. How often had he wished for someone who shared his unique dilemma, someone who understood the anguish of a past that eludes their best efforts to remember it? How often had he sought the companionship of isolation rather than endure the torment of having his loss ground in his face by those who knew their heritage and remembered their childhood, their families, their upbringing?

Too often, was his answer. Every day for five years, in fact.

But what set the hairs to rising on Trell's arms and the back of his neck was wondering how this stranger could know these innermost thoughts—for clearly *this* was Náiir's implication.

Náiir was gazing at him neutrally, waiting for a reply. Trell held his gaze, wondering how to respond, until it occurred to him that Náiir would likely welcome any response without questioning it. "No," Trell admitted, choosing truth in the end, "I quite understand you," and Náiir acknowledged him with a nod of approval.

"Rhakar and Ramu," Trell said then, his mind jumping to a subject it had never really left. "Will they be here tonight?"

"Ramu is attending the Mage," Náiir answered, "but Rhakar is that man there," and he nodded to the man Trell had noticed playing Kings.

Trell was surprised and excited to find that one of the men responsible for his rescue was close at hand. "I should thank him," he said, and rose to do so.

Náiir propped one elbow upon the chair arm and rested chin in hand. His eyes followed Trell as he stood. "You can certainly try," he noted with quiet amusement.

Puzzled by this statement but hardly discouraged, Trell approached the two men in the opposite corner. Rhakar's raven-haired opponent lifted dark green eyes as Trell neared, but there was no friendship in his gaze. Rhakar did not look up from his assessment of the board at all, though he clearly took notice of Trell, for he muttered, "What do you want?"

His harsh manner caught Trell off guard. "I'm the man you pulled from the well," he offered in reply, thinking that perhaps Rhakar didn't recognize him.

Rhakar lifted his yellow-gold eyes from the board and leveled them on Trell.

There was no kindness in his gaze, and even less interest. He asked again, emphasizing every word, "What-Is-It-You-Want?"

"Only to thank you," Trell told him, trying not to let the man's rudeness arouse his ire. "Just to thank you for saving my life, you and Ramu."

"We didn't save your life," Rhakar muttered as if the mere mention of it was an insult. "The Mage did that. We just pulled you from the water." His eyes flicked over Trell as he added, "I didn't even get wet. You can thank Ramu for that part. If you like." He turned his attention back to his game and seemed to forget Trell altogether.

Trell glanced at Rhakar's opponent, who was watching Trell with a distinctly smug expression. There was something decidedly unnerving about the other man, something that inspired nothing if not distrust. Trell arched a brow in direct challenge, made a point of turning his back on the man, and rejoined Náiir.

The latter was suppressing a grin, but his manner was so amiable that Trell wasn't offended. He even broke into a chuckle as he retook his seat, and Náiir shared in his amusement.

"A bold attempt, Trell," Náiir complimented. "I applaud your tenacity."

Trell sat back in his chair, still smiling in bemused wonder. "I cannot say you didn't warn me," he admitted.

"Not what you expected, eh?"

Trell shook his head. "Everyone else here has...well...exceeded expectations of hospitality."

"The Mage keeps good company," Náiir agreed. His gaze flicked toward the stranger sitting with Rhakar, wherein he added as an afterthought, "That is...more often than not."

"Speaking of the Mage..." Trell broached a subject he'd been meaning to mention to Vaile when he saw her next—for Balaji had too easily evaded Trell's attempts to elicit explanation. "Loghain called the Mage something different when last we spoke. 'The First Lord,' I think he said. Do you know what he might have meant by that?"

Náiir waved a dismissive hand. "Mages go by many names to many people. That you knew he was speaking of the Mage when he named him so, this is all that matters, I should think."

"Why not answer him truthfully, Náiir?" came a familiar voice from behind Trell. He craned his neck to see Vaile standing there. "Náiir would have you believe he knows nothing of the term," Vaile told Trell, "which serves no purpose, it would seem to me, save to dangle a carrot before your eyes." She turned her emerald gaze on Náiir, looking disgusted. "You *drachwyr* and your mysteries. You are so stingy with your knowledge."

Náiir burst into laughter. "And *your* kind are any more forthcoming, Vaile?" he inquired through his mirth. "Oh, no. *That's* right," he added, pressing a forefinger across smiling lips, "only when it suits your *motives*."

Vaile gave him a black look. As if to prove him wrong, she turned to Trell and explained, "The title of 'First Lord' is an ancient one, translated from Old Alaeic, the mother language of your northern Common tongue—*ma dieul tan cyr im'avec*," she supplied, "which means something akin to 'My first and only lord, owner of my heart.' It is a title we all use for the Mage—a name he is more widely known by, actually."

Trell glanced from Vaile to Náiir, who was looking amused, and back again. "I thank you for the explanation."

Leveling a cool look at Náiir, she replied, "It was nothing."

Náiir chuckled.

Vaile came around to stand beside Trell so he might better eye her appreciatively. She wore a black silk gown of the same revealing cut and design as her green one before, yet her lithe form looked far more elegant in the black. Strange that a simple change of color could have so profound an effect, but then, women of all races were experts in his art of subtle manipulation. "You look lovely, milady," Trell complimented.

Vaile arched a brow, and her green eyes flicked to Náiir. "He thinks me a lady. I have tried to correct him, but he seems incorrigible on the matter."

Náiir was relaxing with chin in hand again. "There are worse crimes," he murmured, and winked at Trell.

Vaile grunted in a manner that sounded unconvinced. "If you are finished here with this charmer of snakes, Trell of the Tides, there is someone I should like you to meet." Trell looked to Náiir. He waved him to depart. "I hope we shall have time to speak again, my new friend Trell," Náiir said, echoing Balaji. Perhaps it was a ritual saying among their race.

Drachwyr. At least Trell had a name for them now.

He stood and looked to Náiir. "Thank you again for the warning," he said in parting.

Náiir winked, smiled. "Any time." He returned his attention to his book.

"Come Trell of the Tides." Vaile took his hand with the usual tingle at her touch, and he followed obediently.

Noting Trell's gaze as they passed the hostile pair playing Kings, Vaile arched a brow and murmured knowingly, "I take it you met Rhakar."

Trell glanced back at the man over his shoulder before following Vaile through the parting of drapes. "Not an especially hospitable fellow is he?" he muttered as they headed into another tent.

"Srívas'rhakarakéck." Vaile said the complicated name with ease. "His name means The Shadow Of The Light. He can be...difficult."

"That's one way of putting it," Trell muttered. He was just about to ask her what sort of race the *drachwyr* were when she pushed through a curtain of colorful glass beads into another tent. Trell recognized the sitting room where the two women had been seated earlier, though there was only one woman seated there now, writing in a small book.

"This is Jayachándranáptra," Vaile said, holding a hand to the woman who was carefully penning her thoughts and so far ignoring their entrance. "Her name means Rival of The Sun."

Trell thought he could see why. The woman had flame-gold hair like the burnished color of the setting sun, and it was piled atop her head and held with tiny, opal-studded pins. She wore a desert gown of tangerine silk, ornately beaded along the wide hem and embroidered with thread-of gold, and a delicate headdress that dangled tiny citrine stones across her forehead.

At last she finished her sentence and glanced up at them, wherein Trell saw that the yellow-orange stones perfectly matched her eyes. Her face was pretty in an odd sort of way, for she had a long and slightly rounded nose and almond-shaped eyes set beneath artfully arched brows. Her smile, however, was perfection; it filled her face with light. "Vaile," she greeted. She set her book and quill aside and stood to receive Trell's raven-haired companion.

"Jaya," returned Vaile.

They embraced.

Withdrawing, Jaya shifted her peculiar yellow-orange eyes to Trell with curiosity.

"Jaya, this is Trell of the Tides," Vaile introduced, holding a hand to him. Then she flashed a devilish grin and added, "Or perhaps we should call him Trell of the Well?"

Trell gave her a pained look.

"Oh, *that* one," Jaya murmured, eyeing Trell with new appreciation. "Ramu wasn't sure if you'd make it when he pulled you out of the water. He said you were quite blue." She looked him up and down with one arched brow, as if surprised that he was that color no longer. "It seems the Mage took a liking to you," she decided. "This is great luck for you, Trell of the Tides.

"Yes, my lady," Trell murmured. Everyone was telling him how lucky he was to have gained the Mage's favor. Either it was true, or a lot of people wanted him to believe it was.

Jaya offered a hand to Trell to take a chair across from her. The she took Vaile's hand and pulled her down beside her on the settee. "Did you just arrive?" Jaya asked Vaile, to which the latter nodded. "My, what a long week it has been," Jaya lamented with a shake of her bejeweled head. "I have only just returned myself. The battle intensifies, you know."

Vaile's smile vanished. "Tell me."

Jaya squeezed the other woman's hand. "We lost Abu'dhan."

"No! *When?*"

"Last night. Now Radov's army marches on the Qar'imali."

Trell knew this was terrible news, though not as terrible as if Raku itself was threatened. Still, the Qar'imali was an important stronghold that ensured the safety of the Emir's supply lines.

Vaile shook her head. "I cannot believe Abu'dhan fell. What happened?"

"A team made it past the lines beneath the protection of a glamour," she paused to purse lips as if to hold back a curse, adding in a quiet hiss, "Radov's wielders have begun to put their talents toward truly appalling uses. The team were all hunted down and slain, but not before they succeeded in poisoning the spring."

Trell felt as if a cold fist clenched around his heart. "But the well at Abu'dhan serves everyone traveling the Kairo-Lubaiyd road."

Jaya turned him a tragic look. "Just so, Trell of the Tides."

Trell worked the muscles of his jaw and tried not to think about the ramifications of a poisoned well that was a major water source for thousands. Vaile meanwhile asked, "What's happening along the Cry?"

"The Converted are still firmly ensconced in the hills. Without the bridges at Orlan and Fayle, the Veneisean army remains on the west bank. They'd need to retrace their steps all the way back to the Haden Gorge to gain the eastern side—a fully untenable step for an army of that size—knowing all the while that they would meet the same opposition once they regained their current position. The commander of the Emir's Converted is a bright man. I am told he ordered his team to destroy the bridges at Orlan and Fayle only seconds after the last of the Emir's troops had crossed the Cry, long before the Veneiseans marched from Tregarion. A gifted man, to have such vision."

Trell felt relief wash over him upon hearing that Raegus' men were holding their own. Of course Jaya had no idea that she'd just complimented him, and he wouldn't think of mentioning it.

"Surely the Veneiseans won't risk the trek back to the Haden Gorge," Vaile said. "Not this late in the season."

"Indeed not," Jaya confirmed. "Baron D'Lacourte has ordered his men to rebuild the Orlan bridge near Corinth Falls instead." She shook her head. "It is another massacre waiting to happen. What is it about these Northmen that makes them so careless in sacrificing their men? Does the gift that is life mean nothing to them?"

Neither Vaile nor Trell had an answer for her.

Jaya sighed. "Radov's wielders, Veirnan hal'Jaitar and his minions, are proving troublesome and beleaguering but pose no real threat to us, as there are none among them who can work the fifth."

"The fifth, my lady?" Trell inquired.

Jaya turned him a puzzled look. "Why, the fifth strand, of course," she supplied, as if this explained everything. Then she frowned at him.

"This is all news to me," Vaile said, regaining her attention. "The last I heard, the battle was stalemated."

Jaya grunted. "At the Sand Sea perhaps. But the fighting along the southern escarpment between Dar'ibu and Chamaal is terrible—so many are dying each day, and the Nadoriin attack anything that moves! Livestock, refugees, innocent children! They have no respect for the established trade routes followed by the nomadic tribes, even though these routes have always been held inviolate. Only the Silk and Ruby Roads are safe to follow, providing one can reach them. Radov should be beheaded and befouled for allying with that Saldarian prophet, Bethamin. The Veneiseans and Northmen are tenacious, but at least they deploy honest men who respect the old ways. But these Saldarian mercenaries are treacherous heathens whose only interest is in the rape and plunder Radov promised them. I cannot abide it—many of the victims are Radov's own people!"

"What does the Mage say?"

Jaya tossed a jeweled hand into the air. "The Mage refuses to do anything about it, *of course*, when just a simple command from him could..." She bit her lip even as she bit back the words and scowled down at her lap instead. "He has his reasons, I know..." she whispered. Her eyes lifted to fasten on Vaile again, and both expression and voice were tormented. "But what does he expect from us, Vaile? We cannot win *all* of these battles for him! And it seems such a futile war. I do not understand its purpose."

"It is a holy war, my lady," Trell advised, wherein Jaya shifted her gaze to him. Trell knew it was ill news that Radov had allied with Bethamin, but the fact didn't change the conflict, only contributed to its escalation. "The Kutsamak is sacred to the Basi, and the Nadoriin exploit their riches. They destroy and desecrate sacred shrines with their mining—all to feed the Northmen's greed."

Jaya arched a pale brow. "It seems to me that the Northmen hold no monopoly on greed, Trell of the Tides."

"Perhaps not, my lady," Trell admitted, "yet the Northmen's desire for the riches of these mountains seems insatiable."

Jaya's look changed to one of surprise. "But you're a Northman yourself!"

Vaile explained, "Trell has spent the last five years in service of the Emir."

"I see. Then you are Converted?"

"No, my lady."

Jaya really looked puzzled then.

"Trell remembers nothing of his past," Vaile told her. "He heads to the west in search of it."

Both of Jaya's wispy brows rose that time. "Indeed," she murmured. She considered him for a moment then, looking him up and down with those strange, tangerine eyes. Then she sighed despondently, and leaned back on the settee. "I do not like wars," she complained. "That we were recalled from isolation and set to this task chafes at me."

Vaile cast her a dry grin. "No doubt the Mage hopes to keep the six of you out of trouble."

"*Trouble*," she grumbled. "Trouble! *Malorin'athgul* wander the land and he wants to keep *us* out of trouble!" She shook her head and narrowed her gaze in vexation, muttering again, "I do not know what the Mage hopes to accomplish with this war."

"The shrines—" Trell tried once more to explain.

Jaya cut him off with an upraised hand and a flash of orange-gold eyes. "Spare me your propaganda, youngling," she returned bluntly, surprising Trell with her change in manner. "There are reasons for wars, and then there are *reasons* for wars." Turning back to Vaile, Jaya muttered in a frustrated tone, "Balaji knows the Mage's mind, but he will not say."

"Balaji is too often close-mouthed," Vaile agreed. "I have long wondered if he took lessons in the art of ambiguity from the Mage's zanthyr, or if the Mage's zanthyr took lessons from him." She rolled her eyes heavenward and added, "The Creator knows both are older than the sun."

Jaya looked sour. "They are equally infuriating creatures."

But Trell couldn't get past her last words. He knew Vaile had meant it figuratively, but he could have sworn that Balaji was little more than ten and six at best. He blurted before he could stop himself, "Impossible! Balaji can't be any older than me."

Both women gave him such a look of wide-eyed wonder...and then they burst into laughter, leaving Trell perplexed and embarrassed while he watched them fall into each other's arms consumed by mirth. Their enjoyment lasted far too long for Trell's ego, which had taken quite a blow.

"*Oh*...oh my," murmured Jaya as she finally straightened and dabbed at her eyes with ebony-nailed fingertips.

Vaile released her only to fall back on the settee in another fit of laughter. "You... haven't...the...gift..." she managed as she tried to catch her breath. "You haven't the gift at all, Trell of the Tides!"

Eventually Jaya took pity on him, perhaps noting the dejected look in Trell's grey eyes. "Oh...in all truth, young Trell," she said rather breathless but still smiling, "we are not sure who is older—Balaji or Ramu. Nor are we sure which one is our leader, for sometimes Ramu takes orders from Balaji, and sometimes Balaji takes orders from Ramu. So we listen to both, as should you, if ever they bid you to task."

She sobered then, and straightened the lay of her silken gown across her slim knee. "Speaking of Ramu...he and Rhakar have just been given new assignments," she told Vaile, "which leaves the rest of us with twice the area to patrol. It is difficult enough as it is."

"More is expected from the talented," Vaile observed with a droll smile.

Jaya settled her a sooty look. "You would not be so tolerant had your own task been less appealing."

Vaile's grin softened beneath a flush of her creamy cheeks. "Admittedly."

Trell took advantage of the break in conversation. "I am told Ramu was responsible for my rescue," he said. "Will he be coming here tonight, my lady Jaya?"

"Ramu is attending the Mage," Jaya replied, glancing curiously at him. "There is no telling when he will return, though I do expect him before morning. But Rhakar is here now, and he also aided in your rescue."

"Our Trell of the Well has met Rhakar already," Vaile advised.

"Oh?" Jaya looked to Trell expectantly.

"Yes," he admitted, "I met Rhakar, but our conversation went...poorly."

"Rhakar is volatile," Vaile observed sympathetically.

"He's temperamental," Jaya corrected. She gave the other woman a disapproving look. "*Moody*. Not volatile. We are none of us volatile. The *Malorin'athgul* are volatile. Whisper Lords are volatile." She eyed Vaile up and down. "*Your* kind are volatile."

Vaile gave her a very feral sort of grin. "True."

Trell wondered of which 'kind' Vaile was. He knew Jaya must certainly be one of the mysterious *drachwyr*, but what was Vaile?

Why not just ask them? he wondered. *Yes, but would either of them tell me if I did?*

Their conversation continued while Trell sat in thoughtful silence, immersed in his own questions and mysteries. In the end, he decided to watch and listen and ask no questions of the ladies. Whisper Lords, 'Vaile's kind,' and *Malorin'athgul*—whatever in Tiern'aval *they* were—might be volatile creatures, but it was Trell's experience that there was nothing more volatile than a woman whose dignity had been insulted by a poorly phrased or ill-conceived question, no matter how innocent or of good intent the hapless man that posed it.

TWELVE

'If you live in the river, make friends with the crocodile.'

– Bemothi adage

Trell's evening after leaving Vaile and Jaya went splendidly. Náiir invited him to dine with him, after which they played a close game of Kings and shared far too much *siri* even for Trell's head—which said a lot for Náiir's capacity for the drink. Trell retired around midnight with the *siri* warm in his belly and a promise from a triumphant Náiir for a rematch when Trell was 'feeling better.'

Trell climbed into the Mage's bed and shut his eyes with great relief, but to his surprise, sleep wouldn't come. It was his last night at the sa'reyth. Tomorrow the moon would be full, and he was meant to be away, and his mind could not be at rest. His head was full of questions, of thoughts of the people he'd met and the things he'd heard. A comment Náiir had made earlier kept teasing at him. '*...it is my experience that people of magic prefer to own things of magic, just as they prefer to associate with other races of magic.*'

Trell got out of bed and turned up the lamp. He looked at all the books stacked in piles on the floor, on chairs and chests, on the ornate table the Mage used for a desk. Balaji had given him leave to read any of those books...the Mage's books. Magic books. Somewhere, in one of them, might lay the key to the identities of the mysterious *drachwyr*, one of whom was said to be 'older than the sun.' Now that his departure was nigh, Trell wished he'd spent more time perusing those books.

He wandered to the table and looked over the volumes there. He saw from their spines that many were written in Agasi, which he spoke fluently—it was just one more disjointed piece in the puzzle that was his life. He was quite surprised to discover that the language of those books didn't change when he picked them up. In contrast, those that were written in obscure tongues shifted to the common tongue the moment he opened them.

Fascinating, he thought. *The books know I can read Agasi, but they also know it's not my native language.* It wasn't a huge surprise—most everyone he met thought he was from Dannym or Veneisia—but it was a boon to have a thing of magic confirm it thus.

And then Trell realized the significance of these thoughts and chuckled to himself. *A thing of magic...* Imagine, trusting to such a thing to tell him about himself. If only Ware and the others could see him now...conversing with *drachwyr* and Whisper Lords and reading magic books that belonged to the Emir's Mage.

Trell moved to the Mage's desk. The first two books he picked up were the heaviest books he'd ever held, especially for their small size. They shocked his hand the moment he opened them, actually making a spark that singed his fingers and drew a muted curse, and since they were just full of drawings of strange designs, he put them right down again—albeit more carefully.

He next reached for a pile of matching books bound in blue leather, each with a strange entwining pattern embossed on the front, but upon opening one he got a different kind of surprise. The journal was written in Agasi in a smooth, flowing script. The words at the top of the page captured him immediately, but they also brought a flush of embarrassment as he realized this was the Mage's personal journal.

'I would regret the lives snuffed like candles by the rising west wind had I only the time for such indulgences; I would apologize deeply for denying these men choice, had I still the luxury of remorse. They are needed. T'was mercy my solitary guide, I might excuse them from their duty, for surely they've paid penance in loss enough. But the need is too dire, the moment nigh after so many years of waiting, and all I may allot to them now is my compassion.'

Feeling guilty about reading even that much, Trell closed the book and gently put it back on its pile. He was sure *these* writings were not meant for his eyes, no matter what Balaji said. It would be dishonorable to read any more… yet he felt so strong an urge to do so that it disturbed him.

Glancing down, Trell saw the corner of another blue book, this one open on the desk beneath a large canvas inscribed with a jumble of intersecting black lines. He pushed aside the canvas and read the open page. It began in the middle of a sentence.

'…so different in temperament, yet they are brothers to the core. One has the mind of a master tactician; his skills need polishing, but the talent is there. The other has Returned, and has been long awaited. Much is expected from him.' The next line read: *'The time has come to hone them both, these, my kingdom blades. They can no longer go on being mere pieces; they must become players.'*

There was no more, and the next page was blank. Trell pushed the canvas back in place and leaned back in the velvet-upholstered armchair, pushing one forefinger to his lips. He felt…unnerved. Who were the two men the Mage referred to as his 'kingdom blades,' and why did he feel so certain that one of them was him? *And if I am one of the two of whom he speaks, then I have a brother…somewhere.*

As he was pondering this, he heard voices outside.

"Thank Epiphany you've returned!" a woman exclaimed from just beyond the draperies that formed the exterior walls of Trell's tent. Trell thought at first it might be Jaya, but he soon realized it was another. "You cannot let them do this. The sa'reyths are sanctuaries for all!"

"Which is why these traitors must not be allowed to enter, Mithaiya," replied a male voice that Trell didn't recognize, though there was something about it that caught his attention.

"How can this not be skirting the boundaries of Balance, Ramu?"

Ramu!

Trell came alert upon hearing the name. More than anyone, he wanted to meet this Ramu, the apparent leader of the *drachwyr.*

"Mithaiya," Ramu returned, sounding vexed, "I haven't time for a philosophical discussion on cosmic disparities."

"But the *Balance*—"

"*Amithaiya'geshwen,*" Ramu rumbled, and that time there was an edge to his tone that brooked no argument. Gaining her silence, Ramu continued more gently, "Trust me, dear one. The First Lord knows what we are about this night."

There was a pause, and then the woman submitted. "*Cuithne*," she whispered. "*Ythllia'nea ma dieul im'avec*."

"I know," he whispered gently. "Now, let me go. There is someone I must see."

Trell listened for more, but none came. He jumped into action. If he was going to speak to Ramu, it would have to be now, knowing how these *drachwyr* vanished on a wink and a whim. As he made a frantic search for his britches, he heard Jaya's voice from outside his tent, asking, "Where are they now?"

And Balaji replied, "They were spotted on the trail in from Jar'iman Point. Rhakar and Vaile have gone to apprehend them before they can claim sanctuary."

Still tying the laces of his britches, Trell rushed for the heavy drape closing off his room—

—and drew up short, face to face with a man who was just reaching for the drape from the other side.

The stranger had the same dark hair and features as his *drachwyr* brethren; though unlike Balaji and Náiir, he stood of a height with Trell, and his eyes were as dark a brown as any Basi's. There was something else different about him, too, something Trell noticed immediately: the man held himself with an air of authority that the others did not affect.

"Oh good, you're awake," said the stranger in that commanding voice Trell recognized as the one that had so captured his ear. "Náiir told me I might find you here." He extended his hand and locked wrists with Trell in greeting. "I'm Ramu. The Mage thought you would be awake despite this late hour. I am shamed to say I doubted him."

Trell came alert as he shook Ramu's hand. "The Mage? He's here?"

"No. I have just come from attending him."

"Then how could he know...?" Trell let the words fall away, for Ramu was smiling at him.

"There is an old desert proverb," the leader of the *drachwyr* offered, "that says that a man who can sleep before an important journey has nothing to gain from his travels. He might as well stay home."

"And you think that's how the Mage knew I would be awake?"

Ramu looked amused. "I do not know how he knew it, Trell of the Tides," he admitted, eying Trell quizzically. "You can ask him, if you like, when next you meet. But let me look at you." Smiling warmly then, Ramu took Trell by the shoulders in a powerful grip. "You certainly look much improved. When last I saw you, you were quite blue."

Trell's heartfelt gratitude was evident in his smile. "I cannot thank you enough. I owe you my life."

Ramu shook his head. "I did what anyone would have, under the circumstances." His manner was affable, and his gaze was cordial, even perhaps affectionate in the way friends might look upon one another. Trell felt very much at ease in Ramu's company, and he thought he knew why: things of magic might be drawn to things of magic, but men who were used to command were *definitely* drawn to men of the like. Looking admirably humble, Ramu added, "I am just glad we got to you in time."

"Not nearly so glad as I," Trell assured him.

The tall leader of the *drachwyr* barked a laughed and then glanced over to an ornate chest and the crystal wine service resting there, the liquid cold enough to make the glass perspire. Trell wondered if it was Wildling magic that kept the *siri* so cool.

"Come," Ramu said, taking Trell by the arm, "let us share some *siri*, and you can tell me about your recovery."

Trell could only accept. "I don't remember much," he admitted while Ramu went to pour the drinks. "If you don't mind, I'd rather you told me about my rescue. Rhakar said you were the one who pulled me from the water..."

"You spoke with Rhakar?" Ramu sounded surprised. "You don't look the worse for it."

"I've had a few hours to recover."

Chuckling Ramu turned, goblets in hand, and said with a knowing wink, "Well spoken, Trell of the Tides."

Trell studied him as he approached. He wore loose black desert pants tucked into high boots cuffed at the knee, and a grey tunic beneath a quilted black vest hemmed with silver. He also wore a greatsword strapped to his back, the black stone hilt extending diagonally above one shoulder. The hilt was impressively carved into the image of a dragon with the cross-guard fashioned as the dragon's spread wings. Trell could appreciate the superior workmanship; undoubtedly the blade was an ancient weapon—older than he cared to speculate—and he couldn't help but wonder if Ramu had been its only owner.

Ramu handed Trell a drink and motioned him into the same armchair where he'd conversed with Balaji that first day. Ramu took Balaji's chair.

"You were just with the Mage, you said," Trell began as Ramu was adjusting his sword behind him. "One day I hope to be able to thank him for his help. Will he be coming here?"

Ramu shook his head. "Alas, his duties do not permit, but I will relay your thanks."

"I'd appreciate that." Trell tasted the *siri* and discovered it was wine. *Red* wine. *Strange*, he thought, glancing over to the decanter of colorless *siri*. Hadn't Ramu poured both glasses from the same decanter? And if he hadn't, where had the wine come from? Shaking his head, Trell took another sip. The wine was very good; probably an Agasi vintage, knowing the Mage's penchant for things Agasi. Eyeballing the wine curiously, Trell posed, "He's not just the Emir's Mage is he, your First Lord?"

Ramu was reclining in his chair regarding him with candor, an intense sort of gaze. He sipped his wine and answered, "He is a great man with many roles."

Trell could accept that. After a moment, he asked, "The night of the cave-in... how did you find me?"

Ramu picked at the faceted red crystal of his goblet with one black fingernail. "We'd been searching for you, Rhakar and I. We felt partly responsible for your trouble, you see, and of course the First Lord was furious."

Trell looked up sharply. "Furious? Why?"

"He thinks very highly of you, Trell."

Trell frowned and shook his head. "I didn't realize the Mage knew much of me at all."

Ramu arched a curious brow. "Are you not the man responsible for the Converted holding the River Cry against the Veneisean force?"

Trell cracked a modest smile. He'd forgotten that his deeds were praised in the highest echelons. "I am rather pleased about that," he admitted.

"As is the First Lord," Ramu said, returning Trell's smile. "And as are we. We rarely need patrol that quadrant now, which makes our duties easier. You have helped us all immensely, Trell of the Tides."

That was the second time Trell's ears caught on Ramu's words, but by the time he realized what had bothered him the first time, he was already asking, "What kind of man is the Mage?" The words from the man's journal were still fresh in mind. "Everyone I've met seems so, well…devoted to him. Several of my—well, men who used to be in my command are now pledging themselves to his service."

Ramu settled him a sage look. "You find that disturbing, do you?"

Trell was surprised at his perceptiveness. "Well, yes." He hadn't put his finger on it before, but it was very unlike Ware to pledge himself to any one man.

Ramu shifted in his chair while holding Trell's gaze. "In the case of your Converted, fortune may be behind their interest. The First Lord believes you cannot put a price on a man's life. No mere treasure can replace the loss of a son to a father, or a brother to his sisters. Every life is priceless, and therefore all rewards for service are great—something on the order of Agasi silver, and Bemothi rubies as well, I believe."

"The Mage pays them such treasure personally?"

Ramu nodded.

Trell gazed at his goblet. What a discordant belief from the man who'd decimated an entire army on the Khalim Plains, the Mage himself claiming the lives of over a thousand men with a power that dared not be named aloud, even now. Trell had ridden through the gruesome scene. He'd witnessed the grey faces of the dead who littered the fields. It was as if the very life had been sucked out of them. If the man truly believed as Ramu said, then what price of conscience must he be paying even now to have taken so many lives?

'I would regret the lives snuffed like candles by the rising west wind had I only the time for such indulgences…' Could he have been referencing the Khalim Plains in his journal entry?

Ramu was eyeing him knowingly. "You asked what kind of man he is, Trell of the Tides? He is the kind of man even you would line up to serve," and there was only compliment in this statement. "The kind of man who—"

But his words were cut short, for just then Náiir appeared in the parting between the drapes. He'd changed into garments much resembling Ramu's, and he also now wore a dragon-hilted greatsword on his back. "Ramu," he said. "You are needed." He glanced to Trell and gave him a bright smile. "Well you look much improved." But then he frowned at the goblet in Trell's hand. "What's this? More *siri*? Did you not learn your lesson, Trell of the Tides?" Náiir turned and cast Ramu a reproachful look. "I told you not to give him any more of that."

"I didn't," Ramu protested, grinning innocently. "His is wine."

Náiir looked to Trell. Trell looked taken aback. "Wait. Mine is…what?"

"Oh," said Náiir, turning back to Ramu. "Let me guess. One of the Solvayre reds?"

Ramu was reclining in his chair like a king. "I was trying for a Volga. How did I do, Trell?"

Trell shook his head again. If he understood them correctly... "You changed *siri* into wine?" he declared. "Right in front of me?"

Ramu winked at him. "Couldn't have you making yourself sick on my account, and Náiir said you'd already had too much *siri*."

Trell still couldn't believe it. "You changed *siri* into wine?"

Ramu looked back to Náiir and shrugged helplessly. "He seemed to like it."

Náiir made to go. "Are you coming?"

Ramu nodded and stood. Then he cast his gaze on Trell, considering him. "Why don't you walk with us?"

That drew a curious look from Náiir, but he said nothing, only motioned them on.

Trell stood and set down his wine. "Well I'm no expert," he offered as he followed the two *drachwyr* from the room, "but that could have been a Volga."

Ramu laughed. He had a robust sort of laugh, the kind of laugh that was bequeathed to a man who would use it often and enjoy it immensely. "A little too dry?" he inquired with a glance at Trell.

Trell grinned. "A little."

Ramu snapped his fingers and shook his head. "I just can't get that right."

"Balaji says—" Náiir began helpfully.

"I know what Balaji says," Ramu grumbled. "But his is too sweet to be a Volga."

Náiir leaned to Trell and said conspiratorially into his ear, "Some say there has always been war in the Kutsamak, but it is truer to say that the oldest feud lies between the greatest of the greats: Ramuhárikhamáth, Lord of the Heavens, and Dhábu'balaji'şridanaí, He Who Walks The Edge of The World, arguing over who conjures the better wine."

Ramu turned him a frustrated look. "You always make it sound so trivial."

Náiir grinned in a flash of pearly teeth. "That's because it *is*, Ramu."

They passed through the common tents, empty by then of all guests, and headed outside into the night. Two torches marked the entrance to the complex, but the world beyond was dark, for heavy clouds covered the waxing moon, just shy of full. "I'll go see about the traitors," Náiir murmured. He headed off, and the darkness soon swallowed him.

"Traitors?" Trell inquired.

Ramu turned him a considering eye. "Tell me, Trell of the Tides. What do you know of the sa'reyths?"

Trell thought of Vaile's explanation. "That they're sanctuaries for...well, I guess for anyone who knows where to find them?"

"Better to say for anyone with the *ability* to find them," Ramu corrected, "but yes, you get the idea. The sa'reyths have their own rules, yes? Honor being foremost among them. We honor the rules by honoring each other's rights, and in doing so, we honor the First Lord, without whom these sanctuaries would not exist."

"Makes sense," Trell remarked.

"Yes. Yes it does. And yet there are those who have no honor, who seek to abuse the First Lord's own generosity twice within their time—first by neglecting the tasks he gave them, though he spared their lives for that very purpose, then by standing with his enemies against him in his absence. Now they think to escape his justice by seeking refuge beneath his own roof and hiding behind his own rules of safety. They think to abuse the gift of his sacrosanct honor when they themselves exhibit none."

The Lord of The Heavens drew in his breath and let it out again slowly. His eyes narrowed. "It does not please me, the task that lies ahead, but these traitors go too far. They think to pollute the First Lord's sa'reyth with another of their ill-begotten plans of cowardice." The look in Ramu's dark eyes was as unyielding as stone, as steadfast as the bedrock of the world. "I tell you this," Ramu said in a tone of ominous softness, as if he were the Maker himself speaking, "*never* shall that be allowed, Trell. *Never.*"

The word reverberated like distant thunder, and Trell actually felt it in his gut. He exhaled sharply, and self-control alone overruled the instinct to double over from a clenching pain spreading like a twisting spear inside of him. Ramu had spoken without malice or anger—simply making a declaration of what he considered undeniable truth—but the statement itself had boomed through Trell, rattling the framework of his mortal self. "I…believe you," he managed, gasping around the words.

Ramu's brow furrowed. He took Trell's arm and said in his intense way, "*Oh*, I do apologize."

With Ramu's touch, the pain vanished and Trell's breath returned as if it had never left. Trell lifted a startled look to him.

"I am sorry," Ramu whispered again. Then he made a self-deprecating grunt and released his arm, staring off into the direction Náiir had gone instead. "The First Lord is right to sequester us," he murmured. "We are careless creatures, too long away from the world." His gaze was saddened when he turned his eyes to meet Trell's again. "We can bring harm so easily to those we mean no ill."

"It was nothing," Trell said, amazed and a little shocked at the man's abrupt contrition. "Really, you mustn't—"

Ramu placed a strong hand on Trell's shoulder. "You cannot be the voice of my conscience, Trell of the Tides, though I thank you for wishing it so. Here now," he nodded toward the group just then approaching out of the darkness and dropped his arm back to his side. His gaze hardened. "What's this? Rhakar? What are you doing here?"

The group that was Rhakar, Náiir, and Jaya halted in front of Ramu.

"I told you to guard the traitors, Rhakar," Ramu said.

Rhakar settled his yellowish eyes on Ramu, looking fierce. He had also changed into an over vest and desert breeches and had a dragon-hilted greatsword strapped to his back. "I did," Rhakar protested. "Balaji's with them now—"

"I told you to guard them, Rhakar, not to simply wait there like a dutiful pup pending Balaji's arrival."

Rhakar's expression darkened. He glanced at the others as if to catch them laughing at his expense, and his gaze stuck on Trell. "What's *he* doing here?" he demanded, bristling.

"Keeping me company. Now be off with you before I have to take my displeasure out of your hide."

Rhakar snarled something in an acid tongue. Then he spun and stalked off. Trell thought he almost felt a great buffeting wind propelling Rhakar away and tensed to stand his ground against it, but there was no breeze to justify the sensation.

Jaya's odd, tangerine eyes followed Rhakar as he stomped up the hill. "Must you be so hard on him, Ramu?" she murmured. "He's just a youngling—"

"He is old enough to do what he's told, Jaya," Ramu replied in his calm, unyielding way. He looked at Náiir. "What of the traitors?"

Náiir frowned, as if he, too, found this task distasteful. "Balaji and Vaile are bringing them now."

Jaya bristled like a porcupine. "Did they really think they could stroll into a sa'reyth and expect no one to notice their arrival?" she demanded.

"They've learned a hard lesson by it, Jaya," Náiir murmured. He sounded subdued.

Jaya was just opening her mouth, perhaps to reply to this, when she hissed instead, "Leyd," drawing out the distasteful name as if it burned her tongue.

Ramu and Náiir turned heads to follow her gaze, but Trell was already watching the approaching shadow that solidified into the form of a raven-haired man with green eyes and the sort of toadying smile that irritated Trell to no end. He thought even less of the man upon this, their second meeting, than he had upon their first when Leyd had occupied a chair across from Rhakar.

"Well, if it isn't the great Ramu!" the raven-haired Leyd observed as he sauntered up with thumbs hooked in his sword belt. He gave Ramu a greasy sort of smile, eyeing him up and down like a lustful brigand admiring a wench. "We are certainly blessed to find ourselves in your venerated company."

Next to Leyd, with his oily hair and stained leather tunic, the immaculate Ramu seemed touched by divine grace. "Leyd," the *drachwyr* leader greeted, nodding to him a genteel welcome while ignoring his sarcastic slight. "There is no need for you to join us. This is not your battle."

"I rather think it is," Leyd disagreed.

"What business does a zanthyr have in matters such as these?" Náiir inquired skeptically.

"As much business as Vaile has," Leyd returned, sounding insufferably smug. Trell wanted to strangle the man already. "Or had you forgotten that Vaile is my sister-kin?"

"*Vaile* serves the First Lord," Jaya pointed out, settling the zanthyr Leyd a look that was as dangerous as it was icy. "I don't recall you giving him your oath of fealty."

Leyd shrugged. "I do tonight."

"Very well," Ramu calmly interposed before Jaya or Náiir could incite any more hostility, "you may join us. Rhakar is bringing them now with Balaji. Perhaps you can offer your assistance." His tone hardened as he raised his voice to include everyone, "Either these traitors will give their oaths tonight, or they will face the Maker for their crimes."

"*Oooh*..." Leyd shook his shoulders in a mock shudder while leering at Ramu. "I just feel so...righteous!" With that, he turned his insolent grin on Náiir and Jaya, ignoring Trell completely, then started off in the direction Rhakar had gone.

But Náiir grabbed his arm. "We are none of us fooled by your little charade of allegiance," he murmured, pinning the man with his pale golden eyes, which seemed just then to reflect the fire of the nearby torches—at least Trell hoped this was the cause of the flames that seemed to burn within them. Náiir's voice was as calm as Ramu's, but there was no question of his deadly intent. "If even one of those traitors has decided to swear his oath to the First Lord and suffers from your blood-thirsty blade before he can do so, you will have to answer to me. Best you remember that."

Leyd pretended to shudder again, though his grin rather ruined the effect. "I'm all aquiver, your majesticness." Sneering, he jerked free of Náiir's hold, and in the same instant, two black daggers appeared in his hands. He spun them through his fingers as he held Náiir's warning gaze. "Things have changed since your race ruled the world, Chaser Of The Dawn," he observed through a feral smile. The daggers flipped into his hands, and quick as a flash, he stabbed them toward Náiir's eyes, stopping within a hair of the man's lashes. Náiir's expression was stone. He didn't even blink.

Leyd just grinned at Náiir, spun his daggers back through his fingers, and made them vanish as he finished, "Best *you* remember *that*." Then he turned and sauntered off as if completely oblivious to the viperous stares aimed at his back.

As soon as he was out of earshot, Jaya hissed an oath in a fiery language. Trell did not understand the words, but he gleaned their meaning when both Náiir and Ramu arched brows and turned to her. She lifted her chin. "I'll say it again if you like."

"Once was quite enough, Jayachándranáptra," Ramu murmured. He returned to gazing after the departing Leyd, looking troubled.

"He's up to something," Náiir grumbled.

"A safe assumption," Ramu agreed.

Jaya grunted deprecatingly. "You could say the same about any zanthyr. Not one of the creatures is ever about what he seems to be about."

Náiir was also watching the departing Leyd. "You take your chances trusting a zanthyr in every case," he agreed, "but some really aren't worth the headaches they cause."

Trell took these aspersions with a grain of salt. He held no prejudices against zanthyrs, or really against any of Alorin's diverse races—how could he cast the first stone when he didn't even know his own heritage?—but he wasn't unaware of the zanthyrs' notoriety for self-serving, capricious acts of betrayal. And yet...Vaile was a zanthyr too, Leyd had said. Trell wasn't sure what he thought about that, though it made sense out of the puzzle of her spar with Loghain; a mere woman holding her own against a Whisper Lord was stupefying, but a female zanthyr? Well...

"He is of the worst sort," Ramu agreed quietly and with a sorrowful tone.

Trell looked to him. "Because he's a zanthyr?"

"No, Trell of the Tides," the Lord of the Heavens returned. "Because he feels he is entitled to his immortality and need not earn it. He has no respect for the miracle of life."

Balaji appeared out of the night then. Trell saw that he also wore the same garments as his male cousins and decided it must be some kind of uniform. "Rhakar is leading them in now," Balaji reported as he joined their group. He flashed a smile at Trell, but hadn't time to greet him before Ramu asked, "Who is the Espial among these traitors, Balaji?"

"Rothen Landray."

"Ah…" Ramu nodded. He retreated to his thoughts again.

"I take it this must be his little group of followers then," Náiir observed. "Cecile Andelaise, Sahne Paledyne, Pieter van der Tol..."

"Yes and a few others," Balaji confirmed. "It's one of the things Ramu will have to sort out."

"Sort out?" Ramu said.

"There are a pair of Basi who claim they are not with the others and came to give their oaths."

"Which pair?"

"Usil al'Haba and Pavran Ahlamby."

"Ah…" said Ramu again, as if this explained everything.

"Here they are now," Jaya murmured.

Indeed, a party of three was approaching out of the night: a woman leading two turbaned men. As they neared and the woman came into the firelight, Trell saw that she was Jaya's darker twin. Instead of golden-red hair, hers was black, and instead of orange-gold eyes, hers were blue.

"Who have you, Mithaiya?" Ramu inquired.

"Usil al'Haba and Pavran Ahlamby," Mithaiya replied. "They want to renew their oaths."

Ramu looked at the two men. Their pinched expressions well conveyed their nervousness. "Is this true?"

"Yes, Lord of the Heavens," they answered together, and then the taller of the pair added with an undertone of desperation, "We want to redeem ourselves in the First Lord's eyes. We have done as he bade us."

Ramu arched brows. "Indeed, have you? Very well then. Mithaiya, you know what to do with them."

The Basi exchanged a tense look at this, but they followed obediently as Mithaiya led them away again. They had just vanished into the dark beyond the torchlight when the others came into view. Rhakar and Vaile led a half-dozen men and women. They were lined up single file, and their hands seemed to be bound in front of them though Trell could see no rope or chains. Most of them stared at their feet, though a few of the men glared at Vaile as she patrolled the line swinging her swords. She looked very different that evening, dressed in black leather britches and vest over a longish black tunic, and with her long hair in a thick plait down her back. Trell remembered his initial impression of her as being highly dangerous. Her prowling stance tonight reaffirmed the wisdom of this decision.

"Landray's crowd are the youngest of the lot of them," Balaji noted as they approached.

"Tis a tragic end," Jaya murmured, shaking her head. "Cecile Andelaise could not have seen more than fifteen name days before she was branded a traitor and made to work the Pattern of Life."

Strangely, Trell recognized all of these names, but it took him a moment to call up the recollection from the fog of his forgotten adolescence. He saw a round room lined with bookshelves and a wall of windows overlooking an overcast sea…a dark-haired tutor towering above himself and two other boys, one older, one younger. They were sitting in a row at a table stacked with books…flashes of a hand drawing—*his* drawing of…of a dragon—passed back and forth between himself and his…yes, his younger brother, while the tutor read off a list of…names. These very names. *Yes*…he'd been taught them, and they were called…"The Fifty Companions," Trell murmured aloud as the title came to him.

All eyes turned his way, and there was apprehension in every gaze. "Traitors all," Náiir advised, but there was an edge to his tone that implied his concern that Trell might think otherwise.

Any significance Trell might have placed on the activities of the Fifty Companions, or on their being referred to as traitors by these *drachwyr*, was far overshadowed just then by the recollection of the very moment wherein he'd learned their names.

I was tutored in a tower by the sea.

Trell's heart was near to bursting with the exhilaration of the memory. The images of the tower brought a very specific feeling to his soul, one Trell had forgotten without realizing it was gone, but it came back to him then in a heartbreaking moment of tenderness.

It was the familiar feeling of home.

Home! That was my home.

Though he didn't know where that home lay, he knew there was a tower there, and it was beside the sea. *And I have two brothers*…only…that didn't seem correct. Yet he was sure that the two boys, both with grey eyes and grins so like his own, were indeed his flesh and blood.

He was puzzling over this when he realized the *drachwyr* were all watching him. Jaya and Náiir looked wary, Ramu's level gaze was unreadable, and Balaji was regarding him with a sinuous smile that sent Trell's skin crawling down his spine. Of all the *drachwyr*, Balaji by far had been the most amiable, and yet it was Balaji who made Trell the most uncomfortable, as if at any moment something malignant and deadly with sharp claws was going to burst out through Balaji's perfect white teeth and gobble Trell up in one fell bite.

"Have you a difficulty with this, Trell of the Tides?" Jaya inquired in a tone that wasn't cold but certainly wasn't warm, pulling Trell's gaze to her.

It took him a moment to remember what she was referring to. "Why, uh…no, my lady…I was just—"

"His mind is elsewhere, I do believe," observed Balaji. He settled Trell an ingratiating smile that made Trell's teeth hurt.

"That is well," said Ramu in his quiet but intense way, "for it is time we dealt with this. Náiir."

Náiir nodded and took Trell by the arm while the rest of the group walked off to meet up with Rhakar and Vaile.

"It bodes well to find you among us tonight, Trell of the Tides," Náiir said, "though a possible battle is never a favorable excursion. Take care to stay in your tent now, for we must face some unpleasant things."

This surprised Trell. "I am recovered enough to join you, I should think," he replied with good humor. "You needn't think me fragile, Náiir."

"Fragile indeed compared to us," Náiir returned, shooting Trell a quick grin, "but this was not the intent of my admonishment. No," and his expression sobered. Deep lines furrowed his brow as he continued. "These traitors are wielders and Adepts, not mere mortals to be bested with the hard-worked steel of men. Ramu will give them leave to defend themselves before we claim their lives for the First Lord. They will likely attempt some spineless patterning, but their ill-summoned magic will have no affect on us. You, however…" and here he paused to give Trell a concerned look, "you would be in harm's way, and death this night is not the Mage's intent for you."

Trell arched a brow. "And what is the Mage's intent for me?"

Náiir shrugged. "Who knows the inner workings of a Mage's mind?"

Trell decided he was not fond of that phrase.

Just then, Ramu returned. "Come Náiir," he said. Then he gave Trell one last smile in farewell. "I am glad we had a chance to meet, Trell of the Tides. The First Lord is right about you. You are a good man, and I am thankful that you survived."

"I am thankful that you saved me," Trell said, returning Ramu's smile though he felt an old frustration welling.

Ramu waved absently. "Well, we felt responsible, as I said." He turned to go, but Trell grabbed his arm, suddenly remembering what had captured his attention before. "Wait, please—I have just one last question: how can you have been responsible? I thought the cave-in was the result of a battle of magic between Radov's wielders and the Mage's Sun…dragons..."

It struck him even as he said it.

Ramu's lips spread in a slow smile, which Náiir echoed, and there was something about those smiles that made Trell's hair stand on end. He realized in that moment that while these creatures—all of them, Vaile included—seemed genteel and quite civilized, there was a side to their nature that was decidedly feral.

Then whatever it was that had bothered him about Ramu's smile vanished, and it was just a smile again—amiable, if still partnered with his typical intensity. The Lord of the Heavens clapped Trell on the shoulder, and his gaze was warm. "May fortune bless you in your search, Trell of the Tides."

Then he and Náiir turned and walked to meet the others, who had halted perhaps twenty paces away, just at the edge of darkness.

Trell watched them until they disappeared into the night with the traitors in tow, then he wandered back inside the complex feeling unnerved. *Sundragons.* Six of them.

Why hadn't he put it together before?

Because none of us knew they were shapeshifters. No one knows!

The sudden realization that he'd been conversing rather intimately with creatures who could, in their animal form, squash him with a single toe was quite unsettling.

Sundragons, he mused again, shaking his head.

Trell marveled that he wasn't more disturbed. He'd seen these beings in their animal form; he knew their deadly nature and their power. Strange…and yet not so strange. *Not now,* he realized, for he'd admired them as dragons, and now…now he admired them as individuals. When all the pieces were considered, Trell knew he had nothing to fear from them.

Back in the sitting room, Trell picked up his wine. *Ramu's wine*…and studied it before downing the last few swallows. *Amazing that he did this,* he thought as he gazed at the goblet in his hand. But hadn't Jaya said they were of the fifth strand? Now the reference made sense to him—he vaguely recalled something about the fifth strand of *elae* being the one that controlled the elements themselves, the one nobody could work…and something else…a story from the Age of Fable where a Bemothi wielder used the fifth strand to command the earth to rise up and form itself into a grand castle. Or had it been a palace in Agasan?

Where did I learn about the five strands of elae? he wondered, remembering again that tower room and the drawing he shared with his…brothers.

I do have a brother. I must! Despite his earlier doubts, somehow he knew it was true, knew it in the depths of his soul. He could see both of their faces so clearly in his mind now. One with grey eyes so like his own, the other blue-eyed and stern-featured but still similar enough to remind him of himself five years ago. Again with the image came the understanding that one brother was lost. But which one remained?

Trell knew then that if it took all of his days, he would find him.

Regaining the Mage's tent, Trell threw himself onto the bed and clasped hands behind his head. He thought of Ramu's proverb. Perhaps there was truth in those words. His journey had already proven valuable, and he knew there was much yet to be gained in making it.

THIRTEEN

'One does not 'have' faith. One knows faith.'

– The Fifth Vestal Björn van Gelderan

"I **know** *Hell, for I have died there. Hell is a blessing compared to what awaits us all if he fails.*"

Ean spent the better part of the next day pondering the Shade's words. No matter how he tried to put an explanation to them, however, no sense ever came of it. He finally concluded that he wasn't meant to understand, that the man had just been speaking with his own anger, not foretelling some cataclysmic eventuality.

Still, Ean couldn't stop wondering who *he* was.

The only bright side to that morning's events was that Ean was still allowed some measure of freedom—no doubt the Shade was certain, and rightfully so, that Ean wouldn't attempt another escape. The prince had quickly determined that the Shade had somehow replaced his old crew with an entirely new one—for not one face was the same. The new crew seemed more concerned with protecting him than with holding him hostage, which was somehow more unsettling. Ean slept in a tent that night, and knowing how silently the assassin had slipped up on him the last time, for once he didn't begrudge the guards standing watch.

It was after midnight when Ean was jerked out of sleep by someone shaking his shoulder. He opened his eyes and a hand clamped down over his mouth. "Speak not," warned a deep voice quietly.

Ean nodded.

The hand released him, and Ean sat up.

"We must go," said a shadowed form barely discernable in the darkness of the tent. "There's little time."

Ean didn't question him as he rushed to don his boots, but a thousand thoughts raced through his mind. Surely this was rescue, yet how was it possible? Who could've found him here? Where was the Shade? What of his guards?

The latter was answered as Ean followed the stranger from the tent and found eight shadowed forms lying scattered in the night. "*What in Tiern'aval…?*" His rescuer appeared to have single-handedly eliminated his guards.

Ean spun a stare at the stranger, who more than matched him for height. He knew they'd never met, for he would remember such a man: raven hair falling in loose curls to his shoulders, sculpted features equally statuesque and stern, and compelling emerald eyes. The man was staring back intently. "I see you are well enough," he murmured as he ran those emerald eyes over Ean. "That is a blessing."

"Whole, at least," Ean managed, thinking of his near escapes from death. "But who—?"

"Keep your voice down!" the stranger hissed, glancing around. There was no sign of the Shade, but in the distant night, Ean saw men walking their patrol, and other huddled by a far fire engrossed in dice. An excited shout erupted from the gaming group, and the stranger took the prince by the shoulder and urged him forward. "Stay close. We must hurry."

Ean went, somehow never thinking to suspect the man or his motives. "Who are you?" he whispered as he matched the other's long, fast stride. He took hold of the man's arm, urging, "Why are you risking your life for me?"

"I risk nothing," the man grumbled. He jerked his arm free and upped his speed toward the forest.

They moved silently into the trees catching brief glimpses of the waxing moon in a clear sky. Ean fell into step behind the stranger, watching his heels as they brushed and lifted his heavy dark cloak that seemed to be congealed of night. Everything about his rescuer inspired confidence, but he was bursting with questions and his impatience again got the best of him.

"Please," the prince said after they were well inside the trees and ducking to avoid low branches, "you must tell me. Who are you? How did you know I was here? Who are these men, and what—what *business* brings a Shade to task with me? Please—" he grabbed the man's arm, but released it again, shocked. The stranger's flesh might've been marble for all it yielded to his touch.

"Do I look a Shade to you, Prince of Dannym?" the man growled, oblivious to Ean's surprise. "My business is not his business, and his is not mine. Where our paths intersect, we cross without touching." He turned a penetrating gaze over his shoulder, adding, "and there is nothing I *must* do."

"The safety of my father's kingdom may depend on what information I can gather," Ean pressed. "If there is nothing you can tell me, then I will be forced to return and attempt to question the Shade's men."

Abruptly the stranger stopped and spun, forcing Ean to draw up short lest he run into him. He leveled a hard look at the prince and declared with the darkest conviction Ean had ever witnessed, "Don't be a fool! Your life is more important than you know!"

The words stunned him.

The stranger grabbed him by the shoulder and pushed him into the lead. Ean stumbled into motion, feeling oddly chastised, unexpectedly childish, and keenly aware of the man's presence just behind.

A pale and distant horse grew substance in the moonlight, and Ean focused on it, his face brightening. *Caldar! Something familiar, thank Epiphany*. Motion behind the horse of a darker sort, and Ean saw it was yet another great stallion, as shadowed as its master. They soon gained the horses, and Ean felt his hopes surge. *We've really done it! We're going to escape!*

"We're not out of this yet," the man warned as if reading the prince's thoughts. Almost in answer, the grating bellow of a horn erupted in the night, sending a nearby flock of birds scattering out of their slumber from the limbs above. Ean spun with a sharp intake of breath.

But the stranger wasted no time; he bounded in silence onto his saddleless horse—just the creak of leather britches as they stretched with the tightening of his thighs. Taking up the reins, he swept his cloak behind him and gave Ean a frightening and humorless grin. Tiny fang teeth glinted in the far corners of his mouth, teeth Ean would never have noticed had the man not smiled just like that.

Ean froze.

A *zanthyr,* he realized only then. Strangely, the truth seemed somehow appropriate. A mortal man stealing into the Shade's camp to whisk him away seemed impossible, but a zanthyr… they were Alorin's most ancient race and harbored two distinctly separate forms; one human, one animal. Both as elusive as the wind.

Ean reminded himself to breathe.

"Hurry," the zanthyr urged. "They know you've escaped now." He swung his stallion around and charged off through the forest.

Ean mounted quickly and set his heels to Caldar's flanks. He pushed the warhorse to catch up, hoping above hope that the animal could see where he could not. The zanthyr's black cloak billowed behind him as he rode through the night, making him look very much the part of the famous specter of All Hallowes Eve. The horses surged down a hill and splashed across a stream. Back up the other side, the zanthyr turned them hard to the north.

They rode for hours, sometimes furiously, sometimes carefully, but always pressing unfailingly northward. By the first twinge of dawn, barely more than a grey lightening of the sky, they'd gained a trail where the horses fell into an easier, loping canter.

Ean had taken advantage of the silent riding, and he'd decided a few things in those quiet hours, not the least of them that his companion had to be working some kind of magic to replenish their horses' strength.

To think that zanthyrs can wield elae! That was something no one knew, surely. The creatures were already relics by the turn of the current Age and they'd only grown more elusive as the centuries passed. Humankind knew little enough about them, but the one thing everyone seemed to agree upon was that zanthyrs were notoriously disloyal. Stories of their capricious acts abounded throughout the kingdoms of man; tales of a zanthyr pledging his fidelity to each of two warring kings, only to sell each monarch's secrets to the other and make fortunes off the both. Since the dawn of their creation, the creatures had apparently been betraying someone.

And while this zanthyr may have been saving Ean's life, that very fact troubled him. He would have to be daft indeed not to realize that any matters involving Shades, zanthyrs, and elusive assassins were quite beyond his ken. Why *he* was involved in them was the realm problem, and quite too much to make sense of. He meant to get to the bottom of it.

The prince brought Caldar alongside the zanthyr as they walked the horses beneath the grey dawn light. He wasn't sure what to ask the creature, though his mind was overflowing with questions. He decided to start with the most obvious. "Tell me," he began in a sharp whisper, "why are you helping me?"

The zanthyr turned and gave him a withering look. "Be grateful that I am and leave it at that."

Deflected, Ean was brooding over how to elicit some kind of answer from the creature when the zanthyr offered, "I don't know if you noticed that I repaired your sword for you."

"My sword?"

He indicated Ean's saddle. Frowning, the prince spared a closer inspection and caught the glint of a well-known jewel. He retrieved the weapon from its secured place, but his eyes widened when he pulled the blade from its scabbard. *It can't be!*

The sword had disintegrated into dust right before his eyes, yet the steel gleamed as true as the day of its forging. He swung the weapon, cutting the air with precision, and then placed two fingers under the tang. The sword was better balanced than before. Now he was truly astonished. He turned to the zanthyr. "How could—how did you do this?"

"You will have need of that sword yet," he replied gravely. "Much need."

They traveled in silence after that, the man's comment having sent Ean back to his brooding. *A zanthyr, by all that's holy*, and a particularly dangerous one from everything Ean had seen. The prince wasn't sure why he was so in awe of the zanthyr. Perhaps it was simply that the man was so...*impressive*. Killing eight men was no easy task, but this creature had done it without gaining so much as a scratch, without a spec of mud upon the trim of his immaculate cloak...without making a sound.

Staring at his mysterious and silent companion, Ean couldn't help but wonder how the zanthyr might fare against the Shade and his terrible power, and then he cursed himself for such a thought.

At daybreak, as the sky was turning a chill purple and mist began to rise from the earth, the zanthyr led Ean toward a thicket of oak saplings and dark hawthorn bushes growing in such close proximity that night seemed to remain there, trapped within. The zanthyr dismounted in front of a small gap in the hedge and bid Ean do the same. "We will camp here and rest today," he informed the prince as he looped his reins over a fledgling branch.

Ean dismounted and looked around, trying to ascertain their location. "Do you know where we are?" he asked as he bent to rub down Caldar.

The zanthyr had also begun attending to his horse. "Near the duchy of Stradtford."

"Stradtford?" Ean all but laughed at him. "You jest, surely. We were just in the Eidenglass."

"What's your point?"

Ean hunched down on his heels in order to view the zanthyr from beneath Caldar's girth. "It's impossible that we traveled all that way—"

"Nothing is impossible," the zanthyr interrupted, sounding irritated.

Ean didn't want to argue with him. "Stradtford then. But surely you don't expect trouble any longer?"

The zanthyr grunted. "They are looking for you, make no mistake of it." He pinned Ean with a disquieting sort of look. "You have a significant price upon your head, Prince of Dannym. Be glad I am not in need of coin."

Ean pressed palms to tired eyes. *Who? Who is behind all of this?* "Tell me what you know of my kidnappers," he said thickly, "and I will see you rewarded for it. My father will be most interested to know the identity of those plotting against the throne."

The zanthyr looked Ean up and down with a critical eye. "This is no mere plot against a throne, Prince of Dannym. Be forewarned: Cephrael's Hand glows in the heavens. The cosmic Balance once again has shifted, and only the condemned may defeat the forbidden."

Ean glared at him in exasperation. "What does that even *mean?*"

The zanthyr knelt to draw something in the dirt and then stood and announced,

"Let's go in. Morning approaches." With that, he disappeared into the thicket.

A groan escaped as Ean got to his feet. He was beginning to feel truly ragged—not just physically but mentally. He bore the burden of avenging Creighton's death, but to do so properly he had to understand the forces at work. Unfortunately, every word out of the zanthyr's mouth only left him more confused. He was constantly fighting back the wrenching ache of loss by focusing instead on the present, but the pain of Creighton's death was always right there, lurking beneath the surface of his thoughts, waiting for any opening to strike him with waves of crippling sorrow.

Ean gave Caldar one last loving stroke and ducked to enter the thicket, but the zanthyr's drawing stopped him. It was an intricate, looping pattern scribed in the bare earth, and there was something about it that caught and held his attention…

A rough hand grabbed him by the shoulder and pulled him through the bushes. He barely noticed falling on hands and knees. After a moment, he shook his head to clear his gaze and looked over at the zanthyr. "What…what happened?"

"It's a mindtrap. Don't look at it."

Ean shook his head again, surprised by how fast his thoughts had gone far astray. "A mindtrap," he repeated, never having heard of such a thing but understanding now of its power. He thought about how easily he could've been stuck staring at the pattern for hours and cast the zanthyr a sour look. "Nice of you to warn me."

"I just did."

Frowning at the creature, Ean scrubbed at his beard again—it really itched—and looked around the tiny grove. The zanthyr had cleared a small space and dug a fire pit lined with stones so that the glow of the flames might not be seen.

The zanthyr was choosing a spot to spread his cloak. "There are deadly forces about," he said without turning from his task. "The mindtrap will keep them at bay while we sleep."

Ean nodded in understanding. "The Shade, you mean."

The zanthyr cast him a narrow look, as if deciding whether Ean was worth the trouble of an explanation. He must've decided in the prince's favor, for he blessed him with something close to an answer. "Shades are not the greatest threat to you. They serve the Fifth Vestal and thrive in his shadow."

"The Fifth Vestal." Ean blinked. It was a title out of legend, though surely the man had once existed. Now it was only heard in stories, certainly not in casual conversation. The zanthyr might've been speaking of long dead kings or the defunct Cyrene Empire, two-thousand years vanished from the realm, for all the name registered with Ean.

Had the information come from anyone else, Ean would've laughed at him outright, but this was a zanthyr who spoke to him, one of the oldest of races; his very nature gave certain credence to his words. "You speak of Björn van Gelderan?" Ean said, feeling ridiculous just saying the man's name in earnest. The Agasi wielder was a storied villain, perhaps the most infamous in recent centuries; yet the prince felt the heat of the zanthyr's gaze and knew that this news was somehow of vital importance. "So you're saying that…Björn van Gelderan has returned to Alorin from…well, from wherever he's been for what—three hundred years?"

"Yes."

"And?"

The zanthyr frowned disapprovingly at him.

Ean gave him a black look in return, but he tried to piece things together all the same, lest the creature become disappointed with him and refuse to answer any more questions. "So the…Fifth Vestal is behind the Shade's appearance, but…" and here he hesitated, quickly thinking through what he'd been told. "But someone else is searching for us," and here his tone grew sardonic, "and they're somehow *more* dangerous than the worst traitor Alorin has ever known or his army of inhuman drones that work the blackest magic and command man-eating hounds conjured out of thin air."

The zanthyr shook his head resolutely. "No, my prince. They're not searching for *us*. They're searching for you."

Ean barked a laugh, but his expression quickly sobered. "You're serious."

"As the sun sets west."

Dumbfounded, Ean held the zanthyr's gaze. After a moment, he concluded, "You're not going to tell me any more, are you." It wasn't really a question, so he didn't really expect an answer. In that, he wasn't disappointed. "So the mindtrap will protect me today. What of tomorrow?" *What of when I'm home in Calgaryn? What of the rest of my life?*

"Tomorrow is a new day. Rest now. At twilight, we ride." With that, the zanthyr lay back upon his cloak, draped a leather-clad arm over his eyes, and did not stir.

Letting out a ragged sigh, Ean fell onto his back and pushed his arm over his eyes, mirroring the zanthyr's position. He expected to lie there for hours tormenting over all the things he didn't understand, but instead fell fast asleep.

That evening, as Ean was saddling Caldar in preparation for resuming their travels, his eyes kept straying toward the mysterious pattern called a mindtrap—though he was careful this time not to look directly upon it. The wielder's art of Patterning was something he'd always wanted to better understand.

'*All things are formed of patterns,*' his mother had explained to him once. Though she was but a novice historian of the Art, she knew more than most. '*Like the intricate lacework of a snowflake, or the infinitely complex veins that form a single leaf. One can learn to see these patterns and recreate them using elae. Only when a student has mastered the pattern of a thing can he then control or compel that thing. Only then does he embark upon a wielder's path.*'

Frowning as he adjusted his stirrup, Ean asked the zanthyr, "Is that a wielder's pattern or an Adept's pattern?"

The zanthyr was holding his midnight stallion's head in both hands and staring into the horse's eyes as if somehow communicating with him. He did not turn from his odd task as he answered, "It is simply a pattern."

Ean wandered over to it. "But don't Adepts and wielders work patterns—work *elae*—in different ways?"

"Yes."

Ean braved a direct glance at the looping design, but finding no mental pull in the doing that time, he allowed himself to look at it more closely. The zanthyr must have done something to it, for it seemed nothing more now than a pattern in the dirt. While studying the intricate design, he tried to puzzle out the hidden meaning that he suspected lay behind the zanthyr's laconic *yes*. "So Adepts and wielders work *elae* differently," he posed, "yet they use the same patterns?"

"It is not so simple as that, my prince."

Ean frowned at him. Then he turned back and frowned at the pattern. If all it took to be a wielder was a mastery of Patterning, then he imagined he could be a wielder too. He had a knack for patterns—had he not chosen an equally intricate design for his own personal seal? The zanthyr's pattern didn't look that difficult to remember, and Ean expected he could draw it as well as any man.

Suddenly the zanthyr was right beside him, speaking low into his ear, "Thinking of trying your hand at the Art?"

Ean started. He turned the man a peevish glare over his shoulder. "It doesn't look that hard."

"You think not?" The zanthyr cast him a shadowy smile. "Look as long as you like then. Memorize it."

Ean was keen to the challenge. While the zanthyr finished saddling Caldar for him, Ean stared long and hard at the looping design. *It's not too different from a number of scripted L's strung together in a circle,* he decided, trying to find something it might remind him of. He sent his mind whirling through the loops as if trying to memorize the steps of a Court dance. *Right loop, right loop, left loop, down loop, right loop…*on and on.

"Ready?"

Ean blinked and looked around. Everything was ready, the horses were saddled, and all evidence of their stay had been erased. How long had he been staring at the damned thing again? "Yes," he answered after a moment. He thought he was.

The zanthyr gave him a fiendish grin and swept his boot across the dirt, erasing the pattern.

Ean knelt to redraw it, and—

"Gone!" he exclaimed, straightening up again in surprise. "It's gone!"

The zanthyr was still grinning at him. "So you noticed."

"No, I mean in my head! I can't—"

"No," the zanthyr finished for him. "You can't. You are not a wielder, Ean val Lorian." He turned and walked back to his horse.

"But…" Frustrated, Ean jumped to his feet and joined him by the horses. He couldn't tell if his aggravation was with himself or the other man. "So, what…? A wielder could've remembered?"

The zanthyr mounted his horse with the same graceful ease with which he seemed to do everything. "A wielder first learns to accurately recall the pattern," he replied as he took up his reins. "Then he learns to draw it. Finally, he must learn to create it substantively with his mind alone."

Ean swung into his saddle as he considered that. "So what is an Adept?" All he knew was that an Adept was born with the talent to work one of the five strands of *elae*, whereas a wielder had to learn Patterning to do it.

"An Adept forms the pattern with his mind, only he does it innately as he wills the strand that governs his power to do his bidding. He does not envision the pattern, nor does he mentally draw it, yet the pattern is there when he works *elae*, for the pattern is the way he thinks. The patterns that enable his magic are so ingrained in the fiber of his being that he works them with as little thought as breathing."

"An Adept *thinks* in patterns," Ean concluded. It was impressive, he had to admit.

Taking reins in hand, he sent a curious look toward the zanthyr. "So what are you?"

The zanthyr flashed a grin and spun his horse to the north.

It was a drizzly morning that greeted them as they reached the southernmost boundaries of Gandrel Forest and began looking for a place of shelter. Ean had finally admitted that they were where the zanthyr claimed, though he still couldn't fathom covering as much ground as they had on that first night. But the Gandrel was familiar to him, as was the line of distant mountains along the coastline, and there was no doubting that they neared Calgaryn.

The forest felt more forbidding that morning, its usual beauty subdued beneath grey skies. As they passed within the sheltering trees, night fell again. If Ean turned and looked beyond the tree line, he could see the gradual brightening of the grey morning, but within, it remained dark and silent, as if the forest was sleeping late.

After walking the horses for the better part of an hour, the zanthyr finally dismounted and set up camp beneath the low-bowing branches of an ancient balsam fir. Soon thereafter, they laid down to rest, and as before, Ean was falling asleep even before his head touched his arm.

He woke at twilight to the smell of rabbit roasting. Sitting up with a yawn and a stretch, he found the zanthyr sitting cross-legged beside a low fire. The skinned rabbit was browned where it hung from three crossed hickory limbs—green, so they wouldn't catch the flame—and wispy tendrils of smoke from the fire funneled up the tree trunk to dissipate among the higher branches. Rain was falling beyond their tent of fir limbs, but either the broad tree or some spell the zanthyr had worked kept them snug and dry.

As Ean pulled a water flagon from his pack, he watched the zanthyr remove the rabbit from the spit and slice into the breast with one of his dark knives. He placed the meat on a cleaned strip of bark and handed it to Ean, who thanked him.

While Ean ate, the zanthyr settled back on one elbow and rubbed his thumb along the dagger he held. It was a cold looking weapon, with both blade and hilt fashioned of a singular black stone which Ean couldn't place. *One of their enchanted blades, no doubt—Merdanti weapons. At least that legend is true.* The dagger was polished smooth, yet the stone cast no shine; rather, it seemed to absorb the firelight into its core. Seeing it reminded Ean of his own blade, and the mystery surrounding its repair. "Might I ask a question of you?"

The zanthyr glanced up between the spill of his raven hair. "You may," he granted with a shadowy smile, "though I may not answer it."

Ean smiled through a mouthful of rabbit. "It's my sword," he posed. "You wielded *elae* to mend it, but everything I've learned about the power denies such workings. My understanding is that *elae* can be compelled to alter the forces of life, but none can command it to alter the state of inanimate objects." Ean stopped and gazed at the zanthyr. "But you did."

Though the zanthyr's expression showed no change, yet Ean sensed that he was amused. "Yes," he confirmed as he cleaned his dagger on a corner of his cloak, "I did."

"And how is that possible?"

The zanthyr considered his answer before replying. "In my day, there were a great many wielders who commanded the fifth strand of *elae*, the elemental strand called *Elorindael* by my race. The fifth is the most powerful of the five strands, for it compels the elements themselves."

Ean nodded; it was as he'd suspected. He pinned the zanthyr with his own level gaze. "I knew this. I just didn't think there was anyone alive who could work the infamous fifth strand."

The zanthyr cast him an elusive sort of smile. "There are a few," he returned. "The Agasi wielder Markal Morrelaine is one, if he lives, and Malachai ap'Kalien was a fifth strand Adept—he had to be, to do…what he did. And of course, the Fifth Vestal," he added with an off-handed wave of his dagger.

"Björn van Gelderan," Ean murmured, feeling strangely uneasy about speaking the man's name aloud now, though for no reason he cut put his finger on. It wasn't as if Ean expected the wielder to appear at the mention of his name. Still, the zanthyr claimed the man had returned to Alorin along with his Shades. Who knew what he could do?

There was something else that puzzled Ean, however. History taught that Björn van Gelderan had betrayed his revered position as one of only five Vestals chosen to protect the realm, so the prince was puzzled to hear the zanthyr name him by that title still. "How can Björn van Gelderan remain a Vestal after all he's done?" he asked.

"All he's done…" The zanthyr repeated slowly, looking up beneath his wavy dark hair with a narrowed gaze. "What do you mean by that?"

Ean missed the dangerous shift in the zanthyr's tone. "It was the Fifth Vestal's duty, and that of the other four Vestals, to protect our realm from the misuse of *elae*, was it not?"

"It was and is."

"So what do you call the Adept Wars, and the treasonous role Björn played? He took up Malachai's banner and waged war on his own race. His betrayal was the worst of all, they say."

"*They* say," the zanthyr repeated slowly, his dagger suddenly clenched in his fist. "What do *they* know of the Adept Wars?"

Ean drew back from him in startled response, unsure what he'd said to irritate the zanthyr but sorely aware that he now tread on dangerous ground.

"What do any of you know about it?" he growled. "Mankind bears the wars like a banner proclaiming their victimization, but *mankind* was—" Abruptly, he stopped, paused, and then idly waved his dagger to dismiss the subject—and his ire—completely. "You asked how the Fifth Vestal can still be the Fifth Vestal," he said, all green-eyed calm once more, "and the answer is simple: because the new Alorin Seat, who you know as the First Vestal, Alshiba Torinin, has no one to replace him. It will take none other than a fifth strand Adept of Björn's caliber to assume his position, and as you correctly stated, my prince…" and here he paused, his tone taking on a terrible and unexpected sorrow, "Alorin has no fifth strand Adepts any longer." He added more quietly, "None have Returned for generations."

Ean could tell from the gravity of the zanthyr's tone that this circumstance was far more serious than he understood. "In the North, we still follow the old ways," he offered. "We honor the sacred festivals and speak the rites, though I don't know how many truly believe and how many do these things out of mere tradition. We believe in the Returning, and we say the Litany for our lost ones, and we...hope." He managed a smile that didn't quite touch his eyes. "We hope we might someday meet them again, and somehow know them though they look different to us. But *you* speak of these things with more...meaning."

The zanthyr looked him over critically, and once more he deigned to grant him the boon of an answer. "There is Balance in all things. Life and death fall easily within the scope of this Law. The Adept races are the true children of this realm, their lives tied to the realm's life, all living patterns inextricably intertwined. Always before, those Adepts who died yet Returned, and always they maintained their Adept gifts in their next life, for death changes nothing of their true nature, only the corporeal aspect of their existence. Thus the race continued. But now...now the realm is dying."

"And so dies the Adept race," Ean concluded heavily. He didn't know what to say, so he apologized without knowing why. "I'm sorry."

The zanthyr gave him a tolerant sort of look. "Eat your dinner," he grunted, pointing his dagger at the rabbit.

Out of respect more than lingering hunger, Ean complied. But first, he asked, "The uh, Shade...did he use the fifth strand to destroy my blade?"

"No."

Ean shook his head and chewed his meat. *So many mysteries...*

Yet the zanthyr seemed in a conversational mood, for he exhaled a thoughtful sigh. "Your humankind was a different people before the wars," he told Ean. "Magic was an integral part of life in many of the kingdoms. Wielders, Adepts, warlocks from the Shadow realms, shapeshifters and Sundragons...once all the races lived in tandem with the civilization of men."

"Terrorizing civilization, you mean," Ean countered, then he grimaced at his own obvious ignorance and added by way of apology, "Or so I've heard."

The zanthyr opened palms skyward. "A subjective conclusion." He fixed Ean with a quiet stare. "What is it you hope to hear from me?"

"Only the truth."

The zanthyr laughed softly. "Ah...truth is it, my prince? And whose truth would that be? My truth? Malachai's truth? Perhaps the truth of the Sundragons who were banished to the nether-reaches of the realm by the First Vestal simply because they'd once served her ex-lover. Do you expect those dragons, who thrived in the warmth of the desert kingdoms, to think their banishment to the icy edge of the realm was justified?" He shook his head. "There is only one truth in this universe."

"Which is what?"

"There is Balance in all things."

Ean frowned. "Balance again," he grumbled, not daring to take that one up, as the zanthyr had already proved he'd no intention of explaining the subject. "But what of the histories—"

"Since when did historians concern themselves with facts, much less objectivity?" the zanthyr challenged. Leaning back again, he waved his dagger and remarked,

"Once in a while some historian will stumble over the truth, but most of the time he'll pick himself up and continue on as if nothing has happened. And some things..." he settled Ean a stern look then. "Some truths are better left to myth and legend, prince of Dannym."

It was a sobering thought.

Ean set aside what was left of the meal, his appetite lost. "What of our plans?" he asked. "Do we sti—" but he left the words unfinished, for the zanthyr had raised his hand, demanding silence. In the next moment, he was on his feet with sword in hand and was slipping through the branches.

Bemused, the prince made haste to follow, but as he pushed through the veil of fir limbs behind the zanthyr, he came up short. Two men stood before him with upraised swords, their frozen blades dripping rainwater, their eyes downcast at a looping pattern scrawled in the mud. Ean returned his half-drawn sword to its scabbard and exhaled his captured breath. He squeezed around them and joined the zanthyr, who was standing next to a large oak, his gaze scanning the dim forest through the rain.

Ean's gaze kept straying to the men behind them. "How long will they stay that way?" he whispered.

"Until someone pulls them off."

"What if no one does?"

"Then we'll have two less swords to worry about."

Ean forced himself to turn his back on the living statues and followed instead the zanthyr's line of sight as he peered into the twilight gloom. But Ean's eyes were not so keen as the zanthyr's, and he saw little more than long sheets of rain pouring down through the mist and the trees. "Is it the Shade that follows?" He was surprised to discover that he almost hoped it was; at least the Shade was a known commodity.

The zanthyr glanced Ean's way. "Stay close."

He started off into the night.

The forest was quiet—too quiet, Ean realized. No ravens called from their evening roost, no crickets sang, only the rain pattering on dying autumn leaves. A fog was rising too, dampening the earth as much as the evensong, so that Ean heard all too clearly his breath coming faster than he would've liked.

The dagger struck without warning.

Ean felt the sharp pain in his chest, just below his right shoulder, and staggered back, crying out first from the shock of the encounter and next from a searing pain that numbed and immobilized as it radiated outward from the wound. Right away he found he couldn't move his right arm, and in the next heartbeat he collapsed to his knees, laboring to suck air into lungs that refused to fill.

He watched in the detached way of the dying as the zanthyr deflected two more flying daggers with his dark blade and then advanced on a far tree with murderous intent. When the next dagger flew, the zanthyr snatched the knife right out of the air and spun a tight circle, slinging it back whence it had come with a whip of his wrist. Ean heard a cry, and then a man tumbled from high limbs. He struck the earth and bounced once, only to then lie still.

The zanthyr streaked through the darkness. Abruptly he bent and took the man by the throat, staring into his eyes. "Geshaiwyn," he growled. "You, at least, will travel no more."

The assassin smiled and whispered with his dying breath, "A *halál csak az'eleje.*"

Ean meanwhile knew something was dreadfully wrong. His shoulder was an agony of burning flesh, and his muscles were twitching so uncontrollably that he couldn't even grasp the hilt of the dagger to pull it free from his chest.

Poison, he thought as he watched the growing circle of blood soaking his tunic. *Poison on the blade.*

The foul stuff burned with the fire of acid in his veins. He opened his mouth to yell to the zanthyr, but suddenly he felt a wrenching pain in his stomach and pitched forward into convulsions. *Poison*, he was all he could think as he gagged and choked into the mud.

Ean sensed a shadow approaching and managed to turn his head, but before he could see the man, his insides convulsed again and he vomited. He was hardly aware of what happened next—even when the zanthyr yanked the dagger from his flesh, the scream he emitted sounded far away. Only the pressing of hands upon his wound brought a moment of clarity. Ean saw the emerald eyes of the zanthyr looking into his own. Then another wave of nausea overcame him, and he rolled onto his side and vomited until he blacked out.

It could have been seconds or minutes later that the prince found himself aware, only partly knowing he'd been unaware moments before. The zanthyr's eyes were pinned on his, and holding the man's gaze helped Ean focus.

"You were lucky," the zanthyr said once he saw that Ean had regained himself. He pulled the prince to his feet.

Ean reeled; his world spun, and he passed out again.

When he came to, he was sitting atop a black horse—a running black horse. It was daylight, and they were deep in the Gandrel surrounded by sky-scraping hemlocks whose trunks were broader than a horse was long. Caldar paced along beside them, strangely at ease playing second to the zanthyr's stallion.

Pale-faced, Ean looked back at the zanthyr, who held him securely against his own body with one strong arm wrapped around the prince's chest. "He got me again," Ean managed with a rueful smile. It was hard to form his thoughts into words, and his tongue felt heavy and thick. "But how…?" Ean couldn't understand. "Poisoned… yet I'm alive?"

The zanthyr silenced him. "You will die yet if you don't get that shoulder tended to," he growled. "I am no Healer. See to it that you don't die before we can get to one, or I will be quite vexed with you."

Ean blinked at him.

"And mind you keep your mouth shut along the way, Ean val Lorian," the zanthyr warned irritably. "This is just the beginning of your Return, and I cannot follow along forever silencing you."

Ean stared at him. He had never known such awe, such gratitude…or such impatience to understand. "I…I owe you my life," he managed.

"You owe me much more than that," the zanthyr muttered as they rode beneath the wide, majestic trees.

The prince didn't know what to say. He leaned his head weakly against the zanthyr's broad shoulder and offered, "Somehow I will return this. I pledge you my service, my trust—"

"No!" The zanthyr's response was ferocious enough to call Ean back to full awareness. "Do not trust me!" He locked eyes with Ean to reinforce his command. "I will not have it upon my conscience!"

The warning seemed a strange sort of farewell. Ean felt darkness calling like an old friend. He managed a weak nod, already forgetting what he was committing to, and went to greet it.

FOURTEEN

'If courage is the seed of conviction, then faith is its life-giving water.'

– Errodan val Lorian, Queen of Dannym and the Shoring Isles

"Do you wait to see him, too?"

Franco turnedfrom the window at the sound of a woman's voice and saw a vision framed in the archway. He blinked, but the vision remained, a tall, lithe creature of amazing beauty dressed in a desert gown of tangerine silk, her long raven hair bound at the crown by a net of firestones, her braid three times caught with citrine-crusted bands. Franco finally found his manners and bowed with a polite, "Milady."

Her dark eyes showed the faintest surprise. "You are not the Vestal."

"No," he confirmed with a self-effacing smile. "I am but his humble servant."

Her eyes swept him assessingly and then held his gaze, her lips rising in the faintest of smiles. Franco felt a thrill of desire in the contact, leaving him wanting in a way he was quite unused to. She spoke with the unmistakable accent of Avatar as she concluded, "You are his Espial then?"

Intrigued by the woman, Franco nodded and gave her a sweeping bow. "Franco Rohre, at your service. And may I be so bold as to inquire of you, my lady?"

"I am Ysolde Remalkhen."

Of course you are. He knew now that this was no chance encounter. From everything he'd heard of Queen Errodan's Companion, she would've come for a purpose, but was it her own, or her lady's? "Tis an honor, Princess," Franco replied with an even deeper bow.

They both then looked to the towering double doors at the far end of the antechamber. Easily twenty paces tall, they were carved with the val Lorian eagle and barred from the inside. Beyond stretched a long corridor and a formidable host of the King's Own Guard, red-coated and immutable. Past them, lay the apartments of the king. Admiring the large eagle artfully carved with wings and talons outstretched, Franco murmured, "You asked if I waited, too, Princess."

"Yes. I thought you were the Vestal. Now I realize he has already been admitted."

"Only just. I was surprised the king didn't keep us waiting longer."

"Indeed." Ysolde's eyes flashed as she turned back to the doors, but Franco had the sense that her angered gaze speared well down the passage beyond. "Her Majesty has been waiting on the king's pleasure for nigh on two cycles of the moon."

She did not have to say, *and here this Vestal gains his ear without hesitation,* for Franco heard it well enough.

Her eyes shifted back to his, and he felt that thrill of contact again. The woman was simply electrifying. In all his long years, only a handful of women had such an effect upon him, and most of those encounters had turned out disastrously. Still…

Ysolde looked Franco over again as if deciding whether or not he warranted further communication. She must've decided so, for she said to him, "Perhaps you would accompany me to the queen's audience, Mr. Rohre. I believe her Majesty would have words with you instead."

So here we go at last. Franco gave her a terse nod. "Of course, milady."

She spun an elegant retreat and led away.

Franco admired her as he followed. She seemed to float down the hall in her luscious silk, but it was the curve of her hip and its graceful sway that most attracted his eye.

Ysolde Remalkhen, he mused.

What did he know of her? Unfortunately little enough; his knowledge of the current royal lines was cursory at best. He knew she hailed from Avatar, a princess from the Fourth Line of Kings. She'd apparently become Companion to Errodan n'Owain when she was in her teens. She was said to be a woman of powerful intellect and unquestionable loyalty. She was also rumored to harbor lustful desires and was said to have taken many lovers. Franco was most curious about the qualifications of the latter.

The passage eventually ended in a wide stairway that opened upon a vast marble-sheathed room large enough to house a small town. Easily hundreds of people walked, talked, milled or mused among its sky-scraping columns, each demarking another passage leading elsewhere in the vast palace complex. A crystal-domed ceiling cast a diffuse glow. Ysolde waited for him at the steps, unerringly standing in a shaft of sunlight, and Franco joined her side inquiringly.

She smiled at him, a glory to behold—truly, she looked a woman in her prime, though Franco had heard that she neared her fiftieth name day. Franco knew the intimacies of the Pattern of Life and the immortality its routine working rendered; he quite suspected that Ysolde Remalkhen was no stranger to it either. "They call this the Boulevard—informally of course," she said, holding out a hand to the cavernous room before them. "No doubt you understand why."

Franco but swept his gaze once across the vast chamber to understand. "Indeed, Princess. I am grateful you know the way from here."

She nodded politely, and then headed down the staircase. For all its bustling activity, the Boulevard was strangely muted once one passed within, as if the vastness of the room swallowed each conversation long before it reached another's ears. They'd barely reached the main level when a flash of gold caught Franco's eye, and he looked again for the source. Two men draped in white togas with gold bands at their necks and wrists stood next to three figures shrouded from head to foot in ghostly grey silks. They'd been stopped by six palace guards and seemed in heated conversation.

Ysolde caught Franco's gaze. "Two of Bethamin's Ascendants and their Marquiin. Would that his Majesty had seen fit to turn them away at the kingdom border. Now they have no doubt spread their filth as they came in and will do so again as they leave."

One of the gold-collared Ascendants looked up as Franco was staring at him.

You don't know I am an Adept yet, do you? Franco thought, letting his own gaze slide indifferently past the man, *and if you did, would you send your ghostly goons to question me? They'd be in for quite a shock, I fear.* The thought made him smile, but his eyes had strayed beyond the Ascendant, so he didn't see the man frowning after him.

Beyond the Boulevard and down the wide hallways of the palace, Ysolde led the Espial. By the time they came to a pair of tall doors not unlike those demarking the king's chambers, Franco was quite lost. He wondered how Raine would ever find him but wasn't so naïve as to think his passing went unnoticed, being as he was in the company of the Queen's Companion.

The doors opened inward as Ysolde approached, and Franco followed her past two green-coated guards, down a flight of steps and into the open air. The late morning was still brisk, and the sea air was fresh if slightly damp. Franco strained to listen for the sounds of the waves impaling themselves against the cliffs that formed the northernmost wall of Calgaryn Palace; he imagined he could just hear their faint whisper on the breeze.

"This is the Queen's Garden," Ysolde informed him as they tread down a stone-paved path. Franco was searching for something innocuous to say about the overgrown 'garden' when Ysolde continued, "I noticed your interest in the Bethamins. Last month, another five of them came here—two Ascendants and their trained hounds. His Majesty refused to see them, thank Epiphany, and provided an 'escort' to ensure a quick traverse back to Saldaria. Bethamin is dull-witted, however, and sends his creatures with annoying persistence."

A smile twitched Franco's lips. "I take it you are not a devotee of the Prophet's teachings."

"I am a Daughter of the Sand," and from the way she spoke it, she clearly felt nothing more need be said in answer. She turned her dark eyes upon him as they walked side by side. "And you, Franco Rohre? What god or gods do you follow?"

The sanguine kind that come in dark bottles.

Do shut up.

"I am a practical man, Princess," Franco managed despite the mad voice in his head. "Gods don't interest me overmuch."

"*Khoob*, that is well for the sun. There are far too many gods seeking footholds in the minds of men these days."

Franco grinned admiringly at her. "Princess, I couldn't agree with you more."

As they walked beneath a promenade of apple trees trained over arching trellises, Franco heard the flinty sound of a hoe striking the earth. He soon saw the elderly gardener wielding it, and just beyond him, a woman in a servant's blue dress was bent over pulling weeds from a flower bed long gone to seed. A large section of the garden here had been recovered back from wilderness, and flowers bloomed despite the lateness of the season.

"The queen works to restore the beauty of her garden now that she has returned to court," Ysolde explained. "It is an arduous task."

The serving woman turned at the sound of Ysolde's voice and straightened, pushing the back of a dirt-encrusted glove across her brow to clear fine wisps of hair from her eyes—green eyes beneath cinnamon hair woven in an elaborate crown of braids, and Franco realized he was staring upon the Queen of Dannym herself. He flushed and quickly bent the knee with a hasty, "Your Majesty."

Errodan tossed the weeds she'd been holding into a pail and cast an inquiring look at her Companion.

"The Espial Franco Rohre," Ysolde supplied.

Errodan arched brows in understanding. "Ahh…then you travel with the Fourth Vestal?"

"Indeed, your Majesty."

"Please—please be on your feet, Mr. Rohre. There's no sense dirtying your britches on my account."

Franco complied, but not without surprise. The queen seemed nothing like the wild-tempered, vitriolic woman of reputation, and her Companion was almost ethereal. *What a curious pair.*

"The Vestal is already in chambers with his majesty," Ysolde explained, "but I thought his Espial might prove of help."

The queen looked back to Franco, and the hint of a smile graced her lips. She was a woman of deep beauty—not as fine-boned or as exotic as the willowy Ysolde, but sculpted honestly as if by an artist's loving hands. They were marble and alabaster, these two.

More like onyx and obsidian, he belatedly cautioned—*penetrating beauty that could just as easily turn into a razor-sharp spear to pierce a man's heart.*

"No doubt you've rarely seen a queen doing her own weeding, have you, Mr. Rohre?" the queen asked. She had lovely teeth and a mother's warm smile; there was nothing in her figure to show she'd birthed three boys, and yet…

Franco hastily met her gaze lest she catch his eyes straying. "No, majesty," he replied with a quirk of a smile.

"I find that gardening calms me. Even when the world seems to be falling to pieces, I can find some measure of peace in my garden." She added with a wry smile, "Sometimes it's the only activity that quiets the noise in my head." She removed her gloves and handed them to her gardener, who had stopped his hoeing upon their arrival and now stood attentively. She made several quick motions of her fingers as he watched, and then he nodded and shuffled off.

"Jeremiah, my gardener, lost his tongue in the War of the Lakes, about twenty years ago," the queen said, coming toward Franco as old Jeremiah vanished beneath the apple trees. "His hearing only abandoned him in the last ten years. It's what saved him his position, really." She motioned Franco and Ysolde to join her and led down a path deeper into the garden.

Franco had never walked in such close proximity to a queen and a Fire Princess. He found it not at all an unpleasant experience. "And how is that, your Majesty?"

She gave him a gentle smile. "Being that he doesn't know the finger language, my husband found great difficulty communicating to Jeremiah that he no longer had a job, so he let him stay. Now it is up to the two of us to tame this wilderness."

Franco let his gaze float across the vast park she called a garden and couldn't help but remark, "That is a monumental task, my lady."

She laughed. "You speak Raine's truth, Mr. Rohre."

"Please call me Franco, your Majesty."

"Very well. But I *know* of your name, Franco," she said, turning him an inquiring look. "You are quite famous among certain circles. You're one of a number of survivors they call the Fifty Companions, are you not?"

Fifty and one, he thought, suppressing a grimace, *but Markal Morrelaine will never consider himself one of us.*

"Yes, Majesty."

Ysolde had fallen behind them—much to Franco's disappointment—and she inquired then, "You survived the fall of the Citadel, Mr. Rohre?"

"Franco," he corrected gently.

"Franco," she obliged.

Can you really call hiding in the Citadel's catacombs survival? Isn't it truer to say you 'avoided' the fall? Might as well have slept through it for all you did to help—

"You *were* at the Citadel, were you not?" the queen meanwhile inquired.

"Yes, I was."

She shook her head. "A tragedy beyond measure; the very island of Tiern'aval lost and the Citadel and all its learned halls along with it? Tell me, how did you escape?"

Yes, tell her how you did it.

"There were a number of us who fled before the fall," he said evasively.

"And well that you did," Ysolde remarked, "else the entire Adept race may have had its end upon that very day, as doomed as the island."

"What did happen there?" the queen questioned and Ysolde asked, "Are the stories true? There are so many of them, and every one seems but in conflict with the others."

Go on, tell them all about your experience hiding among the dead while Malachai rended the sky and Shades butchered your masters and Death walked unhindered laughing with wild abandon. Tell them why you were really hiding there…

Over the years, the number of people who'd asked Franco these same questions outnumbered his long span of life. They always wanted to know about his past, about the true story, about the part he played in the Battle of the Citadel. Where once his face had reddened in shame, now he knew better how to school his expression into impassivity, how to dissemble, how to compartmentalize his thoughts and emotions.

Now he had a renewed purpose, one he was finally coming to believe in; yet this purpose brought with it a whole new set of problems replete with their own complement of dreadful, soul-binding secrets.

Franco stopped their walk amid a path bordered in cherry trees. "I mean in no way to seem coy, your Majesty, Princess," he confessed as if the conversation was as innocuous as it seemed, as if he wasn't in fact evading the subject of his life's ruin and ultimate disgrace, "but I would you understand that the battle's events were in fact so terrible that no retelling—no matter how artfully crafted—could do justice to the memories of those slain. I beg you, do not make me sully them further with my own inept attempt to recount the atrocities of that night."

Both women looked slightly taken-aback. Ysolde dropped her eyes, and the queen seemed contrite as she replied, "It was most ungracious of us. We should have realized…"

"I have many times been asked," Franco reassured her, "and many times denied to speak of it. Perhaps some day my resolve will fail me, and I will find solace in the retelling."

"It must be an immense burden to carry the weight of so many souls," Ysolde observed, regarding him compassionately. She cupped his cheek with soft fingers. "I would that you might find peace someday, Franco Rohre. You seem a decent man who should not have to suffer so."

Little do you know, Princess!

"But here now," the queen forced a smile, trying unsuccessfully to lighten the mood, "I do not believe I have ever had the occasion to converse so candidly with an Adept of your caliber before, and there is one question I have longed to ask. What is it like to work the Pattern of Life? I have heard stories of its use to achieve near immortality, but never first-hand."

Unbidden, the memory of the first time Franco had worked the pattern flooded his mind, a host of unwanted images that brought with them a swell of turbulent emotion despite his strongest attempts to block it. The image of himself kneeling at the Fifth Vestal's feet staring at the blood that soaked his boots all the way to his knees, at his gaze—his dreadful, accusatory gaze—standing in judgment as Franco begged for forgiveness, for mercy. And the image of the pattern itself, forever seared into his memory, into his very being, warping his soul. Once learned, once wielded, there was no undoing its power, no altering its course short of suicide, yet a single working did not mean an endless lifetime in the prime of one's existence; the pattern must be continually renewed to maintain youth.

In the moment directly after working the pattern, as he lay gasping for breath, Franco had sworn through his tears never to do it again; but over the years, he'd found himself intent upon the deed time and time again.

Gods, I am doomed. Why do I linger in this life? Why have I not ended it as I swore to do?

Because you fear death so fervently that even a pattern as violent as that *one is preferable to the blackness beyond.*

It was true, he did fear death, but for very different reasons than those that had driven him into the Citadel catacombs as an adolescent. Yet in his heart of hearts, Franco didn't think this was the reason he remained. He had been a craven once, yes, but cowardice did not yoke him still.

Franco emerged from his internal reverie to find both women gazing inquisitively at him and realized only then that it had been many a long moment since the queen asked her question. "My gravest apologies, your Majesty, Princess," Franco said, nodding to each of them. "My thoughts sped fast astray."

"It must be a very powerful working to have so profound an affect on you," Ysolde remarked. Was there something knowing in her tone?

But the queen was regarding him shrewdly, a newfound glint in her gaze, and she surprised him with the observation, "We all have regrets, do we not, Franco Rohre?"

Franco held her gaze for a moment longer than intended, both of them searching the eyes of the other as if to read the secrets of their souls hidden just beyond. *What an extraordinary woman.* "Indeed, your Majesty." It was a bare whisper.

At first, the company of two lovely women in a pastoral setting had seduced Franco into mistaking himself among common company, but this was Calgaryn Palace and the lovely women were the daughters of kings.

Franco surprised even himself by suddenly taking the queen's hands into his own and asking directly, "How may I assist you, Majesty?"

She must've experienced something in the prior moment as well, for she studied his face as if committing it to memory and did not pull away from his impertinent touch. "My son has been taken," she confessed then, her gaze revealing the emotion she schooled so well, her voice now stricken raw with fear. "I don't know by whom or for what purpose. He was due to arrive days ago but was ambushed on the road. My husband's men have learned nothing, despite all efforts."

Franco squeezed her hands in heartfelt sympathy. "How many knew of his arrival?"

"The whole world," said Ysolde. "Her majesty invited over four-hundred dignitaries from seven kingdoms to attend a banquet in the prince's honor. No doubt you saw the parade preparations as you arrived."

"But his ship put ashore in secret," the queen explained, unable to hide the frantic undertone in her voice. "We took so many precautions...yet still, they found him."

"Do you have reason to fear someone means him harm?"

"Only the premeditated death of her other sons," Ysolde replied.

Franco conceded she had a point. He looked back to the queen, who was gripping his hands as tightly as he held hers. "What can I do?"

"Entreat the Vestal to read the currents in search of Ean," the queen answered immediately.

Franco blinked. "Do you believe magic was involved in your son's capture? Because otherwise—"

"We understand how the currents work," Ysolde remarked, which was enough of an answer to alert him that indeed they suspected that very thing. "What you must understand is there is no *raedan* in the king's employ, no one qualified to read the currents. Your timely arrival with the Fourth Vestal seemed Fortune's gift."

Errodan suddenly pulled free of his touch and walked to the edge of the path where it opened upon a fountain choked by weeds. "We are no closer today to finding those behind the assassinations of my other sons than we are in understanding who has taken Ean—and this despite my husband sending scores of men to scour the kingdom and a host of spies alert for any whispers." One hand found its way to cup her cheek, which was barely in profile to Franco, and she whispered, "I cannot lose Ean to their greed. *I cannot.*"

"Will you help us?" Ysolde asked, drawing his gaze back to her.

Seeing opportunity rising like Fortune's island on the horizon, Franco didn't hesitate. "Princess," he said, boldly taking up her hands and kissing the back of each, "it would be my honor."

FIFTEEN

'I will not believe until I hear it from his lips.'

– The Second Vestal Dagmar Ranneskjöld, to his oath-brothers and sister after the fall of Tiern'aval, 597aV

When Raine D'Lacourte was admitted to see the king, it was with the slightest trepidation. Several things worried him at present, most notably Franco Rohre. He was certain the man was hiding things from him, but the Espial was so skilled at shielding his thoughts that Raine gleaned just bits and pieces of his suffering. Franco had given him no cause to question him at all, however, and Raine was loathe to broach the subject in conversation. If Franco had secrets, well…everyone did. They'd all made mistakes during the War. He didn't wish to hound Franco over his own, for the man surely hounded himself relentlessly. Still, there was a great deal Franco wasn't saying, of that Raine had no doubt.

Another unsettling revelation was the presence of Bethamin Ascendants in Calgaryn Palace. This disturbed him on several levels. He was in a position to know that the king of Dannym had ordered all proselytizers of Bethamin's creed turned back at his borders; to find the priests so deep within the kingdom meant they'd found powerful allies among Dannym's nobility. Raine feared an eventuality that seemed inescapable. The popularity of the Prophet Bethamin was growing at an alarming rate, and while he seemed to preach a 'religion for the people,' in fact Bethamin sewed intolerance among two races that had lived harmoniously for eons.

Then of course, there was the matter which had brought Raine to Calgaryn to begin with. *Björn.*

Raine's oath-sister Alshiba chastised that he worried too much, but he knew that if he let go of any of the myriad threads of concern now woven among his thoughts, he would lose the cohesive whole. Perhaps it stemmed from his years of training as a *raedan*, which undeniably changed the way he viewed the world. One cannot spend centuries studying the currents and remain obtuse to the fact that everything in the Adept world is interconnected—all magical workings, in some way, are connected to one another. The old adage of a butterfly that flapped its wings in Bemoth and caused a snowstorm in Kjvngherad wasn't just a wives' tale. Certain events, no matter how disparate their locations or subjects, were often yet somehow connected.

For Raine, every new piece of information was a thread somehow woven into the whole; his challenge was to find out where each thread fit in the great tapestry of their living realm.

Raine was escorted into the king's private chambers where he awaited his Majesty's pleasure in a spacious drawing room. A feast of refreshments was laid out on a gilded table, and large glass-paned doors opened onto a balcony patio which overlooked the sea. Raine had only just poured himself a glass of wine when the king entered from the opposite end of the room.

"Raine D'Lacourte," he said as his secretary closed the doors behind him.

Gydryn still struck a powerful presence even in his fifth decade. He came and locked forearms with Raine in a gesture of welcome that marked the Adept as his equal. It was something Raine had always admired about Gydryn val Lorian, his willingness to grant importance to others; though he suspected this was an attribute that garnered him as many enemies as it did friends. Good men in high positions always had a difficult time trying to hold together a kingdom comprised of baser men. Few mortal kings knew better than Gydryn val Lorian the sacrifices one made for a crown.

"What brings you to Calgaryn?" Gydryn asked as he motioned them toward a grouping of armchairs.

Raine heard the deeper inquiry in his thoughts and shook his head to the negative: *no, my friend, I am not here to discuss our joint venture; not yet.* Aloud, he answered, "I've been following a trail upon the currents."

Raine D'Lacourte and Gydryn val Lorian had long forged a bond of trust, and while some state secrets might never be shared between them, there was yet a willingness to speak openly of what matters they could. "The trail led me here," he added as they both sat.

Gydryn frowned. "To the palace?"

"In essence—specifically to a harbor tavern in a fishing village twelve clicks southwest of Calgaryn. But I must study the currents from a node in order to better decipher what I found there. As you know, there is a nodepoint beneath the palace, in a room once used as a divining chamber."

"Yes, I'm all too familiar with the chamber you speak of," Gydryn answered with a sour expression. "It has been causing me some concern of late." He thrummed his fingers on the arm of his throne.

In the silence that followed, Raine sensed for the first time the king's state of mind. To say he was troubled would be to speak of a typhoon as an intemperate rain-shower. As his fears came to a head, Gydryn began projecting his thoughts—however unwittingly—loud enough for Raine to pick up on a great number of them.

The Fourth Vestal leaned forward in his chair. "Never-mind my inquiry," he said earnestly. "Speak to me of Ean."

The king glanced up sharply. After taking a moment to garner his emotions, he replied in a choked voice, "I cannot bear to lose another son."

"He's been taken?"

Gydryn nodded. "It was not my intention to beleaguer you with the troubles of a single kingdom when you shoulder the concerns of your entire race."

Raine dismissed his comments with a wave of his hand. He tried to make sense of the impressions and images Gydryn was projecting. The king seemed to be battling against the grief that had invaded his heart, and only fragmented images could be gleaned through his turmoil. "Was...*elae* somehow involved in your son's kidnapping, your Majesty?"

Gydryn pressed his fist into the arm of his chair and settled Raine a heated look all the more intense for the anguish hiding beneath it. "I just don't know."

So it was that Raine pulled the entire story from the king, though Gydryn seemed loathe to speak of the 'imposter' Shade and his 'supposed darkhounds.' All the while, Raine listened in silence with a carefully schooled expression of neutrality. Inside, however, he was furious. And then some. Where there were Shades, there was Björn, for the creatures were bound to the Fifth Vestal in a way Raine had never come to understand. Yet the fact remained: there could not be one without the other, and there was no doubt but that the creatures acted upon Björn's will.

You have much to answer for, my brother, he declared, hoping Björn might somehow feel his threat riding on the currents. *And I will see you called to term for all of your crimes.*

When the king was finished, he looked to Raine as if for confirmation of the absurdity of the tale, but the truthreader could no more reassure him than he could understand why Björn would have taken an interest in a northern prince.

As if I truly understand anything my oath-brother does.

"I would like to tell you that your men spoke only of fiction, your Majesty, but alas, I cannot."

The king didn't ask Raine to elaborate, nor did he ask what the truthreader wasn't saying, in the same way that Raine didn't ask about the many *other* matters he'd gleaned from the king's thoughts. Many things were better left unspoken between them.

"So," the king grunted, mastering his emotion into practiced calm. "How can I help you in your task?"

"By your leave, I would spend a few days in your divining chamber studying the currents. I have an Espial in my service currently, and he would also be helping me."

"Of course."

"And I will look for traces of your son on the currents, your Majesty. If *elae* was involved in his capture, there will be signs still upon the tides."

Gydryn merely nodded. "Thank you for that."

Raine pitied him. To lose one child for the sake of a kingdom might be borne, but to lose three?

Yet if Björn is involved in this, then the prince's disappearance has nothing at all to do with a throne.

Their meeting concluded, the king called for his Guard and a specific lieutenant who would be assigned to assist Raine in whatever way he required.

Bastian val Renly arrived soon thereafter and bent the knee, one fist to his heart. "Majesty."

"Bastian, this is the Fourth Vestal Raine D'Lacourte," the king informed him, as if Raine needed any introduction. "Take him where he desires and assist him in his activities. Oh and Bastian…"

"Yes, Sire?"

"When in the tunnels, inquire of him as to that other matter."

Bastian saluted crisply and turned to Raine. "After you, your Excellency," and Raine led him from the king's chambers. In the wide passage beyond, the Lieutenant inquired, "What is your will, your Excellency?"

Raine pulled himself from his thoughts. "First, to find my Espial, if you will, Lieutenant."

"By your command," replied the solider, and led briskly away.

Franco was just releasing Ysolde's hands when Raine appeared, walking down the path in the company of a red-coated officer of the King's Own Guard. "What's this?" the Fourth Vestal inquired lightly as he joined them. "Princess, are you attempting to usurp the attentions of my Espial for your own purposes?"

Franco glanced at Ysolde and stepped a polite distance from her person. "A favor only, my lord," he answered with a smile. He held one hand toward the ladies. "May I present her Majesty Errodan val Lorian and her Companion."

The queen came forward in a royal manner quite incongruous with her simple clothing. "I had hoped to meet with you," she confessed to Raine while her eyes strayed to Bastian val Renly, "but I see you are about my husband's work. Perhaps another day."

For the briefest of moments, Raine looked slightly indecisive, as if he would stay and speak with the queen, but then he seemed to decide the better of it. He nodded to her. "Another day, your Majesty." Looking to Franco, he said, "Might I ask your assistance, Franco?"

"Of course, my lord."

And they departed.

Franco wanted to ask what had transpired with the king, why the officer came with them though he seemed to follow instead of lead, why the Vestal seemed so preoccupied, but he knew all such questions must wait until their proper time.

As they made their way back inside and began a winding course downward through kitchen levels and storerooms and long tunnels barren of anything save the most inconsequential, flickering light, the lieutenant that walked just behind Raine said to him, "If perhaps, your Excellency, we might first attend to that other matter?"

Franco looked from the Vestal to the soldier. "What other matter?"

Bastian gave him a rather weak smile, as if he didn't relish the task. "I think it is best explained by witnessing it, my lord."

And, as Franco discovered, it was.

"What in Tiern'aval…?" he gazed incredulously at the rock ceiling of the tunnel, which seemed, well…*melted.* Then his gaze lowered to the dead man. There was no putting words to describing him, nor explaining in matters known to nature what could've killed him.

But Raine knew. It was clear from the powerfully anguished look upon his face; clear that he knew too well what had caused the man's death. Franco watched him bow his head with closed eyes.

Franco also shared an understanding of what had been done there, though he relished not the knowledge, and the truth was certainly as far from *natural* as could be imagined. What he didn't know was who could be responsible for the deed. Malachai was long dead, after all. There was something about the dead man that caught Franco's attention, but he couldn't put his finger on what it was.

With his diamondine gaze sternly if tragically settled upon the body, Raine slowly touched the toe of his boot to the man's shoulder.

The body disintegrated in an explosion of ash.

"Shade and darkness!" Bastian cursed, skipping two steps back.

Franco knew he had to tread carefully. *Very, very carefully.*

They were joined just then by two blue-coated soldiers of the Palace Guard who'd been on watch at the end of the tunnel and came running to investigate Bastian's outcry. The Lieutenant waved them no matter, but curiosity kept them from departing too quickly.

"What happened to him, my lord?" Franco meanwhile inquired of the Vestal. Better Raine thought him curious.

The Fourth Vestal turned and looked over his shoulder at a pair of iron doors set into the tunnel wall. It was the divining chamber—out of use for centuries—where the node was yet located. "Someone came in through the node," he whispered. Then he looked to the hole above. "And found his own way out."

Franco noted the two soldiers spitting onto the floor and grinding their boots over the mark. He didn't think a ward against the evil eye would be of much use against *deyjiin*.

"So..." Bastian looked like he was itching to escape. "Do you know what happened here, your Excellency?"

"I have a fair idea." Raine sounded grim. He looked to the lieutenant, "But I will speak of it to no one but your king, and neither shall any of you," and he let his gaze encompass all three of them. They didn't look of a mind to protest.

"Assuredly," Bastian promised.

"I need to study the currents now. Those doors," he said, pointing then. "Are they unlocked?"

"There is no key, I'm told."

"You mean it's trace-sealed," Raine corrected.

Bastian reddened immediately with embarrassment. Obviously he'd forgotten he was speaking to a truthreader. "Your pardons, Excellency. I swore never to speak of it—"

"There is no shame in obeying your oaths, Lieutenant, and I know truth from falsehood regardless."

"Yes, milord. I should tell you that to my knowledge no one's been in that room for decades. I'm not certain anyone even knows the pattern to release the seal—excepting yourself, of course."

Raine looked to the iron doors and studied them for a long moment. Franco watched him frown and then walk over to them. "No doubt I could work the trace-seal. Yet if I'm right..." He reached for the iron latch. It clicked without protest, and Raine pushed the doors inward. They moved on silent hinges.

"Now that can't be good," Franco said.

Raine cast him a telling glance over his shoulder. Then he stepped into the room. Franco followed him into a vast chamber whose floor was gained by way of a curving stone staircase carved out of the wall. Raine was already halfway down it.

The Fourth Vestal stopped on the chamber floor, which was dominated by a still pool, smooth and dark as glass. Globes hung on chains from the high ceiling, their ensorcelled light burning low, and everything was draped in gloom.

"What do you know of Malachai's realm, Franco?" Raine asked, his voice echoing in the vast chamber.

Caught by the unexpected question, Franco paused on the stairs and then shrugged, continuing his slow descent. "Only what everyone knows."

"Have you traveled there?"

It was a direct question spoken in the truthreader's tone. Franco couldn't remember the last time Raine had *required* a truth of him so brutally. "...No, my lord," he replied, startled by the question and yet immensely grateful he could respond with the truth. "No one can travel to T'khendar. It was created from the fabric of Alorin and shares much of our realm's pattern, but the nodes between the realms are hopelessly twisted and their ways cannot be traversed."

"Aye," Raine murmured, sounding vexed, "Yet my oath-brother has returned somehow." He turned and settled Franco a look of piercing inquiry. "I have not asked you about the Citadel, Franco, and how you survived its fall. I have questioned many of your fifty brethren over the years, however, and all have given me different answers. Strange, isn't it, that the fifty of you were supposedly together, and yet each recounting is entirely dissimilar from the next?"

Franco gazed disconcertedly at him.

Abruptly Raine waved a hand. "I care not, really, what you're all hiding. Whatever truly happened there is in the past—you do believe me, don't you, Franco? I want you to understand that the Vestals harbor no ill feelings toward all of you."

"...Thank you, my lord," Franco murmured uncertainly.

Suddenly Raine was beside him with a hand on his shoulder. "But I must know now...*tell me*," and he again used the voice Franco so feared, "how much do you understand of what we've found here?"

This time the truthreader's compulsion hit Franco like a blacksmith's hammer to his gut. He knew to attempt a lie was all but impossible now. "*Deyjiin*," he choked out, and the pressure in his chest lessened. "I know it was *deyjiin* they—he—whoever it was used to kill that man. But that's all I know of it."

"You were at the Citadel," Raine said, his hand still firmly holding Franco fast, his gaze still pinning him just as surely. "But I do not know how much you saw, or what you've learned since. Of those Adepts who followed Malachai into T'khendar, the Paladin Knights sent by the Council of Realms, and many others...do you know what became of them?"

Franco tried not to resist the compulsion in his tone, for to do so was only to strain oneself needlessly, only to cause intense mental pain. "There are many theories as to how they died," he managed.

Raine frowned at him. "There is only one truth. T'khendar killed them."

Little do you know, Franco gritted his teeth. It took all of his self control—all of his many, many long years of practice at compartmentalizing his thoughts—to keep Raine from learning anything, from hearing anything.

The Vestal continued slowly, thoughtfully, "This power you name so carelessly... *deyjiin*. What do you know of it?"

"Only..." he gathered his composure and forced the words, "only that Malachai and his Shades worked it." It was a lie, and Raine would know it so, but Franco felt certain that at least he wouldn't be able to tell what more Franco actually knew.

Raine released him and let his hand drop, exhaling his frustration. Perhaps in his agitated state he'd missed the dishonesty in Franco's answer, or perhaps not. It was worth hoping though.

"Here's what *I* know of this power," Raine offered. "It comes from T'khendar. It was something unforeseen by Malachai, something entirely alien to Alorin and its natives, the antithesis of our *elae*. Very little is understood about it, for it cannot be studied with *elae*. Those who have tried have..."

"Failed," Franco supplied.

Raine settled him a disquieting look. "They have died. What is known of this power, which travels its own channels even as our *elae*, is that it is a consumptive power. Some believe it is the power of the dark gods with whom Malachai supposedly made his pact; others claim myriad other origins. What we do know is what it creates—or rather, I should say, destroys, for it destroys utterly everything it touches." Raine looked back to the doors. "That man was killed with this power, the power of T'khendar, a power we call *deyjiin*, for it means death."

Franco was thinking fast to keep up his charade of ignorance. "Then...then it can be wielded like *elae*?"

"Not like *elae*," Raine corrected severely, "for no known pattern compels it. But yes. Malachai could wield it, and I fear my oath-brother Björn can as well...now."

He looked around the chamber with narrowed gaze, no doubt studying the traces of magic left upon the space. "It is as I thought," Raine concluded, looking back to Franco. "They must've arrived here. Tell me, Franco, where is the weld?"

"A weld?" Franco was honestly confused by the question. "You mean a node. Calgaryn harbors a node, my lord."

"Perhaps once it did. It harbors a weld now."

Such major links in the pattern of the world were immensely rare, and most all of them were known and charted, but Raine was pinning Franco with such a penetrating look that he dared not protest. So he looked. And he saw.

Oh gods, I'm doomed. Doomed!

"There," he said, pointing to a distant space near the center of the pool. To his wakeful inner eye, the portal was as stark as daylight. "But—it's impossible."

"I know," Raine agreed. He looked crestfallen. "Yet it was the only explanation."

Try as he might, Franco could not follow all of the implications to their logical denouement; there were too many things he didn't understand about this discovery.

How in Tiern'aval did a weld come to be here where none existed before?

He pushed a hand through his hair, braving a glance at Raine, but the truthreader was battling his own demons. *Shade and darkness*, Franco inwardly swore. He had to get word to—

That's when he understood—not everything, of course. That was too much to hope for, but enough...enough to wonder if Raine had already pieced things together.

The Fourth Vestal is a good man, an honest and decent man.

Franco hated lying to Raine—he loathed it, in truth—but his oaths were binding. He wasn't certain he could speak the truth even if compelled beyond his own ability to withhold. And then what would become of him?

No. Better to attempt to help the Vestal some other way.

"My lord, what does it mean?" Franco asked, drawing Raine's eye to him. "Who killed that man, and why? Is this the Fifth Vestal's—" he almost choked over the name, "work, or…or was this evil something he intended you to find? Have we…have we perhaps been following a trail not to him, but to…to this?"

Raine looked straight at him. "Why don't you tell me, Franco Rohre?"

SIXTEEN

'Fortune rarely sends excitement in the guise it was envisioned.'

– Farshideh im'Shiavash

Tanis tromped through the Gandrel belligerently in search of 'dandelions, rosemary, lavender or chamomile' for his lady—not one species of which grew in the shade, he well knew, being sun-loving plants all—which was exactly why he was looking for them in the forest.

His lady had been in ill-humor for days, no doubt because Farshideh's health was rapidly failing, but did she have to take out all of her frustrations on him? He reasoned that the longer he spent on this errand, the fewer times she could upbraid him for things that had nothing to do with him, and the fewer tasks she could assign him before the day's end. It seemed a fair solution all around.

Not that he was a lazy boy—no child raised in the Giverny household would ever suffer that affliction!—but her Grace embraced most any laborious task with a frightening enthusiasm. '*A change of work is as good as rest,*' Alyneri always replied if Tanis came to her asking for some time to himself. So he'd learned to take his rest whenever he could in whatever fashion best presented itself.

His belligerence also stemmed in general from the terrible timing of this trip to the country. He understood the reasons for their visit, of course—and to be certain, he loved Farshideh too!—but it didn't change the fact that by now he'd missed Prince Ean's parade, and the banquet, and now Festival had probably begun and he'd be missing that as well. Moreover, he hadn't had the time to learn anything about the Fourth Vestal's visit to Calgaryn, or even to pay him respects, as every truthreader was duty-bound to do.

Raine's truth, but it was so dreadfully unfair! Why did loved ones have to get sick when you were least prepared?

Tanis picked up a fallen branch and swatted at bushes with it as he passed, brooding all the while on the cruel hand of Fate. He knew his thoughts would sound callous if voiced aloud. The truth was that deep down he was scared. Farshideh was the closest thing to a mother that Tanis had ever known. His fondest memories of his childhood included Farshideh—sitting cross-legged on the rug by her fire while she told him stories of the Nine Princes of M'Nador, or standing on a stool to watch her prepare teas for Lady Melisande. Farshideh taught him of herbs and plants and medicinal flowers. She showed him how to recognize them in the wild, which parts to use, and how to clean them and treat them, to distill them for tinctures or extract them for syrups. Indeed, he'd learned far more from Farshideh than he ever had from her Grace.

When the Lady Melisande still received the infirm there at her manor, they'd spent almost all of their time in Aracine. Once, the sprawling mansion and its grounds had truly felt like home; now the country felt too lonesome, and the stillness of the great manor too akin to death.

Cool it was that day, the same as every day in Gandrel Forest, no matter the temperature beyond its borders. In summer, it was a welcome relief from the warmth, but on a blustery Autumn afternoon like that one, as Tanis walked among towering oak and maple and ash, a chill took him. He paused between two sprawling hawthorn bushes and frowned into the gloom, his colorless eyes searching for a reason to explain the hairs rising on the back of his neck. "Shadow take me," he whispered to himself, shaking out his shoulders. "I must be a fool. Are you frightened of shadows now, Tanis?"

He gazed around trying to prove that there was nothing to be afraid of, nothing to justify his apprehension. And yet he felt a…*presence*.

Then he saw him—saw them, materializing out of the gloom between a copse of firs. A dark rider holding a second man before him slumped back against his chest. The rider had one arm wrapped protectively around his charge, who was most certainly injured or infirm. Beside them walked another noble steed of royal caliber, a fine stallion with a silvery mane falling like moonlight against a cream-pale hide—

A Hallovian Grey! Tanis had only heard about the majestic horses, never seen one in the flesh, but the Second Vestal Dagmar Ranneskjöld was said to ride the original sire in the line.

Tanis forgot all of his fears and ran toward the strangers. "Milord, have you come for…?" he began, but the sight of the rider up close took him by such surprise that the rest of the words slipped unspoken off his tongue.

The man was dressed all in black leather, and he had both sword and dagger at his belt—strange weapons, these, which looked to be made of stone. He face bore the chiseled features of the nobility, but he wore his raven curls loose, cropped just above his shoulders; add to this the height and build of a warrior, and he made a striking figure.

Tanis wondered what a man like him was doing in Aracine. *He should be off doing battle somewhere like the Fire Kingdom or the Akkad,* the lad thought immediately.

Only then did Tanis realize he'd been staring at the stranger all this time. The man was just gazing tolerantly back, as if waiting for Tanis to finally finish his sentence. "I—I meant to say…"

"Alyneri d'Giverny," the rider finished for him. His voice was what Tanis imagined a lion's would sound like if the animal could speak the Common Tongue. "Yes, lad. This man has need of her ministrations."

Though he spoke gently, his gaze was penetrating enough to make Tanis feel as if he could see straight through him into his soul. Tanis finally found his voice again. "I—I know the way, milord. I will take you to her."

"Lead on, then," the rider replied.

Tanis took the Hallovian stallion by the bit and led away, but he couldn't help but wonder where the two riders had come from. The injured one looked like flotsam washed up by the sea—as ragged and pale as driftwood.

Tanis led them right through the gardens—he knew the groundskeeper would have conniptions but this was life or death—and around to the closest entry, which was through the loggia off the south wing. As it happened, Farshideh was standing atop the staircase wrapped in a heavy woolen shawl speaking to the gardener. When she saw them coming across the lawn, she turned and went inside. The gardener gave Tanis a scathing look and stormed off.

Moments later, Farshideh emerged again. "I've sent for her Grace!" she called to them while they were still on the lower lawn. She leaned on her staff and came to the edge of the limestone staircase leading down to the gardens. There she waited while the rider dismounted and gathered his charge in his arms. "Bring him up—bring him up!" she waved impatiently.

But as the rider ascended the stairs, Farshideh paled measurably. "You!" she gasped. Her bronzed skin turned ashen, and she leaned heavily on her staff with both hands and swayed in place.

"Tanis, stay and help her," the rider murmured, breezing past Farshideh and on inside the manor as if he knew exactly where he was going.

Tanis hadn't the time to wonder about this strange behavior, or to marvel at how the man had known his name, for his every concern just then was Farshideh, who looked in danger of toppling. He darted to her side and slipped one hand beneath her elbow while placing the other around her waist. "*Sit*," she gasped, barely getting the words out.

Tanis helped her across the patio, and she fairly fell onto a settee. "Farshideh—" the lad began worriedly.

"Leave me, Tanis," Farshideh whispered hoarsely, unable to look at him. "I beg of you."

Confused beyond measure, Tanis yet did as he was tasked. First shouting to the gardener to fetch the coachman to tend to the Hallovian steed, he then ran to join his lady.

Alyneri came rushing down the hallway just as the zanthyr rounded a corner carrying Ean in his arms like a child.

"Quickly!" her Grace ordered, waving him toward her mother's infirmary. "This way."

Alyneri opened the infirmary door and directed the zanthyr to lay Ean upon a long wooden table, which he did with great care. Her Grace took one look at the prince—at his filthy hair and beard and stained, tattered clothing—and exclaimed, "Dear Epiphany—did you drag him here behind your horse?" For a moment she wondered where to begin. Then she waved at the zanthyr, "Well, don't just stand there. Help me get him out of these clothes." The zanthyr dutifully obliged, stripping Ean down until he wore naught but his loincloth.

Alyneri all but shoved the zanthyr out of the way then so she could look him over.

"The wound is—" the zanthyr began.

"I see it!" she snapped. Her hands moved quickly over Ean's unconscious form, touching identical points on each side of his body, at temple and neck, at inner arm and wrist and the back of the knees, at ankles and heels and other places of significance known to those trained in the Healer's craft. In this manner did she move around his entire body. Finally, she asked, "When did this happen?"

"Last night. I created a —"

"I noticed your pattern," she cut in, "but…what is it doing?"

"Keeping him alive."

Alyneri settled him a flat look. "How very helpful."

He grinned accommodatingly.

She bent over Ean to examine his shoulder then, concentrating all her effort on understanding what that pattern was meant to do… "It's…was it…it's containing something?"

"Well deduced, your Grace."

She looked up abruptly. "Was it poison on the blade?" Then she stared at him. "You know a pattern to counter the effects of poison?"

"So it would seem."

Alyneri tried to contain her amazement by turning her attention back to her charge, but her heart was fluttering. *To think that such can be done!* "And where did this happen?"

"Near Stradford."

She straightened and leveled him a stern look. "Do not lie to me, milord. Stradtford is two days' ride from Aracine." She arched a brow at him. "Now the truth. Where did this happen?"

The zanthyr grinned again. "In the Gandrel on the northern border of Stradford."

Alyneri narrowed her eyes at him. "So that's your story and you're sticking to it. At least you're consistent." She returned to her study of Ean's wound. "So who is he?" she asked without looking up.

"No one of import."

"No one of import," she repeated dubiously, "yet a zanthyr works a pattern to save his life and personally brings him to my door. Do you think me a fool? What's your business with this man?"

The zanthyr responded with an almost feral grin, his voice so deep it was almost a purr. "My business with him is my own business."

Alyneri arched a brow at him. "Typical. Well then," and she settled him an icy look, "be on your way. No doubt you'll want to be getting back to your 'own business'."

The zanthyr gave her a polite nod. "Until we meet again, your Grace," he said. Then he simply vanished.

Alyneri let out a little shriek and jumped back two paces, grabbing hold of the edge of the examining table. She shot an affronted glare at the empty space where the zanthyr last stood.

At that moment, Tanis came running in. "Your Grace, is everything all right? I thought I heard a scream."

Alyneri turned with an exasperated look but quickly recovered her composure. "Everything's fine. I just put a kettle on the fire in the kitchen. Bring that and a basin for washing. I'll also need the siphon," she added crisply, counting off on her fingers, "the spice bowl and crusher, one of the bigger ceramic goblets, cheesecloth for his tea, and don't forget the scissors this time." She glanced over at him to make sure he understood. Her eyes had taken on a purposeful, determined look. "Any questions?"

Tanis shook his head. With a tilt of her head, she indicated the door.

He bolted for it.

"Bring the water first!" she called after him.

Alyneri turned back to the mystery man and frowned at the dark wound on his shoulder, the skin of which was badly inflamed.

Impossible that they traveled so far in one day, she brooded while she stared at Ean's shoulder, eyes and mind both probing the wound. Then she caught her lower lip between her teeth and shelved the problem for later. Who could say for certain what a zanthyr could or couldn't do? The only thing anybody really knew about the creatures was that they were utterly insufferable. Abruptly, she turned to the door, calling, "Shadow take me, Tanis! Where's that water?"

On cue, Tanis rushed back into the room with the kettle in his right hand and a multitude of items cupped in the circle of his left arm. He set everything on her work bench and then rushed back out of the room.

Alyneri cleaned the man's wound and followed with the rest of him, all the while wondering who he was. He had the calloused hands of a sailor—*could he have been shipwrecked?* It would certainly explain all the dirt; the man was practically bleeding mud. His teeth and gums were too good to be those of a sailor's, though, and while his nails were shredded, his toes in contrast were nicely trimmed. It was hard to tell his age with the beard and unkempt hair, but he still had the hairless—if well muscled—chest of relative youth. Alyneri thought he was not much older than her. Twenty at most. The funny thing was that he looked *so* familiar. His face was fairly hidden under his unruly beard, but she couldn't help wondering where she might've seen him before.

When she'd finished, her charge was measurably cleaner, but she was no closer to answering who he was or what possible interest a zanthyr could have with him. Finally, she shook out her wrists and placed her fingers to either side of the man's head, closing her eyes.

When she put her hands upon a man, she could see what some called his aura, his energy, that which was peculiarly *him*. It was within the aura that a Healer found each individual's personal pattern, a pattern which, theoretically, should it be unworked, would cause the very man to cease to exist.

All things are composed of patterns... It was the first rule any Adept was taught; whether or not they ever learned to manipulate patterns outside of their own strand, the fundamentals were the same. *All things are composed of patterns,* Alyneri repeated the phrase to herself, and continued on with the Healer's axiom '*...and every life pattern is unique.*'

In order to heal a man, she must first find his own pattern. This she knew, yet she'd been trying for several minutes now to isolate this man's pattern from among the rushing river that was his lifeforce. But she could find nothing. The only pattern she kept coming upon was the zanthyr's.

Impossible! It has to be there—he's alive, isn't he?

She looked again, more broadly this time...letting her awareness perceive him wholly, and saw...she saw...

In the same moment that she found his pattern and heaved a sigh of relief, she was also confronted with an incredible discovery. This man's pattern wasn't *contained within* his energy, it *was* his energy.

His pattern isn't a current within the river, it is *the river.*

"Talk about not seeing the forest for the trees," she muttered.

Alyneri had never encountered anything like this before. In effect, she'd been looking for something small, when the truth was magnificent in scope. It was a startling discovery.

Perhaps this has something to do with the zanthyr's interest in him?

Her mother had never mentioned such a possibility to her, and knowing her mother, that meant the Lady Melisande had never happened upon such a thing in all her long career—nor her mother before. Nor very likely Alyneri's great-grandmother, for such was the method of teaching that the mother-healer taught her daughter *everything* she knew.

Three generations, and none of them ever healed a man whose pattern was his energy.

What could it mean?

Having no answer immediately apparent, Alyneri returned to her task and began repairing the torn threads of the man's life pattern. It was arduous and time-consuming, for each thread must be matched to its appropriate end else the pattern be reconstructed incorrectly and the man die as a result.

It was nearing dusk before she finally withdrew her perception from the man's energy and opened her eyes. Sometime during her work, Tanis had come in to light the lamps and bring her supper; it rested untouched upon her workbench. Looking back to her charge, Alyneri was pleased with her work.

The man looked much better, and she knew by tomorrow his wound would be nearly healed. Now that the threat to him had passed and she could turn her mind elsewhere, however, something nagged at her. Two things, actually. First, the unusual pattern that was this man's life signature; and second, the wielder's pattern which the zanthyr had used to seal out the poison.

Unheard of! Yet so *exciting* to think it could be done. *By Epiphany's Grace—to have that kind of skill…to be able to both heal and manipulate the currents to assist in one's healing!*

It was a lifelong dream, but never more than a dream. Since the destruction of the Citadel on the island of Tiern'aval, there were very few centers of Adept learning. The Kingdom of Veneisea supported the Commune at Jeune, though the Adepts there were mostly focused on scholarly learning rather than application of the Art. Alyneri longed to study Patterning at the Sormitáge in Agasan, but so long as she was commissioned to House val Lorian, and so long as House val Lorian was supporting the war in M'Nador by sending every available kingdom Healer to the front lines, she knew she would not be allowed to leave court.

*I just want to travel as my mother did…*she lamented, catching her lower lip between her teeth and pushing back old feelings of angst and loss. *To see the world, and learn, and help where I can.*

There was always the chance that the Nadori war with the Akkad would end, the kingdom's healers would return to court, and Alyneri would be released of her commission.

There was always a chance that pigs would be born with feathers, too.

Tanis came in and stood behind her, and Alyneri quickly brushed a tear from one eye lest the boy see her crying and start asking questions with that truthreader's voice he'd been working so diligently on. If only he put half as much effort into keeping her herbs stocked…

"Have you any idea who he is, my lady?" the lad finally asked.

Alyneri shook her head as she gazed at the man, but her eyes narrowed as she thought again, *There's something so familiar about him!* If only she could figure out why she thought she knew him. Then again, men with shaggy hair and unkempt beards all tended to look alike to her. "It's puzzling, isn't it, Tanis?" she asked. "He comes wearing neither jacket nor coat of arms, nothing to proclaim his station. I thought at first that he might be a sailor, but if he is, he's not spent too many years at sea. Besides, that zanthyr insists they came up from the south."

Tanis stared at her. "That man was a zanthyr?" He pushed a hand through his ash-blonde hair and scrunched up his comely face as he wondered aloud, "Is that why Farshideh was so upset to see him?"

Alyneri turned him a curious look. "What are you talking about?"

"Farshideh nearly fainted when that man came up from the gardens."

Alyneri frowned. "That's very odd." *I'll have to ask her about that.* "Maybe he owes the zanthyr money," she offered then, returning her attention to her charge. "Why else would a zanthyr try to help a man, save for personal gain?"

"Maybe," Tanis said, but he didn't sound convinced. "You should've seen their horses, your Grace. The zanthyr rode the biggest stallion I've ever seen, and this man rides—well, I assume he rides the Hallovian Grey."

"A Hallovian Grey?" Alyneri caught her lip between her teeth. That ruled out a few theories right there. No man who could afford a noble steed would owe a zanthyr coin—at least, she hoped not. "Oh, well…when he wakes, I suppose we can ask him and the mystery will be solved." She walked to her workbench. Tanis merely stood there, watching her. "By the way, Tanis," she said without turning from measuring out several teaspoons of dark, crushed leaves for a medicinal tea, "where are those flowers I sent you for?"

Tanis blanched and grimaced.

Alyneri didn't have to see him to understand his silence. "I think you know what to do," she murmured. "And perhaps think of searching for the herbs in the herb garden this time, Tanis," she added with a private smile, "for I need you to run into town for a few items once you're done with that and it's nearly sundown already."

Thus with a muttered apology and downcast eyes, Tanis made haste to collect the forgotten herbs.

Alyneri finished up in the infirmary and then called her staff to move the man from the table to the adjoining bedroom. Once she was assured that her charge was resting peacefully, she went to see Farshideh.

She found her Seneschal seated in her sitting room staring absently into the fire. As usual, the room was stiflingly hot, but Alyneri pushed up her sleeves and took a chair across from her friend and mentor.

If Farshideh had looked pale and weak this morning, now she seemed positively ethereal, as if her lifeforce was copiously bleeding out of her with every breath. Alyneri bit back a gasp and forced a smile to cover her shock, though she knew she was fooling no one. She reached to take the other woman's hand. "Farshideh, how are you feeling? Tanis said you nearly fainted in the loggia?"

"I was surprised, is all," Farshideh murmured without lifting her dark eyes from the fire.

"Won't you please tell me what's troubling you? Your name means 'radiance,' and you have ever been a guiding light for me. It pains me so greatly to see you this way."

After a tense moment in which Alyneri feared she was going to be permanently shut out of the other woman's thoughts, Farshideh lifted her sad, dark eyes to meet her gaze. Her next question was as startling as the dismayed expression that accompanied it. "How much did the Lady Melisande tell you of Tanis?"

"My mother?" Alyneri asked in surprise, "of Tanis? She...well, very little actually. We never really discussed it—I mean, I never thought there was much to discuss. She just said she was taking Tanis on as a ward until he was ready for a truthreader's commission. I assumed his parents were—I don't know...dead or indigent, I suppose."

Farshideh barked a dry laugh that erupted into a fit of coughing. She pressed a kerchief to her mouth, unable to hide the blood that stained the linen. Alyneri held her breath for fear of what she wanted to say and do. It was torture having to watch this dear woman die, knowing there was nothing she could do—yet knowing also that others might have the skill...that even that zanthyr might have the skill with Patterning to cure her.

"Dead...to be certain," Farshideh finally managed. "But assuredly not indigent."

Alyneri arched brows, wondering where this was going. "What do you know of him?"

"Not much," she admitted, shaking her head. "Your mother knew more of his origins, but she never spoke of them to me. Only once...once when she'd been up for several days—it was during the Red Plague in M'Nador and you were still a youngling and the boy in swaddling—once she let slip something that I've never forgotten."

"What did she say?"

"We'd just drawn the cloth over four children—an anguished task it is, *soraya*, which I never wish upon you. And the Lady Melisande—I don't think she knew I was listening—she murmured, 'Epiphany's grace the boy is safe in Aracine. Renaii would never forgive me if something happened to him.'"

"Renaii?" Alyneri repeated. "That's an Agasi name, isn't it?"

"Sure as silver." Farshideh fell into another fit of coughing, and the stains upon her kerchief became broad and dark. "Her Grace spent several years in the Empire you know," she managed once she'd recovered herself.

Alyneri blinked in surprise. "I knew she traveled the kingdoms, even to Dheanainn, but...several *years* in Agasan?"

"Her Grace had secrets, she did," Farshideh confirmed. "Well traveled, she was, in her youth. Your grandmother, the Lady Terraine, she was in love with an Agasi all her days, even though she married that Highlands lord."

Alyneri shook her head and smiled. *Amazing what secrets women keep in their hearts*; she knew that well enough. "So my mother spent years in the Empire," she repeated, both thrilled for the fact and injured that her mother never trusted her with the knowledge.

"To be certain, her Grace never studied at the Sormitáge. But she met many an Agasi in her travels with Prince Ryan."

"She traveled with Prince Ryan?" Alyneri was now truly startled. The king's brother had long been gone from Dannym in his role as the Ambassador to Agasan. He made his home now in the Imperial City of Faroqhar and was raising his sons there. "How could she have so many secrets from me?" Alyneri tried to keep the hurt from her voice, but it was there all the same.

"If she kept silent, *soraya*, it was only to protect you."

"But I'm her daughter!"

Farshideh brushed a strand of silver-grey hair from her eyes and smiled lovingly at Alyneri. "Some things…a woman's private affairs, affairs of the heart…these she keeps from everyone—especially her children." She patted Alyneri's hand between her own. "One day you will understand, *soraya*."

As much as she wished to feel injured by her mother's secrets, she couldn't find it in her heart to blame her for anything. She loved her mother too greatly to be angered by any of the choices she made in her life. Just thinking of the intensity of that love brought tears to her eyes and a burning ache in her chest. "Then…this Renaii," she managed, blinking away the tears. "You think my mother met her on her travels?"

Farshideh shrugged. "She never mentioned Renaii save that one time, but I cannot think how else she would have come to know such a woman." She frowned then and looked back into the fire.

Alyneri leaned to try to recapture her gaze. "Farshideh…what does this have to do with what happened in the loggia today?"

Farshideh was silent for a long time. "I never thought…I never thought to see him again," she finally whispered as if to the flames. "The way he said it…I thought it was brazen posturing. I never imagined the day would come."

Alyneri shook her head with bewilderment. "Farshideh, what…?"

"I told him never to come back," she went on, unhearing, speaking the words like a deathbed confession, never lifting her gaze from the flames. "I hated their kind during those years because of…well, because I believed some of the stories and thought them truth. So I told him to get out, that I never wanted to see him again."

Farshideh lifted her eyes from the fire as if with great effort and settled them on Alyneri. She smiled a dreadful smile, entirely mirthless and filled with despair. "He told me, 'the day you see me again, old woman, is the day you will die.'"

Alyneri stared at her. "Who told you that?"

"The man who brought the babe Tanis to us fourteen years ago," Farshideh returned in a bare whisper. "The zanthyr who came again today."

It was well and truly dark before Tanis returned from the nearby township of Bell's Ferry, but the day hadn't been a complete loss, for he'd learned some amazing news. Unfortunately, Mistress Hibbert and her crew—who always had an ear for gossip—had already taken to bed, so Tanis made his way down the hall in search of his lady. He saw a light glowing from the infirmary and poked his head inside.

"Oh, Tanis, there you are," Alyneri said. She was crushing herbs with in a mortar and pestle. "Did you finish up in town?"

"Yes, your Grace." He glanced at the man now sleeping peacefully in the adjoining bedroom. "Has he woken?"

"Not yet. I want you to sit with him tonight so I can be with Farshideh."

Tanis sighed. "Yes, your Grace."

"But pay a call on Farshideh first," she said in a peculiarly emotionless tone. "She's convinced...well, I should tell you, her health is failing quickly."

Tanis ducked out and ran down the halls and upstairs to Farshideh's rooms. She bade him enter when he knocked, and called him to her bedside. "Ah, Tanis, *khortdad*," she said weakly, her deep voice barely a whisper, her dark eyes half-mast, "you come to say goodbye."

"No, Farshideh," he murmured, taking her hand in his. "Just good night."

"What fib is this?" She affected a chiding tone though her gaze was gentle. "A truthreader cannot lie."

Tanis smiled lovingly at her. "Then it must be true."

She closed her eyes and nodded. "You are the dearest child I have ever known, Tanis, *khortdad*, as dear to me as my own Sudi, lost now these many years. I go to rest knowing the sky is big in your future."

Tanis didn't know what to say, mostly because he had no idea what she meant.

"Tanis," she whispered, "do not fear for me. I go soon now to the Path of the Dead. The dead...they see so much. *They know.* I can see now what I should have seen long ago. Tanis, *khortdad*, when I am gone, Alyneri must return to our people—to her family in M'Nador. She has *much* family there, Tanis, family who will love her...her father's people—good people. She must not stay in this cold place, a child of the desert. Tanis..."

Tanis held her hand tightly. "Yes, Farshideh?"

"Tanis, this world is dying. Tanis..." she whispered, but before she could say more, Tanis realized she'd drifted off to sleep.

He stayed with her for a little while longer, but once he was sure she was merely sleeping, he made his way back to the infirmary.

Tanis felt a great emptiness inside. Farshideh seemed so frail, and her words were so...so final; for the first time it became real to him that she would soon be gone.

He took a seat on a stool at the end of the counter where Alyneri was measuring out varied powders into a beaker, but it only reminded him of the many hours he'd spent sitting on that same stool watching Farshideh instead. So he got up and walked to the window. He thought to maybe lighten the mood by sharing his news from town. "Your Grace, did you hear? Everyone's talking about it. Prince Ean—"

But Alyneri cut him sharply off. "Tanis, you know I don't care to hear the court gossip."

Tanis sighed and slouched forward, resting his forehead on the windowpane. The night beyond seemed nothing but sharp shadows full of hate and spite. "Yes, your Grace," he muttered.

Alyneri pushed her flaxen braid off her shoulder, brushed her hands together, and turned to him as she took off her apron. "Our mystery man's tea is all ready for when he wakes. Two teaspoons per cup, and he should drink a cup every hour while he's up—but encourage him to rest. You know where I'll be if you need me." She spun on her heel and left.

Feeling dejected, Tanis walked into the man's room and sat down glumly in a chair beside the bed. It wasn't even a comfortable chair.

In his dream, Ean faced the darkness boldly, but inside he was trembling. The pale certainty of his fate only filled him with fear. Not fear of death—though death was certain—but fear of failure. All those he loved and who loved him…all who had died that he might reach this moment, he felt their presence with him now. Everything rested on his shoulders.

With the support of the lost and the loved, he carried the burden like his family's banner: proudly, with unwavering determination, with certainty of duty.

Before him the darkness undulated as far as the eye could see. Its emptiness was complete, yet Ean knew the darkness comprised something so vast that the mortal mind could not fully embrace its existence.

And every writhing, swirling, vicious inch of it seethed with hatred.

Ean felt its malevolence washing over him in huge waves that stirred and lifted his hair and equally burned and chilled his flesh, but he held fast to the thread in his hand.

It was a delicate silver thing, so ephemeral, so fragile, yet he knew it was the key to the Undoing. So he drew upon it, slowly at first, then with more speed…finally reeling in the thread in voluminous, billowing clouds until the length of thread formed great silvery mountains around him.

And all the while the darkness raged. It beat and tore at him, shredding his clothing, singeing his hair until he stood burned and naked before it. It invaded his body then and destroyed him from within, delving deep into flesh with sharp biting barbs, gnawing voraciously on his living bones. But no matter the agony of Its violation of him, no matter the bloody tears that stained his cheeks, Ean kept pulling on that thread; faster…*faster*, feeling each hand firmly around the string until he looked down and saw that the thread was now attached to him. *His* feet, *his* legs were already gone, Undone, yet he couldn't stop pulling now. The thread kept unraveling at lightening speed, taking him, screaming, with it…

Tanis must've drifted off to sleep in spite of the hard wood pressing into his backside, for he started awake to the sound of the man groaning and thrashing in his sleep. He seemed to be having a bad dream, so Tanis leaned to gently shake him. "Sir… wake up, sir."

The man jerked awake with a startled half-cry, surprising Tanis, who jumped backwards into the beside table and nearly knocked it over. The man pushed palms to eyes and blinked a few times. "Where…where am I?"

"Aracine, sir." Tanis bent and helped him sit up slightly, propping pillows behind his back for support.

The man ran his hands down his face and then turned to look full at Tanis. He had eyes the color of a stormy sea. They seemed in striking contrast to his tangled brown hair and beard. "Aracine," he repeated, sounding more lucid with every waking moment. "At the healer's home? What is it—Fersthaven?"

"Yes, sir."

"Ah…" he said. Then he frowned. "How did I come to be here?"

It was Tanis's turn to be surprised. "You don't know?"

He shook his head. "The last thing I remember is…" He frowned. "Well, it all seems a dream, really."

Tanis wasn't sure what to tell him; it seemed the poor man knew less than they did. "All I know, sir," the lad began, "is that a zanthyr brought you here on the biggest stallion I've ever seen. He brought your horse, too, sir, and if it's not too bold for me to say, well…he's a real beauty, that one."

"No, no it's fine." He ran hands down his face again. "A zanthyr…" and his gaze clouded at mention of his rescuer—or at least Tanis supposed the creature was his rescuer, though there was certainly no proof it wasn't the zanthyr who'd stabbed him in the first place. "Yes, I certainly remember him, and you said…my horse is here?"

"We stabled him, sir. Happy as a lark he is. What's his name, if I may ask?"

"Oh…yes. His name is Caldar."

Tanis nodded his appreciation. "He certainly looks the part, sir."

"He is well named, I'll admit," the man agreed, sounding more lucid with every waking moment. "He hasn't hooves of gold like the Second Vestal's famous stallion, but the name is apt."

Tanis rubbed at one eye. He still had one question. "The zanthyr, sir. Was he a friend of yours?" Tanis wasn't sure why, but he did hope that the zanthyr could be trusted. There was something just too frightening about him should he prove otherwise.

The man scratched thoughtfully at his beard. "A friend? Why…why, yes. I suppose you could say that." Then he added with a little frown, "Though I wonder if he would agree with you."

Tanis looked at him doubtfully, a look which elicited a chuckle from the man. He brightened and gave Tanis an amiable smile. "Well, lad," he said then, "I fear we haven't been properly introduced. Shall I do the honors?"

Tanis gave him a relieved look. "If you would, sir."

"Certainly. I think I remember you—you're the truthreader, Lady Melisande's ward. Am I right?"

"Yes, sir. My name is Tanis."

"Well met then, Tanis. Know me as…" but here he paused and seemed to reconsider his answer. "As…Ean of Calgaryn."

Tanis gave him a curious look. His truthreader's sense told him there was something the man wasn't saying. *But what? Clearly he's not lying.* That much Tanis could easily tell. The lad had quickly discovered that being a truthreader wasn't the easy gift everyone thought. Most of the time he was more confused by the snippets of thoughts and emotions that he picked up than he would've been had he sensed nothing at all. So Tanis asked, "Have you no surname, sir?"

"Ean of Calgaryn is sufficient," the man answered.

"Ean of Calgaryn," Tanis repeated, wishing he understood all of the perceptions feeding into his awareness. "You've the same given name as the Prince of Dannym."

Ean broke into an even broader grin. "Fancy that! How keen of you to notice, Tanis."

Tanis frowned at him. "Are you mocking me, sir?"

"Surely not," he denied, though Tanis wasn't so sure his smile didn't say otherwise.

"I'd best get you your tea," Tanis murmured, and went to attend to it. While he was stoking the fire in the infirmary and setting on a kettle to boil, Ean called from the adjoining room, "And how is Alyneri? I take it she healed me?"

"Yes, sir," Tanis called back. "She had a bit of help though."

"How is that?"

"Her Grace says the zanthyr worked a pattern to spare you from poison and sure death."

"Yes…that zanthyr," Ean repeated musingly again. "Then Alyneri knew him, did she?"

Tanis sat back on his heels while he waited on the kettle. "No sir, not really. She only knew he was a zanthyr. Her Grace is very astute at that sort of thing… spotting Wildlings and so forth. Raine's truth, sir, she rather hoped you'd be able to tell us something about him."

He heard Ean murmur something that sounded much like, *I could tell you many things,* but he didn't think he was supposed to hear that, so he made no mention of it.

When he had the tea prepared, Tanis returned and handed it to Ean. Then he sat down in the chair to be sure to watch him drink it—for as her Grace often admonished, the infirm developed devious tendencies when it came to taking their medicine. But Ean complied without question.

When he was finished, he handed the goblet back and settled Tanis a crooked sort of half-grin. "I find it curious, Tanis," he commented, "that you and Alyneri aren't at Festival. It was my understanding that all of Dannym's nobility—not to mention dignitaries from seven kingdoms—had collected in Calgaryn to receive Prince Ean."

"Lucky for you her Grace had to come to the country," Tanis pointed out, sounding more resentful than he intended.

"Oh indeed," Ean agreed, smiling in such a disarming way that the boy soon found himself grinning foolishly back.

"Truth be told, sir," Tanis confessed then as he settled the goblet on his knees, keen to speak with Ean since he seemed in the mood to converse, "they started Festival without the prince."

Ean raised brows. "Indeed?"

Inspired by his interest, Tanis leaned in and whispered, "The prince didn't show up in port when he was due. Some say he's gone missing!"

"Ah no!" Ean exclaimed. He clapped a hand to his cheek. "What do they say has happened to him?"

Tanis shrugged. "Nobody knows. Some say his ship rendezvoused with an Agasi *draegoon* owned by a princess of the Imperialty, and others say he was captured by pirates, but some think he sabotaged his own homecoming, leaving the ship mid-sail between the Isles and Calgaryn, vanishing in the dead of night."

"Oh indeed, and why should the prince want to avoid Calgaryn?" Ean's eyes glinted with mirth.

"Because of the heiress that refuses to marry him," Tanis answered in a tone that implied everyone should know *that*. At the same time, he almost seemed indignant on the Prince's behalf.

Ean seemed to be having incredible trouble concealing his smile, for it kept twitching the corners of his mouth. "An heiress, eh? That's one I hadn't heard before."

"My friend Tad val Mallonwey thinks it's the only explanation for the prince not being betrothed yet."

"I see. And who would—*ahem*," he paused and cleared his throat, "this heiress be?"

"How should we know? Nobody knows."

"Now quite obviously the prince knows," Ean pointed out in his teasing way. "And the heiress too, I imagine. Too bad we can't ask either of them."

Tanis just looked at him. He was sure Ean was mocking him, but he couldn't decide how, exactly.

"And did you mention this to her Grace, by chance?" Ean asked.

Tanis frowned and rubbed at the goblet with his thumb. "No. She doesn't care to hear the court gossip."

Ean chuckled. "That sounds like her." He stifled a yawn, and for a moment Tanis caught the briefest flash of his thoughts spilling over, full of sorrow and regret, so in contrast to his outward demeanor. His tone betrayed none of his feelings, however, as he smiled and said, "I do believe your lady's tea is working, Tanis. I think I should try to get some rest. But don't fret, I have a feeling you'll have some gossip to spread around none too soon."

It was a clear dismissal, so the boy took his leave, but long into the evening, he couldn't stop wondering what the man could have meant.

SEVENTEEN

'Dare not seek to outwit Fate. It is the rabbit that cannot be caught.'

– origin unknown

F**arshideh im'Shiavash**, daughter of Parviz the Scholar, died that night. The God Inithiya came for her spirit as Alyneri was holding her hand. Azerjaiman claimed her last breath in a passing sigh, and His wind blew outside as the gods left Aracine with Farshideh flying free among them.

"Tanis." Alyneri shook him gently, for he'd fallen asleep in his chair at the foot of Farshideh's bed.

The lad opened his colorless truthreader's eyes, so like the deep waters of a rushing stream, and saw Alyneri's tears. He stood and embraced her, and they remained in this fashion until her shuddering sobs subsided and no more tears would come for either of them.

She wiped her face then and braved a smile. Together, they pulled the sheet over Farshideh's closed eyes. Her body would be returned to M'Nador for the proper rights. Alyneri had promised.

Her Grace sent Tanis off to bed then and herself looked in on her charge. The man was sleeping peacefully again, so she also retired, though it was a long time before sleep came to her.

When she woke, it was with the dawn. Alyneri always woke with the dawn. She made the rounds in Farshideh's stead, nodding approval to the maids as they began their rounds of the occupied rooms, saying good-morning to the cook and her staff and listening attentively to complaints about the gardener. She looked in on the head groundskeeper and his gardeners and listened to complaints about the cook and her crew, but all the while she felt in a daze, like she'd forgotten something important that should've been remembered. She left a note for her Chamberlain, who would oversee Fersthaven until Alyneri could find a new Seneschal, and issued instructions for transport of Farshideh's body. Then she bolstered her courage to face the day and went to the infirmary. Her guest was still asleep, so she set to preparing his morning tea. Tanis had told her last night that he'd woken, but she'd really heard little of the lad's report, being so absorbed with Farshideh at the time. Now for the life of her she couldn't even remember the man's name. *Is that the important thing I've forgotten?* she wondered as she poured boiling water into a goblet, but then she thought, *Honestly, what difference does it make?*

As it turned out, a great deal.

She entered his bed chamber and set the tea upon a coffer chest before crossing the room to open the curtains. As she was tying back the panels—

"Alyneri."

She turned to find him awake and sitting up, and their eyes met…grey eyes beneath cinnamon lashes. She knew those eyes, and now she knew that voice. It was older, yes, but no one spoke her name with quite the same inflection.

"You don't recognize me?" he inquired with a crooked grin. "I was under the impression before I left Calgaryn that you had something of a crush upon me, despite being betrothed to my brother."

Oh yes, she knew him. "Ean," she managed, gripping the curtains for meager support, such emotion evident in the simple utterance of his name. It was a shock, to be sure—not simply that she'd healed him without realizing who he was, but mostly that she'd taken such strides to avoid him yet he was delivered to her doorstep!

Five years—*five years!*—she'd spent trying to rid her heart of Ean val Lorian. Five years wasted, for she felt the pull of him as strong as ever. She grasped for any words to cover her dismay. "By Cephrael's Great Book, what *happened* to you, Ean? You were supposed to arrive in the harbor. There was going to be a parade…"

It was clear from the twinkle in Ean's gaze that her discomfiture wasn't lost on him. "What—that's it? No 'welcome home, your Highness?' Not even an 'I'm so marvelously glad to see you, Ean, might I have a kiss?' I'll freely admit that I've missed kissing you, Alyneri."

Alyneri gathered her shattered composure like shards of broken china, brusquely and without undue ceremony. She released the curtains as if affronted by their proximity and pushed hands primly to her sides. "Were you hijacked," she inquired, all business as she walked to retrieve his tea. "How did you wind up in Stradtford?"

"A bit of chance and a lot of luck," he answered, which wasn't an answer at all. He crossed arms before his bare chest and regarded her with open admiration. "You only grew more beautiful while I was away. I didn't think it possible."

Alyneri grunted skeptically. "Such fawning flattery comes cheap, Ean."

"And abundant," he agreed boldly, "for I can think of nothing I'd rather speak of right now than your beauty."

When she didn't answer him, Ean posed, "There's a certain irony in this, don't you think?"

"Really?" She had paused with her back to him, hands white as they gripped his goblet of tea. "I don't see how."

"Yes, you do," he returned, and she pressed lips together against the truth of it. "You went to great pains to avoid seeing me—coming way out here to the country so as not to be anywhere near Calgaryn when I arrived home, and what happens but I show up as if to spite your best efforts."

Alyneri closed her eyes and forced a swallow. She was ill prepared for this meeting today of all days, what with two nights where she'd barely slept and Farshideh lying cold upstairs…

"Perhaps there's a reason we've been thrown together this way," he suggested.

"Well of course there is," Alyneri answered, finding the strength to face him somehow. She turned with tea in hand. "You're here because you were injured, and I am a Healer. These things just aren't complicated, Ean."

The prince settled her a level look. "Alyneri, you know perfectly well what I mean."

Alyneri arched her right eyebrow in unconvinced response as she walked to his bedside and set the goblet in his hand. He gave her a cheerful grin as he looked up at her. Dear Epiphany, how could she not have recognized him? "You saved my life, you know."

"I am aware of it, yes."

He ignored the cup and held her gaze. "Thanks are in order."

"A note will be sufficient." She tried to move away, but he captured her hand.

"Why do you flee, Duchess? Is my company so loathsome to you?" and he tugged on her hand, all smiles and innocence.

She turned him an annoyed look, though she felt a smile forming beneath it. Ean had always been able to make her smile. "Absolutely," she returned, granting him the banter he seemed to crave, though it took more than she imagined to find the strength for it. "You're a cad and wretch and I want you out of my house immediately."

He laughed. "*That's* the Alyneri I remember. I dare say you had me frightened for a moment."

He released her then, but her escape was bittersweet.

After a moment, Ean said, "We were true friends once, if I recall." He was watching her curiously.

"We were," she reluctantly admitted.

He cracked a smile as he gazed at her. "You do realize you're standing about as far away from me as you could possibly be and still remain in this room?"

Alyneri looked and discovered that she was pressing herself against the wall beside the door to the infirmary. She could do little more at that point than play along, however; so she bit her lip and gazed upon him in consternation. "If...if I may speak openly, your Highness?"

"Please," he offered in earnest.

"It's your breath, Ean," and she pressed fingertips beneath her nose, adding, "I simply cannot bear the stench of it."

"All right then." Ean laughed and held up both hands in surrender. "I will leave you be. If you don't want to tell me what's bothering you, I cannot make you confess. But come, sit with me," he said then, indicating the chair near his bed which Tanis had occupied the night before. "I have so many questions."

Alyneri pressed her lips together and slowly submitted to his will. "I confess, I have questions of my own," she admitted as she returned to his beside.

"Come then. Let us pool our information and perhaps we will find some answers." To humor her, Ean drank his tea and then said as she was sitting down, "I must get word to Calgaryn. Have you parchment and pen, and a bird to send?"

"Of course." She rose to attend to it, but he caught her hand again.

"In a *moment*, please—*seven hells*, Alyneri, do you so despise my company that you can't grant me even a few minutes of your time?"

Alyneri felt her lower lip trembling and caught it between her teeth. She shook her head.

"Well then, *sit*, Duchess." She sat. "Now then, do you know anything of the man who brought me here?"

Alyneri stared at him. "Don't you?"

Ean shook his head. "I know nothing of him beyond his nature. Not even why he risked himself to save me."

"Save you? Ean, I cannot fathom how this all—"

He held up a hand to quiet her. "Yes, yes. I know. I'll tell you everything."

And so he did.

Alyneri listened attentively while Ean spoke of his night landing, of the battle and Creighton's death, and of the days following his capture. She was horrified by the story and the things Ean had been through. While she believed him wholly, it yet seemed so fantastic and unreal, so terrible and tragic, that she found it hard to imagine such things were possible.

When Ean was finished, she sat in silence for a long time just trying to gather herself. She wished for all the world that she might've had fewer involvements with val Lorian princes altogether, for they seemed to court Death while courting her, and Death was a jealous mistress.

Eventually Alyneri pled a moment to herself. She rose and retrieved parchment and pen for him, and wax to seal the missive. All the while Ean wrote, she tried to think of a way out of this...a way to escape from her connection to him. She felt trapped by Fate—for surely there was Fate in this meeting, Ean must be right about that much—but she couldn't see any way to distance herself from the prince short of fleeing the kingdom. Wasn't it bad enough that her heart would always belong to him? Did he have to own her destiny too?

When Ean was finished, Alyneri handed off his letter to her Chamberlain to send to Calgaryn by household courier and returned to Ean's beside, a part of her wondering how long she would have to bear his company in her home, another part wishing it was forever.

While she brooded, he watched her quietly. "What has come between us, Alyneri?" he asked after a moment. "What happened to our love?"

She glanced up, saw his cheeky grin, and gave him a withering look in return. "It was a childhood crush," she told the lie perfectly. "Nothing more."

"Age has wizened you, I take it."

Alyneri sighed. Keeping up the banter was truly draining on her today, for her reserves were so low already. "Life has wizened me," she confessed, unaware that the admission offered Ean more insight into her soul than she would've liked.

"I would that the past had not been, also," he agreed. "If my death could bring back my brothers, I would gladly walk to meet it. But what could've happened to so jade you against *me—oh*...I see..." And he must've truly seen then, for his lighthearted expression faded. "We were all taken from you, weren't we—myself, my brother your betrothed, your own mother... When the *Dawn Chaser* was lost, your whole world changed."

Alyneri turned him a fierce look full of anguish, but her gaze quickly hardened to anger—anger that he'd seen so deeply into her heart, and that it clearly meant so little to him.

She stood and pressed out her skirts. "This was fun when we were children, Ean," she said, "but I cannot make a game of batting words about with you all day any longer." She picked up a package wrapped in sackcloth from atop a dresser, one of Tanis's errands in town yesterday. "These are for you," she said, placing the package where he could reach it. "Tanis will be available for anything else you need."

Ean looked hurt and confused. "Alyneri, I was only—"

"My Seneschal passed over last night!" she snapped, spinning him a desperate look. She'd meant to carry on with proud determination, to show him she was a child no longer, but her voice broke in the speaking of Farshideh's loss, and she could say no more.

"Oh, Alyneri…" and his tone held such sorrow on her behalf. "I'm truly sorry."

Ean's heartfelt sympathy was more than she could bear. She shouted at him, "If you'd never come here, she wouldn't be dead! Tis your fault she was taken from us!" and she fled from the room in tears. Rushing down the hallway, Alyneri pushed past a befuddled Tanis, out through the loggia, and veritably flew down the very steps up which the zanthyr had carried Ean the day before.

Reaching the gardens, she ran.

EIGHTEEN

'If harm needs be done, do so. The sweet well of mercy is brackish with the tears of sacrifice.'

– The Agasi wielder Markal Morrelaine
at the Battle of the Citadel, 597aV

Franco was spared what he feared was certain demise at Raine's hand by—as he decided in hindsight—what could only have been divine intervention.

In the very moment when Raine was reaching for him to no doubt delve more severely and deeply into his thoughts, the truthreader withdrew his hand and clapped his other hand across it. His diamondine eyes took on a far-away look, and he stood for several moments utterly still.

Just when the hairs were starting to rise on the back of Franco's neck, the Vestal shook out of his stupor and dropped his arms to his side. "So." He settled a disquieting gaze on Franco. "We shall resume this discussion at a later time. We must travel immediately."

Franco barely hid his relief, for all the good it did him to try to hide anything from Raine. There was no way the Vestal was ever going to trust anything he said ever again. Franco admired and respected Raine immensely, and it pained him to lie to the man. "I am at your service, as ever, my lord," Franco said with a heavy heart. "What is your will? As it happens, we are in an advantageous place for travel."

But when Raine told him, Franco groaned. They'd just passed through Dheanainn seven days earlier and now meant to return from whence they started! At least with a weld at his disposal, their return would be instantaneous instead of as laborious as the journey north had been.

Raine cracked a smile at Franco's reaction, but despite the discord between them, it was quite without malice. Franco had noticed that the man was ever just in his dealings with others. Very probably, until Raine had proof of some treason, he would go on treating him with the utmost respect and courtesy. "I am sorry, Franco," the Vestal apologized, referencing his request. "You have been very forgiving of my demands upon you these past weeks, and especially in this last trip, and I am probably not paying you enough to compensate for your sacrifice of time and energy."

"You're not paying me at all," Franco pointed out sullenly.

"Oh, yes," Raine cast him a droll smile, "there is that."

Franco frowned at him and then turned and gazed out into the still pool. The weld glowed invitingly. If only he could travel its path to somewhere relaxing, like Jamaii. He had friends on the island, friends of the female persuasion—pirates all, of course, but they got along well enough. Franco sighed as he gazed at the expanse of water between himself and the weld, not relishing wet boots for the next two days. *I suppose there is nothing to be done for it except to walk.*

As if hearing the thought, Raine motioned with his arm. "Lead away, nodefinder."

Grumbling about the state of his already over-taxed boots, Franco sloshed out into the pool with Raine close behind.

"My oath-brother shares your pain, Franco," he remarked idly. "No doubt Björn would as soon turn the water to ice as walk through it. He mislikes getting his feet wet. Once, when we were on a mission in the jungles of Bemoth, he spent two hours building a bridge of air with fifth-strand patterns rather than traversing a river no more than thigh deep at midpoint."

"That seems an awful lot of trouble," Franco agreed. "Why not simply make your boots proof against the water?"

Raine shrugged. "Too mundane, I suppose. He tends toward the dramatic."

"You suppose..." Franco glanced at the Vestal. "Did you not ask him, milord?"

Raine gave him a rueful look. "Clearly you have never met the Fifth Vestal."

"Not under any amiable circumstances," Franco muttered, relieved he was able to answer truthfully about that at least.

"My oath-brother never answers a question directly. It interferes with his passion for lengthy discourse. Add to that an ego so dense that the bedrock of the very realm would shatter against it, and one soon realizes that the fewer questions asked, the better."

"I wonder if that isn't a result of the influence of the fifth upon its Adepts," Franco mused. "Not that I mean to advocate for the Fifth Vestal, milord, it's just that...well, Markal Morrelaine and I are well acquainted, and I'd be hard-pressed to believe *his* ego could be any less immense."

Raine smiled softly. "Perhaps you're right, Franco. I would like to believe it so."

They reached the weld, and Franco held a hand for Raine to wait. "If you will give me a moment to travel ahead, milord, and open the channels."

Raine nodded.

Franco stepped through the portal.

Travel within a weld was not the same as through a node or a leis. It was a central hub for the very pattern of the world, and energy surged around Franco as he moved within its domain. A torrential wind roared in his ears such that communication would've been impossible for him, yet not even the frayed edge of his cloak trembled beneath the ethereal force. Still, every hair on his body stood on end, electrified, as energy pooled and collected around him and then streaked on. He was a rock in the frothing waters of a raging river; without his right of blood and birth to work the patterns of this Traveling as innately as he worked his own breath, he would've been instantly swept into oblivion.

To see with the eyes of an Espial while standing within the hub of a weld was to see an immense net of silvery pathways merging, diverging, converging into infinity. To understand them, to know where they led...this was a journeyman Espial's most arduous—and potentially disastrous—task; but no Espial was admitted to the Master's Guild who had not demonstrated his competence at navigating a weldfield with or without a map.

Standing amid the frothing energy stream, Franco found the path to Dheanainn and then stepped back out of the weld. Raine was waiting patiently for him.

The relative silence of the divining chamber was dramatic to his accosted hearing. Franco took a moment to recover, to find his breath, to still his heart. One did not become the focal point for the energy of the world without being drained by its passing. He pressed hands over his ears and dropped his jaw a few times to clear his ears of the bellowing roar that still seemed trapped within. Finally, he mustered his resolve again and pushed his weariness aside. "This way, my lord. If you would be so good as to place your hand upon my shoulder, as we have done in the past..."

Dheanainn was the largest of the Wildling cities, and like its population, its weather was fierce and unpredictable. As they emerged from the weld into the city of Dheanainn, the air was humid and thick and the streets were wet from showers. A bank of dark clouds was moving off to the north toward the mountains, a swath of jagged granite peaks.

Raine procured horses from one of his many contacts scattered throughout the realm, and they rode east, toward the province of Malchiarr. Malchiarr was Geshaiwyn country, and Franco would have as soon not run into any of them. He made a point of avoiding Shapeshifters when at all possible, and especially Geshaiwyn. As a race, generally, they had an alarming sense of humor.

Raine had mentioned nothing of the nature of their errand, nor who had contacted him in such an unusual manner. Franco was well traveled and knowledgeable in his field, but he admitted that when it came to Patterning, there was a great chasm of knowledge as yet unknown to him. Raine, conversely, seemed to walk with certainty across this vast uncharted terrain.

They were not long out of the city when they came to two heavy, iron-worked gates blocking a shaded drive that led up into the forested hills. Franco recognized the lion crest upon the verdigris metal. "Marc Laven? Last I knew he'd vanished into the wilds of Avatar."

"This is his ancestral home, I believe."

"What is our business here, milord?"

"Alas, she told me nothing of the matter. Only to come straightaway."

She must've been Alshiba Torinin then. The First Vestal, now the Alorin Seat since the Fifth Vestal's betrayal, was the only woman who might command Raine D'Lacourte to attend her heel like a pup.

"If I may ask, milord? How was she able to contact you?"

In answer, Raine held up his hand and the oath-ring he wore on his middle finger.

"Oh, right."

Franco had heard that the Vestal oath-rings were powerful talismans, but their secrets were usually well guarded. He wondered why Raine trusted him with the knowledge. The truthreader dismounted and pushed the gates wide to let Franco through with the horses. It was testimony to the Fourth Vestal's code of honor that he used his own magic only out of necessity and never as a display of power; most certainly not to do something so mundane as opening a gate, though it would've been the simplest thing in the world for him to do.

They rode up the road in silence, sheltered from a rising wind by a border of towering moss-covered oaks, their thoughts following very different paths. Traveling the weld had put memories of Dagmar into Franco's head, and remembering the Second Vestal brought a smile to his lips. Dagmar Ranneskjöld was called the Great Master by his Guild, for his talent at the craft was mastery indeed. *Artistry, even.*

Dagmar could do things with the nodes that *no one* could do.

The Great Master could reroute the pattern of the world itself.

Thinking the thought scared him a little, and suddenly he wondered if it had been Dagmar that moved the weld to Calgaryn. He prayed it wasn't so. He desperately needed to believe that the Great Master remained incorruptible.

Dagmar came to every Espial at some point in his life. The Great Master felt it immensely important to establish personal contact with all of his 'sons'—for it was rare indeed that a female was born to the second strand. As rare as a male born to the first. In addition to his talent at nodefinding, the Great Master was blessed with the additional gift of dreamwalking, a very rare trait found only among Adepts of the second strand.

"Do you miss him, Franco?" Franco turned Raine a swift look, but the truthreader held aloft a reassuring hand. "I do not invade your privacy, I assure you. Your thoughts of my oath-brother were…very strong."

Franco willed his beating heart to settle and nodded. "Yes, milord. I deeply miss his counsel."

Raine gazed at him sadly. "Has he contacted you since…?"

"The Citadel?" Franco shrugged. "In my dreams only." He was grateful to be able to tell the truth about it.

Tis shameful how you take pride in finding anything to say that isn't a boldfaced lie.

Franco gritted his teeth at what he was coming to call his mad voice of conscience.

"I hear tales," Raine said pensively. "Tales that he's come to others in their dreams. They all say he claims to be a prisoner of my oath-brother, Björn. That he's being held in T'khendar." Raine turned him an inquiring look.

"He hasn't said that to me." *Another truth.*

Oh, well done.

"Has he come to you, my lord?" Franco asked. "Has he visited your dreams?"

Raine shook his head. "The nature of our oath prevents us from contact in dreamscape." The Vestal looked as if he wished to say more but just then they rounded a curve in the road and exited the wood, reaching an open drive that circled in front of an immense manor the color of malachite. Gargoyles glared down accusingly from high parapets that edged a steep roof darkened with moss, and the entire place looked tediously grim.

Raine was dismounting as they heard a raucous cry from high above.

Franco craned his neck to spy a hawk soaring down out of the grey clouds. It flew in an arc across the drive, out over the near trees, and circled back down toward the horses with wings outstretched, talons extended. Suddenly gold-bronze flame erupted skyward, engulfing the bird completely. Franco cringed instinctively away, though the flames were quite without heat.

When the fire faded, a man stood upon the road.

Oh gods, I'm doomed.

Of all the Adepts in the world he least admired, it was Seth nach Davvies, called Seth Silverbow, leader of the Avieth Clans, Third Vestal of Alorin. They'd met numerous times, for one of Franco's dearest friends was Seth's great-nephew Mazur; yet Seth had disowned Mazur after the events at the Citadel. Mazur's fate was by far the worst of all.

Seth was a stocky man of average height with shoulders like small boulders and biceps you could bend horseshoes around. Like most avieths, he had fiery red hair, tawny-gold eyes, and an aquiline nose. He wore garments of green leather and had a quiver of silver-tipped arrows strapped to his thigh. He took one look at Franco and scowled.

"What's *he* doing here?" he demanded of Raine.

"Helping me to travel, Seth, or did you imagine I would float here on my magic carpet?"

Seth's gaze flicked dismissively over Franco. "He looks terrible. What did you do to him?"

"Neither of us has slept since last you and I spoke."

"That was a week ago."

Raine sighed. "Precisely."

"Well, did you at least find the bastard?"

"We found something unanticipated."

"No kidding."

Raine ignored his slighting tone. "And you, brother? How did you find this place?"

"Alshiba got an anonymous tip."

"While in Illume Belliel?" Raine looked skeptical.

"No, she was in Agasan conferring with the Empress. But come," the avieth said, waving them off toward the staircase, "they're waiting."

Franco didn't bother asking who 'they' were, knowing he'd find out soon enough, and more knowing such a question would only earn him a scowl from Seth.

They headed into the manor following behind Seth, who navigated the maze of halls and adjoining rooms unerringly. The manor seemed long deserted save by spiders and bats; window treatments had been replaced by cobwebs, and a thick coat of dust covered everything.

"Only the floor is clean," Raine noted pensively, completing Franco's thought. Indeed, the marble tiles shone immaculately, as if swept clear by a powerful wind.

They finally reached a gallery overlooking a courtyard gone to weed, and there Alshiba waited for them. She wore traveling leathers in supple white, and her golden hair was drawn into an elaborate braid down her back. She looked exceedingly ethereal. Beside her stood a tall soldier in chain mail and a white surcoat trimmed in silver. The hilt of a greatsword gleamed over his shoulder.

The First Vestal brightened at their entrance. "Raine." She swept forward to embrace her oath-brother.

"Alshiba." Raine pulled away and placed hands on her slim shoulders. "I have come. What have you found?"

She cast her grey eyes toward a dark doorway in the far wall. It looked to have once been obscured by a faded tapestry—probably by the very one that now lay crumpled in the corner. "Come," she said grimly. "I will show you."

It was the smell that hit Franco first. The stench was powerful, almost overwhelmingly so, an acrid, rotting stench that could only be death in all its viscous decay. Alshiba's Espial and protector led them down the staircase which lay beyond the doorway, conjuring fire in his palm for light as much as to burn away the stench of evil that suffused the place.

He stopped at the foot of the stairs and moved aside. Raine walked further into the gloom and beheld. So did Franco, who saw more death in a single sweep of his gaze than he'd seen anywhere outside of Tiern'aval.

Gods, what has been done to them?

For once his conscience was silent, respecting the dead.

Torture, Franco knew then. What was worse, seeing the dead merely confirmed what he'd been fearing for months. The rumors were true. The time had come.

Soon I will be Called.

Raine looked stricken. "Is...is it all of the missing Companions?"

Alshiba shook her head. "No. All were Adepts, yes, but none were Companions."

"They're not?" Franco blurted, stunned that his suspicions had been wrong.

Alshiba arched a brow at him.

Raine said, "So Marc is still...."

"Missing, yes. And Rothen Landray, Cecile Andelaise, Sahne Paledyne, Pieter van der Tol... many others. Raine..." she called his gaze back to her. "I knew you'd never believe this without seeing it yourself. I fear this is but the first of many such places."

Raine exhaled pensively as his gaze swept the ill-begotten room. "This is not like the ones we've found murdered," he observed. "Joseph and Kedar's were clean deaths. All of the Companions we've found have been such. Nothing like this."

"Why?" Seth demanded as he gazed angrily into the room. "Why did he do it?"

Raine turned him a severe look. "You think *Björn* did this?"

"Who else, brother?"

"Anyone else!" Raine retorted, incredulous. "I cannot believe he's capable—"

"He slaughtered the Citadel Mages in cold blood," Seth snarled. "He took up Malachai's banner! He sent Shades across the world hunting for his own kindred! He's capable of far worse than this!"

"But torture, Seth," Alshiba said coldly, her blue eyes leveled on the dead. "It is hardly his style."

"What then?" Raine asked her. "Who?"

She shook her head. "You will put your many resources to this task, no doubt, but I fear the things they won't find."

Raine pulled a small flat stone from his pocket and began passing it through his fingers, rolling it between each with quick surety. "An anonymous tip," he mused. "Do you think they wanted us to find their handiwork?"

"I suspect a different source," she murmured, "though one no less culpable—if not for this, then other crimes."

Raine looked at her as if knowing to whom she referred. Franco imagined he did as well.

Alshiba exhaled a troubled sigh. "Adepts kidnapped and murdered, others simply vanishing; unrest plagues the kingdoms of man. The Empress says the Danes plan a revolt and expects war in the spring." She shook her head and pressed lips tightly together. "Alorin is out of Balance, and the realm is dying."

Raine worked the muscles of his jaw, clenching and unclenching.

"We *know* when it began," Seth said belligerently.

She turned him a swift look, her blue eyes hard as agates. "Do we? Or are we fooling ourselves, pouncing upon the first helpless ewe that strays from the herd?"

"Björn is hardly helpless, Alshiba," Raine murmured, his gaze staring distantly as if seeing the man in question, "and far from innocent."

"Crimes he has to answer for, yes," she agreed, "and some of them, like the murders of the Mages, are indeed unforgivable. But Seth would have us chase the first hare startled from the brush. All of our actions would be based on wrong assumptions. Raine, what if he isn't behind—"

Seth suddenly raged incredulously, "You are still besotted with him! Three centuries and you remain faithful! He made you his *whore*, Alshi—"

She struck him across the mouth with an openhanded blow that silenced him even as it drew blood. The moment was shocking—Franco never imagined she was capable of such cool dispassion and crude violence in the same motion, or that she dared strike the Third Vestal. That he took it without retribution… Franco realized Alshiba was more of a force than he ever gave her credit for.

"Calm yourself, Seth," she meanwhile warned in a low voice as he glared venomously at her at dabbed at his lip with the back of his hand. "You shout your own crimes."

Silence descended. Franco wished he could've been anywhere else. In the quiet of the gruesome chamber, his fears were given too much voice.

"Would that I could find Markal Morrelaine," Raine finally grumbled as if following his own thoughts in a different direction.

"You won't, brother," Seth remarked after a moment. He spat blood onto the floor, but he seemed calmer. Perhaps brute force was the only way to handle his volatile temper. "Face it, *please,* for all our sakes. Three centuries you've searched for the bloody man. He obviously doesn't want to be found."

Alshiba grunted. "Markal is too simple a solution to this complexity, Raine. He won't tell you what you want to know, even should you find him and delve deeply into his mind. He and Björn were thick as stones. You're foolish to think Markal will share their plans with you—that he *could* speak of them, even under coercion."

Foolish indeed, Franco thought. He hadn't known that Raine searched for the Agasi wielder, and he thanked Epiphany that he didn't know where Markal had gone to ground, awaiting his Calling.

Seth added grumblingly, "Might as well ask that damned zanthyr. He knows *all*—I guarantee you that!"

Raine cast him a weary look, appealing to what modicum of decorum he might posses.

"I have long ago given you leave to try questioning Phaedor, Seth," Alshiba said, glancing his way coolly.

"As if the creature would deign to speak to *me*."

Franco had begun gazing morbidly at the floor of the room, which looked darkly polished in the muted torchlight. "It's blood," he whispered, not realizing he said the words aloud, calling all of their attention back to the terrible scene they'd come to witness. "The floor is covered in blood."

"Two fingers thick," Alshiba said, and there was such powerful fury in her voice that he felt his heart quiver from the force of her wrath. "They bled them all, bled them dry."

"Dear Epiphany, why?"

"I cannot fathom."

Raine flicked the stone through his fingers and then caught it with finality. He observed quietly, "There is one shadowed corner into which we haven't peered for answers. A legend we all know well…"

She turned him a sharp look and pressed fingers to his lips. "We will not name them here," she whispered. "They do *not* exist."

Franco suspected that in this, too, he knew of whom and what they spoke. What little effort it would take to tell her how wrong she was, how indeed, Malorin'athgul truly existed, how they walked the realm, how the First Lord had known of them for eons… He *wanted* to tell her the truth, but he suspected that even should he try, he would choke on the words. There was nothing so binding as an oath to the Fifth Vestal.

"I have said the rights for the dead already," Alshiba said quietly. "I don't know what more to do."

"Fire the room," Raine replied, at once emphatic. "Incinerate everything in this place. You know the working as well as I."

Wordlessly, she nodded.

"What?" Seth protested, grabbing Raine's arm. "We can't destroy the evidence! We must investigate! Find out who's behind this heinous craft since you're so bloody certain it wasn't Björn!"

Raine turned to him impatiently. "If the currents tell us nothing, Seth, then you can rest assured that the villains will not have left behind a note proclaiming their names and whereabouts."

"Nothing is certain, Seth," Alshiba added. "I mean only to keep our vision wide and not limit ourselves to foregone conclusions."

"You're both *mad*," Seth snarled, out-voted and hating them for it. "Wool-brained and fool-witted!" He spun on his heel and stalked up the stairs.

Franco watched him go and wished he could follow.

There was a time—a span of decades, in fact—when Franco had doubted his mission. That day, that first fateful day when he'd groveled at Björn's feet and pled for mercy…it was upon that day that the great battle still before them had been explained in no uncertain terms. He'd been given a task to complete ere the time when he would be Called upon for greater contribution; but all of it was so outrageous, so implausible, that at the time, his misguided adolescent mind simply could not accept it. Oh he took the oath, to be certain—it was that or face a grisly death—but he didn't actually believe a word of it. Not then.

Oh, to be so naïve again, he lamented, *to be an innocent of the world, sheltered from all its tragedies and treasons.*

"Franco Rohre."

He looked up to find her watching him. He'd always thought Alshiba was too Avataren for his tastes with her pale hair and foreign-looking features, but since meeting Ysolde Remalkhen, he realized there was great beauty in Alorin's First Magic, as well as great strength. "Yes?"

"You need not remain for this, Franco."

"Bless you, milady, but I would all the same."

She nodded, accepting his answer without needing a reason, and reached for Raine's hand. "I know the working," she murmured, and set to it.

NINETEEN

'The quest for truth is man's greatest adventure.'

– The Adept Valentina van Gelderan, Empress of Agasan

"**Ho Julian!** Look at this one!"

Julian D'Artenis looked up from the gold necklace he was studying to peer through the sea of heads in search of his friend Liam. It was no easy task. Cair Rethynnea's Avenue of the Gods was packed with travelers seeking the perfect prayer beads, crystals or colored glass for meditation, or just the right sized miniature replica of their chosen god carved from the appropriate stone. City law prohibited solicitation beyond the Pillars of Jai'Gar, the prime desert god, so the merchants had positioned their stands of jewelry, polished prayer stones, figurines, and crystals along the boulevard from Palladium Park right up to the edge of the green jade Pillars.

Julian at last spotted Liam's red head and pushed his way over to him. "What've you got?" he asked hopefully.

Liam held out the necklace to his friend. It was a stunning configuration of cabochon aquamarines set in a chain of delicate platinum roses—very expensive. Which the seller soon confirmed. "Fifty crown!" the merchant barked at Julian.

Shocked, the teen lifted his pale green eyes to the man, only then noticing that the latter was a heavyset, black-bearded Khurd from the Akkad. Julian shot Liam a quarrelsome look that spoke volumes. Everyone knew that bargaining with a Khurd was like trying to bleed wine from a stone. But the necklace *was* what he was looking for... *There's nothing to be done for this, I suppose, save to try*, he decided, wherein in protested in reply, "That's an outrageous price!"

The merchant harrumphed. "Fifty crown!" he barked again.

Julian eyed the man irritably, then turned and glared at Liam. "Why'd you go and pick *his* stand, bungleboy?" he accused.

Liam was unrepentant. "You said you wanted the prettiest stones for your mom, and the Khurds have the prettiest stones—everyone knows. The Bemothi traders give them first pick at the Bashir'Khazaaz—"

"I *know*," Julian grumbled. He turned and stared at the stones again. They really were beautiful, like the clearest water captured in flawless perfection. But it was their shape that was important. *Exactly what I needed.*

Just then, his friends the triplets Rickon, Dickon and Rod arrived in a rush and announced in unison, "Julian! We saw the Keeper of the Bones! He gave us each a shard of the—"

"Put those down!" Julian slapped all three of their outstretched hands, knocking loose the shards of white bone to disappear beneath a dozen feet. The black-haired triplets glared at him. "Do you want to call the eye of the Fhorg Demon God to yourselves, you idiots!" Julian scolded. *Walking around with enchanted bones!* Julian inwardly groaned. Everyone knew how the ebony-skinned Keepers tricked people into converting to their dark worship by handing out bones laced with magic.

Rickon was quick to recover from his petulance when he saw the necklace in Julian's hands. "Wow! Are those sapphires?"

Rod clapped his brother in the back of the head, knocking a black forelock into Rickon's brown eyes. "Those are aquamarines, you dimwitted fop."

Rickon rounded on him, shouting, "*You're*_a fop!" They tumbled off into the crowd, who closed in around them again indifferently. The other three went back to the matter of the necklace.

"It's for your mother, Julian," Liam reminded him—as if he needed reminding!

"Yeah, Julian," the slender Dickon agreed. "You can't scrimp on her birthday present."

Liam added, "And it's not like you can't afford—"

"*Will* you two shut up!" Julian hissed, shooting a look at the merchant. The Khurd was leering at him now, grinning like a bridge troll. Utterly embarrassing.

Liam looked injured. "You said aquamarines," he pointed out in a hurt tone. "You said your mother wanted cabochon aquamarines."

"Fifty crown!" the merchant barked, pointing at the jewels. Julian began to wonder if those were the only words the man knew how to say. He frowned at the necklace again. It wasn't that he couldn't afford it. Fifty Free Crown was barely half that in Veneisean gold, but it was still outrageously expensive.

"You said aquamarines," Liam repeated a third time, "since they're the Goddess Alshiba's favorite, and your mother being—"

Julian leveled his friend a pointed stare. "Liam," he interrupted with forced patience, "I do not need reminding of my mother's station. She does enough reminding for all of us. All right?"

Liam looked injured. He set to pouting.

"That is a certainly necklace deserving of a High Priestess," someone observed mildly from behind Julian. All three boys turned their eyes to the man. He stood half a head taller than the tallest of them and was dressed in an elegant jacket the color of sky. His black curls were cut short, his features were elegant and his manner refined, and he had sparkling blue eyes that complimented an amiable smile. Dickon and Liam grinned back at him like the village idiots, but Julian settled his pale green eyes on the man. Strangers didn't just jump into conversation on the streets of Cair Rethynnea—not when their intentions were honorable.

Seeing that he had the boys' attention, the dark-haired man continued, "But aquamarines are not Alshiba's favorite gem. The First Vestal prefers the firestone—opals."

Rickon and Rod just then shoved their way back into the group, having ostensibly decided the victor of the fight—though a man would be hard-pressed to tell which one of them it was; Rod was sporting a cut brow and Rickon had a bloody lip. Julian ignored the both of them.

"How would you know that?" Liam challenged the blue-eyed stranger. "You're no priestess."

Julian was eyeing the man with cautious reserve. He couldn't help but notice that he wore a silver ring set with a large aquamarine far more exquisite than any stone in the necklace Julian held; it sparkled almost as intensely as the man's blue eyes. "One would think the goddess's Healers would know such things," Julian said.

The man smiled noncommittally. "One would think," he agreed. "May I?" Julian held the necklace out, and the stranger took it from his offering hands and looked it over. "These are fair quality. Probably the best you'll find in this market." He settled his stunning sapphire eyes on Julian again and gave him a knowing smile. "Have your heart set on this one, do you?"

Curious now, Julian shrugged.

"Fifty crown!" the merchant barked.

The man handed the necklace back to Julian. Then, arching a dark brow, he turned to the Khurd and told him, "*Ben pazarlik yatmam. Üç yüzden fazla vermem.*"

The merchant gaped at him.

"You speak the desert tongue?" the triplets chimed in wonder.

The dark-haired man settled the merchant a penetrating look. The merchant blinked, then turned to Julian and barked, "Thirty crown!"

Julian was taken aback. He spun a swift look at the stranger.

"That will be his final price," the blue-eyed man advised. "You should take it." Then he turned and disappeared into the crowd.

Wide-eyed, Julian grabbed for his purse.

Minutes later, the five boys were wandering down the Avenue of the Gods toward the towering jade Pillars of Jai'Gar.

"Who was he?" Rickon wanted to know.

"How'd he learn the desert tongue?" Rod demanded of no one in particular. "I thought only the Khurds could speak it."

"Maybe he was from M'Nador," Dickon suggested.

"He didn't look like a desert man to me," Rod argued. "More like an Agasi."

"Yeah, that's true," Dickon admitted.

Silent among his bickering friends, Julian was walking with his necklace in hand experiencing a sick feeling of trepidation. *Why?* he wondered. *Why did he want me to know that he knows who I am?*

"I thought we were to meet in the Temple of the Vestals," the cloaked man said suddenly into Björn's ear as he walked along the Avenue of the Gods, following a good fifteen paces behind the five teenagers.

Björn did not need to turn to know who now walked at his side. "I was otherwise engaged," he answered in a low voice. He nodded toward Julian's fair head among the crowd in front of them. "He has the gift, though he doubts it still."

"An Adept?" the man beside him asked. His voice was muffled by the deep cowl of his sky blue cloak, which kept his face in shadow. "What strand colors his blood?"

"The rarest one," Björn answered. His eyes never strayed from the five boys ahead of him. They had passed beneath the Pillars and were walking along Temple Row heading for a soaring structure of green glass and white marble that was a scaled-down replica of the Hall of A Thousand Thrones in the cityworld of Illume Belliel—though not a man on that street knew it save himself. "It becomes increasingly clear to me, Dämen," he began, "that none of the Vestals understand what's been happening these past centuries during my absence, lest they'd have long sent others in search of these lost souls."

The Shade's silver features were fully concealed beneath his cowl, but his dark eyes looked sadly upon the five boys. "They're Returning, but not awakening," he remarked with sage understanding. "Is it Balance that prevents the knowledge of their gifts from surfacing?"

Björn shook his head, and his sapphire eyes were granite hard. "I suspect it is merely the force of the others' presence in our world. They need *do* nothing, Dämen," he stressed with sudden fervor, turning to regard his Lord of Shades with concern marring his handsome brow, "nothing but wait, and the pestilence that suffuses their being will gradually dissolve our living realm. But they do not *do nothing*." He cast his Lord of Shades a telling look before turning forward again. "They act. And thus do we."

"Indeed, First Lord," said the Shade solemnly.

Rather than expounding on the troubling subject further, Björn got right to business. "How go the preparations?"

"Everything is ready," Dämen confirmed. Then he frowned. "But First Lord, do you really think this course is wise? What if there is trouble with the node?"

Bjorn cast him a sideways glance. "There will be no trouble with the node, Dämen, and you know my reasoning better than most."

Dämen pursed his lips, frowning beneath his shadowed hood. Clearly something was troubling him deeply. "We find ourselves at the same crossroads, *ma dieul*," he murmured at last. "They will find him again soon—it is assured. Do you not think it prudent to do more to protect—"

"*No*," Björn said in a tone that brooked no argument, his eyes flashing with warning. "Twice before we've reached this crossroads, and twice we've failed. Every time we have tried to help this man, he has died as a result, and do you know why?"

"No, First Lord."

Bjorn cast him a telling look. "Because we overstepped ourselves. Balance plays a mighty role in this man's life. All we can do is keep the Balance on his side, give him time to come to the understanding on his own. It may seem cruel, Dämen—and dangerous—but it is the only way to avert tragedy."

Dämen still seemed reticent. "The Second Vestal has spoken to me on the matter, *ma dieul*," he admitted. "He sees events unfolding on many strands and wishes we might exert more influence over them."

"Dagmar is driven by an insatiable need for action and wants more than anything to return to Alorin," Björn replied, waving off the Shade's concerns. "He would rush headlong as our sole vanguard against the ravening hoards—and would no doubt cut a formidable swath through the enemy ranks—but ultimately, in his haste he would fail." He eyed his Lord of Shades intently. "All things fall in their time and place, Dämen. While we might wish them differently, our wishes cannot change the pace of the game. No, we must ride the river, no matter how interminably slow its current may seem, and trust that the river is taking us where we need to go."

"Yet the river is long and winding," Dämen said disagreeably, "and full of sharp rocks and treacherous falls that we cannot see while riding its current."

Bjorn eyed him crookedly and then chuckled. "Touché."

Dämen bowed respectfully, his point made and taken; it was as much as he could hope for. "What is your will, *ma dieul?*"

"The node is all that remains," Björn told him, "but for the plan to work I must have the services of a Nodefinder. I need your Shades to track down Franco Rohre. He is one of the fifty, you will recall, who swore fealty and were given tasks at the fall of the Citadel." He narrowed his gaze, adding, "The time has come for Franco to prove his troth."

"Your will be done, *ma dieul,*" Dämen murmured with another reverent bow.

"But first I have a task for you," Björn interjected before the man could fade. "A trifling matter for my Lord of Shades."

And as Dämen leaned in to listen, Björn gave him his orders.

Shaded by the cool marble confines of the Temple of the Five Vestals, Julian gazed with reverent awe upon the pristine statue of Alshiba. The statue stood fifteen paces high, a vision of the Alorin Seat holding out her hands, palms down, as if to heal. Many a man and woman had pressed their heads within the cup of those stone fingers while saying a prayer, and later swore their ills had left them. The statue glowed with a wondrous white light, which Julian knew was the result of a wielder's working so long ago. The populace needed no such knowledge, however; often enough, their faith in the statue's power was what drove their own prayers to fruition. *Every one of us works a little magic*, his mother had often told him.

Now Julian knelt upon the velvet cushion at the Goddess's feet and closed his eyes, trying to shut out the fear that gnawed his stomach raw. He'd taken to chewing ginger root to settle it, but he knew the pain would abate only when he found a solution to his problem. *Would that I could tell my mother*...but he dared not, for fear of what she would be driven to do.

Heartsick, Julian opened his pale green eyes and looked down the east wall of the temple. Statues of the other Vestals were spaced in equal distances of fifty paces: Dagmar holding his famous sword, Seth with a hawk on one outstretched fist and five fiery arrows clenched in the other; Raine, whose eyes were set with two diamonds of stunning brilliance, and then...but the last marble pedestal was empty. It was the space where the Fallen One would have stood, Björn van Gelderan, the Fifth Vestal. It was forbidden to create any rendering of him for fear that he could take its form and return to Alorin in this way.

Julian didn't know if such magic was possible or if it was just superstition, but he did know that his mother and all of her priestesses in Jeune believed wholly that fifth-strand adepts were born evil and must be eradicated. Queen Indora supported this belief so completely that any Veneisean child showing even the slightest Adept talent was sent to Jeune for testing. To Julian's knowledge, none of them had ever shown a gift for the fifth, but even the testing was torture enough.

Theirs was a fear Julian didn't fully understand. True, Malachai had been a fifth-strand Adept, as was the Fallen One, and history had seen what they had done—his mother had born first witness, in fact, being one of the few survivors of the Adept Wars and a member of the famous group known as the Fifty Companions. So he supposed he could understand her fear in that sense. But nothing puzzled him more than to see the raw terror that came into her eyes at the merest mention of Björn van Gelderan.

Nor could he understand why so many people found no illogic in this idea—that two men did evil things surely couldn't mean that mean *all* fifth-strand Adepts were born evil? If a prince went mad for power and slaughtered his brother, did that make all princes evil, or all brothers evil? If a mother drowned her baby soon after birth did it mean all mothers were murderers in their hearts? Did not everyone ultimately have a choice in their actions? Couldn't a man choose to do good or ill with his gifts?

Julian had always advocated for the power of choice, but broaching such arguments with his mother had never gone anywhere pleasant, and the latest time had almost brought them to blows.

Now the subject had taken on a whole new and terrifying importance, and Julian dared not broach it with anyone.

Drawing in a heavy breath, Julian lifted his gaze to the statue of Alshiba, who the priestesses of Jeune worshipped as a goddess, and said a small prayer. Then he stood and wandered absently over to the empty pedestal at the far end of the temple where the Fifth Vestal's statue belonged. He gazed at the pedestal for a long time.

His friends were outside granting him a moment alone, but Julian could not be at peace. Just that morning at their inn, he'd dropped a teacup to shatter on the stones of the hearth. As he was cursing his clumsiness, he offhandedly envisioned the cup snapping back together again—in the way one wishes something like that could happen but knows it can't—yet when he'd bent to gather the pieces, he'd found the cup whole and shining as if straight off the shelf. He'd almost dropped it again, he was so startled. And it wasn't the first time this sort of thing had happened.

He'd left Jeune three moons ago pleading youthful wanderlust, but in truth, he'd left because he feared everyone could see what he was—worst of all that his mother could—and if they ever discovered his secret...well, at least for now he was safe in the Free Cities, but he feared he would have to flee to the ends of the realm if anyone from Jeune ever found out.

"Well, I don't see why I can't change my name to Dagmar," Rickon protested as he and the others shared sips from Liam's flask of plum brandy while sitting on the steps of the temple. The afternoon sun had passed beyond the city hills, and the Avenue of the Gods was cast into cooler shadow, for which the boys were grateful. "At least it could be my nickname," Rickon added. He puffed out his chest and observed, "I think I would make a fine Dagmar."

"You'd make a fine bar wench," Rod chastised with a clap on the back of Rickon's head. Rod was the oldest by five minutes, and he took great pains to remind his brothers of the fact.

"Shut up, the both of you!" Liam hissed. He was staring at the hooded figure of a man just then climbing the steps toward them. In the afternoon shadow, the stranger's pale blue cloak seemed to glow with an even paler nimbus. Something about the man made the boys shiver, and though each suddenly had the inexplicable urge to stand and run with sudden fervor, something kept them rooted—perhaps it was pride.

They would never have the opportunity to curse it.

Seeing that he had all of their attention, Dämen lifted his black-gloved hand at the boys. *Look at me but once, and I have the power to bind you, children.* A pity they didn't know that.

Rod was the first to discover he couldn't move, and when he opened his mouth to shout, the sound that emitted was little more than a guttural choke. By the time the Shade reached the step below the boys, they were all wild-eyed and whimpering. Dämen glanced around. The Avenue at his back had a constant flow of traffic, but it was not so crowded as the bazaar beyond the Pillars, and now there was an abundance of shadows to fuel *deyjiin*. "Come lads," the Shade murmured.

They stood obediently and followed him up the stairs toward the deeper shadows.

Dämen took them around to a lush but deserted courtyard between the Temple of the Five Vestals and the black marble temple of the Wind God Azerjaiman. There, he gathered his cold power and focused it into the space of a needle-thin beam, searching the air before him for the finite division between shadows and light. *There.* The spear of power split in two directions, searing a hole in the delicate veil of worldly light. A silver-black line speared down, and as Dämen guided it, the line broadened to reveal a dark, cold nothingness. The fabled dimension of Shadow.

Dämen pushed back his hood, revealing his silver features, and settled his obsidian eyes upon the four boys. "After you, lads," he murmured.

"He isn't the monster people accuse him of, you know," the man said to Julian suddenly.

Julian sucked in his breath with a hiss and spun. He relaxed somewhat when he recognized the blue-eyed stranger, though he wondered why he wasn't more surprised to see him again. He turned back to the pedestal feeling empty inside. "No?" he returned, his voice sounding dull and without conviction even to his own ears. "Björn van Gelderan butchered the Citadel Mages in cold blood and was responsible, even if indirectly, for the deaths of all the innocent inhabitants of Tiern'aval." Julian could near recount each name of the deceased, his mother had been so adamant that he knew and remembered the massacre. "And what of the thousands of Adepts that Malachai and his creatures slew?" Julian looked to the stranger and was startled yet again by the intensity of his blue eyes. "There were other losses too, you know," he went on, though he was too morose to debate with any fire, "the loss of magical knowledge and wisdom that went with the Mages to their graves, the destruction of the Citadel Library, and the near extermination of our—of the Adept race. Anyone would say those are monstrous crimes."

"Yet Björn spared your mother," the stranger pointed out.

Julian's heart fluttered. *Dear heavens, who is this man to know such things?* His mother had never admitted it to him, but Julian had discovered the truth unbeknownst to her. It had been several years past when he and his mother had been guests in Queen Indora's court. The topic of the Citadel and his mother's survival had come up in front of a visiting Agasi truthreader. The lad was barely older than Julian at the time, and they'd struck up a friendship during their winter together in Tregarion. Before the Adept returned to Faroqhar in the Spring, he'd confessed the truth to Julian: that his mother had been lying that night about the circumstances of her survival; that it had been Björn, in fact, who *spared* her life.

Now this blue-eyed stranger was no truthreader, yet he spoke of truths no mortal could know. *Which meant…* Julian turned away from him feeling flustered and shaken. "What do you want with me?" he whispered. "Please…leave me be."

"I cannot, lad." It was a strangely heartfelt admission. "Nor do you truly want me to."

Julian found himself trembling. He had no doubt in his mind now that this man—who was certainly an Adept—had discovered his terrible secret. It was a long moment before he mustered the courage to ask the question he most feared. "How… did you know?" His voice sounded meek and younger than his seventeen years.

Björn considered him gently. "You were going to try to turn the aquamarines to opals, were you not? It was not so hard to guess. We all go through this period of fearful curiosity…that is until we accept ourselves for what we are."

And Julian knew him.

He *knew* him.

Never had he seen his face, or even heard it described, but he knew the man with as much certainty as a truthreader working his talent upon another.

Perhaps sensing the boy's thoughts, Björn walked to the empty pedestal and leaped atop it with fluid grace. "How should I stand?" he inquired as he turned to face the lad with arms spread wide. "How stands the exterminator of an entire race, Julian D'Artenis? Would he stand proudly, unapologetic for his crimes?" and he placed hands on his hips, his immaculate boots spaced a shoulder distance apart, his broad shoulders board straight. "Or should he represent the incarnate of evil, with a pitiless sneer and a bolt of lightning aimed at the innocents?" and into his outstretched hand appeared a streak of sizzling brilliance, which he hurled over Julian's head to vanish harmlessly somewhere behind the startled youth.

Björn lightly stepped off the pedestal again and took Julian squarely by the shoulders. He exuded a confidence that Julian found overwhelming. "This is a vibrant gift, son!" he declared, gazing at the youth with fatherly warmth. The unexpected intimacy was disconcerting. "I can teach you how to use it. I am the only one who can."

Julian stared at the man in front of him feeling confused and heartsick, and above all of these, terrified. To think he was standing face to face with the most heinous traitor that had ever lived, a man who his mother claimed had once tried to kill her. He wondered why he wasn't quaking in his boots?

Perhaps because in some convoluted way, it made sense. *Though my own mother wouldn't have me if she knew, it seems her enemy welcomes me with open arms.* The irony was a bitter pill.

"Go ahead and do it, lad," Björn encouraged, releasing Julian. "Change the stones." Julian flashed him a terrified look at the very idea. "I assure you…you can. At this early stage the power just comes—the less you think about it the better, in fact. The stage passes, as all stages do, and that's when our trials truly begin: once we must understand what it is we do before we can command anything, once we can no longer simply *will* it so."

As if in a dream, Julian reached for the necklace. Everything seemed… hopeless now—as if in coming for him, Björn had confirmed his worst fears and now nothing mattered. He could think of nothing but the fear of what would become of him now that his awful suspicions had proven true.

Holding the heavy necklace in one hand, Julian placed one palm over the other. *How do I do it?* His mind seemed suddenly void, as dark and empty as the heavens on a clouded night. He didn't know how he'd managed it the other times.

"Don't think about it." Björn's voice came soft and close in his ear. There was something about the man's nearness that filled Julian with an unexpected thrill, if still colored with revulsion. *This is a gift,* he tried to tell himself in defiance of his mother's rants, squeezing shut his eyes so as to ignore the truth of the man beside him. *Who else in the realm could do this?* Björn's voice came again, "Don't ponder it, lad. Just *decide*."

With a brave nod, Julian did.

Be.

That was the entirety of his thought as he envisioned the aquamarines as opals, yet it was an all-encompassing entirety, a conceptual postulate, a vision and an understanding of the existential composition of two things together in one split second. It was an understanding intrinsic to a fifth-strand Adept alone, for so much of the Adept's very being came from the same existential strand of the lifeforce. In some way, he *was* the stones.

When Julian opened his eyes, he found opals in his hand.

Ah Cephrael, no! He forced a swallow as the truth struck him, struck so hard that there was no denying it. He *was* a fifth-strand Adept!

Just like the man beside him.

The realization made his skin crawl. Julian slung the necklace away with sudden disgust and shoved a forearm across his eyes as he staggered back. "*No! No!* I—" he groaned, pressing his face into the crook of his elbow so as not to look upon what he'd done. "I *can't* have…I don't even know how…"

Björn extended his hand toward the necklace with an intent gaze, and the jewels flew up and into his palm with a clatter and jingle of links. He looked them over with casual interest. "One need not always understand what one does in order to do, Julian," he observed philosophically. Then he bade the youth look at him and settled his keen gaze on the boy. "Thus is the nature of an Adept's early gift," he advised, "to *do* without knowing how one does. But in not understanding, so lies the danger. There is Balance in all things."

Julian looked numbly at him, unsure what he was feeling.

"Come with me," Björn encouraged. "I will protect you from those who would harm you. I will teach you how to use your gift."

Julian dropped his gaze to stare forlornly at the floor.

"You are not the only one," Björn told him, to which the youth gave him a startled look. "There are others like you who are already being taught. You won't be alone in your studies, Julian." He walked over and placed a hand on the youth's shoulder. "At last, you will have friends who understand you."

Julian looked stricken, for the truth of those words had speared him. Rickon, Liam and the others…he called them friends, but he had always felt an outsider among them, for he knew his true nature was something they couldn't understand. And among the Adept teens who lived in Jeune—mostly Healers-in-training—he wasn't included in their elite number either, for he was a man who could never understand their feminine gifts. So he had forever felt isolated, always caught between two worlds.

Suddenly, he wanted more than anything to go with this man, this very deadly and yet startlingly compelling traitor.

But what will Liam and the others do without me? True friends or no, he couldn't just leave them alone in the Cairs. "My friends, I—"

"The other boys have already been provided an escort. You need have no fear for them foundering alone in the Cairs."

Julian could think of no other reasons to deny him—he didn't *want* to deny him, for the Fifth Vestal's very presence was a commanding force. Björn van Gelderan was the kind of man that men fought each other for the right to follow, and Julian realized that he wanted very much to be one of those men. "I would follow you then, my lord," he said bravely. "If you will have me."

With a look of extreme solemnity, the Fifth Vestal spread his arm before him, and a violet-silver line speared down through the air, widening into a window of blackness that gleamed like polished onyx.

Julian walked forward into the darkness.

TWENTY

'Greed makes murderers like love makes poets.'

– A popular Malchiarri joke

The Marchioness of Wynne was shown into Queen Errodan's public rooms by her green-coated personal guards. One of her ladies-in-waiting escorted the Marchioness into a drawing room whose walls were papered with pale blue striped silk, the same color repeated in velvet upholstered chairs and settee, and there she waited.

And waited.

All the while, Ianthe's disgruntlement grew until she was ready to get up and leave—the sheer effrontery of agreeing to an audience and then making a peeress of the court wait for such an interminable time!—yet she was far too polite, not to mention politically astute, to abandon an appointment once permission had been given. So she sat, and she drank the tea they offered her, though she didn't touch the little biscuits, no matter how fresh the cream upon them. In Veneisea, the Queen served honeyed pastries folded forty times and the rarest of candied fruits from Kroth.

When at last the door opened and Ianthe stood, it was not to receive the Queen at all, but her Companion. This, too, chafed at her.

Ysolde crossed the room in another flowing silk gown, this one the color of dawn, and clasped hands with Ianthe, exchanging a kiss on both cheeks. Still holding hands, both women sat upon the settee, knees close.

Ysolde said, "Her Majesty apologizes for this deplorable wait upon her audience, Marchioness, but she is most bereaved about the late arrival of her son and begs your understanding."

"Of course," Ianthe replied, affecting her most sympathetic tone. "What mother would not fear for her child under such uncertain circumstances?"

"I'm so relieved you understand the fullness of the situation," Ysolde told her with a silken smile. "Do inform me then of the nature and specifics upon which you were hoping discourse with her Majesty, and I shall per force pass on the information to her."

The truth could not have been more plain if Ysolde had spoken it aloud: Ianthe was never going to receive a direct audience with the queen. She might be a grand-niece of Queen Indora of Veneisea and married to one of the richest merchant-princes in Dannym, but she was still only a Marchioness holding a courtesy peerage. Ianthe kept up her polished smile, but her eyes hardened indignantly behind it. "Of course," she concurred with a smile quite lacking for warmth. "I would be most indebted for the opportunity to share my thoughts with the Queen's Companion—indeed, it is befitting that we speak, you and I, for you were witness to the conversation of several mornings ago."

"More tea?" Ysolde inquired.

"No, thank you. I came to speak on what can only be described as the perplexing matter of the Duchess of Aracine."

"I see," Ysolde murmured as she sipped her tea from a delicate gilded cup. "Perplexing in what nature?"

"What to do about her, of course."

Ysolde set down her teacup and regarded the Marchioness steadily. "And what do you propose to do about her, Lady Wynne?"

"I'm sure you agree that it is simply intolerable for the girl to run around the kingdom unchaperoned. She is no longer a child of thirteen but a woman of birthing age who should be being readied for marriage to a suitable gentlemen."

"Her Majesty is considering that matter already."

"Indeed, she would be," Ianthe admitted with an approving nod. "One cannot expect his Majesty to ponder such trivialities, but now that her Majesty has returned to court, tis only seemly that she would...well," and here she made a little chiming laugh, "tie up these loose ends."

Ysolde smiled politely, but the Marchioness was unable to read anything in the smile. "As to the matter of a suitable chaperone for the Duchess's mentorship," Ysolde inquired, "did you have someone in mind?"

Ianthe drew herself up regally. "Why, I was going to offer myself for the position, of course. While it is a monumental task to ensure the proper upbringing of a young lady of the court, I feel that someone must assume the responsibility, lest the poor girl fall into an even more disgraceful state." Ianthe smoothed the skirt of her golden gown across her lap and continued seriously, her fair brow furrowed with obvious concern, "Questionable habits, once ingrained within an impressionable young mind, are difficult to reverse and with dour consequences. She must be educated in the Cardinal Virtues that the Gods of Virtue may look kindly upon her in her childbearing years. In Tregarion, a girl her age would have already chosen a patron virtue and made weekly offerings in the god's temple. I fear it may already be too late for the girl, but I am willing—indeed, I do see this as a service I feel compelled to offer her Majesty—to put forth my gravest efforts to restore the Duchess with some measure of self-respect."

"That is most thoughtful of you, Lady Wynne," Ysolde murmured. "I will be certain to relay all of your charitable concerns and your noble expression of service to her Majesty, who will be undoubtedly grateful."

Ianthe nodded gracefully. "Of course. And thank you, Highness."

The ladies rose, and Ianthe departed with a private smile of satisfaction. As she was leaving, one of the Queen's men entered in a rush to announce, "Princess, this steward has news..." and on his heels came a thin-nosed steward of middle years nearly bursting at the seams as he held aloft a parchment.

Ysolde Remalkhen moved swiftly down the passageway. Though no one was allowed into the queen's private wing without invitation, and at present the halls were quite deserted, Ysolde would never be seen to rush. She was, however, moving as fast as her long legs would carry her, and she pushed through the doors and into an arched gallery without pause. "Errodan," she said in a breathless rush. "We've a letter from Ean."

Errodan dropped her teacup with a clatter of china and stood from her escritoire so quickly that her chair overturned. She let it lie and rushed to meet Ysolde. "Let me see! Dear Epiphany *let me see it!*"

Ysoldehanded the parchment to the queen, and she read quickly. As Ean's words recounted Creighton's death, Errodan gripped Ysolde's hand and read on. Only when she'd finished did her tension lessen, and she spun to embrace her dearest friend, hugging her close. "He's alive!" she whispered fervently, her face wet with tears. "He's safe!"

It was evening in Calgaryn when Franco and Raine emerged from the weld in the pool of the divining chamber. To Franco's surprise, the Lieutenant Bastian val Renly was waiting for them as they sloshed through the iron doors as patiently as if he'd never left.

He roused himself from the far wall and approached smartly. "Your Excellency, welcome back."

"Thank you, Lieutenant," Raine said, settling the man an inquiring look.

He smiled. "Uh, yes, I've been sent to wait for your return. Her majesty has news and has requested audience with you."

"Lead on then, Lieutenant."

After a ridiculously long trek through Calgaryn palace, Franco arrived in the queen's chambers to find a host of others already assembled. Errodan's drawing room seemed a staging area for half the palace, what with green-coated soldiers receiving orders from an older man who could only be the queen's Admiral-father, a score of palace officials hastily discussing plans to resurrect parades and banquets in the prince's honor, a number of King's Own Guard milling about looking out of place, and servants and pages fussing among the melee trying to refresh cups or goblets or fetch a sudden immediately necessary item from elsewhere.

Raine spotted the queen on the far side of the room and made his way over to her, and Franco followed him closely. As he neared, he saw Errodan press hands to her cheeks and heard her lament, "I should've had daughters. I'm certain daughters would not have caused me such intolerable strife!"

"I would be no trouble at all, Auntie," said a man lounging in a nearby armchair. Grey-eyed and black-haired, with a close-shorn beard and a sardonic grin, he seemed a smaller replica of the king. "Why don't you adopt me?"

She eyed him warily. "I'm afraid I couldn't afford you, nephew."

This must be Fynnlar val Lorian, Franco determined. The black sheep of the family and only son of Prince Ryan, Gydryn's younger brother, Fynnlar had made quite a name for himself in the Cairs bartering for the pirates of Jamaii. Franco reckoned they'd even crossed paths once or twice, though they'd never formally met.

Sipping wine from a goblet, Fynn noted pleasantly, "My latest venture is quite affordable, I assure you, Auntie."

She grunted skeptically and settled her gaze instead on a man standing behind Fynn's chair. Morin d'Hain stood with a letter in hand, his brown eyes moving quickly over the flowing script. The queen eyed him quietly. "Do you think to uncover some new meaning from my son's words, Morin?"

"I mean only to read them for myself, your majesty," he replied without looking up. He frowned several times, and then handed the letter back to her.

"Well, what do you think of it?"

He pushed a hand through his blonde hair. "If you will forgive my saying so, my queen, it seems fantastical. Shades, assassins, fell magic, poisoned daggers, and a zanthyr? The Immortal Bard, Drake DiMatteo, could not have fashioned a more outrageous tale."

"I think I could've come up with something far more creative," Fynn offered. "Really, Morin. Shades are so passé."

"Are you saying my son is lying?" Errodan returned, ignoring Fynn. There was a hard edge to her tone, and her eyes were flinty. "His story fully corroborates that of my men."

"I imply nothing of the sort, your Majesty," Morin said soothingly. "I would not presume to question the prince's honesty. I only wonder that he hasn't been through a terrible, trying time and perhaps his recollection has become exaggerated in the retelling."

Shades, assassins, fell magic, poisoned daggers and a zanthyr, Franco mused. He spared a glance for Raine, and they exchanged a look. *Yes,* the truthreader's gaze seemed to answer, *it is indeed curious news.*

The queen meanwhile arched a brow at Morin but let the matter lie. "And what think you about this zanthyr? Surely you don't claim he made that part up."

"A most disturbing development," Morin agreed. "I assure your Majesty that we will be looking deeply into it."

"You will look into all his statements, outrageous or no."

Morin bowed accommodatingly. "Indubitably, majesty." He clasped hands behind his back and adopted a thoughtful frown as he paced a small square. "Much about his report troubles me, in fact. The circumstances of his capture..." Abruptly he looked to her. "I wonder, Majesty, do you have one of the prince's original letters of invitation, those which were sent abroad?"

Errodan gave him a curious look, but she searched her desk and came up with a tri-folded card, once sealed with dark wax but since then carefully opened so the seal remained intact. She handed it to him.

Morin looked it over carefully, paying special attention to the signet used in the wax. "This is the prince's personal seal, I presume."

"Yes."

"It is...unique." He handed the invitation back to her.

"Is it?" Errodan looked at the swirling pattern pressed into the wax and managed a soft smile. "I suppose it is at that. He's been drawing that pattern for years. I'm so used to seeing it...but it is an odd sort of seal for a prince, I'll admit."

Raine interrupted then, "Might I have a look, your Majesty?"

Errodan looked over and only then seemed to notice Raine and Franco. "Oh, your Excellency," she sighed in relief. "Thank you so much for coming. Of course, here you are," and she handed the invitation to him. While he looked it over, the Queen sat down in the chair behind her escritoire. "So, Morin," she said with a sigh, "what's the rumor to be this time?"

"Fortune has graced us that the prince found his way to the Duchess of Aracine," Morin replied, well prepared. "Already my people are spreading word that Alyneri d'Giverny is the mysterious heiress who refuses to marry Prince Ean—it is just one of many rumors we have long been propagating—and that his Highness has spent the past many days in her company trying to convince her to change her mind."

Errodan arched brows. "That actually sounds...plausible."

"With any luck, Morwyk will think his plot a complete failure and wonder what became of his men. Epiphany has delivered us a boon, one saving grace to this tragedy."

The queen's expression grew ever more sorrowful. "Ean wrote of Creighton."

"Yes. I feel we must assume he has passed on, evidence or no."

Errodan sighed again. "Then we are in accord."

"Indeed. A contingent of the King's Own Guard will depart ere morning to retrieve the prince from Fersthaven. Majesty." Bowing without waiting for her leave, Morin spun on his heel and departed.

The Queen looked back to Raine. "No doubt you've surmised that my son has been found, your Excellency, but I would still implore your assistance. The circumstances are so...well..." she seemed at a loss for words.

"I am pleased to be of service in whatever way I am able," Raine replied with his typical diplomacy. He handed the invitation back to her. "Perhaps I might start by reading the prince's letter?"

She handed it to him.

Raine looked it over, frowning several times, and said as he returned it to her, "I confess, your Majesty, I am as confused by the appearance of a Shade as I am by the presence of a zanthyr. The creatures are solitary by nature and typically despise humankind. The very fact that these two creatures are involved leads me to believe that your son is somehow enmeshed in a much larger conflict."

His words both startled and worried her, if told from her expression. "I cannot imagine how he became embroiled with such creatures, but I've no doubt of his innocence! My son is a good man, your Excellency, I—"

"I do not imply the prince is complicit in anything unsavory, your Majesty," Raine soothed.

She looked relived somewhat. "Would you be willing to speak with him? He should be here tomorrow."

"Unfortunately, I must travel at once to Illume Belliel," he told her, which was the first Franco had heard of it. It wasn't a matter of concern to him, however, for he was certain the Fourth Vestal did not mean to take one Franco Rohre to the sainted cityworld; no doubt Alshiba would send her Espial to fetch him instead. Franco was relieved, actually, for it meant time off from this tormenting manhunt that was rapidly giving him ulcers.

As if three hundred years of inebriation had nothing to do with the sorry state of your guts.

Shut up!

The conversation continued, but Franco felt eyes upon him and shifted his gaze to find the Princess Ysolde watching from a chair by the hearth. For such a striking woman, she had the ability to all but vanish in a room, only gaining notice when she willed it so. Franco caught the come-hither look in her dark eyes and complied without hesitation. He hoped he might be arranging his own sort of rendezvous later that evening, but of a more personal and intimate nature.

As it happened, the princess did not disappoint.

It was well after midhaven and the moon was high as Fynnlar val Lorian made his way into a tavern in Calgaryn's Star Quarter, that section of the sprawling, seaside city which catered to those needing companionship of one sort or another. The tavern was neither full nor empty, but the bar was crowded and the two serving wenches looked overworked as they wove their way between the tables of drinking men.

Fynn found his way to an empty table near a corner and sat down with his back to the door. He hadn't been sitting there long when a barmaid showed up toting a tray laden with drinks. "We got wine and we got beer," she said unenthusiastically.

"What kind of wine?" Fynn asked.

"Dunno. It's a red. The master uncorked the barrel yesterday."

"And the beer?"

She sighed impatiently. "It's a black ale from Chesterhouse."

"Ale sounds good."

She grabbed one of the tankards from her tray and plopped it unceremoniously down on the table, spilling a good bit of it. Fynn pulled the tankard in front of him and sipped on it. It was flat.

Figures, he inwardly grumbled. It just wasn't possible to get a decent drink in the north. Their ale was always either flat, sour, bitter, or unbearably sweet, and they didn't seem to know that some of the best wines in the world were grown in the neighboring kingdom of Veneisea, preferring instead the syrupy vintages from Dannym's south-western provinces. And forget about finding a nice Agasi red, or anything from Agasan's famous wine-making region of Solvayre. What were common luxuries in the Empire were utterly foreign in the north.

Not that Fynn was entirely without recourse. His first-cousin-once-removed on his mother's side was the Agasi Ambassador in Dannym, but Anke van den Berg had grown stingy with her stash of wines—especially the Volgas—and especially of late. She claimed Fynn went through bottles too quickly and had just that afternoon cut him off from her cellars. No amount of shameless begging had changed her mind, *the heartless wench*. But how much compassion could you honestly expect from a woman who drowned her own husband in his bathtub?

Fynn sighed and sniffed at his flat ale. The north was so different from the Empire. Why, just that night Fynn had nearly come to blows with the palace guard about going out into the city. And why? It wasn't as if his face was unknown to them, or that they had orders to keep *him* inside the walls—it was more likely they'd have orders to throw him out—but still the soldier held firm that no one came in or out after the hour past midhaven. *The hour past midhaven*, of all the arbitrary times to lock the damned gates—*the guard might as well have drawn times from a hat as choose one hour past midhaven. Why not three hours before dawn? Or the second past luncheon?*

Fynn hated arbitrary rules almost as much as he hated tax collectors. *Come to think of it, Tax Collectors are walking arbitraries*, which was probably why he hated them so much. *Moreover,* he thought, still fuming over the incident, *what gives them the right to tell me I can't go wenching and wining if I so choose? It's my god-given right to be a carousing inebriate!* Fynn had finally pulled rank on the man and threatened to go to his uncle, *the king,* with names. The soldier had let him out then, but not without griping all the while about nobility always insisting the rules didn't apply to them.

"You afraid that beer's gonna bite you?" asked a voice from over Fynn's shoulder. He felt more than saw a man sitting with his back to him at a table caddy-corner to his own, so that their shoulders were nearly touching.

"For a black, it does seem a bit green," Fynn remarked with a sour expression, staring suspiciously at the stuff.

Neither man turned to look at the other.

"I hear your cousin's been found," the man said after a moment. "Morin's people speak of a lover's tryst, but we know he was missing under suspicious circumstances. Fortune must've been with him."

"T'was a zanthyr that was with him, in point of fact."

"A zanthyr? Fascinating."

Fynn grunted skeptically. "I hate zanthyrs. Insufferable bastards, the lot of them."

"But useful in saving princes," the man noted.

"Apparently."

Silence followed while Fynn thought about sipping his ale again but couldn't bring himself to suffer the taste of it. "What do you hear?" he asked after a moment's indecision.

"The Karakurt is active."

Fynn arched brows, but no one noticed, for he was facing the rear wall. "The Karakurt? Here?"

"She is not unknown to work in the north, but we hear whispers of her in association with your prince."

"What kind of whispers?"

"Black strokes on white parchment."

"*What?*" Fynn hissed. "Why?"

"Dunno. Thought you'd want to know."

Fynn was stunned. "I do. I do." He fought the urge to push hands through his dark hair. *The Karakurt has a contract on Ean?*

Fynn was starting to get that feeling in the pit of his stomach, the uncannily prescient one that always meant impending danger and warned him to get out of town. The last time the feeling had visited, he'd fled Tregarion in the middle of the night, only to learn that the inn where he'd been staying had been burned to ash that very evening. Another time, the feeling had saved him from a huntsman's arrow—or so he told others, though he privately suspected it might've belonged to Lord Fallowey and had something to do with his wife's recent infidelity—and in yet a third episode, he'd narrowly escaped capture by the Agasi Imperial Navy, which would've meant a fortune in stolen cargo lost to the authorities. His crew had both sworn him born under a lucky sign and cursed him as being in league with Shadow, but whatever its source, the feeling had never yet led Fynn astray. Unfortunately, this time Fynnlar knew he couldn't heed its warning to flee.

He reached into his pocket and retrieved several gold pieces. Lowering his arm, he reached back and let the gold fall into the coat pocket of his informant.

"Nice doing business with you," the man said into his wine. "Friends and fellows."

"Friends and fellows," Fynn murmured, but his mind was elsewhere. He tossed a couple of coins on the table and got up, carefully not looking at the man still seated behind him.

Out on the street, he called for his horse, but he was immensely troubled now.

Shade and darkness! What in Tiern'aval has Ean gotten himself into? Fynn knew he would have to do a considerable amount of investigating, which was going to hurt his already spare coffer.

But first, to find some place in this damnable city with a decent bottle of wine.

A man had to have his priorities.

TWENTY-ONE

'Veiled women, like zanthyrs and gypsies, cannot be trusted.'

– Prince Radov abin'Hadorin of M'Nador

Trell started awake to find Balaji standing over him, and never a more unsettling experience there was. The youth wore his usual sapphire robes, so bright against his flawless caramel skin, and Trell was sure that Balaji's wheat-gold eyes knew far more than they should—just like his smile. Balaji seemed to hide all the secrets of the universe behind his perfect white teeth.

"Good morning, Trell of the Tides," the youth greeted in his amiable way. "Today we part, I am sorry to say. But the Mage has left you some farewell gifts." He lifted a bundle he was holding and set it down at the foot of the bed. "When you are ready, be pleased to find me outside. No hurry." With that, he left.

Feeling on edge, Trell sat up and rubbed his eyes. It was never a pleasant experience to wake only to find an enemy standing over you, to know they had been there while you slept and could have claimed your life at any moment. But Balaji wasn't an enemy... was he? Trell wondered why Balaji alone made him feel so edgy and uncomfortable when none of his cousins had the same effect.

The idea of beginning his quest in true soon banished these uneasy thoughts, however, and Trell threw off the sheet and got up to join the day. The bundle Balaji had left for him turned out to be—of all things—the *drachwyr* uniform: black pants and a quilted vest, and a heavy grey fleece tunic worked all over with elaborate embroidery—perfect for the coming winter if a little showy for his taste. There was also an oiled greatcloak lined in ermine, which would have been a valuable gift on its own, and a thick wool half-cloak lined in suede, both in a deep charcoal grey much the color of his eyes. The garments were made of expensive silks and heavy, soft-spun wools. Though they were of a utilitarian cut, they felt luxurious.

Trell welcomed the gift. His dun-colored clothes would stand out once he left the desert kingdoms on his way to...where *was* he headed? *The Cairs,* he decided. He wasn't sure why he picked the Free Cities of Xanthe to start his search for himself. They just seemed as good a place as any, and he'd always wanted to visit them. The stories Graeme had told him about life in the Cairs...

Trell dressed and then walked to the water pitcher and basin and splashed some water on his face. Looking into the mirror, he pushed wet hands through his perpetually tousled hair in a futile attempt to calm it down. Then he gave the room one last look, grabbed his satchel and his sword, and swept aside the drapes, belting on his blade as he said his good-byes to the Mage's sa'reyth.

Outside in the bright morning, he looked around for Balaji but found Vaile instead. She was seated with Jaya among a grouping of plush chairs set out beneath a tasseled awning. Both women were sipping Khurdish *kaffe* from little porcelain cups. Vaile wore a simple flesh-toned silk dress that shimmered against her smooth skin. The skirt was slit up the front to mid-thigh, falling to either side of her crossed legs, and as usual, she wore supple suede knee-boots of matching hue. She glanced up when she heard Trell approach, and her elegant features formed into a mysterious sort of smile that beckoned him and simultaneously shut him out. "Good morning, Trell of the Tides," Vaile greeted. "Rough night?" and her emerald eyes took in his unruly hair.

Trell peered up at his hair beneath his brows. He reached a hand to push at a recalcitrant curl that seemed to want to stand up despite his best efforts. "Odd morning," he replied, still wondering why Balaji unsettled him. He sank down onto a chair next to Vaile. A small table before them was set with a pot of the *kaffe* and a number of porcelain cups.

"Please help yourself," Jaya offered, eyeing him in her unreadable way as she sipped at her drink. She wore a different dress but in the same tangerine color, and a similar headdress with its dangle of citrine stones. As Trell was pouring some of the *kaffe,* Jaya smiled and offered, "Balaji walks on clouds. Soundless. Do not let it bother you."

Trell glanced up at her in surprise.

"He wakes all of us each morning," she explained in answer to the question in his eyes. "He is the sentry of the dawn."

"He Who Walks The Edge Of The World," Trell murmured.

"Told you his name, I see." She looked amused. "Ours is an old language, older than mankind."

Trell sipped his drink and watched her over the rim.

She looked thoughtful and held her cup with both hands. "Much has changed since we lived among the kingdoms of men."

"Much has changed even since the wars," Vaile agreed sadly. "There is little magic left in the southern lands, and less in the north. Only Agasan remembers, and the Empress holds tight reigns over the Sormitáge and the Adepts born into her domain."

Jaya sighed and nodded. "The Citadel was a great loss. Now all that remain to teach in the east are the scholars from Jeune with no working knowledge of their craft."

An entering Náiir snorted at that. "Scholars indeed," he commented as he sat down next to Jaya with a long sigh—too long for so early in the morning. He was once more dressed in his usual loose black robes. He winked at Trell by way of hello, then added, "Their black-robed masters are novices compared to the wielders of our day."

Jaya sighed and shook her head. "As ever, Balance plays its hand. The traitors who survived the wars did not stand with those who might teach them; instead, they cowered in the shadows while the war played out. Now shadows are all that is left for them to learn from."

Náiir and Vaile gazed at her with expressions of regret. "It is a tragedy beyond measure that only the cowards were left to carry on," Náiir observed, "and now the realm suffers their demise. This, my friends, is Malachai's legacy."

Vaile shook her head in sad agreement. "Alorin is out of Balance. And magic is dying." She lifted her green eyes and caught Trell's gaze, and her expression softened into a smile. "But this is grim talk for the beginnings of a fair adventure. We have last night still on our minds, Trell of the Tides."

Trell nodded in understanding. "How did it end with them?"

"The only way it could," Náiir said, sighing. "Ramu gave them their options. Save for a few, the rest chose to fight rather than give their oaths to the First Lord. Ramu let them do their worst—"

"Their worst," Jaya muttered, shaking her head. She looked at Trell. "Who throws fire at a dragon, Trell of the Tides? Might as well attempt to stop a charging crocodile by dumping water on it."

Náiir shrugged. "It seemed the best they could come up with."

"Their best just wasn't good enough," Vaile finished, looking almost as if she enjoyed the memory. "Ramu tasked Rhakar to take care of the traitors. It is always his role to play— Srívasrhakárakéck...the Shadow of the Light."

Trell grimaced into his *kaffe*, draining the cup. He could imagine what was left of the traitors once the volatile Rhakar had been at them. "Well," he said, standing and setting the cup back on the table. "I must thank you all for your companionship and hospitality."

"We shall welcome you back, Trell of the Tides," Náiir said. "You owe me another match of Kings."

Trell smiled and nodded.

"Fare thee well, Trell," Jaya said. "Fortune grace you in finding yourself..." She paused, considering him, and added, "...and anything else you might be seeking."

Trell looked at her curiously, but she was merely gazing at him with those odd tangerine eyes.

He looked to Vaile then. She set down her cup and stood. "I will walk you to Balaji. I think I know where he is about." She nodded to the two *drachwyr*, then slipped her arm through the loop of Trell's elbow and led him toward the high hill in the back of the complex.

As they walked from the shade of the awning into the bright sunshine, Vaile murmured for his ears alone, "You must take care to watch yourself, Trell of the Tides."

Trell turned to her. "And why must I do that?"

"You travel within dangerous times and shall come into contact with deadly company...the kind that cannot be trusted."

Trell worked hard to keep a straight face. "And your kind can, milady?"

"Oh no," she was fast to admit, flashing a lovely grin. "None of us can be trusted. But the worthy ones..." She made sure she held his gaze before finishing amid a rather disturbing little smile, "the worthy ones will tell you so. Just you remember that."

"You are kind to warn me, milady," Trell replied.

"Kindness has no part of it," she said seriously.

"I still thank you." With that, he removed her hand from his arm and kissed it while gazing into her greenest of eyes. Then he gave her a genteel bow and turned and walked away. He'd seen Balaji atop the hill near a line of picketed horses, and he made his way to him. He did not look back, though he felt Vaile's gaze following him all the while.

When Trell reached Balaji, the youth was leaning against a tethering post talking to Rhakar. The latter's yellowish gaze fastened on Trell as he neared, and with the long rays of early morning falling across his eyes, the Shadow of the Light seemed quite unearthly, like some sort of alien statue. But it would be a statue with a certain wickedness about it. Like poison disguised as sugar.

Rhakar muttered something in his strange language and walked off before Trell reached them. Balaji looked happy to see him however, and he greeted Trell with a clap of hands on both shoulders. "You have a long road ahead of you, my new friend Trell. We all wish you luck and good fortune upon it."

Trell felt a swell of unexpected gratitude. "...Thank you, Balaji."

The youth took him by one shoulder and steered him along the row of picketed horses. "The Mage has arranged some gifts for you, and he also makes a request."

"What sort of request?"

"One you will not mind, I am most certain."

Balaji stopped in front of a silver-white mare, a beauty of a creature with a mane of pale gold. She was saddled and ready to ride. "Gendaia," Balaji named her as he rested a hand on her flank.

Trell let out a low whistle. "A Hallovian grey," he noted appreciatively.

"She is of a royal line," Balaji told him. "The Mage had planned to sell her at the next market, but he would have you take her instead. She will better serve you."

Gendaia snorted and pawed at the dirt. She really was a beautiful animal, fit for a king, and Hallovian steeds were famous. The Second Vestal, Dagmar Ranneskjöld was said to ride the original sire in the line: Caldar, whose hooves were supposedly cast in gold. Trell placed his hand on Gendaia's nose in greeting. Her bridle was worked all over with beaten silver so that what was not delicate yet seemed so, and her saddle was packed high with supplies.

"Yes," Balaji said, noting Trell's eye upon the packs. "Food enough for a fortnight's journey—about what it will take you to reach the Cairs."

Trell gave him a swift look. "How did you know I planned to go to the Cairs?"

"The Mage thought you might," Balaji said in his amiable way, as if there was nothing at all strange about that. "And now, to your gifts."

Trell shook his head in wonder. "More gifts? The clothes and this horse are so much more than I can ever repay."

Balaji smiled that smile...the one that seemed to hide something savage behind it. "The Mage is generous to his friends, Trell of the Tides. But here," and he slapped one of the saddlebags before pulling the tie that opened it. Inside were three black leather purses and a leather case. "The money is for you, the case for one of the Mage's contacts in Cair Rethynnea. He asked if you might deliver it on his behalf."

Trell took out one of the black bags and pulled it open. Silver coins gleamed back at him, all of them stamped with the royal Agasi crest. *Agasi silver, close to a hundred pieces at least. I could buy an entire village with this.* Trell was overwhelmed. Looking up to Balaji, he whispered, "This is too great a fortune!"

Balaji smiled. "You will spend it well, I trust."

Trell shook his head. "This is too much. Surely the Mage must want something of me—something more than a delivery most anyone could manage." He searched Balaji's face, but the youth just kept smiling benignly. Feeling frustrated and slightly confused, Trell looked at the silver in his hands again and murmured, "There was something I wanted to ask you yesterday."

"Indeed my new friend Trell? How may I help you?"

Trell pursed his lips. "Pieces and players. Have you heard the Mage refer to them before? Or…or refer to me in this fashion? Do you know how a piece becomes a player?"

"Ah…" Balaji nodded, looking highly pleased by the question. He held up one finger as he explained, "This is an old philosophy, the Structure of a Game. A piece becomes a player, Trell of the Tides, in part by learning what game it is in which he plays."

"You imply that I'm playing in a game," Trell said.

Balaji arched brows innocently. "Do I?"

"Don't you?"

Balaji grinned. "Aren't you?"

Trell tried very hard to contain his aggravation; he despised this sort of circular logic, it interfered with his tactical form of thinking. "If I'm in a game," he began, forcing calm, "what game is it?"

"Ah…now that *is* the question, isn't it?" Balaji noted agreeably. "Unfortunately it is a question best addressed to the Mage, Trell of the Tides. You could ask him…if he were here." He grinned irritatingly at Trell then.

Grumbling to himself, Trell returned the silver to its bag and secured his own pack to the others. He placed both hands on his saddle readying to mount, but turned to look at Balaji one last time. "I have this feeling that I can't shake."

"And what feeling is that?"

"The feeling that I'm being manipulated."

Balaji's smile faded. "Why would you think such a thing?"

"You told me to read any book in the Mage's room," Trell said. "Was it coincidence then that I opened a journal that…that I believe spoke of me? Then Ramu lets slip that perhaps my journey of self-discovery is as important as the end knowledge itself. And now the Mage leaves these things with the understanding that I'm heading to the Cairs, as if it was a foregone conclusion…" Trell frowned over his horse at the long grass blowing gently on the hills. "Instinct shouts that there is more going on here…that your First Lord has a plan for me—" He gave Balaji a swift look. "That he's made me into one of his pieces."

Balaji regarded him quietly. "If instinct shouts, you must follow its command, Trell of the Tides. What will you do?"

Trell looked up from under his brows. "I'm not sure that my motives run contrary to your First Lord's, but why doesn't he just ask of me whatever it is he wants?"

Balaji sighed. For what seemed the first time, he actually looked sincere. "Are you familiar with the concept of Balance?"

Trell shook his head.

"Balance is an old, old subject long misunderstood," Balaji explained, "and one far too complex to discuss without a large supply of *siri* and much more time than I believe you'd wish to invest this day," he added with a wink. "But what you must understand about it, Trell of the Tides, is that all of our lives are in the gravest of dangers if the Balance in Alorin is not restored, for in its waning rises a most terrible threat. It is this task that the First Lord labors upon. If you have a role to play in that greatest of games, you must know that you will be aiding a noble purpose."

"A noble purpose doesn't require subterfuge," Trell challenged.

"Ah…" sighed Balaji, nodding heavily, "but Balance often does."

Trell sort of stared at him, for his words held the resonance of truth. While his mind spun, clouds passed over the sun, pitching them into cooling shadow.

"I do not know the Mage's purpose for you, if indeed he has one," Balaji admitted then, perhaps taking pity on Trell, or perhaps because he was struck with a benevolent mood. Or perhaps because it was yet another strategic turn of his hand, all part of the same manipulative game Trell suspected was in play. "But whatever your role, the Mage cannot—*would* not—compel you into it."

Thinking that over, Trell mounted up. He looked down at Balaji still feeling troubled. "I'd already decided to go to the Cairs," he said, "but the Mage was careful to *ensure* that I did by having me deliver this case to his contact there. Doesn't that seem strange to you, Balaji?"

"Strange? No."

"Manipulative, then?"

Balaji grinned at him. "You are suspicious by nature. This is a good trait to have in these troubled times." He took Gendaia by the bridle and led her away from the picket line. "You will always be welcome here, Trell of the Tides, should you ever have need of sanctuary. Take care to remember the trail back, in case you do." And with that, Balaji pointed to a tiny path leading over the ridge. "No doubt you have been wondering what part of the Kutsamak Mountains hides this oasis, no?"

"You could say that," Trell muttered.

"The sa'reyths lie upon the old ways," Balaji explained, "paths which only a second-strand Adept—Nodefinders or Espials—might travel. For your return to the trail near Jar'iman Point, we have prepared the node to carry you alone. Remember the path well. We will keep watch for you, and if ever we see you upon that trail again, we will send someone to help you through the node—though I earnestly hope you never need seek refuge here."

"Thank you," Trell said, meaning it. It was a relief to understand at last where the sa'reyth really was. Though he still had residual feelings of unease, they were necessarily overshadowed by his gratitude for all that he was being given—all that he had been given. He owed the Mage his life, and for that alone, he would do as the man required of him—for at least as long as their purposes were aligned.

"Once you cross the node," Balaji meanwhile advised as he led Gendaia away from the sa'reyth, "you will be within harm's reach. Rhakar and Mithaiya are on patrol, and they will watch your back from the skies as far as they dare, but stay wary of the road before you. Though you can pass for one of them, the Nadoriin and their Saldarian allies shoot anything that moves on two legs."

Trell nodded. Despite his misgivings, he was starting to feel oddly choked up. The *drachwyr* and the Mage and most of the others he'd met at the sa'reyth had shown him unexpected friendship and enormous generosity, and he wasn't one to overlook these things, no matter his personal conflict.

Balaji had walked him to the beginning of the thin path that led away through the field and up over the next rise. "From Jar'iman, make for the Ruby Road. This far west of the battle, it remains inviolate. Oh…and one last thing…"

"What is that?"

"The man you seek," Balaji offered, giving Trell that grin again. "I thought you might want to know…he also rides a Hallovian steed."

Trell stared at him, too astonished to respond.

With a last exuberant grin, Balaji reached up and clasped wrists with Trell. "Fortune bless you, Trell of the Tides! *Llythuin y'ama miathwyn!*"

Trell gave him one last long look, and then Gendaia was cantering away, west, toward his future and—he hoped—his past.

Trell's next two days of travel became a haze in memory, for the trail was long and winding and the terrain looked the same from sunup to sundown. He made the Ruby Road in good time, however, and his travels gained speed thereafter.

It was late afternoon when Trell reined in Gendaia atop a ridge overlooking the Bashir'Khazaaz, the largest bazaar in the Akkad's western mountains. Traders came from as far south as the Forsaken Lands to sell their wares, and merchants traveled from Kroth or even Cair Thessalonia to buy them. There were items to be had beneath the colorful tents of the Bashir'Khazaaz that couldn't be found anywhere else outside of Dheanainn, and it was there that the Bemothi traders brought their famed rubies, by ancient pact giving the desert tribes first pick of their newest and most brilliant gems.

Trell had been to the Bashir'Khazaaz several times on errands for the Emir, but he'd never seen it so crowded, nor the plains surrounding it so mushroomed with colorful tents, every one of them fashioned in the mosaic pattern of a different tribe.

The reason for their gathering was a grim one, however. *Refugees*. Since gaining the Ruby Road, Trell had been passing mile-long caravans fleeing the eastern villages. Long lines of turbaned riders led dark-eyed boys who carried trowels for swords; men too old to fight guided pack mules and leaned on long poles sharpened at both ends; and old women and young mothers held tightly to the hands of their children, infants worn in slings across their backs. These people took with them what few belongings they treasured...or what they could salvage from the wreckage of their villages, and they walked as if with one eye ahead and one behind, their ears listening for whispers of an approaching threat.

A breeze buffeted Trell from behind, causing Gendaia to snort uneasily and paw at the earth. Trell cast a look over his shoulder. The eastern horizon was gloomy and dark, and the burgeoning wind felt charged, as if ready to erupt into lightning at any moment. Gendaia snorted again and flattened one ear. "I know, I know," he soothed her.

The storm was still a few hours distant, but he would need a sturdy shelter that night, and it was also time to refill his waterskins. The Bashir'Khazaaz would provide for both. Trell clicked his tongue, and Gendaia headed down the steep incline of the ridge as if already smelling the sweet water that awaited her.

The Bashir'Khazaaz was always arranged in seventeen concentric circles—one in honor of each of the lesser desert gods—with the towering jade Pillars of Jai'Gar crowning the center plaza. The pillars and the well they marked were the only permanent installations in the Bashir'Khazaaz, for the hundreds of merchant tents shifted with the seasons.

The seventeen rings were quartered by four avenues, each named for one of the faces of the powerful Wind God Azerjaiman, and it was the easterly-most of these that Trell followed as he made his way toward the pillars. Once he passed within the seventeen rings of tents, the noise became cacophonous—catcalls and bellows accosting him from every direction. On an equal level with the noise was the smell, for most any exotic animal was to be had at the Bashir'Khazaaz: eastern elephants, southern lions, northern wolves, and even the bizarre *giraffe* found only in the Wyr'Umjai Crater on the Agasi island of Palma-Lai.

Several times Trell passed black-turbaned Khaz'im, the official peace-keepers of the Bashir'Khazaaz. They wore the traditional *ghoutra,* a wrapped turban covering their head and face, exposing only their deep, dark eyes; and they carried the *ammitar*, a great curved sword three times as wide at the point as it was at the hilt. The Khaz'im were the reason the Bemothi traders came to barter their famous rubies at the Bashir'Khazaaz, for not only was a Khaz'im's word taken as law, but their justice was swift. All thieves caught were summarily executed, and all thieves were caught.

Trell's way finally opened onto the round, stepped plaza leading down to the pillars and their surrounding pool. It was taught in the scriptures that Jai'Gar was never to be represented in body or likeness, but solely with the erection of two enormous pillars of the purest green jade. The pillars had to be constructed to exact specifications, and any impurity in the stone rendered them unfit. There was much symbolism and significance in Jai'Gar's choice of pillars as His representation, and there were just about as many ceremonies to follow when standing in their shadow. Not being Converted, however, Trell observed only the first form of respect.

He dismounted on the second step and led Gendaia to the watering trough, one of many long, low marble basins fed by the spring that served the Bashir'Khazaaz. He then walked to the center of the sandstone-paved plaza and stopped beneath the pillars, which stood in the center of the wide pool. The Pillars were always erected thusly, for Jai'Gar was the giver of life, and a life-giving spring was symbolic of His power.

Before partaking of the water, Trell knelt and gathered sand into his right hand. Standing, he tossed the sand into the wind—there was always sand in the air surrounding the Pillars of Jai'Gar—and said the appropriate prayer. He then turned and bowed low to the pillars, kissed the fist that had thrown the sand, knelt again on his right knee, bowed his head to touch it to his bent left knee, and then rose with both hands pressed together and bowed one last time. This was the minimum expectation of reverence; to do nothing was an unforgivable insult and would mean immediate expulsion from the Bashir'Khazaaz—that is, so long as the Khaz'im were in a benevolent mood.

His duty fulfilled, Trell walked back to Gendaia to retrieve his waterskins and was soon bent over the wide sandstone pool refilling the leather bags along with two score other visitors. It was strange to be standing there, he reflected while the cool, crystalline water bubbled around his hands, when every time prior he'd been traveling with Graeme or Ware. Now his only friends were dead and he walked alone. It seemed a bitter irony that men with families who loved them were taken from this world, while he, the orphan, was left to go on.

No, not an orphan, he remembered. *I have a brother…but does he mourn me? Or was I cast out in shame?*

A shadow befell him, and Trell glanced up to see four Khaz'im standing over him in their black *ghoutras* and baggy desert pants, broad red sashes at their waists. Seeing them, Trell slowly straightened from the well. "*Sa'laam,*" he greeted with a bow. *Peace.* For the ghost of a moment, he feared he must have genuflected out of sequence to Jai'Gar, but then the Khaz'im were bowing in return.

"*Sa'laam*, Ama-Kai'alil," the leader replied.

Peace, Man of the Tides. Trell hadn't heard himself called the simple name in many years. He replied in the desert tongue, "How may I serve the Khaz'im?"

The leader said, "We of the Khaz'im have a message for the Emir. If it please him, the tribe of Libaya al'Ama-Khazaaz supports his quest to purge the sacred mountains of the blasphemous Nadoriin. He need only send for us; we are eager to serve."

Trell nodded and replied with a solemn bow, "I will let it be known."

The exchange concluded, they turned and departed. Trell watched them go with a little frown, Jaya's words echoing in mind. '*...There are reasons for wars, and then there are reasons for wars...*' Trell knew that for a great many people, this war *was* about preserving sacred ground, but he also now knew that Jaya was in a position to learn secrets that would never filter down to the common ear. He wondered what motives could be driving the war if indeed it wasn't about protecting the honored shrines.

Letting out his breath heavily, Trell turned back to his task, only to be hailed once again by the address, "Forgive me, Sir. A word if I may?"

Trell straightened again to find three women dressed in caramel-hued burkhas, just their eyes visible between the folds of cloth; one dark, the other two aqua-blue. The silk hems of azure-blue gowns fluttering delicately beneath their tan burkhas. Color on a woman outside of her home was forbidden among the desert tribes, thus he surmised that they were not Akkadian-born.

He nodded to each of the women and then turned his gaze inquiringly back to the first. "*Sa'laam,*" she said, using the traditional address of peace. She continued in the desert tongue, "Forgive our intrusion, but we noticed you made only the first genuflection at the spring just now. Could it be that you are not Converted?"

Trell noticed her accent immediately. It was neither Nadori, nor Agasi, nor even the usual slurring inflection from those who Converted from the common tongue. It was something else, something decidedly...foreign. Another curiosity. He wondered what this was about, but he answered her, "It is so, madam."

The other two women let out a collective sigh, and the first smiled and murmured under her breath, "Mother be praised." To Trell, she then explained, "We have lingered here for three days in the hopes of finding a guide through the mountains. Thus far, you are the first we have come upon who is not Converted."

Trell's gaze narrowed slightly as he regarded her. "The Converted know the mountains as well as anyone, madam. Have you some prejudice against them?"

She exchanged a look with her two companions, wherein the shortest of the three, the one whose dark eyes seemed the most fearful, replied, "It is just the opposite, milord. It is they who may hold ill feelings towards us. You see, we are from Tal'Shira."

Trell arched brows. He believed she at least was, for her accent confirmed it so, but he couldn't help wondering where the other two hailed from. It was rare to find women unattended in the Bashir'Khazaaz, and even stranger to find foreign-born women there at all—especially ones who also spoke the desert tongue. But surely these ladies had not crossed miles of war-plagued desert by themselves. "How is it you are traveling alone?" he asked the first woman with the strange accent, trying for another chance to place it. "Where is your escort?"

"We travel alone," she told him, and there was an emotion in her tone that he couldn't quite place.

The woman beside her, who had not yet spoken, answered hesitantly, "We are not without our gifts."

"Will you help us?" asked the Nadori woman in a wavering voice. "We are…quite desperate."

"We will pay you generously for your effort," said the first.

Trell frowned as he regarded all three of them. "Where is it you're heading?"

"To Sakkalaah," the Nadori replied. "But we need help gathering supplies for the trek through the gorge…and perhaps securing some guards who can be trusted?"

Trell crossed his arms. Sakkalaah was half a week's journey along a very dangerous road—there might not be thieves in the Bashir'Khazaaz, but they were plentiful on the roads in and out of it. It was no wonder the women desired his aid if Sakkalaah was their destination. Coincidentally, the oasis city was a planned stop for him on his way to the Free Cities, but he was hesitant to commit himself to their service. "And from Sakkalaah, madam?" he inquired guardedly. "Where then do you head?"

"To Duan'Bai," answered the dark-eyed girl.

Now Trell was truly shocked. He could only imagine the reception they would get, these three tribeless women, as they rode unaccompanied beneath the sanctified walls of Duan'Bai. "Madam," he said seriously, "forgive me, but you will not be welcome there."

She nodded solemnly. "And yet, that is our road."

Trell frowned as he gazed into three pairs of beautiful eyes, two as clear as spring water, the other dark as night. Instinct told him there was more to this story, but the question was, did it matter? They were foreign women in a friendless kingdom, and he felt unfortunately that he must aid them. Much against his better judgment.

Sundragons, zanthyrs, Whisper Lords, and now…what? What race of women travels alone into a hostile kingdom fraught with war, bandits, and marauding soldiers? He seemed destined to meet a representative of every known race upon this quest; was it coincidence, or the hand of a higher power?

Follow the water, Trell of the Tides…

He could almost hear Naiadithine's whispered blessing, if it was a blessing at all. He looked to the spring of Jai'Gar, its waters glittering in the strong afternoon light. Was the water—was Naiadithine—leading him still?

The women were watching him anxiously from between the rectangular slit in their hoods. He knew their hopes now rested on him, their next breath hinging on his reply. He retrieved his waterskins and capped them. "As it happens," he said, still not quite believing the words were leaving his mouth, "I am headed for Sakkalaah."

All three woman visibly deflated with relief, and the Nadori girl threw her arms around his neck, exclaiming in the Common Tongue, "Oh, thank you!" Then she backed away looking embarrassed.

The first woman said, "I am Fhionna, and this is my sister Aishlinn," and she indicated the second woman with eyes so like her own. "And this is—"

"Lily," said the Nadori girl.

"Well met, my ladies," Trell replied, keeping to the desert tongue. "They call me Trell of the Tides."

He carried his waterskins back to Gendaia and replaced them among his packs. The women followed. "What supplies will you need?" he asked them while tending to his own things.

"Everything," answered Fhionna. "Our things were lost in a storm three days ago."

"Horses too?"

"Everything," Fhionna confirmed.

Trell arched a brow curiously, but he didn't challenge her tale. He took up Gendaia's reins and led the women through the crowded bazaar acquiring what things they would need for the journey to Sakkalaah. He also spoke to the Khaz'im, inquiring about four men who could be trusted.

While the Khaz'im spread the word for new guards for the women, Trell found and purchased a large tent for them and a smaller one for himself. He acquired four desert horses from a Maudin, whose tribe was renowned for its fine-bred stock. Next he purchased additional waterskins, a variety of food stuffs, bed rolls and blankets, and a camel to carry it all. When Fhionna protested the smelly animal, Trell explained that while a mule would do fine through the gorge to Sakkalaah, it would not survive the trek overland to Duan'Bai, where a man could walk for days and encounter neither water nor shelter nor another living soul.

They were readying to depart when a Khaz'im arrived with four stone-faced men in tow. He told Trell in the desert tongue, "They are Khurds."

The laconic statement yet told Trell much. The Khurds were the largest of the seventeen recognized tribes—so large, in fact, that outsiders often used the one tribal name to describe all desert folk. But recognized members of any of the tribes made the men fully trustworthy, as they would be held accountable to the tribe for any wrongs committed. The Khaz'im continued, "For a hundred *denar* apiece, they will make the journey to Sakkalaah, but not beyond. It is the last threshold."

"I understand," Trell replied. Sakkalaah was the westernmost city in the Akkad. Beyond its borders lay the Assifiyah Range and the boundaries of Xanthe, and the Khurds would not walk those lands. He had not told the Khaz'im about the women's intent to travel to Duan'Bai. It was best that they kept such knowledge to themselves for the time being. The men's price was high but fair; it was a dangerous road.

The Khaz'im departed, and Trell nodded to the four new guards. "*Sa'laam*," he greeted.

"*Sa'laam*, Ama-Kai'alil," they returned in unison.

Trell walked over to the waiting women and explained, "They require a hundred *denar* apiece." If the women didn't have it, he was prepared to cover the cost—after all, he carried a fortune in Agasi silver and could do with some guards himself. The women nodded, however, and Fhionna replied, "You believe this is a fair price, Trell of the Tides?"

"Indeed, madam. For what you are asking."

"Then we shall pay all of you now," and she reached for her coin.

He stilled her hand with his own. "You shall pay *them* when we reach Sakkalaah," he told her in a low voice, "and me nothing at all."

Her eyes went wide. "But surely, you—"

Trell shook his head. "I cannot accept anything from you in good conscience."

Lily gave him a look of wonder. "Truly, Fortune must bless you for such generosity, Trell of the Tides."

But Aishlinn had been studying him, and she shook her head. "No," she disagreed softly, peering at Trell with a thoughtful gaze. "He cannot accept our coin, but it is not generosity that drives him...though I think honor does."

Trell nodded silently to her. Indeed, she was correct. Honor bound him to help these women because of their grave need, and more so since they followed his own path, but he felt he would be compromising his allegiance to the Emir if he accepted their coin for it, as if somehow that would constitute contracting for the enemy.

Fhionna and Lily gave Aishlinn a curious look, one they then turned back upon Trell, but he only motioned for them to mount up and he did the same.

Thus did they depart.

The sky was darkening dangerously and the wind picking up as the group made their way west with two guards leading on horseback, followed by Trell riding Gendaia, then the women, and then the last two guards and the camel named Sherba. They didn't get far, but they didn't need to, only far enough beyond the bazaar that its noise was drowned by the high ridges of the gorge—the Bashir'Khazaaz only shut down when there was nothing left to sell; even the coming storm would only drive the merchants inside their tents until the worst of the winds died down.

They were following a dry riverbed to the ominous rumble of approaching thunder when one of the leading guards, named Kamil, pulled his horse alongside Trell's. "Sayid says a campsite is just ahead," Kamil reported in the desert tongue, indicating the other guard with a nod of his turbaned head. "You can see the site there, halfway to the canyon rim."

Trell sighted down Kamil's pointing finger to a flat outcropping a few hundred paces up the side of the steep incline. "Thank Sayid for his effort," he said. "We will stay there for the night."

Kamil put heel to his horse and cantered ahead. Trell turned to the ladies, who were riding just behind him, and reported, "We've found a campsite where we can stay the night. It is just ahead, halfway up the canyon. A good site, from the looks of it."

Lily followed his gaze, but her brow furrowed upon spotting the site. "What is wrong with this very spot?" she inquired, indicating the flat expanse where their horses walked. "Why must we labor up so steep a hill with all of our belongings when could just camp here?"

"This canyon was carved by a river, milady," Trell explained. "It remains a flood channel. To spend the night here would be our death with the storm that approaches."

The women looked somewhat disturbed to hear this, perhaps because they'd have likely made that very mistake had it been up to them to decide.

Lily offered then, "We are indeed blessed to have you as our guide, Trell of the Tides."

"You are blessed to have Kamil and Sayid, madam," Trell corrected, "and Radiq and Ammar. I serve only as facilitator."

He could tell from the startled expressions on their faces that this was not how they'd considered him, but it was the only capacity in which he was prepared to serve.

The first droplets of rain had begun to fall by the time they made camp. The men rushed to set up the women's tent, and thereafter the ladies waited inside while the men picketed the horses and Sherba beneath a protective tarp and erected their own smaller *cadirs*, one-man tents of oiled wool just large enough for a bedroll.

The women were sitting close together when Trell ducked through the multilayered flaps that sealed the tent from the storm. They'd traded their burkhas for desert gowns not unlike Jaya's in design. The sisters wore identical gowns in a variegated sea-blue, and Lily wore a gown of the deepest green. It was the first Trell had seen of their faces, however, and he drew up short in surprise. The Nadori was almond-skinned and younger than he'd thought—surely not a day past ten and six, while the sisters were...older, but nearly ethereal in their beauty. Fhionna's honey-brown hair was held back from her lovely face by a cap of firestones, while Aishlinn was blonde and fairer with angular features that reminded him of a fragile bird. He would never have known them sisters if not for the identical color and shape of their eyes.

The ladies looked equally startled by his mud-drenched appearance. "What happened to you?" Aishlinn asked.

"The storm, milady," Trell answered. He set down the bundle he'd been carrying and went to his own packs to find a cloth to wipe his face. "This is the desert. It rains mud." He splashed some water from his flagon onto the cloth and began the systematic procedure of cleaning up—over the years, he'd learned to do it with as little as a single glass of water and one piece of cloth a foot square.

Without thought to current company, Trell tore off his muddy tunic and received a harmony of feminine laughter for his effort. He looked up to find Lily and Aishlinn whispering with bright eyes. Only the lovely Fhionna was watching him with a smile of admiration. "I beg your pardons," Trell said, feeling foolish for not remembering his protocol around highborn ladies. "While the rain persists, I fear there is nowhere else for me to clean up. Might I use this corner of your tent?"

"Of course, Trell of the Tides," Fhionna replied, eyeing him in so arousing a way that she stirred warmth into his loins. "Your company is welcome." While Trell began wiping down his chest and arms with his bit of cloth, Fhionna joined her two companions in whispering. He glanced their way occasionally, only to find three sets of eyes regarding him over a myriad of hands concealing whispers and laughter.

After several extended moments of this, in which Trell managed somewhat nervous smiles in response to their whispers, Fhionna rose and approached him.

Trell regarded her openly. Her large, aqua eyes were framed by chocolate lashes, and her heart-shaped face was perfection, with a goddess's smile and lips as full and red as a blood-kissed rose. Her body was all curves where they should be, and her long legs made him think only of how they would feel firmly secured around his hips. Quite unexpectedly, Trell found himself lost in her eyes and confessing breathlessly, "Milady, I don't believe you can be human."

Fhionna laughed, and the sound was music to his ears. "You are quite right, Trell of the Tides," she murmured. Then she gave him a little pout that was nearly irresistible, making him long to taste of its perfection. "But why have you stopped?" she inquired innocently, a single finger caught between her perfect teeth.

Trell looked down at his bared chest, cleaned now of mud, and then to his lower half, which was still awaiting ministration, though the throbbing warmth he felt longed for ministrations of a different variety. He lifted grey eyes back to her; the others' presence was all but forgotten in the thrall of Fhionna's aqua gaze. "To move further at this juncture might be dangerous, milady," he answered breathlessly.

She came closer and trailed a hand down the line of his muscular chest. "For me?" she whispered. "Or for you?"

Aishlinn suddenly appeared beside her sister. "Fhionna, you must stop this," she scolded in a hushed voice. "It is unseemly to take advantage of Trell when he offers us his service so selflessly!"

Fhionna's eyes flashed, but then she reconsidered her anger and looked gently upon her sister. Much to Trell's disappointment, she stepped away from him, leaving his body aching for her touch. "You are right, Aishlinn. It is unseemly of me. I do apologize."

"Not to me—to *him*," Aishlinn whispered.

"Yes, to Trell," Fhionna repeated, shifting her sultry eyes back to his. He thought he caught more than a hint of invitation in her gaze, but then she was clasping her hands before her and bowing her head. "I entreat thee for forgiveness, Trell of the Tides. I fear I have enchanted you without your awareness, and it was wrong of me."

Trell arched brows. It was the last thing he expected to hear. "You...*enchanted* me?"

"Yes," declared Aishlinn. "She cannot help it, and yet she *must*," and this latter was stressed with a stare of reprimand. "Please, Fhionna."

Fhionna turned away from Trell without another word, but she did spare one last glance over her shoulder, and this time there was little doubt of the desire in her eyes. As he watched the women turn their backs politely, Trell scratched his muddy hair and wondered how he kept stumbling into such unusual companions.

He made haste to finish cleaning up. He hung his soiled clothes to be washed in the river in the morning, dressed again in his usual dun-hued desert pants and a clean, knee-length tunic, and gathered up the bundle he'd brought before joining the sisters.

They shifted positions at his arrival, making space among them, and he held up the bundle as he folded his legs to sit. "Dinner, my ladies."

They let out exclamations of joyful surprise as Trell set down the cloth and unwrapped it. Within were strips of lamb, hunks of goat's cheese, heavy unleavened flatbread, some dates, figs and olives, and a paste of beans and spices wrapped in palm leaves. Trell helped the ladies to their share and then sat back to eat his own.

While they ate, Trell asked the inevitable question that had been foremost on his mind since meeting them. "If I may ask, Fhionna, Aishlinn, where are you from? Clearly Tal'Shira is not your homeland as it is Lily's."

"I was born in Malchiarr," Fhionna said.

"Malchiarr, truly?"

She nodded with an elusive smile. "Yes, Trell of the Tides."

He stared at her in wonder. "I've never met a woman from Malchiarr."

She gave a throaty sort of laugh. "We do exist, I assure you."

He continued, still holding her gaze, "But I have met a man from Malchiarr. He was speared through in the Emir's palace. He laughed as he died."

"Death is only the beginning," she murmured.

Trell eyed her curiously. "Yes, that's what he said. The thing is…this man looked uncannily like the Emir."

She leaned back on one hand and regarded him coolly. "Did he? And did you see his death?"

"I am the one who speared him, my lady."

She laughed. "How very bold of you."

He cast her a rueful grin. "Yes, as I discovered. I was almost beheaded. Fortunately the real Emir arrived in time to prove my valor instead of my treason."

"You were young, I suspect," she said.

He settled her a curious look. "I was. How did you know?"

"The young ones often see Geshaiwyn for the Shapeshifters they are," she returned. "The eyes of the young are not yet veiled by the horrors of the world. They don't try to trick themselves. Men too often wear sackcloth before their eyes, seeing only what they want to see, the mind inventing explanations where none exist."

Trell regarded her steadily. "You're not like him then. Not Geshaiwyn?"

She shook her head, still smiling.

One race down. A dozen more to go…

"And you, Aishlinn? You were born elsewhere, I take it?"

"I was born near Mt. Pisah," she replied endearingly.

"Our mother traveled widely in her youth," Fhionna supplied. "She visited many Wildling communities."

"Choosing suitors in each," Aishlinn said with a suggestive smile.

Trell was beginning to think himself somehow caught in a den of wolves in sheep's guise. What had become of the innocent, helpless women he'd met that afternoon? They'd seemed to grow fangs with the fall of night. All, that is, save the diminutive Lily.

"And you, my lady?" Trell asked her. "What is your story?"

"Oh," she flushed. "I am…I haven't a story to tell, really. My mother is dead and my father is…not."

"Why not tell us of yourself though, Trell of the Tides?" Aishlinn cut in with a telling glance at her sister. "How came you to know the desert tongue and walk the Emir's palace?"

Trell drew in a deep breath and looked at the sisters as he slowly exhaled. He'd hoped to avoid discussing his history and current quest, but he felt obligated to share something of his story in kind. So Trell told them how he'd awoken in Duan'Bai knowing nothing of his past, how he met Graeme and Ware and came to run with a company of Converted, and how upon Graeme's death, he'd left to find his past. He made no mention of his close relationship with the Emir, however, nor of his role in the war, for these were things better left unspoken.

The women listened, captivated, and when he was finished, Aishlinn spoke. "Would that we had a 'reader among us," she murmured.

"A reader?" Trell repeated.

"A truthreader," she explained. "They have ways of helping people remember such things. If your memory is merely occluded and not hindered by physical damage, then a truthreader could help you." She quickly added in response to her sister's arched brow, "Cast me not that look, Fhionna. I am the first to admit the fourth-stranders have their uses."

"Even were it possible, milady," Trell replied, staying well clear of the sisters' private conflicts, "I think I would have to refuse."

They all looked surprised to hear this, and Lily asked, "But why?"

Trell gave her a soft smile. "A...well, a friend of mine once told me that a man who can sleep before an important journey has nothing to gain from the trip. By this he implied that my journey is equally as important—if not more so—than the prize I seek at its end."

Fhionna regarded him quizzically. "Do you truly believe that, Trell of the Tides?"

Trell gave her a solemn nod. "Indeed, milady, and based on my experiences thus far, I am starting to think that I shall not find the one without the other."

"You speak with great wisdom," Aishlinn said, giving him a kind smile. "We are blessed to have you among us."

Ever uncomfortable with praise, Trell gave her a modest nod of thanks and then got to his feet. "I must take leave of you now, my ladies. My shift approaches."

"You stand watch tonight?" asked Fhionna.

Trell nodded. "There are always bandits about after a storm, hoping to catch people unawares. Sleep well, my ladies. We'll leave at first light."

With five men to share the night hours, Trell's watch went quickly, so that when he awoke to the first grey light of approaching dawn, he didn't feel lacking for sleep. He tended to Gendaia and then went down to the flooded stream to wash his clothes of the night before. He was still there when he heard the women coming out of their tent. A muted commotion was soon followed by exclamations of surprise—though he'd told them the dry rock bed would flood with the storm, they apparently hadn't expected to find a rushing river where only dirt and stone had been on the eve before.

Trell returned to camp still wringing out his clothing and found the women lined up along the hill waiting for him. They looked a bit rumpled but otherwise seemed in good spirits. "Good morning, ladies," he greeted them. "How did you sleep?"

"Well, thank you," Fhionna answered for the group. "This was the first night in many that I've not been plagued by ill dreams."

"Truly," Lily agreed. Then she teased with a smile, "You must have dosed our water to make us sleep so soundly!"

"Tis the water of Jai'Gar," a passing Sayid commented, his deep voice adding an unexpected richness to his words. The tallest of the four Khurds, Sayid had a competent air about him, and his dark gaze was quite compelling.

The women followed him with their eyes as he continued on toward the horses. Then Lily whispered, "What did he mean?"

Trell explained, "The water from the springs of Jai'Gar is said to heal the ills of mind, body and spirit, milady. That is the water you carry in your flasks."

"And you think this is why we slept so well?" Lily sounded skeptical.

"I didn't say it was the water, milady," Trell replied, casting her a shadowy grin. "You did." With that, he bowed to the women and made his exit, following in Sayid's footsteps to the post where Gendaia was tethered. To his surprise, Fhionna followed after him with Lily in tow.

"Do you believe it's true?" Fhionna asked as her long legs easily matched his stride. "Does the water heal?"

Trell turned to her and opened his mouth to reply, but her unanticipated beauty captured his breath. "...I don't know," he managed after an embarrassing pause.

"You don't subscribe to the desert beliefs, do you?" Lily inquired, leaning around Fhionna to peer at him with her lovely dark eyes.

"That's the thing about Jai'Gar, milady," Trell remarked, glancing her way, "He doesn't require that you believe in Him before He works His miracles. I haven't seen the spring-water heal, but I have seen other things that I cannot explain."

"Like what?" Lily asked with keen interest—perhaps too keen.

Trell shook his head. "A story for another time, perhaps." With that, he managed to extract himself from their company and devoted his time instead to helping the Khurds break camp.

The orange-gold sky had faded into pale blue by the time they departed, with Sayid and Kamil leading everyone up out of the canyon before turning westward to ride along the rim. The wind was chill and brisk on the open ridge, and the autumn sun held little warmth. Trell almost missed the fire of the Nadori desert. The canyonlands surrounding the Bashir'Khazaaz were higher and colder than the Kutsamak, and it would get colder still as they neared the Cry on their way into Sakkalaah.

Gendaia was as surefooted in the pebbly soil of the canyons as she had been along the rocky paths of the Ruby Road, and Trell felt her a boon companion. A bond was growing between them; Trell was learning to read Gendaia's signals, and she was responding to his in kind. Hallovian steeds were known and bred for this trait, but Trell had never had the privilege of riding one before—at least not that he remembered.

'The man you seek...he also rides a Hallovian steed.' Trell thought of Balaji's haunting words.

Was it insane that he'd left the sa'reyth without at least trying to find out if the Mage spoke of his true heritage? Should he have tried to learn something more about the stranger mentioned in the Mage's journal? Would any other man have walked away from the knowledge, especially when he might've gained it by simply turning the page of a book? Trell asked himself these questions repeatedly, but the fact was that it didn't matter what other men might have done; his own honor forbade it.

Which led him to wonder... Who *had* instilled in him such an unshakable sense of right and wrong, such that he always knew which choice to make even under difficult and confusing circumstances? It wasn't the Emir, though Trell admired him as a generous and noble leader, but often times Trell's idea of the moral right was not the same as the Emir's. Much of this was due to the teachings of Jai'Gar, which were laden with consequence and spare on compassion, but beyond this, there was a definite difference in the way he looked at honor and the way the Basi viewed it.

His thoughts turned to the other man again, the second of the Mage's 'kingdom blades.' What kind of man was he upon whom so much depended? And he thought of his brother from the tower, whose eyes were as grey as his own.

Where are you now, my brother? Trell wondered as he rode into the west, *and what is the game in which we both play?*

TWENTY-TWO

'A man makes his own luck, but it never hurts to pray on the off-chance somebody is listening.'

– Fynnlar val Lorian, Prince of Dannym

Tanis woke with a start right at the crack of dawn. He sat up feeling grateful for the dawn, relieved to be free of the dream that had him in its clutches just moments before. Still sandy-eyed, he climbed out of bed and shuffled over to his nightstand to wash his face. Beyond his window, the sky was flamed a solid orange-rose, and birds chirped in welcome of the day. Tanis glared out at them several times as he threw on a grey-blue tunic and charcoal leggings and cloak and fought with the laces of his boots. But if the birds saw his scowl, they cheerfully ignored it, as if knowing that Tanis wasn't a 'morning person.'

Unlike her Grace. No matter what time Tanis woke—and it had taken years to train himself to wake before noon—her Grace was already at work in her infirmary, or studying some dusty text in her solar, or out for a morning ride. She called herself a 'morning person,' but Epiphany save the one who tried to converse with her before she'd finished her first cup of tea.

Yawning wide enough to bare his tonsils, Tanis shuffled down the hall to check on Ean, wandering into his room in such a daze that he nearly collided with the prince, who had just finished washing up. The lad squealed in surprise, and Ean reached to calm him.

"Whoa—sorry there, Tanis. You okay then?" As Tanis nodded, Ean clapped him on the shoulder, saying, "I'm glad you're here. You can help me with this mane I seem to have acquired," and he shook his cinnamon head like a wet bear.

So tasked, Tanis retrieved scissors and razor and a pan of warm water and helped Ean cut his hair and shave his beard. When this was done, the prince opened the package of clothes Tanis had purchased for him in town.

"I hope they fit," the lad said, looking sheepish. "It was all the tailor had on his shelf, and your other clothes were quite ruined."

Ean had the britches on already and was slipping into a loose forest-green tunic. "They'll do nicely, Tanis," he said with a look of appreciation as he laced the shirt. He threaded his belt around his waist and then held out both arms. "Well? How do I look?"

Tanis was impressed. As Ean stood there in his new tunic and britches, clean and shaven and with his cinnamon hair brushed and cut, he seemed a different person altogether. Royal even.

"Look better, do I?" Ean observed with a grin.

Tanis nodded. "Do you leave us then, my lord?"

Ean must've caught the disappointment in his tone, for he gave him an apologetic look. "I wish I could stay, Tanis, but I'm well and healed, thanks to your lady, and in light of what's happened, I cannot justify further delay no matter how I'd like to stay and relax here in your pleasant home."

Quite without warning, Tanis felt an overwhelming desire to ask Ean to take him with him, just anywhere...wherever he was going. There was something about being in Ean's company that made Tanis want to remain there, like he would be safe so long as he was. He knew he could trust Ean, despite the secrets he was keeping; in fact, he'd never felt so strongly that anyone could be trusted. These feelings were quite inexplicable, and Tanis made a mental note to ask Master O'reith about them.

Yet for all the strength of these desires, the lad had no idea how to request such a thing, even should he find the courage to do so. He lowered himself onto the edge of the chair and asked instead, "Will you be waiting to say good-bye to her Grace? I don't know where she is. She's usually up by now."

Ean was sitting on the bed donning his boots, which the maids had cleaned and polished. He paused long enough to exhale a sigh. "I doubt she has much interest in seeing me off." He shot the lad a perplexed look. "Is she always so... unpredictable?"

Tanis shrugged. "Pretty much." He thought of her Grace rushing past him in tears in the hall the day before and wondered... "What did you do to upset her so, sir?"

Ean cast the lad a rueful look. "Oh, I've managed to start off our relationship with my typical explosive charm." He rubbed his shaven chin, looking thoughtful. "You'd think I'd committed one of the Veneisean Cardinal Sins, though to save my life I couldn't tell you what it was. All I did was tell her how sorry I was—and am—about your Seneschal passing, and she just..." and he shrugged.

"Farshideh was a great lady," Tanis said. The great burden of her loss was a mountain of stone upon his chest. "She was like a mother to her Grace." *And to me...* "It has been hard on us seeing her health failing this past year. Her Grace...well, I think she feels responsible for being unable to help her."

Ean regarded him with honest sympathy. "Tis a terrible thing, our impotence against the wishes of Fate," and from the way he said it, Tanis knew that Ean felt this truth in a personal way. They held each other's gaze for a long moment, as if both pondering Fate's capricious desires. Then the prince pushed to his feet and made a show of walking in his new clothes. "Well, they're a little big, Tanis, but I think I'll manage. Thank you for all of this."

"You're welcome, sir," Tanis said glumly. He wished he was brave enough to ask what he so desired, but the words just wouldn't come.

Ean tucked thumbs into his belt and fastened his grey eyes on the boy. "You know...she said something odd to me yesterday before she left all in a flurry of skirts."

"What was that?"

Ean frowned. "She said if I'd never come, Farshideh wouldn't have died. It seemed like there was more than mere spite behind the statement. Do you know what she could've meant?"

"I've no idea, sir." Tanis pushed hands solemnly between his knees. "As I said, Farshideh's health was poor, and after seeing that zanthyr, well..." He paused and caught his bottom lip between his teeth. "Well, she just seemed to fade away..."

Ean considered the lad for a moment and then placed a warm hand upon his shoulder. "Will you come and show me to my horse?"

Tanis jumped up. "Of course. It's—"

The rumble of galloping horses interrupted further conversation, and Ean moved to the window. Two long lines of at least three dozen horsemen were cantering down the long drive toward the house. "It's the King's Own Guard," Ean said after a moment's study.

"What would the king's men be doing in Aracine?" Tanis asked. He went to the window and peered out beside Ean.

The prince gave him a rueful look full of apology. "Tanis...there's something I need to tell you..."

At work in her laboratory since long before dawn, Alyneri was disturbed by the clatter of hooves along the quarter-mile of paved drive leading to the front of the manor house, a route nobody used save those who didn't know any better—which usually meant some tiresome noble from Calgaryn.

This can wait, she thought to herself, setting down the vial of peppermint oil she was extracting and dampening the little burner beneath it. She took off her work apron, hung it on a hook behind the door as she passed, and lightly lifted her blue shantung skirts as she marched down the long hall.

"Tanis!" she called out while turning the corner on her way to the front hall. *Now where is that boy? If I have to go searching for him...*

Fersthaven's front doors were carved from two massive pieces of solid oak. Normally her Chamberlain and Seneschal would attend visitors, but nothing at all was normal about her life just then. She thought she had a good idea who was approaching and why. Unfortunately, a meeting with Captain Rhys val Kincaide never improved her mood.

Not that much was going to. She'd barely slept the night before, what with both mourning Farshideh and berating herself for not knowing Ean when he lay in her own house. It wasn't any solace to her that he'd been a thirteen-year-old boy when he'd left, tall and lanky, all bones and sinew and not a pinch to spare. The intervening years had broadened him, hardened his physique. He was a man now. *Still...I should have known him!* Alyneri couldn't decide what bothered her more: that she hadn't recognized Ean though she was supposedly in love with him, or that his identity had eluded her even while in rapport. They both seemed equally repulsive facts.

Suddenly grateful for the chance to be justifiably ill-humored, Alyneri threw open the doors and then stood square in the middle of the portal, squinting into the bright morning. She watched the king's men trot their horses into the turnaround, and glanced down as a large tabby cat fled from underneath a shrubbery and darted up the steps to hide itself beneath her skirt. She shook her silks away from the creature. "Traitor," she accused, giving it a hard look. "You destroyed my mint last night. No milk for you today!" The cat flattened an ear irritably and turned its tawny eyes to gaze out at the newcomers.

The men reined in their horses in the drive, giving Alyneri the opportunity to frown down at the Captain. Rhys sat tall in the saddle of a great chestnut warhorse. As ever, he sported his chain of office in prominent view. *No doubt he's come for Ean at last,* she thought, regarding him narrowly, *and none too soon!*

The man in question dismounted in one swift leap and ascended the steps toward Alyneri with long, determined strides, looking as if he meant to push right past her; but the cat began hissing at his approach—not to mention the affronted glare in Alyneri's eyes—and one or the other kept him at bay. For a moment, the captain and Alyneri stood deadlocked in an impasse of contrary gazes that her Grace seemed content to prolong indefinitely.

At last the captain gripped the hilt of his sword in aggravation. "*Well?*" he barked. "Where is he, woman?"

Alyneri regarded him imperially. She was in no mood to be trifled with, and especially not by the Lord Captain Rhys val Kincaide, who held permanent residence on her bad side. "I'm afraid there are a few matters we must rectify here at the outset, my Lord Captain," she began with supreme disregard for his obvious haste. "First, I never answer to the address of '*woman.*' I do have a name, but *your Grace* or at least *my lady* are most appropriate, and you may address me as such any time. Second, you are standing on my land, bestowed upon my family by King Aaryn, First King of Calgaryn. I know you are aware that you're speaking to a Duchess. I will overlook your obvious disregard for my station because you seem distressed. Should you choose to apologize, I might have a powder that will help you with that temper."

The captain's eyes bulged, and he made to reply, but Alyneri pushed on. "Along those lines then, I am loathe to imagine you had the intention of barging into my home—without even observing a shadow of the respect one bestows upon a peeress of the Court—just because there's no moat surrounding my front door," and she crossed her arms and stared at him beneath a dangerously arched eyebrow.

The captain's face went crimson, beard bristling. "*Do* you know what this means?" he barked, shoving his chain of office toward her face.

"Of course, my Lord Captain," she replied, meting his hostility with indignation. "I am prepared to offer the Captain of the King's Own Guard all the hospitality at my disposal—that is, if you intend to stay," and her tone implied that she hoped he did not. "I must warn you, however, that we observe the well-established rules of etiquette here in Gandrel Forest just as in Calgaryn Palace, and I expect no less of you here than His Majesty would expect in Court. That includes appropriately dressing for meals—I will not have my dining room smelling like rusty mail and unwashed bodies, nor will I allow any of you to sleep between my linen without bathing first. If bathing is too much of a burden, of course, you can lodge in the stables with the other unwashed creatures."

By this time the captain was making strangling noises.

"Third, and last of all," Alyneri continued without pause, "and getting back to your original question, I'm afraid you will have to be more specific. I treat many an injured man, and I haven't the least idea of whom you refer." This was a lie, of course, but it was quite edifying to watch the captain's jugular vein bulging dangerously along the side of his neck.

Once Rhys' countenance matched the color of his beard, he responded in a gruff, barely-controlled voice, "*Your Grace*, I search for his Highness, Ean val Lorian, Crown Prince of Dannym, and whose personal letter arrived by way of *your* courier just last night!" Then he shouted, "*Now is he here or not!*"

Alyneri nudged the cat away with the toe of her shoe and stepped aside, gesturing to the captain. "Why, yes, now that you mention it. I do believe he is."

"My prince!" one of the King's Guard cried just then, and Alyneri turned to see Ean and Tanis approaching from behind her in the hall. Her heart skipped a beat to see him, so like she remembered from their youth. *Why must you be so ridiculously handsome?*

Suddenly all the soldiers were dismounting and falling to one knee with a massive shuffling, chinking and clanking. To Alyneri, it sounded like a great clock had heaved one last, dying sigh and collapsed.

"Your highness," the captain said, straightening, "it is good to see you well and whole. You gave us all quite a fright."

"It's been a long time, Rhys," Ean replied with a warm smile, including all the men in his greeting.

"Tis a godsend that you came safely through it all," the Captain commented, clearly still not quite sure what to make of Ean's report.

"Yes, Fortune graced me," the prince agreed, but there was deep sorrow in his tone.

The king's men kissed their thumbs for continued good luck, and the Captain seemed to want to do so though he managed to restrain himself. "We need to return to Calgaryn at once, your Highness," Rhys said instead.

"Very good," Ean replied. "Her Grace was kind enough to stable Caldar with her own mare."

Rhys waved one of his men to retrieve Caldar from the stables and looked to Alyneri. "*Your Grace*, their Majesties bid you return to Calgaryn with us that they might properly thank you for your service to their son."

"I plan to return ere Festival is completed, Captain. I'm sure my role is small enough that—"

"Unfortunately, your Grace," and his tone reflected his opinion that he thought the matter quite unfortunate indeed, "their majesties require that you return with us."

Alyneri frowned as she considered the order. In the end she decided defiance would be too emotionally draining—however gratifying it might've been to annoy the captain. "Very well," she replied with a sigh. "I suppose if that is their Majesties' desire, there is nothing to be done for it. We can leave for Calgaryn as soon as I am packed. My Lord Captain, please have your men help Tanis with my things." She turned to the lad and counted off, "I'll need all of my herbs, of course, my leather bag, Tanis, and also a few necessary personal things...pack my usual trunk."

She turned back to the captain, who clearly was not used to being ordered by anyone save his Majesty and looked a trifle indignant, and continued, "You'll have to send one of your men to saddle our horses as well. My groomsman is occupied with preparations for transporting my Seneschal's body—I doubt you could know that she passed over yesterday, but these things do happen and one must attend to them. Tanis and I came with the coach from Calgaryn, but we'll return with you. I vow, the air of a morning ride will do me good."

The captain turned from Alyneri to a smiling Ean and back to Alyneri as if battling to reconcile his orders to bring the Duchess against the necessity of meeting all of her demands in order to do so. Finally, he heaved a ponderous sigh and grumbled, "As your Grace wishes," and dispatched his men appropriately.

Ean grinned even wider. "Fabulous then!" he exclaimed, clapping hands together. "Why not make a real event of it? Perhaps tour around a little, I can show you the ins and outs of Calgaryn Palace—"

"I'm quite familiar enough with Calgaryn Palace, thank you, your Highness," Alyneri remarked tersely. She was still furious with him and certainly had no intention of spending *extra* time in his company. "I have, after all, spent the last five years in residence there during your notable absence. Well, move along then, Tanis," and she waved the lad off to pack her things.

Within the hour, they were riding north.

It was afternoon when Ean and the others came into view of Calgaryn city and its stately palace crowning the ocean cliffs. They were spotted immediately, and thirty or so of the palace guard soon came cantering to meet them upon the road—as if the thirty-plus soldiers of the King's Own Guard that currently flanked the prince weren't nearly enough.

The man leading the party, however, was as unlike a soldier as Ean was like a shepherd. He was dressed in the velvet doublet and cape of the nobility, though in a foreign cut and of a rather garish violet-red. His wavy black hair was unfashionably long to his shoulders and looked as if it hadn't been brushed in a week, but he wore a precisely-manicured moustache and chin beard with flair. "Welcome back, cousin!" the man called as he neared, leveling Ean a wide smile somewhat reminiscent of a tomcat who'd just enjoyed a meal of the Queen's treasured doves.

Ean reined in with a grin splitting his face from ear to ear. "Shadow take me! But what is Fynnlar val Lorian doing back at his ancestral home?"

"Licking wounds, cousin," Fynn replied with easy humility. He reined his horse to a halt before Ean, adding, "And I hear you have a few of your own that recently needed tending." He lifted val Lorian grey eyes to view Alyneri and the others, who were just then joining them, and added lustily, "but I must admit, I much prefer your nurse to mine," and he sent a sideways nod to a bull of a man mounted just behind him.

Ean turned his gaze to the latter. "Surely you must rival the gods for patience, Brody, to put up with this black sheep for so long."

"I do as my lord Prince Ryan requires," the bull-shouldered man named Brody replied in a voice like grinding gravel.

Fynn gave the Bull a withering look. "Yes…well, we all have our gifts." He looked around then, and noting that everyone had collected, he motioned to the others to follow. The men behind Fynnlar cleared way for the two princes as the royal pair led on to the palace. "So what's it like being poisoned?" Fynn wanted to know as they set off.

"That's a morbid question, my lord," Alyneri observed, riding just behind them.

"Yes, death has always fascinated me, your Grace," Fynn declared, turning her a grin over his shoulder. He made no secret of his gaze as it fell with appreciation upon her bosom and only lifted his eyes again as he suggested, "Mayhap such a respected Healer as thyself could have something to add to my studies?"

Alyneri arched a brow at him.

"And might I add," Fynn went on, "it is such a pleasure to see you again after these many long years. I recall so fondly our childhood days of tormenting one another with vindictive aplomb."

"They shall remain fondly in your memory alone, Lord Fynnlar."

"I fear Alyneri has outgrown us, cousin," Ean explained. "She no longer has the time to engage with us in mundane banter."

Alyneri shot him a vexed look. He winked at her.

Fynn put on another of his feline grins. "We'll have to manage without her then. But what of my question? I am most curious."

The Prince shook his head. "Cousin, I thought my uncle taught you better manners."

"Ah yes, *manners*, the lubricants of society," Fynn agreed. "But I rather like being the grindstone. You were about to say?"

Laughing, Ean answered, "In all truth, the entire episode seems but a blur to me now."

"See, I knew it so!" Fynn banged his fist upon one knee. "I told that fool of a Veneisean, Lord Aigelmort, that he ought to use arsenic in his wife's tea, but he insisted an overdose of laudanum was better. The awful woman was sick for days before the end."

Alyneri turned Fynn a reproachful glare. "You are a horrid man, Lord Fynnlar."

"Ah, but such a necessary component of society, your Grace," Fynn pointed out.

"And what society would that be, exactly?"

"So what brings you home, Fynn?" Ean interposed.

Fynn tore his eyes from Alyneri's. "Oh trifling things, really. Some loose ends—and of course, I really wanted to be here for your parade."

"You ran out of money, didn't you?"

"Yes," the Bull answered before Fynn could lie about it.

"I did *not* run out of money," Fynn declared indignantly, shooting the Bull a fiery look. "I need more capital for my latest business venture, that's all. I thought dear Uncle Gydryn might want to invest."

Ean laughed. "I doubt it."

"More likely his Majesty would pay you just to leave again," Alyneri observed.

Fynn broke into a wide grin and replied with a wink, "I'm *counting* on it, your Grace."

A blaze of trumpets sounded as they were heading into the tunnel that led beneath the palace's outer wall. The trumpeters raised their silver horns again when Ean's group exited the tunnel on the other side, and they continued their bursts of revelry until the party reached the Promenade.

Thanks to the trumpeters' valiant efforts to rouse the entire kingdom into awareness of the prince's return, by the time Ean and his companions reached the First Circle, half the nobility on hand had collected to welcome the Crown Prince home—most notably the female half. When Ean turned Caldar through a row of arched columns crowned with a flying eagle to begin that final leg across the parade yard to the palace entrance, a cheer rose up from the assembled masses, many of which threw flowers in his path.

"I didn't know you were so well loved," Alyneri observed blandly as she rode along to Ean's left.

"Don't be ridiculous, your Grace," Fynn interposed from Ean's right. "They're cheering for me, of course." He puffed out his chest like a strutting rooster and grinned.

She gave him a withering look.

"In all honestly, Alyneri," Ean admitted while being bombarded with flowers, "this far exceeds my expectations."

The assault of cheering grew louder the closer they came to the palace entrance, and as they passed a group of teenage girls, five of them broke away from their matronly chaperones and rushed up to take turns kissing Ean's boot. One auburn-haired girl, who showed promise of becoming a great beauty, pulled an embroidered lace kerchief from within her décolletage and shoved it off into Ean's hand. Even Tanis knew the significance of that gesture.

"Subtle, aren't they?" Alyneri noted.

Ean's reply was a stoic look only slightly marred by the half-grin twitching the corners of his mouth.

And then they were halting before the palace's towering doors amid welcoming hands and open arms of family friends, his father's ministers and council members, the highest ranking nobility in a rainbow display of velvet and silks, all the palace staff lined up in neat rows, and then, suddenly, the King and Queen.

A hush spread like wildfire through the assembled crowd, broken only by the rustling of silk as hundreds curtsied or bowed. So it was in silence that Ean dismounted and turned to look up at his father for the first time in five years.

The King stood atop the stairs framed by the immense marble portal, black-clad and statuesque beneath the gleaming silver crest over the doors. With his dark hair greying at the temples and his hand on his silver-hilted sword, he seemed the subject of an impressive painting.

On first seeing him again, Ean was returned to the little boy whose eyes always filled with pride and even awe when he looked upon his father. Gydryn val Lorian was a powerful presence, a presence that was always far more indelible in memory than even the handsome face of the man who possessed it. Ean had not expected to feel so honored by his welcoming—he half feared the years away would've changed the relationship between them. But it seemed his father was as eager to renew their bond as Ean was.

Unable to conceal his emotion, Ean climbed the stairs and walked into his father's open arms. A cheer rose up from the crowd, the loudest yet. "My son," the King murmured into Ean's ear. He held him in a rough embrace, and for once in his eighteen years of life, the Prince didn't mind feeling the child in his father's company. "Epiphany blesses us that you return whole and safe," Gydryn confessed with such relief that Ean choked back tears. It was so meaningful to him knowing that his father cared, but it shouldn't have come as such a surprise. Twice Gydryn had lost a son; the loss of his third and youngest child might have proven the final straw.

"Ean..." the prince lifted eyes and saw his mother standing just behind the king, and he moved to embrace her with even greater emotion. While Ean was taller and broader than his slender mother, it was clear from the way Errodan held him so dear and close that he would always be her youngest child.

"My dearest, *dearest* son," Errodan breathed into Ean's ear while she held him enfolded in her arms and the crowd cheered on and on. For a brief moment as Ean returned her hug with his cheek pressed warmly against hers, the terrible events of the past week were forgotten.

Ean kissed his mother lovingly, then pulled away smiling. Errodan cupped his face with both hands, was about to say something, but then grabbed him back into her arms again. "Dear heavens, if anything had happened to you, my darling boy..."

"I know..." Ean said, laughing in her arms, "there would've been hell to pay." Errodan laughed softly beside him, and even the king smiled and reached a hand around his son's shoulders.

And the world started again. The guards and nobility were all crowding for placement near the prince, the rest of Ean's companions were dismounting and handing off their horses to the pages, squires were rushing down the steps to take their things, the Mistress of Apartments was loudly declaring where everyone had been quartered, the onlookers began to disperse...Tanis was being jostled this way and that and found himself climbing the steps beside Lord Fynnlar.

"And what's your name, lad?" the royal cousin asked.

Looking pleased that Fynn had taken notice of him, Tanis replied with a smile, "Tanis, my lord."

But when their eyes met, Fynn gaped at him. "Burn me proper!" he declared. He put a hand on the boy's head and turned his colorless eyes away. "You'd best not be reading my mind, lad. I wouldn't want to put you through such torture."

"I'm only in training, my lord. I can't read minds yet."

"Oh? Well then. So long as you don't go poking around in anyone else's head—and specifically mine—we'll get along splendidly."

Walking beside them, Alyneri observed imperially, "A guilty conscience, Fynnlar, is a firmer imprisonment than any dungeon could ever prove."

Fynn gave her a look of surprise. "How strange, your Grace; my conscience has never bothered me at all."

They reached the royals then, and Errodan took notice of Alyneri. "Alyneri d'Giverny," she said in her most stately of voices.

Alyneri curtsied and came forward. "Yes, your Majesty."

"You have done us an invaluable service. We shall talk later in private of your reward."

Alyneri curtsied again and kept her eyes lowered respectfully. "I am pleased to perform my duty as healer to the crown and ask no favor."

"All the same, you shall have a place of honor at tonight's banquet table."

"Your Majesty is too kind," Alyneri murmured.

Ysolde held out her hands and took Alyneri's in her own. "As soon as we learned the prince was in your care, we had no more fear for him," she said.

Alyneri was taken aback by their gratitude and praise. Her face flushed beneath her caramel skin, and she nodded as she stepped back with another curtsy.

The King came over and put a hand on Ean's shoulder. "I would speak with you, son. There is much to discuss."

Ean winced at the skepticism in his tone. "Father, I—"

And someone screamed.

Ean felt more than heard the second arrow whiz past his head as panic ensued. Someone grabbed him from behind and thrust him against his father, who in turn was being mobbed by his guard, all of them forcibly pushed backwards through the portal inside the protection of the palace. People were screaming and shoving to get out of the way, guards shouting to regain order.

The palace doors slammed with a reverberating thunder, but inside was no less chaotic. A breathless Ean finally freed himself from the mass of guards, looked around, and demanded of the confusion, "What in Tiern'aval *happened?*"

It was Fynnlar who stood at Ean's side. "An assassin's arrow, Ean. Didn't you see it strike some poor doomed porter straight through the eye? Epiphany's hand alone guided it on a hairline between you and her Majesty—Raine's truth, only divine intervention could've kept it from striking you both down together."

"Thank you for that colorful recounting, Fynnlar," the Queen said, coming up behind him with her green-coated guards looking formidable in a half-moon formation around her. She pressed a handkerchief to her cheek, its linen dark with blood.

Ean blanched. "Mother—!"

"It's nothing," she soothed, though he could tell she was shaken. She gave him a reassuring smile. "Just a scratch, my darling. Nothing our Alyneri can't easily mend."

Ean was suddenly overwhelmed by an onrush of guilt. He grabbed her into his arms fiercely. *My brothers, Creighton, and now my mother was nearly taken from me!*

"It's all right," she soothed into his ear, hugging him close.

"*No*," he growled, choked by fury, consumed with grief for those already lost. He barely kept the two emotions at a brimming boil, their disparate flavors melding into something fierce and malevolent.

Errodan sensed his mood, and her expression turned grave. "Don't do this, Ean." She took his face between her hands and captured his gaze with her own. The arrow's trail was an angry welt marring her perfect ivory skin. Ean was ready to tear off the archer's head with his bare hands. "Don't take on this guilt, my son," she told him in a low voice while people milled around them and the King's Guard shouted to regain order. "We are all victims here, and none of us culpable save in too naïve a belief in the goodness of men."

"It's too late, mother."

"No—*no!*" She gripped him tightly. "We never wanted you to don this burden. We kept you safe in Edenmar—"

"A brief respite." He gently extracted himself from her, but his gaze was steely as he watched Morin d'Hain spearheading through the melee trailing a host of black-coated men. He stopped smartly at the King's side. "We got the archer. He's being prepped for questioning. Your Majesty…" he added emphatically, and his brown eyes turned and settled on Ean.

"Indeed," the King remarked, clearly fuming mad. "Ean…" he said, "we must talk." He turned and headed off.

The prince willingly followed, his expression as dark as his father's as they headed through the palace together surrounded by a swarm of guards.

They convened in the King's study, where two floors of bookshelves overlooked a wall of windows and the churning sea beyond. Alone together, the King walked to a sideboard and poured two glasses of wine for himself and his son. Handing one to Ean, he stared out the windows, one fist resting behind his back. "This is not the homecoming I had hoped for you, Ean," the King remarked, his tone hot with the coals of his fury, "but I confess there is no surprise in it."

Ean found something reassuring in his father's anger; as a child it had terrified him, but as a man he felt the vengeance that infused it, and it was a glorious thing.

"We'd hoped to keep you free of this fight. Your mother took you to Edenmar knowing none would dare touch you there. We hoped that our enemies might attach themselves to a new target."

It took Ean but a moment to understand. "Yourself, father?"

He cast his son a rueful look. "But it was not to be. I am not so formidable that they daren't make an attempt on my life. It is just that they know how much they can weaken me first by slaying my sons." Gydryn turned back to the window, but Ean saw the way he worked the muscles of his jaw, holding back his emotion.

"First my blood-brother," Ean ground out the words, "and now my mother. Who *dares*—"

"Morwyk," said an entering Morin, just then walking through an interior door from an adjoining room, obviously having taken a different and less well-known route from the dungeons back to the King's apartments. "It *was* Morwyk, your Majesty. We have the archer's confession."

"Fast work, Spymaster."

"It seemed the man was rather attached to his fingers and valued them over his allegiance to the Duke."

"But you'll behead him for this crime," Ean said, both a demand and an order.

Morin replied with a grim smile. "Eventually, your Highness. But hope is an interrogator's greatest ally. The apathetic man has nothing to lose, and therefore no inspiration to share the truth of his crimes."

"Morwyk must be getting desperate for him to go so public with his treason," the King noted. He and Morin shared a knowing look.

"What am I missing?" Ean said.

Gydryn turned to his son. "The Duke of Morwyk has long connived against the Eagle Throne, Ean. We believe he was also behind the failed attempt on the night of your return."

"Partially behind it," Morin corrected. He perched on the corner of the king's broad mahogany desk and folded hands in his lap. "The introduction of a Shade rather shattered his plans for a graceful coup."

Ean realized he'd drained his goblet. He set it down on a near table feeling unsettled, his anger rising. "If Morwyk is to blame," he said, the image of his mother's damaged face looming large in memory, "why is it he still lives?"

"It's not so simple, Ean," Gydryn remarked regretfully.

"Even if it were that simple," Morin offered, "Morwyk isn't at court. He claims fears for his southern border, that trouble with Saldaria necessitates his staying east and raising an army to protect his lands."

"He raises it against *you*, father," Ean declared.

"No doubt," the King agreed.

His dispassion set Ean's anger alight. "Then why haven't you stopped him? If you've known all this time—*seven hells*! My blood-brother might still live!"

"It was my understanding from all reports, including yours, that the purported Shade killed Creighton," Morin pointed out tactlessly.

Ean turned him a scathing look. "It *was* a Shade," he declared, enraged by Morin's skepticism, "and he speared my blood-brother in cold blood. How dare you challenge my report, Morin d'Hain. Tis a matter of honor that his death be avenged!"

"Yes, if only we had his body we might lay it at the feet of any number of seditious factions."

Ean bit back a retort in surprise, looking from Morin to his father and back again. "His body?"

"There were no bodies at the scene, your Highness—not a one. Not a single dead traitor, nor any evidence of Creighton Khelspath…when the King's Guard arrived, they found only the survivors, who'd bound each other and themselves for no apparent reason save madness."

Ean stared rigidly at the Spymaster. "I saw what I saw."

"No one challenges your account, Ean," the king murmured.

"Then you're looking for him?" Ean demanded of Morin. "Your spies are turning over every stone in search of that hell-spawned Shade?"

Morin gave him a compassionate look, one of the few he ever mustered. "We might as well chase our own shadows, your Highness," he said gently. "You must understand that as well as I. When passion no longer rules your head, you too will see the illogic in sending men on such a search."

Ean felt such hatred for Morin in that moment that his eyes burned with it. Never mind that the man was right.

"Legendary monsters, notwithstanding," Morin pushed on, "Morwyk is a very real, very tangible threat to your person, your Highness."

"One you're apparently doing nothing about," Ean growled.

Gydryn turned solemn grey eyes upon his son. "There is much you don't understand, Ean."

"Keep your friends close and your enemies closer," Morin murmured.

"Close enough to stab you in the back?" Something inside Ean snapped, and he could hold his anger in check no longer. "Mother was right!" He glared incredulously at his father. "All those years, she was right. You sit around and do nothing while evil men claw for the throne and those dearest to you fall prey to their avarice."

"Your Highness goes too far." Morin's said sternly.

"No, not nearly far enough, Morin," Ean snarled. "But I intended to go much farther." He looked to his father. "If you won't look for the damnable Shade, be assured that I will!"

He threw wide the study doors and stormed out. But while Morin's call to stay went unheeded, he couldn't ignore the rational side of his conscience, who cautioned not to alienate his father upon the very instant of their reunion. Suddenly indecisive, Ean paused just outside the door, his shoulders hunched against the anger fighting to explode.

He heard Morin calling him from the study again, and then, "Let him go, Morin," came his father's calm reply. "He's grieving for the last of his brothers. Let him go."

A moment of silence followed while Ean deliberated returning with an apology, the idea battling against his rage at their inaction. Just as he was about to turn and go back inside, Morin said, "Having now met your son, Sire, I feel ever more unsettled by your intentions. From all accounts the prince is reckless and brash, and I've seen nothing to convince me otherwise. Such a man is liable to make....incautious decisions. Telling him could imperil everything you've worked so hard to gain."

"Knowledge is power, Morin," the King replied, "as you of all people well know. I won't deny my son the truth any longer. When the Vestal returns, we shall tell him."

"As you will, Sire," Morin said in acknowledgement, and before Ean realized the conversation was done, the Spymaster was passing him with a nod of hello and not even a flicker of surprise at seeing him standing there.

"Ean," called his father from the study.

Realizing they'd known he was listening, Ean turned and walked to the middle of the open doorway. The King stood before the windows looking impressive with a gathering storm for a backdrop.

"Father?"

"If you want to search for the man who slew Creighton, you have my blessing."

Ean stared in surprised silence.

"But promise me you won't leave just yet. I would have your company for a few hours at least after all these years."

Shamed, Ean dropped his gaze. "Of course, father." He turned to go.

"And Ean..."

The prince looked over his shoulder. "Father?"

"Welcome home."

TWENTY-THREE

'The heart and head are seldom in accord.'

– Morin d'Hain, Spymaster of Dannym

Alshiba Torinin, First Vestal of Alorin, sat behind her broad marble desk with fingers pressed painfully to her temples, eyes closed. Her realm was crumbling within her hands; her race approached extinction within three generations unless something could be done to alter the Balance, yet all her efforts changed nothing. She was in a constant battle with her own self-doubts, yet this only made her conscience heavier, for she knew so many placed their hopes and prayers upon her.

More and more of late her thoughts were tormented by memories of Björn. He was more than just the Fifth Vestal; as the Alorin Seat, Björn had navigated the politics of Illume Belliel as easily as he conjured handfire. It was a simple game to him. *Maybe that was the problem,* she thought with a derisive grimace. *This game was too easy.*

As always, with thoughts of Björn, her mind turned eventually to *that* night, the night of her own near death three hundred years ago, the night she should have and *would* have died if not for one man. He'd shattered her hopes and spared her life in the same wrenching moment. Alshiba would have given anything to change that past, to see Björn still as the Alorin Seat, with or without her at his side. The knowledge of what he'd done was a constant thorn in her heart. Centuries passed and she lived on, but she'd never recovered, neither from Bjorn's betrayal, nor from the loss of his trust.

Alshiba recalled with vivid clarity the moment she learned of Björn's betrayal, the moment she turned her back on him to walk her path alone…

"The Overlord awaits, your Excellence," the Shade told her as he stood in the open doorway of the room where she lay dying.

Alshiba blinked against the light streaming in behind the man—could he still be thought of as a man when he was raised from naught but dust and darkness? She shielded her blue eyes with her hand and struggled to rise from the bed, but no sooner did she set feet upon the stone floor than her head began to swim and vertigo threatened again. As she began falling, the Shade moved to her aide. He looped her arm across his strong shoulders and slipped his hand around her waist to support her. How strange that this creature of smoke and shadows could also have such substance.

She'd been just days in T'khendar, but every day she was closer to dying. Whatever force sustained life there, it was stingy and partial to its own.

With the Shade's support, Alshiba concentrated on putting one foot before the other. She was grateful for the strength of the creature beside her, but she couldn't help but wonder how many of her race this one had killed, this one who showed her such odd and unexpected compassion.

She wanted to question him, but her head was pounding as hard as if she climbed through thin mountain air. "How is it," she managed breathlessly, "that you can survive in my world, but I cannot survive in yours?"

The Shade answered without malice. "T'khendar is newborn, your Excellence, birthed as you know from the womb of Alorin. It suckles within the thin shroud that separates existence and nothingness, so we its first children touch both."

"You can work both powers, live on either of them, while we cannot."

"Just so."

The halls they walked were made of existential rock, basalt and granite, bedrock of the world, but as they traded the cathedral-sized passage for the garish light of open air, Alshiba marveled yet again at what Malachai had done. His city was a spectacular feat of architecture—palaces, mansions, temples and towers, all of them interconnected by hundreds of arched bridges. The sere, red rays of T'khendar's sun made everything a stark contrast of shadow and light. There was beauty here, but it was a harsh beauty.

It was Björn that had taught her to see such things, to appreciate the varying shades of aesthetics. But thoughts of Björn brought hated tears, so she forced her mind back to Malachai instead. "You know," Alshiba whispered, for that was all the air her lungs could manage, "you know he's quite insane, your Overlord. The same power that sustains you has driven him mad."

She didn't know how the Shade would respond, but he only smiled. "Perhaps he is insane," he admitted. "But his children are not."

"No?" she challenged. "It was wholly rational then, this genocide of his that you and yours participated in?"

"We are but pawns in the game, your Excellence," the Shade returned somberly, "prancing to the Players' dictates, prey to their delusions."

"No," she disagreed in her bare whisper. "You have a choice. There is always a choice…to do or not to do, to act…or not."

"If the only choice is between life if you obey or death if you do not, is that really a choice?"

"Yes! There is the Returning," she gripped his arm and stared into his depthless obsidian eyes as she gasped to draw breath. Was there hope? Could he be turned to her cause? "Death is only the end of *one* life," she whispered. "The choice should never be one of death and life, but to choose the *right* thing, the *right* path." It was what Björn had always taught her, *yet what path does he walk now?*

"And which is the right path, your Excellence?" the Shade inquired sadly, holding her in his arms like a limp ragdoll yet treating her with the utmost gentleness and respect. "How does a mere pawn determine the right path when only the Players know where the paths may lead? When the Players can twist the paths so each seems true, or alter their course so each ends where the Players want despite any choices made?"

"You speak as if Fate controls us all," she managed, even more breathless than before. Her head was spinning so violently now that the Shade was nearly carrying her.

"Not Fate, your Excellence," the Shade replied quietly as they walked slowly across the bridge. "We aren't fated to an end—would that it were true, for Chance plays in the game of Fate, and sometimes Luck as well. No, tis the Players that control our choices, and they are infinitely harsher taskmasters than Fate."

Reaching the far side of the arched basalt bridge, they entered another building through a row of beautifully crafted stained-glass doors. As soon as they were inside, footsteps approached, and the Shade stopped and looked down an intersecting passage. "*Rad nath,* First Lord," he said with a reverent bow.

He's speaking the Old Tongue, Alshiba thought with surprise. She hadn't heard the language spoken since she was a child. She slowly managed to turn her head to see who this First Lord was…

And her heart leapt and shuddered in the same moment.

Epiphany give me strength—tell me he's not here!

But she knew her eyes didn't lie, and when the tall man with the dark curls and the vibrant blue eyes came to a halt before her, she even smelled his familiar scent, reminding her of their intimate moments together and vanquishing all her hopes in the same breath.

His betrayal was the worst of all.

The Shade was wholly supporting her, but she had forgotten he was there. To see Björn walking of his own accord, his shoulders so straight while she struggled to draw every breath…her oath-brothers had told her that Björn had betrayed them, but she had prayed there was some mistake.

There was no mistaking the man standing relaxed in front of her right now, and there was no mistaking the reverence with which the Shade had addressed him. "I'll help her, Dämen," Björn offered.

The Shade bowed off.

No, please! she thought, choking back tears. *Anything but to be near him now…*

Alshiba had no choice but to let herself be lifted into the arms of her long-time lover. Björn was as strong as ever, his breath warm upon her clammy skin, but never had the feel of him brought her such anguish. *I'll die before I let him see me cry!* she promised herself.

As Björn headed off, following along five or so paces behind the Shade, she gave him a scathing look. "How *could* you?" she demanded with every bit of fire she could muster. Perhaps it was the anger, but she began to feel a little of her strength returning.

He turned his gaze upon her with that look of his, the one that always made her breath quicken—even then, even hating him as she did, she felt her desire for him stir and waken.

Björn brushed several strands of blonde hair from her eyes and gifted her with a droll smile. "Was that a rhetorical question?"

"You had all the power you could have desired as the Alorin Seat, Björn," she protested, her voice near to tears. She was so hurt, so frustrated and confused by what he'd done. It was numbingly difficult to comprehend his betrayal.

Björn gazed down at her sadly as he carried her. "You think this is about power?" he inquired quietly.

"Of course it's about power!" she snapped, regaining enough of her breath to raise her voice, enough even to want to stand on her own. "Put me *down*," she snapped, struggling against him.

He dutifully lowered her gently to her feet.

She straightened her skirts and glared at him. "In love with you, I might've been, Björn, but I've never been a fool. If this wasn't about power, what was it about? Who blasphemes the Maker—*by Cephrael's Great Book!*—by daring to create an entire realm, Björn? Who *does* that if they aren't raving mad for dominion?"

The Fifth Vestal gazed sadly upon her, his eyes so incredibly blue, his face so godlike in its perfection. "If that is what you truly believe, Alshiba, you should be grateful for this betrayal. After all, I've given you the chance to claim what you've always wanted: the Alorin Seat."

Alshiba gaped at him. "I never—" she gasped, stunned. "I've…that's never been my goal!"

"Not in so few words, perhaps," Björn agreed, "but do you really think I didn't know the thoughts in the back of your mind? Those little whispers that told you if you can't sit the throne, at least bed the Seat."

Alshiba felt as though she'd just been stabbed. "I…loved you," she choked out, hastily wiping tears from stinging eyes lest they fall and betray her promise.

"*Loved*, is it? Not still?" He settled her an innocently inquiring look that was yet somehow so lustful that she found herself blushing—and hating him even more for it.

"Save your wiles for those who desire them," she said, wishing her voice betrayed less of the terrible ache she felt, the agony of a breaking heart. "I am the First Vestal, by the Maker's grace," she managed, drawing herself tall, "not some mortal woman aching for the gifts of your loins!"

Björn chuckled as he gazed down at her. "No, dearest," he agreed, "I expect you've had enough of my loins to last you several lifetimes."

Alshiba stared at him. Amazing that one statement from him could make her feel so empty inside. Her eyes stung again, and a lump formed in her throat. Finally she turned, picked up her tattered skirts with stoic resolve, and set off behind the Shade, who was now at least twenty strides ahead down the black stone hallway.

Björn easily fell into step with her. "You do me an injustice, Alshiba," he protested. "I am not this monster you accuse me of. You know me better than that."

"You stood up to be counted with every monster imaginable!" she retorted, not daring to look at him. His countenance was too precious to her, his near presence too forceful upon her heart. She stared ahead as she added, "Dagmar said he saw you decapitate Jarell hal'Benniman even as he pled for mercy."

"Jarell was the worst sort of river slime to ever work the lifeforce, Alshiba, and you know it," Björn argued. "I did you a favor."

"Yes, you're full of favors, it seems," she quipped bitterly.

Abruptly he took her arm and halted her. His fingers lifted her chin to meet his gaze, and she trembled at his touch. She loved this man more than life, and he'd shattered her, broken her over his knee like a brittle branch.

Björn trailed a hand down her cheek. "There is so much I wanted to tell you… want to tell you still…if only you could find faith in me..."

Tears finally flowed as she hit his hand away. "Why now? Why do you seek my understanding *now* when all is irrevocable? Why not before, when you shut me out of your life?"

He gazed at her in that manner she'd come to despise, his eyes so distant…as if he saw all that had ever been and would ever be, yet didn't see *her* at all. Björn's lips curved in a tragic smile. "Trust is a fragile thing, isn't it?"

Unable to bear his gaze, she turned and followed the Shade through one of three sets of double doors, all thrown wide, into a sweeping hall where at least fifty of his brethren had gathered. It was intensely unsettling to see silver face after silver face, all of them exactly the same—the same features, the same icy indifference, even the same velvet coats. It was like looking upon a hundred mirror images come to individual life.

Björn was catching up to her, so she assumed a stature of proud resolve, both for the benefit of the horrid Shade clones—to see they had not broken her—and for herself, that in looking the part of bravery, she might start to feel a measure of it.

Her heart leaped when she saw her oath-brothers waiting at the front of the hall. Dagmar stood as tall and broad as ever in his characteristic black. Raine seemed calm, quietly accepting, with that lock of soft brown hair falling unassumingly over his colorlessly crystalline eyes. Beside Raine stood the avieth Seth, as always a quiet storm just waiting to explode. And then there was Björn—*damn the man!*—who settled off to the side with his effortless elegance. Björn watched her until she came to a halt between Dagmar and Raine, and then he blessedly turned away.

Just being in the company of her oath-brothers was immediately reassuring; and yet, as Alshiba tried to push thoughts of Björn from mind, she realized her sudden recovery of strength could be attributed to no other.

"Have you tried to work?" Dagmar asked in a low voice.

She nodded grimly. "The moment I arrived here. They tell me I was unconscious for two days."

"So was I," Raine noted without turning his gaze from the dais and its towering basalt throne fashioned in the shape of two bestial demons tearing out each other's throats. Alshiba didn't want to know if such horrors actually existed, if Malachai had *created* the things depicted on that throne. Still staring forward, Raine added with odd indifference, "We're dying, you realize."

Alshiba looked at him; she was starting to feel rather numb herself. "They've treated me well," she admitted, somehow unable to vilify Björn to the others, even then. "It was my reaching for *elae* that left me in such pain."

Standing on Dagmar's left, Seth grunted caustically. "What need for torture when we can do it to ourselves? Saves them the effort."

"They could have killed us if they wanted us dead," Dagmar pointed out in his calm way. He noticed a hangnail on his thumb and absently pried at it with his teeth. Alshiba had never seen him bothered by anything.

"We're *dying* already, brother," Seth reminded him sootily. "It's hardly a mercy to draw it out."

"Malachai visited me," Raine confessed in his quiet way. "Else I'd not have been able to walk at all."

Hangnail caught between his teeth, Dagmar muttered, "Björn came to me."

Seth grunted disagreeably again. "Belloth take the both of them."

Alshiba cast him an irritable look. The avieth made a practice of naming the worst sort of beings at the worst sort of times. Who knew if Malachai didn't actually make his pact with the legendary Lord of the Underworld himself? And naming the Demon God was never a fortuitous habit.

A hush suddenly spread through the room, followed by a great shuffling, and Alshiba looked behind her to see the Shades prostrating themselves on the marble floor. She turned back to the dais just as Malachai entered from behind the throne. *Oh, my*...It tore at her to see him so, even after all he'd done. Unending compassion was a Healer's curse, and on first glance, all Alshiba saw was a tortured soul.

"Rotted to the core," Seth muttered ungraciously.

Raine shot him a sidelong look full of immediate annoyance.

Malachai was still dressed in his small-scaled armor that looked much like the luminous skin of a green viper. His pale hair hung wildly about his shoulders, and his brown eyes hid in shadowed hollows, as if fearing what they would see should they be touched by light. There was a fierceness to him that had not been there when last Alshiba saw him a month before he began his genocidal rampage, and as he entered, he seemed to bring a terrible chill into the room.

Alshiba's heart quickened, and the fist of fear clenched around her heart. She had effectively ignored the truth for a brief few hours, but there was no escaping it now. She was mortal here, and as a mortal, she would die.

Malachai seated himself stiffly onto his throne and settled his empty eyes on the four Adepts as if wondering why they were there. Two Shades entered from behind him, and one leaned to whisper in his ear.

"Oh...yes," he said, and he lifted those hollow eyes to Alshiba and her oath-brothers. "Your Excellences, I have a parting gift for you." He waved the Shades off to enforce whatever command he'd already given, and then seemingly deflated back against his throne. "It's over, you know," he told them in a voice that seemed paper thin. "The war, I mean."

"This war won't be over until you and all of your abominations are seared from the face of the realm!" Seth retorted scathingly.

Malachai simply stared blankly at him as if he was a tree that had suddenly spoken.

Alshiba glanced around the wide room. She couldn't help but wonder if the Shades were ever going to stand up again. It was highly unsettling to be surrounded by a sea of velvet-clad bodies lying face down in silence.

Just then a long procession of Shades entered through the doors. Alshiba caught her breath upon seeing what they carried.

Heads.

Cleanly severed, jaws agape, dead eyes staring. A terrible understanding set upon Alshiba as she recognized the faces of the dead. She felt her newfound strength evaporating, and she dug her nails into her palm to keep herself lucid, to keep from shrieking.

"*Dear Epiphany*," Raine muttered as the Shades paraded by carrying the severed heads like horrid ornaments.

"That was Gerald hal'Gere," Dagmar noted grimly. He continued in a low murmur, "Vivienne d'val Bartheon, Jasyn ryn Tavenstorm, Scar Whitmore...Willem Stonewall."

Dead! Alshiba shuddered and a moan escaped; her vision began fading at the edges. *The Hundred Mages! All dead!* "They were supposed to be safely in the Citadel!" she said, her voice a bare whisper.

"Björn," Seth hissed.

"He wouldn't!" Alshiba gasped.

Seth gave her an incredulous look. "Who else, sister? The strongest of us are dead or standing before you! The Citadel was impregnable, but not to *him*. Never to *him*," and he slung a venomous glare toward the Fifth Vestal.

Feeling hopelessness like a heavy blanket, suffocating and black, Alshiba admitted the truth. Only Björn could have breached the Citadel's defenses.

Then, suddenly, she understood that this must've been Malachai's plan all along. He'd sworn to destroy Alorin's magic and all who worked it out of retribution for the Council of Realms' vilification of T'khendar. By slaying the Mages, and after such a long genocidal war, who would be left to teach Awakening Adepts?

She felt the world closing in on her, blackness descending with the swiftness of shadows, but then strong fingers were cutting into her elbow, pushing her to stay on her feet. She blinked to clear her vision and felt Björn next to her. His fingers were cutting into her arm, but the pain dissipated the faintness.

Seeing that he had her attention, he opened his right hand, and Alshiba saw him weave a vision for her eyes alone—a small band of travelers winding through a wintry mountain pass. There were perhaps fifty faces she recognized, maybe a few more, and these Adepts traveled with their families and their belongings. *Safe!* A wave of relief passed through her. A man led them through the dangerous pass, a dark-haired man with fiery emerald eyes that seemed to light the way with their glow. She knew him, too. If there were these fifty, surely there were more, pockets of others who'd survived Malachai's scourge.

Alshiba lifted her gaze to meet Björn's. *How?* she mouthed the words. *Why?* And she seemed to hear his answer echo in her mind: *I am not the monster you accuse me of.*

Then why…?

"Alshiba. *Alshiba.*"

The Alorin Seat roused with a start and lifted tired eyes to her oath-brother Raine. In their centuries of friendship, he had always been the one she called upon when she needed support and reassurance…or a shoulder to cry on after Björn's sharp tongue had wounded her, bringing tears. But the latter was lifetimes ago, what still seemed like yesterday.

She noted that the sun had risen while she ruminated, more hours wasted on thoughts of Björn. He was the puzzle she could never solve. No matter how many myriad ways she put the pieces together, they never formed a whole.

"I apologize for my late arrival," Raine said as Alshiba pressed palms to her eyes, shaking off another sleepless night. "On the way here I sidetracked your Espial on an excursion of grave importance. I had to know, you see…*Alshiba*," and he stressed her name to gain her attention, "so much has happened that I haven't been able to brief you on—"

She held up a hand to quiet him. "I know." Pushing up from her desk, she walked to the sideboard and poured mint-infused water into a goblet. Draining the glass, she poured another. "Now then," she said, feeling a bit more like herself, "tell me of your recent quest for our oath-brother."

Raine followed her outside onto a long, porticoed balcony overlooking the azure ocean beyond. The morning was cool, but the sun was warm. The 'city at the center of the universe' had a perennially temperate climate. As they seated themselves at an alabaster-topped table, Raine began, "The quest for Björn led me ultimately to Calgaryn. I confess, until I arrived there, I was quite befuddled by the chase. I'll spare you those details, but it made no sense to me that the Fifth Vestal would allow his presence to appear on the currents unwittingly."

"Certainly not. I told you as much when you set off after him."

"In which presumption you were quite justified," Raine admitted with a humble smile, "but I had to follow his trail, nonetheless."

"Of course you did."

"He knew I would."

"No doubt he was counting on it."

They held each other's gaze for a long moment, each recognizing the other's understanding of their oath-brother's nature, acknowledging their own tragic predictability in his machinations.

"So." Alshiba smiled.

Raine glanced out to sea. "I've no idea how *he* discovered it, but what I found at Calgaryn..."

"What did you find?"

With unerring prescience for her needs, Alshiba's steward entered with a breakfast tray for two. Raine gazed out to sea while the man silently set out the meal, and Alshiba observed the truthreader in turn, her gaze following the clean line of his brow, his pointed nose, his lovely lips. He was a handsome man in his own right. Why couldn't she have fallen for the Fourth Vestal instead of the Fifth? No doubt Raine would have treated her better.

The truthreader turned his diamondine gaze on her as the steward bowed and left them. "I sense our dear brother in your thoughts. Another nightmare?"

She rolled her eyes and grunted. "When I find the luxury of sleep, he dominates my dreams."

"Foretellings?" Raine asked hopefully.

She shook her head. "Hauntings."

"Ah..." He poured her a cup of tea from the service set before them while offering idly, "There is a prince in Calgaryn, the youngest val Lorian heir. In the midst of an attempted assassination in a vie for the Eagle Throne, the prince was abducted by a Shade, later stabbed by a Geishaiwyn assassin while still the Shade's captive, and finally rescued by a zanthyr."

She arched a brow at him. "Is this some new bard's tale?"

He gave a sardonic chuckle. "Not yet."

Alshiba furrowed brows curiously. "What interest could Björn have in a northern prince? Truly—he sent a *Shade* to capture him?"

"I asked myself the same question, and then I saw the boy's personal seal."

She shook her head, uncomprehending.

"His seal mimics the Pattern of Life, Alshiba—or at least his personalized imprint of it. The boy has Returned. But what is truly exciting is that he's recently Awakened."

She sat back in her chair. "That's impossible. The youngest val Lorian heir has to be nearing twenty."

"He's ten and eight, but apparently he's been drawing the pattern for years. Long enough to make a signet of it."

"What makes you think he's Awakened?"

"It's the cause of my delay. I needed to study the currents from a nodepoint downstream of Dannym, so I asked your Espial to first take me to Tregarion. I found two things in my study of the currents there. First, that the prince became present on the currents many days ago, while he would've been in the Shade's custody, and second..." he paused to level her a telling look, "that Björn is in the Cairs."

Alshiba reached for her tea, considering. "Tell me first of the prince. Is there any chance you misread—" then she realized just who she was questioning, for Raine's ability at reading the currents was unmatched—and shook her head. "Never mind," she said, setting the tea absently back in its saucer. "Just tell me what you found of him."

"The working was short and closely centered—so likely aimed at one person. There was only the faintest trace of it left. The working would've likely been intrinsic to him, something recalled from his prior lifetime, lest he'd never have been able to work it so soon upon Awakening."

Alshiba pressed fingers to her lips. "If it's true, Raine...if Björn knows how to trigger an Awakening in later life..."

He held her gaze. "I know. It could mean the revival of our race."

She pushed the backs of her fingers against her face to cool her cheeks as her heart raced, knowing well the import of this revelation. So much knowledge was lost to them when Björn betrayed them—he alone knew the *Sobra I'ternin* as if he'd written it himself. The most skilled Patternists in all of Illume Belliel had yet to decipher even half of the sacred book.

"Do you think it was an accident that the prince Awakened?" It seemed a ridiculous question, but she had to explore every avenue no matter how she wanted to jump at the hope.

Raine knew her mind, but he played along. "He just happened to Awaken while in the care of one of Björn's Shades? I think that's too coincidental, even for a skeptic like me."

Oh, please, please, let it be true!

But there was something else to consider. "Could it mean...is it possible the Balance is turning, Raine?"

The Fourth Vestal sighed heavily and shook his head. "I don't think so, dear sister, as much as I wish it were true."

She took up her tea again, sipping pensively. "So Björn is in the Cairs. Doing what?"

Raine shrugged. "Your guess is as good as mine."

"How did you find him?"

"He worked the fourth—a broad illusion."

"Careless," she said, frowning as she set down her cup. Her eyes flew back to Raine's. "The Fifth Vestal is never careless."

"Indeed not," Raine agreed.

"Burn the man." Alshiba pressed fingertips to forehead and closed her eyes. "What are you doing in Alorin, Björn? What game drives you now?" After a moment of silence, she looked up between her fingers at Raine. "Do you have any idea how agonizing it is to have the Sight and yet find it so useless against one's enemy? It's worse than not having it at all! I don't understand how he manages to hide from the Sight—it's like he's hiding from the eye of the Maker Himself!"

Raine just gazed at her, knowing the cycle of her moods, expecting more.

Alshiba sank forehead into hands. "Sometimes," she whispered, "sometimes I feel so inept here. All the politicking, the insidious whispering." She lifted eyes to meet his, already ashamed of her next confession. "The horror of it is, Raine...I find myself wishing that Björn was here—even after so many long years...even after his betrayal. He handled the position so effortlessly. I spend days trying to discover a plot that, in the same amount of time, Björn would have entirely unraveled such that it fell to pieces long before it affected Alorin."

"He was bred for this game, Alshiba," Raine reminded her gently, "birthed into the Prime House of Agasan, for the sake of the Creator. Is there any family more conniving?" Shaking his head, he turned and gazed out at the azure swells of Illume Belliel's great ocean, sipping his tea in silence.

She watched him brooding and knew that whatever news he avoided discussing, it was only to spare her pain. She'd never known a man so compassionate as Raine D'Lacourte. He was considerate to a fault. "Are you ready to tell me what you found in Calgaryn?"

He glanced at her briefly, but his gaze was troubled. "You won't like it."

"I gathered that much already."

He looked back to her, and his diamondine gaze became intensely troubled. "I saw evidence at Calgaryn that would indicate..." he shook his head, lips pursed. "I daren't even speak it, lest my fears prove correct."

She reached lean fingers to touch his hand, gaining his eye. "We made the mistake of hiding our eyes to the truth once before, brother, and look what resulted." Refusing to believe Björn had betrayed them had ended in the slaughtering of the Mages and the deaths of thousands during the cataclysmic loss of Cair Tiern'aval. With those images as fresh in mind as the day of their making, Alshiba continued, "We must learn from our mistakes, Raine. Hiding from the truth only shames us." When the Vestal merely gazed unhappily at her, she pressed, "What did you find in Calgaryn?"

He exhaled a slow breath. "Someone twisted a path into Alorin, perverting the very pattern of the realm. The body I found on the scene had been devoured by *deyjiin*. Above the dead man, the rock of the cavern roof had dissolved, but it's the node that troubles me most."

"The node at Calgaryn," she clarified.

"Yes, but it's a node no longer." He held her gaze as he spoke the terrible truth. "Now it has become a weld."

Alshiba caught her breath. "Who...?" she whispered. "Would—would even Dagmar have that ability?"

"Him and him alone. Unless…"

She nodded with understanding. These were bitter facts indeed, for only two choices remained to them: either to believe that Björn himself had become twisted by the deadly forces of T'khendar, as ravaged now by madness as Malachai, or that mythical creatures had appeared in their realm. She wasn't sure which choice was worse, but she was certain which one was more likely.

Oh, Björn, what have you done?

She looked back to Raine feeling threadbare. For all her sermonizing, there were still truths which she wouldn't admit even to herself. "We have to find him, Raine."

Raine barked a cynical laugh. He flung a hand toward the sea. "You might as well say we have to stop the sun from rising, Alshiba."

She gave him a long look, wishing she had the wherewithal to argue the matter with him. *When will you stop acting the fool?* she scolded herself. *Björn never loved you, yet you remain true to him. When will you believe yourself as capable as* he *believed you? When will you stand up to him and declare that you can outwit him, that no man shall ever again have the better of you?*

But she knew that day was not this one.

Alshiba stood and walked to the railing, resting her hands on the smooth baluster as she gazed out over the blue-green sea. It was easy to forget her home in Alorin after so many years in the pristine cityworld. Illume Belliel was a carefully cultivated utopia that felt false in all the important ways.

She hated feeling so disconnected from Alorin; she hated how long it had been since she'd laid hands on a man to heal him. And she hated Björn—for his freedom, for his utter unwillingness to conform to any man's rules but his own. Most of all, she hated him for his ability to so completely sever himself emotionally from everything he held dear.

Mustering her resolve, she turned to Raine. "I do not envy you your task, my brother, but you must find him and discover the truth. If he is behind these crimes, he must atone for them."

"Seven hells, Alshiba," Raine growled. "I haven't even discovered how he's traveling between the realms! The nodes to T'khendar are so twisted, I can't believe even Dagmar could navigate them. So how in Tiern'aval is Björn traveling back and forth?"

She shook her head.

Obviously frustrated, Raine took pains to gather his composure. "You're right, of course," he admitted after a moment, lifting his sincere gaze back to meet hers. "We are shamed by our own fear if we believe ourselves already defeated. Knowing the power of our enemy only gives us an advantage."

Alshiba smiled her relief, infinitely grateful for Raine's strength of character.

"I will do everything within my power to track him down," he promised then. "He's in the Cairs, that much I know."

"It's a start," she agreed.

The Fourth Vestal smiled crookedly. "You remember Björn's favorite saying?"

"How could I forget?" she answered dryly, quoting then, "*The only way to discover the limits of the possible is to go beyond them into the impossible.*" She frowned at him, understanding his implication in broaching the subject. "Perhaps it is an impossible task I've given you, but who else will stand up to him if not us?"

Raine gave her a wan smile. "Yes," he agreed. "Who else?" He stood then and bowed low from the waist, a polished, elegant gesture. Straightening, he pressed fingers to his lips. "I bid you *adieu*, sister. I go now to begin my traverse into the impossible."

"Epiphany's blessing on your quest," she replied as she watched him go, praying he would somehow achieve the unachievable. What she did not say was, *For without her Graces, we don't stand a chance.*

TWENTY-FOUR

'Wherein doth honor best reside: in generosity, self-sacrifice, or in the strength of one's own conviction?'

– Istalar, a Basi holy man

Trell's fourth day on the road to Sakkalaah dawned cold and damp, a sure sign that they neared the Cry. He was up with the first paling in the eastern sky, opening his eyes even before first light as he had long made a habit of. He roused Kamil, and together they rode out to the edge of the ridge where the earth fell away into the canyon lands. Banded rock rose in irregular patterns, a labyrinth of passes and valleys and ravines that dead-ended unexpectedly; and throughout, the Cry wound like a twisting snake in and out of view, its waters churning charcoal in the early light. It was the northern rim of the Haden Gorge, and the beginning of their trouble.

From their high vantage, Trell and Kamil mapped their intended route. The trail followed the Cry most of the way to Sakkalaah, but Trell had a bad feeling about it, and he wanted to keep to the higher passes whenever possible. Kamil and Sayid had traveled that part of the Gorge several times, and Kamil pointed out several ravines—little more than shadows near the horizon—where bandits were known to attack.

That was the trouble with bandits, however; they were never where you expected them to be.

The company breakfasted on dried dates and figs, nut cakes, olives, small white onions and hard goat's cheese. It was desert fare, but the ladies didn't complain. Trell was grateful for that, and for the way the women helped to set up camp each night and break it down each morning.

Even with the women's help, however, the day was fully upon them before the company started the long descent into the canyon, once again with Kamil and Sayid in the lead. They made the Cry by mid morning, and Kamil turned them ever west, following downstream.

Trell was uniquely aware of both of sisters as they rode, but especially Fhionna. The willowy Wildling had captured his attention, and Trell found his gaze straying her way more often than he would've liked. All three women had abandoned the burkhas they'd donned solely for the Bashir'Khazaaz, and that day they wore layered silk desert gowns the color of flax, earth and sky. While the diminutive Lily was lovely with her dark hair wound in a twisting braid, she was too young to appeal to Trell. The sisters however, had taken root in his consciousness, and he had difficulty getting them out of his thoughts.

That day Fhionna wore her honey-brown hair unbound beneath a woven circlet of seed pearls, while Aishlinn's blond tresses were braided loosely and tied through with ribbons the color of fire. These differences in styling were subtle reminders of the variance in their ages, though Trell was hard-pressed to place even Fhionna's above his own. He was not so foolish as to hazard a guess, however. Even were Fhionna not a Wildling and likely older than he thought, he'd never yet met a woman that took pleasure in revealing her true age.

There was little talk, for the gorge made a channel for the wind, which gusted erratically, whipping the churning charcoal waters into icy spray and stealing away voices to be heard miles downwind. Dark clouds blew overhead, threatening more rain. The weather seemed as inhospitable as the river, which was the deepest on the continent and at most times the widest. The Cry could not be crossed without ferry or bridge, for its hunger was insatiable, and its waters were swift to claim any who strayed too deeply.

Trell was watching the churning water and thinking about Graeme when anxious whispering from the women caught his attention. He turned over his shoulder and peered at them as they rode. "Care to share your thoughts, ladies?"

They all looked to him at once, like a nest of startled birds. "We *must* tell him," Lily insisted.

Her urgent plea notwithstanding, it was the obstinate looks the other two wore that made Trell uneasy. He whistled to Kamil, who was closest to him, and signaled the need to stop. While Kamil flagged down Sayid, Trell reined in Gendaia and pulled around next to the women. "Tell me what?"

Fhionna's expression became grave as she turned her gaze to Trell. "We should not go any further down this trail, Trell of the Tides. It isn't safe."

Trell eyed her with growing suspicion. "How do you know this?"

The sisters exchanged a look, and Aishlinn shook her head emphatically *no*, her gaze angry.

Trell looked to each of them, but they'd become strangely mute. "Very well," he decided, spinning Gendaia in a tight circle. He dismounted and handed off his reins to Kamil. "We stay here until someone starts talking."

"But—" Lily protested.

He turned her an inquiring look.

She pressed her lips together and stared sullenly at him.

As the others collected, Trell made a routine inspection of their packs and horses and ignored the women completely, especially the distractingly beautiful Fhionna. He'd completed his inspection and was crouched over a dirt map conferring with the Khurds when she approached.

"May we speak, Trell of the Tides?"

Trell lifted his gaze to her. "That depends," he said, pushing to stand a head taller than her.

"On?"

"On whether you plan to tell me the truth or another contrivance."

She looked at him warily. "I'm sure I don't know what you mean."

"I'm sure that you do."

Fhionna exhaled her displeasure. "Why do you insult me this way, Trell of the Tides?"

"Milady," he replied evenly, "we are putting our lives in your hands. The least you can do is tell us honestly what threat we face on your behalf."

"Bandits," she retorted exasperatedly. "We told you from the beginning—"

"You told me a carefully crafted lie," he cut in, holding her gaze. "I didn't believe it by the Springs of Jai'Gar and I don't believe it by Naiadithine's Tears."

Her eyes flew wide, and she drew in her breath with a hiss, staring at him. With one hand across her mouth, she whispered, "You speak the river's sacred name."

Now it was Trell's turn to falter. The phrase had just found its way onto his tongue. He had no idea whence it had come.

Stunned, Fhionna lifted slender fingers from her own mouth and placed them gently across his lips. Her touch sent tingles through his flesh, waking inconvenient stirrings of desire. "The Mother reveals herself only to those most worthy of her daughters' trust." Trell kept his silence as she searched his eyes with her own. "My astonishment knows no bounds, yet now I understand why the Mother led us to you in the bazaar. Naiadithine has taken favor on you, Trell of the Tides."

Trell was increasingly surprised by the things that no longer surprised him. There was something about conversing with shape-shifting Sundragons that changed one's perspective on the world and everyone in it. He knew somehow that Fhionna spoke the truth, and he wondered what he could have done to so gain the goddess Naiadithine's eye. Surely his meager offering was not worth her favor.

Still clearly startled but recovering, Fhionna let her hand drop from his lips—much to his disappointment—and turned her gaze upriver where the dark water tumbled and frothed. "It is not to protect ourselves that we spoke untruths," she confessed at last, casting him a demure gaze full of entreaty, chocolate lashes framing her water-clear eyes. "I would you to know that, Trell, for there are some who say our motives are ever selfish, and it is unfair to bespeak us thusly. Our sister-kin is as dear to us as our own flesh and blood, and..." her tone hardened as she added, "and we will do whatever we must to protect her."

"Fhionna, if I'm to help you three, I must know what really happened and what you still fear. I need to understand the enemy we face."

Fhionna caught her lip between perfect teeth and nodded. Turning upriver, she took his hand and led them along the banks until they were quite alone. She found an outcropping of stone to settle on and beckoned Trell to sit beside her.

"Lily, our sister-kin," she began as he moved to her side, "is the daughter of a powerful Nadori lord. Her father planned to sell her in marriage for personal gain, as so many of you mortal men do, but Lily had already pledged her troth, unbeknownst to her father, to a young man from a family currently out of favor with the ruling princedom. When Lily's father learned of her interest in the boy, he did everything in his power to see the young man banished. Lily was devastated. Aishlinn and I couldn't bear to see her in such a state, so we...we offered to help her stay in touch with Korin."

Fhionna tucked a lock of her honey-brown hair behind one ear and turned her aqua eyes to Trell. There was something so unbearably alluring about her in that moment that Trell found it hard to breathe. Perhaps she *was* enchanting him, as she claimed. The closer he was to her the less self-control he seemed to posses, and every motion she made aroused and enticed him. Even Vaile had been resistible, but Fhionna was...electrifying. The desire to *possess* her was nearly overpowering.

"...other reasons as well," Fhionna was saying, "but she realized she had to flee the pal—that is, I mean, her home. Aishlinn and I helped Lily send word to Korin, who'd taken refuge in Xanthe, and he agreed to meet us in Sakkalaah. We all traveled safely into the Akkad, as we were able to follow the rivers, but three days out of the Bazaar her father's men caught up to us. We escaped with our lives into the river, but only just. When we dared return to land much later, they had ransacked our packs and run off with our horses."

"And they hunt for you still?" Trell asked, trying to look at her without also seeing images of her face looking up at him, her body pinned under his own, her gaze rapturous.

"We think so," Fhionna said. She looked up at him, and suddenly he saw his own desire reflected in her gaze. Her breast rose and fell with her quickening breath, and a budding flush came to her cheeks. Their eyes locked.

Trell's entire body came alive, his craving to possess her resonated with Fhionna's own yearning to be possessed. His member bulged, pulsing painfully against his britches, swollen with his need.

"*Fhionna,*" Trell breathed, astonished.

"*Trell,*" she whispered.

And then his mouth was on hers and they were in each other's arms. Trell cradled her as they tumbled into the dry grass, wanting her with every fiber of his being. The taste of her was a feast for his senses; her tongue was berry sweet, the skin of her throat scented with vanilla, and her breasts—his mouth longed to suckle them, to feel her nipples harden beneath his tongue even as they hardened now beneath his thumbs.

Fhionna's fingers were tangled in his hair, her tongue seeking his thirstily. They clung to one another breathlessly; Trell felt the beat of her heart pulsing, her breath feeding him as she straddled his hips, grinding against him. He found her breast with one hand, the other buried in her hair, and—

His desire vanished.

Stunned, appalled even, Trell fell still in her arms. A barrel of ice water upended over his head could not have done a better job of quenching his desire. Even as he struggled to understand what was happening, he heard a whisper echo in his soul, though the message was for Fhionna.

He is not for you, daughter.

Fhionna sucked in her breath with a gasp and jerked abruptly free of Trell's embrace. Her tongue left the taste of cinnamon in his mouth as she rolled off him, mortified and shaken. Her cheeks were flushed from their passion, but she couldn't have looked more dismayed.

Perplexed, Trell pushed up onto his elbows.

Fhionna drew her knees into her chest and covered her face with both hands. It took a moment for Trell to realize she was crying. He sat up and gathered her into his arms. This time there was no flame of desire, no tingling in his skin, no lustful thoughts. She cried into his shoulder as he gazed confusedly over her head at the rushing river.

Goddess, do you protect me from your daughter's spell? As much as he'd wanted Fhionna only moments ago, he felt no sorrow that the spell had been broken, no longing for what might have been; only a fond feeling remained, strangely without regret.

The entire encounter was so baffling that Trell didn't even attempt to seek understanding, much less an explanation. He wasn't sure he really wanted to know; the idea that the river goddess could extinguish such heated desire—that a god could have more control over his body than he did—was unnerving.

Finally Fhionna lifted her face from his embrace, pressed her wet cheek against his own and hugged his neck. "*Forgive me*," she begged, a bare whisper. "Please, *please*, forgive me."

Utterly bemused, Trell yet replied, "On the condition that one day you will explain this to me, Fhionna...I forgive you."

Her aqua eyes seemed liquid as she smiled gratefully and took his hand. "I will," she said, pressing a chaste kiss to his palm. "Thank you."

Trell ran a hand through his unruly dark hair and gave her a crooked grin. "Well...," he said awkwardly. Pushing to his feet, he offered a hand to help her up. "Where...uh, where were we?"

"We need to speak with my sister."

As they walked back toward the others, Fhionna said, "Please know, Trell...Lily wanted to tell you from the beginning, but we...my sister and I...our kind..." She turned him a look of sudden fury. "There are terrible, evil men who hunt us for sport and others who delight in torturing a daughter of the river by seeing how far from her source they can take her before she expires, every moment of it in unbearable anguish. So we are wary of trusting men with our secrets."

Trell imagined he would be too.

They met Aishlinn and Lily coming looking for them. Aishlinn regarded her sister warily as she neared. "What happened? I heard—"

"I told Trell everything."

"Fhionna!" Aishlinn was incensed. "We—"

"He spoke the river's sacred name, sister," she cut in emphatically.

Aishlinn closed her mouth with an audible clap.

Lily looked shocked. She reached tentatively toward him and whispered, "Naiadithine spoke to you?"

Trell looked to the river rushing cold and deep beside them. Rather than answering, he said, "You said this trail was unsafe, Fhionna. Is that because you think the men are near, the ones chasing you?"

They all exchanged a worried look, and then Fhionna nodded.

"And how do you know?"

"The river...told me," Aishlinn said hesitantly, yet there was a stubborn look in her eyes, as if she expected Trell wouldn't believe her. "I...listen to the riversong."

Trell regarded her thoughtfully. After a moment, he asked, "How much can the river tell you?"

"Only as much as she knows."

"But these men are careful," Fhionna explained. "They know we can follow their movements if they drink from the river, or cross it, or travel close to the water's edge, so they stay as far as possible from the Cry and her fingerlings."

"The streams feeding—" Lily tried to explain.

"I get it," Trell said, cutting her off. "So what can you tell me, Aishlinn?"

Her expression fell. "Only that they're near."

"Downriver? Upriver?"

She shook her head. "I'm sorry. The river doesn't know. She had the barest sense of them, and..."

"This isn't particularly helpful, Aishlinn."

Her haze hardened. "It's not an exact science!" she snapped. "Riversong is cacophony. You try sometime and see how well you do!"

She spun on her heel and stalked off.

Trell gazed after her, bewildered.

"She is frustrated," Fhionna explained gently as her eyes followed her sister. "She wants to help—we both do." She wrapped a slender arm around Lily's shoulders and pulled her close. "We can't bear the idea of anything happening to our sister-kin. We feel impotent, and we aren't...used to these feelings."

Trell turned her a discerning look. "Aishlinn said you had gifts. Can they be of use to us?"

"Not if the men stay far from the water. Our power lies within the Cry."

Lily turned and buried her face in Fhionna's embrace. "I never should've run away!" she lamented. "I've endangered all of you—and now Trell of the Tides and these good men also!"

"No Lily," Fhionna said, firmly taking her by both shoulders. "It is not wrong to love, and you should not be executed for daring to give your heart to one of your own choosing."

"Korin waits for you in Sakkalaah, milady," Trell said. "We must get you to your true love."

Lily lifted her eyes to his. "These are dangerous men, Trell of the Tides. They are well trained in warcraft and willing to trade their lives for their liege lord's cause."

"That's to be expected," Trell said with a shrug.

Lily gazed wondrously at him. "Do you really have no fear, Trell? You ask for nothing from us to risk your life for me. Are life and limb meaningless to you?"

Trell took no offense at her words, for her tone was one of honest inquiry. He let his eyes stray back downriver toward the Khurds. He could just make out glimpses of their dun-hued turbans moving about. "The reasons men fight are myriad and many, Lily," he returned quietly, thinking of the countless men he'd known, commanded, befriended and buried. "Sometimes they think of life and limb, as you say, but mostly I think their motives lie elsewhere...beyond themselves, really. Some fight for gain, of course—or revenge—but among true fighting men, self-serving causes are few. Of those I've met, some fight for honor, others for faith, but...I think many men fight in the hopes of just finding something they can believe in."

"And you?" Fhionna said, her beautiful eyes searching his. "Why do you risk your life?"

Trell held her gaze and answered simply, "Because you asked it of me, milady."

The day passed slowly after such a morning, and the company traveled in silence wrapped in their cloaks against the chill afternoon wind. Trell conferred with the Khurds, sharing what he'd learned, but they decided to continue on the same path, for it was the most direct route to Sakkalaah. They agreed to stay alert, however, and two of the four Khurds were always riding at a distance ahead or behind, scouting for signs of trouble.

The wide river was cold and forbidding, at times looking angry where it fell into whitewater, but more often seeming to hold a dense and terrible secret in its swirling, twisting depths.

Naiadithine.

She lurked there, everywhere and nowhere. *Naiadithine's Tears*, Trell had named the Cry; the true name of the river had been the goddess's gift to him, that her daughters would trust in him. It was said the tears of thousands fueled the Cry's savage current, but Trell wondered now what the real story was, what man or child Naiadithine mourned in every drop of her water-blood.

Trell spent far too much of the day watching the depths and pondering the nature of his own intimate connection with water. It was a strange feeling to know oneself as the object of a god's interest. There were some who said gaining the eye of Angharad or Thalma, what goddesses the Northmen named their Ladies Fortune and Luck, was a boon beyond imagining; but Trell rather suspected that gaining a god's notice only meant a lot of trouble on the horizon. He didn't imagine the gods looked upon mortals with much respect—*What are we to them but frail and inconsequential creatures?*—and he didn't relish the idea of dancing to the puppet strings of any immortal. Rumors of those living happily in the thrall of a god must've been spread by men who'd only dreamed of the encounter. The real thing was disconcerting at best.

Yet Naiadithine seemed to have no agenda of her own for Trell, and he couldn't help but wonder why she'd brought his cause to her breast as her own. He found himself growing ever more grateful to her even as he rooted deeper into her debt.

Sensing Trell's pensive mood, the women kept to themselves. Fhionna was still contrite over their noonday encounter, and Lily had taken to casting Trell unreadable looks, most of which he missed on account of his own brooding disposition. The Khurds took turns scouting ahead and behind, ensuring their safe progress.

It was only once, late in the afternoon, that Kamil came to Trell with news.

"I found signs of passage," said the Khurd in a low voice, reining his mount in close so their horses walked flank to flank. "More than a dozen horse."

Trell gazed ahead. "Bandits? Or Nadoriin?"

Kamil shrugged.

He turned to him. "Show me."

Kamil heeled his mount forward, and the two of them broke away from the party to canter a mile or so down the trail.

At the edge of a branching canyon, where a smaller river flowed into the cry and the earth remained soft from the recent flashflood, a sandy hill was trampled with hoof prints.

Trell dismounted and bent to study them.

"Nadoriin," he declared after a moment. He waved Kamil over. "Here, look." He pointed to the prints. "See, these are all large horses. Their hooves are as wide as my hand. Like Gendaia," he added, nodding to her. "Not desert-bred."

Kamil hunkered down at Trell's side. "Bandits often take the horses," he pointed out.

"Yes, but they'd have many different breeds among them. These are all uniform from one to the next, with no variation in the size of the prints. Likely Saldarian warhorses."

Kamil regarded him appreciatively. Then he straightened to peer down the canyon, which curved away to the south, the view obscured by trees.

"Do we follow them?"

Trell studied the route. It looked too inviting. "No," he said, his gaze flinty. "We move on."

The sun was nearing the rim of the gorge when they stopped to make camp. Trell was concerned, but he kept his thoughts to himself so as not to frighten the women. Twenty horses could mean twenty men, and he didn't like those odds. The campsite they chose had a clear view in all directions, but on a cloudy, starless night like that one, it wouldn't provide much of an advantage.

They set up minimal shelter and picketed the horses and Sherba close-in, to better utilize their keen senses for any warning they might provide. They made no fire to preserve their night vision, and the men ate in silence while the ladies took their food into their tent. Trell took the first watch, but as the night grew on with nothing untoward happening, his apprehension began to abate. Perhaps his fears were misfounded.

Still, sleep wouldn't visit him even after his watch was over, so he lay on his pallet with hands behind his head gazing into the deep dark sky and brooding over his future as much as his past.

Her footsteps drew his attention, but he recognized her light step. "Hello, milady. Come to bewitch me again, have you?"

She settled down beside him, drawing her knees in close. "Never again," Fhionna replied, still sounding embarrassed. "You have my heartfelt promise."

"That's a shame," Trell said, turning her a wink and a grin.

She broke into a smile, admiring him openly. "The Mother knows what's best for her daughters," she confessed with a wistful sigh, "but I couldn't have chosen a better man for a mate than you, Trell."

Trell exhaled heavily. "I have no idea of my own birth. I would not will the same fate upon my own child."

"No daughter of mine would live a bastard's life," Fhionna told him seriously. "And your blood is pure."

Trell was stricken by her words. "You cannot know that."

She took his hand and bade him sit to better look into her eyes. Pressing his palm to her bosom, she said breathlessly, "But I do. My body tells me what the mind denies. I will honor the Mother's wishes, but she cannot control what I feel for you. I am only attracted to men of noble blood, Trell of the Tides, and I cannot say…" She closed her eyes and finished, "I cannot say when I was last *so* attracted to a man. You must be *very* noble indeed."

Unwilling to accept her words, Trell retrieved his hand from her grasp. "The bastard son of a nobleman is still a bastard son, Fhionna."

"Nobility is not merely a blood-right, Trell," she argued. "It is honor-embodied, and that…that *is* you." When he said nothing, she took a deep breath and forced a smile. "Come," she offered, holding out her hand. "I want to show you something."

Trell resisted. "It isn't safe to leave camp—"

"We won't go far." Her smile was so alluring, her hand so warm and soft, her face so beautiful... She'd promised not to enchant him, but he didn't think she needed magic to claim a place in his heart.

So he remitted, against his better judgment, and went with her toward the river. They headed downstream together until Fhionna found what she was looking for, a rockfall of large boulders jutting out into the river, its rushing waters falling in a smooth but terrible wave that churned the raging water into mist about ten paces below.

With Trell's hand tightly in her own, Fhionna led him out onto the rocks, to the very edge of the waterfall where the rocks were wet. "Now then," she said. "Sit here, beside me," and she settled casually onto the damp and slippery stone.

Trell was more careful, but he soon found himself knee to knee with her. "And now?" he asked.

She smiled. "Now we listen."

"Ah...riversong. You think to teach me to hear it?"

She gave him an approving smile.

"But I am just a man," he argued lightly.

"A man with Naiadithine's blessing is not just any man." She took his hand and interlaced their fingers, settling their joined hands into her lap. "Close your eyes," she murmured.

Trell did as he was bidden, enjoying the moment, the closeness of her. It was a relief not to feel that unbearable need, to know only the natural desire of a man for a beautiful, intelligent woman. This was true, real...not a trick of Wildling magic. And Fhionna had promised to keep him free from further interference of that nature. He felt his body rising at Fhionna's touch, but he had spent many years coexisting with Desire in all her myriad facets. He knew her like an old friend.

"You're not listening, Trell," Fhionna chided.

He darted a glance at her and smiled sheepishly. "Sorry."

She sighed. "You are such a beautiful man."

"And you, milady."

They gazed into one another's eyes for a long time, and then finally Fhionna laughed and shook her head. "Now neither of us is listening. So..." She settled herself again more purposefully. "Let us try again."

They closed their eyes together and listened. Trell heard only the roar of the waterfall, and then Fhionna whispered in his ear, "Riversong is cacophony...discord and noise to the inattentive ear. It roars, screams, rages."

"Yes," he murmured, eyes closed.

"But what is a cacophony but a merging of too many harmonies for the ear to separate?" she continued, her breath soft on his skin. "To learn to hear the song of the river, one must shut out all but one note. So, Trell," and she gripped his hand tightly for encouragement, "you must try to find one note among the roar; listen for just that one sweet sound. Let it linger in your ear, on and on...on and on. The river sings all notes at once. Listen..."

Trell cleared his mind, pushing away everything but the sound of the churning water, even distancing himself from the feel of Fhionna close beside him. Only the water, rolling, falling, tumbling... The constant rushing became hypnotic, lulling Trell's senses... and finally, once he'd long lost track of time, he did begin to hear beyond the noise. He couldn't separate the notes, but he *could* perceive that there were many of them.

The river sings all notes at once.

Something about the roar of the waterfall triggered a memory, but it was so deep and distant from his consciousness, so hard to get hold of. He swam toward it. There was a luminous haze far off, too far to reach. His eyes and chest burned, and his head throbbed violently. He felt hope leaving him, floating away toward the light, and he reached for it with longing and regret...with apology.

Then he saw her. She coalesced above him from the liquid sea, her water-clear features lovely, long hair like ocean waves...barely visible, only a mirage. Her lips moved, speaking without sound.

Trell of the tides...

Beside him, Fhionna gasped. "Oh no! *No!*"

Her alarm instantly brought him back. His eyes flew open.

Fhionna was already on her feet and pulling him to come. "Hurry, oh please, Trell. Hurry!"

He jumped up. "What happened? What did you hear?"

"Hurry!" she urged, and as they made land, they ran.

They met Kamil and Radiq halfway back to camp, the former trying to pull the latter out of the Cry, both men drenched and bare-headed, long hair like vines around their shoulders. Trell rushed to help rescue Radiq from the icy waters, slipping himself on the slick rocks, but they managed to get him to safety.

"It's my knee," he gasped as he collapsed onto the sand. "Twisted."

Kamil looked to Trell. "Nadoriin," he said, catching his breath. "They chased us down, drove us into the river. No doubt they thought us lost, but Naiadithine carried us safely, because we are your companions, Ama-Kai'alil."

Trell was horrified. How could he have been so careless with their lives! "And the others?"

Kamil shook his head. "I do not know."

With a look of profound apology, Trell left them and ran back to camp. The site was in shambles when he reached it, the ladies' tent trampled, their things scattered. He began to feel the fingers of panic but pushed them away, cold anger descending in their place.

A moan from afar drew his gaze, and he sprinted toward the sound. He found Sayid crawling out from beneath the collapsed tent dragging the unwound cloth of his turban behind him. His head was bloodied, but he seemed otherwise whole.

Trell grabbed his elbow and helped him up. "What happened?" he asked, desperate for news.

"A dozen horsemen," the Khurd answered. He pushed a fold of cloth to his bloodied head, looking dazed. "They charged down the hillside from above, scattered us. Took the girl."

Trell cursed his lack of foresight. The Nadoriin had probably been watching them for days, waiting for the chance to attack. "Fhionna was with me," he told Sayid, "and we met Kamil and Radiq downstream, injured but whole."

"*Khoob*, that is well for the sun," the Khurd said. He sat down uncertainly and checked the cloth from his head. The wound seemed to have stopped bleeding. "Ammar was guarding the little Lily," Sayid told Trell then, seeming more alert. "The Nadoriin struck him down. It may have been mortal, I do not know. The blonde *nymphae* Aishlinn dragged him unconscious into the river with her."

Trell looked around angrily at the ruins of their campsite, his breath coming hard. He felt it an unconscionable mistake; if Lily came to harm, he might never forgive himself. Sherba was idling among the trees, but there was no sign of their mounts. "Did they take the horses?"

Sayid cracked a grin, his teeth very white in the night. "Your mare, the Hallovian Grey, she broke free before the Nadoriin could grab her. Nearly trampled two of them as she fled. The other horses escaped in her wake, followed her upriver. I suspect they will all return if you call her back."

Trell placed a hand on his shoulder. "What can I do to help you?"

He shook his head. "Do what you must, Ama-Kai'alil."

Weighted with regret, Trell walked to the river's edge, put two fingers to his lips and whistled for Gendaia. He waited a minute and whistled again. As he was rejoining Sayid, Fhionna and the other two Khurds arrived with Kamil supporting a limping Radiq.

"Sayid," they greeted laconically. He nodded to them.

Trell frowned at their condition. "Kamil, how fare you?"

"I am unharmed, Ama-Kai'alil, save for my pride, which requires retribution at least in kind." He helped Radiq to sit and then squatted to inspect the other man's knee.

"The Cry is hungry for Nadoriin," Fhionna murmured mercilessly, her blue eyes hard as agates.

"Good," declared Trell. "I'd like to feed her tonight. Feed her well."

The Khurds took some time to collect themselves while Trell and Fhionna salvaged what they could of their things. Trell's packs lay miraculously untouched, and most of their food remained, though their water stores had been found and the bags slashed. The women's tent was destroyed, but their things were merely scattered. It wasn't long before Trell and Fhionna had put things right again.

They were at the river refilling waterskins when the horses returned. Gendaia was in the lead, and she announced her approach as she came over a rise. The others filled in to either side of her. Seeing her, Trell was unexpectedly choked with gratitude, both for the treasure that Gendaia was to him as well as the gift of her. *Balaji, your Mage again has saved me, it seems.* He stood and clicked his tongue, and Gendaia pranced happily across the distance to join him, pressed her nose into his chest, and nickered a hello.

"Oh," said Fhionna, coming to stand beside him, "she adores you."

"The feeling is mutual." He stroked Gendaia's neck. "Thank you. Thank you so much."

She nickered again.

Within an hour after the attack, order had been restored. Kamil lit a fire to dry their soaked clothes, and they all collected around it. Trell rejoined the Khurds, taking a seat beside Sayid. He was quiet for a long moment, and then he leveled

Sayid a serious look. "I have to go after Lily."

"Indeed so."

"I cannot ask you three to accompany me on this endeavor."

Sayid nodded sagaciously. "You know us well, Trell of the Tides. To *ask* for our aid would be insulting."

A smile twitched in the corner of Trell's mouth.

"You'll be risking your lives," Fhionna said imploringly. She was fretful and full of ire, and they knew she feared for Lily. "All to save a Nadori girl. You could be walking to your deaths! Is that really what you want?"

Sayid's dark eyes settled on her evenly. "Are not our lives just as worthy as Trell of the Tides'? Why do you ask one man to make a noble sacrifice and not ask the same of his companions?"

Fhionna looked taken aback. She dropped her eyes to her hands. "Your honor shames me, sir."

"Let not the politics of kings invade your heart, princess of the waters," the Khurd replied. "All men may find brotherhood in their hearts."

"Well spoken, Sayid," Trell murmured, glancing compassionately at Fhionna. He could tell she was feeling fragile.

"We will find your friend," Kamil reassured her, "and rescue her from the heathens. Be at peace, Naiadithine's child."

Fhionna braved a smile and brushed a stray tear from her cheek. "Forgive me." She looked them all in the eyes. "I am overwhelmed by the nobility of the men who surround me tonight. The Mother's blessing on your quest." Her aqua eyes lingered on Trell.

Trell looked to Sayid inquiringly. The de facto leader of the Khurds nodded. "So. Radiq will stay with the *nymphae* and the horses. We two will go with you."

"Let it be so," Trell replied quietly.

TWENTY-FIVE

'Death is only the beginning.'

– An old Wildling saying

Ean found his Queen mother in her apartments surrounded by a host of clucking hens, most notably his Admiral grandfather, who fussed ridiculously over her state, quite in contrast to the way he treated his sailors—verily, a man took his life in his hands bringing anything less than a mortal wound to the Admiral's attention, for Cameron L'Owain swore by the healing powers of the sea and was more likely to send a man to naptha the hull while the ship was afloat than to call a healer to attend his injury.

To her credit, Alyneri seemed oblivious to the commotion surrounding her as she healed the queen's cheek. Neither woman noticed Ean's arrival, so he stood back and watched intently, hoping to see some outward proof of Alyneri's talent, in part to assuage his confusions over his own wound that had healed so quickly while in the Shade's captivity. Sadly, his mother's wound looked no different when Alyneri finally dropped her hands to her lap and smiled at the queen. "Tomorrow it will be much improved, your majesty," she said. "There will be no scar."

"You are a blessing, child," the queen returned, gracing Alyneri with a kiss on the cheek. Errodan's eyes lifted then and fixed on her son, and something ineffable came into them, that look of joy and love and adoration that only a mother's gaze can truly comprise. The adoration didn't fade though she noted Ean's ill mood with a furrowed brow. "I was going to ask how it went with your father," she said to him, "but I see now I shouldn't have wondered."

Ean's frown deepened. He glanced around the room at the many eyes now upon him. "It's not…it's not what you think. I hadn't known of the…missing dead."

"Ah, yes." She held her hands to him, and he came and took them as she stood. Errodan looked him up and down, and then she flashed another adoring smile. "Let's go for a walk. Alyneri, dear, why don't you come, too?"

Alyneri looked startled. "Me?"

"Unless you know of another Alyneri in the room," the Queen suggested.

Looking disgruntled, Alyneri dutifully got to her feet, but Ean noted that she made a point of walking on the other side of the queen. They followed her Majesty into a tower staircase, and after a spiraling climb, arrived in Errodan's circular solar. The bay windows seemed to place them in the center of the growing storm. Ean thought the dark, roiling clouds perfectly mirrored his mood.

Errodan walked to one of the windows and placed her hand on the glass. It could have been a trick of the light, but Ean thought the gash on her cheek looked slightly better. "You three were educated in this room, do you remember, Ean?"

The prince nodded. It had been many years since he and his brothers studied together, long years since his eldest brother spoke with excitement of going to M'Nador as an ambassador for peace.

When Errodan turned from the window, there were tears in her eyes. "We have all three of us lost those most dear to our hearts. In that we are bound together."

Ean glanced at Alyneri, but her gaze was fixed upon his mother.

"In the Isles we do not speak the names of the dead. Did you know that, Alyneri?"

"I heard something of it, your Majesty—certainly that you wouldn't speak the names of your lost sons."

"It is so. Do you know why?"

Alyneri shook her head.

Errodan walked to Ean and took his face between her hands. He gazed tragically down at her, choked by his own emotions and the memories she'd evoked. "We do not name them," she said as she looked upon her last and youngest son, "unless we are ready to forget them."

"Does that mean..." Alyneri began, "if you do name them, then can you—"

Errodan released her grieving son and looked to the girl. "We can never speak their names again."

"Then what difference does it make?" Alyneri protested.

The Queen smiled crookedly at her. She slipped her arm around Ean's waist and hugged him close. "The difference is in our hearts. Some prefer to keep the dead close forever, always thinking of them, never naming them aloud. Others prefer to let the dead go, believing it helps the departed move on, believing in the Returning, that with Epiphany's Grace they will know them again some day. These rituals are from the old ways, and many of the mainlanders practice them no longer, but they have value."

Pulling away, Errodan cupped Ean's face and kissed his cheek. "What happened with your father?"

"I told him if he wouldn't look for the Shade, I would."

"And what did Gydryn say?"

"He gave me his blessing."

"That's folly, Ean," Alyneri blurted before the queen could reply. "To go in search of such a creature—he could be anywhere—or nowhere!"

Ean cast her a surly look. "Then I'll hunt down his master—*someone* will pay the price of my blood-brother's death, Alyneri."

"It could very well be you if you go in search of a *Shade*, Ean," Alyneri retorted haughtily.

"Either way, the price is paid!" he snapped.

"Ean," his mother's gentle voice drew his gaze to her, inviting calm. "Wait until you've spoken with the Fourth Vestal before you storm off after this creature—that's all I ask of you. His Excellency promised to consult with you upon his return from Illume Belliel."

Ean glared at Alyneri as he replied, "I don't intend to go storming off into the night with no plan of attack nor even any trail to follow. I am not so reckless as that, no matter what *some people* say about me in Court."

"Don't look at me," Alyneri sniffed indignantly. "I hardly speak of you in Court at all."

"No doubt when you do it is simply to malign my memory."

Errodan stifled a smile as she inserted, "I hate to interrupt such lighthearted banter, though I see you've both easily regained your old roles with one another, and they don't seem to have evolved at all between ten and three and ten and eight. How charming." She cast them both a droll smile. Then, to Ean, she said, "I know your mind, my darling. You will spin yourself in knots over this Shade and all that happened in his wake. Might I suggest finding your way to Ysolde's chambers when you're finished here? There is an Espial sharing quarter with my Companion, and he has most recently been in the employ of the Fourth Vestal. Perhaps he may prove of some help to you in planning your search for the Shade."

Ean let go of the tension in both mind and body. He took his mother's hand and kissed her palm. "Thank you," he murmured. "Thank you for always understanding me."

Alyneri sniffed indignantly again, as if knowing the comment was aimed at her.

Errodan let her gaze fall across both of them. "Now, dear children, to the reason I brought you both here. Morin d'Hain has circulated a rumor that you, Alyneri, are the heiress who has long refused to marry my son."

Alyneri stared blankly at her. "What? Marry Ean?"

"It's a famous rumor, Alyneri," Ean said, trying not to grin at her baffled expression, "but I know how you hate to listen to court gossip, so let me fill you in. There has long circulated a rumor that the reason I am not yet betrothed to some worthy princess from a faraway land is due to the mysterious heiress who refuses to marry me."

"Nonsense!" Alyneri looked affronted. "And I'm supposed to be this heiress? Who would believe that?"

Errodan exchanged a humorous look with her son. "Why...everyone believes it, dear. You *are* the daughter of a Nadori prince. You were, after all, betrothed to my treasured middle son."

"Yeah, about that, mother," Ean said, his dark mood lifting at last. "If your middle son was the treasured one, and my eldest brother was the wondrous one, what does that make me?"

"My irreplaceable one," she said adoringly.

"Irrepressible, you mean."

"That, too," she said with a wink. "Well, I shall leave you two to work out your story. Make sure it's convincing, as you will most certainly be asked about it. No one must know that Ean was injured and in your care, Alyneri, only that he came to Fersthaven to beg for your hand. His life depends upon this rumor taking on a life of its own." She placed a hand on Alyneri's shoulder, adding before she departed, "I know I can count on you, dear girl."

"Yes, Majesty," Alyneri said with downcast eyes.

But as soon as the queen was gone, she speared Ean with an affronted glare. "How *dare* you!"

"*Me?*" he protested, throwing up both hands. "*I* didn't have anything to do with this!"

"You *knew* all about it—"

"Which doesn't automatically make me complicit in its creation!" he retorted.

"Then how did you know about this 'famous rumor' from across Mieryn Bay when I've heard nothing of it?"

"As a point of fact," he said smartly, "Tanis told me two nights ago."

"Don't you dare bring Tanis into this, Ean," she hissed. "He's an innocent. He would never make up such a thing!"

"I never said he made it up," Ean snapped exasperatedly, "only that—"

"This is clearly of your devising," she interrupted with prim disdain. "Very well. I will go along with it, but do not think to claim any *privileges*. As far as we are concerned, I still refuse to marry you, and that's my final answer. You offered me a throne, and I turned it down in order to travel the world. After much discussion, you relented and promised to release me from my service to the crown once you claim the throne, as proof of your unconditional love for me."

Ean stared at her, fuming. "Alyneri," he growled through clenched teeth, "sometimes I really don't like you."

"Now, now," she chided, "that's not the attitude of a man in love."

"Then what is?" he challenged, throwing out his arm. "Utter subservience to a woman's whims, no matter how…how *insane* or illogical?"

She shrugged. "I really wouldn't know, Ean. I've never seen a man truly in love." With that, she spun on her heel and marched primly from the room.

Franco Rohre opened his eyes to the rumble of thunder shaking the windowpanes of Ysolde's bedroom. He turned his head to find her pillow abandoned and realized that it must be late afternoon. It had been a long night. After maintaining a sleepless vigil with the Queen's Companion in which they'd bestowed hedonistic pleasures upon one another, he'd finally drifted off to sated sleep as Ysolde dressed in preparation for Prince Ean's arrival.

Franco was grateful for the night spent with Ysolde. The Fire Princess was one of the most remarkable women he'd ever had the pleasure of bedding. Her intellect was cunning, as he'd discovered over an early game of Kings which she'd very nearly won, and her lovemaking was positively primal. The experience had proven cathartic for his troubled conscience—hour after hour focusing upon someone else's pleasure instead of his own ill-fated decisions—even if he'd gained little in the way of much-needed sleep. No matter, he'd caught up on it now, and there was always tonight…

Smiling at the thought, Franco sat up—

And froze.

The curse that escaped him would've made a sailor proud. He forced himself to continue getting out of bed, though his eyes never left the man sitting in the armchair across the room. "How long have you been there?" he asked in a somewhat choked voice as he slowly bent to retrieve his pants from the floor.

"If you're asking did I witness your wanton lovemaking all night, the answer is no."

Franco swallowed. "Have we…met? I mean, you know…before?"

The Shade shook his head. "My name is Reyd. Reyd Kierngedden…once. I see you are well informed of our origins. The Second Vestal has no doubt advised you of the inevitability of this meeting."

"Something like that," Franco muttered as he donned his pants feeling chilled to the bone.

The Shade stood with fluid grace, a motion more like the up-pouring of dark water, melting and reforming from sitting into standing. He drew himself solidly tall, fastened his depthless obsidian eyes on Franco and announced formidably, "This is your Calling, Franco Rohre. Do you accept it?"

Franco actually *felt* the power threatening in the Shade's announcement, but he had long since accepted his fate. "I do."

"Well and good," the Shade replied, and some of the menace left his manner. "The First Lord despises the taking of life, though it has been sadly necessary of late."

Franco had waited a long time for this moment, and though he dreaded the answer, still he found himself asking, "What is...my Calling?"

"Tis not my place to say, even should I know the answer. Make your way to the First Lord's sa'reyth. You will find the node in the Kutsamak, three days west of Raku. Tell those who watch that you have done as you were bidden. Wait there for further instruction."

"What of my affairs here?"

"You have one day to arrive at the sa'reyth or someone will be sent to retrieve you, and under those circumstances, Franco Rohre, the First Lord's messenger will not be so amiable."

This is amiable?

"I am in the employ of the Fourth Vestal," Franco blurted before he could stop himself. He wasn't sure why he felt compelled to confess that truth; whether it was because he knew in saying it to a Shade that the First Lord would learn of it, or whether it was in conflict over abandoning Raine.

"Have you some quandary over your allegiances? Do you renege on your Calling and choose to serve the First Lord's enemies instead?"

"No, it's just—"

"Then we have nothing left to speak of." He began fading even as he added, "One day, Franco..."

Then he was gone.

Almost as if timed, a tentative knock came upon the door. "Milord," murmured the voice of Ysolde's chambermaid. "Milord, are you up?" She tapped lightly again, "Milord?"

Franco shook himself from his stupor and went to answer the door. He poked his head through, trying desperately to remember the maid's name. "Emma, is it?"

"Eva, milord."

"Right. What is it you needed, Eva?"

She looked a bit round-eyed. "Milord, it's—"

"I am sorry to bother you, Mr. Rohre," came a male voice from behind the girl. Franco shifted his head to see a man standing across the room. From his cinnamon hair, so like the Queen's, and his angular features, so like the King's, Franco surmised this could only be the young Prince Ean. For all he'd already been through, he seemed barely a man. Did those broad shoulders have the strength to withstand the coming months? *He's no younger than you were when you took your oath,* a voice reminded Franco.

Ean stepped further into the room. "Might I have a moment of your time?"

Your moments are numbered. Count them carefully.

"Of course," Franco answered. Then he grinned. "I confess you take me by surprise. If I could have just a moment to dress..."

"Of course," Ean said, looking embarrassed that Franco had even thought to ask. Franco looked to the chambermaid. "Eva, might you bring us some wine?"

"Right away, milord." She curtsied and fled.

The Espial closed the bedroom door and rummaged around in his things until he found a clean shirt, all the while wondering what business Prince Ean could have with him.

The prince was seated at a table in the arch of a bay window when Franco reentered Ysolde's sitting room. He observed the boy carefully as he approached. He hadn't read the prince's letter himself, but from all accounts, he'd been through hell. Who knew if it wasn't the same Shade that just visited Franco that had killed the prince's blood-brother? Franco had no doubt Ean's tale was true, though he was both baffled and intrigued as to why the Fifth Vestal would have any interest in this northern prince.

He took a seat across from Ean while rain lashed the windowpanes. "How can I be of service, your Highness?"

Ean's gaze shifted from the storm to settle on the Espial. On first inspection, Franco thought the prince seemed the genuine sort, with wolf-grey eyes and cinnamon hair framing angular features, a fine looking young man by any standard. "I came in the hopes of a candid conversation, Mr. Rohre."

"Call me Franco."

"Franco, then. I—" but he paused, frowned. Franco waited patiently while the prince seemed to grapple with his own thoughts, clearly embroiled in some inner struggle. Finally, Ean lifted eyes to him again and continued, "I don't know how much you know of what happened to me, but I've no doubt you heard a Shade was involved."

"Indeed."

"There was also another man, an assassin. Three times he tried to kill me. Twice he almost succeeded. The third time, the last time I saw him, he fell from a tree to his death, impaled by his own poisoned dagger loosed by the zanthyr's hand."

The zanthyr. Franco noted Ean's inflection; already the prince was speaking as if there was no other zanthyr in the world. Knowing the creature that served Björn van Gelderan, however, Franco wasn't surprised; no doubt Björn's zanthyr felt the same way about himself.

"The zanthyr named the assassin," Ean continued. "He called him Geshaiwyn."

It was the last thing Franco was expecting. "*Geshaiwyn*," he repeated.

Ean noted Franco's expression. "What are Geshaiwyn, Mr. Rohre?"

"Franco," he corrected absently. He pressed lips together and looked up beneath his brows at the prince, intensely curious now. "Geshaiwyn are a Wildling race. They hail from the province of Malchiarr, near Dheanainn. I don't know how much you understand about the Wildling races, but it is a peculiar trait among some third-standers that they can shapeshift. Some, like avieths, are accepted among the races of man. Geshaiwyn not so much. Besides their...unusual sense of humor, they are particularly troublesome because they can also travel like Espials. Do you follow my meaning, your Highness? Their nature crosses strands with the second. They can travel the lesser portals, what we Nodefinders call *leis*. Geshaiwyn can change the shape of their faces to mimic anyone. Their mimicry is never perfect, but it is often close enough to pass a cursory glance." He grunted, adding, "The fact is, no one is certain what any of them truly look like."

Ean received this news with thoughtful silence.

Franco offered, "Can you be certain that the man who died was the same one who attacked you the first time?"

"Not exactly," Ean muttered, gazing off with a troubled frown. "He was a lunatic, kept going on about his dagger named Jeshuelle. I thought they caught him after his second attempt on my life, but I didn't see him well the third time."

"But this zanthyr killed him, you said."

"Assuredly."

"Well then. That's a boon."

Franco considered the prince in the following silence, wondering what question he really wanted to ask but dared not yet broach, for it was obvious that the young man was chewing on something gritty and raw. "Your highness," Franco posed, hoping to help things along, "I wonder…have you any idea why a Shade would come to your rescue?"

Ean blinked at him. "My *rescue*?" Ean shook his head and declared somewhat hotly, "Clearly you know nothing of what transpired."

"I know enough," Franco pressed, holding the prince's gaze. "And I know something of Shades. Perhaps you know a little of me?"

The prince shrugged. "I know your name, of course, along with the names of forty-nine others. You survived the fall of the Citadel."

Franco cast him a grim smile. "Would that I might say it so cavalierly..."

Ean's expression instantly shamed and he held up a hand of apology. "I'm sorry. It is…odd…to speak of these things. They are just events in a book to me."

The chambermaid Eva arrived with the wine and goblets and set them on the table between them. Franco nodded to her, and she curtsied and left them.

"As I was saying," Franco said as he poured their wine, "it's true, I didn't read your letter, but I know enough of Shades to understand that if they'd meant to kill you, you wouldn't be here now."

Ean shook his head. "It was the zanthyr—"

"That zanthyr could be in league with the Shade for all we know, your Highness. You can't rely on anything a zanthyr claims, and especially that one. His motives were ever his own."

Ean grabbed Franco's wrist with sudden intent. "You *know* him?" he asked urgently. "How can you know him?"

Franco silently cursed his loose tongue. "There are not so many zanthyrs who fraternize with Shades," he hedged lightly, trying to cover his mistake, "or dare to take them on. If this zanthyr is the one I suspect, he cannot be trusted."

Ean released the Espial and leaned back in his chair with a grunt. "Yes, he said as much himself."

Franco regarded him steadily, wondering… If Ean had traveled with the First

Lord's zanthyr, how much had the creature already told him of the conflict? *And what role do you play in it, Prince of Dannym?* "Your Highness, did that zanthyr by chance mention to whom the Shades are bound?"

Ean held his gaze intently. "He said they thrived in the Fifth Vestal's shadow."

Franco was relieved that he didn't have to broach the truth himself. "Might I ask you then, have you put any thought into how the Fifth Vestal knows of you? Why would he be interested in you?"

Ean grunted. "I have no idea." Suddenly he pinned Franco with a look of naked torment. "So much depends upon my solving these riddles—if I can't...if I can't, I shall never be able to avenge my blood-brother's death. I've wracked my brain for days with these questions, trying to imagine why anyone like Björn van Gelderan would take an interest in me."

Exhaling a frustrated sigh, Ean pushed a hand through his hair and then pressed palms to his eyes. "I can see the moment I set foot upon the path that led me to today," he confessed in a choked voice, "and I rue every step I took between then and now. I can't help wondering, what if we never landed on that beach? Would it have been enough to change our paths to now? Would my blood-brother still be alive if we'd anchored in Calgaryn harbor, if I'd cared less for my own safety and more for that of others?"

Franco regarded him compassionately. He knew too well the hazards of regret How long had he treaded the knife-edge of reason wishing he could undo the choices of his past, wondering if he'd only done this or that, would things have been different? Might he have lived a normal life and died a natural death? Might he have been spared the suffering of three centuries of self-abasement, or the shame of a single catastrophic choice which could never be unmade?

"Don't follow those roads, my prince," Franco advised, hearing the ache in his own tone though he'd tried to speak dispassionately. "They lead to dark places, caverns so deep and twisted that a man can lose himself in them forever."

Ean lifted grey eyes to meet his. After a moment he exhaled and shook his head. "I know...you're right. It's just...this all began when I returned from Edenmar. I can't help but wonder where we'd be now if we'd never come home."

Franco eyed him inquisitively. "Did it?"

"Did what?"

"Did it really begin with your return? It would seem quite a few people had already taken an interest in you before you set foot upon Dannish soil. Such things take time to orchestrate."

Ean immediately saw the truth of that.

"Did anything happen before you returned?"

The prince thought hard, retracing steps... "Not really. I was aboard my grandfather's ship for six months. I only saw land one week out of that time, and all of it was spent sealing invitations—"

"Invitations, yes!" Franco snapped his fingers and pointed at Ean. "Morin d'Hain was quite curious about your invitation, and his Excellency also looked it over. There was something about a signet—"

"I sealed all of the invitations with my personal seal instead of using the val Lorian crest."

Franco nodded, remembering. "Morin d'Hain said it was unusual."

Ean shrugged. "I suppose. I can draw it for you if you like."

"I would very much like to see it." Franco retrieved parchment and pen from Ysolde's escritoire and set them before the prince. Ean bent and began sketching the pattern at once. Although the twisting design could have been created by drawing a series of connected loops, Ean began the pattern at one corner and followed the winding and maze-like path with his quill as though he walked it in his mind. Minutes later, he connected the end of the path back to its beginning and spun the parchment toward Franco.

Dear Epiphany!

It was all Franco could do not to visibly recoil from that pattern, he knew its like so intimately and yet so dreaded the knowing. There was no hiding his dismay, however, and the prince saw it at once on his face.

"What? What's wrong?"

Franco looked up at the prince. "Ean..." he said, calling him by name, all protocol forgotten. His face was ashen. "Ean, do you have any idea what this pattern reveals?"

Disturbed by Franco's manner, Ean shook his head.

"*Yaşam örnek*," Franco said in the desert tongue. "That's what the Khurds call it. In Agasan, where I hail from, we call it *Patroon van Leven*, and the *Sobra I'ternin* names it *Vivir Illuminar,* literally 'Life Illumined.'"

Ean stared at him uncomprehending.

"This pattern, Ean...the one you just drew for me, it is the infamous Pattern of Life—or at least something close enough to it that the bones are there for all to easily recognize."

Ean looked baffled. "But that makes no sense."

"The rendering of the Pattern of Life is slightly different to everyone who works it, but...truly, the bones of this pattern are unmistakable."

Ean narrowed his gaze, considering all that he'd heard. "How can I draw the Pattern of Life?" he inquired slowly. "I'm no wielder. The zanthyr—" He paused and looked somewhat desperately at Franco. "One morning the zanthyr drew a pattern and challenged me to remember it, and I wasn't—I couldn't even remember the first line of it."

Franco knew he had just crossed a threshold into uncharted waters. This changed everything. Obviously this prince played some vital role in the First Lord's plans, and he knew enough of Balance to know he could greatly disturb it if he spoke out of turn—if he so much as hinted at something that sent the prince in a new direction, one he wouldn't have chosen on his own...well, who knew how terrible would be the consequences? Franco couldn't take that chance. He dared not, knowing what hinged on the play of Balance.

"I fear I cannot advise you in this, your Highness," he said, hating the look that came into Ean's eyes. *What's another betrayal, more or less? You've long lost count.*

Shut up!

"Can't?" Ean said quietly, "or won't?" He regarded Franco keenly, waiting for a reply.

Franco sighed. "Both."

"But why?" It was a heartfelt plea, Ean's gaze beseeching his with touching frankness.

He deserved an honest answer. Franco truly didn't know if he'd be able to give him one, but he wanted to try. "Oaths," he said first. "Binding oaths requiring silence. And of course, Balance is part of it."

Ean shook his head and grumbled, "The Balance has shifted."

"Yes," Franco agreed, surprised to hear the prince knew of the subject.

Ean looked sourly at him. "The zanthyr told me that. But what does it mean?"

Franco considered how to answer. How could he explain such an all-encompassing Cosmic Law when he barely understood it himself? "Balance is..." But failing that attempt, he pursed his lips and tried again. "The universe has laws, Ean. Adepts work *elae* and bend those laws. If we bend them too far, it disturbs the cosmic equilibrium on some level, big or small. Balance is a term coined among my race which we use when discussing how far an Adept can stretch the universal laws before they snap."

"What happens if they do?"

Franco arched brows. "Typically? You're never heard from again. If you upset the Balance, that's the end of you. It doesn't always happen right away, but it always happens."

"Then how do you know how far to push?"

Franco grunted. "You don't. That's the rub. That's the risk we all face when we decide to work *elae*. There is always some risk involved. The greater the area you try to affect, the greater the risk."

Ean gazed intently at him. "Are you taking a risk right now, in telling this to me?"

"Yes."

"Then I thank you."

Franco nodded. Then he drained his goblet. Ean's sat untouched upon the table.

"Just out of curiosity," Ean posed quietly, "who *would* be able to tell me of these things?"

"Well, the Fifth Vestal, of cou—" Franco blurted before he realized what he was saying. Desperately, he tried to correct his error. "But I don't advise you in any way to seek him out, Ean," he said emphatically. "He is known as a traitor to our race and is a most dangerous and fearfully...uncompromising man."

"Of course," Ean murmured. "No, I would never do that."

The outer door opened then to admit the striking form of Ysolde Remalkhen, her willowy frame alluring in a red silk gown. "Ean, what a pleasure!" she greeted warmly as she approached. "But shouldn't you be readying for your banquet?"

"Indeed," Ean admitted. He stood to greet Ysolde and planted a chaste kiss on her cheek. Then he looked back to the Espial and nodded his thanks.

Franco nodded in reply.

Good luck, my prince, he thought as Ean showed himself from the room. *Whatever role you're meant to play in the First Lord's game, if he sends a Shade and his zanthyr to protect you, you're likely going to need it.*

TWENTY-SIX

'Do not offer me flattery or gifts, offer instead your good deeds and noble sacrifices.'

– Queen Indora of Veneisea

E**an exited** Ysolde's apartments to find Morin d'Hain leaning against the opposite wall, waiting for him. The Spymaster pushed himself tall and walked to meet Ean. "You're a hard man to track down, your Highness, even for me."

Ean glanced at the two pairs of soldiers of the King's Own Guard who stood barring each end of the passageway, ensuring privacy, and then looked back to Morin d'Hain. "I'm kind of in a hurry, Minister."

"It's quite all right," Morin replied, "we can talk as we walk." He motioned to the guards, and they fell into place in front and behind as Ean headed off. Morin shrugged a lock of blonde hair from his brown eyes and fell into step easily with Ean, their boots treading softly on the thick Veneisean rugs that lined the royal wing. The spymaster was just slightly shorter than the prince, but otherwise they had a similar build—broad-shouldered and long-legged. "Did you find Franco Rohre's conversation helpful?"

"Somewhat." Ean was hesitant to divulge the details of their talk, but he knew Morin d'Hain's reputation. When the man wanted an answer, he got one. Ean was loathe to call undue attention to Franco after the Espial had gone to such pains to help him, so he offered Morin a portion of the truth. "He, uh, explained what a Geshaiwyn was."

"Geshaiwyn," Morin repeated. "Why did this topic come up?"

"It was the name the zanthyr called the assassin whose dagger nearly claimed my life." Ean gave him a narrow look. "I see you know the term well enough."

Morin regarded him seriously. "Geishaiwyn assassins have made their way into Dannym before, your Highness, but their involvement is never a light matter. When their Guild takes on a contract, they guarantee it." He cast Ean a shrewd look. "You take my point? With Geshaiwyn, you are not just dealing with one assassin, but as many as it takes to get the job done—mind you, it's rarely more than one."

Ean bit back a curse at this unwelcome information. He gave Morin a sidelong look as they walked. "What did you want to speak to me about, Minister?"

"I've brought you an honor guard, as you can see," Morin said, indicating the King's Own Guard hovering close.

"Bodyguards, you mean. Why?"

"In light of this morning—"

"I've been walking around alone all day," Ean cut in suspiciously. "Why now?"

Morin cast him a look of begrudging respect. "Very well. The truth is we caught a man lurking about the palace grounds not long after your ordeal earlier today. He carried a pair of daggers and spoke in a foreign tongue. We have him locked up in the dungeons, but who knows how many more sellswords are out there. You have a significant price on your head, Ean. Morwyk may not be the only one who wants to see you lying cold in a grave."

Suddenly it was all too much—Creighton, the Shade, Alyneri, the truth about his pattern, unknown assassins... Ean's temper flared and he rounded on Morin, demanding, "Why won't you believe it was a Shade that killed my blood-brother?"

Morin assessed Ean's sudden mood swing with a quick once-over and deftly steered the prince through the closest door he could find, which turned out to be a servant's pantry full of linens and candles and smelling strongly of a large vat of dried lavender. He shut the doors behind them and turned to Ean, his face barely illumined by a thin, mullioned window at the far end of the long room.

"There is so much you don't know, Ean," Morin advised in a hushed voice, his hand still firmly holding the prince's arm. "Your father and I...you may think we abandoned the search for your brothers' killers, but it would be a lie. Everything we do now—*everything we do now*—is integral to that hunt." Morin pulled Ean further into the pantry and dropped his voice to a bare whisper. "The treachery we've uncovered in this plot is rooted deep and broad. It would take hours to recount to you the hundreds of threads we've followed. We cannot know that this latest attack on your life isn't part of the same scheme. There are always new actors on the stage, but this play has but one director."

"But of the Shade—"

"It probably *was* a Shade, Ean," Morin cut in tersely, intensely. "Raine's truth, it's hard to mistake the damnable creatures, and a man certainly knows once he's met one. But that's not the point. The point is that *everything we do*—"

"Is involved with finding my brothers' killers," Ean repeated, feeling strangely numbed by the Spymaster's words.

Morin acknowledged this with a nod of approval. "So you begin to see."

Ean did, though he wasn't at all sure that any real picture was forming.

"I cannot tell you more than this now," Morin whispered. "Your father has given me explicit orders on the matter."

Ean felt his anger fading, replaced only with a dull ache. "Is there anything you can tell me? Do you know anything about the zanthyr that saved me? Or why a Shade would be involved? Franco Rohre thinks the Shade was sent to protect me." He pushed a hand through his hair and looked toward the window. "I cannot bear the thought of it."

Morin regarded him for a long moment, his expression unreadable. "As with all things, this too had a beginning," he said finally. "Should you find it, the rest will become clearer. That is all the advice I can offer you now. That and a warning: please, your highness—*please* do not venture anywhere without your guards, and for now, do not leave the palace. The danger to you is real. It is great. And the threat is mortal."

Benumbed, Ean just nodded.

Morin ushered him from the pantry. His guards took up their positions before and behind him again without question.

"I bid you farewell, your Highness," Morin said, touching fingertips to his brow and affecting a tidy bow, "until we meet tonight at the banquet."

Ean watched him spin on his heel and retreat down the passageway.

'As with all things, this too had a beginning...'

Morin's words seemed somehow to echo another's.

'It would seem quite a few people had already taken an interest in you before you set foot upon Dannish soil...'

So when *did* it begin? Could the pattern have been the beginning? And what did it mean that he could draw the Pattern of Life? *No,* he realized. *What does it mean that I've seen it since I was a child?*

"Are you unwell, your Highness?" one of his guards inquired.

Ean pressed palms to his eyes and then focused on the men who were risking their lives to protect him. It seemed so strange. Just weeks ago he and Cray had been working elbow to elbow with common deckhands, scampering up masts to fix the rigging of his grandfather's ship, tarring the waterline below decks while off-duty sailors diced at tables behind them...and now loyal kingdom men were standing guard at his back to protect him from a fate that had already claimed his brothers.

"I'm—" But 'fine' was no longer a word he could glibly use. "I'm sorry. I have a lot on my mind."

"It's just that we're pretty exposed here, your highness," said the guard.

"Yes, of course." Ean headed off down the passageway, immediately lost in thought again.

When *had* it all begun? If his pattern was somehow involved...

Then he had it. Or at least he thought he did.

The one thing he did know was how the Fifth Vestal had learned of his pattern. *Invitations sent to every corner of the globe...*

Why the pattern mattered was the mystery.

Somewhat reeling from the day but feeling a bit more focused, Ean reached his rooms and began to ready himself for the banquet with a renewed purpose. He almost felt as if he could enjoy himself. At least, he intended to try.

The Grand Hall in Calgaryn Palace was a vaulted room bordered on one side by towering mirrors interspersed with life-size paintings of val Lorian kings, and on the other side by a series of tall double-paned glass doors that opened onto a long balcony overlooking a sculpture garden. Running the length of the room, six long rows of banquet tables had been set for the coming meal. Each ended near the foot of the wide dais where the King's table rested, itself draped in a blue velvet cloth embroidered all over with thread-of-silver. The centerpieces of the King's table were identical ice sculptures of Dannym's flying eagle. A stunning display.

As Tanis entered through a pair of the silver-fringed, blue velvet drapes that adorned all the entrances and exits, the grand hall's sunken floor was an undulating sea of color. Ten chandeliers brightened the impressive room, illuminating the guests who stood chatting between the tables. No one would sit until their Majesties arrived.

Because her Grace was still preparing and Tanis had gone on without her, he arrived feeling very out of place. He began looking for anyone he knew, and spotted Prince Ean at once. His Highness stood upon the dais next to Lord Mandor val

Kess, his Majesty's Minister of Culture, and was surrounded by an entourage of bodyguards. The prince was receiving a long procession of nobility who had lined up to pay their respects.

Tanis felt overwhelmed by the crowd, and he wondered how he'd ever find his seat among so many. He was still searching for any other familiar face when a steward in liveried blue came up to him wearing a knowing smile. "Ah, young Tanis. Looking for your seat, are you? Would you like me to take you?"

Tanis looked much relieved. "Oh yes!" he answered. "Could you?"

The steward nodded and led away. Glancing back over his shoulder, he commented mildly, "You must've turned some heads, young man. You're seated at the royal table with their Majesties."

Tanis felt his heart flutter. "I am?" He'd never eaten at the King's table before. Though her Grace often dined with his Majesty informally when she was at court, Tanis was usually seated with Tad and the other boys. He wondered why his seat had been moved. "Was it her Grace that requested it?"

The steward shot Tanis a wide grin over his shoulder. "No, lad. T'was the prince who ordered it."

His Highness! Tanis's eyes widened in wonder. *His Highness wanted me to sit with him?* He couldn't believe his luck.

The steward left him on the dais at the end opposite where Prince Ean stood, and took his leave with a wink and a grin. Tanis soon became uncomfortable standing there, however; he felt as if every gaze was upon him, perhaps wondering why a common boy would be sitting with the King. Every couple that passed out of the line after greeting Prince Ean would eye Tanis before walking off with a rather indignant tilt to their heads. But the one saving grace of his high vantage point was that Tanis was quick to spot Tad val Mallonwey among the crowd. He rushed off to meet his friend, relieved to have an excuse to leave the dais before anyone else could glare at him.

When Tanis caught up with Tad, the young heir to Towermount was chatting with the black-haired, blue-eyed Killian val Whitney, heir to Eastwatch. Tanis had always admired his two noble friends and wished he could be more like them, so he was quite surprised when Tad said by way of greeting, "Look at you, Tanis. Have you been adopted by the royals then? First I hear you've taken apartments in the royal wing and now these," and he held a hand to Tanis's own garments. "The King's colors no less. You're looking more the nobleman than me."

"Aye, that's a certainty," Killian agreed with a taunting grin. Though he'd spent half his life at court, Killian spoke with the lilt of a Highlander, a manner inherited from his father, the King's General of the East. "Have ye happened upon a royal birth of a sudden then, Tanis?"

Privately, Tanis did feel smashing in his new boots and velvet doublet in the king's colors of silver and blue. The new clothes had been laid out for him when he got to his rooms and were quite finer than anything he'd ever owned before; he had no idea who sent them. Perhaps they came with the room? Tanis grinned and whispered, "Tad, can you believe it? I'm seated at the King's table!"

Tad punched him good-naturedly. "You jest!"

"No! It's true! The steward said his Highness ordered it."

"What'd ye do to so claim the prince's favor, eh Tanis?" Killian inquired. His tone implied Tanis must have done something sneaky.

"Oh, speaking of! My sister says—" Tad began, but then his expression fell.

Tanis thought he knew his friend's mind. The whole of the nobility was talking about Katerina val Mallonwey, who apparently was refusing even to leave her apartments after hearing of Creighton's death.

Killian placed a hand on his friend's arm. "She'll yet recover. Kat has ten suitors standin' in line for her hand."

Tad smiled and nodded. "No doubt you're right."

Tanis wondered if Tad wasn't mourning more the loss of his special status as 'brother to the girl being courted by the prince's blood-brother.'

Tad offered, "I was going to say, Tanis, I think I've an explanation for your Lady Alyneri's rapid exodus from Calgaryn a few days past."

Tanis's ears perked up. "What is it?"

"Kat says the Duchess of Aracine had something more than a crush on the prince when they were young."

"But she was betrothed to his brother," Killian pointed out.

"Thus the rub," Tad concluded, adding dramatically, "The painful thorns of fate, separating star-crossed lovers."

"I don't think they're star-crossed lovers," Tanis noted, thinking of the scowls and glares her Grace had been casting Prince Ean every time they were in a room together.

"The way I hear it," Killian said, "her Grace has long refused to marry the prince an' he spent his time at Fersthaven wooing her."

"Is it so, Tanis?" Tad asked hopefully. "Is her Grace the mysterious heiress?"

Tanis was careful in his response. He'd been instructed to perpetuate the gossip to protect Prince Ean, but a truthreader couldn't lie. "I'm not sure. If she was, I don't think the negotiations went very well. Her Grace isn't speaking to him at present."

"See," Tad elbowed Killian in the ribs. "I told you she wasn't the heiress in the story, no matter what they're saying in the kitchens. No, my theory is better." Tad grinned, his imagination in full gallop. "The heroine pines for her lost love, promising her troth to him as the long years pass, only to find upon his long-awaited return that his heart now belongs to another."

"I think ye missed your calling, Tad," Killian said with a grin. "Ye should've taken up the lute and become a minstrel. Tis more to your nature than orderin' soldiers hither and yon."

Tad puffed out his chest indignantly. "I'll make a fine general."

"Ye'd make a better minstrel. Plus, ye've got the looks for it. Like that Espial whose been hangin' about, what one as came with the Vestal."

Tanis came suddenly alert. "What?"

"Oh, didn't I tell you, Tanis?" Tad said, scratching his head. "I must've forgotten. You were right. That *was* the Fourth Vestal we saw, after all."

Tanis's excitement grew. "Is he still here?"

"As far as I know. He comes and goes like the wind, you know, and seems to be spending most of his time in conference with their majesties or down in the cellars or something. Don't ask me what could interest him there."

Tanis thought he knew. *A mysterious hole, a dead man and a set of iron doors leading to....what?*

"So anyway," said Killian, resuming his thread of conversation, "the man who's with him—"

"Franco...Rohre," Tad supplied, snapping his fingers as it came to him.

"*Franco Rohre?*" Tanis gaped at the familiar name.

Killian looked surprised. "You know him, Tanis?"

Delanthine Tanner, Rothen Landray, Gannon Bair, Franco Rohre... Tanis was suddenly grateful that Master O'reith had made him memorize so many strange names. "Franco Rohre is one of the Fifty Companions," Tanis told his friends in a hushed tone. "He's one of the few who survived the fall of the Citadel."

"He was on Tiern'aval?" Killian looked amazed.

"And to think I thought the man just some wayward Nodefinder," Tad confessed, looking stricken. Tanis knew his friend prided himself on his information; no doubt this news came as quite a blow to his ego. "I've only ever seen him following the Queen's Companion like a puppy, or entertaining her with a lute and a song. I never imagined he was someone important."

"He's a famous Espial," Tanis informed him with no small measure of satisfaction at finding *something* that his friend didn't know. "He's worked the Pattern of Life."

The Pattern of Life! Even as he said it, Tanis thought about how wondrous it was. Just the legendary pattern itself was intriguing enough—moreover a man who'd actually worked it. Not that Raine D'Lacourte and the other Vestals hadn't all done the same, but the Vestals seemed utterly unapproachable, while Franco Rohre was merely a man. Tanis added conspiratorially, "He's over three-hundred years old!"

Just then, the trumpets sounded. Tanis spun toward the dais, worried about the time, but it was only the first fanfare. Two more would sound before the king and queen arrived. Still, he knew he'd best depart. "I'd better get going," he told his friends.

Tad clapped him on the arm with a grin. "I'll expect a full report, young man."

"Aye, Tanis, all the juicy details from the King's table," Killian added, rubbing his hands together and leering lustily.

Smiling, Tanis rushed off through the crowd and—

Ran right into Fynnlar val Lorian.

The royal cousin looked almost presentable in a muted grey doublet with slashed sleeves lined in silver and with his shoulder-length wavy hair actually brushed. He stood talking to two noble ladies, one blonde, one brunette, neither of them memorable. As Tanis tried to slip by, he heard one of the ladies say, "But surely my lord agrees that such butchers must be punished. Did not the barbarians murder our Prince Sebastian, thy own cousin, while he lay sleeping?"

Before Fynn could answer, the other woman interjected with, "Tis a shock his Majesty has not already sought like retribution for Prince Sebastian's death. I know there are some who speak against it, but indeed, if ever there was a justified reason for war, my Lord Fynnlar, you must admit his Majesty has it."

Fynn arched a dubious brow and sipped his wine. "No one ever goes to war for the right reasons, my lady," he murmured, wherein he spied Tanis trying to slip by unnoticed. "Well, hello there, Tanis, truthreader-in-training. Come to fetch me for my uncle, have you?"

Tanis gave him a bewildered look.

Fynn clapped him on the shoulder and laughed. "Enjoying the banquet, I see."

Tanis was worried about getting to the dais. His eyes kept straying there. "I suppose, my lord. And you?"

Fynn smiled wanly. "Immensely. These noble ladies and I were just discussing the merits of war, of which I discovered few." He drained his goblet with two long gulps, belched, and announced then, "Dear heavens, I seem to have finished my wine. Do excuse me, ladies." He darted off into the crowd dragging Tanis behind him.

Both women glared at their retreating backs.

As they made their way toward the dais, Tanis confessed to Fynn, "My lord, I didn't actually come in his Majesty's name."

"Oh, I know, Tanis," Fynn reassured him. "I was eager to escape." He glanced over his shoulder, but the women were lost in the ever-shifting crowd. Fynn shuddered. "They were just like little parrots—do you know what a parrot is, Tanis? It's a tropical bird they have in Jamaii that repeats everything you say without understanding a word of it. They were little parrots, those women, perpetuating the same drivel fed them by their lord husbands. At least they were loyal supporters of the crown. I suppose one must grant them that."

Tanis was puzzled. "Should we *not* be fighting the Khurds, my lord? I've heard of some speaking in dissent, but I thought his Majesty was firm in his decision to support M'Nador."

Fynn eyed the boy as if discerning his loyalties. Finally he grunted. "War is sometimes appropriate—so long as you're actually fighting the people you ought to be fighting, which is rare."

Reflecting on that bit of cryptic wisdom, Tanis wondered if there might be more to the royal cousin than first met the eye. "Lord Fynnlar," he asked then, "do you really sail with the pirates of Jamaii?"

Fynn snagged a full goblet off the tray of a passing steward and winked at a lovely lady in a pink dress. "Something like that," he murmured as he kept walking and drank his wine at the same time, all without spilling a drop.

Tanis was quite impressed. "Is it true that they sail their ships into caves to hide them?"

"I could tell you lad," Fynn answered with a conspiratorial wink, "but then I'd have to kill you."

Halting at the base of the dais, Tanis gazed in astonishment as Fynn continued up. "Really?"

Fynn grinned. "*No*, Tanis—ye gads, no!" He pulled Tanis on up the steps. "I'm only teasing you."

"You've got to be careful about that, cousin," a familiar voice observed, and Tanis turned to find his Highness approaching. Ean ruffled the lad's hair affectionately as Tanis topped the stairs, and then he added, "Our Tanis is perhaps the last true innocent, Fynn. T'would be a tragedy to jade him."

While Fynn said something into his wine, Tanis gazed admiringly at his prince. Attired all in black, Ean was resplendent with silver filigree decorating each velvet sleeve and his Kingdom sword with its sapphire pommelstone gleaming at his hip. Tanis had never felt so common in any man's presence. He thought he should be kneeling, and might have had Ean not asked first, "Is the jacket to your liking, Tanis? You could pass for a noble yourself now."

Tanis was startled. "You—*you* sent them, your Highness? I thought—"

Ean chuckled and clapped the boy on the shoulder. "The coat was mine, Tanis, long ago. I thought it might fit you and had it sent over."

Tanis fell mute with gratitude; that the prince had worn the coat himself made Ean's gift even more meaningful.

"I must speak with you, Ean," Fynn meanwhile said more soberly than his usual wont.

Ean selected a crystal goblet of sparkling wine from an offering steward, and took a sip, murmuring, "Go ahead."

"I've heard talk, Ean," Fynn said, glancing around to make certain no ears were close. "My sources say his majesty intends to send you south with Duke val Whitney when the General returns to Tal'shira by the Sea. There are rumors of a parley with the Khurds."

"My father and I still have much to discuss, Fynn," Ean replied, and his gaze seemed shadowed by whatever memory suddenly infused his thoughts.

"You mustn't go, whatever you do," Fynn admonished. "We all know what happened at the last parley with Abdul-Basir."

Taking another sip of wine, Ean murmured his agreement as he turned and surveyed the room.

Alyneri was just then arriving on the arm of the black-haired General of the East, Loran val Whitney, who was almost a to-scale enlargement of his son Killian, but far more terrifying in demeanor. Tanis eyed him uncertainly.

"Ah, if it isn't their Graces, the Lady Alyneri and Duke val Whitney," Fynn welcomed with a leering grin. "What a pleasure it is indeed to be among such esteemed company."

"Fynnlar," Alyneri and Loran said together, and their tones were equally wanting for warmth.

"My cousin and I were just discussing your war, in fact, General," Fynn went on. "Or rather, I should say, his participation in it."

"I know of no plans to allow his Highness to go to war, Fynnlar," Loran assured him while nodding a gracious hello to Ean.

"Really?" Fynn challenged, "Because I heard Ean was meant to represent the king at the upcoming parley with al'Abdul-Basir."

Loran did a poor job of hiding his astonishment. Clearly this information was meant to be held in the utmost secrecy. He seemed uncertain whether to deny Fynnlar out of hand or demand to know how he learned information that was only known to a select few.

Fynn advanced relentlessly into Loran's startled silence, declaring, "Tell me, my lord Duke, do you expect to lose the last of our princes at this next parley with the Emir?"

"Lord Fynnlar!" Alyneri protested in outrage as the General's face darkened.

"Because, you see," Fynn continued, "I am running out of cousins, and if you let the Khurds murder my last one—"

"You go too far, Fynnlar," Loran growled.

"—then I'm afraid *I* might be next," Fynn continued, adding, "though I cannot imagine anyone wanting to kill *me*. I can understand the whole Sebastian thing, of course—sorry, Ean but you have to admit he really was an insufferable snot. Never would lend me any money—"

"*Enough*, Fynn," Ean warned.

Fynn turned to him looking injured. "I was only saying…"

The General's expression was fierce, but he confessed to the charge with admirable calm. "*Should* his Highness accompany me to the parley—and I am by no means advocating any plans to this affect—he would nonetheless be kept quite safe. Prince Radov has ample forces at Tal'shira, and every possible precaution would be taken to ensure his Highness's continued wellbeing."

"*Mmm*," Fynn murmured into his wine, and for a moment, everyone thought the uncomfortable conversation was blessedly at an end, until—"Ah, but you see General," the royal cousin announced with his head tilted sideways and a ponderous look upon his face, "I have often found that if you know something can go wrong and take due precautions to prevent it, then something *else* will go wrong."

Before the General lost his temper, Alyneri interjected coolly, "I was speaking earlier today with the Princess Ysolde, who brought up a most interesting notion, Lord Fynnlar."

Fynn tore his eyes from the General's to turn her an inquiring gaze. "Is that so, your Grace?"

"She proposed the convention that our nobility should uphold a certain standard, and were that standard to dip below an acceptable level…" She gave him a pointed look. "Mayhap said noble should be deemed unfit for his title." Alyneri cast Fynn a lovely smile. "Don't you find that a unique idea? The Princess said the Avatar nobility have truly embraced the concept."

Fynn glared at her over the rim of his goblet and muttered, "Quite so, your Grace," into his wine.

Several others ascended the dais then, with the Queen's Admiral father, Cameron L'Owain, in the lead. Cameron and his group joined Loran, Ean and the others, and there followed a round of quick greetings. Tanis's gaze, however, was drawn to the man who stood just behind Admiral L'Owain. He might have changed his clothes from chestnut to fawn grey, but his countenance was unmistakable, as were his colorless eyes.

"Ean," Admiral L'Owain addressed his grandson, "have you met the Vestal?"

Ean shook his head and he extended his hand to clasp wrists with Raine. "No indeed. I have been most anxious to meet and speak with your Excellency."

Raine held his gaze. "As am I, your Highness."

Loran said to Alyneri then, "Your Grace, have you met the Vestal Raine D'Lacourte?" Loran held a hand to the man Tanis was staring wondrously at. Raine nodded a polite hello, murmuring, "A pleasure, your Grace."

"I do believe we've met, your Excellency," she said pleasantly. "I was quite young. You may not recall."

The Vestal responded with a smile, one that held a rather elusive quality. "That is indeed correct, your Grace," he murmured. "I applaud your memory."

Alyneri allowed a steward to refill her empty goblet. Then she explained to the rest of the group, "His Excellency came for the swearing-in ceremony of the truthreader Kjieran van Stone. I was in attendance with my mother and father. I couldn't have been more than four."

"Whatever happened to that van Stone character?" Loran asked. "When I left for the front, he was all but attached to his Majesty's hip."

"I have been wondering much the same, Duke," Raine admitted, and his tone implied he was quite displeased about it.

"You've been at the front for over two years, your Grace," Fynn pointed out to Loran. "Much has changed in the fair kingdom of Dannym since you left."

"I am told that Kjieran van Stone has been missing for several months," Alyneri explained to the Vestal as Loran looked on. "Rhys val Kincaide, captain of the King's Own Guard, seemed verily displeased about his absence and the mystery of his disappearance."

Loran's expression hardened with a frown. "It seems unlikely that the man ran off."

"It is unthinkable," Raine declared, and there was a cold edge to his tone. "A sworn truthreader in the service of a king? Absolutely unthinkable."

Alyneri gazed at him for a moment with an unreadable expression. Then she smiled and tried to lighten the mood, asking, "And what brings you to Calgaryn this time, your Excellency?"

"Something dark and sinister, no doubt," Fynn interjected, but at the glares he received, he added indignantly, "I didn't mean *he* was dark and sinister. I'm certain his Excellency is only upon the most honorable of missions—as befits his reputation."

"Thank you, Lord Fynnlar," Raine said with an enigmatic look, settling his diamondine gaze upon the royal cousin. Fynn reddened beneath his steady stare and covered his unease with a hasty gulping of wine.

Tanis could restrain himself no longer. He had so many questions for the famous Vestal, but surprisingly the one that made it first to his tongue was, "Your Excellency, do you really command the Brotherhood of the Seven Stones?"

Raine turned to him with a smile, but even when benign, his gaze was difficult to hold. Looking into the Vestal's eyes, Tanis felt as if he stared into the very center of the starry heavens where no truths remain hidden. His head even began to swim a little, as if he'd had too much wine.

"And you must be Tanis," Raine said. "Vitriam mentioned you with fond regard. He says you are learning our craft well."

Tanis blushed and dropped his eyes to his boots. "Thank you, your Excellency."

"I do not lead Veneisea's Brotherhood, young Tanis," Raine answered then, "but I have many allies within its ranks." Then he added, "Actually Lord Fynnlar is not unfamiliar with our network."

All eyes turned to Fynn, who belched gratuitously and then looked injured when everyone glared at him.

"Indeed? How so?" Alyneri inquired, seeming unconvinced that Fynn could have anything to do with a profession that didn't include debauchery as its main pastime.

"Yes, you *are* mistaken, my dear Vestal," Fynn responded. His words were becoming slurred, which didn't serve to improve his standing with present company.

"The only dealings I've ever had with your Brotherhood of the Seven Spies—I mean," he paused to belch again, "Stones—is the time they beat me unconscious and left me for dead in the streets of Cair Thessalonia."

"A shame they left the job unfinished," Loran muttered into his wine.

Fynn cast him a sooty look.

"Alas, I fear that was a case of mistaken identity, Lord Fynnlar," the Vestal apologized, though he sounded more amused than contrite. "Our operatives were seeking a certain scoundrel who was trading in Agasi artifacts stolen from a frigate that had been overtaken by pirates. Of course, an upstanding nobleman like yourself would brook no dealings with pirates. Once they learned of your identity, of course, they released you. The leadership was quite embarrassed over the entire affair."

Fynn grunted skeptically.

Trumpeters sounding the imminent arrival of the King and Queen quieted further conversation. The court herald walked to the edge of the balcony above the dais and announced: "His royal Majesty, Gydryn val Lorian, High King of Dannym, Protector of the Northern Isles." Tanis and the others made their way to their seats and stood attentively. The horns blew again, and the herald cried, "Her royal Majesty, Errodan Renwyr n'Owain val Lorian, Queen of Dannym and the Northern Isles." The trumpets sounded for the last time, and everyone bowed.

Gydryn and Errodan, dressed in coordinating blue and silver, entered from opposite sides of the dais, followed by Rhys val Kincaide and Ysolde Remalkhen respectively, the latter with Franco Rohre in close tow. Servants appeared to help the queen sit, fanning her great robe of blue velvet trimmed in silver sable around her throne, but Gydryn remained standing and took up a sapphire-crusted goblet brimming with ruby wine from an attendant. This he held aloft to the assembled nobility, announcing, "To my son, and his long-awaited return!"

The crowd took up their goblets and intoned, "To his Highness, Prince Ean!"

Everyone drank.

There followed a long succession of toasts from nearly all of the nobility present—or so it seemed to Tanis as toast after toast was offered to the prince's return, to his continued well-being, to his health, to his prosperity, to his future, to the kingdom's future, to the king, to the queen, and so on.

Finally, the King drank the last of his wine and declared, "Let the feasting begin!"

The room soon reverberated with the clink of china and crystal and thousands of individual conversations as everyone took their seats and the stewards began the immense process of serving the food. As Tanis took his own seat next to Fynn and smelled the amazing aromas wafting up from the table, he realized just how famished he was. His only focus became how to keep his hands in his lap until the King and Queen and Prince Ean had been served. When it was finally his turn, he pried a leg off a roasted turkey and couldn't remember anything ever tasting better.

Once he'd finished the fowl, a heap of apple-chestnut dressing, and two plumb and pheasant tarts, Tanis felt satiated enough to take a breath and look around. At some point during the meal, Prince Ean had changed places with her Grace, such that she now sat between the prince and the king. At least she was speaking to his Highness again. As Tanis tried to listen in, he heard her Grace saying in a low voice,

"...something wrong about him, Ean, I'm telling you."

"I'm not disagreeing with you, Alyneri," Ean repeated. "I simply asked why you thought so."

"I told you I don't know," she stressed in her courtly whisper. "It's just a feeling I have about him. He knows too much about everything that's going on."

"It's Morin's job to know things, Alyneri."

"He knows about *Adept* things, Ean. I heard him talking about the strands as if he had personal experience with them."

"Lots of people are knowledgeable about *elae*, Alyneri," Ean pointed out in a low voice. "Even my mother gives Morin her trust and begrudging respect."

"How can anyone trust a man who trades in lies for his living?" Alyneri demanded crossly.

Ean grinned. "I submit to your point, Duchess. Maybe it's just that he knows more than he can ever safely speak of. You could be sensing that."

"I can't believe you're defending him, Ean. Have you heard nothing of what I've said—"

"I'm not defending him, Alyneri," Ean calmly interjected. "I merely require more than your 'feeling' to declare a man a traitor."

Alyneri settled him a frosty look. "Are you trying to get back on my bad side?"

Ean cast her a shadowy grin. "I hadn't realized I ever moved out of it."

"I didn't think you *had* a good side, your Grace," Fynn chimed in from Ean's right.

She shot him an icy look. "Fear not, my lord Fynnlar, you shall never have occasion to see it."

"Well, that's a relief."

"So what's your point, Alyneri?" Ean returned them to the subject at hand.

Frustrated, Alyneri sat back in her chair. "I don't know. I just don't trust him."

Ean gazed at her for a long time. Then he decided, "You are the oddest woman I think I have ever met."

At that, Alyneri harrumphed indignantly and turned to engage in conversation with his Majesty instead.

"She's certainly got the royal dismissal down to an art," Fynn observed from Ean's right.

Ean gazed over at him wearing one of his famous half-smiles, just that quirk of a grin twitching the corners of his mouth. "For all her venom, cousin, she has several redeeming qualities."

Fynn looked unconvinced. "Indeed?"

"In fact, I'm thinking of courting her."

"That doesn't seem in the best judgment to me."

"Good judgment comes from experience, cousin," Ean observed sagaciously. Then he added with a crooked grin, "and a lot of experience comes from bad judgment." He raised his wine to Fynn and finished with a wink, "Lead me to wisdom, I always say."

TWENTY-SEVEN

'Ideas, not greed, drive men to war.'

– Gydryn val Lorian, King of Dannym

Morin d'Hain was troubled as he headed through the underbelly of Calgaryn palace on a course for the dungeons. His conversation with Ean had been unexpectedly illuminating. Knowing Geshaiwyn were involved was significant, but that fact alone engendered concerns over his latest prisoner.

Geshaiwyn. The word was a hiss in Morin's thoughts. He'd dealt with assassins aplenty in his long life, but Geshaiwyn were by far the most troublesome. He felt confident—as confident as one could ever feel in his line of work—that the Duke of Morwyk knew nothing of Geshaiwyn. If he'd known of their existence, he'd have long ago contracted with them. No, the Geshaiwyn had been sent by another, someone who wanted the prince quite definitively dead; someone with knowledge of Wildlings and their varied talents. That ruled out anyone in the north. Morin had never lived in a kingdom so cut off from *elae.* That Gydryn employed only two truthreaders...well, it would've been unthinkable before the War.

But fewer are Returning every year to fill the vacancies left by their ancestors.

He knew it, most Adepts knew it, the Vestals knew it. What no one knew was why.

'There is no afterlife, there is only the Returning...'

The northmen repeated the sacred phrases glibly. What people like Gareth val Mallonwey didn't understand was that Adepts were *inextricably* tied to their strand. For an Adept, death was yet another beginning, because every Adept Returned, reborn again as an Adept, again of the same strand. Their talents reawakened as early as their first childhood steps or as late as adolescence, but for millennia the Returned had always awakened.

Since the War, however, either they weren't Returning—which begged the question of where they *were* going—or more likely, they weren't awakening. Morin rather suspected the latter. Either situation was equally grave. No one knew how to reawaken the Returned if their talent didn't manifest in adolescence, and as for finding out where the dead went if they weren't Returning...well, he certainly wasn't volunteering to follow them to find out.

Wearing a brooding expression that mirrored his thoughts, Morin passed a palace soldier heading the opposite way in the tunnels. The man didn't meet his eye, and Morin made a mental note to have him investigated. Whatever he was hiding was probably nothing, but Morin didn't ascend to his position by giving people the benefit of the doubt. Suspicion, a keen eye and a shrewd intellect were what kept him alive.

And a great many years longer than most, at that. Spies had a short life expectancy—even Adept ones—and Morin was no stranger to certain patterns...the kind that extended a man's life long beyond his natural span of years. The list was few who'd tread the world of shadows longer than Morin d'Hain.

Which brought his thoughts back around to Ean val Lorian.

Morwyk's plotting notwithstanding, that Geshaiwyn, Shades and zanthyrs could be named in association with the prince made Ean just about the most interesting case that had ever crossed Morin's desk. The prince had made no mention in his letter of Björn van Gelderan, but Shades made no move but at his bidding. It was clear the prince didn't understand why the Fifth Vestal was interested in him—and for that matter, neither did Morin.

Oh, he'd instantly recognized Ean's pattern for what it was—no doubt Raine had also—but he couldn't fathom why the Fifth Vestal would be intrigued by it, nor why he'd sent a Shade and his zanthyr to protect the prince from Morwyk's trap and then abandoned him again knowing a Geshaiwyn assassin followed.

But Morin had his hands full enough with the things he did understand about Ean's situation, and those were threats such that he didn't bother to concern himself with Björn van Gelderan's involvement as well. If there was one thing as certain in their realm as the Law of Balance, it was that no mere mortal could understand why Björn van Gelderan did the things he did.

Morin swept through the double-barred doors that opened into the dungeons and descended a flight of steps with quick surety. His keen gaze missed nothing—from the neat state of the two guards who jumped to attention at his entrance, to the single lamp that had gone out above a dungeon door, to the faint odor of sickness wafting out from deeper within the hallway. So it was that upon entering the cell block where his prisoner was being kept, he noticed immediately what had changed.

"Duncan! Caol!" he shouted for the guards without breaking stride—in fact, picking up speed as he headed down the long, narrow passageway toward a cell at its end.

The guards Duncan and Caol came running to attend. "Milord?"

"Why was the Bemothi thief moved from his cell?" Morin demanded as he walked.

"Didn't Farris find you, milord?" Duncan asked as he fell into step to Morin's left with Caol on his right. "We sent him to report—"

"No, obviously he did *not* find me. Why was he moved?"

Duncan and Caol exchanged a troubled look, and the former said, "It was because of the flooding, milord."

Morin drew up short. "Flooding? We're a hundred paces below solid rock, man. What flooding?"

"In the cells at the end of the hall, milord," Caol reported.

"It was the damnedest thing," Duncan said, looking mystified. "When we opened the door to move the prisoner, it was near up to the man's chin, and him chained to the floor and all."

Morin grabbed the guard by his surcoat, chain mail clinking within his fist. "You moved *my* prisoner?"

"We had to, milord!" Caol insisted at the same time that Duncan said, "The man would've drowned in there, though where in Tiern'aval all that water came fr—"

Aghast, Morin gripped Duncan's shoulders with both hands. "Where did you put him?"

"He's chained safe and sound, milord," Duncan insisted, though Morin's expression was clearly making him uneasy. "Just two cells further down, on the left there—"

Morin dashed for it. "Open it, man! Hurry!"

Caol rushed to comply, hastily pulling the key ring from his belt as he exchanged a frantic look with Duncan. Clearly neither man relished landing on the bad side of Morin d'Hain.

He got the door unlocked and Morin threw it open.

"See, mi—" Duncan began.

But the cell was empty.

"Yes," Morin said, turning on him with a sudden dangerous calm. "I quite do."

It was well into the quiet hours of the morning before Ean escaped the banquet in his honor. The revelers would continue through the night, toasting him every hour as was tradition, but Ean had too much on his mind.

Morin had said if he found the beginning, things would become clearer. Well, Ean was fairly sure his pattern was central to his troubles, but no matter what steps he took—no matter the direction in which he tried to seek answers—the mystery only deepened. Ean felt somewhat like his other self, the one in his dream that faced the darkness knowing only death awaited him at the end of every avenue. He was trapped in a maze fashioned of Shades, zanthyrs, assassins and mysterious forces more dangerous than all—*lest we forget!* There were a half-dozen paths leading away from him, but follow all or none, he met only with a dead-end of confusion.

"Ean!"

The prince looked up to find Morin approaching from the other end of the hall, looking uncharacteristically cheerful. Morin waved Ean leave his bodyguards behind, and Ean gave them a curious look before walking to meet Morin further down the wide corridor.

"What is it, Minister?" Ean asked as he neared.

Suddenly Morin's face turned ashen, and he pointed urgently at something behind Ean. Ean spun, but he saw only his guards, who were suddenly running toward him—

And Ean understood in the split second that was all he had to react. He dove forward, tumbling into a roll, the dagger missing him by mere hairs. He kept rolling as the Geshaiwyn assassin made another stab for him, striking the marble floor with a metallic scrape as he dove after Ean like a butcher in the hen yard. Ean scrambled for his footing but the assassin was fast on his heels, so Ean spun to his back and brought up both feet. He smashed the man in the chest, sending him sprawling backwards, but the assassin catapulted himself off his shoulders and onto his feet, landing catlike with bent knees. No longer wearing Morin's features, the Geshaiwyn grinned at Ean with a face the prince recognized too well.

Ean's bodyguards were footsteps away when the assassin fled and sprinted back down the hall. "Not this time!" Ean growled, scrambling to his feet after the man. He yelled to the near guards, "If he makes it to his node we'll never catch him!"

Ean pushed his legs to new lengths as he chased. He was quickly well out in front of his armored bodyguards, and he took a flying leap, only just snagging the Geshaiwyn by his ankles as they both tumbled to the floor with legs and arms akimbo.

The assassin wriggled like a fish while flailing maniacally with his dagger. Ean managed to save his thigh from obliteration but the blade took a chunk of flesh out of his palm before he finally grabbed hold of the offending dagger and wrestled the Geshaiwyn for ownership. They fought, rolled and kicked, and then, finally, Ean's bodyguards arrived and the Geshaiwyn was pulled off him hissing and spitting belligerently as he struggled and squirmed.

Panting with fury as much as from the brief but frenzied fight, his hand and clothes bloody, Ean got to his feet and glared at the assassin. "Who hired you to kill me?" he shouted.

The assassin struggled as he glared at Ean, but Ean's bodyguards had his hands and arms pinned behind him and were already binding them.

"Ean!"

The prince turned heatedly, once again to find Morin d'Hain running to meet him. Wary now, he drew his sword and held it a threatening stance. "Stay back!"

Morin slowed and held up his hands.

Ean's blade was a slice of deadly silver poised for a strike. "What advice did you give me today when we spoke?"

"I told you to seek the beginning," he replied without hesitation. "That in doing so the rest might become clearer."

Ean lowered his blade and exhaled an exhausted sigh.

"I accept full responsibility for this terrible mistake, your Highness," Morin said as he approached, eyeing the Geshaiwyn critically. "I made a grave error in judgment allowing this man to be imprisoned inside the palace walls. Perhaps it was ego, though I would take more comfort in believing that my skills are becoming rusty."

"You didn't know he was Geshaiwyn, Morin," Ean said.

"The fact remains, I should've been more thorough."

Ean looked back to the assassin. "*Who* sent you?"

"I'm just the messenger," the man said with a grin.

"Ah, so he does speak our tongue," Morin said critically. "And what is your message?"

The Geshaiwyn leered. "Your days are numbered, Prince of Dannym."

"Was that all?" Morin inquired with a steely gaze.

"No, your lordship," the man replied tartly. "My daggers have a message too."

"Indeed," Morin said quietly, and he drew his sword and ran the man through in one swift and startling motion.

"Why did you do that!" Ean shouted in fury. "We could've questioned—"

"You never question Geshaiwyn," Morin calmly explained as he jerked his blade free of the man's chest, his gaze pinned inexorably on the assassin.

The man smiled at Morin, uttered, "A *halál csak az'eleje,*" and died.

Morin frowned at him. Then he lifted brown eyes to Ean's silent but dutiful bodyguards who still held the man's hands behind his back. "Just leave him here. I'll call my people to attend to his body. You go on with the prince."

"Milord," they intoned with a smart clicking of heels and promptly dropped the dead man on his face.

Ean was starting to feel the aftereffects of his brief battle; mentally he felt slightly numb around the edges, while his bleeding right hand ached and throbbed. He looked to Morin. "Is that the end then? Or should I expect another of them to appear in my room tonight?"

"He was Geshaiwyn," Morin said heavily. "More will come. For tonight, though, you should be safe enough." He glanced down and only then noticed Ean's bleeding hand. "I'll send for the healer to attend—"

"No, this is beneath Alyneri's skill." The Duchess was the last person Ean wanted to deal with. He held up the gash and eyed it critically. "Some water and linen is all it needs."

"Very well," Morin remitted.

Ean turned to go, but he looked back at Morin over his shoulder with one last question. "What did he say just then?" he asked, his eyes shifting to the dead man. "When he died."

Morin's expression was unreadable. "He said 'death is only the beginning.'"

"I see." Though in truth he saw very little. A thousand tiny fragments seeming to have no connection with one another.

"Your Highness," Morin called the prince's gaze back, looking upon him with lines of concern deepening his frown, "this man may be dead, but please—for my sake if not your own—please be careful."

Ean managed a humorless smile. "I'll do my best, Minister. Good night."

Much later, and after bandaging his hand, Ean finally found slumber, but it would not prove restful…

In the throes of a heated dream, Ean felt for the thread of Unraveling. His hands and feet were cold—*so cold!*—and his bare skin burned. The only sounds were the pounding of his heart, the rushing of blood in his veins, the uneven hiss of his breath. He felt power in the darkness that surrounded him, the electrified air pulling the tiniest hairs on end, a thousand needles pricking flesh. He felt hatred in the nothingness, and the intensity of it made his insides churn.

They were at an impasse.

He feared the darkness, but he knew *It* feared him also.

Why? Why does it fear me?

The silver thread in his hands cut sharply into his fingers. He hissed a curse and almost released it, but he knew he mustn't. *I mustn't!*

Clenching teeth, Ean resisted the pull of the darkness on the other end of the thread, drawing it closer instead. The razor-sharp silver sliced deeply into his flesh, cutting until he felt it hit bone. Blood gushed down his hands and along bare arms, making the thread slippery, but still he held to it. *It's slipping! Slipping!*

Ean held to his thread until he felt it sawing bone. *Oh, the agony!* Yet he knew this pain was pale compared to what he faced if he failed. This he knew like his life depended on the understanding

Yet it was too much. The power against him was too great.

Suddenly his fingers were useless things. The tension snapped, and the thread spun out of his control. Ean flailed, falling backwards grasping for purchase in the emptiness, the wisp of silver melting out of sight. He watched it go with a desolate sense of failure. When the pain in his hands finally drew his attention, he looked down at his fingers and saw only bloody stumps—

The prince uttered a muted cry as he sat up roughly in bed, soaked linens clinging to his bare skin. Motion across the room made him jump for his sword, which he'd placed at his bedside in prudence for his life. He knocked into the bed table as he grabbed the weapon.

"Quiet, you royal idiot!" hissed the figure that approached out of the shadows. Fynn pushed back the hood of his cloak. "You'll wake the neighbors and get me in trouble."

Ean kept the blade leveled threateningly on his cousin, though his injured right hand was pounding and he felt blood soaking through the binding. Perhaps he should've let Alyneri tend it after all. "Tell me something only Fynn would know," Ean demanded.

"My penis is bigger than yours," Fynn replied, grinning broadly.

"Wrong." Ean faked a thrust, but he didn't have the energy to carry through with the feint and lowered his sword as Fynn neared.

"Seven hells, what'd you do to your hand?"

"It was the Geshaiwyn," Ean complained, holding up his bleeding appendage to eye it in annoyance, "or hadn't you heard."

"Oh that. Didn't you see Alyneri afterward?"

Ean gritted his teeth. "No."

"See, obviously you need a little help with this whole courting thing. You're supposed to take advantage of any chance to see the girl you intend to court, and letting her tend a wound gained on the field—or hallway—of battle, is always a boon. Girls like that sort of thing."

"Alyneri would only find a way to blame me for the band of relentless assassins that are after my life."

"Yeah, and you're courting her why?"

"I said I was *thinking* about courting her," Ean grumbled, shooting Fynn an irritable look. "Why are you here anyway? This is *my* room."

"Hey, don't shoot the messenger," Fynn protested with raised hands. "You're to pack your things and come with me. Don't ask questions because I don't have any answers. Someone came to my room with the same damned line, and I'm only repeating it. It's a game, I think. Next it'll be your turn. I suggest waking your dad. He'll like that."

"Pack? You're serious?"

Fynn turned reluctantly sedate. "They'll be here any moment, Ean. Truly, you must hurry."

The prince rushed to comply then, but even with his cousin's help, he only just crammed the last of his things into a canvas bag before he heard his guards entering through the adjoining room.

"Your highnesses," one whispered. "If you would come with us…"

They traveled in silence through the royal wing, encountering no one. The guards finally stopped before a door Ean had never been through before—*come to think of it, I've never even seen that door. Isn't there usually a tapestry in this hallway?* "Go ahead, your Highness," the first guard said, and the other added in a bare whisper, "Epiphany's blessing on your quest."

Both curious and wary, Ean opened the door and entered, followed by an uncharacteristically restrained Fynnlar. Beyond lay another door, and beyond that a staircase spiraling down, the worn stone steps dimly lit by oil lamps hung in sconces on the wall. It was a long way down, but neither prince spoke.

At the bottom of the last curving stair, Morin waited. He pressed a finger to his lips and bade them follow.

It was a long time of silence walking the dim, twisting passages with only the sound of their footsteps to keep them company, but Ean could sense the desperation behind this endeavor, so he was careful not to compromise them in any way.

At last Morin reached a door and opened it to usher them inside.

Ean drew up short at what he found there.

The round stone-walled room was warmed by oddly smokeless braziers, which illumined three faces Ean never imagined finding together. Gydryn sat in an armchair close beside his mother, holding her hand in his lap, and the Fourth Vestal stood before them. He turned at Ean's entrance.

"Welcome, son," the king said, and with the slightest tinge of annoyance, he added, "Fynnlar."

"Uncle," Fynn replied cheerily.

"Please, come in, both of you."

Morin closed and bolted the door behind them, and then the Vestal walked the circumference of the room with his eyes closed as if listening to the stone walls. Reaching the point at which he'd begun, he opened his eyes and nodded to the king.

"Ean," said his father, "Fynnlar, what you are about to hear can never leave this room."

"Because of the nature of this information," the Fourth Vestal added, coming toward them, "I must have your agreement to submit to a binding."

Fynn blanched. "Thanks, all the same, but I've already eaten—"

"Fynnlar," the king rumbled, "if you speak another word while in this room, I will ask the Vestal to bind your tongue as well as your will."

Fynn looked sickly at him.

"Do I have your agreement, gentlemen?" Raine asked.

Ean nodded. He had no idea what a binding would entail, but if it meant getting the answers he'd been promised, he could endure it.

Raine stopped before Ean and placed a hand on his shoulder. The Vestal's eyes looked starry in the muted light of the room. "Relax your mind, Ean. You'll feel strange, like something crawling in your head. Don't fight it or it will become very painful."

Ean nodded, holding his gaze.

And then he felt exactly what the Vestal had described. A mouse crawled and scratched inside his skull, making random muscles inadvertently twitch. Here a finger, there an arm, down low at the back of his other knee…his thigh. It was intensely unsettling and required a great deal of self-control to keep from trying to push the mouse away. Finally he heard Raine's voice, but he could see that the Vestal's mouth wasn't moving. This, too, was disquieting.

You will not speak of what you hear tonight, came Raine's voice eerily inside his head. *If questioned directly about what you hear tonight, you will not be able to remember the question. If interrogated, you will make up plausible truths but will not be able to speak of what you hear in this room. If truthread, you will remember only my words and present no memories of what comes hereafter. If forced, the memory of what you learn tonight will retreat to the furthest reaches of your consciousness and will not return save by command of my own voice, which cannot be imitated by another. In such a case, you will continue to act on anything learned here without knowing why, only knowing that you must.*

Thusly are you bound, Ean val Lorian, until such time as I alone may remove this binding from upon you.

Ean blinked out of his daze. He saw that Raine had removed his hand from his shoulder and was watching him inquisitively.

"Is…is there more?" Ean asked.

Raine smiled. "It is done." He turned to Fynnlar.

"Couldn't we, I don't know, just skip this part?" Fynn whined. "I'm getting really tired of having you in my head."

"Not nearly as tired as I am of being there, Fynnlar," Raine returned.

Ean gazed curiously at his cousin, who shrugged and grumbled, "As if I could *tell* you about it."

Then Raine had his hand on Fynn's shoulder and the royal cousin's eyes glazed over.

Morin approached holding out a goblet of wine. Ean stared at it uncomprehendingly until he realized the man was offering him a drink. The gesture seemed so extraordinarily misplaced, having Morin d'Hain offering him anything pleasant…

"Ean, come and sit," his mother said, indicating the armchair to her left.

He felt a little dazed.

"It passes," Errodan advised. "Drink your wine."

Ean looked down and realized he was holding the goblet Morin had handed him, though he didn't remember taking it.

"It passes, dear," his mother said again. "Drink. It will help."

Ean did, and by the time Morin was handing a goblet to Fynn, he did feel more himself. There was no time to reflect on the experience, however, for his father began at once.

"There is much to tell, and little time to tell it, for ere morning comes you must depart."

"Where—" Ean began, but his father cut him off.

"All questions in their time, Ean. For now, you must listen." He took a moment to gather his thoughts then looked around the room at those assembled. "Five years ago," the king began, "soon after your brother's ship was lost, the Fourth Vestal came to me," and he looked to Raine.

"As you know," the Vestal offered, "I have ties to the Veneisean underground, a group known as the Brotherhood of the Seven Stones. Many years ago, the Brotherhood heard rumors—whispers only—of a plot to overthrow the Eagle Throne. Normally, I would not become involved in such matters, but in short order, this plot was linked to a certain growing religious movement that threatened the stability of our race."

"You speak of the Prophet Bethamin," Ean concluded.

"Indeed. We had no evidence, of course. And when I say whispers, Ean, I do not mean the kind spoken aloud. The link to Bethamin was a tenuous thread so fragile I could barely afford to think of it. I knew it must be investigated, however, for this was the kind of whisper that resonated with too much truth."

"His Excellency came to me," the king continued, "at a time when every lead we'd investigated had withered into hopelessness. It was clear that the conspiracy was deeper than we imagined, but it wasn't until the Fourth Vestal spoke to us that we realized just how deeply rooted it was."

"We formed a plan, the three of us," Errodan said then. "I was to take you safely across the bay until you were grown. It had to look like a rift had formed between your father and I. Only then might you be safe enough to avoid the eye of Death which had already found your brothers, my sons."

"You see, Ean," the king clarified with a heavy sigh, "we now understand that this plot is centered on the succession." He grunted sardonically and shook his head, adding, "It seems *I* am easily dispensed with at any opportune time. It is the succession which concerns them. We still aren't sure why."

"You had to seem out of favor, Ean," Errodan explained. "If there was a chance Gydryn would not support your claims to the throne, we hoped you might be safe from their schemes—at least long enough to grow up." She squeezed her husband's hand at this and brought it to her lips, and they exchanged a look of longing, adoration, and love.

Ean realized only then the sacrifice his parents had made to protect his life. That all of this time they'd truly loved one another, that everything said and done was only to ensure his future…

In a choked voice, he asked, "Why now? There must've been a reason you brought me home now. It couldn't have been about my coming of age."

"No," the king agreed heavily.

Morin came and refilled Ean's goblet. "We still haven't confirmed the mastermind behind your eldest brother's death," the Spymaster said. "I am not without means and ways, as you may have heard, but even I have been unable to discover the truth of his murder."

"I thought it was the Emir," Ean said, looking to his father for clarification. "It's the whole reason we went to war on M'Nador's behalf. The *Dawn Chaser*—"

"At the time, we believed in the intelligence we'd received," Gydryn interrupted resolutely, long accepting of the truth that he had sent both his sons to their deaths. "Now, we have reason to suspect the information was false—due in no small measure to Morin's effectiveness."

Ean frowned at the Spymaster, to which Morin smiled. "You are no doubt wondering now how I came into the picture."

"Something like that."

"His Excellency, the Fourth Vestal, enlisted Morin's aide on our behalf," Errodan told Ean. "As you and I were sailing to Edenmar, Morin was traveling here." She cast Morin a grateful look, adding, "Morin's considerable experience has proven invaluable."

At Ean's wondering look, Morin confessed, "I am not *quite* as young as I look, your Highness."

To which Fynn choked into his wine, making a mess of his jacket.

Morin arched a brow at him.

"Three moons ago," the king continued, "we received word from Duke val Whitney that he was returning with a document from Emir al'Abdul-Basir requesting parley."

"The kind of parley where my brother was slain?" Ean asked darkly.

"Indeed," Morin murmured.

Ean remembered Fynn's warning from earlier that night—what now seemed ages ago. "And you want me to go," he realized.

"No!" all four of the adults denied so desperately that Ean drew back in his seat from the force of their reply.

"No, Ean," Raine stressed again. "We want you very, very far from this parley."

"Radov has agreed to attend," Gydryn said, "but the truth is, Ean, we don't think we can't trust him any more than we can trust Abdul-Basir."

Morin said, "It has come to our attention that Radov has granted Saldaria its independence."

Ean stared at him, stunned. "I thought after the War of the Lakes..."

"He swore on his father's grave that Saldaria would never be a free province, tis true," Morin said, "and never a more obstinate bull of a man was born than Radov abin Hadorin."

"What could make him renege on his vow?" Ean wondered.

"Tis a safe assumption that the Prophet Bethamin had something to do with it," Morin muttered, "since he rules the province and has the most to gain from its independence."

"This knowledge is a closely guarded secret, Ean," Gydryn said. "We don't believe Radov is aware that we know of his close association with the Prophet, or of Saldaria's newfound freedom, and we need to keep it that way."

"Of course," Ean murmured. He frowned at the goblet in his hands. "Then... what will you do?" He lifted his gaze to his father.

"I will go to the parley," Gydryn said, and he squeezed Errodan's hand again. She in turn looked pale, but resolved.

Ean immediately understood the peril inherent in this decision. "But surely Loran—"

"It must be me, Ean," his father said. "It must be me because Morwyk is growing desperate."

"Morwyk." Ean had forgotten all about him. "How does Morwyk play into this?" he asked, but then he remembered Morin's admonishment, *There are always new actors on the stage, but this play has but one director.*

"We suspect he is allied with the Prophet," Gydryn explained. "Bethamin's Ascendants are mysteriously finding their way inside our borders despite strict commands to the army patrols. My men have been ordered to stay clear of Morwyk's lands. It is the obvious answer."

"So he shouts in fear of Saldaria while dealing with them in secret."

"A tried and true tactic of the seditious," Morin pointed out. "Quite predictable, actually."

"And now we come to you, my son," Gydryn said in a tone of aching sorrow. "I must travel to the parley to give the Duke of Morwyk his chance to claim my kingdom. We believe he will stage a coup in my absence. It is nearly as certain as the trap that awaits me in Taj al'Jahana."

"But why, father?" his plea sounded that of a much younger boy, and indeed, Ean felt his father's imminent loss as acutely as the day five years gone that he'd first set sail for Edenmar.

"In order to reveal Morwyk's alliances," Raine said after a brief silence in which the king and queen both seemed choked for words.

Ean looked to the Vestal.

"Events progress," Raine told him, "around the world. It becomes increasingly important to reveal the network of Bethamin's allies."

"And you'll sacrifice my father in the bargain?" Ean challenged hotly.

"Bethamin is a scourge upon the land!" Raine replied with uncharacteristic heat, pinning him with such force of will that Ean felt the declaration rumble through his chest like near thunder.

"I do not walk blithely toward death, my son," Gydryn assured him. "There is one other who knows of our undertaking who will be there to help me, one who makes the ultimate sacrifice, for he walked knowingly into the Prophet's embrace."

How Ean connected it so quickly was a surprise even to himself. "Kjieran van Stone," he murmured. "You sent your truthreader to spy on the Prophet."

Raine cast him a respectful look as he nodded. "I bound Kjieran to this quest, even as I bound you and Fynnlar, and everyone else here, though with a binding much more intricate and penetrating, for such was needed if any part of him meant to withstand Bethamin's 'purifying' fire," and the scathing disgust in his tone left little question of how he felt about the latter.

Ean couldn't imagine anything *more* penetrating than the bond Raine had just instilled in his head. He didn't envy Kjieran his task.

"So you begin to see," Raine surmised from the grimace on Ean's face. "Even so, I do not know how much the binding will protect him."

"Surely Bethamin isn't more powerful than yourself, my lord," Morin said.

Raine turned him a dire look. "I have never so much as laid eyes upon the Prophet. He hides like a snake deep in his temple in Tambarré. If he is merely a truthreader like any other—"

"A truthreader?" Ean said, startled. "The Prophet is an Adept?"

"If he is a truthreader like any other," the Vestal repeated more firmly, "there is no fear, but if he is more..."

"More?"

Raine shook his head, unwilling to expound on his fears. "Bethamin's influence is corruptive, Ean. The longer Kjieran stays bound to him, the more imperiled he becomes. Only time will tell if my working can withstand the test. It is a chance we are forced to take."

"Bethamin threatens us all, my darling," Errodan said. "Not one kingdom, but many. We must do what we can."

"So you will go to M'Nador," Ean said, looking back to his father.

"And you must be far, far away from Dannym when Morwyk moves on the throne," his father replied in turn.

The king looked to Raine, who nodded once. Ean felt something in his mind, like the light snapping of fingers, and instinctively knew Raine's time of binding had ended. Gydryn stood, helping Errodan also to stand. They came toward, Ean, who rose as well.

"This is farewell, my son," the king said. Ean saw tears in his eyes.

Errodan threw her arms about her son's neck and peppered his cheek with motherly kisses. In his ear, she whispered, "I love you with all that I am."

Ean managed a swallow, confusion welling. He hugged her tightly in return, and then moved to embrace his father.

"Not the homecoming I desired," Gydryn murmured.

Ean held his gaze though his eyes stung with unshed tears. Gydryn took his hand and placed something in it, and Ean looked down to see an ornate silver ring lying in his palm. The sapphire it contained sparkled even in the muted light. "You are a val Lorian son," his father said in a choked voice. "This has always been and will always be yours."

Ean stared at his family's royal ring feeling conflicted. Both of his brothers had worn such a ring to their deaths. Swallowing, Ean slid the ring on his first finger and looked back to his father.

Gydryn gave him a tragic smile. "One day, with Epiphany's Grace, we will have time to learn each other's ways again."

"I pray it so, father," Ean said, his chest tight with emotion that he strangely found no outlet for.

Morin unbarred the door to let the king and queen leave, and then locked it again behind them.

Raine walked to the table to pour himself a goblet of wine. "You can speak now, Fynnlar."

"*Blaarghh!*" Fynn blathered, shaking his jowls as if to dispel a foul taste. "I *hate* it when you do that!"

"I'd no idea you had such a history with the Fourth Vestal, Fynn," Ean observed, suddenly grateful for the levity Fynn could be counted on to provide.

"Oh, we go way back," Fynn grumbled.

"We are quite well-acquainted, your cousin and I," Raine agreed. He motioned to Ean to retake his seat and came to sit in the chair opposite him, with Fynn between. Morin hovered in the shadows, but Ean remained aware of his presence. He was intensely curious to know who Morin d'Hain really was.

"Your highness, Morin tells me you spoke to Franco Rohre."

"Yes."

Raine took a sip of his wine, murmuring, "He's vanished, you know."

Ean blinked at him. "I just saw him at the banquet—"

"He took leave of Ysolde before midnight and didn't return. I don't expect that he will."

"I thought he was in your employ."

Raine cracked a humorless smile. "I believe his loyalties to me were preceded by those to another." He crossed booted ankle over knee. "What did you and Franco speak of?"

"I told Morin already—"

"Yes, the Geshaiwyn. That was more helpful than you know. Geshaiwyn are contracted through only one agent at present."

"The Karakurt," Fynn supplied. At Ean's curious look, he shrugged and added, "I heard there was a contract on your life, cousin. I didn't know Geshaiwyn had accepted it until tonight."

"I am more interested in the other things you spoke of," Raine murmured. His expression became solemn. "This is very important, Ean. Please, you must trust in me."

Ean felt he was betraying Franco to say anything at all, but it was difficult to know who to claim allegiance to anymore. If Franco served another… "He…we talked of my pattern," Ean reluctantly confessed, glancing at Morin, "and he told me it was… he said…"

"The Pattern of Life," Morin finished when it was clear that Ean could not, or would not.

The prince turned him a rigid look. "Just so. But I don't understand any of this."

"Yours is the Pattern of Life, and it isn't," Raine said. "The truth is complicated and requires an understanding of Patterning. As for why you can see it, surely you must understand what that means…"

Ean shook his head.

"Seven hells, Ean, don't be so obtuse!" Fynn complained. "Once you work the Pattern of Life, it forever becomes part of you. Even I know that much."

"But I've never worked any pattern, Fynn."

"Not in this lifetime, maybe," Fynn muttered. He downed his wine in one gigantic gulp and looked around for more.

Ean heard the words but somehow couldn't comprehend them. "Do you mean to say…you think *I* have…Returned?"

Morin and Raine exchanged a look, and the former asked, "Ean, do you recall anything strange happening while you were a captive of the Shade?"

Ean leveled him a flat glare. "Seriously? You're asking me this?"

"Something unusual happening around yourself—something not caused by others," Morin clarified.

Ean thought back to those crazed days, but he could think of nothing. He shook his head.

Raine looked disappointed. "Returned," he confirmed, "of that you can be certain." He settled the prince a tragic look then. "Our race is dying, Ean. Perhaps you don't know, but the concept of the Returning, as mentioned in your Litany for the Departed, comes directly from the *Sobra I'ternin*, the Adept race's most treasured text."

"There is no afterlife," Ean quoted, "there is only the Returning."

"Just so." Raine looked troubled. "An Adept is inextricably tied to his strand,

and when we say inextricably, we mean even death cannot sever the link. Adepts are reborn as Adepts. This is known as the Returning. Typically an Adept is either born knowing his gift or grows into it during adolescence. Over the past several centuries, however, the race has been dying. We Vestals have long suspected that Adepts are still Returning but not awakening."

"This is just one part of the problem," Morin said.

Ean felt these facts were certainly problematic enough on their own. "What's the other part?"

"My oath-brother is a grave threat, Ean. His return can only herald terrible times to come. Franco's disappearance is a perfect example of one of many inauspicious events since his return. You probably know Franco was one of the Fifty Companions—you're familiar with them, surely."

"Yes."

"Recently—since my oath-brother's return, in fact—many of these specific fifty Adepts have vanished."

"Or *have been* vanished," Fynn muttered into his wine. He'd somehow managed to refill his goblet without Ean noticing. "You know, more *permanently*."

"Your oath-brother," Ean said slowly, holding the Vestal's gaze. "Do you mean the Fifth Vestal?"

Raine settled him a telling look. "The very same. It was he who sent his Shade to claim you and slay Creighton Khelspath. Ean," Raine said, stressing the prince's name with an undertone of caution, "your father told me you wish to seek out this Shade. Is this true?"

"I haven't had a change of heart since this morning, if that's what you mean."

"What he means, Ean," Morin inserted, "is to know that you understand the peril you are in should you undertake such a foolhardy quest."

"I think I have a fair idea, Morin," Ean said caustically.

"I cannot forbid you from seeking the creature, Ean," Raine said, his gaze compelling, "but I implore you not to do so. It matters not in the end whether your life is claimed by Morwyk's assassins or the blade of another; in either case, Bethamin's dark work is done."

Ean regarded him carefully. "Yet I cannot stay here, you've made that plain." Looking around at the others then, he asked, "So. Where do we go from here?"

"To hell," Fynn muttered and belched gratuitously.

TWENTY-EIGHT

'One does not long bask in the glow of a god's favor; 'tis a perilous transient state indeed.'

– The Agasi wielder Markal Morrelaine

Trell had a fair idea where to find Lily, and he and the Khurds reached the canyon with its little river as dawn flamed in the eastern sky. Stopping the horses in the shadow of a high cliff, Trell conferred with his two unlikely accomplices. "They'll be expecting us," he warned. "We'll have to take out their sentries or we won't stand a chance of surprising them. Which of you is the best knife-fighter?"

"I am," said Kamil.

"Good. Climb to the canyon rim and follow the ridge. We'll be counting on you to eliminate their guards."

"It would be my pleasure, Trell of the Tides."

"We will give you a quarter-hour to precede us."

Kamil drew a thin dagger from his belt, clenched it in his teeth, and scrambled agilely up the jagged canyon wall. Something about his movement reminded Trell of Istalar, another good man who had willingly traded his life to save another's.

They waited in silence to give Kamil time to find and dispatch the guards. As thin violet clouds striated the blue sky, Trell nodded to Sayid and they headed into the canyon. The tributary flowed to their right as they followed a footpath single file, the desert horses surefooted in the rocky sand.

They came upon Kamil's first victim at the top of a rise. The man lay broken across a bolder jutting from the hillside about ten paces above them. The bodies of two more guards littered their path as they continued deeper into the ravine, whose walls were narrowing with every step.

Trell took the time to prepare himself, a ritual he'd done many times in his short span of adulthood; while Ware and the others teased him about spending too much time dwelling in his head, they'd never had occasion to fault his mental preparedness. Trell could clear his mind and find a state of alertness in mere seconds if conditions required it, and once focused, nothing disturbed his singular concentration.

He heard the Nadoriin long before he saw them, though he didn't need his heightened awareness to do so, for their raucous laughter echoed harshly off the ravine's rocky walls. Hearing it disturbed Trell, for the laughter seemed to hold a vicious, jeering undertone.

The moment they came in view of the camp, Trell knew why, and the sight turned his stomach, rousing a sense of moral fury.

A dozen Nadoriin gathered in a semi-circle around Lily. They were tormenting her, making a game of tearing off her dress a few strips at a time, and there was little enough left of it now. As Trell watched, a man grabbed a handful of her shift and pulled her into his lap while the others goaded him on. He fondled a crying Lily like a common whore, then roughly shoved her back into the center. A bald man grabbed her around the waist and pushed his hand up her skirt, forcing his way with her.

Trell looked to Sayid and saw the same cold fury in his dark eyes. The desert tribes held women in the highest regard—though Trell was sometimes at odds with the way they displayed their respect—but Lily was a nobleman's daughter and a slip of a girl at that. Their treatment of her was unconscionable.

Four men turned as Trell and Sayid rode out of the canyon shadows into the pale morning light. Trell saw the first Nadoriin hand reaching for his dagger even as his brethren turned to see what had caught his eye.

The bald man slung Lily into the dirt and stood. "Well, well," he gloated in the desert tongue, resting hands on hips where a scimitar gleamed at his wide belt. "So this must be the young and very stupid, soon to be dead, Korin Ahlamby."

In that moment Trell understood the dynamics of this meeting, and he shifted tactics instantly. "I *am* Korin," he returned with just the right touch of indignation in his tone. Using an inflection of the desert tongue that farmers used when calling their pigs, he continued, "Unhand my betrothed, you bastard son of a camp whore, and I will offer you a clean death, however undeserved it be."

The Nadoriin's expression hardened, replaced by a steely glare that could only be a thirst for blood. As if by silent signal, eleven men stood as one and drew weapons against Trell and Sayid.

Well, Trell had seen worse odds, but not lately.

Trell pulled his sword and Sayid his scimitar.

The Nadoriin rushed them with a blood cry.

Trell heaved on his reins and Gendaia reared angrily, bringing her hooves down upon the skull of the closest Nadoriin while Trell slashed at another, his sword opening the man's chest. Two more grabbed for him, and Trell kicked and elbowed them off while managing to gouge a fourth in the neck before someone pulled him backwards off Gendaia.

He twisted as he fell, taking an elbow in the mouth but yanking free of their hold. Swearing as his hip landed on a rock, he rolled beneath Gendaia, who reared again with a scream of protest and then tore away from the man who was making a grab for her reins. On his feet again, Trell drove his sword into the gut of the closest man just as the latter was raising his own blade. Trell maneuvered as his attacker crumbled, elbowing the next man in the nose as he was approaching from behind. Even as the latter fell back, Trell spun and speared him through the heart. He skipped aside as two more men flung themselves toward him, then he rushed in again to close blades. His fist found the jaw of the first, sending him sprawling in a splay of blood, and his sword claimed the other. Another man barreled into him, and Trell brought his sword hilt down on the back of his head, hearing the bone crunch.

As he fell, Trell swung to block the advance of yet another Nadoriin. Their blades clashed to the hilt, and their eyes locked.

The leader of the Nadoriin was not a handsome man. His face was marred by a long scar that pinched the corner of one eye, dragging it downward in a slant that exposed part of the inner lid, but his sword gleamed with a deadly edge, and his shoulders were solid as a bull's. Staring at Trell in close proximity, the man's expression flicked from surprise to anger as he realized Trell wasn't the proclaimed Korin.

"Northern Pig!" the leader hissed. "You'll pay dearly for your interference."

Trell pushed the leader off him and danced back. For a moment, they stalked each other, and Trell used the time to catch his breath and judge the remaining resistance; he could hear Sayid fighting behind him, but at least seven of the Nadoriin lay dead or dying.

The leader advanced, and Trell met his assault with careful precision, the steel of his sword singing true as their weapons met, shared a deadly caress and separated again. Trell weighed every move the older man made, gauging...calculating. The Nadoriin lunged with a forceful sweep, but Trell easily sidestepped the blow and returned with his own, marking the man's shoulder with a gouge that drew blood. The Nadoriin swore and advanced on Trell with renewed force and attention, and Trell went on the defensive, parrying blow after blow until his arms ached.

Yet with every motion, Trell learned something about the Nadoriin. He noticed that his opponent favored his right, and each time he led with his left, he overextended, leaving himself open. Trell took a calculated risk, knowing from years of experience that knowledge gained with minimal bloodshed was worth the price. He let the other take him on the defensive again—though Raine's truth, the power of his strokes threatened to knock his blade from his hands—but he held true despite a near fall, and in the right moment let the man's blade cut him. Fire flamed in his upper arm as the wound bled, but he knew too that it was superficial. As he'd suspected, the Nadoriin thought he held the upper hand now and in his haste to finish Trell he overextended his reach. With sudden unwavering intent, Trell moved inside his guard and drove his blade into the hollow beneath the Nadoriin's ribcage, expecting it would be the death blow.

But he had underestimated the man's strength. With a cry of rage, the Nadoriin wrenched Trell's bloodied blade out of his abdomen and flung it aside. He lunged for Trell, throttling him as they slammed into the earth. The Nadoriin quickly pinned him, and Trell struggled against his hold, kicking with both knees to try to knock the man off, but the Nadoriin's position was superior. Glaring down at Trell, he coughed blood, growled an oath, and yanked a dagger from his boot. "Shall I start with your ears, or your eyes?"

Ever grateful for the training so ingrained in him, Trell swung up his legs and caught the bigger man around the chest. His boots caught beneath the joining of neck and jaw, and one powerful thrust pitched him backwards. Trell dove for his sword as the Nadoriin was righting himself and swung it up just as the man let out a blood cry and jumped onto him again. Trell grunted from the impact, seeing a brief flash of sparks before his eyes, but that time his sword impaled the man all the way through, the bloody tip extending beneath his right shoulder. The Nadoriin's eyes bulged, his face turned crimson, and then he collapsed.

Trell shoved him off and got to his feet, blood-drenched and breathing hard.

"Trell—"

Trell looked toward Lily, but just then Sayid cried out and Trell spun to see him falling to his knees. A cascade of rocks alerted him to the two Nadoriin scrambling down the steep side of the ravine. One of them paused to reload a crossbow. As Trell was deciding how to deal with them, Kamil appeared behind them, higher up on the ridge. He sent two daggers flying. The deadly steel soared straight and true and sunk deep into each man's back. They fell from on high, dead before they landed in a puff of dust. Trell exhaled in relief, fervently hoping they were the last of them.

He rapidly turned back to Lily. She stood in the center of the clearing hugging her arms, her eyes wild; clearly she was just managing to hold herself together. She wore only her shift, torn and ragged, and her dark hair was a mass of tangles, but she maintained a noble bearing that denied the degradation she'd just endured.

Trell quickly took her into his arms. "Ah Lily," he whispered into her hair as she pressed her face against his chest. "I'm so sorry."

Safe at last, she burst into tears.

Kamil and Sayid approached, the latter pressing a wad of cloth to his thigh. "The bolt passed through," he told Trell in the desert tongue, having noted his concerned look.

"What do you want to do about them, Ama-Kai'alil?" Kamil asked, nodding to the dead.

Trell knew what he would do, but he deferred instead to Lily. "What say you, milady? What death shroud do these men deserve?"

Lily drew away from him and wiped her eyes. She looked at the two Khurds who'd come to her rescue, and her lower lip trembled. "The blackest, Ama-Kai'alil," she whispered.

"The lady has spoken. We leave them unblessed and unforgiven."

"Let it be so," Sayid declared darkly, nodding his assent.

"Let it be so," Kamil agreed.

While Kamil reclaimed his daggers from the fallen and Sayid hastily bound his leg, Trell tied a strip of cloth around the wound in his arm and then set loose the Nadori steeds. His shoulder was beginning to ache from the gash he'd taken, but he knew from experience that a good cleaning with a saltwater wash would restore it good as new.

Lily watched him quietly the whole time, hugging knees to her chest. When he returned to her side, she turned frightened doe-eyes up to him. "I c-can't…s-stop sh-shaking," she said. She wiped tears from her face again with the back of both hands. "I c-can't stop crying…either."

He helped her stand up. "You've been through a lot tonight."

"So have…you," she stammered as he swept her into his arms, "b-but you're not even sh-shaking."

"I am bleeding, though," he said with a grin.

"As if that p-proves anything other than your b-bravery," she said, but she gave him a weak smile.

Trell felt her shaking in his arms. "Hold on a minute." He set her back down and returned to the Nadori campsite where he rummaged through their packs, eventually returning with a thick woolen blanket. "Here, Lily." He wrapped it around her shoulders and pulled her close again. Trell suspected the night's terror, more than the chill, was affecting her now, but sometimes little gestures could calm the mind. And it wasn't seemly for a highborn lady to ride around in naught but her shift.

Kamil approached with Gendaia and his own mount in tow. "We should leave this place, Ama-Kai'alil," he said. "Death begets death."

Trell nodded. He looked Lily up and down in a single sweep of grey eyes. "Are you sure you're fit to ride?"

"J-just so long as I'm n-next to you."

Trell picked her up and placed her on Gendaia. He swung into the saddle behind her and wrapped an arm protectively around her waist. Sayid led the way out of the ravine.

They made most of the trip in silence. Trell hugged Lily close as they rode, his thoughts dwelling darkly upon a father so bereft of compassion that he would send such dishonorable men in search of his own daughter.

They were safely out of the canyon and riding again beside the Cry to the hum of riversong when Lily gave a long sniff, wiped her eyes and asked, "Why do the Khurds call you Man of the Tides?"

"Kai'alil is the name of the fishing village where they found me," he said into her ear, "before I was taken to Duan'Bai."

"What do you mean?"

Trell had forgotten that he'd only told the women part of his story.

Lily mistook his silence for hesitation. "I'm sorry. It's just…twice you appeared at a time when I thought all hope was lost, but you're such an…an unlikely hero—if you'll forgive me, Trell. I only mean, well…you're a Northman who speaks the desert tongue—but with a Basi accent—and you risked your life to save a runaway Nadoriin from her own father's men. You must admit these are strange and…conflicting facts.

Trell conceded her point. "The truth is, Lily," he answered quietly in her ear, "I've spent many years in service of the Emir."

She turned to him wide-eyed. "But you—you fight with a *kingdom blade.* Are you not of a noble line?"

Trell caught his breath at the familiar phrase.

'The time has come for them both to flower, these, my kingdom blades.' Words from the Mage's journal took on new meaning.

To cover his surprise, he said, "As I mentioned before, my heritage has somewhat eluded me, Lily."

Lily was still contorting her neck in order to stare at him. "So how does a Northman come to personally serve al'Abdul-Basir without converting?"

Trell wasn't wont to talk of his story yet again, but Lily had just been through a terrible trial, and if his tale took her mind off the Nadoriin… So he told her of waking in the village called The Tides, being taken to Duan'Bai and raised as the Emir's adopted son, and his subsequent life with the Emir. Why he felt he should trust Lily with this knowledge when he hadn't trusted the sisters with it wasn't something he could explain. He seemed to make strange decisions in the presence of Naiadithine's waters.

Lily absorbed the newest details of his story raptly. When he was finished, she asked, "So they found you just lying on the beach with nothing but your sword?"

He gave a rueful grin, remembering how he'd swum through an underground river without giving up that sword.

She stared at him. "It's…incredible."

"I'm sure many have endured similarly unlikely circumstances, Lily."

She shook her head. "No, I—"

But the words were lost, for just then they rounded the rise and came in view of the campsite. Fhionna and Aishlinn both came running down the trail, and soon the women were embracing. Cries of joy were mixed with exclamations of dismay at Lily's condition, and they quickly rushed her off without another word for Trell or the men, though none of the latter took offense.

Trell dismounted and let Kamil see to their horses, for with Aishlinn returned, he was anxious to learn of Ammar's condition. He found Radiq and Ammar sitting together around the fire, the latter looking slightly peaked and somewhat round-eyed but otherwise whole.

"Ammar." Trell placed a hand on his shoulder as he knelt down beside him.

Ammar turned with a beatific smile. "Ama-Kai'alil," he greeted, "you must someday nearly die so that the Goddess may heal you. All men should know such ecstasy."

Trell shifted his gaze to Radiq, who shrugged. "He's been that way since the *nymphae* Aishlinn brought him back. She says it will pass."

Trell placed a hand in thanks on Radiq's shoulder, then he excused himself to wash up in the icy river. After donning a clean shirt, he rejoined Radiq and Ammar. The former handed Trell a bowl of spiced beans and flatbread warmed at the fire. While he ate, Trell allowed Radiq to tend his arm.

The sun was falling low in the west when Lily and the sisters joined them at the fire. The spicy stew had warmed Trell's belly, and his arm felt better since being tended. The cut was deeper than he'd thought, and he felt some numbness in his fingertips which he hoped would fade as the wound healed.

Lily looked much improved after the sisters' ministrations. They'd clearly helped her wash body and hair, and now she wore a proper dress again. She sat down very close beside Trell and pulled her long skirts down around her feet. "Oh…thank you," she said in her accented desert speech as Radiq offered her a bowl of stew.

"How are you, milady?" Trell asked, grey eyes looking her over.

"I've been better," she confessed, then added with a rueful grin, "but lately I've been much worse. I have you to thank for the improvement."

"There were three of us who came for you, if memory serves."

Lily glanced at Radiq. "I meant no disrespect," she told him.

"None taken," he said.

She switched to the common tongue. "Do you prefer this language over the desert tongue, Trell of the Tides?"

He shrugged and answered in kind, "They are the same to me."

"I would think you would find one tongue more comfortable, more uniquely you," she said.

It took Trell a moment to realize she'd spoken the second line in Agasi. He grinned at her and replied in Bemothi, "Are you testing me, milady?"

She laughed happily and replied in kind, "What language don't you speak?"

"Avatari has proven troublesome," he said with a wink, switching back to the desert tongue.

She smiled, but her expression sobered as she gazed at him. "Would that I could properly reward you—all of you," and she included the Khurds in her gaze. Looking back to Trell, she frowned and said, "Are you certain you will accept no coin from us?"

Radiq lifted his dark eyes to Trell upon hearing this news, but Trell only replied evenly, "None, milady."

Lily sighed and nestled the bowl of stew in her lap, its steam drifting up to mingle with her unbound hair. "Once I might've rewarded your bravery with any wish, but now...now I've been disavowed. My father's men made it clear they were only keeping me alive as bait for Korin. *Him* my father wants returned for torture."

Trell lifted brows, surprised by the cavalier manner in which she spoke such words. "Surely they meant only to scare you, Lily."

She shook her head, and her dark eyes were resigned. "No, in this I think they spoke Raine's truth. My father is not a forgiving man, and I have too many times betrayed him—or so he certainly believes."

Kamil and Sayid joined them at the fire, silently taking seats beside Radiq, their eyes dark beneath their turbans. "But it's—it's better this way, I think," Lily went on, sounding immensely frail, as if she tried to convince herself more than Trell. "Korin and I can be together now, and...and so long as my father is occupied with his war, he may not even remember to send men to hunt us down."

The finality in her tone, the utter conviction that her days were numbered, made Trell only feel that much more protective of her. He wondered if she was truly so bold, or if she spoke the words glibly, without actually acknowledging the terrible fears that inspired them. He dared not touch upon such deep wounds while more recent ones still healed, however, so he asked instead, "Your father is involved with the war?"

She gave him a strange look. "But of course, don't you...?" Her eyebrows made a little V that lifted with her surprise as she looked around the fire at all of the Khurds and back to Trell. "You...you don't know who I am?"

"Should we?"

She looked worried now and turned to Fhionna. "You said you told him everything, so I—I thought..."

"About Korin," Trell clarified, lifting his gaze suspiciously to Fhionna, who was looking extremely culpable. "She said your father was a nobleman."

Lily covered her mouth with her hands and turned from Trell to Fhionna and back again. "It...I guess it doesn't matter anymore, does it?" she whispered. Her eyes flitted around the fire, taking in the many foreign faces who watched her with unreadable dark eyes. "After all, I'm not Leilah anymore. I am just...Lily now."

But Trell had heard her given name, and the realization came as a shock, even to him. "Leilah," he repeated, staring at her. "You're Leilah n'abin Hadorin?"

The Khurds hissed an oath, but Lily gazed at Trell unblinking. "No, Trell of the Tides," she whispered. "I'm just...Lily. Leilah n'abin Hadorin died in the Haden Gorge at the hands of her father's guard."

Trell lifted his gaze to the Khurds across the fire. From everything he'd seen of them thus far, he suspected they would keep this confidence, and in that he wasn't disappointed. Sayid met his gaze with an almost imperceptible nod. So. He looked back to Lily. "Very well. You are Lily, soon to be wed of Korin Ahlamby." He settled a long disapproving look on Fhionna before saying, "Rest tonight. At dawn we ride hard for Sakkalaah."

Three pairs of feminine eyes watched him as he stood, and he felt their worried looks follow him until he was out of their sight.

Feeling the need to be alone, Trell walked to the river's edge and followed upstream until he came to a grove of stunted trees overhanging a deep pool. The riversong there invited of peace, so he knelt down and washed his hands and face. The water was icy and instantly numbed his fingers, but it was somehow cleansing to his troubled mind—Raine's truth, he was going to need absolution after this. Saving the daughter of the Emir's mortal enemy...he wondered if the Emir would understand; he prayed that he would.

Trell pushed wet hands through his hair and then dropped his arms and stared at the dark water. He feared with ever growing certainty that there would come a day when he would be forced to choose one loyalty over another. Already his convictions had been tested several times, and he was a long way from finding his family. If he knew anything at all about them, however, it was that they were not the Emir's subjects; what if they required him to denounce his allegiance to the Emir?

More troubling even than this: could he really be loyal to two opposing masters? If his new-found family did require him to forswear the truths he now held, *could* he do it? Was it possible for him to resume the beliefs he'd been taught as a child if they conflicted with the convictions he upheld as a man?

It was dark when he returned to camp. The women had retired into their makeshift tent, which had been haphazardly pieced together from the remnants of their first one, and the Khurds were playing a game of *mancala* salvaged from the attack. Trell offered to take the first shift, and he settled in beneath a twisted tree to watch the moon rise. It seemed like only minutes before Kamil came to relieve him, however, for he was preoccupied with thoughts of the many unusual women in his recent life.

Trell took a moment to check on Gendaia, another of his females, and then he found a solitary spot to toss out his bedroll and stretched out with his hands behind his head. The stars were brilliant; Gorion the Archer was rising in the east and Adrennai's Harp hung at midhaven, yet he found himself searching the sky for another constellation, one that had never held much interest to him until a midnight conversation with a Whisper Lord.

But Cephrael's Hand didn't appear that evening, and after a while the rushing roar of the river began to soothe his tangled thoughts. He found his mind drifting, until it landed, like it always did, on the mystery that was both his past and future.

What will life be like outside of the Akkad?

He knew just from speaking the common tongue that the culture of its peoples was very different. In the desert, as in the language itself, there were nuances—huge disparities, actually—in what was said and what was understood. Like the way the Khaz'im had introduced the Khurds by their tribe alone. Trell's knowledge of the ways of the desert peoples allowed him to make the leap from a simple, laconic statement to its complex meaning.

If language reflected the culture of its civilization, then the Akkad was a kingdom of great history, where wisdom was passed down through parable, fable and poem, and learning was substantive and experiential rather than gained through the written word.

The common tongue, in contrast, was explicit almost beyond question, leaving little to no room for interpretation. Its attention to detail bordered on the mundane, and while its cumbersome vocabulary allowed for great creativity in terms of elocution and poetry—clearly a language invented for the written word—so also did it encourage thoughtless, inane speech, people voicing their thoughts in a careless rush. Thus were its peoples of a similar nature, Trell thought: too often outspoken, too often declaiming without thinking about the impact of the words they chose; too often quick to judge and slow to forgive.

Lily had asked him which tongue seemed more natural to him. Trell really didn't know, but he did prefer the desert tongue, which most Northmen considered difficult to master because of these very aspects of its use. In the desert tongue, a simple phrase had a plethora of meanings—meanings often derived from the parable in which the phrase was first used, thereby necessitating an understanding of the kingdom's history as well as the language itself. With the common tongue, in contrast, a plethora of words were used in place of a simple phrase.

Thus, though it wasn't his first language, Trell had come to find the implicit desert tongue far more appealing than its explicit counterpart—as any thoughtful, scholarly mind would, he felt.

"Deep thoughts, Trell of the Tides?"

Trell opened his eyes to find Lily standing over him. He hadn't heard her approach. "I thought I told you to get some rest," he chided gently, closing his eyes again.

"If I but could," she murmured as she settled down beside him. "It's strange…all of this time I've been so afraid, knowing they chased, yet I slept soundly each night. But now that I'm able to be truly free of fear, my mind won't be at peace."

He turned his head to regard her. "What troubles you, Lily?"

She watched him with an anguished gaze, her expression despairing. "You," she whispered.

"Me?" Trell pushed up onto one elbow. "Why?"

"Yesterday…the Goddess of the Rivers spoke through you."

He grimaced. "Yeah…I don't understand much about that."

"But it's true?" Her tone was anxious, her gaze searching his own. "Naiadithine has spoken to you before? You've heard her whisper?"

Something about the way she said that alerted him to the truth. "You've heard her, too," he said even as he realized it.

She collected her silken dark hair in her hands and pulled it around one shoulder to play with the ends. "When I was nine," she said, not looking at him, "I fell from my father's ship and nearly drowned. I don't remember much about the event, only… only I remember *her*. She was so beautiful. She reached out to me. She told me..." Her voice broke, and she brushed a tear from her cheek as she finished with a wistful smile, "Naiadithine told me to look for the light."

Follow the water, Trell of the Tides.

Trell felt a chill take him.

Lily held his gaze, her expression entreating. "Was it the same for you?"

Strangely unable to find his voice, Trell nodded.

They stared at each other for a long time. Finally, Lily pressed lips together and offered tentatively, "Do you…do you think you may have drowned once, Trell? Could Naiadithine have found you in the sea, even as she found me?"

Trell closed his eyes, thinking of a lovely face floating above him. "It could be so, Lily."

Lily fidgeted with her fingers in her lap. "Naiadithine is compassionate, the sisters say, unlike many of the other desert gods. Most of the time she ignores mortals like us, but on occasion…on occasion a heart opens to her, and she listens."

Trell considered this wisdom. "You're saying that when I was drowning, she heard the…well, the song…in my heart?"

She lifted eyes to meet his. "Yes. Like she heard me, and since our heart-songs gained her notice, she listened."

Trell's brow furrowed as he asked, "Do you know such things, or are you only guessing?"

"Oh no," Lily assured him. "The sisters say it happens all the time. Naiadithine hears and listens a lot, only she very rarely interferes."

"Yet she interfered with you." *The daughter of a prince.*

"And you, Trell of the Tides," Lily returned, her sad, dark eyes mirroring silver in the moonlight. "You she took a special interest in."

TWENTY-NINE

'Do not face Fate with quiet surrender, go boldly forth and claim it.'

– The Second Vestal Dagmar Ranneskjöld

Alyneri and Tanis remained at Ean's banquet until the very end. Early on, her Grace had become involved in discussion with the king's Lord Chamberlain, Matisse val Orin, about the safest means and methods of travel to M'Nador. The Lord Chamberlain had proven a knowledgeable ally and had gracefully offered to handle Farshideh's transport back to Kandori as well as prepare a list of suitable replacements for the position of Alyneri's Seneschal.

Tanis had spent most of the night listening to Fynn's stories of the pirates of Jamaii before the King's Own Guard came in the wee hours with a message for the royal cousin and he begged Tanis's leave. The lad found her Grace again as the hall was clearing. They were headed to their apartments when her Grace was called aside to attend several noblemen who'd been injured in a drunken brawl, and now it was nearing sunrise as they walked wearily back toward the royal wing.

Tanis yawned prodigiously as they neared the massive central chamber often colloquially referred to as 'the Boulevard.' "Your Grace?" asked the boy, his excitement only slightly dampened by his heavy eyelids, which kept trying to close of their own accord, "did you know that the pirates of Jamaii wear silver rings pierced through their ears the way we wear circlets of status? And they pierce a gold ring through one nostril if they've earned the right to captain a ship."

"A pirate ship," Alyneri amended, wishing Tanis had spent the evening with more suitable company. Even that insouciant Tad val Mallonwey was preferable to Fynnlar val Lorian.

Tanis frowned at her tone. "The captain of a pirate ship has to be twice the captain of a naval ship," he pointed out.

She eyed him doubtfully. "Is that so?"

"Yes, your Grace. Fynn says it requires much more skill to command a pirate vessel because of all the battles and thieving and sneaking up on other ships."

"I didn't realized Lord Fynnlar was so experienced," Alyneri muttered.

"He's sailed often with the pirates, your Grace," Tanis said, missing her undertone of disapproval. "Once he was captaining a ship that was almost caught by the Agasi Imperial navy. He had to do some crafty maneuvering to evade them. He told me all about it!"

"Clearly he is a fount of invaluable information."

Tanis frowned at her again.

They came to the Boulevard and headed down the steps and across the wide plaza with its crystal dome still dark in the early hours of morning, but as they neared a group of men wearing the livery of House val Rothschen, the crowd parted and a woman emerged.

"Well, if it isn't the Duchess of Aracine and her noble escort at last," drawled

Ianthe val Rothschen d'Jesune, Marchioness of Wynne.

"Lady Wynne," Alyneri murmured without breaking her stride, but when Ianthe's men fanned out across her path, she slowed and regarded them suspiciously.

"A moment of your time, *Duchess*," said the Marchioness. Her blue eyes were as hard and cruel as the large aquamarine pendant gleaming in the hollow of her throat, the famous stone of her husband's House.

Alyneri paused, noting with some trepidation that the Marchioness' men began encircling her. "What is it, Marchioness?" Alyneri asked impatiently. "We've had a long night."

"Tell me, *Lady* Alyneri," Ianthe said as she neared, "do you have your little 'reader boy undress and wash you, or does he merely sleep on the floor beside your bed like the besotted puppy he portrays?"

Alyneri's eyes flashed. "Lady Wynne, that is most inappropriate."

The Marchioness barked a scornful laugh. "Inappropriate? You wish to lecture me on what is *appropriate? You?*" She clucked critically and looked to her men. "Do you see how she is above herself? She has all the propriety of a camp whore and thinks to instruct me in matters of decorum! This very night she sat beside the king like a courtesan, flaunting her *service* to the crown before the entire assembled nobility!"

Ianthe's men began closing in, and Alyneri's pulse quickened as she viewed the tightening circle. Tanis stiffened beside her. "What is the meaning of this, Lady Wynn?" she managed.

"Has her majesty not told you, my dear? You are to be entrusted into *my* care for a proper upbringing in a true lady's courtly ways." While Alyneri gaped at her, Ianthe looked to her captain, who was closest to Alyneri, and ordered, "Take the boy back to his rooms for the night. We have no more use for him."

"Don't you dare lay a hand on him!" Alyneri demanded in outrage.

"Do it!" snarled the Marchioness.

The captain dutifully reached for Tanis, but the lad was faster. He ducked beneath the captain's grasping hands, sidestepped the soldier beside him, swerved to avoid a third's reach, and free of the circle, sprinted for the royal wing.

Alyneri watched with her hands clenched at her sides, feeling such immeasurable relief that he'd gotten away, yet wishing in some small part that he'd remained to offer her support.

Ianthe snarled an oath at her captain, and Alyneri stared at her, horrified by the encounter. *The rotten, evil, conniving woman!* Alyneri had never experienced such outright hatred for another living being, and she found herself quite unprepared for it.

"Oh, just let him go," Ianthe declared contemptuously as her men turned to chase. "He's just a harmless boy," but her tone clearly declaimed their ineptitude, as well as her own irritation at it. She walked to stand in front of Alyneri and boldly brushed a stray strand of flaxen hair from her shoulder. Alyneri suppressed a chill and held the woman's cold-eyed gaze.

"We have such good times ahead, you and I," Ianthe murmured, and abruptly she slapped her.

Alyneri felt reflexive tears spring unbidden and tasted the salt of blood on her tongue. The moment was so shocking, so appalling, that she had no idea how to react. Anger and grief battled for purchase of her thoughts, but fear had the upper hand. Had the queen really promised her into this hostile woman's care? It seemed an impossibility, yet Ianthe claimed it. *Would she dare pronounce such a thing if it were untrue?*

Ianthe smiled and stepped back to better view the red mark flaming on Alyneri's cheek. She mistook Alyneri's confusion for subservience. "Good. So you understand already who is the mistress and who the pupil. I must admit I had expected more defiance from you, but this submission is far more proper. I am pleased."

Alyneri wanted to scream. She fought back tears and a sense of desperation that constricted her chest, choking her. Her thoughts rapidly sought recourse of action, her eyes darting from face to face, but she found no purchase, saw no escape.

"Tis well you choose to accept your fate," the Marchioness declared, standing tall and triumphant before her, "for the Princess Ysolde is not here to save you this time, secluded as she is no doubt with her new paramour. So you see where you fall in the order of importance. Best you not forget it." She looked to her men. "Let's go."

Ianthe spun and headed off, and her men moved in close to Alyneri, their expressions immobile, clearly at the ready to take her in hand if she disobeyed.

And would she have me flogged should I defy her? Alyneri wondered as she followed numbly, her feet seeming to move of their own accord—for surely she was not willingly doing so.

It all seemed so unreal. She thought of Ean's recounting of his capture by the Shade and realized that he must've felt much this way. How had he found the strength to do battle in the face of such desperate fear? Alyneri felt overwhelmed by it. Her despair was so palpable that her breath came in little gasps, which she tried to conceal from the Marchioness, knowing that she'd already shown herself a pitifully inept opponent.

They were nearing the far side of the Boulevard when—

"Oh, Marchioness?" came a male voice slightly echoing from across the cavernous hall.

Ianthe stopped and turned with an indignant look as if to say, *what now?* But when she saw who approached, her expression hardened and then...softened, but only on the surface. Alyneri watched the transition with startled fascination. That the woman could so easily mask her feelings behind a façade of civility...*she truly is a monster!*

"Yes, Lieutenant?" Ianthe smiled sweetly.

Her heart fluttering, Alyneri maneuvered for a better look and saw the Lieutenant Bastian val Renly approaching with a host of red-coated King's Own Guard. It wasn't until they neared that she caught sight of a sandy-blonde head behind them, and her hopes soared. *Oh Tanis, you dear, dear boy!*

"Lady Wynne," Bastian announced as he stopped smartly in front of the group, his men fanning out behind in formation. They looked a sharp patrol in their red coats with the val Lorian eagle in gold upon the breast. Bastian looked over the group in front of him, and he did not seem pleased by what he saw. "Explain, if you will, Marchioness, why you have the Duchess Alyneri d'Giverny in hand like a common thief."

Ianthe laughed musically. "How dramatic of you, Lieutenant. It is nothing so untoward, surely. The Lady Alyneri is merely accompanying me to my chambers for a late cup of tea—or perhaps an early one, however you prefer to look at it."

"I must've been misinformed," Bastian replied, looking appropriately perplexed. "It has nothing to do then with your claim that Her Majesty has ordered the Duchess into your tutelage?" At this pronouncement, Tanis peeped out from behind a tall guardsmen and glared daggers at Ianthe, reminding Alyneri very much of the barn cat who'd stared down Rhys val Kincaide back at Fersthaven.

Ianthe's eyes flashed, but she recovered her composure with barely a ripple in the mask. "Indeed, Lieutenant," she confirmed primly. "Tis true."

"I should very much like to see the letter," he said pleasantly.

Her expression fluttered slightly as confusion battled against the pretty smile which held back the force of her hostile temperament. "What letter would that be?"

"The letter of assignation," he explained with patient calm. "Such matters of importance are always put to pen in our fine kingdom—or didn't you know that, Marchioness?" He paused to eye her discomfiture at the revelation, adding, "I understand Queen Indora prefers oral agreements in matters of this nature that she may more efficaciously change her mind about them later."

"How dare you, lieutenant!" Ianthe drew herself up. "Queen Indora is my dear cousin, and I shall have her know of such an outrageous declamation of her charact—"

But the lieutenant wasn't to be waylaid from his purpose. His gaze hardened, matched by his tone. His hand went to the hilt of his sword, an indication of his disposition toward her, as he cut in forcefully, "Marchioness, did you really think you would succeed in this farce? The Lady Alyneri is an Adept Healer in the sworn service of the crown and would under no circumstances be given into your tutelage."

Ianthe gasped her indignation and made to protest, but Bastian pressed on, "If their Majesties felt the Lady Alyneri in need of instruction, I assure you they would beseech the highest houses of the realm, not House val Rothschen, who attempts to make up for what it has lost in nobility through the accumulation of wealth."

Ianthe was veritably panting to voice her outrage, and her men looked ready to do battle, their faces dark with fury, but all knew it would be their own deaths should they lift a hand against the King's Own Guard. Bastian continued ruthlessly, "House val Lorian has its own wealth and needs not purchase its nobility," and then he placed a final dagger into Ianthe val Rothschen's heart as he added, "Likewise her Grace Alyneri d'Giverny, who is the only daughter of Prince Jair of M'Nador and heir to the Kandori fortune."

Ianthe sucked in her breath and paled as wan as the moon.

Bastian smiled innocently. "Oh, you didn't know? I am not surprised, for there are few who do, in order to protect the fortune's ten heirs." He looked to Ianthe's guards. "You men, stand aside," which they did as surely as if the king himself had commanded it.

Bastian held a hand to Alyneri, and she accepted with a grateful look. He freed her of the circle of Ianthe's men and handed her off to another of his own, who took her elbow with due regard and glared at the val Rothschens in a fiercely protective fashion.

Bastian's hand now rested easily on the hilt of his sword, and it occurred to Alyneri just how much of his emotion was communicated by these subtleties of stance. Though Ianthe looked beaten now, with her hand collaring her throat, the Lieutenant made certain of it as he continued in a critical tone, "Surely you didn't think their Majesties would betroth their royal son to the Duchess simply out of the goodness of their hearts—" he spun to Alyneri, adding, "forgive my bluntness, your Grace, for you have surely proven yourself worth far more than gold through your loyal service to the crown."

Looking back to Ianthe, he addressed his own men. "Take her to her lord husband, order that she does not leave his sight, and assure him that I will send a full report of how his wife brings shame upon his house and his name."

His men filed out to surround the val Rothschens, and they departed with no more fanfare than a dog shamed by its master.

Alyneri was suddenly overcome—relief, gratitude, lingering fear, so many emotions welled. She threw her arms around Bastian's neck with a little squeak. Then she blushed and stepped primly away again, drawing herself to her tallest though her own face flamed as red as Bastian's. "I thank you, Lieutenant."

Bastian gave her a polite bow. "Your Grace, it is young Tanis you should be thanking. He sought me out in a fury and would not be turned away."

Alyneri looked gratefully to Tanis, but before she could thank him, another guardsman in red and gold rushed up. "Lieutenant," and he whispered something in Bastian's ear.

Bastian's expression turned grave. "Indeed," he said as the man pulled away. He looked apologetically to Alyneri. "Your grace, I must beseech you to accompany us at once."

"Of course, lieutenant. Tanis…" she added in a tone which the boy well knew meant 'accompany us please.'

Thusly, they headed off.

Ean and Raine waited for dawn in the secret circular chamber deep within the bowels of Calgaryn palace. Morin and Fynn had both been sent to set events in motion, and now there was no going back. Ean sank deeper into his chair while the Vestal slowly walked the circumference of the room running a flat round rock back and forth between his fingers.

Reckless and brash. Ean brooded over Morin's declaration. Not that it mattered, for he wouldn't know where to even begin searching for a Shade. So why did Morin's barb sink so deeply? Was it because Ean felt the truth in it?

Now he'd agreed to flee to the Cairs. What new perils awaited him there? Raine had explained that there was safety in numbers, in anonymity, in hiding in plain sight in a country that played host to dozens of races. But what would he do there? Ean gritted his teeth and wondered, *And how will Creighton's death ever be avenged?*

"There will be time enough for vengeance when this is done," Raine advised, looking over from the far side of the room. At the Prince's startled look, the truthreader smiled softly and said, "I wasn't eavesdropping. You should know that thoughts have force. Some of them are...very loud."

Ean stared hard at him. "I take exception to fleeing my enemies in the night."

Raine held his gaze for a long time. Then he came over and sat down across from the prince, his expression troubled. "Ean...you *are* in grave danger. Geshaiwyn are relentless. Whoever hired them through the Karakurt's network is actively plotting your death. Leaving the kingdom may keep you safe from Morwyk's schemes, but have a care at every turn that you don't fall prey to another's."

Ean wished people would stop telling him that. He was well aware of the dangers he faced. He stared broodingly at the Vestal and after a long moment of silence observed, "Do you believe he was sent to protect me?"

Raine sat back in his chair. "The Shade, you mean?"

Ean nodded. "Franco Rohre thought it so."

Raine looked noncommittal. "I dare not speak as to my oath-brother's motives, Ean. I think it safe to say only that when the zanthyr came to your rescue, he saved you from an uncertain fate."

"The Shade *did* save my life," Ean admitted, more to himself than to Raine. Until Franco spoke the words, Ean had forgotten the ache left by the man's fist striking his chin, as well as the reason for it. "Why would he heal me if his master only meant for me to die?"

Raine cracked a humorless smile. "Again, I do not presume to understand the Fifth Vestal's plans," and he added resolutely, "though I vow to unravel them, thread by thread." He settled Ean a penetrating look. "Who knows if my oath-brother merely gave the creature an order to bring you back alive? A Shade follows his master unquestioningly; such an order would easily have necessitated his healing you of any injury."

"And why would the Vestal want me alive?" Ean pressed, feeling frustration constricting his chest and a welling anger threatening behind it, his emotions so potent and fierce and held back with naught but a fragile shield, already many times cracked.

Raine grunted. "If only I knew. My instincts tell me your Return plays some part in it, but to say more than this would be mere conjecture."

Ean looked away and stared angrily into the fire working the muscles of his jaw, clenching and unclenching. "I should just ask him, I suppose," he remarked bitterly.

"*Ean*," the intensity of Raine's reply made the prince turn back to him. The Vestal looked upset by his words. "Ean, my oath-brother is a very dangerous man—the most deadly wielder ever known to have walked the realm. Please, I entreat you—*please* do not seek him out." When Ean still looked defiant, Raine continued, "Perhaps if you will permit an illustration?"

Begrudgingly, Ean waved a hand to proceed.

"I'm sure you've heard many versions of the story of the Last Battle of the Adept Wars, where the other Vestals and I were captured and brought to T'khendar to witness Malachai ap'Kalien's imminent victory. But there is a part of the story that is never told, and I think you should hear it now."

"I'm listening."

Raine pushed out of his chair, reached into his pocket and pulled out his smoothly rounded, flat black stone, which he began twining through his fingers again with skillful ease. "During those last days of the War," he began, "I was fighting in western Agasan—the Sunset Battle, it has come to be called. The Adept forces *were* losing—that much is often told true. We might have stood united against Malachai alone, but when Björn turned against us…" he paused, glanced off into the shadows. "When Björn betrayed us," he continued after a moment, "many good wielders fell. The Fifth Vestal was more than our spearhead of strength, he'd been our hope. He took both with him when he broke his oath."

Ean could only imagine the sense of betrayal Raine must have felt—must still feel. "I remember the story of the Sunset Battle of Gimlalai," he said, hoping to spare the truthreader its retelling. Under any other circumstances, Ean would have loved to hear it straight from the man who fought the battle. He said instead, "I remember it told that you combated Shades and a…a Sundragon, I think?"

Raine nodded. "Five Shades overtook me as I fought the Sundragon Şrivas'rhakárakek, who had allied himself with Björn. After the Shades captured me, they took me to T'khendar where I spent several days in Malachai's palace—a hellish time, for in every conscious moment I endured the agony of life in a realm without *elae*. I was on the brink of death when Malachai paid me a visit." He paused and fixed his crystalline eyes on Ean in a pointed manner. "You see, Ean, an Adept breathes *elae* like humanity breathes air, and we cannot live without the lifeforce to sustain us. I'm not sure what Malachai did to bring me back, for I felt none of the working—whatever it was—but after he left, I was much restored."

"If it wasn't *elae*," Ean asked, "then what was it?"

Raine frowned. "T'khendar touches both the outermost edge of the living realms—those fueled by *elae*—as well as fringes on what might be considered the end of the universe, what lies beyond the veil of life. There, in that place of nonexistence, a different power rules, a consumptive power created to destroy everything it touches. We call this power *deyjiin*, which means 'death' in the Old Tongue."

"*Deyjiin*," Ean murmured, remembering the violet-silver sheen that destroyed his sword, *the one the zanthyr remade…*

"After Malachai visited me in my room," the Vestal continued, "I was taken to a hall where half a hundred Shades waited. I was joined by the other Vestals—Seth, Dagmar, my oath-sister Alshiba—and we were made to line up before the dais like penitents awaiting sentencing. That day was the first time in many weeks that I'd seen Malachai, for he'd long sought the safety of T'khendar while Björn won his war for him in Alorin." Raine paused and shook his head sadly. "To see the change in him… Malachai was mad by then—beyond madness, really. There was little left of the man I'd known, just a haunted shell dominated by the darkness that had usurped his soul. You couldn't even see his eyes, so devoured they'd become by his dark power, so afraid of the light. It was…it was tragic."

Raine flicked the stone off his thumb, a dark sparkle slicing the air. Then it was back in his hand and flashing through his fingers again. "Things happened then… terrible things. You've heard the stories—the sacrifices, the parade of heads."

Ean felt a pang of disgust. "That's all true?"

Raine's look was telling. "While we watched, a parade of Shades passed us carrying the heads of the last of our kind, the Mages who'd sheltered in the Citadel on Cair Tiern'aval. Only Björn had the wherewithal to breach their defenses." He paused and shut his eyes. Even the stone became still in his palm. "Until then, I don't think I really believed Björn had betrayed us," he murmured, "but that parade of death was a statement, *Björn's* statement." Raine lifted his gaze to hold Ean's and shook his head bitterly. "You never could fault the bastard for efficiency. By sacrificing the Mages, Björn had, in one fell stroke, broken his oath to us and likewise proven his troth to Malachai. Tis Epiphany's grace the Adepts known as the Fifty Companions lived to speak of it. They were the only survivors of the Citadel."

Raine closed his fingers around the stone and gripped it against his palm. "Soon thereafter, Malachai began his craft—that most famous of workings, the story told often and best by the Immortal Bard, Drake DiMatteo. Can you know how helpless we felt, Ean? To stand and watch first the flaunting of the murder of such sage souls—wiping out all hope for the advancement of Adept magic, which was Malachai's fateful promise to us—then the imminent destruction of our home, and realize there is *nothing* we can do! Without *elae*, we were impotent as wielders, and as Adepts…as Adepts, we were dying. I myself could barely stand. But stand we did. Dagmar, Seth and I stood by and watched as Malachai struck down our oath-sister Alshiba, *watched* as he opened a weld into the Citadel in Tiern'aval, as Tiern'aval itself started crumbling..."

Ean's eyes were glued to Raine. "Until…?"

Raine stared off for a moment. Then his tormented expression melted away. "Until the Balance shifted," he answered, once more composed. "Malachai's working had stretched the limits of Balance too far, and the Cosmos pushed back…but at a great and perilous cost." He sighed regretfully. "It was over so quickly after the shift occurred that it seemed the next thing I knew we were standing on the beach, soaking wet, looking out over the Bay of Jewels and wondering where Cair Tiern'aval had gone." He shook his head as if he still couldn't quite believe it. "To this day, no one knows what happened to the island. It vanished like a vapor, and while there are some who believe it sank, it is more probable that it still exists somewhere between the realms, wrenched out of Alorin as a result of the terrible forces worked in its vicinity."

Ean felt slightly numbed to hear this tale told true. Barely escaping Malachai's dark work in T'khendar and finding themselves stranded on a beach was a far cry from the storied ending, where the triumphant Vestals banished Björn van Gelderan to the tainted realm. *No wonder the bards tell a different tale.* The truth was far too disheartening.

"So. It was there on that beach that Dagmar vowed to return to T'khendar."

As far as Ean could recall, no mortal knew the reason the Second Vestal had embarked upon his quest to find T'khendar, though speculation abounded. All that was known was that the phrase 'Dagmar's dungeon' had its root in fact. "Did he return in order to kill Björn?" Ean asked.

Raine gave him a tense look. "No," he confessed. "He went back to salvage him."

Ean let out a low whistle. "And he never returned."

"No," Raine answered grimly, coming back to retake his seat, "nor have any of the Vestals ever heard from him again. We know, of course, of the many testimonies of Dagmar coming to others in dreams, but he has not contacted any of us." Raine seemed troubled again. "To his credit, he might have tried to reach us and found that the nature of our magical oaths prevented contact in dreamscape. I just do not know."

Looking thoughtful, Ean set to piecing things together in his mind. "Before… you said you were dying," he recalled, "that you couldn't live in T'khendar without *elae* to sustain you. Returning there would seem certain death. Why would Dagmar risk his life to salvage a traitor?"

Raine spread palms to either side, leaned back in his chair, and settled Ean a telling look that seemed to ask, *Whyever indeed?* But he replied only, "Dagmar has an elevated code of honor that is both his strength and his weakness. He did what he did because he felt it was the right thing to do. Now, if indeed he lives, it will be by Björn's graces, and there is no telling what loyalties Dagmar will have been forced to betray to gain Björn's goodwill."

Ean drew back in surprise. "You think he's joined the Fifth Vestal?"

The truthreader looked regretful. "I fear it is more than a possibility. To have lived this long in T'khendar…Dagmar has either sworn new oaths to Malachai's dark gods, or he has sworn an oath to Björn. In either case, he is suspect…but Dagmar is not the point."

"What is?"

"Ean…" he pursed his lips and frowned. "What I wanted to impress upon you with this story is that yes, while Björn has an interest in you, you may be safe from him—and I say only *maybe*, for this is far from certain. But Ean," and he settled the prince a penetrating look, adding fiercely, "never allow yourself to believe that the Fifth Vestal is not a traitor, that he doesn't work toward his own ends *wholly*, that he cannot betray you in the ninth hour, or that you are indispensable to his accursedly complicated plans."

A knock came three times upon the door, and then twice more. Raine rose to unlock it, and Morin swept inside. "All is readied," he reported as Ean also got to his feet. "Ten minutes ago, the Duchess and the truthreader left on a coach drawn by six horses, your stallion Caldar among them."

Ean wondered what they'd told Alyneri to get her to go along with him, or if they'd simply ordered her without any explanation at all. He supposed if he couldn't stand up to Alyneri d'Giverny, however, what chance did he have of bringing Björn van Gelderan and his Shades to justice?

Morin meanwhile continued, "The Captain headed into the city on a task for the king and will rendezvous with you at Fersthaven by midday."

"The Captain?" Ean said, startled out of his brooding by the news. He'd agreed to taking Alyneri and Tanis along with him—there were a number of good reasons to have their talents at his disposal—but he knew nothing of Rhys val Kinkaid coming too. He rather dreaded traveling with the hotheaded Captain of the King's Own Guard. "But why Rhys?"

"Your father agreed to this plan with that caveat, Ean," Morin told him. "He was explicit in his terms." To Raine, Morin said, "We must hurry. Fynnlar is in place to flag down the Healer's coach, but Ean must be there to make a quick entry."

Raine nodded and looked to the Prince. "Leave word for me at the places I mentioned should you need my aid. Good luck, Ean. Epiphany's blessing on your journey."

Ean nodded to him, grabbed up his bag, and followed Morin out into the dim tunnels. Morin led him with swift surety through the maze of passageways until they came to a door that opened onto a narrow stone staircase spiraling up into darkness.

"Here is where we part ways, your Highness."

"Thank you…I think."

Morin placed a hand on the prince's shoulder. "Remember all that you've been counseled. Knowledge is power, as your father said."

Ean turned to the steps, but Morin called his attention one last time. "And Ean?"

The prince turned over his shoulder.

"Keep thinking on your time with the Shade, on that question of strange things happening."

Ean shrugged. "Sure."

Morin nodded. "Good-bye then. Fair skies and safe passage."

After what seemed an interminable climb, Ean reached a landing and an iron door so rusted that it took at least five minutes to work it open enough to slip through, and even then he had to push his pack through first and suck in his breath as he followed it.

The door opened into a well house that was dim and damp and smelled slightly of dandelions and wet leaves. Fortunately the door to the well house was ajar, and Ean emerged to a brilliant day. He followed a path from the well house through the forest until he unexpectedly emerged upon the King's Road.

"Ean!" Fynn called in a loud whisper.

Ean looked around, but didn't immediately see his cousin until he spotted a vagabond curled up beneath the golden autumn leaves of a maple sapling.

"Don't stare, you fool man!" Fynn hissed while trying to look as if he slept soundly. Ean thought he did a fair job of it. "Get off the road, will you? Hide over in that thicket. The Duchess will be along any moment."

Ean cursed his own stupidity. Raine and Morin had both impressed upon him the importance of keeping a low profile and remaining as anonymous as possible, and here he was standing in the middle of the cursed road for anyone to shoot at. *Fool man, is right!*

He rushed across the road toward the thicket of bushes Fynn mentioned and worked his way within it. Once in the center, he had a fair amount of room and was able to crouch down and watch the road.

Fynn was right in that a coach and horses could soon be heard coming down the road, which was shaded by Winter Oaks whose leaves would keep their loam-green color long after the first snow. As the coach came into view, Ean saw that it was drawn by six horses, and Caldar was unmistakable among them.

Fynn jumped up and ran to wave down the coachman yelling about alms for the poor and could they possibly spare some rum? While the driver had obviously been briefed, it was evident that Alyneri had not, for she immediately poked her pale head out the coach window and demanded, "Why have we stopped? Who is that man? What does he want?"

Ean knew that was his cue. He emerged from the thicket with his bag slung over one shoulder, threw open the coach door and ducked inside before Alyneri could protest. Fynn climbed aboard with the driver and the coach lurched into motion again, tossing Alyneri quite indelicately backwards into her seat.

"You!" She glared at Ean as she grabbed for a handhold in the swaying coach. "So *that's* what this is all about! You're still perpetuating Morin d'Hain's drivel, trying to pretend we're in some kind of lover's tryst? Well, I won't be part of it, Ean! When we get to Fersthaven, you shall continue on without me. I will simply tell his Majesty that I cannot countenance this charade any longer—"

"Alyneri," Ean quieted her with a steady look, amazed by his own sense of calm.

She seemed equally surprised, at least enough to close her mouth.

Ean looked over at Tanis, who was somewhat crunched into the corner on the seat beside him. "Hi, Tanis."

The boy flashed a smile. "Hello, your Highness."

Ean looked back to the Healer. "Alyneri, this is not about perpetuating any gossip," he told her solemnly and firmly, "though I am relieved to know that you acknowledge the terribly offensive rumor was Morin's doing instead of mine. This is about the future of my father's kingdom, and much more besides."

When she only glared at him, he became suspicious and asked, "What were you told?"

"What does it matter?" She turned and stared out the window.

"We were told this was about the future of the kingdom and more besides," Tanis dutifully supplied.

Ean suppressed a smile. "Thank you, Tanis."

"And her Grace jumped at the chance to travel," the lad went on, "and...and they told me..." he flushed and dropped his gaze, nearly whispering, "They said I'm to be your truthreader if...if you'll have me—not being trained much at all."

"I would have you in any capacity, Tanis," Ean told him the heartfelt truth.

Tanis beamed.

Alyneri sat amid a black cloud on the opposite seat staring out the window.

"I don't mind your coming on your own terms, Alyneri," Ean confessed. "I'm just glad you came."

She spun him a querulous look. "Why? Why do you care? Just so you can have a Healer along to patch you up after every ridiculous, foolhardy risk you take with your life?"

"That would be nice," he said, grinning at her, "but no. That's not why, not even close."

His honesty cooled her ire. She held his gaze finally, her dark eyes so serious, so fragile beneath the prickly shell. "Then...why?"

Ean leaned elbows on knees. "Alyneri," he breathed, giving her a somewhat incredulous look, "my brothers are *dead*. All *three* of them. Outside of Fynnlar, you're my oldest friend. Who can I trust on such a dangerous journey if not yourself? Who else can I count on for support, for encouragement, to defend me and question my decisions and remind me who I am when all looks grim? Who else can play that role, if not you?"

Alyneri turned her face away to stare out the window again, but not before she brusquely wiped a tear from her cheek. She murmured something Ean didn't catch.

"I'm sorry, what was that?"

She spun him an injured glare. "I said 'no one.'"

Ean smiled and took her hand to plant a kiss upon the back. "That makes me very happy. Thank you."

"I will too, your highness," Tanis chimed in, "for what it's worth."

"Thank you, Tanis," Ean said, flashing the lad a grin and ruffling his hair. "I know I can count on you. On both of you."

"Just don't count on her Grace to do the cooking," Tanis said.

"Tanis don't be rude," Alyneri grumbled, but a smile had come back into her eyes.

Just then the coach door opened and Fynn swung inside, forcing Alyneri to slide to the far end of the cushion or get pounced on.

"Well, we're off!" Fynn announced cheerfully. "And what luck your destination is the Cairs. Ah, to enjoy a real Volga again." He rubbed his hands together lustily, oblivious to Alyneri's affronted glare from the corner.

"Is there anything you wouldn't do for a good bottle of wine, cousin?" Ean asked with a grin.

"Nothing. If a good wine is life, a good life is a Volga."

"You are a dissolute man of dubious morals, Lord Fynnlar," Alyneri remarked.

"Why thank you, your Grace." Fynn seemed genuinely pleased to be so complimented.

"And thus do the fools play out their roles upon the stage of life," Ean quoted the bard Drake DiMatteo with a thoughtful expression, "and the Gods sit among the heavens and laugh at the farce."

THIRTY

'A love that can end has never been real.'

– Jayachándranáptra, Rival of the Sun

First light arrived far too quickly for Trell, who awoke in darkness to find Sayid standing over him wearing a toothy grin. Trell thought the man wasn't quite as unnerving as Balaji, but he had his moments. Seeing Trell awake, the Khurd turned without a word and headed off again into the grey dawn.

Trell sat up and rubbed his neck, becoming keenly aware of parts of his body he'd forgotten he had. Battles like the one last night left their card of calling even if he'd escaped relatively unscathed. He took a moment to stretch aching muscles and then scratched at the fuzz shadowing his jaw. His scruff was getting long enough to warrant the title of a beard, though a little extra insulation would no doubt serve him well as he headed across the high passes between Sakkalaah and Xanthe.

They headed out into a chill morning with frost cloaking the earth and a prevalent wind stirring the high clouds into wisps of gauze. The trail led ever up and away from the river at last, but they still caught glimpses of the Cry twisting and frothing as they slowly climbed out of the canyon.

By midday, they'd left the Haden Gorge behind them, trading ravine for mountains and arid dirt for forested hills. Sakkalaah lay in a high valley of the Assifiyah range, where the mountains leveled into a broad plateau before shooting up again into the cresting, snow-capped peaks that formed Cair Palea'andes and Cair Thessalonia's impressive backdrop.

To get to that valley, however, entailed navigating several dangerous passes, the first of which opened onto the Cry winding over a thousand paces below. The opposite side of the chasm was gained by way of a hanging bridge, which could only be crossed in the best of weather, and even then, success depended greatly on first receiving the blessings of Angharad and Thalma, the goddesses the Northmen called Fortune and Luck. There was much evidence of those who'd tried to gain such favor; the trail on both sides of the Cry was littered with offerings—the remains of food, prayer beads, broken idols, and spattered wax. As Trell and the others called a halt on the north side of the bridge, he thought he could still smell the incense permeating the air, as if the rocks were stained with it.

All four Khurds dismounted and walked to the edge of the chasm to peer down. Trell sat Gendaia and regarded the bridge with a pensive frown. Lily reined in beside Trell and rested her hands on the pommel of her saddle. "The Ashafani Bridge," she said with a hint of awe. As Trell turned her an inquiring look, she commented, "It's quite famous, you know."

"Infamous, I'd say," Trell returned quietly.

"Yes. Infamous," Lily agreed with a frown.

The sisters had dismounted behind them, and they walked to the cliff's edge and peered down with the Khurds. "Bless me, will you *look* at all of that?" Aishlinn exclaimed.

Testimony to the fools who'd attempted to cross the Ashafani bridge without gaining Fortune's graces were the shattered remains of crates and wagons—not to mention half-clothed skeletons picked clean by ravens—which lined the jagged cliffs like flotsam in a choppy sea. Gold, silver and precious gemstones glittered and gleamed among the wreckage, a tantalizing decoration for the ashen cliffs.

Fhionna turned her sister an impish grin. "Now we know where Caoilfhinn gets all of her jewelry."

Aishlinn grinned in return.

"Why doesn't someone go down and retrieve some of it?" Lily asked. "It's sure to be a fortune. You'd think at least the bandits would claim it."

Sayid turned to her, his dark eyes intense beneath his dun-hued *ghoutra,* the protective face flap left to dangle at his ear. "Tis forbidden," he told her.

"Forbidden?" she replied. "Forbidden by whom?"

Trell explained, "That treasure belongs to Angharad and Thalma. *These* offerings are for them as well," and he extended an arm to include the surrounding jumble of tokens, "left here by the prudent. Those offerings," and he nodded toward the chasm, "were taken as toll by the goddesses from those who were not so wise."

"Do you mean to tell me," Lily returned skeptically, "that the only ones who've successfully crossed that bridge made an offering first?"

"If by 'successfully' you mean gaining the other side without losing precious cargo, then yes."

Lily frowned down at the chasm again.

"The Khurds and I will make an offering for the group," Trell said. "If you'd like to participate, Lily, a simple coin tossed into the chasm will suffice."

"You mean like…like a wishing well?"

"Yes, milady, it is much the same." He dismounted and walked to the cliff's edge. One by one, he tossed eight pieces of Agasi silver into the chasm, watching them until they vanished out of sight. The Khurds all did the same, albeit with Akkadian *denar*. Then Aishlinn made her offering, and Fhionna as well. Finally Lily dismounted and walked to the edge. She closed her eyes and tossed her coin, her lips moving soundlessly. Regarding her with a half-smile, Trell wondered what she wished for.

Their offerings thus made, Trell motioned everyone to gather their horses, and Kamil led the way across the bridge, leading his horse on foot. The others followed one by one.

As Trell headed across, after Sayid and before Lily, he paused midway. The bridge swayed gently in the wind, the weather-hardened wood firm beneath his feet. He looked down at the river far below with a pensive frown. He wasn't sure why the moment seemed significant, but it felt as though he was crossing more than just a rushing river; rather, this crossing represented some part of him that he was leaving behind, though he was hard-pressed to say which part that was.

Gendaia nudged him with her nose. He turned away from the deep chasm, and feeling as if the moment would be indelibly imprinted in memory, he took that next fateful step toward his future and his past.

Once they had safely gained the far side, Lily brought her mount alongside his. "May I ride with you a while, Trell of the Tides?" she inquired softly.

"Of course, Lily." She gave him a pleased smile, and he asked her, "Are you excited to see your betrothed?"

She brightened considerably, yet he saw a shadow still behind her eyes. "I am," Lily answered. "Very. Only..." she dropped her eyes. "I wonder if he will...want me still."

"He would be a fool not to," Trell reassured her.

She gave him a grateful look. Then she pressed her lips together and regarded him hesitantly. "Trell...?"

He knew that look; it was one shared by women around the world. *What now?* "Yes, Lily?"

She pulled her braid over her shoulder and played with the end, rubbing it beneath her chin and not looking at him. "I know you said your journey was as important as your destination, but..."

He gave her a tolerant look. "But...?"

"But I think I know who you are—I mean, who your parents are."

As much as he tried, he couldn't contain his shock.

"If I did know," she said nervously, noting his dismayed expression, "would you want me to tell you?"

Exerting admirable self-control, Trell turned grey eyes to her. "I...don't know."

She gazed at him worriedly. "I won't tell you if you don't want me to. I promise. I won't even hint at it."

He turned his eyes away, for they were suddenly burning. "If you were wrong," he said in a low voice, his throat and chest tight with emotion, "if I was given hope, and then it was taken away...Lily, this is too important to me. I...don't know how I would handle that."

"I'm not wrong, Trell. I'm certain of it."

He shook his head and looked away.

After a moment, she said, "You have your reasons, which seem almost like—like a religion to you—but if not for yourself, think of those who love you still. Couldn't you find compassion enough for them? To know that you still lived...?"

"If they have thought me dead for five years, Lily," he said quietly, "is it a mercy to come back into their lives? If they've moved on, if they've grieved and named me and forgotten?"

Lily looked at him strangely. "What do you mean by that?"

"By what?"

"You said if they've 'named you and forgotten.' What does that mean?"

Even knowing he'd said it, Trell couldn't explain its meaning. "I don't know. The phrase just came to me." He turned to stare off down the trail ahead, the muscles of his jaw working.

After a long silence, Lily leaned across the distance between their horses and placed her hand on his. "Why does it matter so much?"

He gave her a tormented look.

"Trell, I'm...*grateful* to leave behind my name. My father is a vicious, vindictive man. He claims nobility, but what nobility lies in him is only in his bloodright. I have never met a man more noble than you, Trell, blood or no blood. Why should it matter so much from whence you came?"

He respected her enough to consider her question honestly. After a moment's thought, he replied, "I'm not sure, but it does."

"But I don't *want* people to know—"

"I know," he said, interrupting her gently, "but it's easier to give up a name when you have one. You're not the first person who's asked this of me, Lily," he added. "I've lived and fought with hundreds of men who've given up their names for a variety of reasons. Many of them thought as you do." He shrugged and finished, "All I can say is it's not the same." But Trell didn't want to talk about himself anymore, so he asked, "I have questions for you, also. Why Duan'Bai? Why aren't you and Korin returning to the Cairs?"

She cast him troubled look. "It's a long story. Oh, Trell, there is so much happening in the world. So much you can't understand."

"Try me," he murmured.

"It's not that you can't," she corrected quickly, noting his slightly dangerous change of tone, "but that there is too much to tell. My father is involved in…evil things. I won't be a part of them. I can't be. It's just…" She whetted her lips nervously and added in a whisper, "I daren't tell anyone of the things I've seen. I dare not!"

Trell cast her a narrow look. "Why Duan'Bai, Lily?"

She noted the suspicion in his tone and replied in frustration, "You really are too perceptive for your own good, Trell."

His lips twitched in a smile. "You mean to expatriate."

She sighed. "Yes."

"And because you're headed to Duan'Bai instead of Raku, you must feel the information you harbor is best heard by al'Basreh."

She drew back with her surprise. "You know him?"

"Lily," he said with admirable patience, "I lived in the palace of Duan'Bai as the adoptive son of the Emir. How exactly could I *not* know al'Basreh?"

Her face flooded with hope. It was the first time he saw the shadow truly retreat from her gaze. "Would you…could you…is there any way—"

"It would be my pleasure to write a letter on your behalf. But Lily…"

Her elated expression sobered at his tone.

"Prime Minister Rajiid bin Yemen al'Basreh is a very dangerous man. To bring yourself to his notice means putting your life in his hands. If he thinks you duplicitous—if he suspects you in any way, regardless of the truth of things—you will die."

A determined look overcame her. "I would rather die than do nothing to stop my father."

Trell shook his head. "Then I will write you a letter of introduction."

"Oh, *thank you*, Trell!" Lily exclaimed clasping her hands beneath her chin. "You are a most precious gift!"

As if to make the dramatic finish complete, they reached the top of the hill they'd been climbing and came in view of Sakkalaah.

The valley that spread before them was a lake of flaxen gold interspersed with evergreen. The River Cry cut a swath through the fields, its basin deep and walls sheer. Ten miles across the valley, the Assifiyah mountains reared, forbidding and vast, huge craggy peaks blanketed by snow. At the center of the valley on the palisades of the river, framed on either end by forbidding mountains, lay Sakkalaah.

It was a great walled limestone city, designed in a perfect circle around two towering jade pillars that stood higher than any other structure inside the walls, dwarfing even the glittering gold dome of the Sultan's palace.

"Sakkalaah," Kamil said as he brought his horse to a halt beside Trell's. "We shall eat well tonight."

Trell cast him a wry grin. If his friend Krystos had room at his inn, they would eat well indeed, and more besides. Casting a still beaming Lily a quiet look, Trell clicked his tongue, and Gendaia led away down into the valley and its jewel of a city.

Trell's friend Krystos was an Agasi nobleman from the province of Solvayre, and he did a fine business importing his family's famous wines through Sakkalaah to Duan'Bai and beyond. He ran an inn near the Pillars, which also did a fine business overcharging the tourists coming in to see the old Cyrenaic ruins—for Sakkalaah was built atop the remains of a much older civilization that thrived in the days when the Cry was still navigable by ship to Cair Thessalonia, in those times known as the kingdom of Thessalos. The cataclysm that had destroyed Thessalos also altered the Cry's path, dooming a dozen cities to eventual obscurity and ruin. The Emir was said to be a direct descendant of the old Cyrene kings, a claim that had helped him unite the warring tribes of the Akkad into the Emirates he now governed.

All of these connections Trell revisited as he led his company through the ancient, narrow streets of Sakkalaah, finally arriving at the Inn of the Four Faces as the sun was setting in fiery splendor. He hopped off Gendaia while the others were dismounting and ran inside to find Krystos, hoping the man was there and not off on one of his wildly dangerous expeditions in search of ancient treasure.

As luck would have it, Krystos was in the cave he called his office. Krystos was a tall man with the blue eyes and olive-tanned skin of the southern Agasi. He wore his long black hair pulled back in a thick plait and always carried a jeweled dagger at his hip, one of his many unearthed treasures. He looked up from the armillary he was studying when Trell barged in, and his lean face split in a grin. "Trell of the Tides!" he exclaimed. He leaped out of his chair and rushed around his desk with open arms, grabbing Trell up in a bear of a hug before kissing him on both cheeks. "Am I glad to see you!"

He took hold of Trell's shoulder and dragged him around behind his desk. "Look, see what I've found. This text," and he pointed to a dusty looking tome lying open on the desk to reveal its incomprehensible script, "is the foremost reference on the treasure of Amuth-Ra, which it is said was lost in the third century after the cataclysm when the palace of the Caliph of Ishtan was sacked by invaders from—"

"Krystos," Trell cut in laughingly, "I want to hear all about Amuth-Ra, I assure you, but I'm here with others who are waiting with great patience after a long trek from the Bashir'Khazaaz. We need rooms, and a meal, and then you and I must talk of important things."

Krystos shook his head and leveled Trell a reproving look. "What could be more important than the treasure of Amuth-Ra?"

Trell took his friend by the shoulder. "I will tell you soon. Have you any rooms for us?"

"Of course I have rooms!" he exclaimed. Then he peered at Trell out of the corner of his eye. "How many rooms do you need? The Empress's cousin, Dinar van Gelderan, is coming with his entire entourage in a week's time, and—"

"We'll be out of your hair by then," Trell assured him.

Krystos rubbed his hands together. "Good. I'm to make a fortune off of his Excellency's visit—they want the whole tour, out to the Ashafani bridge and the Cyrenaic ruins and even the Temple of the Winds on the Faisal escarpment—but I must be able to accommodate them all under one roof or the deal's off. Belloth's balls, the man travels with an army of attendants—guards and cooks and stewards and footmen and practically a Sheik's harem of females. Have you met his Excellency, Trell?"

Trell was having a hard time keeping up with Krystos' quick desert speech, all of it spoken with a horrendous Agasi accent. "No," he managed. "Uh, when would I have met him?"

"He's been in Duan'Bai since the summer solstice—the man's braver than I, spending the hottest months of the year in the hottest city in the realm. His agent explained that his Excellency uses the heat to purge the impurities from his skin, and that's how he keeps his youthful physique." Krystos winked, elbowed Trell, and posed, "I'm sure it has nothing to do with the host of wielders he's got traveling with him, eh?"

Trell gave him a quiet smile. "The rooms, Krystos?"

"Oh, burn me, yes, you must be impatient. How many rooms did you say you needed?"

Trell negotiated the rooms and rate as they headed out of Krystos' office and found the others waiting in the elegant courtyard. The Inn of the Four Faces was a four-story, four sided establishment of limestone and marble built around a lavish courtyard where fountains sang their crystalline song among towering palms, feathery ferns and lush pink bougainvillea. Low, cushioned dining settees were hidden among the fronds and shaded beneath the scalloped edge of wine-red draperies; and quartz-paved paths wound through a maze of cobalt-tiled pools where bathing was not only permitted but encouraged—clothing being equally optional.

Krystos snapped his fingers for his staff, and Trell's company was soon being whisked away to bed chambers and bath house and a special meal prepared in their honor.

Trell found his own accommodations more than generous, and he soon made his way to the men's bathhouse and stripped down, sinking into the steaming water with a sigh. It had been half a year since he'd allowed himself such luxury, and the mineral-rich hot springs leeched the stiffness from his muscles, leaving him rejuvenated in both body and spirit.

He moved from the hot baths to the larger cooling pool and swam a few laps, the last length entirely under water. He surfaced at the stairs to find a pair of feet in his line of sight. His eyes flowed upward.

"Aishlinn," he breathed, both startled and unexpectedly aroused. "You can't be in here."

She wore a plush white robe tied at the waist, the kind the staff handed out to everyone upon entry to the baths, and her pale hair hung loose around her shoulders.

She began untying the knot as she descended the stairs, the soft robe billowing out behind her upon the surface.

Trell surged out of the water to stop her undressing. "You can't be in here," he urged in a low voice as he wrapped his arms about her waist and maneuvered her around, "and you most certainly can't be doing that. Krystos might have a liberal sense of propriety, but there are some customs that *must* be followed."

Aishlinn let Trell hustle her out of the pool, though she gazed at him all the while with a frown marring her fair features. "I do not understand you, Trell of the Tides," she confessed when they were walking down the tiled hallway away from the pools. "Most men would—"

"Most men would take you without question, I know," he interrupted, "but I am not so quick to plant my seed—especially in a Wildling's garden."

She shook her head. "You could not impregnate me unless I willed it, Trell of the Tides." She moved close to him, her hands slipping around his bare waist, her bosom against his chest as she whispered in his ear, "Have you no knowledge of the *nymphae*?"

Trell retrieved her probing hands from his naked backside and pushed her gently away from him. "And how am I to know that you don't will it, Aishlinn? I seem to recall a similar conversation with your sister not two nights ago."

"The Mother said *Fhionna* was not for you," she insisted, "that doesn't mean *I* can't claim you—"

"I am not a prize horse to be claimed, Aishlinn."

"—and after what you've done for Lily," she pressed on, ignoring his distrustful tone, "it is only right that I offer you *some* reward."

"Your thanks is reward enough," he said.

Three times shunned, she wrapped her arms around herself. "Why do you resist me so? I can see your arousal, I feel your body's response to mine. Is it so terrible what I propose?" She eyed him inquisitively.

Trell was suddenly very aware of his nakedness, that and the fact that while he was refusing Aishlinn, he was also undeniably attracted to her. It wouldn't do for the double doors to open unexpectedly and reveal him and *all* of his assets in bold delineation. "It is not so terrible," he admitted, because he owed her that much, "but even did honor not forbid it—which it does, for reasons I will not explain—a more pressing concern is that I don't trust you, Aishlinn, and I make a point of never bedding a woman I cannot trust."

She dropped her gaze. "I suppose that's fair."

Seeing her heartfelt disappointment gave Trell an idea. "If you will promise to leave before we're caught here, I will share a secret with you," he offered.

She lifted desirous eyes. "A secret? What kind of secret?"

"Your oath first, madam."

Aishlinn looked injured at his impatience with her, but she finally replied, "I give you my word, Trell of the Tides. I will leave at once and vex you no more with my affections."

Trell smiled. "Thank you." He took her by the shoulders, turned her squarely to face the doors, and whispered into her ear from behind, "In a week's time, the Empress of Agasan's cousin will be staying in this very inn. You and Fhionna would have a hard time getting more noble than that." Without waiting for a reply, he pushed open the door and prodded the *nymphae* through, his hand in the small of her back. Then he closed the doors and returned to the pools, that time for a cold bath.

Once he'd recovered from Aishlinn's unexpected visit, Trell returned to his room, dressed in clean clothes and went to find Krystos again. His plan for Lily's trip to Duan'Bai depended on Krystos' generosity in using his contacts on her behalf, and he needed to secure Krystos' agreement to help. More than this, though, he just wanted to spend some time with his friend. It had been two years since Trell shared Krystos' company, and he wanted a few moments alone with him before dinner and the duties of that evening called them both away.

That time he found the Agasi embroiled in discussion with his head chef, a squat Bemothi with a jutting beard and narrow eyes leveled, at the moment Trell entered, at Krystos. The chef spouted off something quick and fast in the South Bemothi dialect, one of the few languages Trell did not speak well, to which Krystos replied calmly in the desert tongue, "Then scour the markets for pomegranates—or pay the local witch to conjure some up, I don't care how you go about it. They *will* be served *chilleas nogada* tonight."

The Bemothi shouted a curse and shook his fist in Krystos' face before spinning on his heel and shouting at his staff instead. Krystos turned to Trell with a smile and a gleam of satisfaction in his sparkling blue eyes. "You will enjoy this dish immensely, Trell of the Tides," he told him as he put a hand to Trell's shoulder and walked him out of the kitchens. He kissed his fingers and added in Veneisean, "*C'est savoreux!*"

Trell chuckled. "I get the idea your chef will not enjoy making it so much as I will enjoy eating it."

Krystos waved him off. "I do not pay the man to be cheerful. I pay him to create works of art with every meal—and I pay him out the nose to do it, believe me my old friend! But look at you," he observed as his eyes swept Trell, "you must be two shades lighter at least!"

Trell smiled. "So what's this about the treasure of Amuth-Ra?"

Krystos beamed at him. "Let me tell you!" And tell him he did, all the way back to his spacious and elegant apartments where he served Trell a traditional Sakkalaah aperitif of apricot brandy and regaled him with the intricacies of his most recent treasure hunt and his deductions on its location. While Trell admired the numerous ancient treasures already decorating Krystos' luxurious apartments, the Agasi explained how he was using the armillary in tandem with several arithmaic equations he himself had developed to deduce the positioning of the stars in the passing millennium prior.

"Thus, you see," Krystos finished as he reclined in a low-slung chair with his long legs extended and feet crossed at the ankles, "by calculating the exact position of the constellations during the last year of the rein of Mephistoles III, then the descriptions given in the Cyrene text can be used to decipher the locations on the map!" He downed the last of his brandy and gave Trell an exuberant smile. "To think, that map has been sitting on a forgotten shelf collecting dust because no one knew the coordinates of Adrennai's Harp in the fifth century," and he added with a wink, "until now."

"You do seem to have found your true calling, Krystos," Trell complimented.

The Agasi rose and walked to an ornate chest where his collection of liqueurs awaited. He refilled his glass and carried the decanter over to Trell to do the same for him. "But tell me, my good friend," he began as he looked down at Trell with an affectionate gaze, "how is it you've come to me in the middle of a war...and with such *unique* companions?"

Trell had no doubt that by 'unique' Krystos was referring mainly to Fhionna, for the Agasi had barely been able to take his eyes off of her earlier as he was arranging for their rooms. "It was our success at the Cry that started it all," Trell began, and over the course of the next hour, he explained the circumstances that brought him to Sakkalaah with the ladies in tow.

Krystos was an eager listener; he hung on Trell's every word as he spoke of the disaster in the cave and then his time in the sa'reyth, and he groaned when he learned of the Nadoriin and the scene at their camp.

When Trell was finished with his tale, the Agasi came over, pulled Trell to his feet, and hugged him tightly. Pulling away, he said, "I thank the Creator you have finally embarked upon this path, Trell of the Tides. Would that I could accompany you. It is the greatest of treasures that you seek."

It was only then that Trell noticed they were speaking Agasi, and he smiled as he realized that he had no idea when the conversation had crossed over from the desert tongue. It seemed to hold an odd sort of significance to him, the ease with which he'd switched languages during conversation. He wondered if his new life would come so naturally.

Krystos cast him a keen sort of look. "You are always thinking, Trell of the Tides," he observed, shaking a finger at Trell's nose. "Sometimes too much, I believe."

Trell laughed. "You could be right, I freely admit."

Krystos got up to pour them another drink. "I sent word to the Inn of the Lotus for the young Lily's betrothed with orders to move him here—free of charge, of course."

"No one can fault your generosity, Krystos," Trell said by way of thanks. Glancing around, he noticed the deepening darkness beyond the windows and knew it was time to take leave of his friend. Motioning Krystos to walk with him toward the doors, Trell said, "There is one last thing I must ask of you," and he proceeded to outline his needs on behalf of Lily and the sisters.

Krystos nodded as he opened the double doors for Trell. "But of course I will do this, my old friend. I would do anything for you."

Trell suspected Fhionna's enchanting beauty might also have played into Krystos' easy declaration, but he thanked him all the same.

Then he was walking back to his own rooms feeling a warmth in his heart that he had not experienced since Graeme's death.

Trell donned his best garments for dinner that night, knowing it would please Krystos to see him so, and he used the inn's provided toiletries to neaten his beard and trim his hair, which had grown ever shaggier since he left Raku. So it was that he seemed a new man yet again when he arrived in the courtyard; in the least, he certainly felt a good deal cleaner.

The meal was set on a low, round table surrounded by velvet cushions. A four-poled tent had been erected over the circular sitting, each pole hung with blood-red velvet draping from a peak into elegant folds on the marble floor. Inside, candles in ornate glass globes hung by chains, casting flickering lights in a myriad of colors upon the marble table where a host of delicacies had been placed to delight both the palate and the eye.

Trell was not the first to arrive; he found Lily already seated beneath the sanguineous hanging, and beside her sat a youth of ten and eight, with longish dark hair and almond eyes so like her own. They both stood in honor of Trell's arrival.

Lily was beaming. "Trell of the Tides, this is my betrothed, Korin Ahlamby."

Trell clasped wrists with Korin. The youth had a firm handshake and held Trell's gaze, though he seemed slightly in awe. "Well met, Korin," Trell said quietly.

Korin did not immediately release his hand. "I cannot thank you enough, milord. Lily told me—" and he glanced at her, adding, "well, she told me much. I'm overwhelmed with gratitude and forever in your debt."

Trell released his hand and took a seat across from them. "Lily is very brave. It has been my honor."

Lily blushed and Korin gazed wonderingly and Trell, made uncomfortable by their adoration, wished he'd had more of Krystos' brandy to take off the edge.

It was not long before the sisters arrived, minus the four Khurds, who'd chosen to spend the night carousing with the blessing of Trell's coin. Aishlinn and Fhionna wore exquisite matching gowns in gold and silver, the silk worked all over with crystals that seemed on fire in the muted light. Each sister wore her hair atop her head in a bevy of waves held in place with jeweled pins. They looked a vision of unearthly beauty.

Trell rose and made a gallant bow upon their arrival. "Those gowns have Krystos written all over them, my ladies," he murmured with a smile.

"You are correct, Trell of the Tides," Fhionna replied. "T'was a gift we found upon returning from the baths. I confess I cannot say why he felt compelled to such generosity," and she added with a darted look at her sister, "for *I* have never properly met the man."

"No doubt he thought you would look a vision in it," Trell replied as he helped first Aishlinn and then Fhionna onto a cushion to either side of him and then retook his seat. "And I must say, save for our little Lily, I cannot remember ever having the opportunity to enjoy the company of two lovelier women."

"*Now* you flatter us," Aishlinn muttered, catching his eyes with her own as she adjusted her gown around her. "Now that you have my hard-given oath, that is?"

Trell smiled. "The lady is most perceptive."

"You strike a hard bargain, Trell of the Tides," Fhionna murmured. "I hope you do not live to regret your choice."

Trell eyed her appreciatively, always conscious of her beauty. "So do I, madam," he admitted, sighing. "So do I."

No sooner had they all been seated than Krystos' watchful wait staff appeared to begin serving the meal.

Dinner was thus a pleasant affair of engaging conversation supplemented by a delectable menu. Roasted peppers were stuffed with beef and pork mixed with spices, raisins and almonds and smothered in a walnut-pomegranate sauce; lamb with potatoes and carrots were served smothered in a peppery golden sauce, and a baked dish of roasted eggplant with vegetables, dates and figs had a wonderful flavor. There was a host of side dishes, of course, and a never-ending supply of warm, toasted flatbread and excellent wine.

Krystos came with the dessert, himself striking a stunning figure in an embroidered red velvet coat and black brocade pants, his boots spit polished, his long braid doubled up into a plaited club at the base of his neck. After inquiring as to everyone's comfort and satisfaction with the meal, Krystos turned his blue eyes on the sisters. "My ladies, you are the image of the goddess in those gowns," he said. He held out his hand to help them rise, and they accommodated his lustful gaze by turning a circle for his pleasure. "These gowns were last worn by the Cypher of Myacene during her rule of Avatar in the eleventh century of the Fourth Age of Fable," he told them. "I found them among other treasures hoarded by Myacene's twenty-third Emperor Titanias the Conqueror, and I have been saving them as a token gift for just such divine creatures as you."

"You are Agasi," Aishlinn replied then, eyeing him as alluringly as he was eyeing her, "and I believe from a noble house?" He nodded.

"And tell us, my lord Krystos," Aishlinn said, "have you the Agasi gift?"

Krystos looked startled at first, but then a smile lit his eyes. "Why…*yes*, my lady, as a matter of fact, I have." If the aspect of this gift was neither apparent from the question nor the response, it was certainly implied in the way the two of them looked at one another after that.

Trell cleared his throat. "Krystos, might you show the ladies to the Tea Room? I expect they would prefer to take dessert there while Korin and I speak of other matters."

Krystos bowed low from the waist. "It would be my pleasure. He extended a hand to help Lily stand and pressed her fingers to his lips with a murmured, "My lady."

Lily beamed at him.

As the group made their way along a path through the gardens, Fhionna fell into step with Trell and said in a low voice, "Lily told me of your conversation with her, Trell, and of her knowledge of your bloodline. Are you certain you won't hear what she has to say?"

Trell turned to reply, but his response was momentarily halted by her beauty. In her dress of diamonds, she seemed otherworldly. He took her hand, feeling the stirrings of desire with her touch and enjoying the freedom in it. Fhionna was like an addiction; part of him craved her desperately while another part screamed in warning. "Before I even began this journey, I was given the opportunity to learn who I was—at least, I believe the information was there."

"Before you even left?"

"Indeed. It was afforded me through the expedient means of an entry in a book. The page was there before me, lying open upon the table. I had even been given leave to read it."

Fhionna stared at him. "Why did you not?"

"I thought about it, certainly, but in the last…well, I couldn't bring myself to look—under the circumstances, honor forbade it. Soon thereafter, I was advised in an indirect manner that my *journey* might just be as important as the object of my quest, a sentiment I relayed to you." He stopped just shy of where the others had gathered. "I have since looked back upon the moment and decided it was a test, a test of my convictions, of my honor, of my very nature. I passed the test there." He pressed his lips to her palm and finished quietly, "I dare not fail it here."

The other women, and even Krystos, looked on as Trell said this, their own conversations paused in deference to his. Korin said to him seriously, "Your quest could be very dangerous, milord. Without the information Lily has about your birthright, you cannot know if you will find success or if you will die trying."

Trell regarded him patiently, only guessing at the trials ahead for both Korin and Lily. "Death takes all of us when it wills," he advised. "While my life is mine, I choose to live it, not to live in fear of losing it."

Krystos applauded him. "And such is why we love you, Trell of the Tides!" he declared before turning his brilliant smile on the women and extending his elbow to Lily, his other being already claimed by Aishlinn. "But come ladies, let me show you to my Tea Room. I have collected over four hundred varieties of the finest teas from across the realm..."

Lily kissed her betrothed on the cheek and hurried to take Krystos' offered arm, waving an excited goodbye as Krystos led them away while regaling them of his more civilized adventures in the discovery of tea. Fhionna trailed behind, her gaze lingering on Trell until fountains and date palms obscured her from view.

Trell turned to Korin, who was gazing after Lily with a troubled frown. "Will you join me in the library, Korin?"

The lad turned to him looking distracted. "Yes," he murmured. "Yes, I ...the *library*, milord?"

"Please call me, Trell," he corrected, for the lad's assertion of his 'birthright' made him uncomfortable. "Krystos has a fine library. It's quite a nice collection of important works, for its size." He guided the youth through the maze of gardens, fountains, and pools toward the west wing where the library was located. As they walked, Trell explained, "Should you choose to spend some time there during your stay here, you will find a number of works that I think will be to your liking. DiMarco's *Voyeur*, for example, is an autographed first edition, and Krystos' copy of Guillaume's *Il Grande Alliance* has been beautifully illuminated."

Korin turned to him in wonder. "*Il Grande Alliance* is one of my favorite works!"

"Guillaume's masterpiece is a timeless example of Veneisean literature," Trell noted diplomatically. In truth, the boy's admiration for the piece was a foregone conclusion—Trell had yet to meet an educated boy of fighting age whose favorite work of literature was anything other than Guillaume's colossal novel of betrayal and treachery in the Veneisean Court.

Reaching the library, Trell motioned Korin within and then entered behind him, signaling as he did to the steward who waited in the corner. The man approached with impeccable civility. "My lords, a drink perhaps? We have a fine collection of liqueurs to offer tonight. Krystos' family Port is in an excellent year. Or I might suggest a Veneisean brandy, perhaps one of the rarer Nadeaux varieties?"

Trell noted Korin's blank expression and offered, "If I may..."

He nodded gratefully. "We'll have the *Frangelicoste*."

"But of course, sir. An excellent choice."

Trell and Korin settled into a pair of armchairs beside two tall windows opened to the evening breeze. The steward brought their liqueurs in crystal snifters and then seemingly vanished, giving them the impression that they were quite alone. Trell had always admired the man for that very talent.

Trell sipped his liqueur and regarded the young man seated across from him, who in turn was watching him uncertainly. "I thought we should speak of your impending trip to Duan'Bai, Korin."

Korin took a rather large gulp of his liqueur by way of reply.

Trell had to be certain of the boy before he sent Lily off in his care. "Are you prepared for what it will mean to marry the expatriate daughter of the Ruling Prince of M'Nador?"

Though the question was a direct challenge, the youth was quick with his answer. "She is my life, sir. If living in Duan'Bai—if dying in Duan'Bai—is what she needs to chase the shadows from her soul, then I will be there at her side every step of the way."

Trell was unexpectedly pleased with his answer. He'd become protective of Lily during their days together, but he saw that this Korin truly loved her. "Then you too have seen the shadows behind her eyes."

Korin nodded.

"What has she shared with you about her secret?"

"Very little," he admitted. "Only that she saw something…horrible…and she feels strongly that certain people should know."

"That certain person is Prime Minister Rajiid bin Yemen al Basreh, a very dangerous man."

"She told me you agreed to give her an introduction."

"Indeed, but *you* need to understand the threat. A letter from me will get you both an audience, but it will be up to Lily to convince al'Basreh of her value to the Emir—something beyond selling her back to her father."

It was clear from the horrified expression on Korin's face that they hadn't envisioned that possible outcome.

Trell considered the youth thoughtfully. "Is this what you want also, Korin? You seem ill at ease here in Sakkalaah."

He swallowed. "It's too like home here, and—and at the same time not like it at all. The Cairs are—well, they're so unlike Tal'Shira in every way except the sea that it's easy to forget all that lies behind me."

Trell had spoken with countless boys of Korin's age who were running from their past…or future. Most of those interviews had been prior to their taking the Oath and becoming Converted, but what Korin and Lily were planning wasn't much different. "And are you ready to make the commitment to the Akkad? Can you renounce your heritage fully? Are you prepared to take actions that will forever sever all ties to M'Nador? These are things al'Basreh will require of you both."

Korin downed the last of his drink in one gulp. His gaze darkened as he lowered his glass, and for a moment Trell saw the savage hatred which the boy tried hard to conceal. "Radov abin'Hadorin had me banished for daring to love his daughter

Leilah," he said, "and that *mercy* was only because my father bartered two of my sisters in exchange for my life. Radov sold my sisters to an Avataren slaver and then stripped my father of his title and lands for the insult and shame of my actions." He clenched his teeth and looked Trell in the eye. "I assure you, milord, I harbor nothing but hatred for the man and everything he represents."

"A man isn't a kingdom," Trell advised quietly.

"I will never go back to M'Nador, sir," Korin declared vehemently, "neither of my own accord, nor bound and tied, nor dragged in shame. I would sever my own wrists before I set foot in the kingdom again."

Trell set down his glass, and the steward appeared to refill them both. "In that case," he said, "I have made arrangements for your travels. Kamil and Sayid, Ammar and Radiq, these men can be trusted. They work for coin, yes, but they were sent to me by the Khaz'im of the Bashir'Khazaaz. This is the highest of recommendations, and I believe you will be safe in their care."

Korin shifted in his chair. "Lily said these men were only hired for the trip to Sakkalaah."

"I thought it wise at the time to keep her final destination unknown to them, but I have since traveled with them, and they've earned my respect." Trell looked down and studied his glass, brimming with the amber drink. "I have spoken with Kamil, who speaks for all. Their fee will be great, and they will want to procure four additional men for additional fees. But yes, they will do it."

Korin had that awe-struck look again.

Trell tossed down his drink and got to his feet, setting down his empty glass on the table. "I depart on the morn, Korin. The fate of three women is now in your hands. Krystos is prepared to assist you with whatever else you might need for your journey. Don't hesitate to impose upon his generous nature. He has many contacts in Duan'Bai and is a valuable resource to you."

Trell made to go but Korin launched out of his chair and grabbed his arm. "My lord, won't you reconsider?"

"Reconsider what?"

"Lily's offer of...of knowledge."

Trell gazed at him sadly. "I cannot."

With that, Trell left the brooding youth, nodded his thanks to the unobtrusive steward, and headed back to his rooms. He had much to do before he could sleep, however, for there were supplies to gather for his journey tomorrow and of course, the letter for Lily.

He was in his rooms repacking the last of his cleaned things when a knock at the door heralded the maid with his requested parchment and quill and a tray with the tea service. Trell thanked her with a coin in Agasi silver. Her eyes widened, her curtsy deepened, and she told him to call upon her at any hour should he need *anything* at all.

After the fawning maid departed, Trell sat back in his chair and began mentally composing his letter to Prime Minister Rajiid bin Yemen al Basreh. Picking up the quill, he began with the usual niceties, inquiring as to the minister's health and that of his two sons, who commanded important outposts along the Akkad's southern border with the Forsaken Lands. That done, Trell introduced Lily and outlined her intentions in brief, allowing that she would detail her thoughts in person, and focused in the last on an idea he hoped al Basreh would consider.

He wrote, '*...while I do not presume to dictate who can or cannot be trusted, my lord, I believe the girl is truly out of favor with her father and could prove useful to us even if the information she harbors is of no value to the kingdom. Respectfully, I ask of you, if your needs do not require her service, let the lovers retire to my holdings in the east. I would that they might know peace together for some small span of their lives.*"

Trell sat back and reread his words. The Prime Minister was one of a select few who knew that Trell had been irrevocably deeded certain holdings along the Akkad's eastern coastline in return for his years of service to the Emir. Trell hoped Lily and Korin would find happiness together, wherever their paths led them.

Satisfied, Trell finished off the letter with the required courtesies, sanded and blotted it, and then sealed the parchment with a bold smudge of Krystos' favorite vermillion wax.

Thoughtful as the wax hardened, Trell frowned down at the smooth circle; he knew that its lack of a signet stamp announced his hand to the Minister as well as—if not better than—any personal seal of his own, yet that very fact held such torment for him. He wondered what crest might one day fill that empty circle and whether or not it would indeed be a noble crest, as so many had intimated of late.

'*The bastard son of a nobleman is still a bastard son...*' Trell thought of his words to Fhionna, spoken so bluntly in rebuttal of her assertion, belying how much it stung him to speak them. More than anything, he wished for an honorable birth, yet more and more it seemed the other was the only answer. Lily had told him he carried a 'kingdom blade,' whatever that implied, and Fhionna had insisted his blood was noble. What else could explain these traits were he not the bastard-born son of a nobleman? Or perhaps even worse, the illegitimate child of a Lady, cast off by her Lord husband and exiled as a youth lest he bring the Lord dishonor.

Even as Trell's throat constricted with the thought, a memory came unbidden; the image of three boys, himself one of them, studying together in a high tower overlooking a charcoal sea. Strangely, the memory didn't fit the explanation of a bastard birth—he would not have been educated with pure-born brothers, and the one truth Trell held to was that the two boys *were* his brothers. He *felt* it was true in his heart of hearts, yet he also knew that he had only one brother now.

How strange, these disjointed memories, he thought, *broken pieces of a missing life.* The puzzle picture that was his past had taken tentative form, yet at best it was only a border or a rough outline; the whole picture was still frustratingly absent. Empty before his vision.

Trell focused on the folded parchment in his hands again and its simple ring of wax. Would he share a seal with his brother one day? The selfsame brother to whom he felt so closely and inexplicably bound, the other of the Mage's 'kingdom blades'? Or would he be cast off again by his blood, forced to go his own way with no name to call his own, his future once again holding the same darkness as his past, forming a black and featureless harmonic connected by shame and dishonor?

'*Our past sculpts us, Trell,*' the Emir had often told him, '*but it does not define us completely. A dishonorable birth makes not a dishonorable man if he decides he will live an honorable life. In every waking moment, it is our next choice that makes us who we are.*'

Trell knew the Emir believed that. It was this very opinion which had spurred him to create the Converted, allowing men of any race to earn rank and fortune rather than be classified by birth or shamed forever by misdeed. Their slates were wiped clean in his eyes, and those of Jai'Gar, upon giving their oaths. Their future was in their hands thereafter; and in truth, it was rare that a Converted crossed the Emir or the boundaries he'd set for them. Having been given a second chance—or often times any chance at all—to make an honorable name for themselves with fortune to boot, these men embraced the Emir's rules and his gods; no more loyal or steadfast a soldier there was.

Conviction and purpose. That's what so many of the world lacked. Trell knew the Emir had provided for both in the creation of the Converted.

Letting out a pensive sigh, Trell set the completed letter upon the writing desk and reached for his tea, which was cool enough now to drink. Not long thereafter, he blew out the lamp and laid his head upon his pillow already anticipating tomorrow.

But he'd barely begun drifting off when he heard a key turn in the latch of his door. He let his right hand fall alongside his bed where his sword waited at the ready, pinned between the mattresses, but when the door opened and he saw who entered, he released the weapon, if not his guard.

"Fhionna," he said, sitting up. "You promised."

"I promised you that I would never again use enchantment against you," she agreed as she closed and relocked the door, "and to the Mother, I swore to make no children of our union." Coming toward him with her unbelievably beautiful face flushed with her desire, she declared with tender honesty, "But I made no promise to anyone not to love you."

"I have a long way to travel tomorrow," he protested, much against his body's desire.

She settled him a velvet smile. "Did you not say that a man who can sleep before an important journey has nothing to gain from the trip? I have merely come to ensure your travels are fruitful."

Trell watched her helplessly as she set down the lamp she carried and turned to him. He needed no enchantment to desire her as fiercely as he'd ever wanted any woman.

One pull on the robe she wore released its sash, and the silk floated to her ankles, revealing all of her perfection as she slipped into his bed. "Thief of my heart," she whispered as she slid her leg across his hips and climbed on top of him, pinning his swollen member beneath her silken nether-lips. "Tonight is for you...all for you." Trailing kisses down his neck as her hips began to move in rhythm with his beating heart, she breathed lustfully, "Whatever your pleasure is my pleasure." She sat up again, baring her breasts as her hips continued their slow dance. "That is...if you will accept my parting gift."

Trell's fervent kiss was his answer.

They made love through the night, until the first glimmer of dawn lightened the sky. Fhionna left him then but not without regret. Their fierce and passionate lovemaking was a harmonic of the bond they'd forged in their week together, and they both knew that it was a different kind of magic that bound them now.

"A love that can end has never been real," she whispered into his ear as she stood at the bedside. "You will always own a part of my heart, Trell of the Tides."

He pressed a parting kiss to her palm.

She looked down at him as she slipped back into her robe. "Do not forget me."

He laughed. "How could I?" Suddenly he grabbed her around the waist and pulled her back into his embrace. Pressing a kiss into her hair as she hugged him close, he murmured again, "How could I possibly?"

Then she slipped from his grasp and was out the door before he could find more words to say.

Rising and readying for the day, Trell paused for a moment before he dressed, looking down at a quilted overvest and a grey felted wool tunic, the latter worked all over with elaborate embroidery, both of them gifts from the Mage. The garments were fine enough to wear to Krystos' table, but Trell had chosen them for a different reason that morning. When paired with black britches tailored trim in the northern fashion, the outfit was presentable anywhere in the north. *Not just presentable,* he thought as he donned the garments. *Noble.* Indeed, the clothes were expensive both in fabric and construction—too expensive to be worn by a man of common blood. It made him wonder why the Mage had given him such fine attire...the Mage who surely knew his family name.

Trell belted on his sword and then stood looking in the full-length mirror for a long time. The deep grey of the tunic brought out the color in his eyes and made his dark hair seem that much richer in hue. *I look entirely different,* he realized.

Not that he'd ever looked much like the darker-skinned desert tribesmen, but now, in the slim pants and trim, tailored clothing...now he saw in himself what others often had: the height and sharp features of a Northman. And in his grey eyes...an image of the ocean flashed to memory, a different image than before, but the same sea, richly mercuric beneath an overcast sky, dark waves crashing violently against chalk-white cliffs, their waters murky near the shore where the milky chalk mingled and remained. All of this mirrored in his storm-grey eyes.

Trell knew that he stood at another milestone, much like his crossing of the Ashafani bridge; his donning of northern clothes somehow marked a turning point in his life. He was about to take a vital step toward his past, one that placed him across that line he both anticipated and feared...the line across which there was no turning back. East of Sakkalaah was the life he'd known for the past five years. West, was the life he'd been born to live.

That morning, he traveled west.

Trell looked at his bearded face one last time. Then he slung his packs over his shoulder, picked up the letter for Lily—which he planned to leave in Krystos' care—and headed out the door.

He imagined a silent departure, expecting to slip through the gates of the Inn of the Four Faces before his recent companions rose to greet the day. Thus it was to his great surprise that he found an assembly waiting for him as he descended the stairs and came into the courtyard.

Krystos and Aishlinn, Lily, Korin and Fhionna all stood waiting, the ladies garbed in colorful silk robes, the youth in a loose desert tunic and pants—all no doubt compliments of Krystos, who himself wore his same resplendent coat of the night before.

"Thought you'd escape without saying goodbye did you, my old friend?" Krystos' blue eyes sparkled above his smile. "Not a chance!"

Trell lowered his packs to the limestone tiles and smiled at the others, feeling unexpected gratitude to find them all come to see him off. He shook his head, not quite knowing what to say, and then remembered the letter in his hand. "Oh…this is for you," he told Lily, handing it to her.

She received it with a nod of thanks and then leaned forward to place a kiss upon his cheek, warm and soft, chaste and sweet. "And that is for you," she murmured abashedly as she pulled away. "For luck."

"I willingly accept," Trell said, smiling down at her.

Korin shook his head. "I get the idea we are somehow not exactly on the same side," he remarked quietly, "and yet you are helping us. Why?"

Trell thought about Jaya's admonishment again, her declaration on the truth of wars; the statement troubled him as much as it mystified him. To the youth, he replied, "Honor does not always hinge upon which side you support, Korin, and wars are not always fought for noble reasons."

"Trell is a man guided by conscience," Krystos observed cheerfully, casting Trell an admiring smile even as his easy good humor broke the tense mood. "He is, I believe, as noble in deed as he is in blood."

Trell shook his head and said to the others, "Krystos would like to think I'm some kind of lost prince—"

"But of course I would!" Krystos interjected, waving his hand in typical dramatic fashion. "Think of the story I might recount! History is rife with romantic tales, but there is always room for one more, Trell of the Tides," and he finished this with an affectionate wink.

Trell smiled and held up his hands in surrender. "Far be it from me to deny you a good story."

Krystos took him by the shoulders and kissed him on both cheeks. "Fortune guide you, my good friend," he said, "and may she one day lead you back to us."

"I will it so," Trell agreed as they parted.

Aishlinn leaned to kiss his cheek, her gaze unreadable, and Fhionna hugged him fiercely, daring not to speak.

Then he was hefting his packs over his shoulder and waving farewell to all of them.

Lily came running after him as the others were dispersing.

"Trell—wait!"

He turned to receive her curiously.

She held out a vial on a long silver chain and bade him drop his head that she might hang it around his neck.

"And what is this?" The engraved silver vial was sealed with dark blue wax. Trell studied it curiously.

Lily regarded him with her sad, dark eyes. "It is the truth, Trell, should you ever decide to know it."

Understanding, Trell held her gaze for a long time. Then he tucked the vial into his tunic, nodded one last farewell, and headed off into the future to find his past.

Part Two

Emergence

THIRTY-ONE

'Only the nightingale understands the rose.'

– The Fire Princess Ysolde Remalkhen

The coach carrying Tanis, Alyneri, Ean and Fynnlar reached Fersthaven as the sun was nearing its zenith. The manor drive led through a yellow-leaved apple orchard, and with the sunlight shining through the branches, the trees seemed to be made of gold. Prince Ean was gazing out the window with a solemn look on his handsome face, while Alyneri alternated between staring out the opposite door and casting affronted looks at a loudly snoring Fynnlar.

"Is something wrong, your Highness," Tanis asked him.

Ean turned and gave the boy a smile. "No, Tanis, not really. I was just…" he shrugged and smiled, "I was just thinking about how I might never see this place again, and it made me sad, because it's quite lovely here."

"Don't be maudlin, Ean," Alyneri muttered.

"Why wouldn't you be able to come back here, your Highness?" Tanis asked.

Ean looked back out the window as the last of the orchard was passing by, giving way to the tall red-gold maples that lined the drive. "No reason, Tanis. It was just a passing feeling." He turned the lad another smile. "Heading off on a journey such as ours, who knows when we'll be back?"

Tanis forced a smile in return, but it made him sad. He knew his prince was lying; he just didn't know why.

As the coach pulled to a halt in front of the stairs and the assembled manor staff, Alyneri veritably flew out the door and vanished inside with her Chamberlain before Tanis even set one foot upon the earth. The lad likewise left the two princes to their own devices and went to gather his things as he'd been bidden.

Prince Ean's strange mood notwithstanding, Tanis was excited almost to bursting. To think of going on an important quest with the prince as his very own truthreader—well, the thrill of it was nearly more than Tanis could bear. If only he'd been able to share the amazing news with Tad and Killian, but they'd had no time for farewells—Morin d'Hain had practically pushed them into the coach after the briefest of explanations and an ultimatum that originally had her Grace fuming. Tanis was surprised that he wasn't more tired, what with being up most of the night—and what a night it had been, too!—but he couldn't stop thinking about what lay ahead for them.

Tanis finished packing and looked around his room. It seemed barren without his things, yet there had been very little of him in it to begin with—just a wooden sword he'd used for practicing and some books Killian lent him. No doubt the Chamberlain would see them returned. Seeing his packed bags lying on the bed, Tanis couldn't help but think of Farshideh. Surely she'd be so pleased to know of his new and important position with the prince.

You take care of him now, Tanis, khortdad, she'd say. *He's your most important ally;*

he'll protect you even as you protect him from those that would infect his reign with lies and deceit.

Tanis thought he could almost hear Farshideh, her words seemed so clear, and he fought the urge to look around to see if she was somehow standing behind him. "Farshideh," he whispered, just in case she was somehow watching. "I love you."

And I love you, Tanis, dearheart. Now get a move-on before Alyneri winds up in a fuss.

Carting his heavy bags on either shoulder, Tanis found her Grace in her Infirmary preparing her vials of extracts, powders and tinctures for the trip. She looked up as he entered and gave him an annoyed look, though the lad quickly surmised that her irritation was in fact aimed at Prince Ean, who was lounging in the far doorway watching her with a crooked grin.

Tanis realized he'd walked into the middle of a conversation when Prince Ean remarked after a moment, "Are you sure about this, Alyneri? It will be dangerous—more than you know. What if I can't protect you?"

"And who shall protect you, your Highness?" she countered, casting him an arch look. "Surely you don't expect to go gallivanting off without even a Healer at your side? What happens when the next assassin finds you?"

"When? When?" he complained.

"Thanks for the vote of confidence." When her only reponse was a dubiously arched brow, Ean dropped his gaze and admitted, "I do plan to be as cautious as possible. I'm the first to recognize the danger. People *are* looking to kill me."

She harrumphed irritably at the truth of that. "All the more reason for me to be there, like it or not. If something happens again, Ean, you won't have that zanthyr—"

"No, Alyneri," he interrupted, his gaze adoring now, "you misunderstand. For all I fear our lives on this endeavor, I couldn't bear the thought of going without my beloved at my side."

"*Do* stop that nonsense!" she returned irritably, shooting him a hard look over her shoulder. "I'm certainly not going because of any affection for you. As Morin d'Hain so mercilessly pointed out earlier this morning, it is my duty as Healer to the Crown to protect the heir to the throne. That's why I'm going along."

Ean gave her a shadowy smile. "Of course. That must be it."

She responded with a withering look.

"Well, I'm all packed," announced an entering Fynnlar. He held two bottles of wine in each hand and carted a satchel brimming with more.

"We won't be that long away from civilization, Fynn," Ean said with a grin.

"What do you mean? These are for tonight."

"Fynnlar," Alyneri posed without turning from her task, "have you never stopped to wonder what you might accomplish with your life if you spent less time worshipping in the temple of inebriation and more time actually focused on some form of productive contribution to society?"

"Fill what's empty, empty what's full, and scratch where it itches, your Grace. That's my motto."

"You live up to it so completely," she murmured.

"One must have *some* principles," Fynn advised importantly.

"Fynn," Ean said, "I was just filling in Alyneri on our plans."

"Oh? Do we have a plan then?"

"Only in the barest sense of the word," Alyneri muttered.

"Alyneri, be nice." Ean gave her a chiding look. "We have a destination," he said then, "and we have a direction in which to travel to reach it. That's plan enough for now."

Alyneri arched a pale brow in unconvinced response.

"I hate to agree with her Grace, Ean," Fynn remarked, "but with all the people trying to kill you, you're going to need a better plan than that if you mean to take any of them down."

Ean crossed arms and settled him a level look. "Really? You think so?"

Fynn frowned at him. "Sarcasm and mockery are *my* territory."

"Speaking of territory," Alyneri cut in exasperatedly, "*mine* is feeling infringed upon. Why don't you both go see to your horses or whatever it is princes typically do before embarking on ridiculously perilous and ill-conceived quests that stand about a snowflake's chance in hell of resulting in any sort of happiness for anyone even remotely connected with them."

Ean grinned at her. "Alyneri," he sighed happily, "I didn't know you cared so—"

"Out!" she snapped, waving at him with her marble pestle. "Out—both of you!"

"See," a pouting Fynnlar said as he followed Ean from the room, "I told you she was maniacal. Did you see the way she brandished that club? And this is the girl you're 'thinking about courting'..."

Tanis watched the princes leave and then came over to observe Alyneri grinding a mixture of dried roots into a powder. "Your Grace," he posed after a moment, "why don't you want to go with Prince Ean?"

She turned him an astonished look but then apparently remembered that he was, after all, a truthreader. This seemed to annoy her. "What does it matter what I think, Tanis?" she said, exhaling a weary sigh. "We're going, and that's that. I know it makes you happy."

He grinned eagerly. "Yes, and it would make Farshideh happy too. She always wanted both of us to get out into the world, to travel and see things, and have... adventures."

Alyneri's look softened. "That's true," she admitted. She set to grinding her herbs again.

"She wanted you to go home, too."

Alyneri's hand froze. "What do you mean?"

"To M'Nador. She told me the night she died. She said you have a lot of family there who...who will love you...your father's people. She said you mustn't stay in this cold place because you're a child of the desert."

Alyneri stared down at her hands. "She said all that?"

"Yes."

"What else did she say?"

Tanis thought back. "Only...I don't know, it was strange. She said the dead can see so much and now she could see what she should've seen before."

"Which is what?"

"That this world is dying."

Alyneri frowned. "What an odd thing to say."

"Yeah. So anyway, I think Farshideh would be really glad that you're leaving Dannym on a great and grand adventure with Prince Ean."

Tanis's enthusiasm must've been infectious, because Alyneri finally smiled. She turned and placed a hand on his shoulder and looked him in the eye. "It is going to be a grand adventure, isn't it?"

Tanis nodded brightly.

She leaned in conspiratorially. "Then Tanis, do you know what we need?"

He shook his head, colorless eyes large.

"For a grand adventure," she whispered, "...we're going to need a lot of Avataren Yellowroot." Turning back to her mortal and pestle, she finished primly, "Might you bring me the last of it from the cellars?"

Thus tasked, a grumbling Tanis set off to retrieve the roots for his lady.

Alyneri finished packing her bag of herbs and then turned to lean back against her workbench, exhaling a long sigh as she gazed around the infirmary. She had so many memories of that room. It seemed she could see all the varied moments overlaid upon each other—her mother and Farshideh tending the sick, mixing herbs, cleaning the windows with lemon water so they shone in the morning sun...her father sitting with his darkly handsome smile, watching as her mother made a bouquet to hang for the Beltane festival, Tanis as a babe, a boy, a young man...

Alyneri had grown up in that room, and now as she prepared to leave, she wasn't sure if she would ever see it again. Oh, she'd criticized Ean for his earlier comments, but she'd known her own hypocrisy even then. No matter what happened on this journey, Alyneri had a feeling she would not return to Dannym. Her future was in Kandori, or perhaps elsewhere, but the heavy ropes that once bound her to the Eagle Throne were mere threads now and those already fraying at the edges.

She had a strange and lonesome feeling that everything had changed, that it was not merely a new chapter of her life opening to her but an entirely new book altogether. When exactly the shift had occurred she couldn't say. Perhaps it was losing Farshideh, yet she'd felt a stranger in her home long before her Seneschal passed away.

Oh, Farshideh... Alyneri lamented, swallowing back hated tears. *What shall become of me without you?*

You must go home, Soraya, Farshideh seemed to answer, *to your real home, to your people. You are loved in Kandori. Do not forsake what family is left to you for this cold and faithless kingdom.*

Alyneri sighed at the thought. She knew the North wasn't entirely without faith. They believed in the old ways, and in the Returning, and they upheld the sacred festivals; but she also knew that few understood the deeper meanings of their fetes anymore, preferring to admire the trappings without embracing the faith they hung upon. Alyneri had been raised with an understanding of her mother's beliefs as well as instruction in the pantheon of her father's desert gods, but neither dogma seemed to fit her very well. Nor did the Veneisean gods of Virtue and their endless rituals and rules hold any answers for her.

You truly are without a home when even the gods are alien to you.

Alyneri shook her head as if to dispel her dire mood and took up a bundle of lavender and hyssop that she'd tied together with honeysuckle vine. She walked to the brazier, lifted the cover, and laid the bundle upon the coals, inhaling with closed eyes as violet-grey smoke began drifting up.

With her offering, Alyneri prayed for Ean, for Tanis, and for a blessing upon their journey, but most of all, she prayed that she might somehow, at the end of it, find her own place in this world.

By the time Tanis returned from the cellars with the jar of Avataren Yellowroot, Rhys and the others had arrived. Tanis found Prince Ean and Fynn in the courtyard speaking with the Captain, who was accompanied by the Lieutenant Bastian val Renly, two other guardsmen, and Fynn's man Brody. They all wore traveling leathers in nondescript hues of ochre, russet, or charcoal.

Prince Ean was looking at the pack horses laden down with supplies, and he didn't seem pleased by their presence. "Do you know something I don't know, Captain?" he asked, indicating the horses. "That's enough to last a month on the road, but it's only three days to Devon."

"No boats," Rhys grunted, clearly knowing the prince's mind in mentioning the port city. "His majesty was clear."

Ean bristled. "No boats? I just spent half a year on board the *Sea Eagle*, and my father's concerned about my safety at sea *now*?"

"Now you are the target of several aggressive factions, your Highness," Rhys pointed out.

Ean cast him a narrow look.

"Ships are easy targets," Rhys went on, "and their crews are too easily infiltrated."

"The Admiral would beg to differ, I think," Ean disagreed.

"But you wouldn't be on one of Admiral L'Owain's ships, your Highness," said Bastian val Renly with his usual neutral calm, "which is an important distinction in its own right, for your enemies would certainly expect your grandfather to oversee your travels at sea. His ships would be the first ones they'd suspect. No, their majesties were very much in agreement that boats should not be considered an option for this journey."

Mollified by this logic but clearly still displeased about it, Ean clasped hands behind his back and looked to Rhys. "No boats, then. Any other orders I should be aware of, Captain?"

"Have you brought burlap hoods, perhaps?" Fynn posed critically. He'd managed to stash his bottles of wine and now held the ever-present goblet instead. Tanis wondered how much he'd already consumed, because he looked a little unstable on his feet. "You know, just to complete the look. It is *the* accessory for captives. Or perhaps Morin d'Hain will have us donning dresses," he posed as an aside to Tanis, "to be carted south in shackles like kept women." He belched and swung back to Rhys, adding, "I prefer the pewter cuffs if you have them."

At Ean's you're-really-not-helping look, Fynn gave him an apologetic shrug and explained, "The brass shackles chafe, Ean."

"No one is going anywhere in shackles, Lord Fynnlar," Bastian assured him.

"Oh, very good. Just the dresses then? May I have a blue one? It brings out the color in my eyes—"

"Fynnlar," Ean warned.

"What?" Fynn protested.

Ean cast him a long, steady stare.

Bastian posed then, "Anonymity *is* important, your Highness. Minister d'Hain mentioned that you agreed to travel incognito as we head south."

"And there's the matter of the horse," Rhys reminded him.

"Yes, he's quite noticeable," Bastian agreed. "It might be better to—"

"I'm not leaving my horse!" Ean declared, fuming.

"Whose quest is this anyway?" Fynn complained.

Rhys drew himself tall. "Prince Ean is very much in charge."

Fynn grunted dubiously. "Sure he is. Why don't we go ahead and call a spade a spade, Captain. Admit it—my horse gets a say before Ean does."

"Fynn—"

"Be quiet, Ean. No—really," and he held up a firm hand. "You are a terrible negotiator. It's important to establish your boundaries at the outset, otherwise they spend all your traveling money on useless trinkets and you're left begging relatives for handouts."

Brody nodded to the wisdom of this advice.

"My lords, if I may," Bastian posed, raising a hand entreating their patience. When he met with silence all around, he continued, "I was not suggesting that your Highness leave Caldar behind, only that we might do our best to disguise the horse as much as your own person."

"Go on," Ean said, crossing his arms.

"Minister d'Hain has prepared a story to explain your absence from court as well as that of her Grace," and he nodded politely to a just then arriving Alyneri, who came to a halt behind Tanis looking suspicious. Bastian continued, "Your Highness has retreated into the customary fortnight's mourning period over the loss of your blood-brother, staying in your apartments and seeing no one." Bastian looked to Alyneri. "During this time, your Grace has taken a last pilgrimage to Jeune."

"Accompanied by the King's Own Guard?" Ean posed dubiously.

"I have several times been accompanied by the King's Guard in my travels, Ean," Alyneri muttered, sounding less than pleased to have their acquaintance once again.

"Under the circumstances," Bastian continued, nodding his acknowledgement of her point, "it is even more appropriate, for a rumor is being spread that your Highness and her Grace will be betrothed upon completion of your period of mourning—"

"*What?*" Alyneri protested in outrage.

"—hence her Grace's timely pilgrimage to Jeune."

"I am not chattel to be handed off like inheritance from one brother to the next!" she declared hotly.

"Tis only a rumor, your Grace," Bastian soothed.

"But the best rumors have their basis in fact," Fynn pointed out through a belch.

She glared at him.

"The guise of a pilgrimage also explains our overland route south," Bastian added, "as well as any spare conditions we might be keeping."

Fynn grimaced. "By spare you no doubt mean spending an inordinate amount of time communing with nature."

"As in bedrolls and campfires," Brody clarified.

"I know what it means!" Fynn snapped.

"Tis an important aspect of pilgrimages," Bastian told him, "that one travels as an ascetic, which would account for her Grace not visiting the usual nobility and foregoing certain comforts on her travels south."

"Yes, how perfect," Fynn complained.

"As to the matter of your Highness's disguise," Rhys said then.

"Should I grow a beard?" Ean offered.

"No good, Ean," Fynn said, sighing. "You'd only look the spitting image of dear uncle Gydryn then."

"Yes, you are…remarkable in your own way, Ean," Alyneri admitted.

"Minister d'Hain thought it best if your Highness might agree to travel as one of the guard," Bastian said. "Lacking fanfare or elegant attire, it is his hope that you might not be singled out from among our number."

"Better yet," Alyneri posed sweetly, "you can be my pageboy."

"Pageboy!" Ean protested.

"Tis for the best, Ean," she replied with a prim toss of her head, "for whoever looks at servants?"

Tanis thought that Prince Ean would get noticed no matter what he was posing as, but he kept this idea to himself.

"I think I look more the part of a soldier than a pageboy, Alyneri," Ean grumbled.

She shrugged. "Suit yourself."

"Lastly, there's the matter of the horse," the laconic Captain said.

Tanis thought it quite interesting how Rhys let the lieutenant do all the talking yet somehow managed to retain his 'I'm-in-charge' demeanor. He couldn't deny the effectiveness of this strategy, however, for the lieutenant had a way of leading others that people easily accepted, whereas the Captain only engendered belligerence—at least such was true in her Grace's case.

Everyone in the company turned to assess Caldar then. The horse stood between Alyneri's chestnut mare and Fynnlar's Agasi-bred roan. With his gleaming golden mane and proud stance, the silver-grey stallion was unmistakably a Hallovian steed. However to disguise such a noble creature?

It seemed everyone was asking themselves the same question, if told by the many frowns. And then Tanis had an idea. "Ash!" the boy cried. "What's that?" Alyneri asked.

Tanis looked at the rest of the company, but mostly to Prince Ean, as he explained, "We can cover him in ash." Tanis knew too well how difficult it was to remove the damnable stuff from anything it touched—limestone hearths, suede boots, her Grace's favorite linen… "We can darken Caldar's mane and hindquarters with ash," he went on. "He'll look just like any other warhorse then. Plus, there's always plenty of ash to be had anywhere we go, so if it begins to fade we could easily darken it again."

Ean brightened considerably. "Brilliant, Tanis. Well done."

And so it was decided.

It was still a late start for the expedition south, however, for Alyneri was quite specific in how her medicines must be stowed in order to preserve their various packages, essences, properties or delicate states of readiness. Rhys was nearly apoplectic by the time they headed down the drive leaving Fersthaven, but Tanis was elated to be on the road; his happiness was elevated to a level nearing ecstasy by the sack of nutcakes Mistress Hibbert pushed off on him with a wink and a smile just as he was mounting up.

So it was that the first few days of their travels passed almost pleasantly, even though the long hours of riding had Tanis sore each night. Beneath the Gandrel's variegated canopy, they found adequate shelter, and the group soon fell into a rhythm in their routine of setting up camp. Rhys and his men were excellent marksmen, securing rabbits and pheasants aplenty for their meals rather than break into their stores of smoked meat, which would be needed in sparer conditions; and Tanis was in charge of collecting firewood, which he made a game of to see if he could stack up fallen branches and limbs faster than Brody could break them into fagots. Bastian did most of the cooking, but Alyneri provided herbs and spices that made the stews more than palatable.

Each night, therefore, Tanis fell asleep with a full belly snuggled beneath a sleeping fur that kept him almost too warm but would be welcome in the highlands to come, his hopes high and his heart light at the prospect of his grand adventure.

THIRTY-TWO

'All you have is a man's will; a slave who owns nothing still possesses his power of choice.'

– The Fifth Vestal Björn van Gelderan

Andrus Vargha, Agent of Malchiarr, unobtrusively patted his various knives in their hidden locations as he followed the Avataren down a dark hallway. The bald man was a giant if ever he'd seen one, standing near seven paces tall, and he had an even bigger scimitar at his hip.

Vargha felt confident he could take the Avataren should such misfortune befall them; people always underestimated him because of his height—or rather his lack of it—and especially the giant ones, who expected their brute force to overwhelm any smaller opponent. Still, Vargha was somewhat on edge, for he'd already been played the fool once that day. The first time was when he'd gone to meet the Karakurt's coach alone and found the Avataren waiting to receive him instead.

Should've known she wouldn't be there.

It was true. He should've known. No one saw the Karakurt without her veil and her screens and her countless bodyguards.

It was the bodyguards that made him uneasy now. These men had cut out their own tongues in a ritual of loyalty to their mistress. It was rumored that she ate the flesh raw to seal the bond, but this was only a rumor. What Vargha did know was that the mutes were vicious fighters and ready to die for their mistress.

Vargha had been an agent for the Geshaiwyn of Malchiarr for a long span of years, and he'd worked with most of the underground agencies at one point or another in his career. Some were more predictable than others. The Pirates of Jamaii, for example, could always be trusted to keep to the Code, while the Veneisean Brotherhood of Seven Stones held to a rigid standard of neatness and prided themselves on never spilling a single drop of blood; even Agasan's Order of the Glass Sword had their weaknesses, though they were few and far between.

But the Karakurt…she was as capricious as the wind.

The Agents of Malchiarr had contracted with the Karakurt several times in more recent years, though always through intermediaries. She was the most unknown of their associates, the most difficult to treat with, the most elusive to contact—every bit as dangerous and erratic as the poisonous desert spider that was her namesake. Though he misliked revealing himself to her now, the message he must deliver today was one that had to be given in person—an appalling message he'd never before had to relay in his long career—and then there was the matter of the Agasi silver…

The hallway led to a door, the door to a spiraling staircase, and the stair to a subterranean passage, this one dank and smelling of mold. The Karakurt was always on the move. She had a small army of followers—rich lords and ladies from powerful families spanning numerous kingdoms—who were practically killing each other for the chance to host her and her entourage in secret, in silence. Vargha had no idea who owned the house he walked in now. When the Karakurt was staying in your home, you didn't show your head.

Not if you value it.

They finally reached a heavy door, and the Avataren banged on it with the pommel of his scimitar while Vargha stared at the spider tattoo on the back of his shaved neck. Vargha listened as the latches were drawn back, and then he was being ushered inside a luxurious room. Layered Akkadian carpets covered the floor, patterned silk draped the bare walls, and low tables and pillows were strewn about, most of them embellished by the Karakurt's entourage of veiled ladies-in-waiting. The Karakurt's bodyguards stood at intervals around the expansive room, most of them near the furthest end where a silk screen had been erected, behind which glowed a lamp that illuminated a seated figure. Vargha could see nothing of the Karakurt except her shadow on the silk, though the ornate headdress she wore was clearly fashioned in the shape of two long-necked birds.

"Ah, Agent Vargha," said a dark-haired man just then approaching. His name was Pearl—Vargha had treated with him before—and he fashioned himself Epiphany's cousin or some such, adopting the ostentatious title of Speaker of the Karakurt's Will. The Karakurt's spider sigil was tattooed in the middle of his forehead, and he wore kohl liner around his dark eyes and a silk robe of crimson overspun in silver thread, patterned in the image of the same tropical, long-necked birds. Vargha noticed that all the Karakurt's women also wore garments of similar material.

Pearl took Vargha's elbow, drawling, "We are most interested in hearing the news that requires such an unusual meeting with Us." The man always spoke in capital letters. It annoyed Vargha to the ends of his patience. "Quite against Our protocol," Pearl continued, affixing the Geshaiwyn an oily smile. "We felt certain, when you accepted this task and Our initial investment of silver, that you understood all of Our requirements. Why then, this meeting?"

Vargha made a quick glance about the room. The giant had taken a position by the room's only door, barring any normal means of escape, but Vargha was Geshaiwyn. He'd already scanned the room for leis and found one that would suit his needs, providing he could reach it. Vargha briefly envisioned himself fighting his way through the Karakurt's line of crimson-clothed guards to the leis behind her screen, but the mere fact that they'd let him keep his weapons said much for the expected *efficacy of that avenue. Probably Shi'ma sleeping darts, he thought, guessing the most* expedient means of eliminating himself with the least amount of bloodshed. It was well-known that the Karakurt misliked bodily fluids on her carpets, and any one of the mutes—*or all of them*—could be harboring a blowpipe up his sleeve.

"Three of our agents have attempted to kill the prince," Vargha finally replied, resigning himself to face whatever outcome resulted from the news he meant to deliver, "and lost their lives in the bargain."

"*Yes*," said Pearl, drawing the word into a hiss through a mirthless smile that said this news did not come as a surprise. "We were warned by our client that the contract might be difficult, which is why we contacted your people for the job, Agent Vargha."

Because Geshaiwyn are effective…or expendable? "The last of my agents lost track of the prince two days ago," Vargha admitted.

"We heard the prince has gone into mourning."

"More likely tis another of Morin d'Hain's rumors."

"But of course," Pearl said, as if this was a foregone conclusion. "We have contacts in every town from Tal'Shira to the Free Cities, and all are on the lookout for this northern prince. He would need Fortune's blessing indeed to avoid Our notice."

"The boy survived the blades of three of my assassins," Vargha pointed out darkly. "I would say Fortune is definitely with him."

Pearl sneered. "Have you so little faith in your own people? What happened to the great Geishaiwyn reputation?"

Vargha cast the man a black look. For a moment, he reconsidered their choice and the reason he'd come to see the Karakurt—but only for a moment. Ultimately the price had already been too high. The Adept race was dying, and his people could ill afford the loss of any more of their kind. Reaching into his coat, Vargha withdrew a bag of Agasi silver—the Karakurt's payment for the contract. This he tossed at Pearl's feet with a heavy *chink*. "Geshaiwyn don't wager against Fortune's graces," Vargha grunted, but there was little boldness in him truly. They were, after all, reneging on their agreement—something never done by the Agents of Malchiarr.

Pearl's dark gaze took on an air of accomplishment, and he cast a look toward the woman behind the screen. "So," he said, smiling coldly, "it is as We suspected. You crawl to Us in shame like a beaten dog."

Vargha grimaced at the truth in his words. No good to deny it. "The loss to us is too great," he said. "If our fourth fails, we will not send another pair. We will not complete the contract."

Pearl drew in his breath with an affronted hiss.

A tinkling of bells and rustling silk drew Vargha's eye to the screen. The Karakurt was standing now, her headdress towering above even the giant at the rear door. Pearl and the others bowed obsequiously. Vargha frowned.

Another form moved behind the screen then, emerging from the Karakurt's silhouette, shadows giving birth to shadows. He was tall and slim of waist, and as he rounded the edge of the screen, Vargha saw that he was elegantly dressed. His long ebony hair was slicked back from a noble's peak and clasped at the base of his neck with a gold band. Three red-gold bangles pierced each ear, but he was no Jamaiian sailor, this one. Vargha was hard-pressed to say if the man was Avataren or Bemothi, for his rounded nose, caramel skin, and slanted almond-shaped eyes belonged to both races. What surprised him, however, was the way the Karakurt's minions shied away from the man; even the insufferable Pearl looked wan as he stepped aside. Not a good sign.

The stranger stopped before Vargha, and a cold gaze regarded him plainly if distantly, as if Vargha was but a smudge upon the window which he desired to look through. "A contract with us is a contract to the death, Agent Vargha," said the stranger with the trace of an accent as foreign as his dress. "You will complete it or suffer gravely for your failure."

Vargha wasn't so easily intimidated as they must've thought him. "The Council of Malchiarr has decided," he returned firmly, staring the stranger in the eye though the man's serpentine gaze brought the uneasy sensation of snakes slithering under his skin. "Even Agasi silver can't replace the lives of three of our agents. We will not commit any more pairs."

The Karakurt chuckled from behind the screen, her deeply resonant voice filling the room. "You don't understand, Agent Vargha. It matters not to us how you kill the prince—whether your agents do it personally or if his death comes from the hand of others you contract on our behalf—but you *will* complete your contract."

"Or face extermination," the stranger asserted.

Vargha felt a cold chill at the threat. This wasn't how things were done. *Extermination?* It was a bold declaration, yet Vargha believed the man meant it. The utter emptiness in his smoldering dark eyes made anything seem possible.

The stranger's ill gaze swept over Vargha, and then, quite without warning, he licked his thumb and pushed it against Vargha's forehead. His touch burned like ice held too long against bare flesh. Vargha shuddered backwards, one hand instinctively reaching for his blade, and though the link was severed as he withdrew, still his forehead flamed with icy fire.

The encounter left him shaken. Vargha knew magic was being worked here—fell magic like none he'd encountered, and he wanted nothing more to do with it. "Threaten me all you like," he managed, barely getting out the words without stuttering over his own urgent desire to flee the stranger's empty-eyed gaze, "but our position stands."

"I am sorry you feel that way, Agent Vargha," said the Karakurt, sounding just the opposite.

Vargha spun and made for the door, yet still he was unprepared for the words that followed him out of the room.

"You are a marked man now, Agent Vargha," the stranger said.

Vargha felt a tingling in the tips of his fingers, an itching that made him want nothing more than to drive his blade through the man's heart and gut him like a pig. Instead, he squared his shoulders and rushed out, heading down the long tunnel, up the stairs, and out into the night.

When the Geishaiwyn was gone, the Karakurt walked to her screen and swept it aside. Her servants immediately prostrated themselves, faces pressed to the floor, eyes tightly shut; each recited a humming chant that ensured their mistress's privacy.

All, that is, save the stranger. He watched her with a gaze as still as death, while from within the sleeve of his coat he retrieved a single feather the color of flame. This he rolled between his fingers, a bit of captured light.

"We will make this right, Lord Abanachtran," the Karakurt said.

The Lord Abanachtran's gaze flicked over her like the sharp edge of a blade, and though she was fully clothed, she felt its deadly touch mark her naked flesh.

"We will redouble our efforts," she promised, now an urgent appeal. "Your master can depend on us, my lord. Please—please assure him of this."

The Lord Abanachtran looked down upon her. He was nearly as tall as the giant. He brought his feather up under her chin and lifted her face to his with a jingling of headdress bells. "You should pray it be so," he murmured. "My brothers are not so forgiving of failure as I."

Then he was gone, flowing out of the room like oiled water, vanishing into the dark.

The Karakurt pressed a hand to her belly, taking a moment to still her beating heart, to quiet the riotous nausea tumbling her stomach. Every time the Lord Abanachtran visited he left with another piece of her soul. Composing herself, she walked over to Pearl. "Get up!"

He scrambled to his feet, eyes downcast. "Mistress—"

Her slap stole the words from his tongue. "What a farce you've made of this!"

He glared at his shoes with injured defiance.

Her next slap was harder and left upon his cheek a white handprint and a biting sting. "See that the val Lorian prince is found and his head delivered to me," she snarled as she returned to her seat and closed the screen again roughly, "and perhaps something can still be salvaged of this fiasco!"

What she did not say was, *Perhaps something can still be salvaged of us.*

THIRTY-THREE

'A man from afar says what he will.'

– An old desert proverb

Ean's company traveled steadily southward over the following week, trading the Gandrel's bright autumn reds and siennas for the long golden grass of the hill country.

While the days passed without trouble, Ean was plagued with doubts. He doubted his instincts, which had failed him abominably the night of Creighton's death. He doubted his decisions, which were 'reckless and brash' if Morin d'Hain was to be believed. He doubted his reasoning, knowing so much of it was born of vengeance, and he doubted his ability to lead his ragtag company of loyal companions. He *doubted*, and the doubts opened a door to indecision, indecision weakening to fear.

The fear he held off with strength of will, but the indecision was miserable.

A week had passed without incident, yet he was no closer to seeing the pattern woven by the many threads connecting through him. What did his pattern—his *Return*—a Shade, Björn van Gelderan, Geshaiwyn assassins, the Duke of Morwyk, and a zanthyr have in common? Where did their threads intersect and why? And why was Raine D'Lacourte so keen to aid him? Raine had sent him south for his safety, but Ean worried that if he didn't come to understand these things, his safety would be the least of his problems.

As if these matters weren't troubling enough, Ean bore the responsibility not only of his own safety but also that of his companions. This weighed more heavily on his conscience now that he'd witnessed so many people offer up their lives to protect him. He felt a grave burden in this knowledge, for he had such nobility in his father to aspire to—Alyneri may have previously traveled with the King's Own Guard, as she said, but Ean suspected Rhys was traveling with them now for a different reason altogether: his father would soon be knowingly placing himself in harm's way, and the king would not willingly do the same for Rhys and his men—knowing that they would so readily offer their lives in trade for his own. So he sent them instead to protect his son on an equally dangerous journey, suspecting however that at least Ean stood a chance of survival.

Just the thought was a cold fist around Ean's heart. That his father was so prepared to die… Every time he thought of it, Ean pushed it away. He couldn't bear the idea of losing his father, too.

Keeping company with his thoughts during the quiet hours of riding, Ean found himself watching his companions more and more. Alyneri rode in a shroud of thoughtfulness, self-contained in her blue cloak, her expression somehow sad; Tanis remained ebullient, his colorless eyes brightly shining as they took in the scenery; Rhys and his men rode in silence, stoic but intense, focused on their task, while Fynnlar complained incessantly to a silently loyal Brody.

The prince wished so much that he could send all of his friends away, to safety, to live out their lives in peace; it angered him that he knew he couldn't, that he needed their council, their support…their protection. So also did he realize that every decision he made would affect their future, their survival. He felt far from ready for that responsibility however it had been thrust upon him.

A week into their journey, while the others pitched camp in the bosom of grass-covered hills, Ean pulled Alyneri aside. He took her hand and led her upstream, following the little brook that pooled near their camp. When they'd climbed out of view of the others, he bade her sit beside him at the water's edge.

Alyneri had warmed to him only slightly in the past week—mostly due to his leaving her alone—but she regarded him suspiciously as she settled down in the grass across from him. "So what's this about, Ean?" she asked, looking around. "Why all the secrecy?"

"Privacy," he corrected, casting her a troubled gaze. "I just want your opinion on something."

"Yes, you need a bath," she confirmed. "There. That's done. Can we go now?"

Ean gave her a sooty look. He cleared a space of dirt between them, smoothed it with one hand, and then picked up a stone and began drawing with a pointed edge. Alyneri was about to voice an irritable comment when the drawing itself caught her eye, effectively silencing her. When the prince was finished, he rested elbows on knees and regarded her startled expression with a sober frown.

She lifted wide brown eyes from the pattern scrawled in the dirt and met his gaze. "Ean…"

"I know," he muttered.

"Do you?" she challenged, straightening to better look at him. "Do you know how impossible it is that you're drawing that pattern—or that you can even see it?"

"So you recognize it too?" For a moment her response gave him hope. If somehow she saw the same pattern…

Alyneri caught her thumbnail between her teeth and shook her head, looking amazed. "When I healed you," she said, staring at the drawing, "it was this pattern I finally found. I'd almost forgotten how strange that moment was…"

"How do you mean?"

She lifted her gaze to meet his. "This is *your* pattern, Ean. That which is uniquely you—the very pattern that is the framework of your existence. A Healer's first task upon any healing is to find a person's pattern, for without that, no healing can begin."

"What was strange about mine?"

She frowned at him, looking uncertain. "Usually finding the pattern is akin to… well, somewhat like searching for a leaf within the waters of a rushing stream. But your pattern…that pattern…it *is* the stream." Abruptly she gave him a hard look. "But you're no Healer," she challenged. "How can you see this pattern at all?"

Ean hadn't been sure how to break the news to her. There didn't seem to be any easy way to go about it. He looked her in the eye. "Because, Alyneri…I've Returned."

For a moment, her brow furrowed. Then she burst into laughter.

"Thank you for understanding," Ean muttered crossly.

"Oh!" she finally managed, pressing tears of mirth from her eyes, "but it's so—so ridiculous!"

He was beginning to find her response vaguely irritating. "Why?" the prince demanded, crossing his arms. "Why is it so unbelievable to you?"

Hugging her belly as she tried to stop laughing, Alyneri finally managed, "Because you haven't any talent whatsoever, Ean!"

The prince gazed darkly at her and tried not to let her chiming laughter chip too many chinks in his ego. "Nevertheless, Alyneri," he cut in deliberately, "it *is* the truth."

His decisive tone dampened her amusement, and she composed herself long enough to look him in the eye. She frowned at him then. "You can't really be serious about this, Ean."

"I was hoping you might have something to offer in the way of advice," he remarked testily. "Returned, but not Awakened. That's what the Fourth Vestal told me. That's what I've recently admitted to myself as truth, and that's why—I'm fairly certain—Björn van Gelderan sent his Shade after me."

She'd fallen silent at mention of the Fourth Vestal.

"So," Ean said. "Have you any knowledge of the Returning, Alyneri? I fear my education extends to the Litany for the Departed and no further."

She steepled fingers before her lips and stared incredulously at him.

"What usually happens?" Ean pressed. "How do you Adepts know of your talents? Is it always from birth?"

She shook her head slowly. "...No," she admitted after a moment. "Oftentimes the gift comes with adolescence. In my case—I mean, Healers always pass on the gift to their daughters, so I always knew."

"What about Tanis?"

She shrugged. "The same, I believe. His eyes, you know—colorless eyes are a sure sign of the gift. Certainly we knew from the moment he joined our household that he'd be a truthreader, but he didn't begin his training until this year."

"And if they don't Awaken during adolescence?"

Alyneri, for once, looked compassionately upon him. "I've never heard of it happening in later life. I suppose it's possible, but you'd think it would be mentioned somewhere if anyone had done it."

Why then? Why does the Fifth Vestal care what happens to me?

"Perhaps when we get to Jeune—"

"We're not going to Jeune," he told her, swallowing his disappointment that she'd nothing else to offer. "That's just our story."

"Then where?"

"Straight to the Cairs. Fynn has contacts who can...hide us," he almost choked over the word, "until things smooth over."

She gave him a troubled look. "And you're at peace with that?"

He glared at her. "No, I'm not at peace with it!" he snapped, moving to his feet lest he expend too much emotion toward her, which she did not deserve. He stood glaring at the little brook with crossed arms instead. "But what choice do I have? My advisors either know nothing or else know nothing more that they're willing to share. People are trying to kill me, and my death means only...only destruction to my father's kingdom."

Abruptly he spun her a tormented look. "What else *can* I do?"

She considered him for a long moment in silence. Then she looked to the brook, a faint frown furrowing her pale brow. After a tense silence, she took a measured breath and offered, "Farshideh always told me that a donkey who pretended himself a horse was sure to falter on a stony path, but a donkey who thought himself a horse would be surefooted in any terrain."

Ean looked heatedly at her. "What is that supposed to mean?"

She chuckled. "It was a lesson that took me a while to decipher, too."

"And did you?"

"I think so," she admitted with a modest smile. "In essence, she was trying to tell me that you cannot act against your nature—your true nature—and hope to succeed. Not that we can't overcome faults in our character—such as being reckless or…or prone to emotional outbursts," and here she lowered her eyes, clearly meaning herself. "But that we have a deeper nature lying beneath our faults, and to the former we must be true."

Ean swallowed.

Alyneri lifted her eyes to meet his once more. "What does your heart tell you to do?"

"To seek out Björn van Gelderan and all of his Shades and incinerate them," Ean growled.

Her expression fell into disappointment, and she dropped her gaze to her lap. "I hoped that you had recognized that taking one more life won't bring Creighton's back," she whispered, "that sacrificing your life won't change anything and only adds to…the loss. Life is such a precious and fragile thing, Ean. No good man claims another's life without regret."

He thought she'd meant to say something else there at the end, but he didn't want to press her. Forthright communication with Alyneri was hard to come by; the Duchess hid her true feelings behind steel barbs that drove all but the most stalwart suitor away nursing wounds.

"Is that your intent then?" she asked, looking up at him beneath dark lashes. "Will you seek vengeance despite all reason?"

"If you would have me follow my heart," he returned evenly, "that is where it leads."

She turned away. "Then you're a fool."

Ean's gaze hardened. "What do you want from me, Alyneri? You tell me in the same breath to follow my heart and then criticize me for it. Would you rather that I do nothing while others slay those who mean the most to me? You would have me continue on a deliberately craven path?"

She stood to face him. "I would have you show some foresight! I would see you think before you leap to your death in a stunt that accomplishes nothing! I would rather believe you a man of intelligence and restraint than a rash and hapless fool!" Her voice broke with this last, and she spun on her heel and stalked back to camp, leaving Ean smarting from the sting of her words.

He was still brooding when he found his pallet that night, but despite his compounding worries, the moment his head found its place, he fell quickly asleep.

The dream came in the early morning hours.

It was one of those dreams where Ean was not himself—the man in the dream looked nothing like him—yet he recognized something of his own being beneath the unknown face.

In the dream, a man sat across a table from him. Ean knew him in the same way he knew himself—the unlikely faces were but shells for their true identities, and neither of them were entirely fooled by the façade. While he didn't know the man, he knew they were enemies. Of this he was certain.

"You cannot hope to succeed," said the man, who stared at him from beneath heavy brows, his dark eyes coldly calculating.

"That's not true," Ean heard himself reply. He knew there was a history to this conversation—it was like he'd dreamed this before, as if this scene was but a continuation of an earlier dream wherein all of what had come to pass was remembered.

The man barked a laugh, but there was only malice in it. "You deny it?"

Ean regarded him calmly. "I deny your right to determine what hope exists and when or where I may lay claim to it."

This retort earned him a hateful stare. "You are a pitiful people," he declared, though it was clear from his tone that Ean's words had found their mark. "*Hope.* What is *hope?* It is nothing. A word, a symbol of an intangible dream, yet your kind *cling* to it, revel in it, but you cannot avoid the truth."

"And what do you know of truth?" Ean returned. "I dare say none of you have known it intimately, nor suffered its restrictions."

The man's eyes grew hot. "You lead a *purposeless* existence," he snarled, and the word seemed both curse and incantation.

Ean held his serpentine gaze. "But it is *ours* to lead."

The other's eyes flashed, and suddenly he was launching over the table grabbing for Ean's throat. They tumbled to the ground with the stranger's hands grinding into Ean's neck, choking him. He saw spots and his lungs burned as he struggled vainly, somehow knowing that this was the moment he'd been expecting all along, that this dream always had the same end. With fingers like a vice around the prince's throat, the man struck Ean's head against the floorboards. The prince cried out as pain lanced through his skull and blackness cloaked his vision.

"You-Can-Not-Win!" the stranger shouted, each time slamming Ean's head viciously against the rough wood floor. Ean heard his skull crack, and white heat seared through him. When at last he managed to focus, he saw it was not a man who throttled him so viciously but a fiery-eyed creature with a mouth of flame.

Ean woke with a start, jerking straight up on his bedroll to a grey, misty dawn, the sunrise just spawning a paling on the far horizon. The rest of the camp remained at rest save for the two men on watch. Exhaling a ragged breath, Ean laid back again feeling shaken. The dream had seemed too real, more like a memory than a dream.

It stayed with him the entire day, in fact, so that he was still unnerved when the day's travel brought two coinciding events of ill fortune. The first was that one of the pack horses fell lame, her fetlock swelling quickly from an unknown malady: the second was that it happened upon the Stradtford Plains.

While the soldier Cayal tended to the lame horse, Ean sat Caldar staring across the vast expanse of highland moors. In the near distance, the Eidenglass range thrust upward, snow-capped peaks cloud-pale beneath what had become a perpetually overcast sky. To the west, the coastal mountains formed another blue-hazed line, their tall pines tearing the chalky clouds into fingerling streaks as a heavy cloudbank tumbled into the valley.

Ean remembered the scene from a different perspective, from a wild ride in the zanthyr's wake; he'd still been amazed at the speed with which they rode, a ground-eating pace fueled by the zanthyr's mysterious power. He remembered seeing the coastal range with wonder as they headed into the Gandrel. It had been his last night with the zanthyr.

Now Ean faced the moors with indecision.

His company had two choices. They could leave the horse and divide her load among the rest in order to push on, but this would place undue stress upon the other horses, especially while crossing the pass between Dannym and Veneisea. Alternatively, they could trade the horse to a farrier and acquire another for the remainder of the trip south—by far the more prudent option. Yet this meant a visit to the closest town, which happened to be the city of Acacia.

Rhys rode over to the prince. "Nothing between us and the mountains now save Acacia," he grumbled, mirroring Ean's thoughts as he reined in on the prince's left.

Fynn brought his horse around to Ean's right. "You'd be safe enough in Acacia, I would think," the royal cousin mused. Then in response to Rhys' glare, he added, "Certainly no more exposed in a city of Acacia's size than pitching camp in the middle of the damned heath where a fire can be seen for miles. Besides, you well know that horse won't make more than a few clicks today, Captain."

"It's too risky heading into Acacia," Rhys disagreed. "There's bound to be someone would recognize his highness."

"Raine's truth," Bastian observed, joining the conversation as he drew alongside the others. "Yet with no disrespect, Captain, it would equally draw unfortunate attention to us by staying in the open. We should expect a visit from the city guard at best. Anyone watching from the walls of Acacia would see our camp—a great temptation for bandits, if no other. And we *must* acquire a new horse, my lord. Perhaps you or I could go alone into the city—"

"Yes, that will assuredly go unremarked," Fynn muttered, "the Captain of the King's Own Guard on private business in Acacia? I can only imagine the questions *that* will raise, questions that will inevitably lead back to the rest of us." At Rhys' responding glare, Fynn added, "Chain of office or no, Captain, your face is too well known. Even the Lady Alyneri is unmistakable to any who've made her acquaintance. Raine's truth, the only one of us *not* known on site by the guards of Acacia is Ean."

All eyes looked to the prince then.

"What say you, your highness?" Rhys asked.

The prince worked the muscles of his jaw, clenching and unclenching. It seemed they were likely to face untimely questions no matter which choice he made, though there was at least a chance that his presence might go unremarked in a city the size of Acacia. And with everyone going into the city, the company would stay safely together. He knew Alyneri would appreciate sleeping between clean linens, and Fynn had begun complaining about his lessening stores of liquid sustenance since one day out of Fersthaven.

"Acacia," he said finally, though once pronounced, the decision felt uncomfortably like the wrong one.

No one protested, however, which only rankled more. Ean would that Rhys might argue the point, that he'd press his position and force the matter. Instead, he deferred to his judgment, *to the judgment of a reckless and brash young prince!*

Ean realized in that moment that he truly was in command, that those who followed would do so unquestioningly, and it only served to heighten his distress. He didn't want idle followers! He needed their opinions, their experience, their advice! In no way did he feel qualified to lead this group, and the situation embittered him toward Morin d'Hain, whose words of chastisement haunted his every waking hour.

The walled city of Acacia hugged either side of the Glass River and boasted a bustling river port, but the city also sat on the main east-west thoroughfare in the southern half of the kingdom. Accordingly, it was the most prosperous dwelling in the duchy of Stradtford and the largest jewel in old Duke Thane val Torlen's ruby-studded cap. Though the city was under the rule of its own governor, soldiers in the livery of House val Torlen were a presence inside the walls, and many held stations at the city gates as well.

They reached the city as the sun was falling behind the Eidenglass, long rays casting the range into violet shadow and limning its snowy peaks with vibrant gold. Ean's company approached the gates with a bare-headed Alyneri at the front and center, accompanied by Rhys and Bastian to her left and right. Fynn, Ean and all the other men followed behind wearing their hoods low over their eyes. They kept their gazes diverted in varied directions as if alert for threats to her Grace's person but in truth to allow Ean to become just one of many faceless guards.

As Fynn had predicted, Rhys was the first one recognized.

"My Lord Captain!" called a soldier standing at the gate, one of the Duke's men if told from his dark surcoat blazoned with the Torlen archer. He shouted to the others, "It's the King's Own Guard!" while rushing forward to greet them. By the time Ean's company came to a halt beneath the city walls, a veritable bevy of soldiers had convened, fully half of them the Duke's men.

One man pushed his way through to the front, dressed in the garments of a diplomat. "Lord Captain, your Grace," he greeted, nodding to each in turn. "What an honor to make your acquaintance. I am Lord Brantley, Earl of Pent, and the Duke's representative here in Acacia."

The Earl was a diminutive sort of man, with a longish moustache and pointed chin-beard of a style no longer in fashion at court. His brown eyes were shrewd, however, and he wore his sword with a subtle awareness that implied the weapon wasn't entirely for decoration.

"Lord Brantley," Alyneri returned, eyeing him narrowly. "How convenient that you happen to be here at the gates at the moment of our arrival."

"Yes, isn't it?" he agreed. "His Grace is expecting visitors tonight, but their ship was delayed downriver." Suddenly he brightened. "But you must stay with his Grace at Finley Manor—tis but a short ride east of here. His Grace still speaks of your great assistance in healing his niece. He has long wished for the opportunity to thank you in person, but the gout prevents his travels to Court, as surely you know."

"Thank you for your offer, Lord Brantley, but I could not impose upon his Grace's hospitality."

The earl looked less than pleased at this response, but he pressed on tactfully. "Indeed," he said with a smile that didn't quite touch his eyes that time. "What then brings you to Acacia, if I might inquire?"

"Her Grace is on pilgrimage to Jeune," Rhys barked.

The earl's eyes widened appreciatively. "Ah, then 'tis true," he murmured, casting her a knowing look that was far too direct for his station. "We've heard the rumors of a betrothal. Congratulations must be in order—"

"Please save them for a later date, my lord," Alyneri interrupted stiffly, her indignation at his presumption all too clear, "for I must maintain my focus upon the purpose of my pilgrimage."

"Just so, just so," he clucked, taking note of her displeasure. He lifted his gaze to her hooded companions. "I don't see the truthreader, your ward," he observed pleasantly. "Is he with you then?"

"We would not have stopped in the city at all," Alyneri pressed on, ignoring his question while her tone stressed her displeasure at his improperly prying remarks, "except one of our pack mounts fell lame."

"Allow me to take care of it," he offered at once, confusingly vacillating between rudeness and gallantry. "Have you rooms for the night?"

"Not yet," said Rhys.

"Might I suggest the Feathered Pheasant, my Lord Captain? I'll have your new mount delivered there shortly after sundown."

"That is most kind of you, Lord Brantley," Alyneri murmured, still eyeing him unpleasantly.

"Courtesies of his Grace, of course," Lord Brantley added as an afterthought.

The earl waved the other soldiers to disperse, and the company moved forward into the city. Bringing up the rear, Ean watched the Earl of Pent from the shadows of his hood. The man was staring after them with a thoughtful expression that Ean didn't entirely trust. As Tanis happened to be riding beside him, he turned and addressed the lad, who perked up at gaining the prince's notice.

"What did you think of Lord Brantley, Tanis?" Ean asked in a low voice. "Can he be trusted?"

Tanis pushed his hood back slightly to better see the prince, his colorless eyes looking grey in the dusky light. "He didn't say anything untruthful, your Highness," the boy replied, though there was hesitation in his tone.

"But…?"

Tanis gave him an apologetic look. "I'm sorry, your Highness. You should have a better trained truthreader to serve you. I get impressions of things from people, but I don't always know what they mean."

"What impression did you get of Lord Brantley?"

Tanis considered the question and then remarked, "That he was a calculating sort of man."

"Yes," Ean mused, turning forward again. "I got that impression, too."

There were still enough people in the streets that their party drew no further attention, for they were just one more company of travelers making their way toward an unnamed end. While crossing a bridge over the Glass, however, they came nose to nose with a party of five hooded travelers heading the other way. Rhys drew rein irritably, for the party did not stand aside for them, though Ean's group was the larger and therefore had the customary right of way.

The man in the lead glared at Rhys with naught but malice in his gaze, a reflection of his obvious ill disposition, while his four companions kept their hooded gazes upon their mounts. Ean wondered immediately what they were hiding, and the realization made him speculate uneasily if his own party had looked the same to Lord Brantley.

"Move aside for the Duchess of Aracine!" Rhys meanwhile barked.

"We are about the Duke's business," the leader hissed in a tone of self-importance that immediately rankled Ean. "Why should *we* defer to *you?*"

"A Duchess in person trumps any duke's lackey," Fynn complained ungraciously.

Rhys didn't deign even to argue about it. "I said *stand aside* for the Duchess!" he repeated more dangerously while Alyneri adopted an appropriately affronted look. Abruptly the Captain stood in his stirrups and reached for his sword. He was instantly mirrored by Bastian and the other two soldiers, Dorin and Cayal, each of them standing tall with hands threateningly upon their weapons in an impressive display.

The man's black-eyed gaze turned sharper still, but he finally motioned his party aside. "The Duke will hear of this," he sneered as Rhys prodded the company forward, his soldiers still standing in their stirrups glaring in outrage.

Bastian drew rein in front of the man while the others passed. "Indeed, he will," he agreed, retaking his saddle without lifting his stern gaze of reproach, "for the Duke is a patron of her Grace, the Duchess of Aracine, Healer to the Crown, and he will be most displeased at your show of rudeness." Then he heeled his mount forward and took up the rear.

Ean nodded in silent welcome as Bastian joined his side, then looked back to the road ahead, but not before noticing Tanis watching the retreating figures with an unreadable expression.

And what impression did you get of that ill-tempered man, young Tanis?

The stars were rising as they reached the Feathered Pheasant, a sprawling, four-story inn bordering the river whose gables were painted a garish, lime-eaten green. To the tune of a lute and hornpipe echoing from the tavern, they dismounted and began gathering saddlebags. Eventually, three lanky boys came jogging up to tend the horses. Rhys handed off his reins to one of the boys and marched up the stone steps and into the common to find the proprietor and secure their rooms.

As Alyneri was dismounting downwind from Fynnlar, she turned to him with a slightly pained expression and suggested, "Perhaps you will take advantage of the bath house, my lord?"

Fynn rolled his eyes. "Oh yes," he drawled, "*bathing* is our first priority—isn't it Brody?"

Brody just grunted.

"Yes, well..." She eyed the royal cousin disapprovingly. "Even on a pilgrimage, personal hygiene should be kept up as a matter of principle."

Fynn snorted. "A matter of principle. There's logic for you."

"Just what do you mean?" she sniffed, looking indignant.

Fynn leaned an elbow on his saddle. "Only that nothing worth doing is ever done as a matter of principle, your Grace. If it's worth doing, it's done because it's worth doing. If it's *not* worth doing, *then* it's done as a matter of principle."

Alyneri gave him a black look.

Ean only half heard the exchange, for his attention was drawn to the heavens and the constellation rising there, four of its seven stars just visible above the inn's moss-covered roof. He recalled all too clearly seeing those stars on the night of Creighton's death, and while then he'd looked down his nose at the superstition, he couldn't quite bring himself to dismiss it so glibly this time.

But was the constellation a warning? And if so, was it a warning to him or to another in the vast city of Acacia? How did one discern for whom Cephrael's Hand glowed?

Ean absently handed off Caldar's reins to one of the stable boys, who was sort of staring stupidly at him, and slung his packs over his shoulder. He was still gazing at the constellation when Fynn approached. The royal cousin stopped beside him and followed the prince's line of sight upwards toward the night sky. "Shadow take me," Fynn muttered under his breath. "Is the bloody thing following you?"

Ean exhaled a measured sigh. "I…just don't know."

Fynn turned him a strange look. "So cousin," he said then, pushing on through his surprise, "I'd like to check something out in town. See you later?"

"Sure," Ean said vaguely. He finally tore his gaze from the heavens and gave his cousin and brief nod. "Do as you need."

Without another word, Fynn sent a look to Brody, and together they skulked off into the darkening city.

Tanis watched Fynn and Brody depart and wished he could have gone along, for he was sure there was an adventure in store. Instead, he waited as his lady gave her mare to one of the boys, but not before admonishing the lad about how best to rub the animal down, what sort of feed to give her and when, that she had a sensitive tooth… Tanis had heard the lecture many times. Yawning, he heaved his and Alyneri's bags over either shoulder, and went inside.

As he found a path through the crowded common, Tanis caught snatches of talk from each table. While passing two men, both dressed in rough leather jerkins, one of them said, "…have everyone on edge. *Sundragons* by all that's unholy! Returned to claim their desert stronghold, some say."

"I heard they were summoned by a mage sworn to the Emir."

"*Mage*," the first spat. "Tis an ill wind blowin' down in M'Nador, as anyone can see, yet his Majesty orders our fine soldiers to their deaths in a fight with a mage? I'll wager there's not a soul in the north as knows how to battle one of them desert witchlords."

"As if dragons weren't bad enough," his friend commiserated.

The first shook his head. "No one can blame a man for keeping well away from M'Nador, even without the dangers of war." Then he noticed Tanis watching him, gave a little start, and seemed to reconsider his prior words, for he added just loud enough for anyone who was listening to hear, "Not that his Majesty—Epiphany bless and keep him—*shouldn't* have sent his army to exterminate the desert bastards. I'm not sayin' that. What with them invading the way they have, and after murdering our Prince Sebastian…"

Tanis frowned and moved on, feeling his talent so often a curse instead of a gift. Being a truthreader wasn't at all as glamorous as Tad thought—especially when your eyes so readily identified you.

"—trouble with the pirates," a mustached Veneisean was saying to his four companions, all of whom were huddled over a game of Trumps as Tanis passed. "You couldn't pay me enough to sail the Sea of Shadows to Agasan, not if it meant crossing the waters near Jamaii."

"My cousin lost an entire hold of cabbages to the bastards," one of the other men added. "They thought his was a galleon ship out of the Bemoth mines…"

"—famous Healer," a woman was noting to her two male companions at the next table along Tanis's way. He glanced over his shoulder and saw that her gaze was fixed on his lady, who had just come inside. "They say she's an important heiress and that the Queen intends to betroth her to our Prince Ean—and this after she was meant to have married the middle brother before his death."

"Can't say I'd trust the girl," returned one of the men. He was sipping his ale and eyeing Alyneri dubiously. "There's probably a curse on 'er—you know how wicked strange those desert folk are. Could be she's the reason the prince's ship faltered in the Fire Sea in the first place…"

Two barmaids carrying trays of empty mugs slipped around Tanis, and as they rejoined in front of him again, he heard one of them whisper to the other, "I tell ye, Lise, he came to 'er in a dream and changed the color of 'er very hair, he did! He made her blonde like she'd always wanted—she says he can do anything in the world of dreams!"

"Really?" the other gasped. "D'ye think the Warrior-God Dagmar would come t'me in *my* dreams and change me into a Lady?" They both set to giggling.

Tanis spotted his Highness then. The prince was leaning on a barstool waiting for Rhys to finish arguing with the innkeeper. His hood had fallen back slightly, and his face was in view from certain angles. Tanis wondered what so occupied the prince's mind that he hadn't noticed his hood. The barmaids certainly took note of him, and one of them whispered, "My heart, but that one's got the devil's good looks, don't he?"

Tanis admitted his Highness exhibited a roguish charm, well looking the part of a hired guard in his muted chestnut leathers—albeit an unusually handsome one. No one else seemed to be paying much attention to him, by Epiphany's grace, though Tanis did notice a man get up and leave after he looked at the prince, but what did that prove? Tanis forced himself to relax about it, though he couldn't quite banish his apprehension; it remained on the fringes of his awareness, making him tense and edgy.

The barmaids eyed Ean as they passed on their way into the kitchen, and he came out of his musing to bless them with a generous smile and a suggestive wink. They giggled even louder and rushed off down the hall amid excited whispers. Still softly smiling, Ean turned his attention back toward Rhys and the others, only to find that Alyneri had arrived and witnessed the exchange. He gave her a wink just for good measure. She replied with a withering look.

"...rooms?" the long-jowled proprietor was saying when Tanis at last joined his friends on the far side of the room near the wide staircase. "Well, to tell you the truth, my lord, we're quite full—every inn in town is the same, I'll wager. What with Festival up in Calgaryn and the Harvest Fair ongoing here and Samhain not but a week away." Then he closed his mouth and settled greedy brown eyes on the captain.

Rhys grunted something uncomplimentary and shoved more silver pieces into the man's hands, which he deftly slipped into his vest pocket. "Now that I think on it, surely we can make room for her Grace's party, my lord—that is if some of your men don't mind doubling up." He glanced to Alyneri, and Tanis thought he saw the shadow of a lewd smile flicker across his lips, but the spark vanished as quickly as it had come, leaving the lad to wonder if he'd seen it at all. "Well then," the proprietor remarked, rubbing hands together. "Please come with me. Tis a long way you've come, your Grace—from Calgaryn, did you say?"

Tanis eyed the man distrustfully. There was something about him that put the boy on edge.

"I wonder," Alyneri asked, "if you might have a private room where we could all dine together. The common looks so crowded tonight..."

"I've a small room in the back," the innkeeper offered as they rounded the landing, "but I'm not sure if it's available..." He looked to Rhys expectantly, like a droopy-eyed hound waiting at the tableside for scraps.

Rhys glared at the man and shoved another silver piece at him.

The proprietor turned Alyneri a winning smile. "I'll have the meal set at once," he cooed.

"You're very kind," Alyneri murmured pleasantly.

Rhys grunted.

Following at the back of the group, Tanis was unable to take his eyes off the innkeeper. *What is it about him?*

Rhys was paying the man for something else when Tanis at last labored past him and on into Alyneri's suite with her Grace's bags. The Captain followed inside soon thereafter, shut the sitting room door with an indignant grunt, then snatched it open again only a moment later and stuck his head out into the hall, ostensibly making sure the innkeeper had returned to his own affairs. After glaring around into the empty dimness, he closed the door, pulled the bolt, then walked over and peered out the window into the darkened street below.

The man would challenge his own shadow, Tanis noted in wonder.

Though there were a couple of chairs set by the mantle, Ean lowered himself to the hearthstone with a dramatic sigh and propped elbows on knees. He looked over to the Captain. "I think perhaps it might be beneficial if you'd see what news you can gather in the Common, Rhys. See if anyone untoward noticed our arrival."

The Captain nodded and stalked out into the hall, and Tanis followed him with a hesitant question. "My Lord Captain," the boy asked as Rhys was shutting the door behind them.

He turned with an automatic scowl. "What?"

Tanis swallowed. "My Lord Captain, did you notice anything odd about that innkeeper? Anything that seemed…well, dishonest?"

"All innkeepers are dishonest," Rhys rumbled. "I've yet to meet a one that wouldn't steal your boots overnight and try to sell them back to you the next morning—and not even polished at that." He turned on his heel and headed down the hall, leaving Tanis staring after him pulling uncomfortably at one ear and trying to put his finger on the feeling that had him so disturbed.

When the boy at last reentered Alyneri's small sitting room, he found her Grace seated in an armchair wearing a rather blushed expression, and became curious about what he'd missed.

"…just admit that you went there to avoid seeing me, Alyneri," Prince Ean was saying as Tanis settled onto a stool beside the hearth to listen.

"Your highness—" Alyneri made to protest.

Ean still sat upon the hearthstone, but now he rested one elbow casually on a pile of wood, long legs extended and ankles crossed. Tanis thought his Highness could make most any position look comfortable. "You're my oldest friend, Alyneri," he reminded her with a wink and a grin. "Call me Ean."

"Your *Highness*," she repeated, "just what do you expect to hear from me?"

"Well, you could start with an apology."

Alyneri's eyes flew wide. "*Apology!* For what?"

"For purposely avoiding me and then refusing to admit that your plans were foiled, that our inevitable meeting was fated to be."

"Ill-fated, you mean," she muttered.

Ean grinned. "Just admit it, Alyneri. What's so hard about this? Don't you know how crushed I am that you weren't waiting to receive me with kisses and flowers on the momentous occasion of my return?"

"Suffering that homecoming at your side was momentous enough," she observed.

He settled her an arch look then. "It was Fate that brought us together at Fersthaven and Fate that keeps us together still. Just admit that you can't outwit Fate, and I'll leave the matter alone."

"There's no such thing as Fate, Ean," she retorted irritably, "and I'm sure I don't know what you mean about any of this." She tossed her head and insisted, "I mislike the crowds at Festival, and Farshideh was in poor health. Contrary to your elevated sense of importance, every decision made in the realm does not pivot around you."

"No," Ean agreed, giving her a devastating smile, "only every decision of yours."

Alyneri's mouth fell open, but her surprise revealed all too clearly the truth of his words. Unable to summon a retort, she pushed out of her chair, glared at him once, and stalked into her bedroom, slamming the door.

Tanis frowned fretfully after her. "If you were trying to irritate her, your Highness," he said, "I think you succeeded."

Ean gave him a wink and a grin.

The prince, Tanis, and a still-fuming Alyneri joined the others downstairs in a small private dining room just as the kitchen girls were setting heavy platters of gravy-soaked lamb upon the long wooden table. Alyneri punctuated her indignation at Ean's treatment of her by disregarding his presence, but every once in a while Tanis saw her glance his way to see if he showed due signs of suffering.

Midway into the meal, Rhys entered, as usual shutting the door and then jerking it open again to check the hall for idle ears.

"What news from the common?" Ean asked as Rhys seated himself. The others paused, even stopped chewing, waiting for his response.

"The usual nonsense," Rhys reported in his typical laconic. He took hold of his sleeve to keep it out of the gravy and served himself some of the lamb, seeming of a mind to say little else on the matter.

Ean contained his irritation admirably. "Might you elaborate, Captain?"

Rhys shrugged as he shoved a hunk of gravy-soaked bread into his mouth. "Lots of talk about the war," he muttered while he chewed. "No surprise there. No one wants their sons or brothers in a foreign land fighting for someone else's kingdom, pact or no." He grunted in a way that said he didn't much disagree.

"Anything else?"

Rhys cast a wary glance at Alyneri. "Talk of her Grace. Morin's lies found their way south faster than we did."

Alyneri sniffed.

Ean cast the Captain a resigned look. "No doubt the Minister was counting on that."

"No mention of you, though, highness," Rhys added more brightly than his usual wont. Then he looked hesitantly at Alyneri and added, "Leastwise…not in relation to our arrival."

Alyneri harrumphed indignantly.

Tanis knew they owed Morin d'Hain their thanks, no matter how her Grace protested. Without the Spymaster's rumors to pave the way, people might've looked much more closely at their party.

A knock came upon the door, and Rhys went to answer it. The innkeeper stood in the portal. "Good evening, Lord Captain," he cooed. "I see your meal was served in a timely manner. Is everything to your liking then?"

"What do you want now, man?" Rhys rumbled. "Her Grace mislikes being disturbed during the meal."

"No, no, I need not disturb her Grace, my Lord Captain. I just received word from the Earl of Pent that he has made all arrangements for your replacement mount, but he requests your presence in choosing a horse."

"It's a pack horse, not a thoroughbred," Rhys complained.

The innkeeper gave him an oily smile. "Even so, Lord Brantley would that you have the best of those available. If he might prevail upon you, my lord, to attend him at the farrier on Longshore, near the river port—"

"That's near halfway back to the gates!" Rhys protested.

"The master there has the best horses in the city, my lord," the innkeeper pointed out, and his disparaging tone implied that he thought Rhys must be too cheap to pay for a good horse.

Rhys' glare lingered on the innkeeper irritably. Then he barked, "A moment," and slammed the door on the man. He looked to the prince.

Ean shrugged. "The Earl at least was as good as his word."

"I don't like it, Ean," Alyneri said. "I don't trust Lord Brantley."

"I don't either, but is there harm in it?"

"We do need the horse," Bastian pointed out.

Rhys looked indecisive. Finally he grumbled, "Fine. Cayal comes with me. Bastian and Dorin, you stay and protect his Highness."

"What am I, chopped liver?" Alyneri objected.

"Last I checked, no one was offering a fortune in Agasi silver to see your head removed from your shoulders, Alyneri," Ean observed.

"How perfectly egocentric of you, Ean," she remarked witheringly. She pushed to her feet and announced, "I for one intend to take advantage of the bathhouse. I would encourage the same of the rest of you, even if you *think* setting a toe in bathwater is certain doom." With that, she marched out of the room, excusing herself primly around the innkeeper, who stood so close to the door that he might've removed his ear from the parting only just in time.

THIRTY-FOUR

'A wielder is limited by what he can envision.'

– *Sobra I'ternin*, Eleventh Translation, 1499aF, *A Discourse on the Nature and Relationship of Patterning and the Currents of Elae*

Ean lingered at the table long after the others had left. After staring for far too long into his empty bowl reflecting on everything he knew and more so over the things he didn't, he finally wandered over to the room's one mullioned window and pushed it open, gazing out into the starry sky.

The constellation couldn't be seen from that angle, but he felt it burning above him as hot as a near blaze. Creighton had given his life under those stars, and Ean had almost lost his own beneath them twice. Someone had to be held accountable for these crimes. But who?

'No good man claims another's life without regret.'

Alyneri's advice had sparked a memory of the night Creighton died, and the more Ean thought on it now, the less it made sense. *'It was not meant to be this way with you…'* the Shade's words haunted him, along with the image of the man's blade angled downward into Creighton's neck.

'It was not meant to be this way with you…'

For the longest time, Ean had no memory of the words at all. Now he couldn't get them out of his head. What had the Shade meant by the enigmatic pronouncement, which seemed now, in hindsight, to have been spoken with regret?

Sighing, Ean shut the window and leaned back against the sill. He wished that Alyneri's criticism didn't strike him so deeply. For that matter, he wished himself inured to all criticism, for it seemed Morin d'Hain's words had truly wounded him.

Reckless and brash...

Could it be that I am the one to blame?

Once it had seemed such an easy truth to fault the Shade who'd taken Creighton's life. Now Ean couldn't help but wonder if *he* was ultimately to blame for Creighton's death? If a king sends a soldier into war, does he blame the enemy who slays the man, or does he take the blame upon himself? Ultimately, who was responsible?

Reckless and brash…

Ean just didn't know anymore.

Disheartened by his own dark ruminations, Ean slowly made his way through the inn and back to the third floor where he and the other men had been quartered. As he gained the landing, however, something gave him pause, and he stopped at the edge of the staircase with wary apprehension.

It took a moment to realize what had changed—such a little thing really, the dousing of a lamp along the wall, but it happened to be the lamp closest to the room he meant to share with Bastian. Moreover, the latter should have been on guard in this hallway, and his absence only confirmed Ean's suspicions.

It seemed a foregone conclusion. Ean drew his sword.

"Show yourself," he said in a low voice.

After a moment, a man stepped from a recessed doorway just beyond Ean's room. There was nothing familiar about him except the style of weapon he held. They walked to the middle of the passage and faced one another.

The Geshaiwyn chuckled. "You seem weary, prince of Dannym. Have you lost the will to fight?"

Ean *was* weary—weary of people trying to kill him; weary of worrying over the impact of his decisions; weary of fearing the loss of those people who were most dear to him. But more than this, he was damned angry. He drew in his breath to challenge the man, but was surprised by the words he heard himself say instead.

"You cannot defeat me," he pronounced, not knowing why the phrase suddenly imposed itself upon his consciousness; it seemed to surface from a deeper memory. What words followed seemed only natural. "Balance is with me, as your brethren have discovered to their peril."

His response gave the assassin pause. He actually seemed to consider Ean's warning for the briefest instant, but then he shook his head. "Death claims us as Fate wills, prince of Dannym," he said, grinning. "Let us see whom Fortune has graced tonight."

As if scripted, the two men moved to greet their fate. Ean swung first, and the assassin parried. Their blades clashed, caressed briefly, and separated with a steel song of parting. Thus followed a deadly melody, each blade ringing, harmonizing, sometimes clashing with a dissonance that suspended as they struggled and resolved as they separated. Percussion came with their heavy footfalls, dancing forward, retreating back; timpani boomed as the fighters spun into walls, cymbals ringing as lamps shattered. Their fighting symphony continued until they reached the end of the hallway where a tall window gleamed darkly, lit by the distant city lights.

The Geshaiwyn got the upper hand as he forced Ean against the window, their blades locked in opposition. Ean gritted his teeth, his entire body rigid behind the effort as the man pushed him harder against the mullioned glass. He heard the metal joinings creak, the glass crackling dangerously with the pressure of their combined force. Ean held, pushing back with all his strength...until at last the assassin's vigor waned. The prince drew strength from sudden hope and launched himself and the Geshaiwyn away from the window, across the passage. They slammed into the wall together and then staggered across to slam into another, except—

Where once the wall had been was only empty space. Ean twisted as they fell sideways, their blades in a deadly embrace. He landed atop the Geshaiwyn with a gruff exhalation, and both their weapons skittered away.

Ean sprung backwards off the man and gained his feet, bracing himself for more, but the assassin didn't rise. As the prince's eyes grew accustomed to the dim room, what had first seemed indistinct grew in substance, and he saw the space was filled with treasures wide and varied. Silver goblets, jeweled swords, boxes overflowing with jewelry, even elegant clothing—all were jammed in the tiny room.

Ean turned to look behind him at the wall through which they'd fallen. Three steps led up from the stone-tiled room, but where the door should've been was only bare wood. He spun back to the Geshaiwyn, who lay upon the floor grinning.

"Where have you brought me?" the prince demanded. If they'd traveled on a node, Ean knew he could be anywhere.

The man chuckled wetly, a dreadful, dying sound. Only then did Ean see the spreading pool beneath him and the shards protruding from his chest. It didn't stop him from grabbing the assassin by his collar. "Shadow take you, man! Where did you bring us? Get me out of here!"

The assassin just laughed harder, coughing and spitting blood in his mirth.

Ean tried lifting the man to force him to comply, but he was already limp as a dead hare.

The Geshaiwyn looked Ean in the eye. "Who did Fortune favor…after all?" he managed, grinning at the prince with blood-stained teeth. "A *halál cask…az…eleje*," he whispered, and then he was gone.

Death is only the beginning.

With a growl of frustration, Ean released the assassin and sat back on his heels. Fortune willing, he was still in the inn and this room was the innkeeper's store of stolen goods. Surely then the man would return at some point, if not to add to his collection then to admire it. But how long would he have to wait there? As if to rub salt in the wound, the room's tiny lamp sputtered futilely and then died, pitching Ean into darkness.

Alyneri dressed slowly, letting the steam from the bathhouse linger on her damp skin, loving the sensation of her bare feet on the warm stone floor. She couldn't understand the male aversion to bathing; a bath was a chance to restore, to contemplate and reflect, to sooth both tangled muscles and mind. *Perhaps men like Fynnlar don't relish time alone with their consciences*, she thought critically. Certainly in the quiet of a bath, particular types of thoughts gained in volume. Alyneri believed Fynn would do most anything to avoid quiet time with his conscience. *But must he really avoid bathing altogether?*

Alyneri loved the solitude and silence of the baths. She'd agreed to travel with Ean—not that Morin d'Hain had given her any choice in the matter—but she hadn't known the price she would pay. For a woman who relished her privacy, she was never now without company, and with the long days of travel, there was never time to collect herself, to organize her thoughts, to recover her composure or even to work up the courage to apologize for speaking more sharply than she'd intended—which was happening more often of late.

That was due to the company she was keeping.

It was a cruel blessing to be near Ean constantly, to *want* to be nearer to him still, and to loathe herself for the weakness of loving a man who would never love her back with the same dedication. Every day she abased herself for these failings, and every day she yearned for a day when Ean might look at her with as much desire as she felt for him.

It would be a kinder fate to hate him than to love him so!

She'd tried pushing Ean away with sharp words and ire, but these were simple obstacles to him, a splay of child's jacks upon the floor. He walked over them with bare feet and barely flinched. It was testimony to his good-nature that he forgave her time and again, so that all of her efforts came to naught, ending not in estrangement but with growing admiration for him. Ean had been teasing her in the room that night, but his words rang with bitter truth; no matter what she did to avoid him or drive him away, unknown forces kept pitching them back together.

Perhaps I am fated to love him.

But she just couldn't accept that—she *wouldn't* accept it.

Exhaling a long sigh as much in longing as in regret, Alyneri did up the laces of her dress. For daily wear, she commissioned dresses that she could put on herself, without the need for a lady's maid. Desert gowns like Ysolde Remalkhen wore were designed with such elegance and could be donned alone, but Alyneri wasn't brave enough to wear the form-hugging silk, though it was certainly her birthright. Still, she thought the fitted blue dress she chose was lovely, if not so elaborate in design as most ladies of the court would wear. *Appropriate for a pilgrimage,* she told herself, but the claim seemed somehow barren and inadequate.

She saved her hair for last, pulling heavy strands of her long, pale locks over her shoulder as she worked her fingers through the tangles. Sometimes, like that time, when her reserves were low, she found herself thinking of Ean with longing instead of angst, wondering what it might be like to share herself with him. She'd seen his bare form; she'd seen his pattern as well, an intimacy that appended her to him in ways she wasn't quite prepared for. She imagined he would be a tender lover, which was right and gentlemanly, yet some part of her yearned equally for a passionate encounter that left them both bruised.

She was flushed by the time she finished her braid, tying it off with a leather cord. She expertly twisted the plait into an elaborate knot at the base of her neck and secured it with a long hairpin that was capped with a tourmaline cut in the shape of a scarab, an early gift from her father which she treasured.

Feeling renewed, Alyneri left the bathhouse. She was walking beneath a covered passage back to the main lodge when she heard someone call out, "Your Grace, a moment?"

Alyneri paused and turned, looking for the voice.

It was the innkeeper who came trotting across the yard, reminding her too much of a droopy-jowled hound with his long cheeks and baggy brown eyes. "Your Grace, I'm so sorry to bother you." He smiled unctuously as he came to a halt in front of her. "Your reputation precedes you—such an esteemed Healer as yourself, and so gracious. I've heard that you've been willing in the past to see certain persons in grave need, and one such has come to our humble inn tonight, a young girl and her mother. Would you be willing to see the child?"

It was true, Alyneri had difficulty turning away those in need. She gave him more of her attention. "From what does the child suffer?"

"The mother preferred to speak with you directly, my lady, but the child looks terribly frail. I'm not certain how long she has—"

"Fine, fine," Alyneri said, wishing the sycophantic man might excuse himself elsewhere, or at least do her the courtesy of falling down a well or something.

She followed the innkeeper along a different path around the back of the inn, through a servant's entrance, and down a hallway lined in dark wood. "They're just waiting in my office," the innkeeper explained with an oily smile when she seemed reluctant to follow. "Just inside here," and he opened a thick paneled door for her.

She moved past him and came to a sudden halt. It wasn't a woman and her daughter that waited inside. Wary now, she turned to the innkeeper, who was closing the door, and demanded under her breath, "What's the meaning of this?"

"A private audience, your Grace," said Lord Brantley, Earl of Pent. "You see, I'm afraid I must insist that you accept the Duke's hospitality tonight. His Grace's guests are quite interested to make your acquaintance. Yours…and that of your ward."

"Tanis?" she asked in confusion.

Lord Brantley smiled, and Alyneri did not at all like what lay behind that smile. "Indeed."

She kept her composure admirably, managing a strained smile in return. "Very well…since you insist. I will just rouse my guards—"

"Regrettably, your Grace," the earl interrupted, still looking upon her with that self-satisfied smile, "your men are not invited."

"I see." She cast the unscrupulous man a steely gaze. "And just what do you hope to gain from this, Lord Brantley? You cannot think to get away with taking me hostage."

"But on the contrary, your Grace, I've done nothing of the sort. Our illustrious innkeeper has arranged everything, complete with witnesses that saw you leaving with a man who could only be your betrothed."

"My betrothed?" she said flatly.

He smiled again. "So, you see, it's all taken care of." He nodded to the innkeeper, who opened the door to admit a host of soldiers in the livery of House val Torlen. The earl held a hand to Alyneri. "After you, my lady."

She turned stiffly and went with the soldiers, knowing protest was futile. How different it felt, this kidnapping, compared to Ianthe's attempt, what already seemed so long ago. Alyneri had no doubt that Ean and the men would find her; and Lord Brantley's contrived story only reassured her that he had no idea of Ean's presence among her company, which warmed her heart considerably. Moreover, she couldn't imagine Duke val Torlen standing for it. When she told him of the manner in which Lord Brantley had taken her in hand, she felt sure he would impart a furious justice.

Even when she saw a worried Tanis already mounted up in the stables and surrounded by more soldiers, her resolve didn't fail her. She held her back straight and accepted her reins politely but with stiff disapproval, and she stoutly refused to look at the deceitful Lord Brantley, even as he led them away.

Rhys val Kinkaid, Captain of the King's Own Guard, reined in his horse just outside the stables of the Feathered Pheasant and dismounted purposefully. He spied one of the stable boys slouching on a stool near the doors and barked at him, "You there! Fetch your master!"

The boy startled awake so frightfully that he tipped backwards on his stool, waving his arms wildly as he grabbed for the near wall. He shot the Captain a sullen glare as he recovered.

The captain was unmoved. "*Now*, boy! Or do you need the flat of my blade for encouragement?"

Looking sullen, the lad got up and slunk past him hugging the doorway. He broke into a haphazard lope as he made for the inn.

"Do you think the innkeeper was complacent in the deception, Lord Captain?" the soldier Cayal asked as he dismounted. He took his horse's reins in hand and untied the lead rope from his saddle, bringing around their new pack mount alongside his own.

"I wouldn't put it past him," Rhys grumbled, "but we'll leave it up to the Governor to decide."

They led the horses into the stables, and Rhys at once noticed the empty stall where last her Grace's horse had been quartered. He turned to Cayal and growled in warning, "The Duchess's horse is missing. Check for the rest."

Cayal looped his leads around a near hook and rushed off to inspect the lines of stalls. Just then Rhys heard footsteps approaching, and he spun and drew his sword in one fluid motion—for such a large and imposing man, he moved with quick surety and grace, not a muscle wasted as he leveled his blade at the doorway.

The second stable boy nearly walked right into it, rounding the corner and halting only just in time. His brown eyes crossed as he looked down his nose at the Captain's deadly steel. "M-my lord?" he inquired meekly.

Rhys lowered his blade and then motioned with it. "Over there, you."

The lad bolted for the corner where his counterpart had been sleeping and stood there wide-eyed. A moment later the proprietor arrived with the other boy in close tow.

"My Lord Captain, is there some problem?" the man asked with a toadying smile.

Rhys had planned to question the innkeeper on the fiasco at the farrier—the horse master had never even heard of Lord Brantley!—but now the absence of her Grace's horse was of more pressing concern. He leveled his blade at the innkeeper and motioned him and his boy inside with it, asking as he did, "Why is the Duchess of Aracine's mare missing?"

The proprietor eyed the steel warily as he shuffled past it into the stables. He held up both hands. "Now, now, my Lord Captain, is there really need for such hostility?"

"Answer my question, man," Rhys warned, holding the heavy weapon level at the innkeeper's thick neck.

He managed a weedy smile. "Very well. Very well. No harm. I'll tell you what I know. It's bound to be out soon enough."

Cayal came running up. "The boy's mount is missing also, Lord Captain."

Rhys' gaze darkened, and he leveled a dangerous glare at the innkeeper. "Where is the Duchess of Aracine?"

"Why, she's gone, my lord," the man replied, his mouth twitching with a pained expression, as if the nearness of Rhys' weapon was giving him intestinal gas.

"Gone," Rhys repeated.

"With the prince," the man said quickly.

Rhys still couldn't process what he was saying. "The Prince of Dannym," he repeated.

"Well it must've been him, my lord," said the innkeeper, affecting a tone of mystery and awe. "You've heard the rumors, no doubt. It seems for once they must've been true. I saw him myself!"

Rhys exchanged a look with Cayal. "You saw the Prince of Dannym," Rhys repeated, turning back to the innkeeper with a skeptical look. "Here?"

"Indeed," the man declared importantly.

"And?"

"And...and he swore to the Duchess that he could wait for her hand in marriage no longer! They left together." Carefully eyeing the Captain's weapon, the innkeeper leaned closer and whispered, "I think they mean to elope."

Cayal asked, "What makes you think this man you saw was the Prince of Dannym? He's to be in mourning for his blood-brother for yet another week."

The innkeeper rubbed his balding head. "Well, I cannot be certain, tis true," he admitted, "for he never declared himself within my hearing, but Raine's truth, he was the spitting image of his Majesty, and there was no mistaking the stallion he rode."

At this news, Rhys spun an inquiring look at Cayal, who shook his head almost imperceptibly. His answer was clear: *Caldar is still here.*

Rhys' gaze narrowed as he looked back to the innkeeper. He advanced on him threateningly. "Let me get this clear," he drawled. Cayal drew his sword and fell in beside his captain, both of them driving the startled innkeeper further down the line of stalls. "You *saw*, with your own eyes, the Prince of Dannym riding away from this very stable on his horse Caldar, and the Lady Alyneri d'Giverny went riding off with him."

The innkeeper backed away as Rhys and Cayal advanced on him. "Yes—yes!" His baggy eyes flitted from one steely blade to the other. "Please, my Lord Captain! You wouldn't slay me for bespeaking what is only Raine's truth, no matter how untimely it may seem...would you?"

Rhys was fuming, so Cayal asked the obvious next question. "And what of the lad, Tanis? Why is his mount missing?"

The innkeeper's eyes darted between them. "He—why he went with them, my lords."

"To elope?" Cayal remarked skeptically.

The innkeeper swallowed. "Well now...now I don't *know* they mean to elope. I was only guessing at the prince's intentions. I mean he—he certainly didn't share them with me."

Rhys angled his blade and drove the innkeeper up against a stall. Inside, Caldar jerked his ash-darkened mane and nickered. Rhys glared darkly at the man in front of him. Clearly most everything he said was a lie, but two facts were certain: the Duchess and her boy were gone. His Highness never would've let that happen willingly, nor would have Bastian and Dorin. So what had actually happened while they were away?

And where was the prince?

Ean felt around in the darkness until he found his sword. Then he used the same technique to find a rounded chest to sit upon. Gaining this, he rested elbows on knees and gazed into the black abyss. As his heart slowed and his breathing returned to normal, he felt strangely focused. Raine's truth, there was no clarity as acute as that which followed a battle. Ean thought he could understand why some men relished a fight—one never felt so alive as after successfully dodging death; while Ean didn't crave combat as some did, he was getting better used to its after-effects.

As his eyes slowly adjusted to the darkness, he eventually began to make out dim shapes. He couldn't be sure, but he thought there must be light somehow leaking into the room. As he stared at the wall, he began to see…something…

Curious, Ean rose and walked carefully toward the steps, picking his way around the dead assassin. Still in darkness, but seeing now a dim nimbus, he climbed to the third step and pressed his hand against the wall where the wood itself seemed to be emitting a pale haze. As his fingers touched the rough wood, Ean began to make out something like the beginning of a design inscribed there. The more he stared at it, the more he concentrated, the better he could see its diffuse glow.

It was a simple, looping pattern that eventually appeared to him. Ean followed it with his finger, and as he watched himself tracing the line, he suddenly understood what he was seeing.

"It's trace-sealed," he realized aloud, his voice a whisper in the dark.

Even a layman like himself knew that trace-seals responded to their mirror-image if traced in the correct order, but something distracted him before he could follow that thought further—it was like a mental nudging, some deeper instinct that yet seemed recently familiar.

Some part of his awareness was drawn to a particular point in the pattern, and he instinctively knew this was both its beginning and its end. Mentally he concentrated on the pattern's point of termination—which piece was the start and which was the finish was somehow indisputable. As he did this, he saw the pattern clearly in his mind—not the dim fuzzy glow that his eyes perceived from the wood, but a golden, clear rendition of the design. Leaning both hands upon the wall, Ean mentally took hold of the pattern's concept, and with a firm grasp of it he…pulled.

He felt something shift beneath his hand where it was splayed against the wall. Nearly imperceptible, yet he didn't doubt that *something* had happened. Too intrigued to wonder, just going with his instincts, Ean sank into rapport with the pattern.

It fit like a tailored glove.

Completely absorbed now, he drew upon the thread of the pattern and watched it curiously with his mind's eye as each strand lifted from the wood. The design might've been made of golden rope, which Ean pealed slowly away until only the end that was the beginning touched the wall, and then…he unwound this, too, and the whole thing dissipated until there was nothing—

Ean pitched forward into the hallway, only just catching himself on knees and elbows.

"Your highness!" Bastian came running down the hall.

Ean looked behind him toward the room he'd just left. A gaping hole remained where once a wall had been. Both puzzled and slightly disturbed by what had just happened, Ean turned to receive the lieutenant, who was bending over him with a nasty gash on his swelling forehead.

Bastian looked immensely relieved as he helped Ean to stand. "I thought for sure—" he breathed, his terrible fears all too clear in his stifled confession. He seemed only just able to refrain from taking the prince into his arms. "After the man surprised me, your Highness, I thought…well, I thought surely—"

Ean put a reassuring hand on Bastian's shoulder and nodded his understanding. Bastian returned a grateful look, thankful that nothing more need be said.

"Are you all right?" Ean asked then. "Your head…"

The lieutenant fingered his temple gingerly and shrugged. "I've had worse." Then his expression became troubled. "There's more. Young Tanis is missing, and I fear her Grace as well."

Ean stiffened. "Missing?"

"Dorin said she never returned from the bathhouse. He's been out to check and there's no sign of her—or the lad."

"Is Rhys back?"

"Not yet, sire."

"What about Fynn?"

"No sign of him either."

Ean pressed his lips together. After a tense silence, he ordered quietly, "Get Dorin. Gather everyone's things and meet me in the stables."

Bastian nodded with a smart clicking of heels and rushed to comply.

Rhys knew he had only moments before the Governor's men would arrive, for he'd called for them upon leaving the farrier's. However, he was now certain that the proprietor of the Feathered Pheasant was complicit in the trick that sent him and Cayal half across town. What's more, the reason for the diversion was evident. He wished he had Morin d'Hain's skill at questioning rather than his own blunt but honest way. Still, it would have to do.

He pressed the point of his blade into the innkeeper's chest, just above his heart. "So," he said in an ominous tone, "describe him to me."

The innkeeper cleared his throat hesitantly. "Describe whom, my lord?"

"The Prince of Dannym."

"Oh," said the man, regaining some of his color. "Well, he was handsome—yes, very handsome. I believe I said before, he looked the image of his Majesty."

"Go on," Rhys murmured.

"Yes, go on," said a voice from the stable's entrance. Recognizing it with immense relief, Rhys' lips spread in a feral sort of grin, which he leveled on the man cowering at the end of his blade.

The innkeeper saw the smile, and from the way his face paled, he'd rightfully concluded that he was suddenly in grave danger. He whetted his lips. "Well, he… uh…had dark hair."

Ean came to a halt beside Rhys, and in their brief glance of greeting, the Captain saw something in his prince's eyes that he hadn't seen before. Ean seemed…different, like a darkness had lifted from him. His countenance was brighter, though his gaze just then was wolf-grey and fierce. He pinned the innkeeper with a predatory stare. "Dark hair," the prince repeated, a soft challenge. "Like mine?"

The man looked hesitant. "I…I suppose, yes."

"And his eyes," said the prince, "were they also like mine then?"

"Well…uh…yes, now that you mention it, they were grey—like his Majesty's," he added helpfully.

"And his sword," Ean murmured softly, drawing his blade. He pressed it into the hollow of the man's throat. Rhys and Cayal backed off but still stood at the ready. "Was it also like mine?" he whispered.

The man looked at him frantically then, for even had he not finally recognized his prince, there was no mistaking a Kingdom blade. Ean raised the hilt, angling the weapon downward, giving him a clear view of the large sapphire pommelstone that pronounced him a member of the royal family of Dannym. The innkeeper licked his lips again, and his eyes darted across all three men. He opened his mouth—

"Don't," Ean warned, his gaze now inexorable. "Your death can still be swift. Tell us what truly happened and where to find the Duchess, and I will ensure you don't suffer…overmuch."

Just then the sound of galloping horses interrupted further questioning, and it was only moments before a host of armed men drew rein in the stable yard. Fynn and Brody preceded them inside, the former coming up short as he arrived upon the scene.

"Oh," Fynn said, looking crestfallen. "So you've heard."

"Rhys," Ean murmured, and the Captain took the proprietor roughly in hand as the prince withdrew and turned to Fynn. The Governor's men rushed inside just behind, and Rhys thrust the man into their ranks as he launched into a report.

Ean pulled Fynn aside. "What did you learn, cousin?" he asked in a low voice.

"Brantley has your betrothed," the royal cousin said.

Rhys joined them with the captain of the city guard at his side.

"We saw Lord Brantley leave the city not long ago, my lords," the captain of the city guard reported. "He was riding hard for the hills with the Duke's men. Likely heading to his estate."

Ean nodded his thanks. "Then so shall we. I trust you have the innkeeper in hand?"

"He'll be taken for questioning, my lord."

"Make sure to ask him about a certain hidden chamber on the third floor," Ean suggested, "as well as the dead man you'll find there."

The city captain's gaze hardened. "Oh, a murderer eh? Well then. We'll be sure to treat him with due regard. Thank you, milord."

Fynn looked to Ean curiously, but the prince shook his head. "Let's be off," he murmured. And upon gathering their remaining companions, they were.

Alyneri's resolve lasted all the way to Duke val Torlen's estates, down the winding drive and until they turned off the road onto a cart path that took them down by the river. There, she admitted, her resolve somewhat fizzled.

Does he mean to take us to ship? she thought with a gulp. This was not a scenario she'd envisioned. She wasn't sure how Ean would ever find her if the evil man took her away aboard an unnamed vessel. But her fears were mollified somewhat when the earl led them instead into the circular drive of a river house of modest size. There her suspicions were proved true.

"Does the Duke know anything of your treacherous machinations, Lord Brantley?" she inquired as they halted in the drive.

The earl gave her a wan smile. "Sadly, the old Duke is no longer a man of vision, your Grace."

"But you are?"

"Indeed. I am a visionary of the highest order." He helped her from her mount somewhat forcefully and held her arm in a viselike grip as he steered her toward the house. "I see where the kingdom is heading."

"And where is that?"

"Into stagnation, my dear Duchess. The val Lorian line has withered. What was once puissant now shrivels with impotence. The three heirs provided by that island wench were none of them fit for the throne. Soon enough, we will be free of the last of her get, and a stronger line will take its rightful place."

This was sounding all too familiar. "I've heard this seditious speech before, Lord Brantley," Alyneri remarked critically.

He cast her a curious eye, his interest piqued. "Indeed, your Grace?"

"Why yes," she said, jerking her arm free of his hold at last. She turned to look him full in the eye. "Morwyk's sycophants all spout the same inane drivel. For insurgents, they've a singular lack of imagination. Perhaps the commonality is what attracts them to the duke as well." She smiled sweetly at him, though there was nothing but poison in her tone. "I've never met so many people who haven't a single inventive thought of their own—"

"Enough, *your Grace*," the earl warned, bristling. He grabbed her roughly by the arm and dragged her up the stairs into the manor. "I would be loathe to hurt you to gain your silence."

"I seriously doubt that, Lord Brantley," she returned, to which he gripped her arm all the harder.

The earl veritably dragged her through the manor after that, his irritation apparent. The place looked deserted, with linens draped over furniture and paintings alike, so it seemed a house of ghosts. Alyneri was not without fear; but while she trembled inside, so also did she hold hope close. Ean and the others would come. They would find her and Tanis, and all would be made right again. She'd almost convinced herself that nothing untoward would happen at all until the earl shoved her through a door into a large room.

When she saw what awaited there, however, her resolve failed her completely.

THIRTY-FIVE

'People who claim something cannot be done should not get in the way of the ones who are doing it.'

– The Second Vestal Dagmar Ranneskjöld

There was a bubble of silence over the table in the corner of the tavern where five men sat hunched over a game of Eastern Trumps, a far different game from the less commonly played Western Trumps. Two of the men had been trumped out of the game, and the remaining players were down to three cards each.

The pirate Carian vran Lea's head was only partially in the game. He could play Eastern Trumps with his eyes closed, and the pot was uninteresting to him, nothing like the games played on his home island of Jamaii, where a man could lose a hand—or worse, his ship—if his attention wavered. Still, it was something to do.

Stifling a yawn while his opponent sweated over his next move, Carian lifted his brown eyes to the window across the room. Snow continued to fall outside, bringing a scowl to the pirate's angular features, the lower-half of which were shaded beneath a perpetual five-day scruff. Carian hated snow even more than he hated the Agasi Imperial navy and Whisper Lords. He wouldn't be anywhere near a climate that allowed for snow if not for his grave need. It was some kind of curse that Necessity could drive a man to uncharacteristic action—bravery or foolishness, brashness or chivalry, *absurd trips to the edge of civilization*, all quite against his nature.

The Khurds probably have a god named for Necessity, Carian thought churlishly. Raine's truth, they had a god for everything else—wind, water, mud, pigs…

The man across from the pirate was a local miner, if told from the pick hooked into the belt of his rough leather jerkin. He didn't seem to have a head for Trumps, for he frowned indecisively at his cards.

Carian inwardly sighed. It wasn't like *he* was snowed in with the rest of these yokels—he was a Nodefinder, by Epiphany's Grace. He could leave whenever he wanted! Carian kept reminding himself of this, for the raging snowstorm outside disturbed his sense of rightness with the world.

Precipitation was not meant to be *white*. It was slate-grey, accompanied by whipping wind and charcoal thunderheads over raging waves three times the height of a man; or it was misty blue, drifting down in the early morning hours to caress a glassy sea; sometimes it was even silver-clear, pouring in great sheets from a tropical sky mottled with storm clouds, sun, and azure blue, rainbows as jewels alighting on dappled waves that spanned from shadowed cobalt to sapphire to warm, aqua-green.

But it *wasn't* white.

If only he'd learned to speak the damned desert tongue, he might be on his way to Veneisea by now.

The man across from the pirate finally threw down a Knave. Carian rolled his eyes, heaved a disgusted sigh, and tossed his cards into the pot dispiritedly. It really wasn't worth playing the game—if the stakes weren't high enough to get your blood boiling in your veins, what was the point?

The map. Remember the map.

Yes, the map. This entire Maker-forsaken trip to nowhere was about the damned map.

And Carian's interest in the map, in turn, was really for a noble purpose. If only the woman who owned it could understand that.

Not that it would matter to the accursed woman!

In his own mind, Carian vran Lea was the second-most talented Nodefinder ever to walk the pathways of the second strand. Besides Carian, only one man in known history had ever traveled to T'khendar and lived to speak of it. That the same man had never returned was no reflection on his skills, however, for Dagmar Ranneskjöld, Second Vestal of Alorin, was the undisputed Great Master to which all other Nodefinders aspired.

That Carian had been forced to say nothing of his own successful—in the sense that he'd actually returned—journey to T'khendar rankled him no end. He bloody deserved a damned medal from the Guild for that feat. Countless times he'd had half a mind to forego his promise to silence and boast of his adventure, but thinking of the consequences of a loose tongue always left him slightly ill—a strange feeling to a man raised on the sea—and each time he'd somehow kept his temper in check. Quite against his nature.

Carian had gone to T'khendar originally intent on finding the Great Master and releasing him from the Fifth Vestal's prison, but things hadn't exactly gone as planned.

That time. But with a Weldmap...

Shadow take the infernal woman! Carian abruptly cursed his current nemesis for the countless time. *Doesn't she understand how valuable that map is?*

Apparently she did. That was the bloody problem.

Trell reached the outskirts of the mountain township of Olivine five days after he left his companions behind in Sakkalaah. He'd traded Sakkalaah's grassy, sun-warmed plateau for the wind-whipped passes and rough trails of the Assifiyahs, and by the time he and Gendaia arrived in Olivine, both wore a coat of snow. Trell was infinitely grateful for his ermine cloak, one of the many unexpected gifts from the Mage who'd saved his life, but he was more grateful still to see the town come into view with its smoking chimneys and golden windows boasting of warmth.

The road from Sakkalaah had been long and surprisingly lonesome after his days with Fhionna, his mind filled with lingering thoughts of her. His body still yearned for her touch, for the singular feel of her skin against his, her hair soft across his face, her lips...

Gendaia nickered beneath him and shook her coat, dislodging an explosion of snow.

Thanks, Trell thought wryly as he wiped snow from his eyes with the back of one gloved hand. Whether the horse perceived his thoughts or just his pensive shift in mood, Gendaia had an uncanny sense for when Trell was reminiscing over the *nymphae*. For a female of the equine variety, she was surprisingly adept at returning him to reality in gentle but effective ways.

There was but one main road through Olivine, which followed along a cold running river that split the town in half. Its banks were edged by a cobbled wall covered in snow, and its waters ran charcoal-dark.

The storm concerned him, because Prosperity Pass was the only crossing in this part of the Assifiyahs. If the storm didn't soon let up, it might be days before the pass was clear enough for travel.

Prosperity Pass, Trell thought, tasting of the name. *And beyond it…Xanthe.*

Technically he was already in Xanthe, but these outlying mining towns were mostly self-governed, imposing their own laws as they saw fit to protect their mineral interests. Olivine was known for its peridot. The gemstones were often mined at night, since it was said that sunlight made them invisible. But no one was mining that evening, not in a storm such as what squatted over these mountains.

Trell easily found an inn on the main road. As he dismounted in the yard, he looked up at its three stories of glowing windows with anticipation of warm relief. The snow was relentless, huge flakes swirling and tossing, a whirlwind of ethereal moths. He was gathering his saddlebags when a boy came running up. The lad was bundled like a babe in swaddling with layer upon layer of wools. Trell could just see a pair of green eyes peering out between the gnarled knitted scarf that enwrapped his head and neck. He reminded Trell very much of the mummified remains of a Cyrene king that Krystos had brought back from one of his expeditions to the deep desert.

The boy took one look at Gendaia and turned immediately obsequious. "Welcome to the Green Frog, milord," came a young voice mysteriously from somewhere among the layers of cloth. "Will you be stayin' the night?"

Trell glanced toward the inn. "Are there rooms to be had?"

"They'll make room for you, milord. The Gov'nor don't like turnin' people away in storm season, and especially not important folk."

A little puzzled by the boy's remark, Trell handed Gendaia's reins to him. "What quarters have you for her?"

"We've braziers in the stables, milord. She'll be warm as a copper on the hearthstone. I wager you'll be ready to move on b'for she is, sir."

Satisfied that Gendaia would be cared for, Trell gave the lad a coin and saw him off. Then he hefted his bags over his shoulder, turned, and trudged through the snow into the inn.

A chain of bells rang as he opened the door and stepped inside onto a broad woven mat that was already soaked with snow. The great room boasted a river-stone hearth big enough to roast a boar and a roaring fire whose heat embraced Trell with welcome warmth as he closed the door behind him. He could hear men's voices off to his left, floating from the depths of a whitewashed hallway, while a wide staircase angled to his right, ending at a balcony that ran the length of the great room.

A rotund woman soon exited from a door beneath the stairs. Her eyes swept him from head to toe and must've found him more than acceptable, for she brightened considerably. "Ah, welcome, milord, welcome," she said, opening her arms to him. "Will ye be taking rooms tonight? Tis a terrible storm that hit us, and so early in the season."

"I would like a room, yes," Trell said, reflecting on how strange it was to be speaking the common tongue, to be in these surroundings, so unlike the desert in every way. "If you have one."

"But of course we do, milord!" she proclaimed, taking him warmly by both shoulders. "An you're a dear, aren't you? My, what lovely eyes. I've a daughter would as love gazin' into eyes such as yours, milord, were she not already bedded up with that loaf of a minstrel, Roark. Never will make nothing of his life when a man can't lift a finger in an honest day's work—talking 'bout how he couldn't make his living if he so much as broke a nail...but come," and she turned him by the shoulder and walked him to her counter, opening a ledger to a page marked with a blue ribbon. "Sign in, milord, and I'll get you a key."

Wishing she would stop calling him 'milord,' which made him uncomfortable, Trell picked up the quill and wrote his name in her book beneath the scrawled handwriting of a man named Jeremiah Gundstrom. He read some of the other names: *Cordell Hait, Rory Tatum, Charis Vogler, Carian vran Lea...* They were western names mostly, northern names, names far removed from the ones he was used to hearing save those of men among the ranks of the Converted.

"Just the one room then, dear?" the woman asked inquisitively, glancing his way as she unlocked a box with a tiny golden key from a chain resting on her ample bosom. "No one traveling with ye tonight?"

"Just my horse."

"An what brings ye to Olivine?" She opened the box, which was full of keys, and began searching through it.

"Just passing through to the Cairs."

The woman turned him a look of sudden compassion. "No, sweetling, I fear that's impossible. The pass has been closed since the new moon. Sorry to be the bearer of ill tidings, but we're as far as you go this winter." She brightened as she plucked a key from its hook. "But we've plenty of rooms, and the Gov'nor is always willin' to give a man an honest day's wage in exchange for room and board. That is if ye run short of coin..." but her tone and her knowing look said she expected *he* would not. She turned her ledger to have a look at his name and frowned. "But what's this? Chicken-scratch! Ye cannot even write? An here I thought ye sure an educated soul."

Trell glanced at his name and realized he'd written it in the desert alphabet. "My apologies, mistress," he said, feeling so strange in this place. Desert-bred women weren't chatty as chickens—at least not with men—and a room in a respectable inn such as that one would be secured by the reputation of your tribe, not by your given name scrawled on a page in a book. He spun the ledger around and struck through his name in the illegible language, penning it again on the line beneath in a smooth, flowing script that felt both incredibly foreign and strangely fitting at the same time.

Trell of the Tides.

How odd to see his name written in the common alphabet. It didn't fill him with as much loneliness as he'd expected. Trell was surprised, actually, to realize there was beauty in the name for him now; it conveyed an intimate connection with the Goddess of the Waters which he never knew existed before his travels with Fhionna. Naiadithine had claimed him as her own, and Trell of the Tides was her name for him, her token of promise, her chaste kiss of blessing.

"Trell of the Tides," the woman read aloud, sounding disappointed that it hadn't been Lord-somebody-or-other. She looked slightly peevish as she looked up at him. "Don't say much about ye does it?"

Trell met her gaze. "Actually, mistress, it says everything I know."

The woman gave him a puzzled look, but she quickly shook it off. "Well then, Trell of the Tides. Let's get ye to yer room, an then I suspect ye'll be wantin some dinner."

In acknowledgement, Trell's stomach growled on his behalf.

As she led him to the stairs, she pointed down the adjoining hall, from which now floated the music of a lute and a male voice raised in song. "The Common's that way. Just opened a new cask of cider—it's still a bit green, so I recommend the mead lessen ye don't mind it a bit sour. We've a bathhouse out back. The Gov'nor keeps the coals burnin bright as the summer sun, but tis an icy walk there and back in this weather."

"Is the Governor about?" Trell asked as he followed the round woman upstairs.

"I'll ask him to find ye in the Common, milord."

On the second floor, she showed him into a smallish room dominated by a wide poster bed. The single window was frosted over. "I'll send Millie up to get a fire started for you, milord," the woman said as Trell walked past her into the room. She handed him his key and strode purposefully down the hall.

Trell closed the door and set his bags on a black lacquered chest at the foot of the bed. The woman intimated her expectation that he'd be here all winter waiting for the spring thaw and the opening of the pass. While he didn't relish the trek back down the mountain, Trell had no intention of staying put in Olivine, not when he carried a fortune in Agasi silver—ripe for the picking should anyone unsavory discover it—and a missive for the Mage's contact in the Cairs. Somehow he had to find a way across the peaks into Xanthe.

With his silver stashed safely in his satchel and it in turn strapped diagonally across his chest, Trell locked his room and found his way to the Common. For all that he hadn't encountered another patron thus far, the tavern was bustling with activity. Tables were packed with men dicing or carding, and the bar was lined two-deep with locals of various sizes and shapes, most of them dressed in rough-spun woolens. A barmaid passed among the crowd, her long wavy red hair a delight to behold among the ocean of ochre and brown. As Trell looked around, he noted that the minstrel who'd been singing earlier now lounged beside the wide hearth entertaining two rosy-cheeked girls of Lily's age who gazed adoringly at him though Trell thought the man of average measure.

It was a scene found anywhere among the kingdoms of men, yet Trell felt misplaced; while the play was the same, all the actors had changed.

Across the room, two men stood and headed for the door, leaving a small table open near the fire. Trell reached it at the same time that the red-haired barmaid arrived to clear the remains of their meal. "Will you be taking dinner, sir?" she asked without looking up from her task.

"Please," he murmured as he lowered himself into a chair.

As she lifted her gaze and met his, she did a double-take, her eyes widening in obvious surprise. She blushed then, a pink color coming up beneath the smattering of pale freckles across her nose. Looking quickly back to the table, she asked, "Anything to drink, milord?"

"Cider," Trell murmured, wondering at her reaction.

She smiled bashfully, curtsied, and darted off toward the kitchens.

Bewildered, Trell scratched his head and gazed after her.

She wasn't the only one to react strangely to his presence. As he ate his meal and drank his cider, he noticed others staring at him. Besides the barmaid, who never again could meet his eye, the two girls that had been fawning over the minstrel kept darting glances his way and then whispering to each other, and a woman in a green dress sitting at a table with three men stared at him the entire duration of his meal. He began to wonder if there was something offensive about his person. He hadn't set foot in the northern kingdoms since he woke in Duan'Bai; who knew what manner he might have adopted in the Akkad that was deemed improper by these females?

The only other person in the room who seemed to garner any attention was a man with long wavy black hair who sat with his back to the wall. The rest of the men at his table were engrossed in a game of cards, but he sat with muscled arms crossed watching the room as if observing a game of Kings, his gaze both assessing and calculating. Trell watched him remove a pouch of tabac from inside his vest and roll its leathery leaves into a fag. He lit it from the lamp on his table and sat back again, exhaling a haze of smoke.

"Is there anything else I can get you, milord?" asked the barmaid suddenly from Trell's right. He hadn't noticed her there. He looked up, hoping to meet her gaze, but she blushed and looked away again.

Trell decided he'd had enough for one night. "No. Thank you." He stood, paid her for the meal, and departed. Rather than return to his room, however, he left the inn to check on Gendaia.

When he reached the stables, he saw that the lad had spoken true: the stable was warm enough to set the long icicles to melting above the wide barn door. Trell eyed them uncertainly as he passed beneath.

How long had it been since he'd seen an icicle? Yet he distinctly remembered icicle sword-fights in a snowbound courtyard, shards of the spikes flying dangerously as he and his younger brother hacked away, laughing as they tumbled through the snow baiting each other with boastful threats...

Trell paused just inside the stables, a sudden lump caught in his throat. For so many years he'd prayed for a memory—any memory—but while he was in the Emir's employ, his prayers had gone unanswered. Now memories came unbidden and with such clarity that they left him feeling stung, even shaken.

With this recent vision, he recalled his brother's face so clearly he might've drawn his likeness! His face was so like Trell's own and yet...different, with eyes of shared color but deeper set. In the memory his brother laughed as they trampled through the snow, both of them wearing only loose tunics and britches tucked into heavy fur boots, their breath steaming in the air. The younger boy gave Trell a taunting grin and beckoned with his icicle, and his name was…

It was…

But it wouldn't come.

The more Trell chased after it the further the vision fled, until even his brother's face began to lose its detail. His memories were fickle things yet, as wild and uncontrollable as the Cry, as deep and mysterious as the goddess who dwelled there.

"Milord?"

Trell focused again to find the stable boy staring uncomfortably at him. He gave him a reassuring smile. "I just came to check on my horse."

The boy's tense expression relaxed. "Ah, she's a rare beauty. I've got her snuggled in as happy as a suckling pup, sir, don't you fret. Here, come and see." He waved Trell to follow as he continued chatting on about how happy the horses were as he walked down the line of stalls.

Gendaia came forward to greet Trell while he was still several stalls away.

"She knows your step, sir, that's Raine's truth," the boy noted with a grin. "Never seen a Hallovian before, m'self, but I've heard fairy tales about 'em. It's a real privilege, sir, I must say. What's her name, if I might ask?"

"Gendaia."

"Well, that's sure pretty. What's it mean?"

"Daybreak," Trell murmured. He took Gendaia's head and stroked her silver-white nose. She nickered and pushed her head into his shoulder. He spoke into her ear, murmuring a welcome in the desert tongue. She tossed her head and snorted, and Trell smiled. He looked to the stable boy, who was grinning eagerly at him. "Well, she does seem happy and warm," he admitted.

The boy beamed.

Trell looked back to Gendaia. "Good night, beautiful lady-horse," he said in the desert tongue and continued in this like, "Enjoy your warm meal and dry hay. Tomorrow it's back to the snow for us, I fear."

She tossed her head in acknowledgement and then pulled back into her stall.

Trell turned to the stable boy and found that he was staring at him in awe.

"You must be Trell of the Tides," said a deep voice from the stable's entrance.

Trell turned to see a heavyset man standing in the doorway. "I am."

"The name's Harmon," said the man as he approached. Harmon had the build of a blacksmith long retired, with a powerful gut where a muscled chest might've once reigned, but his large brown eyes seemed genuine, and his manner was amiable. "I'm the Governor here in Olivine and the owner of this inn."

"Well met," Trell said, clasping wrists with him. "My horse and I thank you for your hospitality."

"Indeed, indeed," Harmon said, emitting a chuckle from somewhere deep within. He glanced at the gawking stable boy somewhat disapprovingly. The lad cleared his throat and rushed off, and then Harmon said to Trell, "Seline, my innkeeper, mentioned you were hoping to head on tomorrow."

Trell nodded. "I was planning to take the pass into the Cairs."

"That's inadvisable," Harmon told him, shaking his head. "The pass is buried under ten feet of snow at last account and more by the time this storm lets up. You'd never get through. Last year a Nadori merchant and his entire company were lost in the pass in snow half as deep and we didn't find them til summer set in. No, no," he shook his head definitively. "The best advice is to winter here and wait for the spring thaw." He settled his gaze on Trell suggestively and offered, "I'm always in need of help this time of year. We're a small community, and it takes every hand to keep the routes clear and the mines running." His little eyes gave Trell a once-over and he added, "I expect you're a man unafraid of honest work."

It was the third time Trell had heard the term. He wondered what these people considered to be dishonest work and how they so easily decided which side of the line he walked. "If the pass is closed," he said, "we'll have to head south to the Ruby Road."

"We?" asked the Governor.

"My horse and I," Trell clarified, only then realizing that he'd spoken of Gendaia as a traveling companion—but one simply didn't think of a Hallovian steed as a mere beast of burden. "We may still be able to get through on the Bemoth end," Trell added as an afterthought.

"And brave the jungles, milord?" the man looked startled. "You must have pressing business in the Cairs!"

Trell couldn't bring himself to confess the truth: that spending three months in the tiny town while the solution to his past lay so tantalizingly before him might prove more torturous than all the years before. Instead all he could offer the man was the simple declaration, "Regretfully, I cannot stay."

The Governor regarded him hesitantly, his brown eyes almost hidden among the heavy folds of his eyes. "Milord..." he said again, and Trell fought the urge to cringe at the title, "I'm not a one to pry, but...is it possible you were speaking the desert tongue just then?"

"Yes. Why?"

"It's just..." The Governor frowned. He glanced around the empty stable and placed a hand on Trell's arm confidentially, explaining, "I've a guest arrived two days past. He's not the type I'd usually recommend to my patrons—that is, we prefer to conduct our business here in Olivine with honest men, so I cannot vouch for him—but he's been asking around for someone who speaks the desert tongue. Tis possible you may be able to...help each other."

Intrigued, Trell shifted his weight and settled his hand absently on the hilt of his sword. "How so?"

The Governor eyed Trell's blade and its gleaming sapphire pommelstone quizzically, but he said only, "Perhaps he should be the one to tell you, milord. If you'll agree to speak with him, I'll introduce you."

Trell saw no reason not to, and soon he was being ushered into a private room adjoining the Common. The room was small, with just four tables arranged around a modest hearth, but the fire was warm and the stout was heady, and Trell figured he had his sword if things came to that.

It wasn't long before the door opened and a man walked in. Trell smiled softly when he recognized him. It seemed only fitting that this would be the man who Harmon had decided walked the other side of the 'honest' line. Neither of them seemed to fit in well in Olivine.

"You're Trell of the Tides?" asked the other man as he closed the door behind him.

"I am."

"Carian vran Lea," he offered. "Of Jamaii."

Of course. Up close, Trell saw that the islander was perhaps thirty and five, but the fine lines edging his brown eyes had been deepened by a life at sea. He certainly looked the rogue, unshaved as he was and with his wavy black hair hanging wild and long about his waist. He wore four silver hoops pierced through each ear and a tiny gold loop in his right nostril.

"So…" said the islander as he swaggered over, swaying slightly as men accustomed to life on the sea often will. He wore a cutlass at his belt as well as dual daggers, but there was nothing threatening in his manner as he sat down across from Trell. Not that the man needed any posturing to prove himself a dangerous opponent. The islanders were said to train in the *mujindar* fighting style, and everyone knew what happened to people who crossed one of the pirates of Jamaii or their countrymen.

The islander considered Trell with the same expression he'd worn in the Common earlier, while Trell gazed neutrally back. After a moment, the pirate crossed his arms and said, "That Hammond fellow—"

"Harmon," Trell corrected.

"Yeah, him," the pirate agreed. He pulled out his tabac pouch and rolled another fag. "So he says you speak the desert tongue. How'd you learn it?"

"I spent five years in the Akkad."

"Huh. You're one of those Converted?"

"No."

The pirate arched a solitary black brow. "Interesting." He leaned to light the fag in the lamp on the table and then exhaled a cloud of smoke. Looking back to Trell, he held out the pouch. "You smoke?"

Trell shook his head. "So the Governor thought we might be able to help each other."

"Yeah."

"But he failed to mention how."

A knock on the door interrupted further conversation. The red-haired barmaid came to the table, curtsied and murmured, "Is there anything I can get you?"

"Two more of whatever he's having," the pirate answered.

The barmaid curtsied again and left—all without looking at Trell even once.

Trell frowned after her. After a moment, he shifted his gaze to the pirate and found him grinning from ear to ear.

"They don't see the likes of you around here much, I'll wager," the islander observed. He drew long from his fag and puffed out three smoke rings in quick succession.

Trell shook his head. "The likes of me…" he muttered, still frowning.

"You know—obviously court bred," the pirate said, waving airily, "sporting a cloak that would cost most of these yokels a year's wages. Plus I hear you ride a Hallovian."

Trell gave him a sharp look. "How did you hear that?"

The pirate barked a laugh. Abruptly he leaned one elbow on the table and eyed

Trell shrewdly. "What you should be asking me, Trell of the Tides, is why it should matter to these folk *what* kind of horse you ride."

The truth of those words made Trell wary, and he lifted alert grey eyes to the door as if desirous to see through it into the Common beyond.

"Nah," said the pirate, waving with his fag as he sat back again. "It's not what you're thinking."

Trell's gaze shifted to the pirate. "How do you know what I'm thinking?"

He grinned. "It doesn't matter what you're thinking. I guarantee you it ain't what *they're* thinking."

"Which is?"

The pirate shrugged inconsequentially. "They suspect you're a mage."

"A mage." Trell was indeed surprised, and even somewhat appalled. "Whyever would they think such a thing as that?"

"There's a rumor going round about a mage in these parts. He's spoken of in reverent tones, like as one of those damned desert gods you say you aren't sworn to, but he's supposed to have dark hair—might as like your own—and speak the desert tongue—same as you—and ride a Hallovian Grey. Also like you, my friend."

Trell received this news with outward calm, but inside he felt dismayed. *What would the Emir's Mage be doing in Olivine?* To the pirate, he said, "How did you hear about this?"

The pirate grunted dispiritedly. "These blaggards talk so much you'd think their mouths were the bellows of their soul. They've no idea how to play a hand of Trumps—*always* talking when they should be thinking and thinking when they should be playing. This bloody mage is all I've heard about since I arrived two agonizing days ago." He exhaled another cloud of smoke and crossed one booted ankle over knee. "Who knows if it's even true, aye? 'These parts' could mean Rethynnea the way rumors spread in Xanthe."

"But you're not worried that I'm this mage," Trell remarked after a moment, gazing now with interest at the islander.

The man shrugged, grinned. "Are you?"

"No."

"Well then."

The barmaid arrived with their beer. She plunked them on the table, blushing all the while, and left with her eyes downcast, closing the door silently behind her.

"Balls of Belloth, if she ain't a pretty poppet on a string tied to you!" the pirate observed with a leering grin.

"The girl can't even look at me," Trell protested.

"Bucko, you're probably the man of her dreams. A pretty chase like you…"

Trell turned him a flat look at his choice of words. "More likely she was confused as to whether you were a freakishly hairy woman she should pity or a mannish woman she'd best guard as a rival, what with hair so long and lovely."

The pirate grinned at him. "I like you, Trell of the Tides," he declared, gesturing with his fag. "So tell me this: how would you feel about taking a little trip to Veneisea?"

"My destination is somewhat south of there," Trell replied. His eyes shifted to the snow blowing against the frosted windowpanes. "They say travel through the pass is impossible now."

The islander leaned back in his chair and puffed a large smoke ring, which floated lazily above the table between them. "What if we needn't travel through the pass at all?" he offered.

Trell sipped his beer. The prospect suited him just fine. "I'm listening."

"I'm in need of a man who speaks the desert tongue to help in resolving a certain conflict with an acquaintance of mine," Carian said. "It's the age-old proposition of 'you scrub my decks, I'll scrub yours.' Come with me to Veneisea, assist in resolving my problem with this acquaintance of mine, and I'll take you anywhere you wish to go afterwards."

Trell was beginning to suspect how the islander meant to 'take him anywhere', but he wanted it plainly stated. "And how would we travel then, if not through the pass?"

The pirate flashed a toothy grin. "On the very pattern of the realm, my fine lad."

Smiling softly, Trell contemplated his offer. While the prospect of traveling the nodes was certainly intriguing—even quite exciting if he let himself think about it—Jamaiian natives weren't known for their honor. It was a brave man who risked any kind of bargain with a pirate captain—Nodefinder or otherwise. Trell sat back in his chair and settled hands in his lap. "How do I know you'll honor our accord?" he asked.

"A pirate can be trusted to keep to the Code," Carian said through a toothy grin.

"What code?"

"The Pirate's Code."

Trell crossed arms and regarded the islander carefully. "Which states what, exactly?"

"I'm not obligated to divulge the secrets of the Code."

"Then how do I know you're keeping to it?"

The islander blew another smoke ring and eyed him sagaciously, a humorous sparkle in his brown eyes.

As much as the man was obviously avoiding the question, Trell had a good feeling about him. The islander seemed good-natured, for all of his pirate's bluster, and he had an uncommon spirit that reminded Trell of Krystos. Trell genuinely liked him. "So...a pirate can be trusted to keep to the Code," he repeated thoughtfully, holding the islander's brown-eyed gaze, "but if I don't know the Code, how do I know if it is in my best interests?"

Carian grinned even wider.

"Ahh, so," Trell returned his smile in good humor. "I think I begin to understand. The Code is probably never in anyone's best interest except the pirate in question. In fact," he added, pressing a finger to his lips, "I'm willing to wager that's all there is to it: whatever is in a pirate's best interest is all your illustrious code bespeaks."

Carian barked an approving laugh and clapped a hand upon the table. He gestured with his vanishing fag, splaying ash as he observed, "You're a brighter torch than I gave you credit for, Trell of the Tides. Most men need a taste o'the cat before smartening up."

Something in the pirate's manner reminded Trell of Vaile's words: *'None of us can be trusted, but the worthy ones will tell you so.'* Trell had already made his decision, so it didn't matter which way the pirate answered, but he was curious to know what he would say. "So, Carian vran Lea," he posed, "can I trust you to keep your word?"

The islander laughed. "As a pirate? Definitely not." Abruptly his expression sobered and he continued with oath-bound solemnity, pressing a fist to his heart, "but as a Nodefinder, on your life and mine."

Trell sat forward and offered his hand. "Then I would say we have an accord."

"Aye," Carian said seriously, clasping wrists with him. Then he grinned victoriously. "And so we do."

THIRTY-SIX

'Thalma cannot be bribed with worshipful praise and flattery; the gift of her luck requires dutiful and repeated sacrifice.'

– Excerpt from *The Elevated Teachings of Jai-Gar*

"How does it work?"

Trell stood facing the icebound wall next to the Nodefinder while snow piled around their knees and Gendaia snorted warm and wetly into his ear. The prospect of heading back out into the storm in the middle of the night seemed a small price to wage against the promise of the relative warmth to be found upon reaching Veneisea. Trell was grateful to leave Olivine, especially after learning of the rumors spreading about him, and of course, the pirate couldn't have been more eager to be off.

"How does what work?" the Nodefinder asked absently as he pulled a long, black silk scarf from his knapsack and began tying it around his head, the fringe mingling with his wild wavy hair. "Nodefinding? *Elae*? Sex?" He winked at Trell, adding, "I'm sure you'll find out about that last option once you grow a little hair on your balls. Girls like pretty boys, but *women* desire *manly* men," and he puffed out his chest to demonstrate his point.

"And yet when salty old men like you tire before pleasuring their ladies, they'll come running to a younger man," Trell remarked, "like me."

The pirate gave him a sooty look. He pulled a dagger from his belt and thumbed the blade. "So this first exit may be a little hairy," he admitted, "especially with that horse of yours. Don't worry though, lad," he reassured Trell, placing a hand on his shoulder. "Stay close to me, and I'll protect you." He took Trell's hand in his own.

"Oh, honey," Trell cooed.

"Don't get any ideas, pretty boy. My boom don't swing that way." The Nodefinder clenched the dagger between his teeth—Trell admitted he looked much the quintessential buccaneer—and stepped through the wall, pulling Trell after him.

Highly curious, Trell followed him into darkness, feeling only the pirate's firm hand around his own and a momentary rushing sensation—like walking through a waterfall without the wet and the cold. Then he felt a jerk and emerged quite ungently into a small bedroom whose only bed was tipped up against the wall.

"Shh!" said the pirate as Trell led Gendaia through into the tiny room.

Trell glared at him in return, for however did one get a shod horse to walk quietly on a stone floor?

It was daylight there, where night had been before, and Trell saw green grass outside the cracked windowpane. The pirate quietly opened the bedroom door, and—

Something colorful leapt upon his back, letting out an angry screech. The pirate swung from left to right trying to dislodge the tiny woman who was clinging to his neck, but this effort was complicated by the two young children who rushed up and began shouting and beating at his legs with sticks.

While Carian yelled curses and pried at the shrieking woman, and the woman in turn shouted in an Agasi dialect and continued trying to strangle him, Trell led Gendaia on into the next room. Three pallets on the floor by the hearth told the story of a frightened family. Doubtless they'd been keeping watch since the last time the Nodefinder visited their abode, perhaps too afraid to sleep in the bedroom lest the inveterate invader return.

The scene was so comical that Trell regretted having to stop it, but intervene he did, coming up behind the woman and wrenching her forcefully off the pirate. The children continued to beat at Carian while Trell dragged the hysterical mother to the other side of the room and pinned her against the wall with one arm.

Clapping one hand over her mouth, Trell leaned close and told her in Agasi, "We mean you no harm." His accent was elegant and refined compared to her provincial dialect.

She stilled beneath him, startled by his educated speech, her brown eyes both furious and frightened.

"Please call your children off my friend," Trell continued. "I have coin to repair any damage to your home, and more to help mend your fear. I'm going to release you now." Holding her gaze, Trell removed his hand from her mouth.

"Ami, Mika!" she managed hoarsely after a moment. "Enough! Leave him be!"

The children lowered their sticks with obvious disappointment.

"Hellions!" a battered Carian complained, yanking the wood from their hands with a scathing look.

Trell suppressed a smile. It was an unlikely scene: a pirate who valued the lives of women and children such that he hesitated to use the dagger plainly in his hand. Trell backed away from the woman, who remained against the wall breathing hard, and opened his satchel. He withdrew ten pieces of Agasi silver—as valuable in the country of their minting as anywhere else in the realm—and handed them to her. It was more than she'd see in a bountiful year, but how did one put a price on feeling safe in one's own home? "For your patience," Trell told her while the pirate continued to scowl at the children, who looked supremely unrepentant, "and for the use of your home on our journey."

Her eyes widened at the coins in her hand, the image of her Empress so clearly stamped upon them. "Milord!" she whispered. "Won't you...won't you stay the night?"

"What did she say?" Carian grumbled. Abruptly he spun and growled like a bear at the children, who jumped with dual shrieks.

The woman eyed him apprehensively.

"We're just passing through," Trell assured her.

She clenched the money to her breast and nodded. Trell motioned Carian toward the door, and he went, but not without making one last jump at the children, who screamed and then started shouting unpleasant things at him. Carian straightened with a triumphant grin and strutted out the door.

"Please come use our...our..." she struggled with the words, "well, you know...

any time you need. But…milord," she added as Trell was leading Gendaia out the door.

He turned inquiringly.

"Perhaps...might we have a little notice next time?"

Trell smiled. "I will mention it to him."

She nodded, and they left.

Trell joined Carian on the lane leading away from the cottage. He cast the pirate a wry grin as they fell into step together, with Gendaia following on her lead. "A *little* hairy?"

The pirate scowled at him. "I didn't know the minx would be lying in wait!"

"That was your idea of protecting me?"

"I was being strangled," Carian pointed out.

"And the children?"

"Hellions!"

Trell laughed. "Remind me never to go into battle with you, old man. My horse could've done a better job of it."

"The woman was freakishly strong," the pirate muttered.

They walked along the lane, which led among grassy hills dotted with sheep. "So where are we?" Trell asked, looking around.

"Somewhere on the outskirts of Sevilla."

Trell arched brows. "Really? I have a friend who was born in Sevilla. You remind me of him a bit, actually."

"Must be a handsome fellow," Carian quipped with a toothy grin.

"He's never lacking for feminine company," Trell replied obligingly, a shadowy smile hinting on his lips. "Where are we headed now?"

"To the next node."

"And where is that, if I might trouble you to inquire?"

"In the city," the pirate said. He shot Trell a sidelong look. "So how'd you come to spend five years in the Akkad if you're not Converted?"

"It's a long story," Trell said.

"It's a long walk to Sevilla," Carian replied with a grin.

"Yet *I* have a horse," Trell pointed out. "I might choose to ride ahead and wait for you at the city limits."

"Then I might choose to take a different node and let you find your own damned way back to Xanthe," Carian retorted.

Trell sighed. "Walking it is. I'll grant you a tit for a tat; you answer my question, I'll answer yours. *D'accord?*" he added in Veneisean.

"Agreed," the pirate said. "What's your question?"

"How do you find your way from node to node? When plotting a course across the realm, is there a chart you can use?"

"The Guild keeps charts," the Nodefinder answered, "but they make you pay out the nose to use them. Most often a Nodefinder just travels a leis or a node to see where it takes him. You try to use portals that you're familiar with, and Nodefinders typically have a repertoire of them. We try to find portals that are easily accessible, but it isn't always possible if there's somewhere very specific that you're trying to go."

"Hence that ugly bedroom scene I just witnessed," Trell said, clicking his tongue reprovingly.

Carian gave him a withering look. "Now you. Fess up. What were you hiding from in the Akkad? You're too young to have caused much trouble."

Trell thought of Korin's fate and knew youth wasn't any sort of protection against the wiles of evil men. "The truth is I don't know how I came to the Akkad..." he began, and as Carian listened, Trell told him his tale.

The Nodefinder was quiet when Trell was done. He thumbed the blade of his dagger thoughtfully as they walked. "So you've embarked upon a journey to uncover your past," he said at last. "Why then the Cairs?"

Trell shrugged. "I hear they're nice in the winter months—that is, if you can abide all the pirates hanging around."

Carian winked at him.

"My turn," Trell said. "What's the different between a Nodefinder, an Espial and a Delver?" He frowned, adding, "Is there a difference?"

"*Pshaw!*" hissed the pirate. "*Is* there a difference, he asks! You're damned right there is!" He gestured with his dagger as he explained, "Espials are kept pets, bilge-sucking courtiers yoked by their balls to a sovereign's whims. All they do is pander to the nobles, carting them around like work dogs on a choke-leash. I'd rather match blades with a Whisper Lord than take a position in any king's court. Nodefinders now," he went on, sweeping a broad arc in front of him with the dagger in his hand, "they're true adventurers! You wanna traverse uncharted territory? You get yourself a Nodefinder. He'll be up for the challenge."

"And Delvers?"

Carian shook his head and gave Trell a warning look. "Well, let's just say if a second-strander calls himself a Delver, you'd best look elsewhere for someone to aid you in your travels."

"Thanks for the tip."

"It'll cost you that horse," Carian said, leveling Trell a rakish grin. "Fair warning: I plan to relieve you of her when our bargain is done."

"Good luck," Trell replied cheerfully. "I rather think you take your life in your own hands, but by all means be my guest at the attempt. You see, she was a gift from a mage."

Carian stared at him. "That wouldn't be the same mage who's rumored to ride a similar Hallovian steed, would it?"

Trell shrugged, grinned.

"And here I thought you an innocent youth," Carian lamented, "only to discover you're in league with wizards."

"And Whisper Lords," Trell added pleasantly. "At least, I believe he would call me a friend."

The pirate looked dubious. "And where did you meet all these marvelous denizens of magic? The Akkad?"

"No," Trell murmured, suddenly reminiscent of his time with Loghain and the others, "...at a sa'reyth."

Carian came to a sudden standstill and grabbed Trell's arm fiercely. "A sa'reyth!" he hissed. "You've *been* to a sa'reyth?" When Trell only gazed neutrally at him, the pirate released his arm and started walking again, shaking his head in wonder. "I heard rumors that they were being established again, but I never…" He eyed Trell suspiciously. "I've never known anyone who's gone to one and lived to tell about it."

Trell thought about all that he'd seen and learned at the First Lord's sa'reyth; the complex might be a sanctuary to some, but it was certainly deadly to those who fell on the wrong side of the Sundragons' loyalties.

"My journey began with the blessing of a Goddess," Trell confessed with a pensive frown, thinking not of his visit to Naiadithine's shrine but to his earlier meeting with her, in the depths of the Fire Sea. "She took a liking to me, I think. Ever since, I've been somewhat under her eye."

Carian cast him a look of flat disbelief. "Assuming I believe you," and his tone said clearly enough that he didn't, "how by Cephrael's Great book did you gain a goddess's favor?" His tone suggested he thought of only one possible route to such a boon, and clearly he didn't think Trell so adept at sailing *those* waters.

Trell shook off his pensive mood and cast the pirate an elusive look. "I'm not obligated to divulge the secrets of my code."

Carian frowned at him. "What code is that?"

"The Heartbreaker's Code."

"Never heard of it," Carian muttered. "You must tell me…"

Trell laughed as they continued down the country lane, the pirate berating him all the while with questions which he was happily not obligated to answer.

They ate what must've been a midday meal in Sevilla, though it felt like a midnight dinner to Trell, and then walked the streets of the sprawling southern city in search of Carian's next node.

"So this next exit might be a little hairy," Carian cautioned as he peered intently into every alley they came to and then shook his head, moving on.

Trell watched him curiously. "Another hostile housewife?"

Carian sucked on a tooth and thumbed his dagger as they walked passed a cobbler's store, a haberdashery closed 'in protest of Guild exploitation,' and a corner fruit-seller boasting pears supposedly blessed by the goddess Aphrodesia. Carian eyed the pears as they passed, replying, "A little more dangerous than our last encounter, boyo—but nothing I can't handle. It'll be important to stay very quiet so nothing happens to your pretty little head."

"Yes, I am quite attached to it," Trell agreed. "The nymphs I met liked it too."

Carian shook his head in wonder, but the confusion behind his brown eyes made him look slightly pained.

After walking back and forth down a particular avenue three times, the Nodefinder finally had an idea. "Stay here," he said before darting into a tavern across the street. Trell watched him vanish inside and waited curiously while the afternoon sun drifted toward the horizon. In the distance, he could just make out the high masts of ships crowding Sevilla's harbor and what might've been the glint of the South Agasi Sea between two far hills.

How long it's been since I saw the ocean with my waking eyes, he realized, knowing that it had once played an important role in his life. If only there weren't so many castle towers overlooking charcoal seas, for knowing he'd been educated in a tower by the sea opened no new doors of his puzzle.

Suddenly Trell heard a crash followed by shouting from an alley across the street. He led Gendaia to the alley's entrance in time to see Carian pitched against a wall. The Nodefinder staggered as if drunk and fell down. "And stay out!" shouted someone from inside the door. An arm reached around and grabbed the handle, slamming it shut.

Curious, Trell led Gendaia down the alley toward the pirate, who was instantly up on one elbow and grinning from ear to ear. "So I was here, like this..." Carian said as Trell approached, "and then I got up," and he jumped to his feet, "and went over this way to throw up," and he walked further down the alley, "and then I turned and saw..." He turned, and his face brightened. "The node!"

When Trell reached his side, he saw another alley connecting into the one they followed. Its entrance was quite hidden from the street. Carian led him to the center of the alley. "Quiet now," he whispered.

"Shall we hold hands again, sweetheart?"

"Unless you'd rather be forever lost within the woof and warp of the realm," the pirate answered with a grim smile.

Trell took hold of his arm.

They emerged from the rush of passage into the dark of night. Trell stilled to let his eyes adjust, but then he blinked at what he saw. He and Gendaia stood on bare earth between two long rows of hammocks strung beneath a thatched roof. Every hammock contained a sleeping form, and the night was loud with the noises of the surrounding jungle, which mingled disharmoniously with the snores of slumbering men. The moonlight illumined a post to Trell's right, which was studded with what on first glance seemed to be shriveled apples but upon closer inspection turned out to be shrunken human heads.

Trell swung a scathing glare toward the Nodefinder, only to discover that he was already far ahead and carefully tip-toeing past the sleeping tribe of Shi'ma.

Of all the fool-brained schemes I've ever heard tell of, taking a node into the heart of Shi'ma territory has to be the most obscene perversion of pushing one's luck ever conceived!

Trell wasn't the religious sort, but as he stood in the midst of the two-dozen sleeping headhunters, he said a quick prayer to Angharad and Thalma begging their forgiveness on Carian's behalf. Then he trod carefully after the Nodefinder, leading Gendaia and cursing the man with every step.

He'd taken no more than two paces before he noticed the thin reeds, each of them five paces or so tall, which leaned against the support poles where the hammocks connected. It didn't take much guesswork to recognize them as blowpipes used to deliver the very deadly poisoned darts the Shi'ma favored. As he passed each pole then, Trell began gathering the long pipes as quietly as he could. By the time he and Gendaia passed out from underneath the thatched roof, he had an armload of the weapons.

"What's all that?" Carian hissed at him as he reached the pirate's side.

"Insurance," Trell whispered in return.

Looking cross, the Nodefinder turned and moved quickly but silently through the village. Trell followed more slowly, searching for someplace to stash the pipes. He found what he was looking for as he passed coals burning low in an open mud oven, and he saw a clay pit just beside it. He shoved the pipes into the soft earth with only a faint sucking noise.

"*Come on!*" Carian hissed under his breath.

Assured that the tubes would be useless for killing them that night, Trell hurried to catch up. They were nearly to the edge of the village when Thalma closed her eye to them and their luck changed.

A group of Shi'ma emerged from the deep forest, six in all. Their low voices were the hum of beetles until one of them spotted Trell. The headhunter opened his mouth and emitted a shrill cackle like the cry of a carrion bird. Then the six Shi'ma were charging and Trell was up on Gendaia and grabbing for the islander's arm, dragging the man up behind him even as Gendaia leapt away into the trees.

The jungle was thinner around the Shi'ma village, for which Trell was grateful. As it was, Gendaia still had a rough go of it as she sped away, struggling through waves of showering vines; Trell and Carian were slapped by limbs and leaves larger than their heads, and Trell was nearly knocked from horseback twice by low-hanging limbs. The Shi'ma were close on their heels—*too close!* Trell heard the spits of deadly darts hitting leaves and trees around them; they seemed to fall in time with the Islander's hissed curses. Only the night saved them, blurring the warriors' aim just enough to keep the darts off their mark. But Trell had no illusions about outrunning the Shi'ma. This was *their* territory.

Carian exhaled a stream of curses in what Trell assumed must be the pirate's native tongue while shouts resounded behind them in the chase and Gendaia struggled through the thick jungle. When she finally emerged onto a path, Trell heeled her into a canter, leaning forward to duck overhanging branches while the Nodefinder behind him was nearly bent in half and holding on for dear life.

"What in Epiphany's name were you thinking!" Trell snarled at the pirate as Gendaia gained in speed. "Shi'ma? Are you *insane?*"

"It was the most efficient way," the Islander returned unrepentantly. "What—are you scared of a few savages?"

"No," Trell growled as he hugged low against Gendaia's neck to avoid the tree limbs lying in wait, "just their darts tipped in poison."

As if to accentuate his point, another barrage of stinging darts whipped past them, shredding the leaves of the trees to either side. One dart struck Trell's saddle just a fingertip from his thigh, and another whizzed past his ear close enough that he imagined he could smell the poison on the needle-thin point. Trell hugged Gendaia closer as she ran and snarled under his breath, "If just one of those bloody things hits my horse, Islander, I'll kill you."

"Easy there, my handsome," came the Islander's response low in his ear. Trell could see his irreverent, toothsome grin even without looking at him. "Don't dive in deeper than you can swim."

In that very moment, Gendaia reared. She shoved all four hooves in front of her in an attempt to stop, but the loamy earth was muddy and slick. Too late, Trell saw the ravine.

Time seemed to slow. Carian shouted something as their momentum carried them forward, and then they were across the edge and falling through the air. Trell spun away from Gendaia, while the pirate launched himself backwards, flipping head over heels, his long hair flying behind him, a variegated pinwheel in his downward rush.

No sooner did Trell hear the river than he was landing in it. He hit sideways, slicing into the water with a stinging slap all along his left side. The river punished him for his lack of grace, spewing water up his nose and ripping the air from his lungs. He felt the current grab him, and he swam with it, surfacing with a gasp.

The barest paling of the sky was enough to illumine the water, which was carrying him swiftly downstream. "Carian!"

"Here!" answered the pirate. Trell caught sight of his head bobbing in the waves, and then they were plunging into whitewater. Trell had time to curse the pirate before the first tumbling wave hit him in the face. He quickly deduced that he'd better breathe at the base of the waves, not at their crest, and he kept his feet downstream as best he could while the water ripped him over the deep rocks. It seemed interminable, what was only a minute at most. At last, the water calmed, and Trell swam for an eddy. Carian joined him there, coughing and sputtering, but Gendaia was nowhere in sight.

Feeling battered, Trell grabbed onto an overhanging limb while he coughed the last of the water from his lungs and caught his breath. The icy water was still too deep to find purchase with his feet, so the two men clung to the branches while the current rushed beneath and around them.

Trell slung wet hair from his eyes with a toss of his head. "How far to the node?"

"Too far," the pirate gasped, still breathless. "We'll have to find another one."

Trell replied with an unforgiving look.

"I know, I know," Carian returned. "If anything happens to your horse… So let's go find her, shall we?" He threw himself backwards into the river and was immediately swept away downstream.

Trell followed, feeling the weight of his sword and boots as cumbersome but necessary accoutrements. As he swam, the image of Naiadithine smiling in the depths of the sea came unbidden to memory. Almost in the same moment, he felt something nudging his back and spun to find a floating log bumping against him. He grabbed onto it, relieved to be able to relax and let the current carry him.

He was getting a stronger hold on the log and worrying over Gendaia when a hush descended over the river. Trell looked around and saw that the river had entered a narrow gorge perhaps fifteen paces wide but easily three-hundred paces high. Dark, shimmering stone jutted upwards on either side, with a pale strip of sky brightening with the dawn in between.

Trell was immensely aware of the deep water beneath him, and he feared for Gendaia so intensely that he felt choked by the emotion. So he laid his head upon the log and prayed as the water carried him along, calling out to Naiadithine to beg her help. He had no idea if she would hear him, or if she did, if she would take pity on his horse. He didn't know if she'd been angered by his union with Fhionna, or if she'd care enough to help when her god-sister Thalma had seen fit to abandon them, but he opened his heart and mind to her as Fhionna had taught him that night on the edge of the Cry, and he poured all of his hope into that tenuous thread.

Please, my Goddess, he whispered. *Please take Gendaia unto your breast and keep her safe.*

He emptied his mind then, just in case the goddess chose to reply—not hoping or expecting really that she would, but more out of respect. Just when he was about to open his eyes, he heard her whisper.

Trell of the Tides.

Her greeting was languid, warm with welcome, a cool embrace received in the waters sweeping about his chest. And in the moment that he felt her presence ebb and fade, he heard the echo of a waterfall.

Follow the water, Trell of the Tides.

"Trell!"

Trell opened his eyes to see Carian just ahead of him. The pirate, for once, looked worried. Trell kicked over to him.

"Madness!" Carian panted as he grabbed a hold of the log. "Is it more rapids?"

"No," Trell said, somehow knowing what awaited. "A waterfall."

"Dagmar's dungeon!" the pirate swore.

Trell cast him a sooty look. "This is what happens when you thumb your nose at Thalma."

"Who?"

"The Goddess of Luck."

Carian slung strands of long black hair from his eyes and frowned at him. "We've got an understanding, her and I."

"I think she's recently reconsidered your accord," Trell muttered.

Carian was about to reply, but then he saw the end of the world approaching, the waterfall's rim. "*Shiiiiite!*" yelled the pirate as they were swept over the falls…falling, falling, until Trell plunged into the depths.

Water rammed up his nose, but the fall wasn't far, and the pool below was deep. He swam for the surface and then headed for a beach just downstream from the falls. Trell pulled himself onto the sand and collapsed on his side. A moment later, Carian dragged himself out of the water and fell to his back with a loud exhalation of relief.

Trell closed his eyes and said a long prayer of thanks, adding a prayer to Thalma begging forgiveness on Carian's behalf. He realized as he finished that he'd suddenly become a religious man. There was nothing quite like communing with a god to illuminate one to the value of faith.

Something wet and warm slopped against his forehead. Trell instinctively swept his arm up to push it off, but his hand met with a familiar warmth that roused him with a leap of his heart. He spun up onto one elbow, wherein Gendaia greeted him with a nudge of her nose against his. Relief flooded him. Trell collapsed back in the sand and gazed up into Gendaia's brown eyes. "Hello, Daybreak," he welcomed her in the desert tongue. "Had a nice swim then did you?"

Gendaia tossed her wet mane. Having apparently assured herself that Trell was fine, she wandered back into the shadows of the clearing, where Trell saw a patch of grass growing out of the rocks as if placed there just for her. When he looked back to Carian, the pirate was watching him. "That's some horse," he observed with a wink. "Can't say as I'd blame you for wanting my life in trade." He broke into a grin. "No hard feelings, eh?"

Trell sighed and pushed palms to tired eyes. "I hope it's worth it, whatever this prize you seek."

"Sure as silver," he returned. He sat up and scratched his wet hair, frowning when his fingers met with something. Using two hands, he disentangled whatever it was from his masses of tangled waves, withdrawing at last one of the Shi'ma darts. "Huh," he remarked, tossing the thing over his shoulder. "Close one!" Then he grinned.

Trell shook his head and looked around in the dim morning light. Ahead, the waterfall was a cascading bridal veil falling from thirty paces above. Trell's eyes followed the flow of shimmering water from its rim to its frothing base. There, a watery figure beckoned.

Trell blinked.

Upon his second glance, he saw nothing in the water, but the image remained in memory.

Carian meanwhile felt around on his person until he found his pouch of tabac. When Trell arched brows at him, he grinned and announced, "Oilcloth. A sailor is always prepared for wet weather." He withdrew a piece of flint from inside the pouch and grabbed his dagger. A moment later, he was reclining on one elbow enveloped in a smoky haze.

Trell found his attention straying back to the waterfall. He couldn't get the image of the figure out of his mind. He left Carian on the tiny beach and wandered into the water, making his way closer to the waterfall. It was perhaps twenty paces wide at its base, a myriad cascade of frothing veils falling from varied heights. One of these veils projected more broadly and widely than the others as the water fell over a jutting boulder midway up the falls.

Whether it was instinct that guided Trell or a vision-gift from his goddess, he dove into the pool on a hunch and swam beneath the plunging waters. Coming up on the other side, he found a deep cave. A dark beach gleamed dimly further within, and Trell swam over to it. He pulled himself out onto the black sand and turned to face the curtain of water. Riversong filled his ears, heady and cacophonous, and in that moment, the sun broke over the jungle rim and set fire to the falls.

Trell caught his breath. In the sunlight, the sheer curtain became a fall of stars, diamonds split with rainbow hues. For the briefest instant, he thought he saw his Goddess's face smiling there, but just as quickly as he saw her she was gone, swallowed again by the raging waters. Trell's heart pounded in his chest, and his throat became tight with gratitude. What had he done to be so blessed?

Perhaps tis not what you've done, but what you will do.

It was Fhionna that seemed to speak the words in his mind, the timbre of her voice rough with her passion as it had been on their last night together. Once again he felt her breath in his ear, felt her body pinned beneath his, her long legs locked around his hips to seal their joining, her bare breasts ripe for his pleasure.

"I love you, Trell of the Tides," Fhionna had promised as she ground against him, her breath in his hair, their skin alive with each other's touch. "My heart will always belong to you..."

Even drenched from the chill waters, Trell grew stiff with the memory as heat flooded him. He lay back on the sand and grinned wearily. *Thank you, my goddess.*

Thank you for these treasured memories. Thank you!

"Trell? ...Trell?" Carian's voice drifted weakly from beyond the falls.

Reluctantly, Trell slipped back into the water, dove low, and came up again in the pool beyond. Daylight bathed the tiny lagoon as he surfaced.

"Oh good," said the pirate as Trell emerged from the water. "I think this is a sacred place. Look." He held up several bone necklaces, each charm carved in a different face or animal. "There's tons of stuff washed up in here. Offerings, I think."

Trell slogged up onto the sand. "There's a cave behind the falls." He walked to check on Gendaia and began looking her over from fetlocks to hindquarters. "I think we're meant to go there."

"Meant," Carian repeated, aiming a skeptical look his way. "By whom?"

"Naiadithine."

"Who is?"

Trell sat back on his heels and looked up at the tall Nodefinder. The man looked fierce with his dark hair plastered around his shoulders and his angular face drawn in contrasting shadows. "Naiadithine is the Akkadian goddess of the waters," he said as he finished inspecting Gendaia. It was nothing less than a miracle that she'd retained only minor scratches—Naiadithine had indeed been watching over her. Straightening again, he added, "The Bemothi call her Thalassa, but I think your folk name her Tethys."

"Tethys." Carian barked a laugh. "Tethys!" He stared wondrously at Trell. "You say you're blessed of *Tethys?*"

Trell shrugged. "So it would seem."

The Nodefinder burst out laughing. He laughed so hard that he eventually fell down. Then he rolled over onto his back and laughed some more, holding his belly as if it would burst. Finally, he composed himself, propped up on one elbow to rest his sand-covered head in hand, and leveled Trell a mockingly serious look. "Okay... well, if Tethys says to swim behind the waterfall, we'd better do it." He made a show then of preparing for the adventure, but he wasn't very good at suppressing his mirth at the idea.

Trell frowned at him. He took Gendaia by the nose and looked into her eyes. "We have to swim beneath the falling water," he told her in the desert tongue. "It is Naiadithine's wish that we do this. Shall I cover your eyes, beautiful Daybreak?"

Gendaia jerked her head out of his grasp and shook herself all over, splattering water everywhere.

Trell took that as a no.

He glanced to the pirate and found him standing with two necklaces in hand as if comparing them. Then he seemed to make a decision, shrugged, and put them both on.

"You can't take those!" Trell protested. "They're offerings to the god of this place."

"The *god* obviously wanted us to have them," Carian returned tartly, "otherwise she wouldn't have brought us here." The pirate gave him one last taunting look and then dove into the pool.

Glaring disapprovingly after him, Trell led Gendaia into the water. She shimmied her coat several times as they walked deeper into the pool, finally feeling the earth fall out from beneath them. She stayed by his side as he swam for the falls, and he felt her near him still as he dove beneath the water, the tension on her reins all the reassurance he needed that she followed. He'd never heard of a horse willingly swimming beneath falling water, but then Gendaia was a Mage's horse and a Hallovian besides. Who knew what she was capable of?

Trell surfaced in the dim cave and saw with relief that Gendaia was still swimming beside him and seeming no worse for the experience. They climbed out on to the black sand beach together, and Gendaia shook her coat with a massive spray of water. Trell drew up short upon reaching the pirate's side, however, for the man stood terribly still, wearing a stunned expression.

"I don't believe it," he whispered, all mocking lost from his tone. "I just...don't believe it."

"What's wrong?"

Carian turned to look at him, and his brown eyes were wide, incredulous. "You really are favored of Tethys," he whispered. "I mean...there's no other explanation..."

Trell took the islander's arm. "Carian, what's wrong?"

The pirate looked thunderstruck. "It's...a weld."

Trell shook his head, not comprehending.

Carian turned back to face the beach. "A weld is a major joining of the pattern of the realm," he murmured, motioning to where it must've been, though Trell saw nothing but sand. "There's only a few hundred of them in the entire world, and most of their locations are hidden without the use of a Weldmap for guidance, of which there are but two left in the known. From a weld, a Nodefinder can travel anywhere. *Anywhere.*" He gave Trell a look of incredulity. Then he burst out laughing. He doubled over to rest hands on his knees as he announced through his laughter, "It's a bloody, freaking *weld!*"

But Trell hardly heard him, for Naiadithine's loving whisper was loudest in his ears.

Follow the water, Trell of the Tides.

THIRTY-SEVEN

'Time means nothing to the gods even as a single life means everything to a man, because he fears he will have only one. Gods know better.'

– The Agasi wielder Markal Morrelaine

The Shade stood staring into the huge, iron-edged mirror with a mixture of horror and fascination on his silver features. He arched his brows and saw the shining chrome face move in concert. He opened his mouth and looked at his teeth—they were normal, white, just slightly crooked in the front, though he didn't remember feeling that chipped molar before…before…

Before I was murdered.

He forced himself to remember this one truth, for all else seemed a hellish fiction. Surely this *was* hell where he found himself now.

I was murdered.

And here he now stood.

I was murdered.

But still he lived.

Reincarnated as a Shade!

The knowledge made him tremble. Yet this was meant to be a mercy.

A mercy!

So they told him, and so he tried to believe.

He watched his reflection in the mirror as he lifted his hands to touch the strange chrome skin, which mirrored his polished silver fingers as they neared. He felt his own touch through his new skin. Metal, and yet living flesh. He looked into his obsidian eyes, seeing the barest glint of amber in their depths. Were his own eyes still there somewhere, or was it a trick of the light?

They'd told him why his eyes had to change, why his skin was necessarily replaced by the alloyed metal. Some few Adepts could handle the terrible power without their bodily forms deteriorating, but most men could not. Since recovering from the death-sleep, he'd felt his own power stirring like an embryo inside him, but he dared not do more with it than acknowledge it was there.

'Once you share the bond with our master,' his mentor had told him, *'you will share the knowledge of how to wield deyjiin.'*

The bond.

More than anything else he'd been told about since waking in T'khendar—and most of it was horrible enough to drive even the bravest man insane—the Shade was most afraid of this bond.

'He will not bind you against your will,' they had assured him, the other Shades who were his blood-brothers now, *but without the bond you will die again, and this death will be forever.'*

It wasn't exactly a heartening choice.

Smoke appeared in the mirror, coalescing behind him, and his mentor, Reyd, soon stood solid in its place. The Shade had learned the trick of disapparating already, but the act scared him immensely. To feel all that was himself dissolving into nothingness was so like unto death that he would reflexively pull all of his particles inwards just at the moment he would have 'elevated to shadows.' He couldn't do it—he couldn't let himself become nothing.

"Comfort in phasing will come, in time," Reyd said from behind him, knowing his mind. Among all Shades, there was a connectivity with each other's thoughts that he was still getting used to, a sharing of knowledge that felt neither an intrusion nor a violation but merely an awareness of others that was sometimes acute—as it was just then with Reyd—but more often seemed as nebulous as his new form. Of the many strange sensations he'd encountered since leaving the death-sleep, the shared mind alone wasn't wholly uncomfortable; at least he never felt lonesome.

Though he heard Reyd's words of encouragement both within the shared mind and through his living ears, the Shade did not turn from his inspection of his reflection. Wasn't there some myth about hellish creatures casting no reflection? It must've been some other kind of demon…

"The First Lord comes," Reyd observed. "Are you ready?"

The Shade turned from the mirror to face his mentor, a living mirror-image of himself. Though in truth, Reyd did not look like him—not really. The Shade could see the vestiges of the other man's own features deep within the metal tissue, even as he could see those haunting reminders of his own former self.

A mercy, he thought, wishing he could still cry. *Is it a mercy to live an eternity without her?*

Reyd gazed compassionately upon him. "There is a saying where I come from," he said.

"What is it?" the Shade asked, wishing he could find hope again, wishing there was a reason to continue on, to accept the First Lord's bond and endure this tragic existence.

"The saying says, 'A love that can end has never been real.'"

The Shade felt his dead heart flutter. What his new brother intimated was too unlikely to be believed. Yet he was surprised to realize that he suddenly hoped—that indeed, he prayed it could be…possible. He lifted his gaze to Reyd, his mentor and only friend so far in his new life. "Will the bond…hurt?"

Reyd shook his head. His hair was also black, like the Shade's own. He'd seen some blonde Shades in T'khendar. They looked…odd. "The bond with the First Lord is painless," Reyd said, "but…"

The Shade saw Reyd's slight frown; he felt his hesitation, he heard whispers of his fears in the shared mind. "But what?"

"But the knowledge you will gain is not."

The Shade swallowed. He'd been told what to expect many times over, but asking the questions again kept his mind off his fear. "Will I see everything he sees and know everything he knows?"

"Only during the binding will parts of his mind be open to you. Thereafter our thoughts and perceptions flow into him but his do not flow to us."

'And without the bond, you will die…'

It didn't seem possible that one man could be the source of life for so many.

"That's too simplistic an explanation," Reyd cautioned. "Do not seek to cache in human terms what is yet beyond you. Once you have seen his mind, you will understand it better."

"And then I must choose."

"Yes. To live in his service, or to dissipate for eternity; for without the bond—without *elae* to pin your living spirit to this shell of shadows—you will move on."

Feeling vestiges of panic at the thought, the Shade looked to his mentor, looked into his eyes so like and yet so unlike his own. "Do you regret your choice?"

"I did…once. But no longer."

"Because of what you learned from the First Lord?"

Reyd looked past him down the hall as he answered, "Because there is no game to be played in death."

"Players and pieces," said a resonant voice from the direction in which Reyd was staring. The Shade turned over his shoulder and saw a tall man advancing down the wide hallway. He wore a coat the color of sky above spotless black britches and boots, and his black curls framed a handsome face with eyes that were impossibly blue.

"*Rad nath*, First Lord," Reyd murmured with a bow of greeting.

The First Lord stopped before them and looked at his newest Shade. "Players know the rules," he said casually, referencing his earlier comment. "Pieces merely obey them. Which would you choose to be?"

The Shade felt power emanating from the First Lord in a way he'd never experienced or even conceived possible. He'd known powerful men, commanding men, robust men of action and noble men of honor; what he felt in the presence of the First Lord was something so far beyond any of these that the use of human terms to describe it seemed simply inadequate.

Swallowing, the Shade met his master's gaze for the first time. His eyes were knowledgeable, worldly, compassionate, interested—but above all of these, they were *intense!*

Blazing intensity, thought the Shade as he trembled inside, *that is as close as I can think of in words to describe him.* "My lord," he managed, "am I meant to choose one of these roles before I choose to swear my oath and…live or die?"

"I meant only to inquire as to your point of view," the First Lord answered with a smile. "Are you a man who would choose to live or die by your own choices, or to play out the choices of another? It was a question of personal ideology, not loyalty."

The Shade glanced quickly to his mentor, who prodded with an encouraging look. "I think," the Shade said then, looking back to the First Lord though it took enormous self-control to meet his gaze, "that if I were given a choice, I would rather be a player than a piece."

The First Lord accepted this with a nod. The Shade couldn't tell if he was pleased or indifferent about it. "Has he been fully briefed?" the First Lord asked Reyd.

"Yes, *ma dieul*."

The First Lord looked back to the Shade. "Are you ready to submit yourself into my control that you might better understand that to which you would be swearing your oath?"

With a mouth gone suddenly dry, the Shade nodded.

The First Lord placed his left hand around the back of the Shade's neck and pressed his right thumb to the Shade's forehead. From the moment he felt the First Lord's touch, the Shade felt also a tingling sensation that soon spread throughout his body. "Be easy and submit to me," the First Lord murmured.

The Shade closed his eyes and saw…he saw…

Images, thoughts, feelings—heartache, tragedy, treason, betrayal, sacrifice, longing, agony, ecstasy, triumph—lifetimes of memories flashed before him. He struggled to keep up at first, but finally he gave in and let the pictures flash by, brilliant, painful, bold…until he began to understand, the story unfolding like a many-petaled flower, a flower that was a pattern, a pattern that spanned the ages…

When Björn released him, the Shade recovered as if from a daze. He felt the wetness of tears on his face, but in the same moment he understood that it was *elae* that gave his body life. Looking around, he realized he'd fallen to his knees, but he hadn't the will to stand. He was overwhelmed. If it was true…but of course it was. He could feel the truth in the very fibers of his soul.

He knew then why the others had chosen as they had. He now conceived of the future in a sense that had never meant anything to him before. "My Lord," he whispered in a choked voice, unable to meet the gaze of this man whose thoughts he now knew too intimately, "I know the binding will tie me to you, and the oath will limit my will…but must I live for you alone?"

The First Lord's gaze was gentle now as he looked upon his newest Shade. "Live for any purpose you desire."

The Shade's eyes flew to his master's. Slowly he got to his feet and pressed hands together before him. The First Lord smiled as he placed his hands to either side of the Shade's.

"*Ma dieul tan cyr im'avec…*" the Shade began the oath as he'd been taught by his mentor, and as he continued to speak the words, every one of them binding him more inexorably to the man before him, he realized that he had never been so proud to be alive.

THIRTY-EIGHT

'There are no real mysteries, only obfuscations.'

– A saying among zanthyrs

Tanis was immensely confused.

He'd been all but abducted from his room at the Feathered Pheasant by two burly men in the livery of House val Torlen and half-carried, half-dragged downstairs, shoved abruptly into a musty closet while someone who ostensively might've helped him passed by, then grabbed up again and carted roughly outside. There he was forced onto his horse and told to wait—all without a word of explanation and only the very real threat of death if he so much as uttered a whimper.

Then her Grace had arrived, clearly a hostage herself, and they'd all made a wild dash out of the city, through the countryside, and to the Duke's lands. But they didn't go to his mansion atop the hill, heading instead for a smaller manor beside the river.

All the while, no one said a single word until her Grace dismounted and started talking to the earl. Far at the rear of the largish company, Tanis could only make out every fifth word or so, but he saw from the earl's darkening expression that the latter misliked her Grace's comments, for which the lad was very proud of her.

"Let's go, you," said one of the men to Tanis.

The lad pulled his gaze reluctantly from his lady, who was vanishing into the manor with the earl, and dutifully climbed down from his horse. He didn't bother asking the soldier what this was about, for he suspected he'd find out soon enough; besides, Tanis knew enough soldiers to know none of them much liked upstart boys who asked too many questions—especially after they'd already been warned not to speak.

So Tanis kept silent and followed obediently and managed to avoid any undue hostility from his guards.

After what seemed a labyrinthine trip through the manor's dark hallways, Tanis was thrust roughly into a room. He jumped as the heavy door was slammed behind him, and then he heard the bolt click into place.

The lad exhaled resignedly and looked around.

"Who's there?" came a weak voice from the room's dim recesses.

Tanis walked toward the voice and soon saw that the room formed an L-shape. Two shadowed forms huddled on the floor in the far corner. They looked up, and Tanis caught his breath, for their eyes were colorless, exactly like his own. The boys were slightly younger than him, but their frightened manner made them seem mere children.

Tanis swallowed his own waxing fear and approached the two boys. "I'm Tanis," he said, kneeling before them.

"I'm Wesley," said a blonde-haired boy. He was holding a dark-haired boy in his arms. The latter trembled uncontrollably. "And this is…this is Piper."

Piper stared into the distance, unseeing, his expression fixed in horror.

Tanis felt cold just looking at the boy. It was like he was caught in a waking nightmare. "What…happened to him?"

"They tested him three days ago," Wesley said, sounding as if he was trying hard not to cry. "They mean to test me too." He gulped. "Maybe even…tonight."

Tanis shook his head, not understanding. "Test you?"

Wesley gave him a terrified look and whispered, "To see if I can withstand…" It took him a moment to muster the courage to finish. "To see if I can withstand Bethamin's Fire."

Tanis recoiled from the heinous words. "Bethamin!" he hissed, staring incredulously at Wesley. "Are you saying there's Marquiin *here*? In Dannym?"

Wesley gazed fretfully at him. "That's who's taken us," he whispered miserably. "The Ascendant is our master now."

His tone was so wretched, so entirely without hope, that Tanis wanted to shake some courage back into him. Instead, he said, "Tell me what happened to you."

Wesley stared at him for a moment and then burst into tears.

The story came out in bits and pieces. How he was taken from his home in Cair Thessalonia and forced to travel with the Ascendant and his Marquiin while they hunted the Free Cities for other young truthreaders, how they kept him in a dark room night and day until it was time to move to the next city; how they beat him if he misbehaved, if he spoke to anyone, raised his eyes in public, or so much as breathed wrong.

"They found Piper in a village outside of Jeune," Wesley told Tanis later. "He was supposed to go next year to Tregarion for his training and a commission to Queen Indora. Now he'll—" Wesley's voice broke again, and he fell into another fit of crying.

Tanis looked at the wretched, horror-stricken Piper and didn't have the stomach to ask if he'd passed or failed his test, mostly because the idea that he might've passed it and yet remain in such a state was too horrible to contemplate. Hoping to distract Wesley somewhat from his fears, he asked gently, "What of you, Wesley? Have you trained at all?"

"No," the boy sniffed. "I'm only twelve."

Twelve!

Now Tanis really wanted to punch something. *A Marquiin would do nicely!* Instead, he clenched his teeth and looked at the trembling Piper, who was only a year younger than him. "Has he spoken to you, Wesley? You know…since…"

Wesley shook his head.

Tanis had an idea. He knew he was taking a personal risk to do what he intended, but if it could spare the other boy some of what must be terrible pain, didn't he have to try?

As it pertains to the practice of healing, Master O'reith had taught Tanis, *a truthreader approaches his craft in three stages: he can draw forth the memories from a man as a voyeur, watching silently from the shadows of another's thoughts; he can diffuse these memories of their power, leeching the life from them so they remain a pale shadow of their former selves; or he can, as a last resort, take them altogether, wall them away behind clouds of blackness such that only another truthreader might restore them to conscious awareness…*

Tanis hadn't the knowledge to perform the third stage of healing, but he'd practiced the second method with his master. The danger was that in order to get to the second stage of healing, he had to first experience the first. He would have to relive the moment with Piper.

"Tanis?" Wesley asked fretfully, for he'd been silent for a long time.

Tanis turned his gaze to the younger boy. "I think I may know a way to help Piper."

"You do?"

Tanis exhaled heavily. "But it won't be easy—for him or for me. Do you think you can hold Piper still?"

Wesley looked uncertain.

"It's just that…if he jerks away from my touch, it could make him worse, not better. Do you think you can do it?"

Wesley licked his lips. "I'll try, Tanis," he whispered. "I'll try really hard."

"Good."

Tanis took a moment to remember his lesson, but mostly to prepare himself for whatever had so terrified Piper. *Remember it's not happening to you,* he reminded himself. *Whatever you see, it's Piper's memory, not yours. It can't hurt you if you don't allow it.*

At last Tanis felt as ready as he'd ever be. He placed one hand on Piper's trembling shoulder and rested the other upon his forehead.

Tanis had once commented churlishly to Master O'reith that he thought the reason only men were born as truthreaders was the impossible finger positioning required for reading another person against their will—that only grown men could possibly have hands large enough to comfortably manage the form.

Master O'reith had made him practice it anyway until he got it perfect every time, so Tanis had no uncertainty in how to position his fingers properly. His thumb went to Piper's temple, his first and middle fingers to the pressure-points at the joining of the bridge of the nose and brows, his fourth and little fingers spanning the eye to press into the opposite temple.

His fingers firmly positioned, he concentrated.

It took only seconds, for Piper's thoughts were a raging torrent, a shrieking gale that overpowered Tanis at once, unprepared as he was for the onslaught. He mentally recoiled, blasted almost entirely out of the other boy's thoughts. He held on by sheer force of will, gritted his teeth and sent his mind spearing back through the wild, spinning madness searching for the memory beneath the mania. Tanis felt buffeted by the maelstrom that was Piper's tortured mind. His was a twisted, toxic vortex of heaving darkness and jagged crackling pain.

How could anyone survive this with any sanity in tact? Tanis thought weakly.

Still, Tanis plunged on, eyes closed, his mind melded with Piper's. In the dark room, Wesley watched Tanis in wordless terror, watched as beads of perspiration formed and fell from his brow, as his left hand gripped Piper's shoulder until his knuckles turned white.

Tanis lost track of the minutes, for it he was soon so lost within the maelstrom that it was all he could do not to spiral off into the madness himself. Standing amid the storm, he was whipped and buffeted with nothing to gauge his whereabouts and nothing to hold onto for support, tossed like flotsam in the dense, malevolent waves of a depthless sea. He felt panic coming upon him. No matter where he looked, he couldn't find the light, couldn't find his bearings. There was only the darkness whipping around him, the terrible flashes of crackling static that were painful and sharp, the churning, raging anger that had no source and no outlet. Tanis searched for anything to lead him beyond the storm, but there was nothing else to see.

And then he understood. Gooseflesh sprouted down his arms with the dreadful realization.

There wasn't some underlying event that had spawned this madness. The virulent storm was *all there was*, and Piper was lost in it. Only, unlike Tanis, Piper couldn't escape by simply opening his eyes. For Piper, there was no escape.

At the same time Tanis realized this tragic truth, he also knew he couldn't help the boy. This was something far beyond his skill, a malevolent working that defied understanding. He slowly withdrew his mind from rapport with the other boy's—

But Piper clung to him. Tanis had a heartbreaking sense of the boy's consciousness, somewhere lost among the madly twisting shadows that had overtaken his mind. *I'm sorry!* Tanis cried. *I'm so, so sorry, but I can't help you.*

Piper strained to hold onto him. Tanis felt his presence as a vague yet desperate pulling against his will, but Tanis couldn't take anymore. He jerked free of the boy's mental pull and released Piper's head in the same instant, snatching his hand away and falling backward onto his hands.

Wesley started at his abrupt motion.

Shaken by what he'd learned and trembling from the experience, Tanis hugged his knees, pressed palms to his eyes and caught his lip between his teeth. He'd never before experienced the grief that flooded him then. To see so clearly into another's madness and know there was nothing—*nothing*—he could do to help him…to give him even a measure of peace…

Wesley saw his shoulders shaking with silent weeping.

"Tanis?" he whispered, truly terrified now. "Are you…are you still…you? *Please*, Tanis—tell me it's so!"

Abruptly Tanis wiped his eyes on his sleeve. He focused upon the younger boy. "It's fine," he managed in a choked voice. "I'm fine. I just…" His throat constricted and his chest felt swollen and tight. "…I couldn't help him, after all."

"Oh." Wesley drew Piper closer. For the first time, Tanis realized Wesley wasn't comforting the older boy but rather was taking reassurance from him—from this maniacally twisted remnant of a once vibrant young life.

There was something so virulently wrong with this scenario that Tanis wasn't sure how to control the anger he felt at it. He jumped to his feet and walked over to the dark window, which was barred both inside and out. He took hold of the cold iron and gripped it until his hands ached, pressing his forehead against the metal bars, trying not to rip himself apart with fury and heartache both. He was still there when the door unlatched and a guard walked in.

"Time to go, you."

Tanis turned to him. "Me?"

"Yes you. Move it."

Tanis spared a parting glance for Wesley. The boy started crying again and buried his face in Piper's dark hair. Right then, Tanis resolved to save Wesley if it was the last thing he ever did.

He walked into the hall after the guard, who grabbed him by the shoulders while his counterpart locked the door again.

Tanis was marched upstairs and through the dim manor, past furniture draped in linen, and finally down a hallway to a door at the end. When they shoved him inside, his mood brightened unexpectedly.

Her Grace stood on the far side of the long room next to the Earl of Pent, and Tanis was so pleased to see her safe and whole that he almost didn't notice the man coming towards him until he spoke.

"Ah then, this must be young Tanis of Giverny."

Tanis turned to face the man, rightfully naming him Bethamin's Ascendant. A tall man, bald and brazen, he wore a wrapped skirt of white linen looped into a gold belt at his waist. His bare chest was collared with a gold torque which matched the wide bands at his wrists. He turned to look behind him momentarily, and Tanis saw that his back was tattooed with a violent design that seemed nothing it not a foul hex. Looking closer, Tanis realized it wasn't so much a tattoo as a brand burned into his flesh, the welts raised and angry. "Come and meet our newest candidate," the Ascendant said, motioning to a form that Tanis had at first thought was a statue draped in linen.

When the statue moved, Tanis knew he was looking at a Marquiin.

He should've gone cold at the sight, knowing what was to come, but his anger warmed him.

"You cannot do this!" Alyneri protested from the far end of the room, her voice near to tears.

But the earl silenced her with a hiss. "If you persist in disturbing this process, your Grace, I will be forced to silence you more forcefully."

Alyneri pressed her hands to her mouth, and Tanis saw tears streaming down her cheeks. If he'd harbored any question of what was in store for him, her desperate tears sealed it.

As the Marquiin approached in his ghostly grey robes, the Ascendant turned back to Tanis. "You are a lucky boy, young man," he proclaimed. "You're being given the opportunity to test for a great honor. The honor of becoming a Marquiin."

Tanis stared at the ugly man. His dark, heavy brows seemed a solid line across his pronounced forehead, and his nose was aquiline and fierce. Looking at him, thinking of what he'd done to Piper, Tanis felt a knot in his gut that turned on the spit of his fury, hardening his resolve. His colorless eyes were hard as agates, and quite without fear as the Marquiin stopped before him.

Tanis could see nothing of his face beneath the layers of grey gauze. There was an unhealthy smell about him, however, and his thoughts were loud with violent force. They bled into the boy's sensitive awareness, and his mind shrank from their senseless fury. Tanis instinctively enwrapped his mind with thoughts of love and laughter to keep out the Marquiin's turbulent thoughts, which were literally spilling forth like an overflowing well, corrupting everything they touched.

The taller man's hand appeared from somewhere among his ghostly robes, and Tanis braced himself for whatever was to come.

Alyneri sobbed a cry and turned away.

The Marquiin laid one hand on Tanis's shoulder, and the other found its way across his face into the truthreader's hold.

Tanis closed his eyes and waited. He felt…

Nothing.

He knew something should've been happening—at the very least he should've felt some compulsion—but he saw only the backs of his eyelids. Then he did feel something strange, only it wasn't at all what he expected.

It was…cold.

Cold that slithered through the folds of his consciousness like the pouring of thick venom. He felt it slowly, inexorably flooding into his mind, its numbing chill cold enough to make his teeth chatter. He forcibly clenched his teeth to keep them quiet, and soon his jaw began to ache from the effort.

"What's happening?" the Ascendant demanded, his voice heated with anger.

The Marquiin gripped Tanis's shoulder tighter…*tighter*, until his fingernails cut into the lad's flesh. Tanis winced, but he dared not pull away.

The sensation of slimy cold worms wiggling through his brain grew stronger still. Only they didn't stop with his mind alone. He felt the chill seeping throughout his very core until he started shivering uncontrollably.

"You're doing something wrong!" the Ascendant snarled, furious now. "Go deeper! Make him see it!"

Eyes still closed, Tanis felt the cold fading. It was like the flow had finally stopped, and now he waited for the rest of the disgusting, malevolent stuff to make its way out of his body, down his spine, past his knees…until it seeped through his heels and out into the floor. Tanis half expected to open his eyes and find himself knee-deep in icy grey-green slime.

The Marquiin released him abruptly and staggered back.

Tanis blinked and opened his eyes.

"Oh, Tanis!" Alyneri cried with both hands covering her mouth.

Tanis looked around in confusion. The Marquiin was holding onto the mantle—*it couldn't be for support, could it?* That didn't make any sense. Neither did the wintry look of fury on the Ascendant's face. He took two steps and backhanded Tanis across the mouth. The lad heard his jaw snap as he was knocked to his hands and knees.

"Tanis!" Alyneri screamed.

Tanis felt blood filling his mouth, tasting strongly of salt, and darkness pressed in on his vision. He moved his head gingerly, but the pain that flooded him with that tiniest motion was more than he could bear. He chose the darkness instead.

Rhys pounded the hilt of his sword against the door of Duke Thane val Torlen's mansion, each strike reverberating like distant thunder. Moments later, the doors were unbolted, and one opened to admit a grey-haired man in a trim black suit.

"Fetch the Duke immediately!" Rhys ordered in a not-to-be-brooked-with tone.

The Steward motioned behind him for it to be done. Turning back, his lined blue eyes swept the captain, and his lips puckered reproachfully as he complained, "Lord Captain, this is most unusual."

"Make way for the Prince of Dannym!" Bastian announced from his position just behind the captain.

The Steward's eyes widened with this announcement, and he did stand back as Ean ascended the steps and swept past him and on inside. Rhys and the others followed, collecting in the vast and elegant entry hall.

The Steward looked distressfully at Ean. "Your highness!" he managed, his lined face pale, "I humbly beg pardon. This is a most unusual visita—"

"I'm looking for Lord Brantley, Earl of Pent," Ean interrupted brusquely. "Is he in audience with the Duke?"

The Steward looked befuddled. "Lord Brantley? Certainly not. The Duke is most displeased with the earl at present."

"Then I've news that won't hearten his Grace," Ean said.

The Steward arched brows at the remark. "How may we assist your Highness? Obviously the matter is pressing. We are at your disposal. His Grace should be here any moment—"

"Indeed," said an entering Thane val Lorian, who was rolled into the room in a wheeled wooden chair by a dark-haired woman of middle age. The Duke sat proudly with an elegant blanket draped over his useless legs, and while his hair was iron grey and his face deeply lined, Ean suspected there was strength in him still.

Thane's brown eyes swept Ean, and then he nodded. "You've grown into a fine young man, my prince. Would that we might've met under better circumstances. Apparently you've ill news for me."

"I do, your Grace."

Ean told him everything that had transpired with the Earl of Pent, watching as the Duke's expression darkened with fury.

"I will have his head, the viperous upstart," he hissed when Ean was finished. At once the Duke called for his captain, and as soon as the soldier learned that some of his men were playing host to Lord Brantley's machinations, he seemed to know at once who and where to find them.

"T'would be the River House where they've taken them, your Grace," the captain told his Duke. "There's been suspicious activity in that area. Several patrols have found tracks around the yard and reported the stables had been in recent use, but we've never found anyone on site."

"Find them tonight, Captain Gerard," the Duke ordered.

The captain nodded dutifully. He looked to Prince Ean. "Your Highness, if you and your men would come with me…"

Ean turned briskly to follow, but the Duke called him back, saying, "Your Highness, a moment?"

Ean nodded for Rhys and the others to go ahead then gave his attention to the duke. "Yes, your Grace?"

The old man looked mortified. "Whatever heinous act Lord Brantley is about this eve, Raine's truth, I did not countenance it."

Ean held the older man's gaze. "You may not be complicit in Lord Brantley's crimes, your Grace, but if you knew he was disloyal and did not treat the matter appropriately, then you are as culpable for your inaction as he is for his treasons."

"I am loyal to the crown," the old man said, looking suddenly as frail as his seven decades would indicate. "You *will* assure your father of that, won't you?"

Ean considered him. After a moment, he returned quietly, "Actions speak louder than words, your Grace. Perhaps it would be better to show him that you are still his loyal subject."

"Of course," the Duke said, his face ashen. "Yes…of course."

Alyneri struggled against the Earl of Pent, but his arms were strongly wrapped around her, and his expression was no longer haughty. Something had gone very wrong with Tanis's 'testing' and now the Ascendant was livid and shouting at his Marquiin in a foreign tongue whose every word sounded a fell enchantment.

"You must release me, Lord Brantley!" Alyneri pled, keeping her voice low. "At least let me see to Tan—"

Looking fierce, the Earl clapped a hand across her mouth and pulled her into his arms. "I don't know what your boy did," he whispered warily into her ear, "but I can tell you what he *didn't* do. He didn't fall to the floor screaming like the others. He didn't tear out his hair in madness. He didn't beg for mercy, and he most certainly *did not* experience Bethamin's Fire as the Marquiin intended it."

Alyneri struggled in his arms, but he only gripped her harder. "Keep *quiet*, your Grace!" he warned. "You don't want to get in the middle of this!"

Indeed, the Ascendant's fury finally peaked, and he struck his Marquiin as he'd done to Tanis. The taller man regained himself with only a motion of his head, and then—much to Alyneri's dismay—he rolled back his veils of gauze to stare at the Ascendant with black, malevolent eyes.

Wholly black eyes.

Dear Epiphany! This was no truthreader. This man was something else, something poisoned and vile. Long lines of symbols had been tattooed across his face, marring even his eyelids; he seemed a twisted, perverted caricature, more a marionette than a man.

"You dare to strike me," the Marquiin hissed, pinning the Ascendant with his inhuman gaze.

Immediately the Ascendant shrank back. "Perhaps I was h-hasty," he hedged. "Perhaps you did in fact administer the test, as you say."

The Marquiin held out his ghostly hand toward the Ascendant. "I poured everything I had into that child," he whispered in a barren and pitiless voice. "The boy *ate* it up. He *ate* Bethamin's Fire!" It came as a desperate plea and shocking accusation in one.

The Ascendant looked to Tanis, his eyes glaring and full of hate. "*Impossible!*" he snarled. "No one is immune to Bethamin's purification!" Abruptly he turned on the Marquiin. "Blasphemy!" he shouted, at once incensed. "*Blasphemer!*" He raised his hand to strike the man down, but the Marquiin was quicker. He caught the Ascendants flailing arm and pulled him into an embrace. Alyneri watched in horror as they struggled against each other, stumbling around the room like drunken dancers.

"Come, your Grace," the Earl of Pent urged, dragging her toward a near door.

"Not without Tanis!" she cried, struggling with renewed fervor.

"Leave the boy!" the earl snapped exasperatedly. "He's done for!" Finally, Brantley picked her off her feet and carried her, kicking and screaming, to the nearest door.

"Let me go! Damn you! LET ME GO!" Alyneri shrieked and struggled, but to no avail. The earl had the door open and launched her through into the dark passage. She stumbled and fell—

And was caught in strong but gentle arms. "Alyneri," a voice murmured.

Her heart leapt to her throat, and she looked up to find Ean's grey eyes gazing into hers. "Oh, *Ean!*"

Alyneri threw her arms about his neck and hugged him fiercely. She heard Rhys barking orders and felt the rush of men pushing past her and on into the room, but she cared only to know at that moment that Ean's arms were firmly around her, taking comfort in the feel of his chin resting on her head, of his strong form close against hers.

It was only a moment, but it could've been a lifetime. Ean reached to take her hands from his neck and stepped back. "Are you all right?" He searched her eyes with his own.

She sniffed away her tears and nodded, suddenly then remembering Tanis. "Oh no—*oh, Tanis!*" She spun and dashed back into the room.

Rhys and a man in the livery of House val Torlen already had the scene in hand. Rhys was holding the Ascendant by his torque with a dagger pressed to his neck, while the other man, who she quickly learned was Captain Gerard of the Duke's household guard, was holding the snarling Marquiin.

Bastian was helping a still groggy Tanis to sit up, and Alyneri pushed her way through the throng of the Duke's soldiers to his side.

"Give him to me!" she said urgently as Bastian finally helped the boy to sit. Alyneri threw herself to her knees and immediately placed her hands upon the lad, sinking quickly into rapport. Healing bones always took its toll on both sides, but she was resolved that the dear boy would not suffer another minute from it. Fortunately, she saw at once that his jaw was only dislocated, not broken, though a tooth was chipped and he'd bitten his tongue deeply. She set to work.

The men convened in the circular drive before the river house. Ean watched with cold anger as Lord Brantley was helped onto his horse, his hands bound before him and a chagrined expression on his face. His men, disloyal to their Duke, had been stripped of their livery and now waited in a circle, bound at the hands and held at sword-point.

Once his jaw began working again, Tanis had told Ean of the other two boys, and now freed, they were being helped onto horses as well. Ean didn't want to entrust them to the Duke's care solely, for the old man seemed somehow broken to him, but he trusted Captain Gerard to see the boys safely returned to their families.

What could be done for the lad Piper had been done; Alyneri gave him a sleeping powder which at least had allowed him fitful rest, but she'd told them after examining him that the boy was dying.

Last to be escorted from the manor, the Ascendant came out snarling and spitting, cursing his captors in three languages, while his Marquiin walked forward with a deathly calm. His face remained free of its veils, free for all to see and marvel over. But this was not what held Ean's attention.

The nimbus that surrounded the man was strangely familiar to him. Incredibly, it seemed somehow like the trace-seal he'd seen upon the wall. But how could it be the same? Intensely curious now and hardly noticing what he was doing, Ean walked toward the man.

"Your Highness?" Rhys asked uncertainly as he watched him pass.

Ean walked until he stood before the Adept, who was clearly an Adept no longer. He gazed at Ean with his coal-black eyes, inhuman eyes, more like a darkhound's than a man's.

How intriguing, Ean thought. *Their eyes are so similar. I wonder what is the connection?* He was barely aware as he lifted his hand and placed it on the Marquiin's chest.

"Why not allow me the same liberty," the man suggested with vile intimations, but Ean ignored him. He closed his eyes to the world and let his mind's eye see.

It was the strangest experience. The pattern he began to sense was very different from that of the trace-seal, yet there was something similar about them. Of course, this pattern and its purpose were very different from a simple trace-seal upon a portal. Far more intricate and complex, Ean found that he could see the pattern only if he didn't try to look directly at it. Without knowing how he knew, Ean was yet certain that the pattern was actively consuming the Marquiin.

While his companions stared in wordless wonder, the prince let instinct guide him, and this time it was easier to find that singular mental focus. The pattern he faced now was much, much larger than the simple twisting trace-seal—easily four times larger. Yet again, he knew where it began and ended without question.

He fixed the pattern in his mind, taking hold of its concept fully. He then very carefully took hold of the end and pulled.

As with the trace-seal, at first he sensed no change. So he pulled harder, concentrated more intently—hard enough to make his head ache from the strain. When the pattern still didn't budge, he let go of it and mentally stepped away, letting the pounding in his head subside. As he recovered, he realized that stepping back from the pattern was exactly what he needed to do, for here he now saw what was stopping it from moving. The single thread of the pattern which he held apparently fed through a tiny hole in a vast dam. Attached to the thread was a wider band that sealed the tiny hole and kept the dam waters from leaking.

It was such a simple solution—taking hold of the thread again firmly, Ean reached out with his mind and widened the hole.

The dam burst.

The Marquiin threw back his head and screamed, startling all but Ean, who stood immobile, one royal hand splayed upon the truthreader's chest. As the Marquiin began to convulse, the startled guards didn't know whether to drop him or hold him fast, but since their prince stood before them with his eyes closed, looking for all the world like he slept on his feet, they decided holding the man up would be best.

Ean felt the vast power behind the dam washing over him, a malevolent storm similar to and yet vastly different from the terrible darkness of his dream; but he knew the only way to survive this flood was to keep pulling on that pattern, drawing the strands in toward himself, letting their now-fragile ends evaporate after leaving his touch, dissipating in his wake. He untied the pattern as quickly as its voluminous folds washed toward him, pealing off the unraveling thread in huge choking gulps.

Unknown to him, for his concentration was complete, the Marquiin shuddered constantly in the arms of his captors. While the Ascendant spouted a litany of vitriolic threats in one ceaseless stream, the others watched in fascinated horror until the Marquiin finally stilled and slumped in the soldiers' arms.

After a moment, Ean withdrew his hand and opened his eyes. He staggered and swayed, but then steadied himself.

"My prince?" a befuddled Rhys inquired in a low voice, stepping closer. "Are you…?" but he didn't seem to know quite what to ask. There was a tense silence among the group, no one understanding what had just happened, least of all Ean.

Finally Tanis walked to the Marquiin. He motioned for the soldiers to lower the man, and they did so gratefully.

The Ascendant hissed at him and shouted expletives. "You filthy brat! Dare not touch the sainted vessel of Bethamin! You befoul him with your unpurified witchery! Evil spawn of Belloth!…"

Ignoring the Ascendant as he continued to rant, Tanis knelt beside the once-truthreader and took his hand. "It's over," he murmured, sounding both fragile and infinitely wise. "You can sleep now. You're free of it."

"Tanis, what—?" Alyneri began.

But Ean silenced her with an upraised hand. "Wait," he whispered. He turned to watch the exchange, desperate himself to understand what he'd done.

Thus followed a long moment of silence, and then the Marquiin opened his eyes.

Alyneri gasped. Rhys hissed an oath. Most of the soldiers spat in the dirt and ground their boots over the mark, and the Ascendant flew into a shrieking frenzy of uncontrollable rage. He tore loose from his bounds and ran, raving and snarling in rabid fury, throwing himself into the fast-rushing waters of the Glass River. By the time the soldiers chasing him reached the edge, he'd vanished among the waves.

Tanis meanwhile smiled gently into the colorless eyes of the Marquiin, who was a Marquiin no longer.

The man opened his mouth, but words wouldn't come. His face twisted in a spasm of pain, but it was fleeting, and soon his expression resolved.

"It's okay," Tanis soothed. He stroked the man's hand. "It won't be long now."

Still not understanding, a confused Ean knelt beside Tanis. The lad turned to him resolutely. "He dies now, your Highness, but he's grateful for death—he's prayed for it for a long time. He wishes to thank you for saving him."

"Saving him?" Ean's face showed his confusion. "But…he's dying."

"He dies as a man, your highness," the boy whispered, dropping his eyes to the man's hand he held in his lap. "Instead of a monster. Whatever you did, you gave him back his humanity—if only for a few minutes."

Ean stared at the man before him unsure how to feel. The Marquiin *were* monsters, yet here this man had been…healed of it? He could make no sense of what had happened, and he couldn't bring himself to pity the man before him, knowing the evils he'd brought down on others. But he held the man's clear-eyed gaze all the same.

They stayed that way, gazing into each other's eyes, until the truthreader sighed his last breath, and his head fell to the side. Only then did Ean realize that there had been some absolution in the exchange.

"It is done," Tanis murmured. He released the man's hand and stood, and Ean stood with him and looked around. Everyone was staring at them.

Abruptly Alyneri rushed up and threw her arms around him, burying her face in his chest. Ean held her for a moment, comforted by her warmth, feeling far, far older than his eighteen years. When she pulled away with downcast eyes, Ean turned to the Captain. "Rhys, are we ready?"

The Captain shook himself as if from a stupor. "Yes, highness."

"And you, Captain Gerard," Ean said, looking to the other captain. "Can we count on you to see these traitors brought to justice and these children safely home?"

The captain was gazing wondrously at him. "Without question, your Highness."

Ean looked to Tanis. The boy nodded.

"Then it's time we moved on." Ean returned to Caldar, mounted up and reined the horse in a circle.

"Seven bloody hells, Ean!" Fynn hissed under his breath as he drew rein at his cousin's side. "I hope you'll explain this to me one day *soon*."

Ean turned him an inscrutable look. "As soon as someone explains it to me, Fynn," he replied heatedly, "you'll be the first to know."

Rhys drew his horse alongside the prince's. "All is in readiness, your Highness."

"Led on then, Rhys."

The Captain heeled his mount forward, and the small company headed off down the long drive of the val Torlen estate as dawn broke into the world in rose-gold splendor.

THIRTY-NINE

'Everything begins and ends with a single thought.'

– The Vestal Björn van Gelderan to his Lord of Shades

The round stone room where the four of them met was cold, cold enough that a layer of ice covered the pale stones, turning what would otherwise have seemed plain into a gleaming crystalline cavern. Cold enough that birds froze to death within moments of coming to that place, and the floor was littered with their tiny, fragile bones. So cold that a human's unprotected flesh would blacken and die before the sand passed once through an hourglass. Still, it was not as cold as their home.

Darshan'venkhátraman's boots rang on the frozen stones as he swept into the room, bones and ice crunching beneath his feet. He walked to the middle of the wide circular chamber and looked up. Thirty paces above, a tiny pinpoint of light heralded freedom. "There now," he encouraged as he withdrew a bird from the folds of his coat, holding the frightened thing gently between both hands. "There is your future. Reach for it—*go!*" He threw the bird into the frozen air and watched with fascination as the tiny creature batted its frail wings, as it struggled to fly higher…higher. But long before it reached the domed roof, the little bird's flight became erratic, bouncing and swerving with a frenzied beating of wings, its goal somehow lost or forgotten. It hit the wall once but recovered, finding again its bearings in a last vain attempt to reach freedom and future. And then without fanfare, it simply froze and fell from the air, plummeting downward to hit the stones with an insignificant *thunk*.

"Why do you bother?" a voice asked critically.

Darshan turned to see his brother Shail leaning against the wall, his dark eyes piercing, the inevitable gilded feather caught between his fingers, spinning… spinning.

"As ever, my youngest brother, you fail to see the greater meaning." Darshan bent and picked up the tiny bird, its feathers already brittle. "With this one act—the little bird struggling to gain its freedom—we encompass the vast cycle of life in this world." He held the broken thing in his palm for Shail to view. "Creatures big or small, intelligent or ignorant, violent or peaceable, all strive toward survival, toward freedom and future.

"Yet is their quest not ultimately for naught? As did the little bird, most creatures lose sight of their puny goals; they pass unknowingly by any window of opportunity, their one chance of future, distracted as they always are by petty trifles and insignificant attachments. Oblivious to the futility then, still they struggle against forces they cannot understand, becoming ever more beaten and battered."

Darshan lifted the bird, twisting it such that the light caught the frost on its body. "As with our little bird, the ice crystallized on its wings." He smiled wistfully at his brother. "If only our little bird could understand the forces at work against it," and his smile grew broader and colder, hinting at intentions that were terrible in consequence, "but you see," he sighed then, waving his other hand airily, "this too is part of the cycle. These fragile creatures are not meant to understand things beyond the scope of their existence, beyond their established ken. They are born, ultimately, to die, and in this purpose, my brother, all succeed."

"How very inspiring," said a tall man just then entering through the room's arched opening.

"Thank you, Pelas," Darshan said, turning with a nod of acknowledgement. He flicked the little bird absently away and looked to his brothers. Though they all wore very different attire, it was clear by their features that they were cut from the same cloth. All had long ebony hair, all were tall and broad-shouldered, and all had very dark, very unforgiving eyes.

"So, we three are assembled," Darshan said. "Who shall begin?"

"I," said Shail. "The man whose pattern I identified has eluded all efforts to eliminate him. His survival is becoming something of a nuisance. The agents assigned are refusing to complete the task."

"So compel them," Pelas spat, as if the matter was beneath this gathering of minds.

"You know so little, brother," Shail returned contemptuously. "Wildlings are useless under our compulsion. Their magic fails—it is too fragile a thing when pitted against our power."

Darshan considered Shail. "Since you bring this matter to our council, you must believe the problem requires a more stringent approach."

"The man *must* be eliminated," Shail declared emphatically, apparently not caring how much his older brother learned of him through the outburst. He sliced the air with his feather to emphasize his point, adding under his breath, "In the past, those who claimed that pattern have created problems for us."

"Problems for *you*," Pelas sneered.

Shail cast him a venomous look.

Darshan frowned. "I cannot say I share your concern, brother, but I applaud your proactive fervor. What then is your desire of this gathering?"

"I would like to put the matter to Rinokh."

Pelas barked a laugh. At Shail's glare, he raised both hands and said, "I have no qualms with calling our eldest brother to the task, but I doubt he will help you."

"The excursion will do Rinokh good. He wastes too much time frying up Avatarens for sport. But Shail," Darshan said, looking back to him, "I cannot condone failure. Those who serve us must learn that obedience is absolute."

"Punishment will be meted as due reward," Shail assured him.

Darshan nodded his approval. He looked to Pelas then. "And you, brother?"

Pelas broke into a feral smile. "I continue my search for the pattern of Unworking."

Shail grunted in disgust.

"Deploy your hypocrisy on those who cannot see through it, brother," Pelas returned. "We all have our games. Darshan's dabbling in religion, your petty politicking with doomed kings. You seem to have fallen prey to your own pretences."

Darshan arched a disapproving brow. "Yet your bloodbaths *are* gaining undue notice, Pelas'ommáyurek. I would not have them compromise our work."

"You have your diversions," Pelas argued with his smoldering gaze pinned on his older brother. "I am allowed mine."

"For now," Darshan returned evenly. He looked to both his brothers then. "Pelas is right: I see no wrong in our little games, but never let us mimic these frail, doomed creatures and lose sight of our greater purpose. Purpose is all."

The three brothers held each other's gazes for a moment longer, trading back and forth among them until all agreed and understood what went unspoken. Then they turned their backs on one another, and though the circular room had but one entrance, they all found different exits.

Standing at the low, crenellated wall of his tower rooftop, the Fourth Vestal Raine D'Lacourte withdrew his consciousness from rapport with the currents to reflect on what he'd just observed. Despite his incredulity, he didn't doubt what he saw—a truthreader learned from his earliest training never to doubt his instincts—yet the truth was nigh to impossible.

Ean had worked *elae.*

Björn did it, Raine thought with closed eyes, a grave relief washing over him. Somehow the Fifth Vestal had found a way to Awaken an Adept after the window of adolescence had closed. The ramifications were monumental.

It means the revivification of our race.

Raine turned from the view without noticing the majestic, snowcapped peaks that were the backdrop of his family's chateau in Vienne-Sur-Le Valle, for his thoughts were already far away. He took the curving steps down from the roof two at a time, exiting the circular tower into his book-lined study. He meant to contact Alshiba right away with the news, but his Steward was waiting for him across the room, standing in the open doorway.

"Your Excellency," the man said with a polite bow, "a visitor requests your audience. He gave his name as Andrus Vargha."

Raine didn't know the name. Walking to his desk, he asked, "Is he a truthreader? Did he state his business?"

"He is Geshaiwyn, your Excellency."

Raine straightened, setting down again the papers he'd just collected.

"There is something else, my lord. The man is clearly unwell."

"Where is he now?"

"He waits in the Damask Room."

Raine walked swiftly from his study, followed by his Steward. "Did you call for a Healer?" the Vestal asked as he traversed the arching, buttressed hallway tiled in pale green marble.

"I thought it best that you saw him first, my lord."

Raine arched a brow, knowing then that his visitor's condition must be dire indeed.

The Damask Room was located in the south-eastern corner of the chateau and had commanding views of the Eidenglass range and the Rogue Valley. It was also usually the warmest room in the house.

Raine found a fire ablaze in the six-foot hearth as he entered the room, whose walls were lined in sanguine damask silk. Even with the roaring fire, his visitor was curled upon a divan just inches from the flames with a heavy wool tapestry-blanket draped across his chest. He inched up as Raine approached, and the Vestal saw immediately what his Steward had seen: a shell of a man not long for this world. Vargha's face was paper-thin and ash-grey, his skin as withered as a lily scorched by the sun, his body emaciated beyond reason or repair.

Raine had seen another man in such a condition too recently for comfort, though at least Vargha wouldn't disintegrate at the touch of his boot. Not yet.

"Your Excellency," Vargha rasped as Raine approached. "Forgive me for not standing."

"I can see your condition, Mr. Vargha. How can I help you?"

Vargha must've caught the double meaning of his question, for he pressed a bony hand to his forehead as if it pained him and answered in a dry, wafer-thin voice, "I should've gone to the Third Vestal, I know, for he is our representative and has always treated with us fairly."

Raine's diamondine eyes fixed upon the man. "You are an Agent of Malchiarr?"

Vargha drew in a shuddering breath. "Yes." His dark eyes held Raine's gaze, though they were so sunken into the hollows of their sockets that his lids looked stretched to cover them. "You probably don't approve of us, my lord," Varga whispered, "and you wouldn't be alone. After the wars, we forged our livelihoods as best we could, trading on the gifts that were our birthright. We may have chosen poorly in this, but the Third Vestal…he understood—"

Vargha fell into a fit of coughing, the sound of wind rustling dry summer wheat. When he recovered, he drew in another wheezing breath, rubbed his forehead with a pained frown and continued in his desert-dry voice, "But I do not know if Seth Silverbow would understand this news I bear, my lord. I heard you were in Vienne-Sur-Le Valle, and it's well known that the Great Master rerouted a node to your front door. After I left our Council in Malchiarr, I wasn't sure how far I could travel…"

"You needn't go on with explanations, Mr. Vargha," Raine said gently. He lowered himself onto the edge of an armchair across from his guest and rested elbows on knees. "Just tell me what you want me to know."

"Yes, my lord," Vargha managed. "Thank you for hearing me, for my news is grave."

Vargha began his confession by describing his interactions with the Karakurt. He told Raine of their Council accepting the contract on a northern prince, and how shocked they all were when their first pair of agents was lost. "When our third failed, our Council agreed we must break the contract. I was the agent who delivered the message to the Karakurt."

He told Raine then of his meeting with her, and finally of the mysterious but deadly Avataren witchlord. "He licked his thumb," Vargha said, closing his eyes and shuddering, "and then he…*pushed* it to my head—here," and he tapped two fingers to his forehead. "It *burned*, my lord," Vargha confessed breathlessly, sounding as if he was truly in agony.

Raine had already suspected this truth. "His touch burned you?"

"Like ice, but…worse. A hundred times worse. It burns still…it won't *stop*.

Yet I'm so cold..." He pressed the palm of his hand to his head again, rubbing a small circle. "The witchlord," Vargha pressed on, "he told me we must complete the contract or face extermination."

Raine drew back in surprise. "Extermination?"

"His words, my lord."

Raine knew of the loyalty of Agents of Malchiarr to their tribes. He could only imagine the Council of Malchiarr's response upon receiving such a threat—*what would any of us do in the same situation?* His gaze was compassionate as he asked, "Did your Council decide to take the contract back?"

"No, my lord."

Now Raine was truly shocked.

"It was toxic to us," Vargha wheezed. "We've never lost so many over a single mark. The Council elected to let this witchlord try to carry out his threat. We do not intend to sit idly by. We have spread the word that this contract violates Balance. We don't think anyone will touch it now, save perha—" but he fell into another fit of dry coughing that lasted nearly five minutes.

Raine let him recover without pressing him, though this information was of grave importance. It was an unexpected boon to Ean's cause to know the Geshaiwyn would no longer pursue him, but if another agency took up the contract in their place... "Mr. Vargha," Raine prodded gently after the man found his breath again. "Who does your Council think will accept the contract?"

"They think only the Tyriolicci."

Raine grimaced. The Tyriolicci were hardly less lethal than Geshaiwyn, but they were better known by a different name: Whisper Lords. He needed to get word to Fynnlar, traveling with Ean's company. *Or better yet...* There were certain Wildlings uniquely suited to battle the Tyriolicci, and he knew one such who had trained all her life for such a mark. *If I can just pry her out from under her uncle's thumb...*

"My lord," Vargha said, calling Raine's attention back to him, "whoever this witchlord is, he is a threat to our very existence—all of us. Just look at me—" he added with a sudden wild madness in his gaze, his voice wracked with grief and fear. "He did this to me with naught but his thumb!"

Raine originally suspected that Andrus Vargha's dangerously lethal 'Avataren witchlord' was actually Björn, but Vargha's description of the witchlord was nothing like his oath-brother. *If it isn't Björn working deyjiin so readily, then who?* It wasn't the first time Raine had entertained the idea of others who might hold such power—it was his duty to explore every avenue in searching for the truth—but never had he felt any conviction about it. Now Vargha's testimony made these ideas worth investigating. But did he dare believe what none of the Vestals would admit aloud?

Not yet.

If Malorin'athgul walked the realm, he would need much more evidence; even more difficult, he would have to prove in turn that Björn *wasn't* behind the many crimes attributed to him. And frankly, *he* wasn't ready to believe that.

"You know, don't you?" Vargha meanwhile managed in his rasping whisper. Raine looked back to him, to the sunken eyes and wasted flesh. His terrible deterioration reminded the Vestal sadly of Malachai in his last hours. Vargha whispered wretchedly, "You know what sort of spell does this...to a man."

Raine's answering gaze was tragic. "It is a power called *deyjiin*," he confessed, "and I fear there is no cure."

Vargha closed his eyes in acceptance of his fate. "My lord," he whispered after a long moment of silence, "would you grant me one boon?"

"Mr. Vargha," Raine said, "you have done the realm a great service by coming to me. I would grant you any boon within my power."

Vargha opened his eyes to hold Raine's gaze. He could feel the man working up his courage to speak, hear the dreadful thoughts that raged within his tortured mind. "My lord…will you…take my life?" He sucked in his breath with three halting gasps. "I have done all…that I can. And I'm so cold…*so unbearably cold!*"

Raine knew the man was only a few paces from Death's doorstep. He needn't do anything, for the task was already done. Yet while he couldn't heal the doomed man, or do anything to stop *deyjiin's* consumptive dance toward death, he *could* wrap Vargha's mind in illusions and make him more comfortable during his last hours.

Raine leaned and placed one hand on Vargha's shoulder, the other hand finding the truthreader's form upon his temples and brow. "Good-bye, Andrus Vargha," the Fourth Vestal murmured solemnly. "May the Maker bless you for your great service to our realm. By Epiphany's Grace, we shall meet again in the Returning."

"The Maker will it so," the Geshaiwyn whispered. He closed his eyes for the last time and submitted to Raine's working.

FORTY

'If you focus on the obstacles, they will be all you see.'

– The Fifth Vestal Björn val Gelderan to his generals at the Battle of Gimlalai, 597aV.

For the next few days, Ean's company traveled under a pall. While Alyneri and Tanis were clearly both still unnerved by their experience, no one in the company was more disturbed than Ean. His mood was apparent to all, yet he seemed ignorant to the many worried looks cast his way.

Day and night, the prince was tormented by his mistake—had they never gone into Acacia, might nothing untoward have happened? Mightn't they have spent a quiet night on the moors and moved on the next day? Might he then be able to live with himself and Tanis sleep without nightmares? Might Alyneri look at him without such fear and concern in her gaze?

Yet what then would you have learned? a voiced asked critically, in defiance of his guilt.

But I've learned nothing!

Yet he knew it wasn't true. Though the happenings mystified him, he'd learned much in the experience, but he gravely regretted the price of that knowledge—Alyneri kidnapped, Tanis's near brush with—and inexplicable escape from—Bethamin's taint…

What price will I be forced to pay in the future? he worried, though this wasn't truly what he feared. No, he feared the price that *others* might be forced to pay, a price extracted against their will and without mercy by a destiny inflicted due to his own ill-advised choices.

It isn't right that I should have such power over their lives!

He truly believed that, yet every time he had the thought, he heard always in reply his mother's voice instructing, *'Such is the mantle of a king, my son: to make a decision and stand by it, to have the courage to face the consequences of these decisions, knowing they may mean the death of his subjects.'*

These matters notwithstanding, Ean also knew that he was dwelling on them in truth because he dared not confront his deeper fears; no, he couldn't even begin to think about what he'd done to the Marquiin.

On the third night, they made camp under sparkling autumn stars with the chill mountain air frosting every breath. They weren't yet above the tree line as they traversed the pass between Dannym and Veneisea, but the ground crackled with frost that never melted, and shadowed patches gleamed white with snow. Brody, Rhys, and the soldiers traded off the watch; Ean had volunteered to join them—Raine's truth he was getting less sleep than the men were with or without holding watch—but Rhys wouldn't have it. So Ean tended the fire, staring into its depths pondering his many troubles that shrouded him like a Marquiin's ashen veils, wishing for sleep that rarely came and only fitfully when it did.

Cephrael's Hand was rising in the east when Fynnlar joined Ean's side. The prince had noted the constellation every night since Acacia, which fact would've mattered little had it been any other grouping of stars. But Cephrael's Hand didn't follow the usual laws. Its course could never be charted, for its stars seemed ever erratic. Astrologers had yet to establish the pattern of its motion—much less understand how the damnable stars moved—which only contributed to the many superstitions about the ill-famed constellation.

"'*A man may rule his household*," Fynn quoted as he settled in beside the prince and joined him in staring up at the stars, "*and a King govern his land, but Death walks in the thrall of Cephrael's Hand.*'"

Ean cast him a weary look. "Can't sleep, cousin?"

Fynn eyed him narrowly. "There's something about bedding in the company of a wielder that makes for less than restful sleep."

Ean tossed another log onto the flames, sending a shower of sparks heavenward among the pale smoke. "I'm not a wielder, Fynn."

"Then what *are* you, Ean?" Fynn hissed. He leaned toward his cousin to better conceal their words, though the rest of the camp was deep in slumber. "You squeezed the black life out of that Marquiin like a rotten fruit!"

"It wasn't like that," Ean growled under his breath.

"Then tell me what it *was* like."

"I can't explain it!" Ean hissed.

"For Epiphany's sake, Ean, *try*. Whatever it was you did, you made a Marquiin no longer a Marquiin!" As the truth of these words settled in, making Ean grimace, Fynnlar leaned his head to capture Ean's gaze with his own. "Look cousin, we don't know if that Ascendant lived or drowned, but if he found civilization…if word gets back to his maniacal sovereign that you can undo his malevolent work…well, let's just say you'll have worse monsters than Geshaiwyn after you."

Ean shot him a tormented look. "Can you pattern? Know you anything of these matters, Fynn, beyond the same rudimentary understanding that I possess?"

"I know little enough," Fynn admitted, leaning back.

"Then what value is this discussion?"

"I might get some rest out of it," the royal cousin grumbled. "At least one of us would be sleeping then."

Ean grimaced and looked away, clenching his jaw.

Fynn put a hand on his shoulder. "Ean…you've got to trust someone with this. Shadow take me if you've slept a solid hour since we left Acacia. We can all see that it's tormenting you."

Ean exhaled a sigh and murmured, "You can see that, can you?"

Fynn leaned back on one elbow and extended his boots toward the fire. "You should talk to someone about it, cousin," he advised, "and that someone might as well be me. I can keep my mouth shut—but *seven hells*, even if I blabbed to anyone who would listen, the whole world knows half of everything out of my mouth is crap anyway. I mean, who listens to me, really?"

A hint of a smile broke through Ean's tormented expression, and he glanced to his cousin. "That's true."

Fynn cast him a black look. "Well, thank you for agreeing with me."

Ean managed a crooked grin, but as his expression sobered, his grey eyes lifted again to the heavens. "It's following me, Fynn," he whispered. "I know it is."

Fynn followed his gaze and made a face. "Maybe it is? What does it matter?"

"It matters because I…I think it's trying to tell me something."

"Oh, for Epiphany's sake—" Fynn threw up his hands and glared at Ean. "Quit changing the bloody subject and tell me what happened with that Marquiin."

Ean pulled knees to his chest and draped his arms over them. He stared hard into the fire. "I don't know—I *really* don't know," he added emphatically. "Twice in Acacia I just saw a pattern and had a feeling that I—Shadow take me, Fynn, it's so hard to describe! It was like a *need*, like I needed to unravel it."

"Twice," Fynn said, eyeing him critically. "Once with the Marquiin. When was the other?"

"When the Geshaiwyn found me at the inn, we battled. Somehow we fell through a portal which I think was trace-sealed. The Wildling died before he could return us to the hall. I saw the trace seal on the wall and…well I…pulled it apart."

Fynn stared intently at him. "You *saw* it? And you *unworked* it?"

Ean picked at the frayed stitching on his boot. "I'm not sure what I did," he admitted. "I saw the pattern. I knew where it began and ended. I had a sense that I should take the end of it and pull it apart. So I did."

Fynn snorted dubiously. "Well, that's definitely not the way I've heard working *elae* described before."

"No," Ean agreed, glancing at him. "Alyneri described Healing to me by explaining that she looks for a person's life pattern and then uses it to heal. What I did was the…opposite…" he trailed off as the realization struck him.

He had *unworked* the trace-seal, *unworked* the pattern that bound the Marquiin to his master; what would happen if he unworked the pattern that was intrinsic to a *person*, that which the Healers used to heal? Would he then be unworking a man's very life?

Fynn was staring uncomfortably at him. "What is it?"

Ean clenched his teeth and shook his head. "Just a thought I had." He lifted grey eyes to the constellation again and swallowed. "It's nothing."

Fynn grunted dubiously, for he had seen Ean's face in that moment, and he'd never seen the prince looked so horrified.

All the next day as they traveled, Ean fretted over his ability. What did it mean that he could *un*work a pattern? Was he then the antithesis of *elae*? Is that why the traitorous Fifth Vestal wanted him—as a weapon to achieve his aims? Could it be that those who desired his death—they who hired the Geshaiwyn—could it be they were actually fighting on the side of righteousness?

They made camp that night on the downhill side of the pass amid blanketing fog. The gaining of Veneisea might have been a moment for small celebration, at least worthy of a shared drink to mark the passing, but the camp remained subdued, as shrouded by their dire thoughts as the night sky was with fog. As the group was bedding down, Ean approached Alyneri.

"Your Grace," he said, affecting an amiable tone though his smile didn't lighten his gaze, which seemed as tumultuous as the sea after a storm. "Might I impose upon you for a favor?"

Alyneri straightened from her task and turned to him. Her eyes were lined with worry, and he could tell that she also had not been sleeping well. For a moment he thought of confessing everything to her—the compulsion was so strong, in fact, that he almost did speak of it. Only the certain knowledge that his fears would burden and terrify her helped him hold his tongue.

"Of course, Ean," she answered, sounding weary and fretful and tense. "How can I help you?"

Ean glanced around, but none of their companions were close. "Have you a sleeping powder?"

Her gaze became even more concerned, and he could tell she wanted to speak to him, but she held her tongue and nodded. She bent to retrieve her bag, but Ean took hold of her arm gently. "If I drink it," he said quietly as she looked back to him, "will you promise to drink it, too?"

Alyneri closed her eyes as if to hold back the many things better left unsaid. Then she opened them again and nodded once, clearly untrusting of words in that moment. Ean released her arm, and she turned to her bag of herbs and sorted through her varying vials until she found the one she wanted. "Valerian root," she told him as she uncorked the vial and measured a small amount into his palm. The dense powder reeked like week-old socks. "Drink it, don't sniff it," she advised with a shadowy smile when he made a face.

Thanking her, Ean crossed camp to where he'd left his own things and mixed the powder into water from his flagon. He drank it fast. Then he laid down on his bedroll and prayed for sleep, refusing to watch Cephrael's Hand rising once again in the east.

He let his mind drift, but only toward pleasant memories…a snowball fight with his brothers in the yard…collecting shells with his mother on Edenmar beach beneath the warm summer sun…swinging brazenly from the mizzenmast with Creighton while his grandfather shouted threats from far below…riding Caldar at top speed with his father and brothers on the heels of his father's hounds during the chase…

These thoughts were all he had time for before the draft took full effect and Ean was pulled down at last into blessed sleep.

With restful slumber, came the dream…

Ean found himself in a three-tiered library warmed by a roaring fire. The flickering flames cast golden shadows on two heavy leather armchairs that were angled toward the hearth. On first glance, Ean thought he was alone, but after turning in a circle to view the rectangular room and its two floors of bookshelves, he turned back to see a man standing at the mantle. He was attired all in black, and though he retained a warrior's lean hardness, he sported no weapon that Ean could see. His blonde hair was swept back from his wide forehead and held in place by a thin circlet of gold, and his eyes were a pale green. He had high cheekbones and a squared jaw, and had the look of the Danes about him—the fair skinned blondes who inhabited the far northern region of Agasan, beyond the mountains of Tirycth Mir.

Upon seeing Ean's bemused expression, the stranger broke into a broad grin. "Welcome, Ean," he greeted. He came over and clapped the prince upon the shoulder.

Ean noted that the man wore a silver ring upon the third finger of his right hand, the azure stone cut deep and square. He'd seen such a ring before on a man with diamond eyes. "At last we meet," said the stranger.

Ean shook his head. "How do you know me?"

The stranger motioned Ean to one chair and himself took the other, explaining, "Even were I not a skilled dreamwalker, I'd have been able to find your dreams."

Ean considered him cautiously, for while the man seemed amiable, there was something in his eyes that belied his words. Ean knew him, however, though the knowledge only made him more apprehensive. How many people had truly been visited in their dreams by the Warrior-God Dagmar Ranneskjöld, Alorin's Second Vestal? And how many just claimed it so?

"Please, join me." Dagmar motioned to a table beside Ean's chair, and the prince turned to find a goblet of wine waiting. When he looked back to Dagmar, the Adept was sipping from an identical goblet.

Ean couldn't stop himself from speaking the first thought that came to mind. "They say you're being held hostage in T'khendar."

Relaxed in his chair, Dagmar eyed him inquisitively. "Yes, so I've heard. 'Dagmar's dungeon,' I believe is the coined term."

"Is it true?"

Dagmar held his gaze. "It is so."

Something inside Ean deflated. He hadn't realized that he'd even being hoping Raine was lying to him about Dagmar's fate until that very moment. Nor did the admission of captivity give him faith in the man before him, for Raine had unwittingly warned him of Dagmar's allegiances. '...Dagmar has either sworn new oaths to Malachai's dark gods, or he has sworn an oath to Björn. In either case, he is suspect...'

Sometimes Ean wondered if Raine had helped him at all; everything the Vestal told him only left him more confused, only warned him against those few who might actually help him. He felt too inexperienced to be saddled with such terrors—murder and sedition, assassins and mysterious fell powers, distrust sewn against his would-be advisors—but for the last five years his mother had done nothing if not schooled him against self-pity. He was eighteen years old, but one day he would be king. There was never a time when he could act as if there was any other truth...any other future.

No matter that I might sell my soul to make it so!

Unsure what to think of the Vestal's presence in his dreams, Ean asked uncertainly, "Why have you come to me?"

Dagmar shifted in his chair, his gaze intense. "My oath-brother talks often of you, Ean, enough for me to know that you're in danger. I came to warn you."

Ean felt a surge of hope. "Then you...you're not sworn to the Fifth Vestal?"

Dagmar arched brows. "Who said I was?"

"It was...intimated," Ean confessed, looking to the near fire. "I wasn't sure who to trust."

"Trust your instincts," Dagmar advised, and his voice sounded tinged with regret. "There is no other sure way to navigate among the reeds of this mire."

Ean turned back to the Vestal. "If he speaks to you...might you know why the Fifth Vestal sent his Shade to capture me? What does he want with me?"

Dagmar considered him thoughtfully, his fair brow furrowed. "My oath-brother mentioned a pattern once when speaking of you," he said after a moment. He shifted in his chair again and crossed one ankle over knee. "Can you describe it to me, or draw it perhaps?" and he motioned to the table at Ean's right. When the prince looked, he found parchment and ink sitting next to the goblet of wine.

Ean took the parchment and drew the whorls and lines of his pattern with fluid ease. He handed the paper to Dagmar, who arched a brow upon seeing its likeness. "Ah, by Cephrael's Great Book," he murmured, shaking his head with a turbulent frown. Lifting his gaze back to Ean, he inquired, "What do you know of this pattern?"

"I have been told it mimics the Pattern of Life."

"Yes, yes that is so," he agreed. "The Sobra I'ternin bespeaks that all living things are formed of patterns. Learn a pattern intrinsic to a thing, and you gain the ability to compel or control that thing. The patterns and the lifelines of living things are therefore interwoven." He released the parchment onto the floor and folded hands in his lap. "When a man works the Pattern of Life, however, it changes his pattern forever, molding itself within the pattern of the man—what is often called by Healers as his 'life signature.' The two patterns remain merged for the duration of that Adept's lifetime, not separating until he ceases to work the Pattern of Life regularly and thereby dies a natural death."

"But my pattern is still merged," Ean said, realizing the truth.

Dagmar gave him an acknowledging and somewhat tragic look. "Just so. I'm afraid there is but one explanation for why your pattern remains merged with the Pattern of Life, Ean."

The prince shook his head, not understanding. "What is it?"

Dagmar's expression was grim. "You did not die a natural death. Moreover, such a death must come swiftly, thus there can be little doubt that your end was brutal—murder or slaying, perhaps in battle."

Ean thought of the dreams he'd been having since escaping the Shade's camp and felt a sickly knot form in his stomach. Like the dream he was having even then, those other dreams felt far too real—more like memories than dreams.

Perhaps sensing Ean's discomfort, Dagmar motioned to the wine at his side, so far untouched. "Please, won't you share a drink with me while we talk?"

Ean gratefully reached for the goblet and took a sip. The wine was surprisingly good and spread radiant warmth where cold unease had been rooting. He almost feared to ask the next question, but curiosity pushed him to it. "Why is the Fifth Vestal interested in me then?"

Dagmar regarded him with a pensive frown. "A certain few Adepts in the long history of our realm have been born with a particular skill," he advised after a moment of silence. Then he settled Ean a compelling look. "Have you an idea of what I speak?"

Ean swallowed. "Unworking," he managed.

Dagmar's level gaze was all the acknowledgement he needed.

"I did that," Ean admitted, staring hard at the Vestal. "I unworked two different patterns just days ago." Forgetting all about his earlier distrust of the man, Ean went on to confess, "And I've been having dreams...dreams about unworking. I never see my enemy, but I can feel his malevolence."

"It could be you are remembering the moments before your death," Dagmar suggested.

"I suppose that's better than forewarning of events to come," Ean said in half-hearted jest, but Dagmar's countenance did not lighten.

"Be wary, Ean," he cautioned. "Our enemies seek you still, for you are a true threat to them. Those with a gift such as yours are a rare breed—especially in these dark times."

Ean felt a pang of unease at his words. "How is that?"

Dagmar looked resolutely upon him. "Alorin is dying, Ean, and the Adept race dies with it. You should know that our enemies work toward this end wholly. If we cannot stop them, if we cannot reverse the Balance, we will all end as shadows and dust."

"Our enemies," Ean said, holding his gaze. "Do you mean Björn?" The question was foremost in his thoughts at all times, and he worried over it constantly.

Dagmar looked hesitant. "Ean…my oath-brother will no doubt reveal himself to you in time, but the most immediate threat to you comes from those who will seek to control or destroy you because of your talent."

Ean pressed a fist against the chair arm. "Who are they? What can I do?"

Dagmar shook his head and smiled sadly. "For now…just stay alive…"

Suddenly the library began fading around him, and Ean realized his dream was coming to an end. "Wait—" he called out in sudden desperation, for there were still so many questions he wanted to ask, but already the Vestal was fading from view. As Ean felt slumber claiming him, he couldn't be certain, but he thought he heard Dagmar say from beyond the curtain of sleep, "…In the end, so much depends on you…"

Alyneri woke to a brilliant dawn, such a contrast from the fog-dampened evening of the night before. From their campsite, they had a clear view of the city of Chalons-en-Les Trois across a distant valley where the Mondes river had carved through the cliffs to create a passage called the Eidenvale. The Glass River of Acacia was a tributary of the Mondes, and had they sailed from Acacia's river port they would have long ago reached Chalons-en-Les Trois. It was a foregone understanding that they would stay the next night in the city, however, for there was no other way through the arm of the mountains into the bosom of Veneisea save to follow them two hundred miles west to the coast.

It was late afternoon when they arrived in Chalons-en-Les Trois, once again traveling under the guise of Alyneri's pilgrimage to Jeune. She was anxious to find an inn, and the closer they drew to the city the more restless she became. More even than the comforts of civilization, Alyneri craved solitude. She needed time alone with her thoughts, time to reflect on what she'd been through, time to heal her own wounds. Watching Ean those past few days had nearly broken her heart, and though he'd seemed in better spirits that morning, she knew he was still tormented.

What had he done to that Marquiin?

For that matter, how had Tanis avoided Bethamin's Fire? The lad had told her all about his experience with the poor boy Piper, though the knowledge had only scared her more after the fact. Tanis had reassured her that he was fine, that the Marquiin's power hadn't harmed him, that he felt no different; and indeed, he seemed completely fine when she'd placed her hands upon him—which she'd done every morning since leaving Acacia, just to be sure there weren't any latent effects. But young Tanis seemed well and truly…himself. It was as if the terrible power had never even touched him.

She'd never heard of any truthreader being immune to Bethamin's malignant power. So how had Tanis escaped its effects?

They reached the city as a long procession of farmers were driving their livestock home from the markets, and they waited in line behind several merchants while a guard at the gates inspected papers.

When at last it was their turn and the guard asked for their papers, Bastian replied in cultured Veneisean, "This is the party of the Duchess of Giverny, Healer to the Crown of Dannym, on her virgin pilgrimage to Jeune. We intend to stay the night in town and replenish our supplies before continuing south in the morn."

"The Duchess of Giverny, did you say?" asked another soldier, who emerged from a door leading deep within the walls while the first soldier was looking over the papers Bastian had handed him.

"So it seems to be," answered the first soldier in his native tongue. He handed the papers to the second guard, who might've been a commander from the gold seal upon his chest.

The latter was older, and more heavily bearded, seeming more like Rhys than Bastian in voice and stature. He looked over the papers and said in the common tongue, his accent thick, "Well zese all look in ordair." He handed them back to Bastian, who returned the papers inside his coat. Alyneri thought he was certain to let them through when he surprised her by saying, "'owevair, I 'ave ordairs to bring ze Duchess of Giverny and her party straight to ze Comte D'Ornay."

He snapped his fingers, and a guard ran up with his horse. As he swung into his saddle, a host of mounted guards appeared just beyond the wall, waiting for them.

"Is the Comte another of your pleased patrons, your Grace?" Fynn posed mildly, but his eyes were hard.

Alyneri shook her head and pressed her lips together tightly. She'd never met the Comte D'Ornay and had no idea why he was requiring her presence. "Perhaps he's in need of a Healer," she whispered back.

Fynn arched brows skeptically as he watched the city guard fall in around them, a mounted escort of twenty men.

The chateau of the Comte D'Ornay was on the eastern edge of the city along the wall of the Eidenvale. Statues in the chateau's stepped gardens were bathed in the red-gold light of sunset as their horses climbed the switchback road to the chateau's walls. The commander spoke in brisk Veneisean to the guards inside the wrought-iron gates, and the latter signaled to his men to open them quickly. The commander then turned to her Grace. "I bid you *adieu*, Madame la Duchesse de Giverny."

With that, he made a sign to his men, and they spun their horses around and cantered back down the long, twisting road.

"*Viens dans*, Madame la Duchesse," said the guard at the gates, sweeping his arm to bid them enter. Still confused and more than a little concerned, Alyneri nudged her mare through, and the others followed. A host of stewards in the Comte's livery took their horses as she dismounted in the yard.

"*Bonsoir*, your Grace. *Bonsoir*, my Lord Captain!" greeted a man coming down the long, many-tiered stone steps that led up to the manse. Unlike the commander of the city guard, he spoke with no accent at all. "I am Antoine, the Chamberlain of Ville La Chesnaye. If you would please follow me, all of your things will be brought up for you. The Comte has ordered refreshments and arranged for any comfort you may desire."

"Monsieur Antoine," Alyneri replied as he neared, "I confess my confusion. I have never met the Comte, and while I am most grateful for his offer of hospitality, I am on a pilgrimage to Jeune—"

"Respectfully, your Grace," Antoine interrupted with a polite smile that said she was wasting her breath asking questions of him, "if you would come with me, I feel assured that all things will be explained in due time."

Defeated, Alyneri forced a smile in return. "Of course."

They followed the indubitable Antoine up the long stone staircase, which twisted and twined through the stepped gardens fronting the manse. Alyneri thought it a cruel torment to make her climb all those steps after such a long day of travel, but she admitted the view was incomparable.

The company was met in the grand entry hall by the assembled staff. Preeminent among them was a blonde woman who stood to the side dressed in a high-necked gown of green and gold, its cut very much in the fashion of Queen Indora's court.

Upon their entry, Antoine announced, "*Madame la Duchesse de Giverny et son entourage*."

The staff curtsied or bowed, all save the blonde woman, who nodded her head politely. Then a thin woman, whose lined face and black eyes looked drawn from a charcoal nib, stepped forward.

"Your Grace, may I present Madame Gilles-Laroque, the *gouvernante* of Ville La Chesnaye," said Antoine. "She will show you to your suite and provide for your needs. His Lordship is in chambers at present but invites you to dine with his household this evening. Of course your ward is also welcome at table." He turned to Rhys. "Lord Captain, his Lordship extends you an invitation, but he requests that your men dine with his guard and promises they will not want for hospitality there."

Rhys just grunted.

Alyneri was beginning to feel light-headed and remembered why she misliked Veneisea—already she felt choked by all the pretension. She darted a glance at Fynn, but the royal cousin shook his head almost imperceptibly. Feeling abandoned, Alyneri put on a brave smile. "*Merci*, Monsieur Antoine. I am most grateful for your assistance. Please inform the Comte that Tanis and I will happily accept his invitation to dinner."

Alyneri fought the urge to look over her shoulder regretfully as she was led away from her companions. She dared not look at Ean lest she draw undue attention to him, though she wished more than anything to know how he was doing. For all that she'd longed for solitude not an hour past, now she feared to let her friends leave her sight. Were they not traveling under such dire secrecy, the offer to stay in a foreign noble's home would have been a true windfall, but Alyneri feared so much for Ean's safety that no boon could be received without suspicion.

She managed the appropriate compliments of the rooms she was given, though she could tell from the housekeeper's pinched frown that she thought Alyneri not nearly admiring enough and no doubt believed her conceited and snobbish simply because she was a duchess in a mere count's 'humble' home—never mind that Alyneri was wont to do her own laundry if she could get away with it.

She was relieved to take a bath, however, and she admitted it was nice to have the chambermaids present to scrub her back and wash her hair; nor did she mind at all the service of tea and biscuits set out for her, or the scented oils the maids massaged her with before wrapping her in a lush velvet robe. It wasn't even unpleasant to let them brush her hair and braid it in the Veneisean fashion. In fact, everything was quite agreeable considering she'd all but been taken hostage by *le Comte*.

Alyneri knew she would've been treated with a tad bit more deference—to put it mildly—if her title had actually set her in line for the throne of Dannym, or if her 'betrothal' to Ean was more than rumor. Not that she desired either; all she wanted was an explanation from the Comte.

Imagine how it must feel to Ean, she suddenly thought as the maids continued readying her for dinner. *To be the target of so many without understanding at all…to be forced to flee his home…to see poor Creighton—Epiphany bless and keep him—slain before his eyes, and all without any explanation!*

It was quite a humbling realization.

The maids had pressed all the wrinkles from her burgundy and gold brocade gown by the time she was ready to dress for dinner. It was a strange sensation just to feel clean after so many days on the road, much less to be dressed so lavishly again.

When it was time for the meal, Alyneri followed a page to the dining room. Tanis was already seated further down the long table, but he seemed happy talking to another boy close to his age. The steward pulled out a high-backed chair for Alyneri, and she murmured her thanks as she sat. As the steward was placing a napkin in her lap, a woman said from her left, "*Bonsoir*, your Grace."

Alyneri had barely noticed the other woman, she was so entrapped in her own net of fears and worries. *What must these people think of me?* Alyneri glanced her way with an apologetic look, realizing it was the same blonde woman in the green dress who she'd noticed upon arrival. "I'm so sorry, I was…worried for my ward. But I see he is fine."

"He speaks with the young truthreader, Alain, a nephew of the Comte who is visiting from Tregarion."

"Oh!" Alyneri brightened. It would be good for Tanis to have another truthreader his own age to converse with.

"And I have heard of you, Duchess, though I believe we've never met," the woman continued. She had the barest accent, though it didn't quite seem Veneisean in origin. "I am Sandrine du Préc."

"*Oh*," Alyneri said again, the surprise evident in her tone.

Sandrine smiled slightly. "And I can see that you have heard of me, also."

"Only good things," Alyneri assured her. "I am acquainted with your cousin, the

Marchioness of Wynne."

"Indeed," Sandrine smiled again. Though she was perhaps nearing forty, she had the same sort of beauty as her cousin Ianthe: the cold, calculating kind. Around her neck she wore a charm depicting the Veneisean goddess of Temperance, clearly her patron virtue. "Come to think of it," Sandrine continued, "Ianthe may have mentioned you in a letter recently."

Feeling her breath coming faster, Alyneri pressed a hand to her throat. "Oh?"

"Something about a recent betrothal, if memory serves." Sandrine settled blue eyes on Alyneri and smiled, though the two parts of her face seemed completely divorced of each other—the eyes saying one thing while the smile conveyed another, neither of them particularly reassuring. "Congratulations, your Grace."

"Please...call me Alyneri." She swallowed and forced a smile. "It's...not official, of course. The betrothal. Not until I've completed my pilgrimage."

"Ianthe seemed to think you would not relish marrying Prince Ean, but you seem pleased by the distinction."

Alyneri managed a little laugh to cover her dismay at the entire conversation. "I...why how could I feel anything but blessed to be promised the hand of Ean val Lorian?"

Sandrine eyed her over the rim of her crystal goblet. "However indeed," she murmured into her wine.

"And what brings you to Chalons-en-Les Trois, Sandrine?" Alyneri inquired, hoping to turn the conversation away from her personal affairs. "Ianthe said you were serving in Queen Indora's court."

"I attend the Comte's wife, Claire, who is expecting twins any day," Sandrine said as she set down her goblet. "It is the Comtesse's fourth pregnancy, and the Queen is concerned for her health. She is a great-niece of her Majesty, the daughter of a favored nephew."

It was then that the Comte arrived. He was not a handsome man, with a jutting nose and a chin too small for his face, but his brown eyes were kind. He greeted his guests politely in his native tongue, and then invited everyone to begin. Thus the meal was served, and Alyneri still had no idea why the Comte D'Ornay had required her presence.

The Comte carried on a conversation with those closest to him, but Alyneri was five seats away. While the rest of the table conversed among themselves, Alyneri felt a strained silence growing with Sandrine. She searched for anything nice to say to the woman, and came up with a question. "Sandrine," she said as the soup course was being cleared away to make room for the next, "might I ask a question of you?"

"Certainly," allowed the older woman.

"Ianthe mentioned that you once saved a man from the poison of a Valdére viper."

Sandrine looked pleased that Alyneri knew of her accomplishments, but she affected an air of humility as she answered, "Indeed, it is so."

Alyneri hadn't considered what else she would say until she heard the words rushing out of her mouth. "Is it something you could teach me?"

Sandrine's blue eyes widened. "Why, it would be my pleasure, Alyneri."

They conversed more easily after that, but still Alyneri was grateful when the meal ended and the Comte at last called for audience with her.

She met him in a gallery filled with paintings of women in compromising positions and only then remembered that Veneisean propriety reigned in the public rooms while in private all manner of indecencies cavorted. Alyneri never could abide the way Veneisean women were expected to follow the Cardinal Virtues to the letter while the men seemed to emulate only the vices. If the Cardinal Virtues were the hinges upon which hung the door of the moral life, Veneisean men seemed content to stay forever on the other side of it.

"Please, your Grace," the Comte invited Alyneri to sit upon a divan as he walked to a sideboard and poured a liqueur into two tiny crystal glasses. "And to finish our meal, my special apricot brandy, which I feel certain you will enjoy." He handed her a glass and sat down on the cushion slightly too close for Alyneri's comfort. She shifted her feet, which allowed her to move her knee out of his reach.

The Comte smiled faintly. "I am so sorry to have detained you and to have made you wait so long for explanation, but I had many guests arriving tonight who required my audience. The truth is, your Grace, I was asked to look out for your welfare, considering the current problems in Jeune."

Alyneri shook her head. "What problems?"

"The city is closed. Three healers have gone missing, not to mention the High Priestess's own son—who was not an Adept—and no one is allowed in or out of Jeune until the Queen's Inspectors finish their investigation."

Alyneri frowned. "I appreciate your concern, my lord. But...if I may ask...how did you know I was coming?"

The Comte gave her a slightly pained smile. "My wife received a letter from Queen Errodan's Companion. She informed us you were on a pilgrimage and would necessarily pass through Chalons-en-Les Trois—for all roads pass through Chalons-en-Les Trois, no?" he added proudly, as if he had somehow orchestrated the Mondes' carving out of the Eidenvale. "My wife Claire entreated me to alert you to the problems in Jeune. I'm afraid the destination is quite out of the question now."

"Very well." Alyneri managed a smile, though the man was starting to unnerve her the way he kept sliding closer on the settee. She sipped her brandy and was surprised to find that it was quite good, if a little strong for her head after the wine at dinner. "I suppose I must go to the Temple of the Vestals in Cair Rethynnea then." The pilgrimage to Jeune was just a pretext anyway.

The Comte considered her as he drank his brandy. "Things are worse in the Cairs, I'm afraid," he said then. "Rumors abound of the missing. Many Adepts are fleeing the Free Cities altogether. Tis a dangerous time indeed for pretty young Healers to be about the realm."

Alyneri shifted to avoid his hand reaching for her shoulder and forced a smile, though she felt fluttery and discomfited by his news as much as being alone with him. "You are too kind, my lord," she managed, "and your lady wife. I truly appreciate such concern for my welfare, but I really must insist. A pilgrimage is not a thing to embark upon lightly, and I would be remiss did I allow myself to be diverted from my promised task out of cowardice or self-preservation."

A crestfallen look crossed le Comte's features, but it was quickly consumed, prey to his insistence. "Surely you might linger a few days to partake of my hospitality and meet my wife?" he asked, slipping closer again. "Claire is due any day, and having a Healer such as yourself in residence would…ease my fears for her."

"Sandrine is a renowned Healer, Comte," Alyneri pointed out. She inched back on the settee, only to realize there was no more cushion to support her. She got quickly to her feet and set down her glass on a near table.

Outrun, le Comte sat back dejectedly. "Yes, but she doesn't really like my wife," he admitted with unexpected candor. "I've no doubt Sandrine will fulfill her service to our Queen, but would she extend herself beyond mere duty to save my Claire?"

His eyes were so sincere in the appeal, his love for his wife so apparent—even if in conflict with his advances toward herself—that Alyneri felt a sudden compassion welling. She didn't understand Veneisean men, who claimed to love their wives yet made passes at anything that swayed when it moved, but it was clear that le Comte did care for Claire. How could she deny him her help? "I must…I must consult with the Lord Captain on the timing of our journey," she replied and added hesitantly, "… but I will ask if we might stay a few days."

With a sudden joyous light in his eyes, le Comte took her hands in his. "Thank you, dear child." To her surprise, he released her without any uncomfortable kissing, for which she was grateful.

Yet as Alyneri made her way back to her rooms, she still felt uneasy, for something the Comte said made no sense: Why would Ysolde have written to the Comtesse about their journey?

Perhaps it was at Morin's behest, another means of propagating his rumors?

But the explanation was out of keeping with Morin's usual wont. Would the Spymaster really have thought it prudent to alert a foreign dignitary with questionable loyalties to Ean whereabouts? Wasn't it safer for them all to simply disappear on a nebulous 'pilgrimage' without a set agenda or path?

Anyone could assume we'd be passing through Chalons-en-Les Trois, she reminded herself. The Comte had been correct—if brazen—in his declaration that all roads south passed through his city. Still, why would Ysolde have written to Claire about it? It seemed a risk the Queen's Companion surely would not have taken.

Perhaps he meant only to detain me in the name of his wife's health. This explanation at least made more sense than Ysolde writing to Claire, but then why the subterfuge?

And who told them we were coming?

What's more, if they knew of Alyneri's pilgrimage, did they also know Ean was traveling among her company?

She thought of sending word to Ean—perhaps calling up her Captain as she'd told the Comte she would do—but it occurred to her that whatever suspicions she harbored, whatever concerns troubled her, Ean was sure to have the same and was better equipped to deal with them. The realization gave her a measure of ease.

Alyneri paused at the foot of the grand staircase absently, seeing only recent memories instead of the wide gilt and marble advance. In the past few weeks, she'd witnessed so many of Ean's better characteristics. It was becoming a trial to be angry with him for anything and an even greater strain upon her emotions. *Why can't I just love and admire him without this awful need to make him mine?*

Heading upstairs, she sighed, lamenting how things would be so much easier if she didn't so wish for the gift of Ean's heart.

To Alyneri's surprise, she found Bastian waiting on the landing when she gained her floor. The young lieutenant pushed off the wall where he'd been relaxing and straightened to receive her, looking ever the proper soldier even in his muted brown traveling clothes. "*Bonsoir*, your Grace," he said, smiling. "If I may be so bold as to comment," he added, blushing slightly, "you look...very beautiful tonight."

Alyneri beamed at him. "Thank you, lieutenant. To what do I owe the pleasure of your company?"

"The Captain wanted to be sure of your welfare."

"The Captain?" she returned with surprised laugh—it just seemed too strange that Rhys would care about her at all.

Bastian looked hesitant. He glanced around the passage. "Well, I mean—"

Alyneri finally caught on. "Oh, of course," she interrupted, giving him an apologetic look. "Yes, that's so very kind of the Captain. The Comte has been quite pleasant. Please reassure him." She motioned for Bastian to accompany her as she headed down the hall toward her rooms. "And what...of your quarters?"

Bastian smiled as he walked at her side. "The same, your Grace. *Le Comte's* men are well fed and housed modestly but comfortably. We have been treated with gracious regard."

Alyneri let out her breath, only then realizing she'd been holding it. "That's reassuring," she murmured. "I...promised the Comte I would speak with Rhys about lingering here another day or two on behalf of the Comtesse. Perhaps the Captain could see me in the morn?"

"I will relay your request, my lady," Bastian said as they gained her doorway. He gave her a nod of farewell, a gentle smile, and withdrew.

Alyneri sighed as she gazed after him. Why couldn't she love someone safe, like Bastian val Renly, instead of a succession of val Lorian heirs who broke her heart? Lamenting her fate, Alyneri entered her rooms and—

Sandrine du Préc turned from the mantle to receive her. The wielder had changed into a deep blue-violet robe worn over a silk dressing gown of fuchsia. "Ah, Alyneri," she said, smiling in a way that seemed more predatory than welcoming, "I do apologize for intruding. I thought I heard a call to enter when I knocked. Imagine my embarrassment when I realized you weren't here at all."

Alyneri slowly closed the door behind her. "I was with *le Comte*."

"Of course. And did he explain his actions to your satisfaction?"

"His concern seemed quite genuine," Alyneri replied, knowing it was true in regards to the Comtesse at least.

"Well then," Sandrine replied amicably.

Alyneri slowly crossed the room. "Sandrine, forgive me if this seems unkindly, but why are you here?"

She gave a little laugh. "For your lesson, of course."

Alyneri frowned. "But...it must be after midnight."

Sandrine opened her hands in a gesture of acceptance. "At dinner you seemed quite urgent to learn the skill of healing which you mentioned to me. I thought surely you meant to begin tonight." Her blue eyes swept the Duchess, and that smile returned. Alyneri did not like that smile. "Come," Sandrine murmured. "Let me help you with your gown at least. The maids are already abed."

"No, thank you—really, I can manage—"

But the woman was already undoing the laces at the back of her dress. Alyneri felt Sandrine's fingers touching her skin, and each time her touch gave her goose-bumps. When the other woman was finished, she slipped her hands beneath the fabric and caressed Alyneri's shoulders as she helped her slide her arms from the sleeves. "There, she whispered, bringing her lips close to Alyneri's ear. Sandrine placed her hands on Alyneri's shoulders then and rubbed gently, her fingers sliding this time toward Alyneri's silk shift.

The Duchess was not so young that she missed understanding the woman's intentions. She spun to face her, clutching her gown to her bosom. "I think—" she managed, though her heart was racing, "I beg forgiveness, Sandrine, but I do think I am too tired to attempt learning a healing tonight." She took a few steps away from the woman.

"Perhaps you're right," Sandrine remitted. She gave Alyneri an admiring look. "Tomorrow then. I will call upon you in the morn."

Alyneri nodded and forced a smile.

Sandrine glided across the room and let herself out.

Only when she was well and truly gone did Alyneri suck in her breath and shudder. She'd never considered lying with a woman before, but she was certain that if she ever did, it would not be a woman like Sandrine du Préc.

Better to lie with the Valdére viper. At least then one knows the fate that awaits.

FORTY-ONE

'Garlic is a powerful ward against golems, but ten cloves taken by the mouth are also efficacious in fending off colds and ill-mannered suitors.'

– The *Hearthwitch's Handbook*

The avieth Gwynnleth nach Davvies walked the peaked slate rooftop as surefooted and silent as a bobcat stalking a meal. Her long auburn hair blew wildly around her shoulders as it was caught and stirred by the rising morning breeze, surrounding her in a diffuse red-gold halo that mirrored the sunrise over Chalons-en-Les Trois. She perched on the edge of the roof and let her booted feet hang over the side, three stories down to the dark alley below, and gazed with tawny eyes over the Veneisean city, watching idly as the townspeople began to stir.

She didn't mind the city so much when it was quiet and peaceful, but she knew that soon enough the entire Eidenvale would reverberate with the cacophony of Chalons-en-Les Trois. Sometimes she swore she could hear the noise of the city all the way in her home on Mt. Pisah, though her uncle claimed she was just being dramatic.

Now…where are you…?

She watched for two men of very different natures that morning. They didn't know each other, but they were intimately connected. She knew she had only to find the one and the other would soon appear, and if he didn't? Well…it was for the best, though she always enjoyed a good fight. Her uncle claimed she enjoyed it too much, but he was wrong about her. Some matters just needed settling, and some men—no matter their race—just needed gentling.

Gwynnleth felt it was a tribute to her inherent good nature that she let them all live. Surely that proved she wasn't fighting just for the sake of a good time. *Ask the elders!* If she'd had her druthers she'd have run them all through—what were a few human men more or less to her? It wasn't like the realm had any grave shortage of them.

Still, she'd been slightly affronted when her uncle Seth made her promise not to harm the val Lorian prince—as if she was completely wool-brained! Raine D'Lacourte sent her to help the man, so *obviously* his life was important. It rankled her that Seth thought her so lacking in self-control as to require an oath on the matter.

I know how you dislike humanity, Gwynnleth, Seth's voice floated to her as if from a great distance. The Third Vestal could sense every avieth's mind, but he rarely intruded on their private thoughts, especially when they weren't in their avian form. Gwynnleth was a 'special case' to him, however. Since her mother died, Seth had become her quite-unwanted, overprotective, hovering, harping and immensely annoying surrogate father.

Go away, Gwynnleth returned vexedly. *I am nearly a hundred years old. I believe I can think without your assistance.*

Ignoring her desires, as was his wont, Seth returned, *Any sign of him yet?*

Gwynnleth sighed. *I only just arrived in the Eidenvale, uncle. I may need a few hours to search him out.*

Raine says the prince should be in Chalons-en-Les Trois by now. His exit from Acacia did not go unnoticed, and it was well known that the Healer in whose party he travels was heading south. It only follows that the company will pass through Chalons-en-Les Trois. No doubt the Tyriolicci who hunts him will expect this also.

Gwynnleth gritted her teeth and kicked her boot heels discontentedly against the side of the gable. They'd gone over all of this before she even left Mt. Pisah.

Fine, Seth remarked belligerently.

A moment later, she knew he'd left her alone with her own mind.

Gwynnleth smiled to herself and stood up on the edge of the roof. The wind whipped at her short cloak, urging her to follow its twisting, capricious path. The sun was just clearing the Eidenglass, casting a brilliant flood of daylight upon the world. She threw her arms out and caught the wind, feeling it pull and tug upon her body in the same way that the call of the form enticed her away from her human self.

It was time to start searching.

Ean woke in the early morning as the Comte's men rose to begin their day. *Le Comte* had given them adequate quarter with his own men and treated them with respect, but when Fynn had tried to leave in the night, he'd been told that all the men were required to stay within the walls. When pressed, the guards had given some excuse about a disturbance in town. Fynn had later remarked, "That lie holds about as much merit as *le Comte's* 'explanation' that his wife received a letter from the Queen's Companion." He'd snorted, adding critically, "As if the infinitely savvy Ysolde Remalkhen would ever be so foolish!"

Ean agreed with his cousin. Ysolde would never have written to anyone about Alyneri's plans, knowing as she did that Ean traveled among the Healer's company. So the question remained, how did the Comte know of Alyneri's coming through Chalons-en-Les Trois, and why did he really detain them?

Rhys found Ean as he was breaking his fast with the Comte's men. "Just saw the Healer," the Captain grunted as he took a seat on the long bench beside Ean and served himself some pear and sausage pie that was still steaming from the ovens. "She says the Comte asked her to stay a few days more. The Comtesse is carrying twins, and the Comte requested her Grace's presence at the birth." He gave Ean a look that spoke volumes, clearly wondering if this might be the real reason the Comte was on the lookout for their party.

"Zee Lady Claire 'as been abed for two moons now," offered one of the Comte's men, who sat across the scrubbed wooden table. He was a clean-shaven man of Rhys' age, with a jutting chin and bright blue eyes beneath a shock of wavy auburn hair.

"Zat's why zee queen sent one of 'er Healers to attend 'er," added another man from Ean's left, his accent strong. "'er name is Sandrine du Préc."

"But she treats zee Comtesse like an insult," noted a third man in a scathing tone. His heavy moustache wiggled as he sniffed indignantly. "Looks down 'er nose at everyone in Chalons-en-Les Trois. Calls our city 'zee fringes of civilization' and claims we've only zee 'barest' comforts."

"*Salope*," cursed a fourth man by way of agreement. "They say she iz a sorceress. Like as to curse a man as to heal him."

"*Prétentieuse*," announced the man across from Ean, shaking his head.

"*Tres vaniteux!*" agreed the other three men, speaking as one.

"But your *Duchesse*," said the auburn-haired man across from Ean, addressing Rhys with a smile, "she is so young to be serving your king, an *ingénue*."

"Her mother died in service," Ean said soberly.

"Ah yes, the famous *tragédie*," said the man. "And now they say she will be betrothed to zee young Prince Ean. You do not think zees a problem?" He leveled a suggestive look at Rhys, adding concernedly, "Perhaps zee mademoiselle is accursed. Is she not from ze dezairt lands?"

"Her late father was a Nadori prince," Ean said, then added in a tone made all the more ominous for its quiet delivery, "but it's the royal family who is cursed, not the Duchess Giverny."

Rhys turned the prince a reproving look, while the man across the table eyed Ean speculatively.

"And does her Grace wish to stay and assist the Comte, Captain?" Ean asked Rhys after a moment, returning them to their original conversation.

Rhys eyed the Comte's men, who were all ears for his answer. "She thinks it would be best."

Ean just nodded, wherein the man across the table seemed to change his mind about where the balance of power rested. His gaze lingered on Ean thereafter.

It was still early when the Comte's men cleared out to attend their various duties. Upon invitation, Ean accompanied the first man on his patrol of the grounds, both eager for a chance to see the lay of the Comte's lands as well as to probe for information. As it turned out, Matthieu was an officer in the Comte's household guard and was privy to quite a lot.

"Your men mentioned Sandrine du Préc," Ean said as they patrolled a lane that fed between the manse's high stone wall and an apple orchard whose rough, barren limbs seemed a graveyard of gnarled bones. A carpet of brown and gold leaves crunched beneath the morning frost as they walked. "What do you know of her?"

Matthieu eyed him knowingly. "A bit of sowing zee wild oats, eh? She is a beauty, Sandrine, but thorny as zee briar towards zee men. Better to cast your eye on zee Comtesse's ladies—they are more amenable to dalliances with zee opposite sex."

Ean's eyebrows rose in surprise. "I see."

Matthieu laughed. "Yes, I can tell that you do. Sandrine had 'er eye on zee little Duchess last eve, yes? Perhaps to send zee Captain to watch out for 'er?"

Ean almost worried more for Sandrine. He didn't believe the Duchess was quite as fragile as Matthieu imagined her.

The two men continued following the little lane, which snaked slowly up the hillside past orchards and fields, until around midmorning they reached the highest point on the property and an unparalleled view. The scene before them was of a massive earthen wedge—the far side of the Eidenvale—where the mountains carried on again westward toward the sea. The Mondes River wove in and out of view in the basin between the cliffs, but the river port was clearly visible along the far western edge of Chalons-en-Les Trois, which seemed a hillside of slate spanning up to the water's edge. To the south of the city lay the great forest of Verte L'eau, nestled against the foothills of the snowbound Eidenglass range, while a long line of snowy peaks formed another crescent to the north.

"Ahh...*le c'est une de toute beauté vue*, no?" sighed Matthieu.

"Yes, it is a beautiful view," Ean agreed.

"Tis a quiet posting here in the service of le Comte," Matthieu confessed, "but a good life. Le Comte, he is not interested in the intrigue, the court rivalries your Sandrine spins like zee spider webs. For a man such as myself, zees is this perfect position. Being in le Comte's household brings certain—how do you say?—benefits..." he paused to give Ean a wink and a knowing grin. "For one such as me, tis better to be zee big fish in zee small pond, no?"

As they walked on, heading downhill to continue their patrol, Matthieu glanced at Ean as he observed, "But you, *mon ami*...you are zee big fish in zee big pond."

Ean slowed, for it had not seemed a question.

"Yes, I know who you are," Matthieu said in response to Ean's wary look, "but I 'ave told no one. My men, zey suspect nothing."

Tense now, Ean murmured, "How do you know me?"

Matthieu waved airily. "I observe, I watch. I see the way zee Captain looks at you for zee answers, and I 'ear the rumors of you and zee Duchesse. I am like you, no?" Matthieu added, elbowing Ean in the arm. "I would not have my betrothed travel zee kingdoms without me at 'er side."

When Ean still looked chary, Matthieu laughed and wrapped an arm around his shoulder. "You can trust me, *mon seigneur*. Your secret is safe." Matthieu started them walking again as he explained, "My sister, Lucie, married a man from Bolton, in your Dannym near zee 'ighlands, yes? His family, zey have zee rivalry with zee neighboring lord, who raids my brother-in-law's estate for his sheep. Always is zee terrible fights between the two lords, and my brother-in-law, he killed a man during a raid, a son of the other more powerful lord." Matthieu paused to give Ean a solemn look as he offered, "A lesser king may 'ave chosen in favor of his crony, but your father, 'e ruled in favor of my brother-in-law, against the other family." Matthieu stopped and turned to Ean. "Gydryn val Lorian gained my loyalty that day, and I extend it now to his son." He dropped to one knee and pressed his fist to his heart.

Ean looked around nervously. "Matthieu," he murmured.

Laughing, Matthieu jumped to his feet and started them walking again. "Zere is no one about to see us, *mon ami*." He spread an arm to the vista. "Only zee trees and zee birds, who care nothing for zee politics of kings. So tell me," he said then, "why do you come with zee little Duchesse in secret? There must be more to zee story, yes?"

Ean knew there was a great deal more, but nothing he wanted to confide in Matthieu. "I will answer you, if you will agree to answer my question first," Ean said.

"Ah, a trade," Matthieu brightened at the idea. "Very well. What is it you wish to know?"

"How did the Comte know her Grace was arriving here? Why did he require us to stay with him?"

"Ah!" Matthieu threw up his hands. "It is as they told you last night, *mon ami*. *Le Comte*, he knew zee Duchesse would be coming through Chalons-en-Les Trois—but 'e never said how 'e knew t'was so—and 'e ordered us to 'ave zee Duchess brought to the manse. But! And I will tell you zis—" Matthieu held up one hand and leaned closer to the prince, "*Le Comte* ordered zat zee Duchesse's party is not to leave zee grounds." He gave Ean a conspiratorial look. "Is curious, no? Why should you not enjoy our lovely city, but no, to be zee chickens in the coop 'ere on zee hill."

The news at least confirmed Fynn and Ean's suspicions, though offered no further insight as to why they were being detained. As Ean mulled over the information, Matthieu said with an elbow and a wink, "So tell me, yes? Why do you travel with zee Duchesse in secret? Do you distrust 'er? She seems not the flouncy to me."

"No, it isn't that."

"Secret lovairz?" Matthieu offered with a broad grin. "You cannot be a day from 'er side? Do you play the voyeur? Come, you must tell me, *mon ami*—I cannot think why zee subterfuge, zee hiding among 'er guard. To what purpose?"

Ean suspected the man wouldn't be satisfied with anything less than the truth, but the truth was far too important to share with him. So he searched for the most outrageous explanation he could manage. "All right, Matthieu," Ean said, affecting a manner of the utmost secrecy, in keeping with Matthieu's dramatic persona. "I will tell you, but the truth must never leave your lips."

"Shall I die a thousand deaths!" promised the man.

Ean glanced around again and then leaned closer to Matthieu as they walked. "I am not here as Alyneri's betrothed," he began in a low voice, "though it is intended upon our unsuccessful return."

Matthieu arched curious brows. "*Un*successful?"

Ean dropped his voice even lower. "It has come to the attention of those in the know that my brother may still be alive."

"*Mon dieu!*" Matthieu gripped Ean's arm. "Which brozaire? Zee one missing at sea?"

"The very one," Ean murmured.

"*C'est incroyable!*" Matthieu gasped.

"My brother and the Duchess are already betrothed, you see," Ean went on, the words coming strangely quick to his lips, "and we must be sure that the rumors are false before she can be mine."

"But you would 'ave 'er, yes?" Matthieu asked with a gentle look. "She is a lovely little *chaton*."

"I would gladly have her," Ean agreed. Then he looked away, adding quietly, "but I would give my life to know my brother lived." *If only there were truth to this tale—any truth at all!*

"Ah, yes," Matthieu murmured. "Tis a terrible loss. So…" and here he smiled once more, "you look for ze brozaire to see if 'e lives, and if so, to return him his 'eritage and to the Duchesse, 'er betrothed."

"Just so," Ean murmured, surprising himself with how much he wished suddenly that this fiction was truly the quest he was upon.

"And it does not bozaire you to give up zee throne?"

Ean's eyes flashed as he turned to Matthieu. "It is my *brother's* throne. If he lives,

I want nothing that is rightfully his!"

Matthieu grinned and clapped him on the shoulder. "Ah, *mon ami*, you are a good man. A very good man!"

They continued their patrol, with Matthieu spending most of the time voicing his suspicions about where Ean's lost brother might be hiding, and finally arrived back at the main gates below the manse. Before they came in range of the other guards, Matthieu turned Ean a knowing look and promised, "*Mon lèvres êtes sceller*," and made the motion of turning a key between his closed lips.

Ean didn't fear for Matthieu's idle gossip, for he'd told him nothing of consequence and had gotten some valuable information in the trade, but he did worry over who else might have put two and two together about his identity among Alyneri's troop.

As they neared the gates, Ean noticed a commotion between two of their company—Fynn's man Brody the Bull and the soldier Cayal—and one of the Comte's guards. Matthieu charged forward purposefully, demanding, "Now, now! Henri, what's zis trouble?"

The guard Henri turned to Matthieu looking relieved and answered in his native Veneisean, "The Duchesse's men, they claim one of their own is missing. I assured them it cannot be so, that no one has been allowed to leave, but they are claiming it is without question."

Ean didn't need to ask to know who was missing. He cast an inquiring look to Cayal, who shrugged helplessly, and then looked to the Bull. "How long, Brody?" Ean asked.

"All night, far as I can tell."

Cayal offered, "I think we all assumed he was sleeping in." He was careful to drop the 'your highness' from the end of his sentence, yet somehow the concept was still communicated in his tone and manner. Ean realized if they ever truly meant for him to travel incognito, he was going to have to train his men to become better actors.

"Have we checked to make certain he's not sleeping in someone else's bed?" Ean posed with a shadowy smile.

"Within reason," Cayal answered with a grimace.

Matthieu grinned. "So zis missing man is missing often, I take it?"

Ean turned him a resigned look. Matthieu was entirely too perceptive—his easy manner belied a shrewd mind.

Matthieu laughed at Ean's look. "Fear not," he promised, "we will sniff 'im out like zee *cochon* roots zee truffle." He turned to Henri and gave quick orders in his native tongue. Henri saluted and rushed off.

As Cayal and Brody left following Henri, Ean's attention was drawn to another of the Comte's men, who was shouting angrily at the gates in two languages. "*S'en aller!* I said be off with you! *S'en aller maintenant ou voyons les Comte's cachot!* Get thee gone or you will see the inside of le Comte's dungeons, you miserable lout!"

Matthieu turned a bemused look to Ean. "Did I say it was quiet here?" He trotted over to the guard at the gates and inquired in his native tongue, "What is the problem, Jean-Marie?"

"It's that beggar over there," Jean-Marie answered irritably, pointing to a shadowy figure lurking in the shade of an alcove of a building across the boulevard from the gates. "He's been there all morning just glaring at me."

"Give him food or something," Matthieu offered.

"I tried that. Philippe took a plate of pie to him and he hit it out of his hands and ran off. But half an hour later he was back again."

"Like the dog kicked too many times," Matthieu sighed.

"It's unseemly," Jean-Marie complained. "Beggars shouldn't take up stations around le Comte's manse. Others might get the same idea."

Ean joined Matthieu at the gates and gazed through the iron bars. "What's the trouble?"

"Just a beggar who doesn't beg. He is probably—how do you say—several cards short of a full deck?" Matthieu looked back to Jean-Marie. "Ignore him, Jean-Marie. He just wants someone to glare at."

"Let him glare elsewhere," Jean-Marie grumbled, but he turned his back on the man all the same.

Ean was about to move on as well when a form appeared, rising over the crest of the hill leading up to the manse. Something about the way the man walked caught the prince's attention. After a moment's study, a grin split his face and he said, "Matthieu, I think you can call off the search for our missing companion."

Matthieu's gaze followed his own, wherein he announced, "*Mon dieu!*" and turned to Jean-Marie. "Le Comte ordered the Duchesse's party to stay within the gates!"

"We've let no one leave, sir!" Jean-Marie insisted.

"Then how here comes this man? Answer me this, Jean-Marie!"

As Fynn neared, Ean saw that he carried a bulging bag over one shoulder. "I wouldn't be too hard on your man, Matthieu," the prince said and then noted blandly, "When it comes to acquiring wine, my cousin has an uncanny knack."

Matthieu frowned at the approaching Fynnlar. "Are you certain zis vagabond is with you, *mon ami?* 'e looks more zee hobo than our beggar across zee way."

"Unfortunately yes," Ean muttered.

Fynn grinned as he neared and saw Ean at the gates. "Oh good, you're up," he announced.

"It's noon, Fynn," Ean pointed out.

"Hey, don't berate me about it," Fynn complained. "*I'd* never wake you at such an ungodly hour."

Matthieu reluctantly opened the gates to admit Fynn, gazing all the while at Ean as if giving him the opportunity to change his mind.

"You can thank me later," Fynn said as he traipsed within the protection of the Comte's lands carting his bag of wine. He looked typically disheveled—rumpled, wrinkled, shaggy and unkempt—but was in fair humor. "I found a lovely Volga and bought every one of the vintage. We really should make another trip into town to stock up. Bring a wagon next time."

"How did you get into town, Fynn?" Ean asked.

Fynn rolled his eyes. "Well it should be extremely obvious that I *walked* there, cousin. Otherwise I'd be riding my horse now, wouldn't I?" He shook his head and headed off, muttering about annoying people that asked obvious questions.

"Hand me that hoof pick, Alain?" the lad Tanis said from under Caldar's broad belly.

The Veneisean truthreader jumped down from his perch upon the stall railing to hand Tanis an iron hook. Alain wore courtly garments of navy contrasted to Tanis's traveling clothes of charcoal and grey, and his fair hair shone like gold, whereas Tanis's had a muted hue. Tanis imagined himself a rather plain shadow of the older boy.

Leaning back against the rail again, Alain watched Tanis clean Caldar's hind hoof and observed, "You know, le Comte has stable hands for this work, Tanis." Though he'd been born and raised in Veneisea, he spoke with no accent at all—a product of his demanding court training.

Tanis lifted colorless eyes to meet the other boy's as he lowered Caldar's hoof. "I know, but Caldar likes being handled by people he knows, and I don't mind the work. Her Grace always had tons of projects to keep me busy. It's kind of strange being here with nothing to do."

"And her Grace had no duties for you this morning? Last night you made it seem there was nary an hour of your day that she didn't require something of you."

Tanis gave him a sheepish grin as he moved to Caldar's other side. He pressed his shoulder against the horse's hip, pushed one hand against the animal's shinbone, and the stallion obediently lifted his hoof. "Her Grace broke her fast with the other Healer this morning," Tanis said while pulling the hoof over his knee to get to the softer underside with the pick, "the one sent by the Queen—"

"Madame du Préc," offered Alain.

"Yes, and now they're sequestered together." Tanis pulled the pick along Caldar's hind hoof and cleaned the packed mud from it in three sure sweeps.

"So, when you might have hours or even an entire day to yourself," Alain observed in amusement, "what do you do but find work for yourself instead."

Tanis moved to clean the horse's other two hooves. Then he straightened and looked at the older boy. "Did you have something else in mind then?"

"As a matter of fact, I was going for a ride in the countryside. Would you like to come?"

Tanis found the idea of unnecessary hours ahorse after weeks on the road less than appealing. "I don't think so, but thanks for the offer."

"We can do something else then," Alain suggested. "Do you play Kings?"

"A little."

"Excellent," Alain said. "Let's take luncheon over a game of Kings. I promise not to smear you too badly across the game board."

"You'd best protect your queen if you mean to play against me," Tanis boasted as they left Caldar and headed out of the stables. "I have a way with the ladies."

Alain laughed. "Do you now?"

"Yes," Tanis said with a sigh, "I send them running for cover."

Alain gave him an empathetic look. "You know it's always like that for us." He shrugged, adding, "Girls are either overawed by the mystique of a man who can read their minds or afraid of what we might discover in so doing."

"Her Grace isn't like that," Tanis pointed out.

Alain gave him a wry grin. "Your Lady doesn't exactly conform to the usual expectations, does she?" When Tanis made no comment, Alain continued, "Truly, she doesn't travel with any ladies at all?" He sounded both surprised and perhaps slightly intrigued. "You'd never see that here," the older boy went on. Then he barked a laugh, adding, "I can only imagine the Queen's face upon hearing a lady of her peerage traveled without an entourage a mile long and a wagon of trunks heavy enough to rattle the earth."

Tanis shrugged sheepishly. "Her Grace doesn't like to be waited on," he said, thinking, *except by me*, "and she prefers to do her own chores," *except when I can do them*, "and she thinks a day's labor is as good as rest." *Well…she really does believe that.*

Alain laughed again. "Tanis, you do realize I could hear *everything* just then, don't you?"

Tanis reddened and dropped a grin toward his feet as they walked. "Was I thinking too loudly?" he asked.

"You've got to learn to keep your thoughts private when you don't want them heard by other sensitives," Alain said. "*Elae* fuels our talent and makes our minds powerful. We can hear a mortal's thoughts when they think them loud enough, but we can also project our own thoughts louder than any mortal can."

"I'll work on it," Tanis promised.

Alain led Tanis to the Comte's game room, a long gallery draped with tapestries depicting men and women gamboling in various states of dishabille. They played one game while a minstrel entertained two ladies who'd arrived with their lord husbands the night before, but the boys left when the three of them started dancing together and took luncheon on a patio in the gardens instead.

"So tell me of your recent adventures, Tanis," Alain said idly as they dined on game hens cooked with leeks and juniper berries, and with the late autumn sun warming their backs.

Tanis's mind, for reasons unbeknownst and quite frustrating to him, jumped immediately to the image of the Marquiin with his hand extended toward Tanis's eyes. The memory was so startling, so frightening in its sudden recollection, that it seemed to leap right from his mind into Alain's. The older boy dropped his fork and gaped at Tanis as the utensil clattered from plate to floor.

"It's not what it seems!" Tanis was quick to deny as the other boy's face turned ashen. "He didn't hurt me." The story came out in a rush then, for Tanis couldn't bear the look of horror on Alain's face.

But when he was done, Alain continued to stare at him. "I've never heard of anyone…" but the thought was too incredible. He shook his head and said instead, "The Queen is incensed by the recent activities of Bethamin's Ascendants—like the one you describe—illicitly searching her kingdom for truthreaders which rightfully belong in her service. I traveled here under guard—for my own protection."

"The Ascendant we met was in league with an Earl," Tanis said, recalling the man as they first met him on the bridge across the Glass River, his eyes black and threatening of malice, his tone dripping with contempt. "I think the Ascendants try to make powerful allies."

Alain sat with his meal forgotten. "What was it like, Tanis?" he asked after a moment of staring unseeing at the half-eaten hen. "He touched you, yet you…you survived the power?"

Tanis pushed a hand through his ash-blonde hair and turned to look out over the gardens. "I don't think it touched me at all," he murmured, "but I can't say why it didn't. It wasn't anything I was doing. The Ascendant was furious. He started shouting at the Marquiin, and then he hit me...and I don't remember much at all after that."

Alain lifted his gaze to Tanis. "My Queen will be very interested in this story, Tanis—you have no idea. Perhaps..." He shifted in his chair to better look Tanis in the eye. "Would you be willing to enter rapport with me...you know, to see if I can find out why Bethamin's Fire didn't harm you?" When Tanis seemed apprehensive, Alain said, "Tanis, if it can be done—and you've proved that it can—others need to know about this. My Queen believes Bethamin has stolen more than twenty of her Adepts. If there's some way to protect them..." His brow furrowed as he gazed at Tanis. "Surely you see the importance."

Master O'reith had told Tanis to always be careful to whom he opened his mind, but Tanis felt Alain could be trusted. He held out his hands, and Alain took them with a look of relief and gratitude. As Tanis had been taught by his master, he opened his mind to the other boy, and soon he felt the expected contact with Alain's thoughts; like the linking of hands, it was a palpable mental touch, gentle but firm. Alain proceeded to guide Tanis back to the vision he'd broadcast so plainly moments before, but this time Tanis felt none of its power, for he was expecting the picture and it did not surprise him. The rapport lasted for many minutes, but Tanis knew as Alain withdrew that he'd found nothing to help either of them understand.

Alain was shaking his head as Tanis opened his eyes. The other boy looked crestfallen. "It must be my lack of training," he whispered. "I'm sorry. I couldn't find anything to help us."

Tanis gazed compassionately at him. "You did your best."

Alain seemed disheartened. "I fear my queen will never believe me." He gazed off toward the gardens. Then he brightened with an idea. "Perhaps it's something in your family line. What can you tell me of your parents?"

Tanis shrugged. "I can't remember anything about them. My earliest memories are of her Grace's mother, the Lady Melisande..." with thoughts of Alyneri's mother came the necessary memories of Farshideh, which always were now accompanied by an ache in his chest. "And her assistant, Farshideh."

"You don't *remember?*" Alain looked shocked. "Why did you never try a Telling with your master to uncover your early memories?"

"I was just a baby when I came to Fersthaven," Tanis said, shrugging. "How much more is there to remember?"

"Tanis..." Alain settled him a chastising look, "did your master never tell you that memories can precede birth? That some Adepts can remember as far back as three or four lifetimes, some even more?"

This was startling news to the lad. Tanis looked to his hands and then lifted his eyes back to Alain, gazing up under ashen brows. "Sometimes I have these dreams," he confessed in a bare whisper, "and I think the woman is my mother...but how can I know for sure? It's just a dream, after all."

Alain was sort of watching Tanis with this funny expression on his face. He held out his hands again. "If there's one thing I am good at," the older boy said, "it's Tellings.

Will you come into rapport with me again?"

Feeling a flutter of anticipation, Tanis once again took Alain's hands.

"Now, Tanis," Alain murmured, and his voice echoed in Tanis's head as they shared each other's thoughts, "I want you to return to this dream of yours, the one with the woman you thought was your mother."

Tanis felt a tendril of Alain's prodding sinking deeper into his memory, stirring images like dust motes behind a curtain of unconsciousness. Abruptly the beginning of the dream sprang to mind.

"Yes!" Alain said before Tanis could even tell him what he remembered. "Yes, tell me about this."

Strange as it may seem, as Tanis began to recall the dream for his friend, the memory became far more vivid to him than some of his recent waking days.

"My mother is holding me in her arms, smiling down at me," Tanis murmured with closed eyes, seeing her face again as if she stood before him, knowing hers was a smile that would remain in his memory forever. "I remember her face!" he exclaimed with sudden excitement.

"Tell me what she looks like," Alain encouraged, though Tanis well knew that the other truthreader could see the image as clearly as he could.

"Well," Tanis began, biting one lip. "She's beautiful. Her face is long and…and yet sort of heart-shaped, and her eyes are wide, pale…they're colorless like yours and—and mine!"

"No—don't open those eyes just yet, Tanis," Alain admonished, for Tanis seemed ready to burst out of rapport. "Keep recalling your dream. I want to see your mother better. Really think of her now. Show her to me."

And indeed, as Tanis let Alain take control, Tanis saw her vividly through their link. Her colorless eyes were lovely in their strangeness—*how unusual to see a woman with those eyes!* Her long hair was chestnut brown, though streaked with gold by the sun, and her face was bronzed. She seemed a strong woman, confident, and she loved Tanis with her whole heart; above all else, that was clear in her smile.

"Now tell me more of your dream, Tanis," Alain prodded gently.

"I know I'm very little," Tanis began. "I can't see myself, but I feel my mother holding me. Then she hands me to someone…my father, I think. It feels like my father. I can't see him except for his beard; it's the darkest ash, and his arms are very strong holding me."

"How do you feel there?"

"Safe. Safe with him." Abruptly, he added, "Now I see my mother's face again. She's smiling and touching my forehead…then my cheek. We're moving, and the air changes."

"Tell me about it?"

Eyes still closed, Tanis frowned. "It's like we've gone outside."

"What's it like outside? What do you hear?"

Tanis thought about that. Then: "It's dark—dusk, I think, and the smell of the sea is heavy in the air—like it is at Calgaryn, but I don't think we're at Calgaryn."

"Why?"

Tanis puzzled for a moment over that. "It's just that…well, I can hear the waves crashing against the shore, and they sound different."

"Like they're crashing against rocks instead of onto sand?" Alain offered.

Tanis shook his head and frowned. "No…more like river stones pouring out of a jar."

"And are they saying anything?"

Tanis nodded. "My father says, 'I must go soon.' "

"All right, Tanis," Alain coached, "I want you to run the conversation through your memory, just like you're hearing it again, and I'll just listen."

Drawing in a deeply excited breath, Tanis did.

"We must part soon, Renaii," Tanis's father said. His voice was rich and deep, and filled with a great sense of loss."I do not think I shall ever see you again, my love…my one true love."

"We always knew this day would come," Renaii said, her voice full of compassion. "But we have Tanis now," and her face appeared in front of him again, smiling, "and he shall grow up knowing and loving the man that is his father, this I swear to you."

Tanis' father sighed with longing, with regret, with the pain of what he must do. "I would have him with me—have you both with me!—if there was any way to ensure…"

Renaii sighed, an aching sigh. "Do not dwell upon it, my darling," she whispered. Her voice was tormented, desperate, hopelessly in love... and strong. Always that. "When we part, I will grieve for you, but not before. I would only love you now, while I have you." She reached to Tanis and pulled the blanket he was wrapped in closer around him. Tanis was comfortable and warm, and he must have fallen asleep in his father's arms, for the dream faded. A wonderful dream.

Tanis opened his eyes and found Alain looking back at him. For a moment, two sets of colorless orbs gazed at each other. Then Alain smiled. "That was no dream, Tanis," he assured the younger boy. "That was your own true memory. You even know your mother's name."

"Renaii," Tanis whispered.

Alain was watching him intently. After a moment, he said in a tone of wonder, "Your mother was a *truthreader*." Alain was looking extremely excited, heady with the information he'd uncovered. "Don't you know what that means?"

Tanis shook his head.

Eyes bright, Alain said, "In the history of the realm, only one bloodline has ever produced female truthreaders."

Tanis just looked at him.

Abruptly Alain laughed and grabbed him by the shoulders. "Tanis, don't you see? Without much searching, you could know who your parents are!"

Tanis wasn't sure he wanted to know. If his dream was true, his father was…gone and his mother—well, something must've happened to his mother, for he felt sure she never would have given him up, even to be a ward of the Lady Melisande. But Alain was obviously very excited to tell him, so Tanis obliged him by asking, "What is the bloodline then?"

Alain eyed him intently, turning suddenly close-mouthed. "It's an Agasi bloodline," he whispered with a conspiratorial grin. "Does that tell you anything?"

"Agasi," Tanis mused, tasting the word in relation to himself for the first time. Strangely, it fit.

"You still don't know?" Alain asked incredulously. "Are you sure you *want* to know?"

Tanis glared and punched Alain in the arm. "Burn you—yes! I want to know."

Alain laughed. "All right—don't say I didn't warn you. But you already know the bloodline, Tanis. Just think—who's the most famous female truthreader in the realm?"

Tanis frowned. For some reason, all he could think of was Raine D'Lacourte, but there weren't any famous female D'Lacourtes. And then...he had it. He looked up at Alain. "But..." he said, unable to countenance putting the two pieces together. "But I only know of one female truthreader: the Empress of Agasan."

Alain looked triumphant. "Valentina van Gelderan."

Tanis sort of stared stupidly at him. Then he barked a laugh. "But you're not suggesting...well that's just absurd!"

Alain crossed arms and gave him a supremely confident look. "Believe what you like, Tanis of Giverny, but your mother could only have been descended from the imperial line of Agasan. Not that this is a narrow field, by any means," he added more to himself than to Tanis, as if he meant to pursue the matter regardless of Tanis' interest, "for the Empress has nine brothers and sisters and twenty-seven first cousins, not to mention her own six daughters and five sons, most of whom have grandchildren by now. Still..." he gave Tanis a smile brimming with confidence. "It's a start."

"This is ridiculous," Tanis protested.

But Alain wasn't to be put off. "It's quite without question, Tanis," he insisted. "Like it or not, *you're* a van Gelderan!"

Alyneri retrieved her hands from Sandrine's for the last time and opened her eyes. What the woman had shown her was...amazing. She was certain it was a different working than the zanthyr had used to save Ean, but she knew it could mean life or death for her future charges. What's more...

I can Pattern!

It was only a single pattern she'd learned—nothing like the repertoire an Adept must accumulate to consider himself a wielder—but she was infinitely proud of that one pattern which she now could command. She drew in a deep breath as if surfacing from the ocean depths and exhaled slowly, feeling immensely tired but also very accomplished. "Thank you, Sandrine," she whispered gratefully, lifting her gaze to meet the older woman's. "Thank you for this gift, and for your help in mastering it."

Sandrine smiled. "My pleasure, *Duchesse*. It is a simple pattern, but one I have found highly useful."

Alyneri nodded to the obvious truth of that. She rose and walked to a table where a decanter of wine and two goblets had been set for them, along with a meal that had gone untouched. Even in her weariness she remained too excited for hunger to take root.

"You should eat something," Sandrine said from close behind her. Alyneri started as the woman's hands found her shoulders again. Sandrine's thumbs moved in slow strokes down the back of Alyneri's neck, and the Duchess admitted it was unexpectedly soothing. "Working patterns that are outside our nature uses our lifeforce in ways to which we aren't accustomed." Her hands moved to massage Alyneri's shoulders. "You feel the thrill of the pattern, an echo of its inherent power. It is invigorating...to some even an aphrodisiac. But it is also deceptively draining."

Alyneri resisted the urge to relax into the woman's capable hands. "Sandrine..." she managed.

The Healer laughed throatily. "I know," she murmured, moving closer still to Alyneri to whisper, "you are staying faithful to your betrothed." One hand traced the line of Alyneri's neck, around to her collarbone, and continued lower still... "But think of this, *Duchesse*," she breathed, her lips touching Alyneri's ear, feather soft, "when you lay with a woman, with whom intercourse is impossible, what infidelity exists?"

As Alyneri tried to fathom that twisted logic, Sandrine turned her so they faced each other. Alyneri blanched—the woman had undone the laces of her dress, revealing her ample bosom. "What happened to Chastity?" Alyneri managed, so startled she could barely think straight. "Is it—is it not one of your Cardinal Virtues?'

"Chastity does not mean celibacy, your Grace," Sandrine returned, placing two hands on Alyneri's hips to draw her nearer. "And my patron is Temperance, not Chastity. I gave you an invaluable gift, did I not," she inquired, letting one hand come to rest boldly on Alyneri's breast, massaging lightly. "It is only fitting that you return the favor—"

"*Madame!*" came a voice at the door, which was accompanied by a fervent knocking. "*Madame la Duchesse?*"

Alyneri gasped in relief and tore out of Sandrine's clutches. "Yes, I am coming," she said breathlessly as she rushed across the room. Opening the door a fraction, she found a steward waiting, a young man of perhaps ten and six. He bowed and then asked, "*Madame la Duchesse, c'est Sandrine du Préc par les vôtres?*"

Alyneri glanced fretfully over her shoulder but was relieved to see Sandrine had fully composed herself. "*Je suis voici,*" Sandrine replied smoothly, coming toward the door. Then she continued in Veneisean, "Is it the Comtesse?"

He answered in kind, "Yes, Madam. The time comes, I am told."

Sandrine looked to Alyneri and arched a brow suggestively. "So. Shall we attend?"

"I think we must," Alyneri said, counting her blessings and making a mental note to thank the Comtesse—or perhaps the twins?—for her excellent timing. She nodded quickly to the steward, and he dutifully led the way.

FORTY-TWO

'I am the night that ends the day. I am Malorin'athgul.'

– *Sobra I'ternin*, Eleventh Translation, 1499aF, *Genesis, Book 5, Verse 10*

Shail'abhanáchtran stood before the mountain as the hot Avataren sunset smeared blood across the heavens. He watched heat waves rising off the scorched sands while he waited on his brother's pleasure.

Shail hated the heat.

Heat was life. Heat was creation. Heat was the energy of motion, motion leading to existence, existence to persistence, persistence to evolution, evolution to survival, survival to infinity.

Toward all of these, Shail was diametrically opposed.

The gilded feather twitched in his hand, a symptom of his malcontent. How did Rinokh stand the damnable place?

When at last the sun had vanished beneath the rim of the world, Rinokh spoke. His deeply resonant voice was the rumble of distant thunder. "What is it you want, Shail'abhanáchtran?"

Knowing how his brother's mind worked, perhaps better than the others did, Shail replied, "I come with a challenge, Eldest."

Rinokh yawned and shook his shoulders as he roused from his sleep. An avalanche of sharp stones tumbled down the mountain, raising dust to blot the bleeding skies. "I am very busy," he replied, the roar of a raging fire, "and you are singularly uninteresting."

"Then let me inspire you, for my challenge is beyond even Darshan."

"I find that unlikely," Rinokh muttered. He sneezed with the avalanche's dust, and the desert shrubs shook with a violent wind.

"Why else would Darshan refuse action except to hide his own ineptitude," Shail countered acidly. "Our brother has become weak, Rinokh, drunk in the adoration of his mindless hoards."

Rinokh said nothing for a long time. A hot desert wind stirred Shail's long ebony hair as he stood before the mountain. The stars were piercing through the dying sun's haze before Rinokh spoke again. Finally then, with the fall of night, he said, "I am listening."

"I have found a man," Shail told him.

"I have found and eaten many of them," Rinokh replied.

"This man can unwork things."

"Good," replied Rinokh, and the ground shook with his pleasure. "Let him be put to task for us and the sooner we shall be done with this tiresome realm."

"He cannot be turned to our cause," Shail said.

Rinokh roared in outrage. Across the desert, sleeping children quailed in their dreams. As the echo of his anger faded, Rinokh growled, "*All creatures may be turned to our cause*."

"I challenge you to try, brother," Shail said with a private smile, knowing his purpose was already achieved.

Rinokh snarled. Across the distant sands, nomadic tribesmen drew their weapons and stared into the night in terror. "You dare to assume I cannot bend these mongrel races to my whims?" Rinokh snapped.

"This man will be different," Shail insisted. He alone remembered the last time they'd found and faced such a man as this Ean val Lorian, for that time it had been Shail who was almost undone. More quietly, he hissed, "You will see."

Abruptly Rinokh laughed, long and deep. The land quaked beneath Shail's boots, and a fissure split the parched earth and splintered away, spearing toward the deep desert sands, lightening trapped within terra firma. "Watch and learn, youngest," Rinokh said then. "Learn well, for there are none who may resist our power."

Abruptly the mountain moved. Shail was battered by gale-force winds as the enormous black shadow lifted from the earth and rose slowly into the sky, blotting out the budding stars.

Shail watched the mountain go. "Good hunting, brother," he said.

FORTY-THREE

'Do not seek to know thy future; seek instead to make it.'

– Attributed to the *angiel* Epiphany

Tanis heard a light knock upon his bedroom door and turned as a chambermaid entered carrying a tea tray balanced on one hip and in her other hand his navy jacket, the gift from Prince Ean, pressed and laundered. "I'm here to help you ready for dinner, monsieur," the young woman said in heavily accented Common as she set the silver tray upon a table and laid the jacket across the bed.

"Oh," the lad replied, frowning. "I told the other maid yesterday that I didn't need anyone to help me." Indeed, much like her Grace, Tanis felt uncomfortable being waited upon hand and foot, and certainly he was capable of dressing himself.

"It's my pleasure, monsieur," the young woman replied, missing the point completely. She walked to the armoire and began selecting clothing to match his jacket.

There was something about the girl that unsettled him, but the lad couldn't put his finger on what it was. Thinking tea would do him good, however, Tanis walked to the table and poured a cup. The aromas of orange and cinnamon filled the room as steam rose languidly from the dark liquid. He sipped it as he watched the girl across the way, fretful of what it was that so bothered him. She was humming as she readied his garments, a somewhat tuneless song. Her thoughts seemed strangely quiet, as if she was purposely not thinking of anything—

The truth came to him just as the cup slipped from his hands and crashed upon the table. He hadn't even felt it fall from his fingers.

"*Bon sang!*" exclaimed the maid, rushing over. She grabbed a linen napkin and began soaking up the spill.

Tanis felt suddenly too lightheaded to confront the maid. He reached for the chair behind him and almost missed it.

"*Par bleu*, monsieur," murmured the girl as she met his eyes for the first time. "Are you all right? Shall I call for the Healer?" yet he knew that her concern was empty.

"*You…*," Tanis managed as the room began to tilt and spin. His heart was racing, and he couldn't seem to find his breath. He leaned back against the chair and shut his eyes, only that made it worse.

When he tried to sit forward again, he found he couldn't move—it wasn't that he was paralyzed; more that the thoughts from his brain couldn't seem to reach his arms or legs.

Tanis lifted frightened eyes to the maid.

"Belladonna," she advised, gazing down at him gently. "Tis a dangerous plant. A little too much and that's zee end of you. But don't fret, monsieur," she added, reaching a hand to brush his cheek. "My mother taught me all about zee Belladonna. You will sleep, yes, and wake with zee head aching but no more the worse for wear."

Tanis felt all fluttery inside, but the racing of his heart and the swimming sensation in his head were almost secondary to the anger and confusion he felt upon realizing she'd poisoned him. "Why…?" he croaked as the edges of his vision started fading to black.

"Twenty shiny gold reasons, monsieur," she replied with a shrug. "Zee man, he says to keep you out of zee way, yes? And he promised me gold tonight." She took Tanis's arm and looped it around her shoulder as she hefted him out of the chair. With a grunt, she half-dragged and half-carried the lad toward the armoire. "Tis enough…to buy passage…to Kroth," she managed as she labored across the room, "and from there? Zee world, monsieur!"

The maid must've been stouter than she looked, for she managed to stuff an unresisting Tanis into the armoire with a minimal amount of grunting and closed the door on the lad, sealing him into darkness. Tanis barely heard the latch click into place, for he was already drifting away.

Ean was just finishing a quiet dinner with his men when Matthieu appeared in the doorway of the dining hall and waved urgently to him. Ean exchanged a look with Fynn, and the royal cousin rose to join him as he walked over to Matthieu.

"*Bonsoir*," Ean said.

"*Bonsoir*," Matthieu replied brusquely. He cast a suspicious gaze around the room and then motioned Ean to follow. "I must show you something, *mon ami*."

The two princes followed the Veneisean officer through the guards' quarters and into the estate's chandlery, which smelled strongly of tallow but was quite empty of prying ears and eyes. Matthieu shut the door and bolted it, then spun to face them. His blue eyes scanned Ean and Fynn, wherein he pulled something from within his vest and handed it to the prince with a flourish of fingers. "This came for you, *mon ami*."

Ean took the piece of cloth and read the inscription penned there in smudged ink.

We know who you are. We have the boy. Be at Les Gros Putain before midnight if you would see him live.

Ean felt a pang of dismay. "Where did you find this?"

"It was tied to *le Comte's* gate." Matthieu clicked his tongue distastefully and shook his head.

"The Fat Whore," Fynn read aloud, translating the last words of the note as he read them over Ean's shoulder. "Sounds like a promising establishment."

"It is zee worst sort of place," Matthieu said, eyeing Fynn doubtfully. "But zee note, it is for you, no? '*We know who you are*,'" Matthieu quoted in a disgusted tone. "Who else could zis offensive note be for if not *le prince déguisé*?"

"I am more concerned about the threat to Tanis," Ean said quietly. "Have you sent men in search of him?"

"*De trajet!* But of course!" Matthieu threw out a hand, declaring, "But *le Comte's* estates are vast, *mon ami*. The young man could be anywhere. I will tell you zis, 'owevaire," he added, leaning in with a stern expression, "zee lad has not left zee grounds. Of *zis* you can be certain."

Ean stared at the note again feeling anger swelling in waves. *We have the boy*... If anything happened to Tanis, he would never forgive himself.

"Ean..." Fynn was staring suspiciously at him. "You're not considering this."

"No, no, no, *no!*" declared Matthieu. "I did not bring zis ridiculous note to encourage you to follow zee dictates of a lunatic! Only to warn you that someone knows you are 'ere. *Mon dieu*." Matthieu snatched the fabric from Ean's hands and shoved it back inside his vest. "Do not think of it, *mon ami*! Zee boy is no doubt off upon an adventure, but my men will find him, never you fear."

But Ean knew too well that the people after him had ways and means at their disposal that were unimaginable to a common soldier; until they found Tanis, the note's declaration could hardly be contested. "I won't compromise Tanis's life, Matthieu," the prince said quietly.

"Ean—" Fynn protested.

Ean silenced him with a penetrating look. "I won't sacrifice his life for mine, Fynn," Ean growled. "I won't do it." He looked to Matthieu, who seemed defiant but ill-inclined to argue. "If you would keep me here, Matthieu," he said in a tone of quiet determination, "you'd best find my truthreader before the time claimed on that 'ridiculous' note, because ere midnight, I will be gone." With that, he pushed past Matthieu, unbolted the heavy door and threw it wide as he stalked through.

Alyneri knew the birth was not going well. The Comtesse Claire had been in active labor before the midwives even called for Sandrine. By the time Alyneri and the other Healer arrived, Claire was pushing; but after several hours of effort, her labor stalled. She'd strained with contractions throughout the rest of the evening, but now even the urge to push had ebbed.

As midnight neared, Alyneri stood watching Claire toss with fitful sleep while Sandrine spoke with the midwives in hushed tones. The Comtesse was pale, weak from the last two difficult months. No doubt it had been a challenge how to ease her pregnancy when her body was so belabored by the two growing babes.

While Alyneri understood the need to keep Claire bedridden lest she lose the twins too early, so also did she know that inactivity weakened the mother immensely. She had not personally delivered many babies—a Healer was loathe to step on the toes of midwives who lived for no other purpose than bringing new life into the world—but Farshideh had spent many years in the profession and 'knew a thing or two about birthing babes.'

'These Northmen with their pampered wives,' Farshideh had always complained. *'Don't they know how much work it is to birth a babe? Would they expect an apprentice blacksmith to pound out the oxen yoke when his arms are bare more than a boy's skinny bone? Would they put the pageboy in the arena with the knight when he could hardly lift a sword? Yet they expect their lady wives to push a melon through a mouse hole—with naught*

but her belly to do the work—when she's been cosseted and coddled so long she can nary lift her own cup of tea…'

Alyneri gazed worriedly at the tossing woman. Perhaps Claire's labor had stalled because her strength was failing her, as Sandrine thought; but what if the cause was another source?

Alyneri moved to the bedside and sat down next to the Claire. The Comtesse was not a young woman, being nearly twice Alyneri's age, and Alyneri could tell just from looking at her that her muscles had atrophied during the long months of bed rest. She took the woman's hand in hers and closed her eyes, letting her mind find the rhythm of Claire's pulse, sinking her awareness deeply into the other woman's body until she felt a part of it, until she heard the thunderous beating of Claire's heart and the roaring wind of her breath.

Finding rapport, Alyneri searched first for the babes. Their hearts were tiny but vibrant drums beating a furious rhythm so much faster than their mother's. She tried to see more of them, but the womb kept diverting her. Her vision slid past and around the womb, water over oilcloth, unable to penetrate its secrets. Frustrated, Alyneri tried several more times to pierce through the lining, but to no avail. She could not reach the children.

Claire stirred, but Alyneri remained deep in rapport. She sought now to know how the mother was faring, sending her awareness into heart and lungs, into her kidneys and bowel. Assured that her functions remained stable, Alyneri pulled her awareness back from the bowels, lingering now in the energy centers, feeling the rush of Claire's very lifeforce along its channels, signals firing from brain to toes, a continuous charge of lightning caught within a single frame. She was always amazed and awed by the majesty that was the human body.

When Alyneri was satisfied with what she'd discovered, she withdrew her consciousness from rapport. She opened her eyes to find Claire watching her with a weary but grateful smile.

"How are they?" she whispered.

"They are well," Alyneri reassured her. "Their hearts beat strong."

Claire nodded, smiled. Then she swallowed and asked, "And how am I?"

"You are stronger still."

Claire exhaled a little cry that was half a whimper and half a laugh. Her gaze was beseeching, tired, fearful. "You…you aren't just saying that to comfort me in my last hours?"

"If it is a comfort, that is well," Alyneri said with a gentle smile, "because it is the truth."

Sandrine approached with the lead midwife, Ghislain, in tow. "Did you find something while in rapport, *Duchesse?*"

It wasn't exactly a challenge, but Alyneri could tell Sandrine did not expect her to discover anything she had not already learned. "Only that her lifeforce is strong," Alyneri answered. "We should encourage the labor to continue."

"And that is exactly what we're going to do," Ghislain declared approvingly as she approached carrying a goblet of dark liquid. "Black cohosh, goldenseal, squaw vine and red raspberry leaf," she told Claire. "A potent cocktail to encourage those babes on out into the world."

Claire pushed up weakly on one elbow and drank the potion in slow sips. Then she lay back again, exhausted. "How long, Sadie?" she whispered after a while.

"Twenty and one hours, my lady," answered one of her ladies-in-waiting from across the room.

"Twenty and one," Claire repeated wistfully. "Jean-Pierre was born in twelve and Lucien in six. Something is wrong, Ghislain."

"Twins have a knack for wanting to stay together, milady," Ghislain advised. "They share everything, even souls, some say. Born of the same egg, their hearts beating as one. Twins must be coaxed into the world."

But Claire shook her head. "No," she managed as her face grew paler still. "No, something is—" but her words were choked off as she sucked in her breath with a gasp that erupted into a scream.

Because she had so nearly been in rapport, Alyneri sensed what was happening even before the blood flowed onto the bed in a sanguineous flood. "She's hemorrhaging!" She grabbed Sandrine's arm with her surprise, and the other Healer rushed to press her hands to Claire's shoulders while Ghislain shouted for linens and water and a mad commotion ensued.

Alyneri quickly shut herself off from the noise and pushed hands to Claire's belly, spearing her awareness down into rapport with an urgency she'd never felt before.

"I have hold of her," Sandrine murmured in Alyneri's ear, but her tone was grim. "You've got to get those babies out *now*."

"*How?*" Alyneri hissed.

"Any way you can!" snapped Sandrine.

Alyneri silently cursed and cast her awareness again toward the impenetrable womb. It made no sense that this one part of Claire's body would remain opaque when all else was so transparent. She tried again to send her sight through the uterine wall, but she might as well have been poking a cow hide with a rounded stick for all the difference it made.

Think! Think! She told herself desperately. *You're smarter than this!*

Alyneri could sense Sandrine in rapport with Claire. The other Healer was a powerful presence, strong as sunlight spearing over a ridge. She had tapped into Claire's energy channels and was monitoring them closely. Alyneri knew if it came to it, Sandrine would push her own energy into and along those channels to keep Claire alive, but she could only push so far before Sandrine would be in danger herself. Alyneri knew the woman would not make that sacrifice.

Then something her mother once told her came to mind. '*The womb is a world unto itself.*'

Of course! Alyneri quit trying to pierce through the uterine wall, which would necessarily be thick enough to survive all penetration save from the sharpest steel, and instead searched for the opening where the placenta fed through the womb. Down, she swept then, following the trail of life-giving blood until—

"It's detached," she whispered under her breath, hardly knowing the words were said aloud. Where the placenta had detached from the uterine wall, Alyneri's awareness spilled into the womb and saw the babes at last. They were curled head to toe and toe to head and filled the sack so tightly there was not an inch to spare. *He's twisted*, she realized, noting how the lowest babe had his head turned in the wrong position and couldn't enter the birth canal.

But what can I do?

"Alyneri, you must *hurry*," Sandrine hissed, the strain evident in her tone. "*Find a way.*"

Alyneri had been so deeply in rapport that she hadn't noticed that Claire had stopped screaming. It was a bad sign.

Alyneri desperately reviewed her craft, images flashing through her mind while she tried to think of anything to help Claire. She could make the woman's body change and grow, but she could do nothing for the babes. She'd never attempted to achieve rapport with a child still in its mother's womb, without the benefit of tactile contact. Yet without this, she knew all three would die.

Alyneri could already sense Sandrine working to stop the hemorrhaging, but the babies would die in the womb without their lifeline and take their mother with them.

Alyneri's head was already aching from the effort, but she pressed on, finding strength in her purpose to save three lives this night. She closed off all sensory perception from her own body until she knew only those of Claire's. Secluded within the quiet of the womb, hearing only the noise of the flowing of blood in Claire's veins, she cast a line for the babe, her own lifeforce seeking that of the unborn child's.

Once. Twice. Again.

Over and over she cast for him, managing only the most tenuous thread, a gossamer wisp that moved on the barest breath; too hard a breeze would banish it. Her head was pounding, and her breath came ragged in her lungs; she climbed a mental mountain that drained her body no less than a real climb would have. But she pressed on, throwing the line, throwing the line, throwing the line.

And then…finally…

It stuck.

She had a sense of him.

Exhaling a ragged sigh of relief as she drew the babe gently into rapport, Alyneri inwardly wept, *If only I had a clue how to make him move!*

Ean walked the length of the Comte's long patio while the last vestiges of sunset bled into darkness and night settled upon the world. As the moon rose from behind the Eidenglass, dense clouds rolled in to obscure it, taking away what starlight lingered, until at last Ean stared into a vast canyon of night. Below him, the twinkling city lights seemed a spread of fallen stars, their celestial homes abandoned for ripe, earthly pleasures.

He had waited as long as he could to give Matthieu's men time to find Tanis—he'd even sent his own men in search as well, though Fynn had equally gone missing when last they scoured the estate—but thus far there was no sign of the lad.

Ean was conflicted by the choice before him. Creighton had already died for him; his companions knowingly risked their lives just traveling with him, and he would be damned if he let anything happen to Tanis merely because someone thought his skin too precious to risk.

Yet...he knew it was certainly a trap laid for him specifically. As much as he resented the knowledge, he understood that his life *was* important—to his family and his kingdom in the very least. T'was the height of irresponsibility then to walk knowingly into a trap and risk his father's kingdom in the bargain. The dilemma leveraged Ean's honor and pride against his deepest sense of duty, and it was an agonizing choice.

Ean pushed a hand through his cinnamon hair and lamented, *If I stay and Tanis dies, I will bear his blood upon my conscience for all eternity.*

Walking to the patio's edge, he gripped the stone railing tightly, battling over what he must do. *If I go, there is a chance we will both survive. If I do nothing, I will never forgive myself.*

And if you die and all is lost? his conscience posed.

Ean gritted his teeth. *Then I shall not die!* he wished to say, but somehow he couldn't bring himself to such glibness. The threats against him were too real—the wound of Creighton's loss bled ceaselessly, a constant drain on his energies. He often pushed memories of his dearest friend from mind, for even the good memories were too painful to recall.

By the same token, he wasn't sure his sanity would survive another such loss.

Ean spun from the railing and made his way down the long, stepped staircase toward the stables, his shoulders hunched against his own dreadful thoughts.

How do you bear it, father? he wondered miserably, the thought coming painfully in his chest, constricting his throat. *How do you endure knowing your failures—your mistakes—meant the end of your sons? How do you keep pressing onward with your life?*

He reached the yard and headed for the stables, his gaze on his boots as they trod dully across shadowed cobblestones. So it was that he nearly ran into Matthieu, who had the prudence to sidestep out of the prince's path.

Ean drew up short, startled, but it was Matthieu who recoiled from Ean's tormented gaze; it speared him, drawing the blood of compassion. "*Mon dieu,*" exclaimed the soldier, his long face caught in a look of sympathy. He took Ean by both shoulders. "Why do you fret so, *mon ami?* I told you, we will find the boy."

Wavering upon the sharp edge between grief and anger, Ean grabbed Matthieu's arm in turn. "My cousin eluded your men, Matthieu," he said tightly. "How can you be certain these others did not also?"

"Yes, yes, we know all about your cousin," Matthieu returned. He took Ean by the arm. "Twice he slipped through our walls, but not without our notice, *mon ami.* Trust that we are watching this spot—a servant's private entrance—and save for your cousin, none but *le Comte's* staff have come or gone through it."

Ean held his gaze with hard, angry eyes. "I cannot risk it, Matthieu." He jerked free his hand and pushed on toward the stables. "The hour has already passed."

"I have my ordairz, *mon seigneur.*" Matthieu sounded grim. "I cannot allow you to leave the walls."

"How do you plan to stop me?" Ean returned not waiting for an answer, and Matthieu did not give him one until he emerged from the stables leading Caldar by the bit. A long line of stolid-faced guards stood barring his way to the gates.

Ean slowed. He settled a penetrating gaze on a dour-faced Matthieu. "So you mean to hold me prisoner, Matthieu?" he demanded bleakly. "Is this how you choose to represent *le Comte* to my father?"

Matthieu grimaced. He stalked forward and hissed in a low voice, "I did not ask for this confrontation, *mon seigneur*, but you 'ave forced me to take sterner measures. I 'ave my ordairz and my duty."

"As I have mine," Ean returned resolutely. He drew his sword with an ominous scrape of steel.

Immediately Matthieu's men replied in kind.

"*Mon dieu*!" Matthieu exclaimed. He spun to his men and ordered, "*Ranger votre tireur d'épée!*" to which they sheathed their swords obediently. Matthieu turned back to Ean looking pained. "*Mon seigneur*, please...tis for your safety that we—"

"*Mon Capitaine!*" called one of Matthieu's men from afar. He rushed up, pushing through the line of soldiers. "*Nous établir les garcon!*"

We found him.

Ean's anger drained away, replaced by a sense of relief that left him feeling empty. "Where?" he demanded, his shoulders sagging as he looked to the man.

Cayal pushed through behind the Veneisean. "In his own armoire, my lord," the soldier reported somewhat breathlessly. Upon seeing Ean's confused expression, he added, "The lad was drugged, but he seems otherwise unharmed. He sleeps still."

Ean turned Matthieu a heated look. For all the man's insistence that the boy remained upon the property, someone *had* gotten to him.

Before Matthieu could respond, more shouting at the gate drew everyone's attention, and just as Ean was lifting his gaze above the line of soldiers to attend the commotion, a huge explosion rocked the court beyond *le Comte's* walls. A ball of flame rocketed skyward, rimmed in smoke; the concussion sent everyone stumbling.

In the next moment, Ean was running for the gate with Cayal and Matthieu's men close at his side. The prince was in the lead as the mass of soldiers pushed through the gates, but Ean drew up short on the street beyond.

The building across from the estate was engulfed in flame. It was as if the entire three-story property had been doused in naphtha. Evil, acrid smoke billowed from third-floor windows and rooftop.

Immediately Matthieu was shouting orders in his native tongue, sending his men scurrying for fire-buckets, brooms and sand, while others rushed to restore order in the street where a host of locals were funneling out of adjacent buildings to mill in confusion and dismay. Ean heard a single scream emanate from among the roar of flames and was off like a shot across the street. He heard Matthieu calling urgently behind him, but nothing registered beyond the sound of terror in that scream and the sense of peril that compelled him to act.

He had the presence of mind to placed hands upon the front door before he kicked it in and dove into the smoke-filled room beyond. Billowing ash burned his throat, choking with acrid heat, but again he heard that scream and pushed deeper into the building. Finding his way almost blindly down a hall, he reached the end and kicked in another door. Blinking tears from his stinging eyes, he finally focused to find a young girl and an even younger boy huddled in the far corner.

There was no sense in their being inside when the rest of the place was deserted, and something of this strangeness registered in the back of Ean's mind, but the terror of the scene was far more compelling. He rushed to gather the children into his arms, murmuring words of reassurance. The girl burst into terrified tears, and the little boy whimpered, but the prince held one in each arm and carried them out into the hall.

"That way," rasped the little girl in her native tongue, pointing toward the back of the building and a door at the far end. Ean rushed for it, coughing in the charred air, feeling the heat singing down from the fiery layers above. He emerged from the building into the rear court just in time. With a scream of timbers, the roof of the hallway collapsed behind them, sending a fury of fiery air billowing out in chase.

The concussion pitched Ean forward onto his knees, and the children went flying from his arms to land harmlessly on a plot of leaf-strewn grass.

"See," said a voice from behind as Ean pushed up coughing and sputtering. "Told you it would work."

Something hard hit his head in a blinding flash, and he fell forward into darkness.

The moon was on its decline as Fynn trod along the Rue de la Fontaine on his way to The Lion and Lamb, a popular gathering place of the gentry of Chalons-en-Les Trois. After their altercation among the candles which Ean cut short by a dramatic exit, Matthieu had been no less demanding that Fynn remain upon the property as he had of Ean, even going so far as to threaten to lock Fynn in his rooms if he attempted to leave. Fynn had let one of Matthieu's men tail him the rest of the night, but he easily lost him when it was time to make his escape. The night called to him as it did to the nightingale, though Fynn was less inclined to sing until round about sunrise.

Usually he enjoyed his nocturnal excursions immensely—the anticipation of wine and women was a heady fragrance—but that night his stomach had that feeling again. What he'd once considered a boon felt more a curse in recent weeks. The only thing that dampened that damnable fluttering was a good Volga, which only increased his urgency to acquire the vintage. Not that he needed any reason for his daily libations—the glory of the substance itself was reason enough—though Fynn admitted that 'imbibing for medicinal value' did have a nice ring to it.

He was testing a fictional conversation with Alyneri in his head when his train of thought was disturbed by a doleful dirge floating from off to the east. Upon the near corner, a crossroad opened into a square filled with seated shapes, the culprits emitting the dismal tune.

In the center of the small square, five roped columns stood atop a pentagonal-shaped marble slab. Though Fynn couldn't see the steps leading up to the slab, hidden as they were beneath a host of candlelit offerings, he knew the roofless temple for what it was—a portal used by Nodefinders. The mourners in the square raised their voices somewhat inharmoniously as the dirge crescendoed to its gloomy end. A cloaked figure stood then and started speaking to the group, but Fynn was too far away to make out the words. He didn't need to, anyway, for the message of the gathering was clear. All around the land people were mourning the Adept race.

That's a black irony, isn't it? Fynn thought disagreeably as he continued on his way, leaving the mourners in the square to begin another lament. *The Adept race is already dying, but now somebody's all about hurrying them along on their way.*

Fynn knew the stories of the missing. Even before he'd left Agasan, the Empress had leveled strident regulations restricting the movement of Adepts in the empire 'for their own protection,' and it didn't take much looking around to see how diminished man's way of life had become. Never mind that mad Prophet Bethamin and his seditious doctrines and freakish Marquiin—they were just salt in the wound. No, it was places like these, ancient places whose purposes had lost their meaning, relics of a better day remembered by a dying few, that really brought the matter home.

Once—long before Fynn's day—the portals were in constant use, run by the Espial's Guild. A man could travel from Veneisea to Faroqhar in a single afternoon. Now such travels required a king's ransom and friends within the Guild. There were barely enough Nodefinders to manage the affairs of queens and kings, much less merchant princes, who were relegated to such old-fashioned means of transporting their wares as wagon caravans and galleon ships.

On the plus side, the pirating had really picked up.

A rising wind accosted Fynn as he neared the end of the Rue de la Fontaine, but the breeze had cleared the heavy clouds off the moon, and Fynn's eyes alighted with pleasure on the moonlit façade of his destination. Thoughts of the Volga that awaited him quickly dispelled his somber mood, and the briskness returned to his step as he went forth to take his medicine.

When Ean came to, he was in the back of a water-wagon wedged between sloshing barrels. Men were talking in the front, and he strained to hear them over the sound of clopping horse hooves, sloshing water, and the slow creaking of wood.

"...hit him hard enough?" one man was asking in Veneisean.

"Yes, I'm sure," snapped a second.

Ean was sure, too. His head was pounding and he felt vaguely sick to his stomach. He closed his eyes and tried to will it to settle.

"The Karakurt claims he's a wielder," said the first.

"And so?" returned the second. Ean heard the scrape of curtain hooks as the cloth separating the two compartments was drawn aside, and he was glad he'd already shut his eyes. "Doesn't matter," said the second after a moment, closing the curtain again. "I bound him so tight, he'd have to be a Delver to get out of it."

"I still think you should've hit him harder," the first grumbled.

In the conversation lull that followed, Ean discovered what the second man meant, for his attempt to move any body part south of his chin resulted in nary the slightest motion. It was quite a different working feeling from the Shade's compulsion. He could feel his toes, he could tense the muscles in his legs and arms—clearly they were still under his volition—but to move them from their position was quite beyond him. *Bound...but how?*

Suddenly it occurred to him that he was *again* being taken—spirited away from his companions, from those who would help him. Again trapped, *again* in mortal peril.

He couldn't allow that. He *wouldn't*.

It was the second time that desperation—that *necessity*—drew out an ability so deeply hidden it seemed merely born of instinct; the second time he began to see the pattern standing between himself and freedom.

This pattern was sharp-edged and knotty, all angles juxtaposed upon one another. It was an ugly, unnatural pattern, and Ean knew it was what he must unwork if he meant to be free of these men.

He concentrated upon his task, but this pattern was not so easily undone. Even the malevolent spell upon the Marquiin had been easier to access—no doubt its owner had never anticipated anyone trying to find and unwork it—while this pattern was clearly created to never be undone. Each jagged knot was painful to explore—as treacherous as a razor-edged barb and just as dense, and there were many of them.

Ean started sweating and his head pounded viciously every time he sent his consciousness again and again along the knife-edged planes, seeking where the pattern began and ended. But he only succeeded in ripping his mind to shreds, and finally he abandoned the task, exhausted and spent, the pain too great to endure any longer.

It was then, as he lay in defeated with his mind bleeding freely upon his frustration, that the pattern suddenly became clear.

It's like the strings of a marionette, all broken and crumbled. But instead of tensile strings, the puppet that was his body had been connected by slender straws, all of them now tangled and bent back upon themselves.

It must be in the center, he realized, *like the whole thing imploded, drawing all of its parts inward.*

So Ean looked there, in the densest mass of mangled straws, his bruised mind probing gingerly among the tangle mess, and at last he found it, that nebulous point where the pattern both began and ended.

He attempted to take hold of the end of the pattern then, but his throbbing skull and the nausea in his stomach kept distracting him, making the thread as slippery as a mud-covered eel. To make matters worse, the wagon swung around a corner, and Ean's head thudded into the wooden side, sending a flare of pain down his neck and spine and nearly pitching him back into unconsciousness. Only by force of will did he hold onto awareness. He clung to the pain, clutching it close, letting its heat fuel his determination. Finally, after several long minutes, he felt some clarity returning.

Drawing in the breath of his will, the prince grabbed the end of that mental thread with fierce resolve, half expecting it to elude him yet again. But this time the pattern held, and after a moment's assurance that he did in fact have hold of it, Ean started his unworking. Without knowing why, as he unraveled the convoluted spell, he wrapped the falling threads around one mental hand, like winding in a ball of string.

It wasn't long before he could move his feet, then his knees, legs, his fingers… finally he had the last of it in hand, the very beginning of the pattern, the final lingering touch of its force holding his head to the wooden boards. Ean pulled with all his determination and strength combined, straining to lift the final piece of the spell…and then it was done. He felt it release him, and he exhaled a great, shuddering breath of relief.

In his mind's eye, he now held a diffuse ball of energy, but in actual fact, he held the entire pattern conceptually within his grasp. He wasn't sure quite what to do with it, so he cast it spiraling away from him with a mental shove.

The men in front were silent as Ean rolled onto hands and knees. Being careful to make no sound, he slithered between the barrels toward the back of the wagon. By providence alone, just as he was climbing over the low rear of the wagon, he caught the glint of a familiar jewel protruding from beneath the struts supporting one of the barrels.

Epiphany must be watching over me after all, he thought and he snatched his sword just as the weight of his falling body pulled him free of the wagon. Ean hit the cobblestones and rolled, hugging his sword flat against his chest. Then he scrambled into the shadows and sat with his head resting against the plastered wall, watching warily as the horse-drawn wagon continued on down the hill and out of sight.

He lingered there long enough to catch his breath and be certain he wasn't going to throw up. While he waited, he fingered his head and found his hair damp with blood. *Not a good sign.* A stupor threatened at the edges of his awareness, and he knew it would be all too easy to slip into its welcoming embrace. *Get up.Get up.Get up.*

Ean pushed to his feet unsteadily and looked around. He was in an unfamiliar part of town, and the merchant street was barren of people, its dilapidated shops shuttered for the night. On a far corner several blocks away, Ean saw the wan light of a tavern spilling across the broken cobblestones. It was in the downhill direction, however, and he knew that the Comte's estates crowned the city heights. Pulling up the hood of his cloak, hunching against the pain he was feeling as much as the weight of the empty night, Ean headed off.

The moon was on its decline as Fynn lounged by the fire in the private game room of The Lion and Lamb. Velvet-upholstered couches and low settees adorned the long room, most of them decorated with local courtesans and their patrons. While Fynn admired the view, he more enjoyed the Lamb's selection of superior Volgas, one of which he was just then appreciating with every long, languorous sip.

He'd closed his eyes to better appreciate the complex flavor—blackberry, stone fruits, the slightest hint of chocolate—when a shadow befell him. He was forced to abandon his vision of bathing in a pool of wine while ten wanton beauties fought over who got to sex him up next—*Because, let's face it, what good is a virgin who doesn't know shite about fellatio?*—in order to see who'd come calling.

Feeling cheated, Fynn opened his eyes with a rebuke on the edge of his tongue, but when he saw the beauty standing over him, he wondered if he was still somehow in the dream.

"Bonsoir, my lord," said the striking brunette. She caught one fingernail in the corner of her mouth and swept him with large hazel eyes, adding in her native Veneisean, "You are all alone?"

Fynn sat up and swung his feet off the couch. "Dreadfully alone," he agreed in the same tongue, "and so sad."

She settled softly beside him, her breasts like pale fruit pressed against the bodice of her violet gown. "Why are you sad, my lord?"

Fynn sighed despondently. "My wife has left me for a minstrel. The tramp." He looked appealingly at her. "You would never leave me, would you? You seem the faithful type."

"I am most faithful," she whispered, leaning her cleavage toward him for his viewing pleasure, "and very, *very* eager to please. But alas," she said, pulling away just as Fynn was starting to salivate, "I, too, am sad."

"Why are you sad, my lovely?"

"It is trouble with my lover. He refuses to let me take another."

"Scandalous!" Fynn clucked.

She furrowed her delicate brows as she gazed at him. "I dare not think...you just seemed so noble, I thought...perhaps..."

Fynn jumped from his couch and even set down his wine. "Where is the scoundrel? Take me to him and I will free you from his treacherous bonds!"

She threw her arms about Fynn's neck. "Oh, my lord!" she cried gratefully as she pressed her breasts against his chest, adding breathlessly in his ear, "Whatever can I do to repay you?"

Fynn placed both hands on her hips looked her over generously. "I'm sure we'll think of something. Now...where is this walking dead man?"

"This way, my liberator...my *hero*," she murmured.

Fynn followed her down a hallway and up two flights of stairs. She reached a door and stood beside it, catching her finger worriedly between her teeth. Fynn grabbed her around the waist and pulled her close, eliciting a gasp and a little laugh. "A kiss for luck?"

She planted a long kiss upon his mouth, sweet with promise.

Fynn released her, squared his shoulders, drew his sword, and kicked in the door, which crashed resoundingly against the wall. He rushed into the room, sword upraised, and—

The door slammed behind him.

Across the room waited not a man, but a woman of indefinite age. She stood with her back to Fynn, dressed also in a violet gown but with a matching cloak trimmed in silver fox. Her dark hair was swept up and held with jeweled combs, and as she turned, Fynn saw the seven-pointed pendant resting upon her bosom.

"Ah, so," he said, lowering his blade. "What is the Brotherhood of the Seven Spies doing in Chalons-en-Les Trois?"

"We are everywhere," she returned evenly, yet settling him a disparaging look in response to his slanderous misuse of the name. "But tonight we act by request of another."

Fynn had no doubt who that would be. Raine D'Lacourte had fingers in every espionage organization in the realm.

She saw that Fynn understood. "Yes," she murmured, "his Excellency would see your cousin unharmed."

"How benevolent of him," Fynn remarked, unimpressed. "But Ean is hardly a child. There are kings his age."

"Young princes are as reckless as young kings," she returned, "and with less protection. Your cousin is in grave danger, my lord."

"Tell me something I don't know."

The woman arched a brow at him, conveying her displeasure with his less-than appreciative tone. "We gave the Comte D'Ornay specific instructions to detain the Duchess of Aracine and *all* of her entourage—but especially the young males among her guard—until the Vestal's agent could arrive."

"His agent?"

"His Excellency has sent an agent to protect the crown prince, but we have neither seen nor heard from him. We thought his Highness would be safe in the Ville de la Chesnaye, but we underestimated their tenacity. Right now Ean val Lorian walks the city streets while a Tyriolicci stalks him for sport."

Shadow take that fool of a man! "How?" Fynn demanded heatedly. "How did he get past the guards?"

"Treachery drew him forth," she replied, her eyes dark jewels in the dim light. "A fire, deliberately set in lure."

"What?" Fynn demanded, flabbergasted by the dangerous turn of events. "When? *Where?*"

"All that matters now, my lord, is that your cousin has fallen from the frying pan into the flames, as you say. The Tyriolicci waits only for the opportune moment."

Fynn swore under his breath again. "What happened to the bloody Geshaiwyn?" he grumbled. *At least they fight fair.*

"His Excellency told us only that the Tyriolicci stalk your cousin. Rest assured, if we've spotted the prince, so has the Wildling. We sent to alert *le Comte's* men as soon as we learned, but—" Abruptly her attention was drawn to the passing of the moon outside. "Hurry, my lord," she urged. "The hour grows late. He may strike at any moment."

Hissing a long stream of invective, Fynn spun on his heel and ran.

Ean hugged the shadows as he tried to find his way back to le Comte's estates. He feared they'd hurt his head worse than he thought, for he was disoriented to the city and uncertain where he was. He was sure he'd passed the last street corner already once, and he had an uneasy feeling that he was walking in circles.

Trying to break the cycle, he turned into a long and shadowed alley, immediately spotting a streetlamp at the other end. He was perhaps halfway through the alley when he saw a strange lump barring in way. Abruptly a form reared out of the shadows, and Ean reached for his sword.

"...Ean?"

The prince halted with his hand around his sword hilt. "Fynn?"

"Balls of Belloth!" Fynnlar crossed the distance between them in a rush and grabbed him by both shoulders, giving him a shake. "What are you doing out here, you wool-brained fool?" he hissed.

"I might ask the same of you." Ean looked past his cousin to the lump lying a few paces beyond. The man must've been dead for some time, for his blood had soaked into the earth, and he was well past odiferous. Pushing a hand to his throbbing head, Ean closed his eyes. He'd seen so much death since the last moon...so many lives lost, and for what? He couldn't fathom the events that spun violently around him, only knowing he was somehow caught in the whirlwind. At least a soldier knew what he was fighting for, but this…this was madness.

"Ean, are you unwell?"

"Hit my head pretty hard," the prince murmured, lifting tired eyes to refocus on his cousin. "I'll be all right."

"I thought he was you," Fynn said, indicating the dead man. He sounded both relieved and immensely annoyed. "It's what drew me into the alley. Come on. We'd best keep moving."

The prince shook off the numbness edging his thoughts and followed, leaving the nameless man to rot in peace. As they headed out onto the street, neither of them noticed the shadow leaping from rooftop to rooftop in silent pursuit, nor the tawny eyes gazing down from a high, shadowed alcove across the way.

The fog began rising from the river as they walked back toward the villa, fat fingers snaking up the hill to leach the color from the night. They reached a corner, and Fynn turned them onto a long boulevard winding uphill. There he paused and looked warily up and down the road. The cobbled street vanished around a bend several blocks ahead, the way lined with three-story flats whose windows were shuttered and dark.

"Fynn, what—" Ean began.

But Fynn grabbed his arm to halt his forward motion with a warning look—and almost too late. Sudden movement directly before Ean made him rear back with an intake of breath in the same moment that Fynn cried, "Wait!"

Something barely missed the prince as it darted past, leaving only the impression of its passing with a breath of wind.

"What was that?" the prince hissed in alarm. His vision sought to find the thing that had streaked by, searching for substance among the night. He could feel blood warming his neck, his head throbbing with every beat if his heart.

Fynn drew his sword wearing a dismal expression of impending doom. "He's toying with us," he growled grimly.

"Who is?" Ean whispered. He drew his sword as well and held it before him, though he doubted his reflexes with his head bleeding as it was.

"The Tyriolicci," Fynn murmured.

"The what?" Ean spared a fast glance at him.

It was then that a strange whispering began, a whisk of silk across the rough edge of glass. It grew into a harsh whisper, angry and abrasive. The sound had prickly tentacles that pierced into the soft flesh of Ean's ears and twisted there, making him cringe.

Fynn hunched his shoulders and gritted his teeth. "*Shade and darkness*, but I hate Whisper Lords!" he snarled.

Something dark flew out of the shadows and darted across the street faster than the eye could follow. Ean swung his head after it in amazement. "What in Tiern'aval was *that?*"

Fynn narrowed his gaze as he held his sword before him. "A Whisper Lord."

Ean never imagined a man could move so fast. He swallowed his apprehension and prayed for clarity. The pounding in his skull seemed to lessen somewhat, but he feared it was only in comparison to the agonizing sound in his ears. And the whispering continued…tormenting, growing soundlessly louder until it shrieked inside Ean's mind, shattering his focus.

The Whisper Lord shot out of the shadows again, but this time Ean saw the man—tall and lithe, dressed in loose garments and a shredded black cloak that hissed as he ran. Ean swung his head to follow the man's path, refusing to blink lest he lose sight of him again. He forced his eyes to focus on the shadows where the man had gone.

There.

He saw him now, lurking against the wall, smiling around big white teeth. His leathery skin was black—so black that it looked charred—and his eyes were golden like the desert sands. His nose was as long and pointed as his chin, a mummer's mask made into flesh. The man locked gazes with him, and—

Suddenly they were nose to nose. Ean felt the heat of his breath in the same moment that the sting of steel pierced his flesh. Only when warmth began spreading across his chest did the prince realize he'd been marked.

Shade and darkness!

"Ean, he cut you!" Fynn grabbed him by the arm, but the prince shook him off.

"It's not deep," he said, startled as he gingerly probed the wound. He looked back to the shadows while his chest stung tightly, adding with grim determination, "He just wanted me to have a taste of what's to come."

"Shadow take the abominable creature," Fynn complained. As if in answer, the whispering swelled in intensity, eliciting groans from both men in unison. "Be ready!" Fynn warned through gritted teeth, and the prince watched Fynn rush to meet the advancing Wildling head-on.

The next few minutes were a blur. The Whisper Lord fought with long, stiletto daggers that speared like claws out of his gloves. His hands crisscrossed with amazing speed, never failing to find their mark on Fynn's person, while his body twisted and spun to avoid each of the latter's thrusts—which in turn only seemed to meet with the slashed silk of his garments. So fast did the Whisper Lord dart and cavort that Ean at first felt helpless to join in, for he could barely see the Wildling move until after it had happened, as if the sight had to bounce off the back of his eyes…as if he could only see the man's reflection.

Then Ean found his focus and rushed to help Fynn. Several fast strides took him into the battle.

The Whisper Lord marked him before he even got his blade around, a long swipe at the joining of neck and shoulder that burned bitterly. Ean realized that trying to use his sword alone would get him killed, so he pulled his dagger and dove in again with dual blades swinging. The Whisper Lord dodged like a jumping spider and managed in the same maneuver to slash a deep cut across Ean's thigh, his daggers flashing first with the silver of steel and then dark with blood. Ean snarled a curse and staggered into the wall, teeth clenched against the pain, for the wound was angry and deep.

Fynn wasn't faring much better. His shirt was shredded, his chest crisscrossed with bloody cuts, and though he fought as Ean did with a blade in each hand, he was tiring. The Wildling dodged and darted like the wind, spinning and striking with the ferocity of a viper with its tail pinned. The sound of their flashing blades connecting was a frenetic click and clatter, the scrape of steel upon steel as fast as a chef sharpening his knives.

Abruptly Fynn hissed a curse and threw himself backwards to avoid a deadly thrust that would've surely speared him through. Those spine-like blades sliced a chunk of flesh out of his side instead, a mortal cut that sent Fynn sprawling onto the stones. The royal cousin clenched his teeth and held one hand to his midriff, using the other to pull himself out of reach.

Desperation fueled Ean, bringing clarity at last through the dulling headache. He dove at the creature with renewed determination, his battered head forgotten in his haste to keep the man away from Fynn. His leg felt sluggish, however, and his foot was hard to control, but he forced through the pain and pushed the Whisper Lord back.

Yet even before they'd made much distance, Ean's arms were burning and his hands were slick with blood. He was perspiring as though they fought beneath the desert sun, and sweat stung his eyes, urging him to blink—but he dared not, knowing such was all the Wildling needed to make an end of him.

The man wore a malicious grin as they battled, and his golden gaze was flecked and sparkling against his face of leathery pitch. Sensing Ean's failing strength, he grinned even broader and began to chant in a voice like sand, "*Tur or'de rorum d'rundalin dalal! Tur or'de rorum d'rundalin dalal!*" Over and over while he pressed Ean now on the retreat; gleefully, like a madman.

And then he made a sudden thrust, and Ean jumped to avoid the slashing daggers that nearly missed his throat. He came down unevenly on his bad leg, and his knee buckled. Faltering, he barely spun out of reach, stumbling and hissing a curse, and still the man bore down on him. A swipe of his hand as Ean scrambled away, and three spiny daggers cut deeply across his back with their sharp fire. The Wildling's other hand darted for his throat again, but the prince veered and twisted so the blades caught his chin and cheek instead. Ean rolled and thrust his sword upward, but the Wildling merely laughed and arched out of his way; the weapon met only the whisper of silk.

Ean was exhausted. His dagger seemed lost along with his will, and desperation was no longer enough to drive him on.

Noting his defeated stance, the Whisper Lord advanced slowly, his grim smile the face of Death above ten spiny daggers raised for the kill. With the shrieking noise still accosting his skull and the loss of blood and nausea in his stomach, Ean felt only numb acceptance. Shaking, he lowered his head—

A tall form pushed past him, knocking Ean aside as it rushed to engage the Whisper Lord, driving the Wildling back and away, taking the battle out of Ean's hands.

Ean fell onto his side, gasping, the last of his strength bleeding out of him. He lay watching his rescuer take offensive control, knowing it was all he could do.

The woman's brown half-cloak floated behind her as she advanced with long, fast strides, forcing the Whisper Lord on the retreat. She wielded two short swords in a flashing figure-eight maneuver that reminded Ean strangely of the zanthyr's battle form.

The Wildling smiled no longer. Every thrust and swipe of his daggers was blocked by the woman's whirling black blades. She matched him stride for stride, spinning when he spun, darting as he did, dodging as he lunged. They performed a ferocious, twisting dance of death where both knew the steps intimately and took them with ease.

As Ean watched, the Wildling slashed his daggered gloves in a motion that would've gutted the woman had she been any less of a swordsman, but she spun out of his reach and opened her stance in a toe-to-toe acrobatic leap, thrusting long as she landed. Her sword met with the flesh of his side, drawing a hiss as he jumped back. He glared malevolently at her and pressed one palm to his side.

"Merdanti," he snarled in surprise, his golden eyes hot as they assessed her black blades. Ean saw then that the short swords were identical in make to the zanthyr's own, if half the size.

Arching brows with a predatory smile, she twirled her blades and lunged for him again, and once more the dance began, the meeting of their deadly weapons a rhythmic beating that seemed in time with Ean's still-racing heart.

And then—

Ean thought he must've dreamed it, his tortured mind inventing an impression for what clearly defied explanation. The woman and the Wildling seemed to shift and slow, their cloaks floating as if suspended on the wind. Then the woman launched out of her turn so quickly that Ean lost sight of her, only to spot her again as she stood squarely before her opponent, blades crossed. With naught but a grimace of effort, she chopped her short swords crosswise through the Wildling's neck, removing his head completely. His body toppled to the stones at her feet, paying respects to her skill.

Silence hung in the street, a palpable blanket sewn of incredulity fringed with pain.

The woman lowered her dripping blades and leveled amber eyes on the prince.

"Ean..." Fynn's voice was faint.

Ean tore his gaze from the wondrous stranger and struggled to rise. Pushing one hand against his bleeding leg, he hobbled to Fynn's side.

The royal cousin looked wan, and he lay in an ever-widening pool of blood. Ean swallowed against the nausea in his stomach, feeling bleak. "What can I do?"

Fynn grimaced, and his breath was labored. "How...bad is it?"

Ean looked at his cousin's wound and found a well into his abdominal cavity. "Well," he managed, forcing a steady voice to cover his dismay, "the good news is you don't have any important organs on that side."

"No—" Fynn gasped, "...just unimportant ones."

Feeling a desperate pain for his cousin, Ean stripped off his tunic and pressed the cloth to Fynn's side, but blood soon soaked through. Suddenly he remembered the presence of the strange woman and turned to ask her aid, but the clatter and rumble of galloping hooves drowned out his words. An instant later, Matthieu, Rhys and a host of soldiers came trampling down the street. Ean closed his eyes as relief swept in. He only prayed they were in time to save Fynn.

Thank you, blessed Epiphany. And thank this stranger, whoever she is.

Rhys was at his side then, and Bastian and Cayal at Fynn's. Matthieu came over as the Captain was lifting Ean in his arms. "*Mon dieu!*" announced the wide-eyed officer upon seeing Fynn and Ean's condition. He spared a glance around, his gaze taking in the headless Wildling and the inscrutable woman standing grim-faced over him. "What has become of my quiet posting? Fires and kidnappings and battles with Wildlings in zee wee hours before dawn…I think you would send me to retire early, *mon ami*."

Ean was too weak to form a retort, but he managed a rueful smile in return. With Matthieu's help, Rhys mounted up and drew Ean close, holding him in his arms. The prince caught the Captain's dour look and knew Rhys didn't trust himself to speak. Closing his eyes, Ean leaned back against his captain and let darkness take him while the horse carried them away.

FORTY-FOUR

'There are three great uncertainties in life: weather, wind and women.'

– The pirate Carian vran Lea

Alyneri lay her pounding head against the cushion of the sofa in Claire's room, willing sleep, but her eyes refused to close, as if in surrendering to slumber she would blot out what had been achieved.

She'd done it.

She'd reached an unborn child without tactile contact, established rapport, and made him move his head into position. To her knowledge, no Healer had ever accomplished such a thing before. The trouble was, she still didn't know *how* she'd done it. Desperation had driven her actions, but now it had left her and moved on, vanished along the winding road that was her past, taking knowledge of what had been done along with it.

"Sleep now, *chaton*, my kitten," said Ghislain tenderly, petting her hair.

Alyneri exhaled a slow breath. Across the room, Sandrine had her head bent in rapport with Claire, who held one babe to her breast while the other, already sated, slept within the arms of its nursemaid. It was a momentous evening for all of them.

"You did good tonight, my lady," Ghislain said, following her gaze across the room. "You and she, you made a fair team."

Alyneri's tired eyes burned and her head ached as she watched Sandrine. She was so exhausted that she felt like she was floating above the sofa while a huge weight pressed her down, but still her heart beat too quickly and she couldn't relax.

It *had* been good working with the other healer. Sandrine exhibited an untempered power when in rapport, and Alyneri suspected she could learn much from the other woman—if only she weren't so frightening to be around.

It's quite like keeping a viper for a pet, she thought, again comparing the Veneisean Healer to a snake, though she didn't exactly think of Sandrine in this fashion. *There's something truly dangerous about her though*, Alyneri decided, *like the viper. You cannot trust that it won't bite you for no apparent reason whatsoever.*

Alyneri had expected Sandrine's gratitude upon finishing her work with the babes and seeing them born healthy and Claire saved as well, but the other Healer had seemed nothing if not annoyed. She'd been sharp with her thereafter, giving her deprecating looks for little to no reason. If not for the urgency with which Sandrine had pushed her to save the babes and thereby Claire, Alyneri might have thought Sandrine *wanted* the Comtesse to die. It made no sense to her—what could she have done to so upset Sandrine?

Alyneri exhaled another long sigh and wondered why she couldn't relax. Her body would not release the tension that held her hostage and kept sleep at bay. But when an urgent knock came upon the door, she knew immediately why she'd remained so alert.

She was off the sofa and running for the door before Ghislain or any of the others in attendance had barely registered the sound. Alyneri threw open the door with a sinking feeling of dread and demanded, "Where is he?"

Bastian stood momentarily stunned, his mouth half open.

Alyneri grabbed him by the shoulders, abandoning completely any thoughts of secrecy. "Where is Ean?"

"The gravest threat is not to your love," said a striking auburn-haired woman who stood behind Bastian. Alyneri hadn't even noticed her there.

"It's Fynn, your Grace." Bastian finally found his voice. "He's bad."

Alyneri couldn't help the relief that flooded her, though it appalled her in the knowing. She drew in a determined breath. "Take me to him."

Bastian spun on his heel and rushed down the hall. Alyneri found herself walking beside the taller woman wondering who in Tiern'aval she was. She studied her profile as they rushed along, noting a nose that was long and straight and fiery auburn hair, which she wore in a thick braid that fell long down her back. She was dressed in mannish fashion in a tunic, leather vest, and britches beneath a heavy russet cloak, with matching boots whose tops turned down above the knee. She had a sword at her belt, too, and blood on her tunic cuffs.

Alyneri pushed aside the mystery of the woman as they reached a staircase and rushed down, asking Bastian instead, "What happened? How were they hurt?"

"It was the Tyriolicci," answered the woman.

"The what?"

"A Whisper Lord," Bastian supplied.

Alyneri gaped at him. "They fought a *Whisper Lord?* Are they both insane?"

"It happened in the city," the woman said. "There was no choice save to fight."

Alyneri glanced uncertainly at her. Who was this woman and why did she keep talking as if she'd been there?

"Lord Fynnlar has lost a lot of blood," Bastian advised as he stopped before a door and swung it open for her. Alyneri walked past him on inside and there found a host of men standing around looking out of sorts and confused.

"At last—tis *le Duchesse*!" announced Matthieu in relief. He pulled Rhys to the side out of her way, and Alyneri saw Fynn lying pale on a bed, with Ean laid out beside him.

"His highness sleeps only," Rhys told her when he saw the color draining from her face.

Alyneri grabbed Bastian's shoulder for support. "They're *covered* in blood, are you certain of—?"

Ean stirred at the sound of her voice. "Alyneri," he murmured, sounding weak but strong of heart. "Help Fynn. Hurry."

Needing no more prodding, Alyneri moved to Fynn's side. The Comte's chirurgeon had cleaned and dressed his wound, but already blood was soaking through the linen. She placed her hands on Fynn's bare chest and calmed her mind, pushing away lingering fears for Ean's condition as well as the image of Sandrine's face, which hovered in her near consciousness. Letting her awareness settle into and sway with the rhythm of Fynn's energy, she found his life pattern quickly and set to the task of repairing the torn threads.

She didn't need to look at his wound to know what had been done to him;

his pattern was frayed and weakened, the strands barely contiguous, its integrity compromised. With immense patience, she gathered each fraying end and smoothed it with the power of *elae* flowing through her. Then she began the puzzle of piecing the ends back together. As she repaired each strand, restoring integrity, she saw the whole pattern begin to shine again.

'Take away the breeze that threatens the candle,' the Lady Melisande had often instructed, *'and the sputtering flame grows bright and strong.'*

Time passed and the men around her settled. The room grew quiet and calm, but Alyneri noticed none of these changes, for her work consumed her attention wholly. She was halfway though Fynn's pattern, however, when a woman's spoken words shocked her almost completely out of rapport. "Why did no one send for me?" Sandrine demanded from the doorway. "Another of your men lies wounded and yet you wait upon *le Duchesse* when I could help?"

"*No!*" Alyneri withdrew from rapport with Fynn as rapidly as she could without harming him and shot to her feet, swaying slightly from the effort. Everyone in the room stared at her in shock, most of all Sandrine. "No," Alyneri said again, not caring that she'd horribly offended the other woman. "Sandrine, it would be best if you took over here. I will tend to the other man."

Sandrine looked skeptical. "You can barely stand, *ma chère*."

"Then it is fortunate I can sit while I heal him, is it not?" she returned testily, and before anyone could protest—not that *anyone* dared—she moved around the bed to Ean's side.

He opened his eyes when he felt her touch, and she had to stifle the whimper that tried to escape her upon meeting his grey-eyed gaze, for he was so precious and beautiful to her. The idea of Sandrine laying hands upon him filled her with a horror so complete that she'd never have been able to find her way back into rapport with Fynn anyway, not while the woman remained in the room.

"My personal angel," Ean murmured, smiling though he was clearly in pain.

"I might say just the opposite of you," Alyneri muttered, but her tone was gentle.

Sandrine watched the exchange with one arched brow, and then she made her way across the room to Fynn's side. She sat and placed her hands on his head, but her eyes did not leave Alyneri. "I suspected when you refused me that your heart had been given to another," she remarked coldly, drawing Alyneri's eye.

Matthieu cleared his throat. "Let us leave the Adepts to their charges," he said in Veneisean, whereupon the men made a mad exodus for the door. Only the red-haired woman remained, arms crossed as she leaned in one corner watching dispassionately.

"I had thought you in love with your betrothed," Sandrine continued, holding Alyneri's gaze, both of them half in rapport with their charges and half-caught by the other, "but now I see you only pretend to the role."

Alyneri tensed at her words, but it was Ean who answered. He turned his head and looked Sandrine the eye, his gaze wolf-keen and fierce. "*I* am her betrothed," he said, and upon observing Sandrine's shocked look, he added sternly, "and I would appreciate your oath to make no more advances towards my fiancée."

Sandrine's eyes widened. "Prince of Dannym," she whispered, staring at him.

"*Mon dieu!*" When she realized Ean was waiting for her oath then and there, she hurriedly replied, "Yes, yes. You have it."

Alyneri gazed incredulously at Ean. It took real effort on her part not to kiss him hard and long.

"I am watching," said the woman in the corner, letting her gaze pass between Ean and Alyneri. "You need not fear on my watch."

Alyneri was so confused by the strange red-head, but Ean seemed reassured. He looked back to Alyneri and winked, and she thought perhaps she had never loved him more than she did in that moment.

So it was that she finally let herself sink into rapport and began her work again, so terribly tired but strangely content just to be near him. At some point during her healing, she knew that Ean had fallen asleep, but Alyneri continued on, weaving the strands of his pattern back together until it shone as brilliantly as the rising sun.

Ean dreamed.

In his dream, he faced the shadows, only now there was a face within them. It remained indistinct, blurred by the fog of time, made hazy by the death that separated then from the now. While he didn't exactly recognize the man, there was something familiar about his rounded nose and dark hair.

"You cannot hope to succeed," the man said, coming closer so that Ean could see more of him. He wore crimson pants and a matching tunic, both cut in the desert fashion, and his feet were bare. "Forswear your oath," he continued as he walked, "and I will give you a quick death. Remain upon this course, and I will cast you out of time. There you will remain, floating beyond the now, dying while eternity passes."

Ean shuddered at the image those words conveyed. He had no doubt that the man could do exactly as he threatened, yet he also knew that this would not be how their battle ended. Ean dreamed with that strange sort of duplicitous half-awareness that one is in a dream while also observing the dream, and that this was a dream one had dreamed before—though the wakeful Ean had no recollection of having ever dreamed it. Still, Ean had the sense that the battle the man suggested had already occurred, thus he knew his end, yet in the dream it had not yet happened, so the end remained unclear to him.

Ean raised a weapon before him, but it was not his own sword. Rather, it reminded him of the zanthyr's stony blade but with a hilt carved in the shape of a dragon, its wings outstretched.

"Do you yield to me?" asked the man.

Ean lifted his gaze, his answer an unwavering stare.

The man snarled an oath and attacked, and their blades met with a deadly song. Ean faced his adversary in an intimate locking of swords, and as their breath mingled, he saw flames behind the man's eyes. The world of dreams seemed to tilt and blur...

Suddenly the fire in his gaze was actually the flames of a brazier, and Ean found himself chained to a low-hanging bar. His back ached from the fiery lashing of a cat-of-nine-tails, and the smell of charcoal mingled with the hot taste of blood across parched and blistered lips. Ean knew this moment, too—knew that he had lived it, or dreamed it, yet the memory seemed somehow too real for a dream alone. The stranger stood across the room staring heatedly at him, and Ean knew that despite the dire scene, despite his quivering legs and the roiling sickness in his bowels, he somehow still held the upper hand.

The cat's nine lashes sliced into the flesh of his back again with sudden vicious abandon, and Ean cried out. His shoulders were a sharp agony, and blood ran down from his manacled wrists to mingle with an ever-widening pool at his feet.

The pain of the lashing reverberated throughout his tortured body, and his gaze dimmed. When he focused again, the stranger stood close in front of him. "Your purpose is to die," he said again, viewing Ean as a curiosity worthy of closer inspection. "Why do you rail against it so? Is not the very foundation of your existence simply to carry forward toward death? Why do you resist what you know is inevitable?"

He lifted Ean's chin with one black-nailed finger and gazed into his eyes, though Ean could barely focus—the man's face swam before him, a thousand-fold flaming eyes. Ean saw him look to someone who stood behind, and he cringed in the split-second before the whips scourged his flesh again, their metal tips finding purchase on bone. He screamed without realizing it was his own raw voice echoing back to him.

The room went black, but the man's voice remained, a vicious, cajoling whisper denying peace. "Do it," came the voice, "release yourself from this pathetic existence blighted by the thing you call life. It is a futile, hopeless thing to fight for when your every breath merely takes you closer to that end. Today, tomorrow, a week of torment from now, I will *still* win, for the end will claim you. It is your destiny. *Embrace it...*"

Ean felt himself slipping...slipping...he knew death was so close... It would be nothing to open himself to its cold, unforgiving kiss...

In the last moment, a face surfaced out of the deep dark. Its brilliance shocked him so greatly that he flew back toward consciousness, regaining himself with a gasp.

Only it was a different scene he found upon surfacing. Though his enemy was the same, there was something very different about the mist-filled plain upon which they both stood.

The stranger glared at him. "My brother is coming for you."

"Coward," Ean said.

The stranger just laughed, and the red sky imploded.

Ean woke with a start.

Never had he been so relieved to know he'd been dreaming. As he lay in bed letting his heart still and his breathing return to normal, he looked around in the gray morning light. He slept in an opulent bedroom with walls paneled in pale blue silk. The frescoed ceiling above him was painted with a scene of nymphs tormenting a shepherd boy. Yawning, he stretched and became immediately aware of a thousand places on his body which he'd never knew existed. Memory returned in a flash, and he exhaled a regretful, "*Oh...*"

"They say the second day of recovery is always worse than the first," came a feminine voice from across the room.

Ean slowly pushed up on one elbow, careful of his head and healing back, the skin of which felt tight and raw. He saw her then, sitting in an armchair by the hearth where coals burned low. Her fiery hair blazed like burnished copper even in the muted light, though it was the only thing feminine about her. Her almond-shaped eyes were set well apart, her nose was long and straight and her cheekbones pronounced—all of the makings of beauty, yet in her the elements seemed too stark. If there was beauty in her, it was the harsh beauty of a hawk, wild and fierce.

He remembered her swishing past him to his rescue—that moment was indelibly imprinted in memory; even now the feeling of overwhelming relief was palpable—but everything after that was a haze. Why she'd come, and why she remained, was a mystery. "I thank you for my life," he said, slowly feeling the numbness of sleep fading. He pressed palms to both eyes and then blinked them again. "Wow... how long was I out?"

"Two days." She stood and approached his bedside. She wore a blood-red tunic beneath a chestnut-hued vest, and leather britches tucked into thigh-high boots, but Ean noted appreciatively that there was nothing at all mannish about her figure. She stopped and looked down at him with eyes that were tawny-amber, like an owl's golden orbs. "How do you feel?"

Ean gave her a rueful grin. "Alive. It feels wonderful. How is Fynn?"

"Alive...like you."

Ean lay back on his pillow and exhaled in relief. "That's a blessing." He stared up at the young man in the fresco, adding, "I was a fool."

"Yes, no doubt," she agreed, "but the Tyriolicci would have found you sooner or later. At least it was only the two of you who bled on his blades. The carnage might've been worse had all of your men been with you. I don't know if the little Healer could've saved so many."

Ean turned his head to look at her. "So you're saying it was actually providential that I rushed into a burning building against all better judgment, was accosted and taken hostage, and somehow managed to escape only to be nearly gutted by a Whisper Lord?"

She regarded him coolly. "I'm saying there is no wisdom in regret."

Ean gazed at her with growing wonder. "Who *are* you?" It was a question long overdue.

"I am Gwynnleth nach Davvies of Elvior."

"Elvior," Ean said, tasting of the strange name. "Where is that?"

"On Mount Pisah."

Now understanding dawned upon him, and he arched brows in surprise. "You're an avieth."

She rolled her eyes. "Well, *obviously*. And that was one."

"One what?"

"One mark against you."

Ean barked a laugh. "How is that?"

She drew herself tall and announced, "I have determined to give you three chances."

"Chances for what?"

Her tawny eyes narrowed as she replied in a steely tone, "To prove you are just like all the other Northmen I've met."

Ean chuckled. "Then I'm afraid you'll be waiting a long time, my lady."

She regarded him doubtfully. "We'll see."

"So, Gwynnleth of Elvior," Ean said, gingerly clasping hands behind his head, "might you be willing to tell me why you came at so fortuitous a moment to save me from certain death?"

She arched a ginger brow at him. "I was sent to your aid by the Fourth Vestal."

Ean lowered his hands in surprise and pushed up on one elbow again to better see her. "Raine sent you?"

"He believed the Tyriolicci had agreed to hunt you—as we both discovered to be true, you a bit more acutely than me." She crossed arms and stared discontentedly at him. "I stayed because, well...you are not as I expected."

The prince lifted a solitary brow in amusement. "I didn't realize you had any expectations of me at all."

"A common failing of men in general, I've noticed." She wandered over to the windows and pushed aside the sheers with slender fingers. "That Raine D'Lacourte sent me to protect you was a curiosity to me," she told him as she gazed out into the hazy dawn, "so I lingered here to see why he would think your life worth saving."

Ean turned his head to watch her at the window, but instead of her slender, leather-clad form, he saw Creighton dying on the blade of a Shade; he saw Fynn rushing to engage the Whisper Lord; he saw the zanthyr spinning to catch a dagger out of the air, his cloak flying on the wind... Exhaling a pensive sigh, the prince murmured, "Isn't all life worth saving?"

She turned him an unreadable look over her shoulder. "I've watched your companions since I arrived," she remarked, turning her attention back to the dawn. "So far I've seen your cousin willingly throw himself in the Tyriolicci's path to save you, and I've watched the Healer—who would bear your children if you but asked—push herself beyond exhaustion to heal you. The young truthreader watches you with awe, even while you sleep, and the King's Guard have such respect for you one would think you already their liege."

Ean felt only regret in hearing these words—except for her absurd assumption about Alyneri. "I am blessed with the loyalty of brave companions," he told her, feeling only the weight of their lives as an endless pressure upon his heart.

She turned him another unreadable look, one ginger brow raised above her tawny eyes. Like the owl sitting upon its high tree espying the whimsical and ordinary with equal dispassion, there was something detached about her, as if she merely observed humankind but had little interaction with or care for them. Something about her manner reminded him of the zanthyr, too, though he couldn't say what it was—the impression of an impression—but he realized he trusted her, much as he'd instinctively trusted the zanthyr.

"So you stayed," he said quietly, "and you observed. And now?"

She walked over to him. "You have two chances left."

"And what outcome are you hoping for? That I should prove you right and be just like all the others of my race, or that I should prove you wrong?"

She regarded him levelly, her strange golden eyes at half-mast. "I have no hopes in the matter at all."

"I'm just a curiosity, am I? Were you bored in Elvior?" He paused and considered her more intently, "Or are you running from something—some*one?*"

Gwynnleth leaned against the bedpost, her expression revealing nothing of her thoughts. "Why is Raine D'Lacourte invested in your welfare?"

Ean slowly sat up and shifted his pillows to rest back against the headboard. If nothing else, conversing with her was much like with the zanthyr—a sometimes elliptical and often warped conversation that never ended where it seemed that it should. "I'm not sure."

She arched a brow at him again.

"What I mean is I'm not sure of his motivations. It seems to me the Vestals have their own agendas which they may or may not share with us, and what they do share may not be the whole truth."

She chuckled. "You are wiser for your years than I gave you credit for, Prince of Dannym. I take back the first mark."

"Well, that's a relief."

"Careful," she chided, narrowing her gaze. "Sarcasm will cost you two marks."

Ean gave her a crooked grin. "I shall endeavor to do better." He peered under the covers then and saw that he was naked beneath them. Lifting grey eyes back to her, he asked, "Have I any clothes?"

Casting him a long look, she walked over to an armoire and retrieved a pair of pants, which she tossed to him. Ean threw back the covers and donned them while she watched, neither averting her gaze for propriety nor seeming to care that he stood with his assets fully revealed to her. She was just so *odd.*

"The Whisper Lord," he said then while walking toward the armoire, feeling every muscle in his body twining and tensing with each step. "At the end, he was chanting something. Did you hear it?"

"Indeed, Prince of Dannym. He said, *Tur or'de rorum d'rundalin dalal.*"

"That was it all right," Ean agreed, surprised to learn she knew the strange words. He shoved his head through a tunic and asked as he pushed arms with care into the sleeves, "How do you know that?"

"I have fought many of them." She looked to him, and a stubborn glint came into her gaze. "Avieths are uniquely suited to battle the Tyriolicci. It is why Raine D'Lacourte sent me to protect you."

Filing that knowledge for investigation at a later time, Ean asked, "Do you know what the words mean?"

"Indeed, Northerner. He was chanting, 'Dare to live fearlessly and fear not to die.'"

Death is only the beginning. Ean recalled too well the Geishaiwyn similar chant. What fascination did these Wildlings have with death that they hired out to cause it and made up chants to mock it? "And what is the avieth battle chant?" he asked as he reached for his belt.

She arched a ginger brow. "We do not toy with our prey before we claim it."

"How practical of you," he remarked. He buckled on his belt and looked for his sword.

"In the corner," she advised, motioning with her eyes.

He gave her a wondering look. "Thanks."

She shrugged indifferently.

"So, Gwynnleth," Ean posed as he claimed his sword, "do I have your influence to thank for the upgrade in quarters?"

"No. It was the Veneisean Healer who required it on your behalf. Something to do with your declaration to her."

Ean slowed in buckling on his sword. "My declaration?"

"Where you proclaimed your betrothal to the Duchess."

Ean grimaced. He'd forgotten all about that. "I see." It had been a foolish error, however noble, for now that his identity was broadly known, they were all in danger. *Two days sleeping, for Epiphany's sake! My enemies might be amassing beyond the gates even now!*

The avieth's earlier words suddenly struck a terrible chill in him—the thought of another Whisper Lord lying in wait and taking down Ean's entire company in the process of claiming his bounty was too much to bear. Shadow take his carelessness!

"You spend too much time in your head, Northerner," Gwynnleth remarked, eyeing him critically. "Wasted time."

"What—I shouldn't think?" Ean protested, glaring at her.

"But you're not thinking, are you?" she inquired with her head caught with that imperial tilt that women of any race seemed to manage so well. "You're regretting."

Her haughty manner roused his ire—that and how completely she seemed to know his mind. He jerked his belt tight and shoved a hand to the hilt of his sword. "I have many lives in my charge, Gwynnleth of Elvior," Ean growled. "Should I feel nothing for their safety? Should I simply shrug indifferently, like you, when my choices place them in danger?"

A half-grin twitched at the corner of her mouth. It was the closest he'd seen her come to a smile. "You clearly care for them, Northerner," she returned, "anyone can see that. What you fail to display is leadership."

Her words were a fiery arrow to his gut, their truth painful and raw. He deflated, feeling bruised and bare beneath her scrutiny. How could she see so deeply into his soul?

"I am perhaps not as young as I seem," Gwynnleth offered as Ean struggled to repair his shattered ego, his eyes burning and his jaw tight as he held her tawny gaze. "I have fought for many great leaders even as I have known pain beneath the command of others. You are the kind of man people want to follow, Ean val Lorian, but true leadership comes at a price."

"And what is that?" he asked thickly, his words laced with a bitter edge. "Their lives?"

"Sometimes. More often it is a personal cost: to bear the largest burden, to put forward the bravest face, to command the greatest courage from oneself for the sake of others. Your regret merely weakens all, for they would depend on you to lead forward, not pin them down mired in past failures, afraid of future missteps."

Ean admitted that most of what she said rang with unquestionable truth, but one thing didn't sit right with him. "So let me get this straight," he challenged. "My companions give their *lives*, but *I* pay the price?"

She came over and handed him his cloak, but he got the sense it was not an offering of a garment but of a sacred trust. "One day you will understand," she said simply.

Ean took the offering and released his angst with forced patience. What good did it do to argue with her? "Is that the day I will prove you right…or wrong?" he challenged.

She considered him. "Perhaps both."

"Then I look forward to it."

Gwynnleth arched a ginger brow and shook her head. "You are not as I expected," she observed again.

Ean shook his head sadly and commiserated, "Alas, milady, the good ones never are."

Tanis felt slightly like a long-tailed cat in a corral of hungry hogs as he lugged his bags down to the yard dodging soldiers and stewards and horses being readied to ride. His highness had awoken only that morning, but already they were heading out. The boy didn't quite understand everything that had come to pass since his chambermaid had drugged him and run off in the night; he was just excited to be off again. To Tanis, their stay at the Comte's villa seemed somewhat caught out of time. It felt as if events in the world beyond needed to catch up with them, and now that they had, everything sprang into motion once more.

As the lad reached his own horse, one of the Comte's stable hands took his bags and shooed him off saying something in Veneisean which the boy couldn't understand. The yard was a fair madness of shuffling packs and bundles and shouted orders in two languages, so rather than get stepped on or jostled or caught unwittingly in the middle of stomping horses or burly soldiers or something else unpleasant, Tanis sought the safety of a marble bench until it was time to go.

In the near distance, Rhys was seeing to his horse while the prince stood near him talking with the Comte's man, Matthieu. They were close enough that Tanis had no trouble hearing their conversation.

"All's well that ends well," Matthieu was saying amiably to Ean as Tanis sat down on the bench. "At least now we know why zee ordair to stay within zee walls, eh *mon ami?*" He elbowed Ean and arched brows suggestively, as if the prince's identity wasn't broadly known by all of the Comte's staff. "I confess I am not so sad to see you go," he added with a grin. "I am too old for all zee commotion! When next I play zee cards with the city guard, they will think me a liar if I tell them zis tale."

The prince said something Tanis couldn't make out save that it was in good spirits, and then Matthieu glanced over at the avieth, who was talking to three of Matthieu's men. From her body position and the glare in her eye, she seemed ready to match swords with them. "And what of zee *heroine?*" he asked in a low voice.

Ean turned to follow his gaze just as Gwynnleth pulled her black-bladed sword and spun it as she split the shaft apart, making two swords out of one. Matthieu tensed, but Ean held up a hand, a shadowy smile hinting on his lips. "Wait," he murmured.

Matthieu's men laughed and drew their swords in turn. They pressed them to foreheads with short bows, and then jested with each other to see who would match blades with the avieth first. One man stepped forward swinging his weapon in challenge.

"Ah, *mon dieu,*" Matthieu exclaimed, shaking his head. "*Idiot!* Now I will have to pay zee chirurgeon to sew 'im up."

The man made a show of swinging his blade and then suddenly lunged at Gwynnleth, but she danced easily to the side and struck his rear with the flat of her blade, sending him pitching forward. He caught himself on both hands in the dirt to the sound of laughter from his fellows. Straightening and brushing his hands against his britches, he settled an angry glare upon the avieth and struck out after her with a snarl. Again she easily deflected his advance, this time spinning as his blade passed harmlessly by to impale sack of flour stacked on a near wagon.

There followed an embarrassing display of humiliation wherein the avieth quickly pinned, disarmed, or struck down Matthieu's men, never losing her composed look of concentration no matter their goading insults or laughter. When each had regained their weapons with black glares, she offered to take them all at once. They brightened at this and formed a line against her while Ean grinned and Matthieu muttered in dismay, shaking his head.

The men rushed her as one, and the sound of the swordplay that followed caused a momentary stilling in the busy yard as everyone turned to watch. The avieth fought with both swords spinning, crossing and uncrossing her arms as she spun the blades in figure-eights. Tanis had never seen anything like it. Prince Ean and Matthieu both watched intently, and Tanis caught a hint of the prince's thoughts as a particularly strong impression bled through, something about the zanthyr that had saved him, who Tanis well remembered.

As quickly as it began, it was over, and Matthieu's men lay in the dirt with thin lines of blood at the base of their throats from Gwynnleth's careful skill, her mark of reminder that humility is the greatest of virtues.

Matthieu stomped over to them and waved them all up amid a florid tongue-lashing, demanding they pay the avieth the proper respects. As the men were grumblingly acknowledging her victory, Fynn arrived with Brody in tow. The royal cousin was walking slightly crooked, still favoring his torn-but-now-repaired side.

"Raine's truth, Ean," Fynnlar complained as he arrived on the scene, "your Healer did something wrong while she was messing with my insides. I've been awake all morning and haven't wanted a drink. What did she *do* to me?"

"Relax, Fynn," Ean said with a crooked grin. "Things could be worse."

"How?" Fynn demanded.

"Instead of taking away your thirst for drink, she might've given you a conscience."

Fynn blanched. "Oh, Belloth's Balls—that *would* be worse!" He dropped the satchel he'd been carrying at his feet and looked around, espying the avieth. "Who's the broad?"

Ean followed his gaze. "That's Gwynnleth. She saved our lives. Don't you remember?"

Fynn frowned at her. "Vaguely. Mostly I remember a lot of blood seeping out of my gut. So what's the deal with her?"

"She's here on behalf of the Fourth Vestal."

"The *Fourth* Vestal," Fynn repeated dubiously, his tone intimating, *Don't you mean the Third?*

Having properly schooled Matthieu's men, Gwynnleth strolled over swinging her blades idly at her side. Tanis admitted she was something to look at. Though she wore a man's attire, it somehow accentuated her feminine shape instead of obscuring it. Gwynnleth spied Fynnlar staring at her and arched a ginger brow. "Does the sight of a woman in pants emasculate you, Northerner?"

Fynn grinned. "*Au contraire, mon chère.* I was just imagining how such pants would look on my bedroom floor."

She arched a disapproving brow and turned to Ean, who held up both hands in protest. "*He's* not included in my three chances."

Gwynnleth grunted and looked back to Fynn. "These pants were made for me by artisans of Doane, Northerner," she told him with one imperially arched eyebrow, "sewn from the skin of a lamb who willingly gave his life in sacrifice. No lambskin is ever so supple as that from an ewe who dies without regret."

"I imagine the skin beneath them is more supple still," Fynn observed with a grin. "I'd be happy to compare the two and let you know."

"Gwynnleth, may I introduce my cousin, Fynnlar val Lorian," Ean said blandly.

She looked Fynn up and down with her tawny eyes and didn't seem impressed by what she saw.

"Fynn, Gwynnleth will be riding along with us until I use up my three chances to prove her wrong."

"Or prove me right," Gwynnleth said, "which outcome I am predicting rather quickly."

Fynn arched brows in surprise. "Can she ride?"

"Of course I can ride," she returned indignantly. "Tis only mankind that need break a creature to its will, for the children of nature see your failings and know you to be toxic to them. Avieths need only ask and a horse will carry us." Pinning her tawny eyes on Fynn's horse, she whistled then, and the animal whinnied and pulled free of Brody's hands, trotting over to her. Gwynnleth held out one hand for the horse to sniff while smiling daggers at Fynn.

"Traitor," Fynn accused the horse under his breath. Looking to Gwynnleth, he said then, "So you speak to lambs and horses too. Was that your mating call just then?"

Gwynnleth eyed him imperiously. "Mankind thinks itself so above the Wildling races, but we must look down our noses to see the tops of your heads."

"Gee, you don't say," Fynn remarked, rolling his eyes. "I suppose otherwise you'd be flying so low we could stab our dinner with a fork. Then again, I don't imagine avieths would make for a decent meal, their meat being hard and tough."

"Better hard and tough than flaccid and fatty," she said with a sweet smile.

Tanis would've stayed to listen to Fynn's retort, but just then he saw her Grace descending the long staircase from the manse, so he trotted over to greet her and see if she needed his help.

The duchess walked with the comtesse, who carried one of her babes in swaddling, and the Veneisean Healer Sandrine du Préc. The comtesse paused halfway down the hillside and hugged Alyneri. Then the duchess and Sandrine continued down together. Tanis met them at the bottom.

"So where will you ride, since Jeune is closed?" Sandrine was asking as they reached the yard.

"To the Cairs," Alyneri said, looking uncomfortable. "I will end my pilgrimage at the Temple of the Vestals in Cair Rethynnea."

"What a coincidence," Sandrine replied. "I was planning to leave for the Cairs next week. Perhaps we should meet in Tregarion and travel on together?"

Alyneri looked a little wan at the suggestion, and Tanis easily picked up on her thoughts. She didn't want to tell the woman that they weren't taking a boat to Tregarion—better she know as little as possible about their plans. No doubt Sandrine would reach the Cairs before they did, even leaving a week later. "A pilgrimage is meant to be a time of penance and reflection, Sandrine," Alyneri returned in a strained voice. Tanis didn't quite understand the depth of tension in her reply, but he saw clearly enough that the other Healer made her Grace very uncomfortable. "I'm not certain our traveling together would allow for enough of either."

Sandrine's returning smile seemed nothing if not predatory. "Perhaps we will meet again in the Cairs then, your Grace. My offer still stands."

Alyneri looked slightly pained. "I am grateful for your offer to continue our tutoring."

Sandrine eyed her humorously. "But…?"

Tanis sensed her dismay and jumped to her rescue. "Your Grace, is there anything I can help you with?"

"Oh, Tanis," she said, looking immensely grateful for his intrusion, "yes, I—where is my mare?" She looked to Sandrine. "It has been a…a pleasure meeting you, Sandrine."

Sandrine looked amused by Alyneri's discomfiture. "And you as well, *Duchesse*." She took Alyneri's fingers and kissed the back of her hand in farewell, all the while staring at Alyneri with a hungry look in her eyes. Then she turned and made her stately way up the staircase to the manse.

Alyneri shivered as she watched Sandrine retreat. Tanis saw her wiping her hand compulsively against her skirts, but he didn't think her Grace realized she was doing it.

They made their way to Alyneri's mare, and because she immediately launched into grilling the stable hand who'd been loading her bags of herbs, Tanis found his way back to the marble bench and sat down with a sigh, resting elbows on knees and chin in hands.

He wished he'd been allowed to do more to help with the preparations. Ever since Prince Ean had come to see them earlier that morning with another thanks for Alyneri and the announcement of their departure, Tanis hadn't been allowed to do anything. *'You're the Prince's truthreader!'* everyone had protested when Tanis asked to help, as if being in service of the prince made him incapable of anything beyond sitting on a satin pillow reading people's minds. He wondered if that's what it was going to be like when he took a commission—never doing anything worthwhile again, being waited on hand and foot, people treating you like porcelain…no wonder her Grace viewed ladies maids like the plague.

"How long have you served your prince?" Gwynnleth asked him suddenly.

Tanis jumped on his seat, turning with a startled breath to find her standing behind him with arms crossed. He hadn't seen her anywhere nearby when he sat down. "Oh…I'm," he whetted his lips and managed, "I'm not commissioned yet. I'm still in training." His nerves settling, he turned to look back out at the busy yard and asked, "Are you…coming with us to the Cairs?"

Gwynnleth blinked and looked around, letting her eyes come at last to rest on Prince Ean, who was adjusting the stirrups on Caldar's saddle. She moved around to sit beside Tanis on the bench. "I think that I am," she answered, sounding as if the words surprised her.

He scooted over to make room for her. "Can I ask you a question?"

She nodded without looking at him.

"How…how did you do that trick?"

"Which trick?"

"With Lord Fynnlar's horse."

She turned him a wry look. "You noticed that, did you?"

Tanis shrugged. "I just knew you weren't telling the truth, but I don't know how you made the horse come to you."

Gwynnleth leaned in, and Tanis realized that upon close inspection, her manner wasn't nearly so unsettling. She almost seemed…nice. "If I tell you, can you keep it a secret?" she asked.

Wide-eyed, Tanis nodded.

"Whenever I come to meet a new horse," she began in a low voice, "I always bring a pocket of grain."

Tanis brightened with understanding. "You had grain in your hand!"

She touched a finger to her nose and nodded sagely.

Tanis beamed.

Just then, Alyneri separated herself from the group that was Ean, Fynn, and several others, and marched toward Tanis as if on a mission. Clearing his throat, the boy glanced sheepishly at Gwynnleth and then got to his feet, just in time to greet her Grace with a respectful nod.

Alyneri gave Gwynnleth a quick once-over and then looked to Tanis. "The prince is ready to leave," she told him, glancing back at Gwynnleth again uncertainly.

The avieth joined Tanis in standing. "Lady Healer," she began smoothly then, "I've a question to ask of you."

Alyneri looked surprised. "You have?" She straightened and pressed out her divided skirts. "Then please do."

Gwynnleth glanced at Tanis with a look that was obviously his cue to leave. Excusing himself, the boy trotted over to join Prince Ean, but before he was out of earshot, he heard the avieth inquire, "Why do you not confess your love to the prince?" to which her Grace's reply was a surprised gasp. Tanis was most grateful to the avieth for her warning glance, which afforded him the chance to escape before the storm.

FORTY-FIVE

'Yield to temptation, it may not pass your way again.'

– Fynnlar val Lorian, Prince of Dannym

Trell rode Gendaia through the city of Tregarion admiring the beauty of the seaside metropolis. The city was built within a mountainous basin, with long tree-lined boulevards spanning the stepped hillside and mile-long staircases as wide as ten horses rising from the bay to the basin rim, where the homes of the elite peeked from dense gardens protected by high stone walls. Myriad stone buildings capped with terracotta tiles paved the lower hills with their russet color, and every street overlooked the sparkling blue bay and its jutting peninsula, where the queen of Veneisea's green marble palace rose in crowning splendor.

High upon the ridge above the bay, and with a commanding view of the entire city, a long line of temples had been erected, each dedicated to one of the Veneisean gods of Virtue: Patience, Propriety, Temperance, Fidelity, and Chastity. Even from a distance, Trell could see people crowding the structures. He marveled anyone would go to the trouble of worshipping at the temples when it required climbing three miles of stairs to get there, but then, religion was a strange bedfellow; he'd encountered many a man who thought the same about anyone bothering to learn the names of the seventeen Desert Gods and their myriad incarnations.

Carian had taken Trell directly from the jungle to the Veneisean city, where they'd spent a couple of days recuperating from their ordeal. For Trell this meant a good night's sleep and time to care for his horse, but for the pirate it translated into a 'real game of Trumps' that was still ongoing when the sun rose the next morning. Now, as evening neared, Trell went to rendezvous with the pirate so they might head off to another node that Carian said would lead them most efficiently to their destination.

Any time the pirate used the word 'efficiently' Trell got suspicious.

Following a map hastily scrawled on a the back of a poster advertising a theater production of the Immortal Bard Drake DiMatteo's farce, *The Illumination of Humbold the Harpist*, Trell found his way into the hills in search of the villa where Carian said to meet him. When he arrived at the end of his map, however, where a large X denoted the supposed location of the villa, Trell found only a path leading away and up into the wooded hills.

Trell clicked his tongue for Gendaia, and she headed up the path and over a little wooden bridge, which spanned a gurgling brook that tumbled and fell around moss-eaten rocks. As they rode, Trell gazed absently out over the glorious landscape and decided it was wholly strange being in civilization. Of course, Duan'Bai was a bustling city, but its outward wash of dun-hued buildings was broken only by the colorful mosaics of its minarets or the occasional date palm extending above the rooftops. Trell had spent most of his time within the walls of the Emir's palace, which abounded with luxuries, but the Veneisean landscape alone—with its glorious bay, lush foliage, and misty streams everywhere—held natural luxuries beyond price.

Trell began to see a high stone wall peeking through the trees long before the trail ended at a wooden gate. Dismounting before the portal, Trell read the sign hanging over the gate, which said, *S'inscrire à là qui être pardonne*—'Enter those who would be forgiven.' Trell puzzled over the inscription, finding it difficult to associate 'penitence' with the pirate Carian vran Lea.

As curious as he was amused by the idea, Trell opened the gate and led Gendaia into a twilit courtyard. Across the way, a large stone house nearly covered in vines seemed to sprout out of the foliage that hugged its foundation. Trell walked to the tall, rounded door and used the iron knocker to announce his arrival.

It wasn't long before an older woman opened the door. She wore a white woolen dress and a long veil attached at the crown of her head with an embroidered black cap. "*Bonsoir, Monsieur*," she greeted. "*Bienvenue aux Villa de Les Soeur de Chasteté.*"

The villa of the Sisters of Chastity? Trell thought with raised brows. *Stranger and stranger.*

When Trell didn't immediately respond, the sister said in the common tongue, "You are here for Monsieur vran Lea?"

Trell shook off his surprise and nodded. "Yes. Is he…here?"

"Yes, monsieur." She looked over his shoulder and saw Gendaia grazing in the yard. "I will ask one of my sisters to attend your horse. I am Sister Fantine. If you would please follow me." She led away without waiting for a reply, so Trell followed her deeper within the manse. Bare stone walls were lit with thick candles that cast wavering shadows on the buttressed ceilings. Trell saw no furniture to speak of; the only luxuries were the thick carpets beneath his feet.

The sister brought him to a set of double doors and knocked twice. Another sister veiled with a blue cap answered. She saw Trell and nodded, stepping back to allow him to enter, and he found himself within a lavishly furnished room. Dense crimson carpets covered the stone floor, and whitewashed plastered walls were hung with tapestries of brilliant color and design.

At the end of the room, the pirate lounged on a scroll-armed divan upholstered in gold damask velvet. Two Sisters sat beside him with their veils thrown back. The first was feeding him fruit from a silver tray held by the second.

"You're kidding me, right?" Trell said upon arriving in front of the pirate.

Carian opened his eyes and grinned. "Oh, good. You're here. Do you like gooseberry fruit? It's a local favorite."

The Sister holding the silver platter offered it up to Trell, who saw an arrangement of greenish-yellow fruits with tiny black seeds. He shrugged and tried one, finding it both tart and sweet.

"We grow loads of them in Jamaii," the islander advised. He opened his mouth and the second Sister placed a gooseberry slice upon his tongue.

"Carian," Trell said, frowning at the man, "what are you doing here?"

The disapproval in his tone must've been abundant, for the islander gave him an injured look. "The Sisters are friends of mine. Trell of the Tides, meet Sister Marie-Clarisse," he said, indicating the woman holding the tray, "and Sister Marguerite. They treat me very well." He gave Marguerite a winsome smile and opened his mouth again. She placed another fruit upon his tongue.

"And in return," offered Sister Marie-Clarisse, "Monsieur vran Lea brings us gifts from his travels."

"A jade scepter from Avatar," Sister Marguerite offered, "which we traded for new beds for all of the Sisters."

"And beautiful silks from Faroqhar," said Sister Marie-Clarisse, "which we sold at market for twice what we paid Monsieur vran Lea."

Trell gave Carian a flat look. It was blatant that the pirate's 'gifts' were either stolen artifacts or pilfered cargo.

Carian seemed to understand his look and shrugged his eyebrows three times saucily, explaining, "The Sisters receive many donations from their vast association of patrons. They often sell them for funds to aid their Order. A gift to the Sisters is never questioned and only welcomed on the open market."

"Monsieur vran Lea is one of our most generous patrons," advised Sister Marguerite. "He brings us many gifts, and we are only happy to purchase some of his more expensive items when he cannot afford to donate them. He gives us a generous price, and we are always able to make money on the sale."

"Is that so," Trell murmured with his grey eyes fastened unfavorably on the pirate.

Carian grinned.

"May I speak to you privately, Monsieur vran Lea?" Trell said.

"We will go see about your dinner," Sister Marie-Clarisse offered. She and Sister Marguerite stood and bowed their heads in farewell. Donning their veils once more, they departed.

Trell gave the islander a look of fierce disapproval. "You're using the Sisters of Chastity to launder stolen artifacts?"

Carian stretched out on the divan and clasped hands behind his head. "You made your bargain with a Nodefinder who happens to be a pirate, boyo," he returned unrepentantly. "Why are you so surprised? A pirate can be trusted to keep to the Code."

Trell grunted. "I suppose I had envisioned you had at least one redeeming virtue."

Carian grinned. "By what crazed notion did you image I would give a rat's arse about the Cardinal Virtues? I don't even think I could name them all."

Trell gave him a flat look. "There's only five."

Carian screwed up his face tying to think of one. "Charity…? No—Chastity. What's the other one? Temerity…tenacity?"

"Temperance," Trell said dryly.

"No, that's not it." He frowned for a moment and then gave up. "Anyway, the arrangement is mutually beneficial—which is more than I can say for most of my dealings…"

Abruptly they heard commotion in the hall beyond and exchanged a look. Then Carian was off the divan and running for the doors with Trell close behind. The pirate cracked the door to find a host of white-clad sisters speaking in hushed tones. That's when they both heard the pounding upon the outside portal and a man's muffled voice yelling in Veneisean, "Open up Sisters! Open in the name of the Tivaricum!"

Carian sucked in his breath with a hiss and pulled back inside the room, shutting the door again. At Trell's curious look, the pirate said blackly, "The kingdom police. We've had a bit of a falling out of late." He began looking around the room somewhat urgently.

"Can't you just escape on a node or a leis or something?" Trell asked as the pirate rushed over to a tall armoire and threw open the doors.

"Yeah, about that..." He began rifling through a store of white dresses hanging within. "Because of the many important 'artifacts' the Sisters have on the property, a certain Nodefinder blocked all the nodes and leis that opened onto their lands—for their own protection, of course."

Trell shook his head and rolled his eyes heavenward. "I'd have left at least one viable means of escape."

Carian shot him an aggravated look over his shoulder. "If I could find the node, so could someone else."

"If you can reroute a node anywhere you like," Trell posed deprecatingly, "couldn't you just loop one so that anyone coming in would be forced to step from one right into another—which takes them right back where they began—but anyone leaving would be able to travel it?"

Carian paused in his search through the gowns to give Trell an astonished look. "That's a damned fine idea! I'm going to use that in the future, poppet. Now, here," and he tossed Trell a white dress and veil. "Put those on."

Trell caught the garments out of the air and gave him a dubious look.

"It's the dress or the dungeons of the Citadel," the pirate said while shoving his head through the neck of another gown. The dress fell to his mid-calves and looked ridiculous on his tall frame.

For a split-second as he gazed at the gown in his hands, Trell considered his options. Distancing himself from the pirate now would no doubt save him time in the dungeons, but he'd given his word to the Nodefinder, and his honor bound him to the man until their bargain was finished. Besides, Ramu's wisdom had become a true guiding force in his life: he believed that his journey was as important as his destination.

None of that predisposed him to wearing women's clothing.

Sighing, Trell shook his head and pulled the dress on over his clothes.

As a veiled Carian came over to help Trell with his own veil and cap, they heard the sounds of soldiers entering the manse. Abruptly, Sister Marie-Clarisse poked her head inside the door. "Oh!" she cried upon seeing them, abruptly stifling a smile. "Well then...hurry, Messieurs. The...um...Sisters are gathering in the gallery while the Tivaricum Guard conduct a search."

Trell and Carian followed Sister Marie-Clarisse to where the other Sisters waited. The two men found their way to the back of the collection of white-clad women, where their boots protruding from beneath their dresses would be less obvious. They were doing their best to blend in when a host of guards barged into the gallery.

The man in the lead wore a gilded breastplate emblazoned with Queen Indora's crest and had a plume of emerald feathers extending from his cap. Carian hissed upon seeing him, but the man didn't seem to notice, for he was just then announcing in his native tongue, "...quite certain it was him. The man is a consummate gambler and just this morning won a fortune in emeralds off the crown jeweler Jean-Pierre

Montrose, which were meant for her Majesty's inspection."

Sister Marguerite walked with another soldier just behind the commander. The former clarified, "Montrose is being dealt with separately, Sister, but we must retrieve those emeralds for her Majesty. The man we seek is a notorious pirate wanted in seven kingdoms for theft on the high seas."

"How dreadful!" Sister Marguerite returned, looking appropriately aghast. Her gaze swept the gathering of Sisters. "I cannot imagine any of our Sisters of Chastity having dealings with a nefarious pirate. Why the very idea of it weakens me, Lord Commander. The Sisters of Chastity seek only to lead a virtuous life—"

"As we well know, Sister Marguerite," the Lord Commander assured her.

"—and I cannot imagine a Sister aiding such a scoundrel. Surely, could you not have received erroneous information?"

"I'm afraid the source is beyond question, Sister," the Lord Commander answered, "for I saw the man heading this way with my own eyes."

Hidden in the back of the group, Trell turned Carian a suspicious look, brows arched inquiringly beneath his veil. The pirate sprouted an iniquitous grin in reply.

Trell glared at him. Whatever the pirate's convoluted plan, he didn't doubt that the man had purposely revealed himself to the Veneisean commander. *Just what are you up to, Carian vran Lea?*

The Lord Commander raised his voice to include all the Sisters as he commented, "Fortunately this vran Lea fellow is a dimwitted louse without an ounce of originality." He began wandering among the collection of Sisters, continuing pontifically, "Like most criminals, his intellect is of the rank and file, and his actions therefore are quite predictable."

Trell could hear Carian gritting his teeth to keep from snarling a retort. He hadn't imagined the islander had such self-control—from all he'd heard of the Pirates of Jamaii, they rarely saw occasion to display the virtue.

"So you see, Sister Marguerite," said the commander as he came to a halt in front of Carian and Trell, "it shall be of no consequence whatsoever to discover the scoundrel among your number." Abruptly he snatched the veil off Carian's head and then skipped back three paces, drawing his sword with a flourish. "*Voila!*"

The Sisters nearest them gasped and drew closer to one another even as the other Tivaricum guard rushed in to lay hands on Carian and Trell.

"Sister Marguerite," declared the commander triumphantly, "I give you the pirate Carian vran Lea."

"The *infamous* pirate Carian vran Lea," Carian quipped with a toothy grin.

"This is *most* unusual!" Sister Marguerite exclaimed, looking shocked. "To allow such an unrepentant man of ill repute within our sanctified walls is truly an outrage. I assure you, Lord Commander, I will search high and low for the Sister who would sully our virtuous Order in such a manner."

The Lord Commander clucked his disdainful agreement while his men bound Trell and Carian's hands. "See that you do, Sister. I pray your virtue be restored quickly with punishment of the miscreants in due measure."

"Indeed, indeed," she said most critically. "They shall certainly be given their due."

The Lord Commander led his guard away without another word, but as Trell was being hustled from the room, he spared a look over his shoulder and saw Sister Marguerite smiling beneath her veil. He couldn't be certain, but he even thought he saw her wink at him.

Outside the villa, the Tivaricum Guard disarmed them and threw the pair indelicately into a jailer's wooden carriage, slamming the barred door and locking it with a heavy iron key. A moment later they were knocked sideways as the horses jumped into a canter and the carriage rocked in their wake.

Looking like a travesty of a bride in his white dress and with his wild black hair long about his shoulders, the pirate pulled out a dagger, fixed it between his knees, and started sawing through the ropes binding his hands before him.

Trell stared at him. "Where did you get that?"

Carian shrugged. "They missed it in their search." He broke free of his bounds and then attended to the ropes binding Trell. Then he found a perch in the corner of the carriage, pulled out his tabac pouch and rolled a smoke. As he exhaled a grey haze, he noted Gendaia on a lead outside the barred window and inquired of a sooty-looking Trell, "Will that horse of yours come when he's called?"

"She," Trell corrected in a somewhat unfriendly tone, "and yes."

"Good. That's good." He eyed Trell curiously. "What's got you so riled?"

"They took my sword, Carian," Trell said in a tone made all the more ominous for its quiet delivery. "That sword hasn't been out of my sight even once since I woke up on the beach in Kai'alil."

Carian blew two smoke rings. "Relax. Everything is going according to plan."

Trell shook his head and looked out the barred window. He really would have to kill the pirate if something happened to his sword. Only Gendaia was more precious to him. *And Fhionna.* But Fhionna wasn't his to claim, though she in contrast seemed to have claimed no small part of his heart. Pushing thoughts of Fhionna from mind—for even just in memory she was uncommonly distracting—Trell looked back to the pirate. "So…emeralds fit for a queen? Where are they then?"

The pirate leered at him. "Hidden in the eyes of a zanthyr, my friend, for nothing else in the realm might overshadow their beauty."

"The eyes of a zanthyr," Trell repeated, thinking of Vaile's predatory gaze one sunny afternoon in the hills above the Mage's sa'reyth. He admitted the pirate had a fair point; certainly no material thing could ever rival a zanthyr's gaze for depth or color.

The pirate looked him up and down. "Were you planning to keep that dress on or…"

Trell had barely noticed that he still wore the white dress. Giving the pirate an annoyed look, he pulled it over his head and let the garment fall. "So what is this all-encompassing plan of yours?"

"Get into the Tivaricum, rescue a pal of mine, recover your sword and your horse and get my prize."

"Prize?"

But the pirate would say no more.

When they finally reached their destination and the doors opened, Trell emerged inside a well-fortified stockade.

"What's this?" protested the Lord Commander when he saw their hands unbound. "Who dares free the scoundrel and his cohort?"

"We didn't touch them, milord," protested the driver. "They come out of the back like unto that."

The Lord Commander glared at a leering Carian. "Search him for blades!" he shouted.

Abruptly five glowering soldiers descended on the pirate.

The Lord Commander turned to Trell then, looking him up and down with pale blue eyes which seemed nothing if not indifferent. "Take this one away."

And off he went.

Trell was ushered into a cell that reeked of vomit and urine and was left there for perhaps an hour. Finally a guard came for him and took him somewhat ungently through a maze of corridors and down a long passage to a room at the end. Inside he found the Lord Commander sitting behind a wide table upon which rested Trell's sword. An older man of middle years sat in one corner with his eyes closed. He wore courtly garments and looked as if he might be sleeping.

As the guard shut the door behind Trell, the Lord Commander looked up at him with a frown. "Now," he said, folding fingers on the table before him, "you shall tell me how you came to possess this sword and what your business is with vran Lea, and if you are honest with me, I will see what can be done to lessen your sentence."

"My sentence?" Trell repeated, not at all liking the Lord Commander's tone.

The Lord Commander eyed him critically. "Any man who consorts with pirates in her Majesty's kingdom shall be sentenced to ten years before the mast."

"Slave ships," Trell snarled.

"A mercy," returned the Lord Commander, holding Trell's incendiary gaze. "So," he declared, sitting back in his chair. He opened his hands toward Trell's sword. "Explain."

"The sword is mine," Trell said evenly. "I would appreciate your returning it to me now."

The Lord Commander leaned forward and placed a hand upon the scabbard. His blue eyes were hard. "This tête-à-tête is a generosity, monsieur," he warned. "I can have others ask the questions in less comfortable conditions."

"The sword is mine," Trell said again less hospitably. He switched to Veneisean so as to ensure the man understood him and continued in his cultured speech, uncompromising and stern, "It has always been mine, it will always be mine, and I would appreciate its immediate return."

The Lord Commander sat back in his chair and frowned at Trell. After a moment's consideration, he asked, "What says her Majesty's Voice?"

The older gentleman in the corner opened colorless eyes and slowly stood. Trell realized he was a truthreader clearly in service to Queen Indora and obviously brought in to divine the truth of Trell's words. "He spoke Raine's Truth," said her Majesty's Voice. "The sword has always belonged to him." His colorless eyes swept Trell, but his expression was unreadable. "Tread carefully, Lord Commander," he added then, glancing back to the soldier once more. "These are matters of grave delicacy." With that, he let himself from the room.

Trell watched him go feeling suddenly uneasy. What was it about his sword that so bothered the Lord Commander? Why would the man require the presence of one of the queen's truthreaders to ensure its ownership? And what was the matter of 'grave delicacy?'

The Lord Commander pondered Trell in silence for a long time. Finally, he asked, "What is your name, monsieur?"

Trell trusted him about as much as a bad-tempered camel, so he answered, "They call me Ama-Kai'alil."

"A desert name," the commander said, looking surprised. "You are... Converted?"

"I have no kingdom," Trell returned, squelching the ache in his soul at speaking the words.

The Lord Commander looked frustrated. "This is most unusual," he declared. He looked Trell up and down again and then stood. "Gregoire, the door!"

A guard entered.

"Put him with the pirate," ordered the commander, "and call for the Magisteré." Looking stormy, he closed himself back up in the room with Trell's sword.

After a long walk, the guard shoved Trell into a room that looked like a dining hall where a dozen guards stood in a circle around the pirate, who lay upon a table. Carian raised his head upon Trell's arrival. "Well, it's about time," he muttered.

"What's all this?" Trell asked the islander as he sat down beside him on the table, indicating the circle of guards.

Carian sat up and swung his legs over the side. "I've escaped from this illustrious establishment eleven times," he said cheerfully. "For some reason, they don't trust leaving me alone in a cell." He looked to the stone-faced Tivaricum Guards. "And how is my old cell-mate Kardashian? I hope he hasn't gone to dance with Jack Ketch since last I visited?"

Carian cast a stony eye upon each guard in turn until one finally answered, "He waits for the hangman's noose on the new moon."

"Ah, good." The pirate smiled a very feline sort of smile. Suddenly he clutched his chest and fell backwards onto the table. Trell reached for him in concern, wherein the choking pirate grabbed his shoulder firmly, and—

Trell was in utter darkness. Only the pirate's firm hold upon his shoulder reassured him that he hadn't been transported into nothingness. He knocked his forehead against something hard as he tried to wiggle out from beneath a heavy weight suddenly atop him.

"*Ow!*" hissed the pirate into the darkness. "That was my skull you clumsy oaf!"

"Where in Tiern'aval are we?" Trell whispered in annoyance. He was so cramped in the tiny space that he couldn't move more than his fingers.

"In an armoire," Carian answered in a low voice. "It was the best I could do on short notice. Their big mistake was letting *me* pick which table to lie upon. This place is riddled with leis. Shhh!"

Trell heard men yelling and the clomping of booted feet as soldiers rushed by. They remained silent until the sounds of men faded.

"Now what?" Trell whispered.

"We're going to weigh anchor out of here, my bonnie lad." Carian pawed around until he felt a latch, and then there was a great release of pressure and they both tumbled out onto the floor.

Carian was up on his feet in an instant. "Smartly now, my handsome!" he urged. Then he was off.

Trell jumped to his feet and hurried after the pirate. Dodging soldiers at every turn, Carian led Trell through a maze of passages, down several flights of stairs, and finally onto an open level of tall, barred cages which emitted an overpoweringly sour odor. Most of the cells' occupants were sleeping in the stinking rushes, though a few sorry sorts eyed Carian dispiritedly as he rushed past. A catcall or two drifted to their ears, but it seemed that these were men who had lost all hope. There were no guards about, and Trell soon noticed that the men were chained to the floor with heavy iron shackles. Most looked too emaciated to put up much of a fight, much less attempt an escape.

Carian finally found the cell he was looking for and pressed his face between the bars. "Kardashian!" he whispered.

A mop of red hair lifted from the straw, followed by the face of a man in his middle years. "About time, you bloody stinking pirate," Kardashian muttered as he stood and wandered to the bars dragging his chains with him. "I was scheduled to dance with Jack Ketch next week." His black eyes shifted to Trell. "Who's your pretty boyfriend?"

"Never mind him," Carian said. "Do you have the map?"

Kardashian eyed him shrewdly. "I've got it. Did you get the emeralds?"

"I told you I would, you gout-brained fop," Carian snapped. "Pass over the map."

Kardashian pulled out a folded piece of cloth from inside his torn vest, while Carian retrieved a velveteen pouch from inside his tunic.

"Where were you hiding that?" Trell hissed in astonishment. "I saw them search you!"

"Trade secrets, poppet," Carian whispered. He eyed Kardashian narrowly. "On three. One…two…three." They exchanged their goods, and Carian's eyes glowed with triumph as he unfolded the cloth and saw the map scrawled within. "You're sure?" he whispered, looking back to Kardashian.

The man grinned through broken teeth. "Sure as silver." Suddenly he jerked his hands, and his shackles fell to the straw. "Let's go." He pushed open his cell door as if it had never been locked. "The food here smells like a camp whore's arsehole and tastes even worse than it smells," he complained. "It's not too late to catch the *Talon* to Kroth, and I'm starving." His tawny eyes gave Trell the once-over, and then he jerked his head, saying, "Follow me."

They rushed behind Kardashian as he led them in a new direction out of the dungeons. Trell grabbed Carian's arm as they ran, whispering tightly, "Who *is* he?"

"Only the greatest thief who ever lived," Carian replied with a grin.

Up several long flights of curving stairs and they emerged into open air across from the stable yard. "Ah!" sighed Kardashian. "The sweet smell of manure. Tis the odor of freedom." He looked to Carian, nodded to Trell and then slipped away into the darkness.

"I'm so utterly predictable, am I?" Carian said, grinning after the thief. Then he looked to Trell. "Smartly now. I've got what we need, so—"

Trell grabbed the man by the chest and pushed him roughly into a near wall. "Not without my horse and my sword," he warned, and his tone left no room for argument.

The pirate gave him a nightmare of a frown, but he didn't argue, possibly because even a pirate of Jamaii knew better than to press his luck with Trell when he got that look in his eye. "Fine," Carian hissed disagreeably. "Let's hope you can whistle loud enough to be heard over the bloody horns, because we're bound to hear them any moment now—as soon as our sainted Lord Commander sets aside his ego in favor of his job, they'll be after me in force. Where's your damn sword then?"

"In a room with the Lord Commander."

"Fortune prick me," Carian snarled. "I—"

But in that moment, horns blared from the stockade walls, drowning out his words. Carian grabbed Trell by the shoulder and shoved him into the shadows as men emerged into the yard from every direction, all of them converging on the main building. Pressing a finger to his lips, the Nodefinder motioned Trell to follow, and in silence, they slipped off again.

It was a strange few minutes that followed as Carian led them across a garland of leis he'd strung for their escape. Their first stop was in the guards' quarters, where they donned surcoats and breastplates and Carian did his best to hide his masses of hair beneath a helmet. Another leis took them deep inside the Citadel, opening upon a dusty room littered with ill-used books. Carian seemed to know the place intimately—which was only fitting, Trell supposed, if indeed the man had escaped eleven times from its confines. Still, he was surprised when they arrived unexpectedly upon the long hallway with its room at the end. They ducked in an alcove and hid behind a dust-laden tapestry as a loud group of soldiers rushed past, and then Carian was loping long-legged down the hall to where Trell's sword awaited. His cutlass appeared in his hand out of nowhere—*how in Tiern'aval is he doing that?*—and then he was barging into the room.

His face fell when he found it empty, though Trell's item of desire remained upon the table. Trell claimed his sword with palpable relief and donned the belt even as they ran out again and—

Met a stone-faced Lord Commander and ten very unfriendly Tivaricum Guards.

Dozier Debardieu pushed up the sleeves of his uniform and settled hands on his scrawny hips. He didn't resent being assigned to the stables, even though he'd joined the Tivaricum Guard on the hopes of participating in grand battles or important missions for his queen. But he never had filled in the way his mama always promised he would, remaining tall and skinny as a barn cat in winter. The other men made fun of him when he sparred, calling him names like Willow Reed and Peach Fuzz, among others which were less supportive of his self-esteem. He knew he wasn't worthy to be considered among their number, so when the Lord Commander offered him the position of Stable Master, he'd accepted with gratitude. The horses were bigger than the soldiers he'd fought in the practice yard, but they were generally of a more even temperament and never called him names.

Except this horse.

She was no doubt calling him all kinds of hateful names, for she whinnied and snorted any time he came near, sounding unpleasantly similar to the laughter of the highborn girls he'd tried to talk to once at the palace while upon an errand for the Lord Commander.

The men who'd gotten her into the small corral had long abandoned him—well, truth be told, she'd struck down two of them in their attempt to unsaddle her and the third said it wasn't worth trying anymore—but they hadn't even managed to get her tack off, and the Lord Commander was sure to want to know what the man carried in his packs. There were ways to break a horse to a man's will, of course, and some of them weren't so cruel that their own Horsemaster hadn't used them on rare occasion, but one didn't think of waging such methods against a Hallovian.

No, indeed not.

Everybody knew Hallovians were nigh on magical beasts and had to be coaxed where they couldn't be convinced. They only went with a man if they deemed him worthy, and no manner of prodding or beating might change their mind. A story was told of a Hallovian stallion that stood his ground whilst his would-be rider beat him til he bled, but still he moved not one inch. Dozier knew he wasn't worthy of riding this horse, but he thought maybe he might convince her to go with him into the stables for her own sake.

He tried again to coax the horse close enough to get a lasso around her neck, if not to make a grab for her trailing reins. "Come now, pretty girl," he murmured. He pushed his hand into his pocket where he'd stuffed some grain and offered it to the mare. She snorted and spun away, running a circle in the corral, her long flaxen mane streaming like moonlight behind her. Dozier was awed by her beauty. It made him wonder yet again about her owner, the one they'd brought in with that pirate.

What kind of man must he be to ride a magic horse?

"Well, if it isn't my old friend the Lord Commander," Carian said amiably as he brandished his cutlass in front of him. "Come for your good-bye kiss?"

The Lord Commander looked pained as he regarded them. Trell couldn't tell if it was due to the pirate's comments, his unfathomable ability to produce weapons out of thin air, or because of Trell. "*Mon seigneur*," said the Lord Commander, clearly addressing Trell, "I beseech you to stand aside and let us deal with this unsavory rogue who has too many times thumbed his nose at her Majesty's justice."

Curiously noting the man's change in manner, Trell replied, "I am honor-bound to complete my accord with the pirate, sir, else I would gladly stand aside for you."

Carian turned Trell a bland look, which he then extended to the commander. Just then a man dressed in an emerald cap and courtly robes pushed through the masses of Guardsmen and stopped at the Lord Commander's side. He was an older man in his middle years, grey-haired and droopy-eyed, but his gaze remained wise. He took one look at Trell and blanched, grabbing the Lord Commander's arm. "It cannot be!" he exclaimed, eyes pinned on Trell like a ghost from the dead. "*Trell?* Is it truly you?"

The Lord Commander looked ill. "Please, my lord," he entreated Trell one last time. "The Magisteré has come to speak with you—only to talk, you understand? We hold no charges against you." His blue eyes shifted icily to Carian, wherein he added, "I cannot abide this treacherous pirate, but I do not wish to see harm come to you."

Trell was caught momentarily speechless—here was a man who undeniably knew him, for he'd given no one his true name. He was staring at them, dumbfounded by their words, when Carian abruptly grabbed him around the neck and pressed a blade to his throat. "That's funny," the pirate remarked as Trell felt cold steel against his flesh and the pirate's breath warm in his ear, "because I'd love to see you kiss the gunner's daughter one of these days, you bilge-sucking, poxed son of a whore. But alas, today I have pressing business elsewhere." He pushed the blade further into Trell's neck, making him flinch. Both the Lord Commander and the Magisteré gasped in dismay, and the Magisteré reached forward as if to halt the pirate with the gesture alone. "Now stand aside," Carian warned, "or this man dies."

"Move aside! Move aside!" shouted the Magisteré with surprising urgency.

The men did so, though the Lord Commander's face was dark with fury. Carian half-dragged Trell past the men, who all turned to follow at a safe distance but with malice in their eyes. As soon as Carian turned a corner of the hallway, he released Trell and grabbed his wrist instead, dragging him in a flat run down an adjoining passage and right through the wall at its end. Trell instinctively threw up his hand as the Nodefinder jerked him across the leis, only to find himself blocking empty air on the roof overlooking the stockade. The horns were still blaring.

Carian turned him an astonished grin. "Balls of Belloth, if you weren't a chase they would've ransomed the kingdom for!" he remarked breathlessly. "Would that I could hang around to discover who they think you are, but we've overstayed our welcome as it is."

Trell felt agonized. It had never been more clear to him that these men knew who he was—or at least they suspected, and certainly the Magisteré had seemed to recognize him at once and had even called him by name! If he but stayed, if he surrendered...the Lord Commander had sworn he was free of any charge.

But the moment he looked to Carian, he knew he could not forsake their accord. *What care have I for a name if I've no honor to back it up?*

"You might think about whistling for your pretty mare any time now," Carian prodded lightly, but Trell saw the tightness around his eyes and sensed the urgency in his voice.

"Right." He whistled for Gendaia.

Dozier was pleased. The mare had suddenly quieted, despite the blaring horns—Dozier would have a thing or two to say to the watch about that once he got the horse stabled—and was now standing still as a statue in the middle of her corral. Surely this meant he was making progress.

Moving slowly so as not to frighten her, he readied his lasso in his right hand and worked the latch on the corral gate with his left. Carefully then, he moved inside the corral, pulling the gate shut behind him but leaving the latch undone so he might leave easily with her in tow.

"Easy girl," he soothed. "There now, that's a good girl—"

Abruptly she tore past him like the wind and was out of the gate and across the yard before he could even find voice to yell after her.

Defeated, Dozier swore an oath and threw down the rope and grain. He wasn't worthy, and that was just Raine's truth. Apparently even the damned horses knew it.

Trell stood in the shadow of a chimney and whistled for Gendaia again.

They'd made a harrowing descent from the roof, Trell mustering incredible self-control to follow the pirate as he scaled bare-handed down a four-story wall. Now, as he crouched in the shadows next to Carian, Trell admitted that if there was one thing he could say for the pirate, it was that his life was not lacking for adventure.

The horns continued to blare, a monotonous overtone that Trell found himself becoming less aware of as the sound wore on, though the yard was no less frenzied than when they'd left it. Groups of soldiers rushed to and fro, while others organized search parties both for the pirate and the escaped thief, Kardashian. Then a combined shouting drew his attention, and the pirate elbowed him happily, saying, "Here she comes."

Sure enough, Gendaia came barreling around the corner, a streak of moonlight pinned to the earth. Trell rushed out to grab her reins with Carian right on his heels, and then they were mounted and Trell turned her to face a long line of soldiers who had amassed in her wake.

"Where is the damnable node, Carian?" Trell demanded through clenched teeth.

"Ride for the gate," the pirate whispered.

"You expect they'll open it for us, do you?"

"No need," he returned.

Trell set his heels to Gendaia, and she leapt into a canter, bowling through the center of the line of men, who scattered like broken pins. Trell saw the main gate, and he leaned close to her neck as she extended her gait to new proportions in a ground-eating gallop.

The islander clung to Trell with his head close enough that his hair kept flying into Trell's eyes. "I forgot to mention," Carian yelled over the blaring horns and shouting men. "This next exit might be a little hairy!"

FORTY-SIX

'Faith is not the question. I have simply seen enough to trust in what I have not yet seen.'

– Ramuhárikhamáth, Lord of the Heavens

Ean's company set out from Chalons-en-Les Trois beneath an overcast sky, following the Mondes as it twisted through the Eidenvale. The days passed smoothly and by the second day, they had climbed in elevation and were traversing the river gorge a thousand feet above the Mondes. The wind was blustery and cold in the gorge, and the high peaks above them were white from recent snows, but the pass was clear and the road remained good.

With the exception of a few caravans and the errant trader headed to Chalons-en-Les Trois, they had the way to themselves, for most people preferred to travel the faster river route; the waterway, in contrast, was busy with sailing craft, ferries and barges on their usual commute between Chalons-en-Les Trois and the Veneisean capital of Tregarion. From the ridge trail so high above, even the larger luxury schooners seemed like toys—which didn't stop Fynn from staring longingly at them.

The weather remained fair, if cold, as they journeyed. The way was clear, the sun was high and provided some small warmth along the blustery trail, and there was firewood aplenty for their campfire each night. For the most part, the company stayed in good spirits—with the singular exception of Fynn, who didn't seem to get on well with Nature in general and bears in specific, and maintained his affronted ill humor even after Gwynnleth had chased the beast away. Still, all seemed marginally well. Gwynnleth assured the prince that the Tyriolicci would not send another assassin so soon, if at all, and thought they should be safe enough in the mountains.

With every new day Ean became more grateful for his companions. Rhys, Bastian, Dorin and Cayal were all capable men, doing multiple duties as guards, scouts, hunters, wood-choppers, cooks, and even story-tellers around late campfires. Alyneri and Tanis pitched in to help like true boon companions, never complaining about any task assigned them no matter how menial, and Gwynnleth was an irreplaceable aid to them, spending her days flying high above to warn of anyone approaching on the road long before they met them, her avian eyes always watchful for those that might bring harm.

Ean was never more grateful for her than on their fourth night.

Because a storm was rising in the west, they took shelter in a cave that seemed to be a favorite among travelers upon the gorge road, for inside they found a woodpile that had been restocked by the cave's last occupants and several fire circles waiting and ready. There was room enough for the entire company, and the single opening meant only one man need stand watch. After eating a satisfying stew of potatoes and lamb from the Comte's stores seasoned with some of Alyneri's thyme, Ean wandered outside with Alyneri in tow.

He'd had little time to speak with her alone since leaving Chalons-en-Les Trois , but he wanted to very much. Though initially he'd dismissed Gwynnleth's words about Alyneri as nonsense, the idea had become a splinter that worked its way deeper into his skin instead of out of it. *Could she really have such feelings for me?* he'd begun to wonder, and if she did, what did *he* feel in return?

While Cayal kept watch from a polite distance, the prince and Alyneri found a spot on a rocky outcropping with an unimpeded view of the western range. The sun was setting in fiery splendor behind bulging storm-clouds heavy with rain, though the sky above the cave was still clear. Far to the south, the rain was already falling in great ashen sheets, blotting out the snowcapped peaks. Ean wondered how Mother Nature knew his mind so well as to create in nature what he battled within.

"Tumultuous," Alyneri murmured from where she sat hugging her knees.

Ean glanced at her. She seemed different after Chalons-en-Les Trois, troubled in a way she hadn't been before. Some of the lightness had left her manner, and because of Gwynnleth's declaration, Ean couldn't now help but wonder if it was because of him. He looked back to the view. "The realm seems truly alive when you see it like this, don't you think?"

She cast him a sideways glance. "I'd never thought of it like that, but yes," she admitted as she focused back on the view. "There's something about seeing all of this—the sunset and the storm—that makes all the world seem like…well, like a living thing."

"They are alive in some way aren't they?" Ean asked. He glanced to her, clarifying, "I mean, all of this we're watching tonight is the fifth strand at work, isn't it? The wind and its storms, the ceaseless motion of the seas, our sun and stars, the earth beneath us. The living realm?"

Alyneri smiled softly at him. "I think maybe you understand it better than some Adepts. The fifth strand is so…foreign to most of us. It doesn't govern life as we understand it, yet as you said, how can anyone look at a view like this and not believe the realm is alive?"

Ean nodded his agreement. They watched the sun setting together then. A dark crimson disk was just disappearing between two far mountains whose peaks tore at the blue-black clouds massing above.

After a moment, Alyneri glanced at him and then dropped her eyes. "Ean, I didn't mean to imply just then that you weren't also an Adept—"

The prince turned with a quick smile to reassure her. "I wasn't thinking about that." He took her hand and twined her fingers within his, remembering days as a boy when they'd sat upon the cliffs together in much the same position; younger days, innocent days, before Death claimed those they loved, one by one. "I was thinking how oddly the scene before us seemed to mirror my mind right now," he said. He shot her a rueful grin, adding, "Tumultuous, I think you called it. That sounds about right… I might say conflicted, also."

"Over your power?" she asked quietly.

He cracked a grim smile. "Over my path." When she offered no input, he asked, "What, no words of wisdom?"

She shook her head.

It was so unlike her not to have an opinion that it actually disturbed him. What had happened to her in Chalons-en-Les Trois? Wasn't *he* the one who'd almost died? Why then did she act as if hope had been stolen from her?

"Alyneri," Ean said, leaning forward to capture her gaze with his own, "if I ask you a question, will you promise to answer me truthfully?"

Immediately he saw a little furrow appear between her brows. "That depends upon the question."

"There should be no secrets between us as betrothed," he said lightly.

But she dropped her eyes again. "Ean..."

Ean held her hand tighter. "I just need to know how you really feel, Alyneri."

"Why?" she asked, biting her lip and staring at her lap. It was both protest and plea in one.

Her question caught him off guard, but he knew she deserved an honest answer. "Well," he said, thinking it through, "so that...so that I can know how I feel."

She looked to him then, and he saw tears welling in her lovely brown eyes. "But you see," she said, forcing a gentle smile, "if you don't already know how you feel, then it really *doesn't* matter."

Ean didn't fully understand that logic, but he didn't want to press her too hard because he could already see that she was upset. "Gwynnleth..." he began, turning to look back at the sunset, which was now fading from red-violet to violet-grey, "she made it seem like I was torturing you."

Alyneri laughed and quickly pressed the tears from her eyes with one hand, but Ean saw with a pang of guilt that she laughed because of the truth in his statement, not because of its absurdity. His expression fell. "I'm sorry," he whispered.

She shrugged and gave him a brave smile. "You have enough to worry about without adding my ridiculous feelings into the mix."

He looked at her with concern. How could she think him so insensitive to her affections? "Alyneri, you are one of my dearest frien—"

Abruptly she touched her fingers to his lips to pause him and then pressed them to her own, her expression stricken. "Don't," she begged, her face a display of emotion. "Don't say it." Swallowing, she looked back to the view. A clump of menacing storm clouds now raced overhead, and all the light seemed vanished from the world.

Ean was about to ask what was so bothering her, when he heard the screaming cry of a hawk and spun his head to the sky instead. The avieth speared down out of the heavens in a headlong rush, missing their heads by mere inches as she streaked past.

Ean stood and helped Alyneri to her feet, turning just as Gwynnleth left the form in a rush of brilliance. Her face was a mask of horror when she turned and yelled, "Hurry—into the cave!"

Ean grabbed Alyneri's hand and ran with her, understanding nothing but the terrified look on the avieth's face and the urgency in her tone.

Cayal met them at the entrance. "What's wrong?"

"Inside!" Gwynnleth hissed, shoving him before her as she ran. "*Inside!*"

She pushed past the soldier and shouted to the others, "Douse the fire!"

Rhys gave her a startled look, but Tanis must've sensed something of her thoughts, for he started scattering the coals with a heavy stick while Bastian smothered any lingering flames with ash.

Seeing that accomplished, the avieth turned to Ean. "Keep everyone inside and away from the entrance," she ordered. Then she ran back out into the rising storm.

"What in Tiern'aval?" Fynn said, coming up beside his cousin.

Ean was equally bemused.

"She didn't want him seeing the light," Tanis offered. The lad approached through the darkness of the cave, backlit by what dim embers remained from the dying coals.

"Didn't want who seeing it?" Fynn asked.

"I don't know—*she* didn't know," Tanis added. "But there's...something out there." Abruptly, the lad shivered.

"Fynn," Ean said in a tone that spoke volumes, and the royal cousin followed as Ean headed back to the cave mouth. He pressed his back against the stone and peered around the rough edge. Beyond, the mountainside fell away into the gorge, a scattering of trees furring the near slopes. What moonlight peeped between the swiftly flowing clouds illumined the gorge in varying shades of charcoal and black.

Ean stared into the gloom letting his eyes adjust. He felt Fynn's near closeness and heard Rhys breathing further behind, all of them trying to discern what had so disturbed the avieth.

Suddenly Ean clutched at his head. It came as an attack on his senses, a shrieking, screaming, raging purge that raped his mind with malicious glee. Gasping for breath, the prince fell to his knees.

"Ean!" Fynn hissed.

Pain consumed Ean, driving the air from his lungs, petrifying their membranes, burning them with sulfuric smoke. Ean clutched his skull and fell forward onto the cave floor, whimpering as he curled into a ball.

While the others looked on in horror, darkness consumed Ean...digested him, and spit him back into the fires to burn anew. He felt the claws of a massive beast shredding his skin, while worms with a thousand spiny teeth chewed their way through his brain. Pain wracked him in vivid color, but despite the assault on his senses, he instinctively knew the attack was waged only against him.

He—means—to—draw—me—out.

It was incredible how hard he had to concentrate in order to complete the thought, for the agony raging within him demanded his full attention. Yet somehow the moment was familiar—as if he'd faced such pain before.

"Get Alyneri!" Fynn meanwhile hissed, and the sound of quickly shuffling feet was Rhys making his careful way back into the depths of the cave.

"Ean..." Fynn grabbed him by the shoulders, but his hands were no comfort. The prince was already putting every ounce of will toward holding in his screams.

Alyneri arrived in a rustling of skirts and threw herself to her knees. Ean felt her soft hands upon his head, and another whimper escaped him. Fire raged up and down his body while unseen claws tore great strips of flesh from his bones.

He burned.

He was being torn apart.

Pain ravaged unhindered, feeding on his flesh with wild abandon.

A low moan escaped his lips, and he managed one agonized inhale. Shuddering, he pulled his knees in closer and rocked himself, clenching his teeth so tightly he feared they would shatter. All his desperation was on trying not to scream, knowing the attack was waged for that purpose alone. *I will not—will not—will—not!*

"What's wrong with him?" Fynn hissed.

"I don't know!" Alyneri sounded close to tears.

"*Lord Captain...*" Cayal said under his breath. He was standing in the shadow of the cave's entrance staring out into the night. "You'd better see this."

Fynn looked up and reluctantly left Ean to join Rhys at the entrance, wherein Cayal pointed to the north.

It was far away and approaching fast, a dark form flying low beneath tempestuous clouds. As it grew nearer, its shape became clearer, though it never seemed more than a shadow. No light illumined it; rather it was discernable only because it blocked other things from view—clouds, trees...entire mountain peaks.

Those who saw it stood frozen, aghast, unable to form words to describe it even had they found their voices.

Abruptly a dark form reared up before them. It was Gwynnleth pushing them back and away, safely into the shadows of the deeper cave.

Even from far within, they saw it fly by, and it was several seconds before all of it had passed. The beat of its wings sent whirlwinds of dirt spinning into the cave, and they all turned their heads away, shielding their eyes. While Ean moaned an unearthly whine and rocked, hugging his head, the creature turned and flew past them again, heading back in the direction from which it had come. They could hear each whacking flap of its wings, a reverberating thump and crack of lightning striking earth.

The thumping faded, and then there was only the sound of quiet rainfall.

After a long silence, Ean released his knees and fell onto his back with a shuddering exhalation.

"Ean—dear Epiphany!" Alyneri hugged his chest, pulling him close as she wept with relief.

Fynn swore a stream of curses. He knelt at Ean's side. "What in thirteen bloody hells just happened?"

The prince laid the back of one arm across his forehead and drew in another shuddering breath. It was hard letting go of the pain—hard to convince himself it was truly gone, that there was no reason for his body to still feel it. Impossible to relax.

"It was looking for him," Gwynnleth said, and turning behind her she added to whoever was listening, "You can get the fire started again."

Moments later a blaze of dead fir limbs illuminated the cave with warm yellow light.

"What was that...thing?" a benumbed Cayal asked her.

She shrugged.

"It was one of his creatures," Ean rasped. He rolled onto his side and shakily pushed himself up. The understanding had come in a visceral way, instinct born of a past life's fatal experience melding now with knowledge recently gained. "The ones who're hunting me. It must've been one of the Fifth Vestal's creatures."

Alyneri got to her feet and helped Ean to stand. "But..." she gazed at him in confusion as he was slowly straightening. "But what gave you such pain?"

"It did," Ean said. "…I think."

"How?"

Ean thought about that as he walked shakily toward the fire, and suddenly one major piece found its place in the puzzle. "It knows my pattern," he whispered, the knowledge coming with a pang of terror as he now understood more about the danger he faced.

Alyneri blanched. "It knows your pattern?" she repeated, aghast. She sounded even more horrified as she whispered, "It can work the lifeforce?"

Ean wrapped an arm around her shoulders—more for his own comfort and reassurance than hers. The last of the experience was working itself from his body, and he trembled every so often, drawing concerned looks from her. "It's hunting for me," he said, "and because it knows my pattern, it can use that to cause me pain."

"That's horrible!" Alyneri gasped. "It's unthinkable that an Adept would do such a thing to another—even a Wildling!"

"I beg your pardon?" Gwynnleth said with one eyebrow arched dangerously. "It's far more likely to see a second-strander abusing his talent than to find a third abusing theirs."

"And I suppose Geshaiwyn are only acting on natural instincts when they hunt men as prey?" Alyneri retorted.

"Girls, girls," Fynn interposed, "if you're going to fight, let it be naked in my bedroom." He looked directly to the avieth then. "I've never heard of any Wildling race that looked like that. Have you?"

Reluctantly she turned to look at him. "I don't think that thing was germane to our world."

"Belloth blow me sideways," Fynn growled. "What in Tiern'aval do we do now?"

Ean looked to him. "Nothing has changed, Fynn."

Fynn threw up his hands. "Oh sure," he grumbled. "'Go with your cousin,' the Vestal said to me," he mimicked Raine's voice and manner fairly well. "'Watch out for him. Protect him from those that hunt.' *Right.*" Fynn spun an irritable glare at Ean. "He didn't say anything about Whisper Lords, Bethamin's Ascendants, Marquiin and bloody freaking *dragons*!"

"It did seem a dragon," noted Cayal in a low voice to Tanis, who sat beside him.

"Calm down, Fynn," Ean murmured. He sat down beside the fire, grateful for its heat, for its warmth. Life-giving warmth. For all the searing pain he'd felt, beneath it, behind it, was a cold so wholly dead it could only represent the end of everything they knew. Trying to shake off the feeling, which disturbed him on a primal level and left his very soul trembling, Ean held his hands to the flames and told Fynn resolutely, "The only difference is that now we know better what chases."

Sometime during the night, the temperature dropped and the rain turned to snow. The company emerged from the cave the following morning into a sparkling white wonderland. Though the day remained cold, the sun hung brightly above them, warming their backs as they continued the long trek through the river gorge.

Ean was reticent to speak with the others about what had happened, refusing to burden them with the same fears he battled constantly. He'd already had altercations with Rhys and Fynn earlier that morning, which resulted in nothing but ill feelings between them, but his position was firm. Better they be angry with him than suffer the same malady of fear and indecision.

Such was his mindset when Gwynnleth came to speak with him.

The avieth rode with them that day, sitting bareback on her chestnut stallion, which had been a gift of the Comte D'Ornay. She offered no explanation for why she rode instead of flying scout far above, but Ean was growing used to the idea that Wildlings rarely explained themselves to anyone.

The winding way alternated between long stretches of high firs and sheer cliffs overlooking the river far below. At one point, the road narrowed as it wound around the edge of a sheer precipice overlooking the Mondes, and the group was forced to spread out. Ean was riding fourth in line, behind Fynn, Brody and Rhys in the lead, when Gwynnleth brought her mount up to join his side. She was quiet for a long while, just gazing ahead with her straight nose and high cheekbones in profile to Ean, her wild, wavy hair pulled back with a leather cord. There was something familiar about her profile—Ean recalled thinking this before, but was still unsure what it was about her that caught his attention—yet while she looked foreign and wild, he didn't think of her as fierce, save in description of her beauty.

"You do them no service, Ean val Lorian," she said suddenly, still gazing forward.

Ean followed her eyes toward Rhys and Fynn and knew she referenced their earlier argument. "What good comes of speaking of things you know nothing about?" he disagreed. "We talk in circles, resolving nothing."

Her attention flashed to him—there were moments, such as then, when she seemed very avian: the way she suddenly jerked her head around, like a hawk spotting prey, or how she might watch for hours unending with an owl's piercing stare. "Perhaps you reach no resolution," she agreed, holding his gaze, "but something is gained."

"What would that be?" he asked skeptically.

She looked forward once more. "You see no value in the conversation because you are thinking only of yourself and your own needs."

Ean bristled. "I am *not* thinking of myself!" he hissed in a low voice.

"Really? A good leader listens to the concerns of his men."

Ean shook his head and stared off angrily over the gorge. "They seek answers that I don't have."

"A good leader listens without the need to solve."

Ean worked the muscles of his jaw, clenching and unclenching. "Is that so?"

"Indeed," she confirmed in her detached way, as if merely commenting upon the weather and not things so close to his heart. "Your men need to speak of these things to you. They're not in search of solutions—as you mistakenly believe—but of reassurance. They need to know you're concerned about the same things they're concerned about, that you're seeing the same dangers."

Her answer mollified his anger but roused his angst. He spun her a pained look. "How could I not be?"

"Of course." She waved a hand airily. "Tis a foregone conclusion that you must have the same concerns. So you should see then that their questions are really just a means of communicating their own fear, and it helps them to voice these fears to you, their leader, even if you are not so similarly aided by the conversation." When Ean said nothing, only stared out at the gorge, she inquired, "Are you similarly aided?"

He turned her a defeated look. One day he would learn better than to argue with the avieth; she had a way of turning all quarrels to her favor while instilling feelings of culpability and guilt more acutely than any of his governesses or even his mother. "How then might I reassure you, Gwynnleth?" he asked bitterly.

She arched a ginger brow at him. "Mocking me will cost you half a mark."

"If my manner seems mocking," he returned, "it is only that I need the reassurance of your continued company. Whoever will lecture me once you leave my side?"

She regarded him narrowly and then turned forward once more. "Why is that creature hunting you?"

Ean thought of denying her the benefit of an answer, but he knew it would only earn him another lecture—perhaps on the ill-advisement of self-serving witticism—so he exhaled a heavy sigh and said, "I believe—and this is only conjecture, for rest you assured I haven't asked—that it wants to kill me because I can unwork patterns."

That drew her eye with both brows raised. "Unwork them? You are a wielder?"

He shook his head.

Her eyes widened. "An Adept then?" She looked him up and down curiously. "Of what strand?"

"I don't know," he confessed, feeling as always the anguish of the mystery turning a jagged dagger in his chest. "The Vestal told me I had Returned. Later I realized that I have recently Awakened, but I've never heard of a strand of Adept who can unwork patterns." He lifted troubled grey eyes to her. "Have you?"

She cocked her head sideways and peered at him. "What can you do?"

Ean thought of the patterns he'd unworked, the trace-seal, his invisible bounds, and the Marquiin. If only he could understand what he'd done. The Marquiin was especially troubling, for his demise sparked questions Ean didn't dare even ask himself. Yet he spoke the words to the avieth as a confession upon his tongue. "I destroyed the hold that Bethamin had on one of his Marquiin."

Far from surprised, Gwynnleth merely cocked her head to the other side and continued staring at him in her unsettling way. After a moment, she turned forward again. "There is an old Cyrenaic legend about a group that called themselves the Quorum of the Sixth Truth," she said. "They lived in the times before the cataclysm, before there were Vestals to watch over *elae's* children. The Quorum was said to boast powerful wielders who could counter even the most terrible spell, undo any magical working." She arched inquiring brows, adding, "Sounds something like you, no?"

"I wouldn't have put it exactly like that," Ean muttered.

"In its nascent years, the Quorum was widely hailed and recognized, for they seemed to live up to their boast and could be called upon for aid in any situation. Alas, their end was not so bright."

"What happened?"

She absently thumbed the hilt of her short sword at her belt. "The legend is unclear. What is known is that the Quorum became splintered; some of its members began practices which were antipathetic to the Quorum's original purpose. There was a grave battle in which their temple in Tambarré was destroyed, and the surviving members scattered."

Ean sighed. *So much for hoping they might help me.*

"You miss the point again, Northerner," Gwynnleth remonstrated with an annoyed look, aptly interpreting his sigh of disappointment. "Adepts are inextricably linked to their strand. They Return—again, and again, and again—always as an Adept of the same strand. I have many times lived and died as an avieth," and she added proudly, "It will always be so."

"I see," Ean said, giving her a peevish look, "so you think I'm a resurrected Quorum member from Cyrenaic times."

"It is not impossible," she confirmed, either missing or ignoring his sarcastic tone.

Ean didn't want to speak of the matter anymore, for it roused too much ire and heartache, so he changed the subject. "The other morning, in the yard at the Ville de la Chesney…how did you learn to fight like that?"

"I have trained for many years."

"In what style?" he pressed, for the matter was a curiosity. There was only one man he'd ever seen swing his blade in a similar fashion.

"I learned from different tutors," she replied evasively.

"You wield Merdanti blades," Ean pointed out. "I have only ever seen one race carry such weapons, reportedly made at their own hands." He eyed her inquisitively.

"Anyone can wield a Merdanti blade," she replied with a toss of her head, which wasn't an answer at all.

The road widened then, for they rounded the cliff at last, and the way opened a view onto the winding path behind them, which followed the line of bulging cliffs. That's when Rhys reined in to wait for Ean. He wore a stormy expression and nodded toward the road behind. "We're being followed."

Ean peered over his shoulder, squinting in the glaring wintry sunlight toward the dark spot further back along the curving trail.

"A lone rider on this trail warrants investigation," Rhys said. "I'll send Cayal for a closer look."

As the captain signaled to the scout, Gwynnleth turned and gazed over her shoulder. "I doubt you have much to fear from that zanthyr," she noted after a moment. "If he intended you harm, you'd have clashed with him days ago."

Ean's heart skipped a beat. "A zanthyr?" he repeated. "You think that man's a zanthyr?"

She arched a brow. "Do you question the eyes of a falcon, Prince of Dannym?"

Fynn rode forward to join them. "What's Cayal off about?"

"We're being followed," Ean told him, nodding over his shoulder.

Fynn turned to look. "I knew it," he complained as he peered at the dark spot that was a horse and rider. "Left to themselves, things always go from bad to worse."

Ean gave him a withering look. "Thank you, Fynn, for that very helpful insight."

"I've said all along we should have taken the river," Fynn pointed out.

"Yes, I remember."

"The trip would've taken half as long and been twice as comfortable," he added. "You have to admit at this point that it wouldn't have mattered, Ean. The whole realm knows you're traveling with Alyneri by now. Might as well go to our deaths in comfort." To accentuate his dramatics, he looked sadly down at his boot, the heel of which was still stained from his treading in something unpleasant that morning, then shook his head again and announced, "Nature abhors people."

Gwynnleth cast him her first smile of the day. "I quite agree with you there, Northerner."

Rhys kept staring at the zanthyr. "Do you think he's a threat, your Highness?"

The prince considered the question and turned another look over his shoulder. "No," he said after a moment. "I think not. As long as he stays only a shadow on the horizon, he's too far to harm us and too far to catch. He just wants us to know he's there."

Ean kept his voice calm, but his heart was racing. *Could it be him?* He looked to the avieth feeling anticipation welling, rising like deep-sea waves to break against his chest. "Why do you say we'd have clashed with him already?"

Gwynnleth shrugged."He's been following us for days."

"Days," Ean repeated slowly, giving her a peevish look, "and you didn't think to alert anyone?"

"I told you, if he intended you harm, you'd already be dead."

And would you have tried to stop him? Ean wondered. Sometimes he really wasn't sure what to think about the avieth.

Still, hope filled him at the idea of reuniting with the zanthyr who'd rescued him what now seemed so long ago; Ean had a sense that if anyone could help him understand his talent, the zanthyr could. *But what are the chances it's the same man?* He dared not let his hopes rise too high for fear of the plummeting fall he would face should it be a different creature. He cleared his throat and asked the avieth, "How do you know that man is a zanthyr?"

"A *zanthyr!*" Fynn repeated in surprise, having missed Gwynnleth's earlier pronouncement. He threw out a hand and proclaimed, "Well that just proves my point! A zanthyr, by Belloth's rotten black balls! What could be worse?" He began muttering to himself about the evils of zanthyrs.

Gwynnleth gave him sour look before turning back to Ean to answer simply, "It's not as though the creatures are hard to recognize."

"Really?" Ean asked. "I guess I wouldn't know, having met only one myself."

"Oh?" she looked mildly interested. "Which one?"

Ean broke into a sheepish grin. "He didn't actually give his name."

She rolled her eyes. "Typical." Casting an ill-humored look over her shoulder, she turned back to Ean and noted, "They all have the same haughty, holier-than-thou, arrogance about them, and not a one but isn't as insufferable a creature as ever walked the realm."

"Wait, I'm confused," Fynn said. "Are we talking about zanthyrs or avieths?"

She gave him a withering look.

"And just how many zanthyrs have you had the pleasure of knowing, Gwynnleth?" Ean asked.

"Even one is one is too many," she returned flatly.

For no reason he could fathom, Ean got a sudden wildly improbable idea that yet seemed the only explanation for her skill with a blade. So he countered with, "Yet, if I'm not mistaken, it was a zanthyr who taught you swordplay."

Gwynnleth stared at him in astonishment. Her mouth opened as if to question how he could know such a thing, but it seemed words failed her.

Ean looked back to the road ahead, grinning from ear to ear. To have perceived one of the avieth's deep secrets was truly gratifying.

"He should get bonus marks for that one," Fynn told Gwynnleth.

"This is not a quiz for extra credit, Northerner," she snapped at him.

"But you'd make such a lovely tutor," Fynn returned. "All the boys would fantasize about you. I'm fantasizing about you right now, actually."

"What a coincidence," she remarked coolly. "I am entertaining a fantasy about you as well."

Fynn grinned happily. "Does yours involve a whip, fudge sauce and a tambourine?"

"No," she replied, narrowing her gaze. "Rather, my swords and a lot of blood—yours particularly."

"See," Fynn said, looking to Ean. "I told you she was the kinky type."

"Fynnlar," Ean murmured. "Behave."

"No one ever tells stories of the well-behaved, Ean," Fynn argued. "I intend to be immortalized in song."

"How shall the verse go?" Gwynnleth posed. She pressed a finger to her lips and said in singsong fashion,

"This is the story of Fynn,
Who partied a little too fine,
He thought with his prick,
And picked up a trick,
Who drowned him in a tub of his wine."

"That was a limerick," Fynn remarked, casting her an indignant look. "Not a song."

"I kind of liked it," Brody offered from behind.

Gwynnleth blessed him with a twitch of a smile.

"Traitor," Fynn accused the Bull. "I should fire you."

"You can't fire me," Brody rumbled. "I serve Prince Ryan."

"Technicalities," Fynn muttered.

As the sun was setting over Chalons-en-Les Trois, Sandrine du Préc heard a knock upon her parlor door and looked up from the letter she'd been penning. She was due to embark for the Cairs the following morning, but thus far her affairs were taking more time than she would've liked to conclude. So it was that she sounded less than welcoming as she called, "*Entrer*."

Her chambermaid poked her head through the parting of the door. "Madame, a courier is here for you."

Sandrine set down her quill. "A courier from whom?"

"He will not say, Madame, but his Veneisean is atrocious."

"Very well. Show him in."

While the maid retrieved the courier, Sandrine rose from her desk and adjusted her gown in the mirror. Assured that her assets were on their best display, she turned just as the door opened again and a man entered. Though she'd never met him, she suspected immediately for whom he worked. All of Morwyk's men had the same ill-disposed set to their jaw, as if intent upon dragging the kingdom by their teeth.

"Well?" she inquired in the common tongue, arching one ice-pale brow. "What have you?"

"A token of my good faith," he replied, withdrawing a card from within his vest.

Sandrine turned it over and saw a violet wax seal imprinted with the signet of House val Rothschen but twisted slightly in a way that only Sandrine would recognize as Ianthe's mark. *So…my dear cousin has placed her bet with the Duke of Morwyk, but has her husband, I wonder?*

Sandrine handed the card back to the courier. "And your message?"

The man glanced around the room. "Is it—"

"We are quite alone, I assure you," she remarked in annoyance.

"Tis well, madam," he replied then, "for my message is one of the utmost secrecy. Your cousin places her faith in our mutual acquaintance and asks that you do the same. Mayhap you discern of whom I speak?"

"Mayhap," she repeated flatly. By the Hand of Temperance but the man was tedious! "State your business and be done with it. I am due to leave upon the morn and cannot spend all evening awaiting the denouement of your visit."

The man looked slightly miffed at her abrasive manner. "The matter concerns the Duchess of Aracine. I was told you made her recent acquaintance."

Hearing this, Sandrine seated herself by the fire, eyeing the man all the while. "I have," she replied. "What of her?"

"Our mutual acquaintance would very much like to meet her."

Sandrine's interest was piqued. "Why?"

"I am not at liberty to say, madam."

"Then I am not at liberty to help you. Good night, sir."

He frowned at her, not moving toward the door.

She poured herself a glass of wine from the decanter at the table to her side and sipped it quietly, regarding him over the rim. After a long moment of this, wherein the courier was obviously weighing his options, he finally snarled an oath and blurted, "His Grace is most interested in the Duchess's…heritage and wishes to question her in more detail upon the matter."

"A letter may be most efficacious to this end," Sandrine pointed out.

"His Grace wishes to do the questioning in person, madam."

"Indeed, and what has this to do with me?"

"It came to his Grace's attention that you may be in a position to help him… acquire the Duchess."

Sandrine laughed. "*Acquire* her?"

"His Grace has heard of your skill and was told you were a woman of... information."

"His Grace is not misinformed," Sandrine confirmed. "I do happen to know whence the Duchess is heading and how best to gain possession of her person without also acquiring her guards. But my services come at a cost."

"His Grace is prepared to reward you for your assistance. Agasi silver—"

"Is not the kind of cost I am speaking of," she informed him with a predatory smile.

He cleared his throat. "I was instructed to gain your help at...any price, madam. Secrecy is of the utmost, and the Marchioness assured us of your fidelity and discretion."

Sandrine's smile widened. "Take a seat," she advised, "and I shall tell you how to snare the sweet little rabbit."

Ean's company made camp that night within the half-mile of forest between road and river. Rhys was edgy, and he led several short expeditions through the woods and back along the road, but he returned each time looking sullen and ill-humored.

"No sign of the zanthyr, your Highness," Rhys grumbled as he retook his fireside seat beside the prince for the third time.

Ean grunted without looking up from studying the flames.

The captain stroked his beard, looking frustrated. "I just don't see how he can vanish like that! One minute there and the next..."

Ean shrugged. "I knew you wouldn't find him," he remarked.

"But we were so close! Three bounds and I would have had him!"

"Three bounds and he would have run you through," Gwynnleth returned, pinning the captain with her hawkish gaze. "Be thankful he didn't want to kill you. Why else would he have vanished, save to avoid confrontation?"

"That zanthyr vanishes at whatever time will most annoy whoever is in front of him," Alyneri observed.

Ean looked at her curiously. "How do you know that?"

She shrugged. "If it's the same infernal creature as brought you to Fersthaven, he disappeared right in front of me for no reason whatsoever. It's not like there wasn't a door three steps away."

"Sounds about right," Rhys grumbled.

Ean regarded her intently. He hadn't realized that she also suspected the zanthyr was the same man, but then it followed that Alyneri would've reached this conclusion; she had a quick mind and could be quite logical when the matter didn't concern her personally or emotionally.

Alyneri looked up and noticed him watching her. She held his gaze. "What do you think he wants with you, Ean?"

"I haven't the first clue." *But I have hopes.*

"You, avieth," Rhys said. "You said you knew the man was a zanthyr. Who does he work for? Why would he be following us?"

Gwynnleth snorted. "He works for no one but himself."

"Every man has a master," Rhys argued.

"Then his master is none but our Maker, for no man upon this earth might order the creature to do anything."

"What about a woman?" Alyneri posed. "Do you have influence over him?"

"Less than the sea upon the shore," Gwynnleth returned with uncharacteristic bitterness. "I might beat and batter and accomplish nothing."

"Not *nothing*," came a deep voice out of the darkness.

The zanthyr entered their campsite from between two trees, from a place several would later swear was empty seconds before. Ean sat up swiftly, and Rhys drew his sword with a scrape of steel, glaring hotly at the creature.

The zanthyr ignored him. He hooked his thumbs in his sword belt and grinned at Gwynnleth, finishing, "Your attempts were at least memorable."

She rolled her eyes and looked away.

'The zanthyr is an elusive creature with questionable motives...' Raine's words sprung to mind as Ean stared at the man he recognized, feeling both relief and anxious unease. He wondered for the hundredth time what kind of creature was honest enough to admit that he wasn't worthy of trust? Ean waved at his bristling Captain. "Sit down, Rhys," he murmured, and he gave him a long, uncompromising look.

Reluctant, Rhys yet sheathed his sword, but he remained standing. Bastian, Cayal and Dorin all rushed back into camp, but each stopped short upon seeing the zanthyr standing there, their faces framed in surprise.

Ean admitted the man was even more impressive than he remembered. In fact, he was downright intimidating.

Taller than the tallest of them, with the powerful build of a warrior, he wore britches and a vest of supple black leather belted over a heavy black tunic. Both a broadsword and a dagger were secured at his belt, and a heavy greatcloak floated like liquid night at his feet. Raven locks fell in loose curls to his shoulders, and piercing green eyes stared out from an ageless face. The strong lines of his jaw and the perfect balance of his features seemed those of an ancient beauty, like a fine statue from a civilization long lost. As he faced them, he was both terrifying and compelling, a powerful combination.

After the prince waved the captain off, the zanthyr smiled a feline sort of smile and brushed past Rhys without as much as a sideways glance. Rhys muttered something unintelligible save that it was derogatory and heatedly retook his seat, all the while eyeing the zanthyr with obvious distrust. Ean, however, was regarding the creature thoughtfully, and Fynn was trying hard *not* to regard the zanthyr at all.

The zanthyr seemed to note all of their reactions, and he chuckled to himself as he took a seat by the fire, across from Ean and next to Tanis. "*Ahh*...my prince," the zanthyr sighed as he settled into a casual pose of relaxation. He spoke with a deep, throaty sort of voice akin to a purr but echoic of a growl. "It is good to see you well and whole."

Ean kept his eyes pinned on the man. There was so much said and not said in that simple statement, so many near-fatal encounters since last they parted. Did the zanthyr know of any of them, or all of them? "Whole at least," Ean replied, "albeit narrowly so." Then he added quietly, "But I suspect you know all about that."

The zanthyr smiled. "Tracking your every move through my crystal ball, perhaps?"

"More like as not he's in bed with your enemies," Rhys grumbled. "Everyone knows a zanthyr will play both sides, and only a fool trusts one of the creatures."

Ean ignored the captain's remarks. "Since that very first day," he said, holding the zanthyr's emerald gaze, "I haven't been able to stop wondering why you risked so much to protect me."

The zanthyr arched a brow in sly humor. "There was little danger to me personally," he replied. His emerald eyes flickered over the remainder of the company, taking everyone in.

"What I want to know," Rhys demanded, "is what was in it for you?"

The zanthyr shrugged. He began tracing an intricate, looping pattern in the dirt with a gloved forefinger. "I was bored and in need of diversion," he answered without looking up. "I offered my services freely; then and now."

"Services!" Rhys scoffed. "What services might these be? What need have we of a capricious creature who knows a few stolen tricks?"

The zanthyr arched a solitary raven brow, untroubled by Rhys' barbs—clearly the captain was beneath his contempt. "How would you know what a zanthyr can or cannot do, Lord Captain Rhys val Kincaide?" He settled the captain a disturbingly cool gaze then. "We are not so different, you and I," he observed. "We have similar purposes."

"And what might those be?"

"My motives are my own," the zanthyr replied, "but it should be painfully obvious that I intend none of you harm."

"And why should we take your word for that?" Alyneri challenged then. She was clearly growing irritated with the creature's haughty ambiguity—not to mention that his history with Farshideh and Tanis made him even more suspect. "You've given us no reason to trust you."

The zanthyr looked Alyneri up and down with a mocking smile. "The fact is, your Grace, I don't require anyone's trust. Though it would be clear to most that at any point I could have claimed the lives of everyone here, there are always some who need more time to reach the obvious conclusion." He looked her up and down again in one smooth sweep, and added with aloof indifference, "Evidently, we cannot all immediately see what is plainly before us."

Alyneri's mouth dropped open. "How dare you insinuate that I am slow witted!"

"On the contrary, your Grace," he returned in quiet amusement, "you take my words as their truth resonates within you, not as they were intended."

Her mouth dropped open again. "Why—why that's no better! I am a Duchess of the realm and a Healer to the crown of Dannym! Have you no respect?"

A dark dagger appeared in the zanthyr's hand—there was no telling from whence it had come—and he tossed it into the air, making it flip three times before he caught it by its deadly point. "As you choose to grant trust only once earned, your Grace," he replied casually, "so do I choose to grant respect in the same manner."

Her eyes really flew wide then.

Ean intervened before Alyneri could retaliate. "So what do I call you? Forgive me, but 'friend zanthyr' is a little too ironic for my taste."

The zanthyr threw back his head as if to laugh but made no sound; only his eyes glittered with amusement. "You may call me Phaedor, my prince," he replied.

Fynn was heard to murmur then, "This is the dumbest decision in the long history of dumb decisions."

Phaedor's emerald gaze looked the royal cousin up and down; he seemed amused. "You could always send me away," he offered with an indifferent shrug.

Not on my life, thought Ean, but he replied, "You are welcome at our fire."

"*Ean*," Fynn protested hotly under his breath, "you can't know the creature isn't working for Björn!"

The zanthyr shook his head. "I am no wielder's minion. You think me a fool."

"More likely he wouldn't have you," Fynn grumbled. Then he added with a glare at Ean, "Far be it from us to follow the example of an enemy, even if it seems wise."

The zanthyr regarded the royal cousin with an aloof yawn.

So why have you really come? Ean wondered, gazing thoughtfully at the creature. *And why do I trust you so completely?* It was the strangest thing he'd ever experienced, this wholehearted belief that, whatever his professed 'motives,' the zanthyr only had Ean's best interests at heart. *It's insane, that's what it is!* He knew he had no reason at all to trust the zanthyr, and every reason not to.

Abruptly Fynn got to his feet. "I hope you know what you're doing, cousin," he said, staring down at Ean with angry, unforgiving eyes. "Almost anything is easier to get into than out of." With that, he turned and left, the ever-silent Brody shadowing his heels.

Phaedor chuckled, the sound a haunting rumble deep from within his chest. "My, my…" he sighed happily as he watched Fynn depart, "this diversion may turn out to be just what I needed."

FORTY-SEVEN

'Patterning is as easily mastered as living an existence free from doubt.'

– Sobra I'ternin, Eleventh Translation, 1499aF, *A Discourse on the Nature and Relationship of Patterning and the Currents of Elae*

Ean and his companions started out again at dawn, but as they huddled in their cloaks and headed off into a frosty, rose-hued morning, there was a strained silence among the group. Tanis caught many furtive glances aimed at the zanthyr, who rode his black warhorse bareback and stayed a good three lengths behind the others. In contrast, Phaedor seemed not at all perturbed, and he wiled the hours in idle contentment, reining his stallion with one hand and flipping his dagger with the other.

Tanis noted that Prince Ean ventured to speak with Phaedor as they rode that morning, but though the zanthyr was accommodating, he rarely seemed to answer the prince's questions to any satisfaction, and maintained his façade of whimsical amusement, as if it was all some kind of grand game. The zanthyr's elusive manner made Tanis twice as curious about him, while Rhys and the other men, Fynn included, maintained their distance, only leveling the zanthyr hard stares which he didn't even deign to ignore.

Driven by adolescent curiosity, Tanis took to riding in the rear, near Phaedor, with hopes that he might be of a mind to converse—for summoning the courage to speak to the zanthyr on a whim was far more difficult a task than Tanis wanted to tackle.

Especially after the episode with Gwynnleth.

It happened around noon. They had stopped beside a chill-flowing waterfall to water and rest the horses. While the others conversed, Tanis wandered off into the woods and happened upon Gwynnleth coming back the other way. No sooner had they said their hellos, however, than *he* was there, all green eyes and black leather. Phaedor's sudden appearance out of thin air gave Tanis a start and earned the zanthyr a heated curse from Gwynnleth.

"*Must you,* Phaedor?" the avieth had hissed after finding her breath again. She gave him a venomous glare.

The zanthyr grinned. "It's always a pleasure to see you, Gwynnleth," he noted with a taunting air. He gazed at her knowingly, looking smug.

"Don't just stand there smirking," Gwynnleth complained. "That's very irritating." She snapped a branch off a nearby sapling in obvious aggravation and began waspishly shredding a neighboring bush with it.

The zanthyr hooked his strong thumbs into his sword belt. "It's just that I'm surprised to find you in Ean's company," he murmured in his goading way. "You were so vocal in your opinions about 'humanity' when last we spoke. I never imagined you would involve yourself with the affairs of a race which you consider so far beneath your notice."

The avieth leveled him an unfriendly stare. "If this is your attempt at teaching humility, Phaedor, it is sadly inadequate. One must have suffered the virtue personally to effectively instruct another in its observance."

"Yet you aspire to instruct Ean in matters of self-sacrifice," the zanthyr countered. "By this logic, how would you ever qualify to teach him?"

Gwynnleth's eyes were tawny daggers aimed at the zanthyr's heart. "You are a spiteful creature," she hissed. "I wish you would leave me be!"

The zanthyr regarded her drolly. "If I have offended you, it was only in my attempt to help you see your own flaws in the same manner as you so graciously assist others to see theirs—"

"Phaedor, what is it you want?" Gwynnleth interrupted. She twitched the twig against her thigh impatiently.

The zanthyr made an obsequious bow and backed away. "I meant only to assure myself of your wellness," he answered. Straightening, he added with a shadowy grin, "And upon seeing this display of your usual choleric disposition, I pronounce you to be quite fit." With that, he fixed his glittering eyes upon her, flashed a wolfish smile, and vanished.

Tanis let out a shriek and jumped back fully two paces, startled out of his wits yet again; he glared in breathless frustration at the place where the zanthyr last stood. The avieth sourly grunted something about spiteful creatures and their infernal gloating, tossed the twig aside with startling fierceness, and herself took the form in a great blaze of golden brilliance without a word of farewell.

As Tanis watched her disappear into the leafy heavens, he pondered the strange conversation with brooding, colorless eyes. They almost seemed old lovers, the way the two of them had snapped at each other, and yet that wasn't quite...right. After a moment, Tanis gave up trying to figure it out, and trudged on back to join the others.

To his surprise, the zanthyr was already there, passing the time reclining on one elbow on his barebacked stallion looking as if he'd never left.

Tanis climbed back on his horse and was working up the courage to speak to the zanthyr when, as if hearing the lad's thoughts about him, Phaedor turned his raven-black head toward Tanis and pinned the boy with one predatory green eye, the other being covered by the spill of his dark hair. Tanis realized he'd been caught staring, and he flushed, raising his hand in apology.

Phaedor grinned at that, and he stared openly back at the boy for a very long time. Tanis felt sure that he couldn't hold the zanthyr's gaze, and yet he found it impossible to look away.

The situation was distressing.

After a long and very uncomfortable silence, Phaedor finally observed, "You have an innocence about you, Tanis, that should you manage to retain, will make you a favorite with the women in later life."

Startled as he was by this observation, Tanis couldn't suppress his smile.

"Ah, yes," the zanthyr said, giving the boy a conspiratorial wink. "That smile will no doubt help you, too."

Tanis really grinned back at him then; the compliments he received at fourteen were few and far between.

They rode on soon thereafter, and Tanis mustered the courage to fall in beside the zanthyr. Phaedor smiled in welcome as Tanis pulled alongside, and he tossed the lad the dagger he'd been toying with.

Tanis looked it over with curiosity. It seemed to be fashioned of a singular onyx-black stone, but how it was forged was quite a mystery, for he could find neither seam nor fold, nor did the stone reflect even the slightest light—not even a glint when he held it to the sun. The lad quickly recalled the legends that told of zanthyrs carrying as many as a dozen of their darkly enchanted blades on their person at one time.

As Tanis studied the dagger, he noticed the zanthyr regarding him with an almost friendly smile. Tanis was taken aback by his companionly manner—so different from what he'd expected.

"You have questions in your eyes, Tanis," Phaedor noted as he watched the boy.

Tanis blinked, startled. *Can he read my mind, or is it just so obvious?*

The zanthyr chuckled and pulled out another dagger to toy with. He pointed it toward the identical one in the lad's hands. "You keep that one. Something to remember me by."

Tanis raised brows at that and asked, rather incredulous, "A gift, my lord?"

Phaedor grinned at him and flipped the hair from his eyes with a casual toss of his head. "Now why does that surprise you, Tanis?" he asked, glancing sideways at the boy.

Tanis flushed at the hinted rebuke. "I'm sorry, my lord. I didn't mean to seem…I just never expected—"

"Now, now…don't be so hard on yourself," the zanthyr interrupted with an offhanded wave of his dagger. "You may decide to dislike me after you've known me for a few days."

Tanis gave him a swift look; he was more than a little surprised at the zanthyr's acute awareness of his thoughts—more aware of them, in fact, than Tanis was himself. "How…how can you know my feeling so?" he whispered. "Have you a truthreader's gift, my lord?"

Phaedor gave him an indifferent shrug. "Does the manner of my knowing make it any less true? Right now you'd like for us to be friends, but fear not that I will hold you accountable to the desire. Emotions are fickle things, just like females."

Tanis observed quietly, "Somehow, my lord, I get the feeling that if I come to dislike you, such a circumstance will have been your intention."

The zanthyr grinned broadly at that. "My, my, I do believe some of your lady's impertinence has rubbed off on you."

Tanis blushed into an embarrassed smile. "I meant no disrespect. It's just that…" he paused, chewed on his lip uncertainly.

"Go on," Phaedor said with a tolerant grin.

"Well, my lord," Tanis began, "it's just that you seem quite in control of the way others perceive you. We see what you want us to see…images, variations of images even. But…"

Phaedor was clearly amused. "But…?"

The lad turned serious then, answering him, "But I suspect you must have loved her…or still do…or something like that."

"Gwynnleth, you mean?"

Tanis nodded.

Phaedor sighted down his dagger, then tossed it into the air and made it flip twice before catching it by the point. "Yes, well…" he shrugged. "Our history is just that. History."

"You say," Tanis countered, "yet you risked her ire just to assure yourself of her wellbeing."

"Is that how it seemed to you?" the zanthyr asked in an amused tone.

Tanis shrugged.

Phaedor shook his head. "There was never any risk involved, lad. Emotion is a woman's most potent weapon, but as soon as a man recognizes that truth, the weapon is all but rendered powerless."

Tanis felt confused by his words. "Were you just trying to upset her for no reason then?"

"You've missed the point completely, Tanis," the zanthyr advised. "How she felt about it is of no consequence whatsoever."

"Then what was the point of the conversation?"

The zanthyr grinned. "Now *that* is the important question."

Tanis gazed at him curiously. "Then you did upset her on purpose—just to see how she would respond." When the zanthyr made no reply, Tanis said, "That's not a very nice thing to do to someone you love."

The zanthyr pinned him with an irritated eye, but it quickly softened to amusement. "You see now why I am such a 'spiteful creature' to quote a recent phrase?" he asked, turning profile again. "Give a boy a dagger, and he thinks he can say anything. You never get respect in response to kindness, and thereafter, your best piercing looks only draw chuckles."

"My lord, that's untrue!" Tanis protested.

Phaedor raised a hand for silence. "Tanis, I fear you are instilling me with attributes I do not possess. Love is a strictly human emotion: frail and transient. The conversation you overheard is but the latest in a long-extant argument; it was no lovers' quarrel. Choices were made many years ago. That is all there is to the story."

Tanis felt strangely hurt by his words, though he saw no reason why they should bother him so. His truthreader's sense told him the zanthyr believed what he said, and yet there was something about his words…as if a more solid truth ran beneath every ephemeral sentence.

Seeing the boy's confused and slightly injured expression, the zanthyr's gaze turned gentle. "Tanis," he began, displaying unexpected patience for the lad, "how can you expect to understand something between two people you know nothing about? My motives are my own, but I assure you, they have nothing to do with love. Our dance is naught but battles waged, won and lost." He flipped his dagger and caught it by the point again. Turning the boy a fast grin, he gloated, "Victory is bliss."

Tanis frowned disapprovingly at him. "Is everything a game to you then, my lord? Is nothing sacred?"

At that question, Phaedor settled the lad with an arresting stare, just a small reminder of whom Tanis was speaking to and that he could frighten the boy at will. "Have you any idea, Tanis, what it's like to be immortal?" the zanthyr inquired quietly, his question all the more ominous for its being softly spoken. "Any idea at all what a curse that is? To know that you will live forever? That only the hand of an enemy your equal can grant reprieve?" He turned profile again and stared forward with an unnatural calm that was intensely disquieting accompanying those words. Abruptly he looked to the boy. "How many times do you think you'd be willing to watch Alyneri die?"

Tanis was horrified by the question. He swallowed, mumbling, "My lord, I don't understand—"

"Do you not?" Phaedor countered, his gaze powerfully intent, as frightening in that moment as a lion readying to pounce. "I think you do. You love her—that is obvious—but if you were immortal and she was not, you'd watch her die…and die, and *die*. Everyone you loved would be taken from your arms in death, until it seemed there was nothing for you anymore but indifference," and he added with terrible deliberation, "because indifference does not hurt, young one. It is cold and steadfast, and like love, it lasts forever in your heart."

Tanis stared at the zanthyr feeling benumbed. He had no idea how to console someone over such a thing as that.

Phaedor cast the boy a sardonic eye. "Dare you ask again if anything is sacred? What could be sacred if love is not? If love is as mortal as a rose, or daylight, or the grass beneath your feet?"

"But it isn't mortal, my lord," Tanis insisted, feeling that he had to change the zanthyr's mind lest he lose his own innocence. "You've shown that even now, for I know you love still in your heart—if not Gwynnleth then others you have lost. The very nature of your anger proves it so!"

The zanthyr peered out of the corner of one eye, a glimpse of emerald caught between wavy strands of his dark hair. "You see deeply for your age," he grumbled.

Tanis returned a sheepish grin; he wasn't used to others admitting he was right. Her Grace never did. He thumbed his new dagger as he watched the creature beside him, who seemed so unnaturally perfect. Pondering how to phrase his next question—one that had been on his and everyone else's mind since the zanthyr's arrival—his heart started pounding so fast he thought it might burst. Finally, when the anticipation was as fearful as any answer might be, Tanis said, "My lord…"

The zanthyr gave him a tolerant look beneath the spill of his raven hair.

Tanis almost dared not ask the question now that he had the zanthyr's attention. "My lord, I know your motives are your own," he braved, not knowing what the zanthyr would say but so wanting the reassurance of his answer, "but have you joined us now because the danger to Prince Ean has grown?"

Phaedor's gaze was both terrible and deeply troubled. "Yes."

Tanis felt the truth of his words resonating back from the zanthyr's own awareness, such that the lad understood this danger in a way that was far more dreadful than his own knowledge would have permitted him to feel.

"And…" he gasped for the words, "are you here to protect him?" Tanis felt compelled to ask, though he dreaded any answer other than the one he hoped for. But he quickly learned that the zanthyr's motives were not so easily exposed.

"Ah, now that is a question much on the order of asking one's future of a Seer," Phaedor cautioned. He stared hard at the boy. "Are you sure you're ready to hear those answers?"

Tanis blanched. "...No," he said with a gulp, though he was surprised to find his head nodding *yes*.

The zanthyr burst out laughing. Turning profile again, he observed with intense amusement, "*Just* what I needed, indeed!"

Making camp that night was something of a spectacle, for none of the men save Prince Ean wanted anything to do with the zanthyr, and if he inadvertently came near them while upon his own affairs, they would drop whatever they were doing or take it elsewhere to do it. As might be expected, this made a fair mess of things while cooking or setting up tents—all to no avail, for certainly the zanthyr made no notice of their efforts of futile protest. Finally he finished tending to his own matters and took a seat at the fire—which was always Tanis's job to get going—and stretched his feet out to the flames.

Tanis grinned in welcome, and the zanthyr gave him an affectionate wink, noting with amusement that Tanis had his new dagger shoved proudly through his belt. Gwynnleth was next to join them, followed by Prince Ean, who sat down cross-legged beside Tanis and began tossing dry fir limbs onto the flames, idly watching each one blaze and dissipate, reminding Tanis of the avieth's transition in and out of the form.

"Gwynnleth," posed the prince after a moment of this, turning val Lorian grey eyes toward her, "you once told me that you're not as young as you seem."

She cast him a wary eye, as if wondering where this was heading. Tanis wondered too. Age was treacherous territory full of pitfalls when its conversation surrounded females.

"I was only wondering at the avieth lifespan," Ean clarified with a grin. "Do you live many years longer than humans?"

Still pinning him with a hawkish look, Gwynnleth nodded.

"Tens of years?" Ean inquired. "Hundreds of years?"

"Hundreds of years is not unknown," she replied, glancing cautiously at Tanis and then to the zanthyr, who yawned. "Some of our elders are nearing five hundred years."

"Amazing," Ean said, giving her an appreciative smile. "And this is your actual lifespan?"

She understood his implied question. "An avieth is proud to live and die in the natural course of time. Avieths don't work the Pattern of Life."

"Not ever?"

She frowned and glanced at Tanis, and the lad was suddenly aware of his talent intruding into the conversation, requiring honesty and candor from those present. He gave her a sheepish look. "There are...some who have done it," she admitted then, looking back to Ean, "but the circumstances were irregular at best. Most of us prefer to let nature guide our lives. When an avieth has lived too long, he loses the ability to change forms and must choose one in which to live out his remaining days."

"Which form do they most often choose?" Tanis asked.

"The hawk, of course," she returned as if there was no option. "I cannot imagine no longer being able to take the form. Living out my days as a *human*," and she shuddered over the word, "for all intents and purposes would be the worst punishment imaginable. It *is* actually our most grave form of censure."

"Are there avieths who have been forbidden to take the form?" Tanis asked wondrously.

"A very few," she answered dourly.

"Five hundred years," Ean meanwhile mused, frowning as he looked into the fire. "I can't imagine living for so long…but I must've been willing to do it once." He lifted his gaze back to her. "Do you remember your earlier lifetimes? You said you'd always been born an avieth."

She gave him an annoyed look, and Tanis realized that she was feeling put on the spot because of his presence at the fire. He wondered what the avieth would've replied had he not been there to gauge the truth in her words. "I spoke more out of faith than empirical truth," she admitted to Ean then.

Ean nodded in gratitude for her candor, even if it was obviously forced. "I wonder about the man I was before," he confessed quietly, pensive and distant. "I wonder what I believed in, what I fought for. I wonder why I chose to work the Pattern of Life." He tossed another dry branch onto the flames and watched it blaze with life briefly and then die. "I wonder if it was vanity that drove me," he murmured then, not looking at the others, just gazing into the flames, "if it was power I sought, or youth, some other purpose that spurred me to make the choice."

"Aging is overrated in importance," the zanthyr observed, "especially by humankind."

"What would you know about it?" Gwynnleth remarked in annoyance. "Your race never ages at all. You need not even work the Pattern of Life."

Tanis looked to Phaedor. "Is it true?"

The zanthyr cast him a look of droll amusement before admitting, "There are some few of us who do not age."

The zanthyr's deep voice carried the conversation beyond the fireside, and as their discussion continued, some of the others began wandering back toward the fire like peasants drawn to an impassioned philosopher espousing his beliefs on the steps of the town square. Alyneri was the first of these, and she came to stand behind Tanis and eventually sat down beside him.

Phaedor observed Alyneri's arrival, and a flicker of a smile touched his lips. "Adepts are tied to the realm," he continued to explain to Tanis. "No doubt your master has spoken of these truths in your lessons."

"He spoke at length about Adepts being bound to their strand," Tanis answered. Then he frowned. "It's a little hard to conceptualize, the way he described it."

Bastian and Cayal were slowly sitting down behind the prince as the zanthyr continued, "Imagine that each strand of *elae* is an element. The second strand would be water, the third fire, the fourth air. Now these connections do not actually exist, you understand, Tanis. It is merely meant by way of example."

The boy nodded his understanding.

"Were there such hypothetical connections," Phaedor went on, noting with shadowy amusement that Fynn and Brody had now joined them and were lingering just beyond the firelight, "then avieths might only be able to shift forms through the use of fire, and Nodefinders could only travel where there was water."

"What of the fifth?" Ean asked with his gaze pinned intently on the zanthyr.

"The fifth is tied to the land," Phaedor answered, "and this is in fact a truth. Whereas the other strands are connected to one aspect of *elae*—one particular current among many, whose patterns are intrinsic to them—fifth-strand creatures derive their existence from the entire world and are therefore linked to every part of it. Where there is air, earth, iron, water, fire—there is the fifth. It is elemental. It is not like other aspects of *elae*. It is life, yet it is not life."

"Tied to the realm itself," Ean mused.

But Tanis understood this more deeply than the others, for his truthreader's sense again resonated with the zanthyr's own truth. Without thinking, only speaking from his heart, Tanis whispered in awe, "You are doomed to this life for as long as the realm shall be."

Phaedor turned him a look of calm acceptance, but Tanis felt a profound sense of loss in his simple reply. "Just so."

The group gazed in shocked silence, for no one could upstage such a tragic fate.

Fynn was heard to murmur then, "I'll take incontinence any day."

After a moment of careful consideration, Ean looked to the zanthyr and said thoughtfully, "Raine D'Lacourte told me that many Adepts went to T'khendar, and it killed them, but the way you describe it, perhaps it was leaving Alorin that actually killed them. Do you know the truth of it?"

"Both statements are...true..." the zanthyr trailed off, for his attention was drawn suddenly to the canopy of fir limbs and the starlit heavens twinkling beyond. Following the zanthyr's gaze, Tanis thought he saw a dark cloud passing lazily overhead, momentarily obscuring the stars.

Abruptly the zanthyr was on his feet. "Get up!" he hissed, and his tone was so commanding that no one dared but scramble to obey. He urged them all away from the campsite into the deeper forest, all save Rhys and Dorin who were on watch. No one said a word as the zanthyr ushered them into the shadows of a massive spruce and bade them collect behind his own form, his left arm extended backwards as if to enwrap them in safety, his right forefinger held before his lips, cautioning silence.

Tanis's heart was pumping; he could sense the zanthyr's tension resonating like the vibration of a string, tightly controlled and extremely focused.

"*Rhys*—" Ean whispered.

"Is in no danger," the zanthyr returned so quietly the words were more an impression on the air than individual sounds.

They waited, but for what none knew. Apprehension filled the space among them, fogging the air with its chilling breath. Tanis looked around in concert with the others, but there was nothing to see. He feared the things he couldn't see then, as did they all.

Tanis felt the stranger's growing presence long before he saw the man, though the lad didn't know this was what he was perceiving; he knew only that the air was growing colder, that the forest had fallen as silent as the grave, that even the wind seemed afraid to move among the trees.

It wasn't until the zanthyr swept his hand slowly before them and Tanis saw the night congealing to obscure the group from sight that he really understood how much danger they were in. The lad had no idea what magic the zanthyr was working, but the air grew colder still as Phaedor encased them in a cloak of night, a haze of shadows that darkened everything in Tanis's vision by several shades. Within this dome, Tanis could barely see the others crowding against the tree, and beyond it, the night seemed moonless and dense.

Then he appeared.

The man who came out of the darkness was a stranger, but he walked as though he owned everything in his path and found it all beneath his contempt. His tall frame was regal in stature, crowned with dark hair and piercing eyes, but something about him was truly dreadful. His thoughts were a riot of malevolence spilling out like the Marquiin's, angry and hateful and hungry for desolation. Tanis had never known such fear as what he felt in this man's presence. He got the sense, too, that the man was more than he seemed, a fiery figurehead upon the prow with the bulk of the ship invisible behind him.

He walked through their camp touching nothing, only his eyes alive and searching, lighthouse beacons scalding the night, splitting the very air into its tiniest parts, leaving no quarter in which to hide. His hands were held at his sides, but his fingers lifted and fell, tentacles tasting the air. And every time the man's attention crossed the fire, the flames sputtered and bent, only regaining their steady heat when he turned away again.

Tanis couldn't tell how many impressions of the man were his own, how many resonated off the zanthyr, and how many came from the others who crowded so closely against him. All he knew was that thoughts had force, and he was feeling attacked by all of the thoughts bombarding him, a cavalry charge of trampling fears. Most of all, he felt the vehemence of the stranger's being; his emotions were piercing and incendiary to Tanis's innocent mind, and the boy felt violated by them.

The lad made a little whimper, and the zanthyr, who was somehow perceptive of his trauma, placed a heavy hand on the boy's shoulder. With the contact, the terrible thoughts ebbed and faded, leaving a tingling numbness in Tanis's mind that was a welcome relief.

Suddenly the stranger turned and looked directly toward them, and Tanis caught his breath. He felt Gwynnleth tense behind him, and heard her Grace inhale sharply. His heart raced as the man walked closer, peering intently into the shadows of Phaedor's spell. His eyes were amber-gold, like the avieth's, but at times Tanis imagined he saw flames reflected within them. Tanis's heart was beating frantically, and he only just held off an overwhelming sense of panic, mostly due to the zanthyr's firm hand upon his shoulder.

When the stranger was close enough to reach out and touch him, Tanis held his breath. He stared at the man, too terrified even to move his eyes, studying his features even as the stranger studied the shadows of Phaedor's spell. He was nearly nose to nose with the zanthyr, whose attention in turn was intently focused if infinitely still. What the stranger saw, Tanis couldn't imagine; he only thanked every god he could think of that the zanthyr was there to protect them from this savage, hateful apparition.

Finally, when Tanis thought he must be turning blue in the face, when his lungs were screaming for air and black spots were creeping in on his vision, the stranger turned away and continued his quiet inspection, fingers undulating at his sides like many-headed snakes. When he was far enough away, Tanis silently exhaled with a massive shudder.

Only when the stranger had been gone from sight for many minutes did the zanthyr release his spell, and the night brighten. Feeling threadbare and mentally ragged, Tanis hugged his arms, only then realizing that his teeth had begun to chatter from Phaedor's chill working. The temperature of the air was noticeably warmer now, as great a disparity as the deep Gandrel to a sunny stone patio on a midsummer's day.

No one said anything about the zanthyr's spell, though upon its release the others began to filter back toward the fire and life-giving warmth. Only Ean and Tanis remained, the latter rooted to the earth, the former staring at Phaedor, who in turn watched the trees intently, focused upon the path taken by the stranger what must've been ten minutes now gone.

"You know his nature, don't you?" Ean asked when the three of them were quite alone. He sounded unsettled, though not nearly as shaken as Tanis felt.

Phaedor did not turn.

"What is he?" Ean prodded, following his gaze.

The zanthyr finally looked at Ean. "He is your enemy."

Ean's expression changed to pained confusion. "Not Björn then."

"Björn?" the zanthyr arched a solitary brow.

Ean shook his head, frowning ponderously. "I thought...I thought perhaps the man was Björn, for I know the Vestal hunts me still."

"Björn hunts you," the zanthyr repeated, giving Ean a sideways look. "And you've reached this conclusion how?"

Ean glanced at Tanis, who watched him with intense curiosity, and then looked back to the zanthyr. He seemed uncertain as he confessed, "Dagmar said the Fifth Vestal would make himself known to me."

"Indeed," Phaedor murmured, sounding unconvinced. He turned to head back to camp.

But Ean grabbed his arm. "He came to me in my dreams," the prince insisted.

The zanthyr eyed him calmly. "I do not doubt you, my prince."

Tanis knew Phaedor spoke truly, yet he also knew that he didn't. It was as frustrating as it was confusing—trying to read the zanthyr was like peering into two streams running on top of one another, each carrying different truths.

Phaedor cast him an amused eye as Tanis had this thought, making the lad wonder yet again if the zanthyr could read his mind.

Ean let go of the zanthyr's arm and frowned after him as Phaedor returned to the fire with Tanis close on his heels.

Rhys was at the fire when Tanis sat down. The captain was grimfaced listening to Fynn explain what had happened, and he kept sending piercing looks into the shadows where Ean remained.

"But who *was* that?" Alyneri asked. She hugged her arms and sat perilously close to the fire. Tanis worried her pale hair might catch the flame.

"One of Björn's minions, no doubt," Fynn declared hotly. He was pacing back and forth, his emotions too riled to find stillness. "He's been behind this from the beginning—from the moment he sent that Shade for Ean up until now."

"Björn van Gelderan?" Gwynnleth said, surprised. "Seth told me he's returned to Alorin and is a grave threat. But what interest could he have in the prince?"

"Something about his talent," Fynn said. "Ean hasn't told me much, only that the Vestals believe Ean poses some threat to Björn and the bastard would see all challengers to his world domination removed."

Phaedor eyed Fynn as he sat down near the royal cousin. "You seem to have everything well sorted," he remarked coolly. "Having ascertained your enemy, all that remains to you is how then to defeat the most dangerous wielder ever to walk the realm."

"Yes, how," Fynn said, glaring daggers at the creature. "You might simply tell us and save us the effort."

"But where would be the fun in that?" returned the zanthyr, though Tanis saw that his eyes were hard and far from amused. It wasn't Fynn that disturbed him, however; this Tanis knew. *So what is it?*

Gwynnleth eyed the zanthyr curiously; she was also keen to his mood. "You didn't see the creature that hunted us the night before you arrived," she said. "A dragon by any account."

"There are reported to be Sundragons in the east," Rhys offered. "Called by the Emir's Mage. Duke val Whitney said the fighting has reached an impasse due to their presence."

"The Emir's Mage," Fynn grumbled, frowning. "I forgot all about that guy."

Bastian said then, "My lord, I need not remind you that the Akkadian Emir was behind the deaths of two of his Majesty's sons, thy royal cousins. Perhaps it is not without reason that we look to his quarter for an enemy as well. Might his Mage have sent a dragon to seek out Prince Ean when earlier attempts upon his life had failed?"

"Who is this Mage to command Sundragons anyway, by all that's unholy," Fynn complained. "All the stories claim the creatures were allied to Björn van Gelderan during the war."

All eyes looked to the zanthyr then, as if for explanation.

His earlier ire seemed to have faded, for he reclined on one elbow and flipped his dagger with his other hand.

"Well?" demanded Fynn in annoyance.

The zanthyr looked up at him beneath his dark hair. "You've nary a need of my input," he remarked. "This storm of fiction is fast creating its own weather. Soon the tumbling snow will become an avalanche quite out of control, burying any truth beyond reclaiming. Pray, continue. I find it a fascinating exercise in futility."

Alyneri abruptly stood and glared at him. "You are surely the most insufferable creature ever to walk the realm!" She stormed off, but Tanis could tell she was just afraid for Prince Ean.

"You seem to think this is all some kind of grand jest, my lord," Bastian said to the zanthyr, uncharacteristically letting his own aggravation show, "but it's our prince's life—and our own—in the balance. If you know something that would help us, why keep it secret?"

"Because he's working for the enemy!" Rhys barked ferociously.

"What was that power you worked back there anyway?" Fynn demanded. "What did you do so the man couldn't see us? Nothing I've ever heard of!"

"Gift horses looked too closely in the mouth may bite," Gwynnleth cautioned. She cast the zanthyr a troubled look, but Tanis couldn't tell if she was worried about the accusations aimed at him or his potential response.

The zanthyr yawned and tossed his dagger, making it flip three times before catching it by the point.

It was then that Ean returned. He looked weary and immensely troubled, but his gaze was hard as it settled on Fynn. "We can slit our own throats just as easily by being too suspicious as by being too trusting, Fynn," the prince cautioned quietly. "I am grateful to all of you for your care and consideration," he added, lifting his gaze to include the entire company, "but if you do care for me, you will cease this fractious talk." He pushed a hand through his hair as the others stared at him, even Rhys holding his tongue, for the prince's internal torment was all too apparent. "I would have some time to speak with the zanthyr alone."

The others rose willingly. To see their prince in such a state was convincing of his need; whether or not they agreed with him, no one would argue.

As Tanis was rising to go, Ean said, "Tanis, I would have you remain...if you like."

But the lad pressed his lips together and shook his head. "Your Highness, my skills are of no value to you here." His gaze rested on the zanthyr as he admitted, "I see only what truths he wants me to see, the same as you, I'll warrant."

Ean held his gaze and then nodded, and Tanis took his leave, finding his way to his bedroll and the blessed oblivion of sleep.

Much later, when all were well abed, Ean finally spoke his mind. "Did you know from the start?" he asked the zanthyr after they'd been sitting in silence for some time just tending the fire. Phaedor glanced up with an inquiring look. "When you rescued me," Ean clarified, "did you know what I was? That I had Awakened?"

The zanthyr regarded him levelly. "Yes."

Ean exhaled and shook his head at the irony. To think how far he'd had to come to gain that knowledge, how much had been endured and lost...and he might've known it from the start if only he'd asked the right questions. It was depressing as hell. "How did you know?" he asked, lifting grey eyes to the man. "Was it the pattern on my invitation?"

"You first gained the notice of others in that fashion," Phaedor said, "but this was no proof of your Awakening."

"What then?"

The zanthyr cast him a sideways look. "Have you no recollection of your first encounter with the Geshaiwyn?"

"Yes. At the beach, the lunatic pinned me and went on and on about his blade named Jeshuelle."

The zanthyr arched a solitary raven brow. "My mistake," he said. "I was not aware that he'd come so close to claiming you once. I am referring then to the second time the Geshaiwyn attacked you."

"Oh." Ean frowned. He remembered the man leaping down into the pit with him and their brief struggle, and he remembered being stabbed, and—

It came to him in a moment of clarity. The dagger flashing again and again toward his bleeding wound *but unable to touch him.*

"Yes," murmured the zanthyr, noting Ean's expression.

Ean lifted troubled eyes to the zanthyr. "But that was—"

"Of your doing," he confirmed. "In that moment, you became present on the currents."

"But I don't even know what I did!"

Phaedor shrugged. "You must've known the working well in your prior existence for its pattern to appear so instinctively to you."

Ean stared hard at the creature. "You're saying…but that would mean I have the ability to work patterns as well as to unwork them."

The zanthyr leaned indolently on one elbow and flicked at a bit of ash that dared alight upon his cloak. "Who told you otherwise?"

Ean glared at him. "*You* did."

"Ah, yes." Phaedor grinned impudently. "I also told you not to trust me, if memory serves."

"As if I could find it within myself to distrust a man who repeatedly saves my life," Ean countered. "*That's* lunacy."

"Suit yourself."

Ean reached over and placed a hand on the zanthyr's leg, capturing his attention with eyes suddenly serious. "But it's the unworking that matters, isn't it?" he asked, a naked, urgent plea. "This is why Björn wants me dead."

The zanthyr considered him for a long time in silence. Finally, he sat up and rested elbows on knees. "I knew you were an Adept when I took you from the Shade's camp, but I realized the nature of your talent when you saw the mindtrap." He leveled the prince a telling look. "For the untrained, to see a pattern at all belies a gift, but to see where it begins and ends…this is unique and rare. This is only part of your gift, though a very important aspect in its own right. But to unwork a pattern is infinitely more dangerous than working one."

Ean frowned at this idea. "Why?"

"An extant pattern holds all of its power charged within it. One must know exactly where the pattern begins and ends to attempt its unraveling."

"Or?"

The zanthyr settled him a disquieting stare. "At best, nothing happens. At worst, however," and here he arched a brow, "at worst, all of the pattern's collected energy explodes. Like the dry fir limbs you've tossed upon the fire this night, the pent-up vitality of the pattern erupts with violent force, taking anything nearby along with it."

Ean went cold at the knowledge. To think he had undone a Marquiin's deadly pattern with curious indifference! Might the entire company have been killed if he'd pulled one single strand of it incorrectly? He forced back a latent sense of panic and tried to find calm and organize his thoughts. It took several long minutes. Pushing on then, he looked at Phaedor intently. "I have another question, if you will do me the service of listening."

The zanthyr gave him a look of tolerant amusement.

"What power did you use to protect us? It wasn't *elae,* was it?"

The zanthyr cast him a narrow look, as if to determine how worthy he was of an answer. "Your enemy searched for signs of *elae* and those who work it," Phaedor offered. "Adepts as yourself, the Healer, the avieth, and Tanis, cannot help but hold *elae* captive within your life energy; you are nets that capture and slow the flowing currents. He searched for evidence of you on the currents, thus I could not use *elae* to protect you from him, for it would only have drawn his eye closer to us."

"Then what?"

Phaedor leaned back on one elbow and flipped his dagger again. "His own power."

"Which is what?"

Phaedor assessed him in one sweep of emerald eyes. "The power that roams freely beyond the edge of the known universe. *Deyjiin.*"

Ean went cold. Raine's warning echoed in memory, *'There was little left of the man I'd known, just a haunted shell...You couldn't even see his eyes, so devoured they'd become by his dark power...'*

What did it mean that the zanthyr could work *deyjiin?* Ean understood that Björn and Malachai worked the power and that both of their minds had been destroyed by its malicious nature—Malachai waging a mad war upon his own race and Björn taking up his banner when he fell. Yet the zanthyr seemed nothing if not entirely sane.

Ean looked back to Phaedor and found the man watching him with a penetrating stare. Unnerved suddenly, Ean swallowed and dropped his gaze. *Shade and darkness!* Everything he knew shouted in warning: *here is danger, here is betrayal, here is certain death!* Yet for all of this, he couldn't find it in his heart to mistrust the creature. The very idea drew such welling rage of protest that he couldn't even conceive of it. So he drew in a deep breath and exhaled his fear, letting it bleed into the air and dissipate with the fire's pale smoke. "*Deyjiin,*" he murmured to himself. Surely then the strange intruder, his enemy, must've been a minion of Björn's, for who else worked the dreadful power?

Only the creature before you.

The thought made him shudder, and Ean decided out of self-preservation to push the thought away. He lifted grey eyes to Phaedor. "So this enemy of mine," he posed, feeling the man's lingering menace like a malaise he couldn't shake. "If he works *deyjiin* and I don't, how can I possibly defeat him?"

Phaedor eyed him sagaciously. "However indeed?"

Ean frowned at him and then turned to frown at the fire. The zanthyr intimated he should know the answer already, but the mystery seemed overwhelming...

"Sleep on it, perhaps," Phaedor suggested, pulling Ean back from a stream of thoughts that were fast rushing him far away.

Ean looked up to find the creature watching him with a peculiar intensity. It was disconcerting to look into those eyes…as if glancing up just in time to see the face of death right before it pounces upon you. "I…I guess I should."

He rose to go, but then he turned back again. There was something he just had to say. "I try not to, for my own sake," he confessed with undisguised honesty, "but *I do* trust you, Phaedor. I'm sorry if the knowledge brings you displeasure. It just happens to be the truth."

The zanthyr's gaze was impenetrable. "Sleep well, my prince," he replied. He arched a raven brow and added quietly, "Tomorrow is a new day."

FORTY-EIGHT

'To know the divine essence of Jai'Gar, look first inside yourselves.'

– Emir Zafir bin Safwan al Abdul-Basir to the newly Converted

T**rell reined** Gendaia directly toward the stockade gates in a ground-eating canter as soldiers shouted in the chase and horns blared with warning, Carian clinging to him from a precarious perch behind his saddle.

"Where is it?" Trell growled, watching the approaching gate with trepidation. "Where's the node?"

"Straight ahead!" shouted the pirate.

Trell gritted his teeth and prayed Gendaia would hold true. Most horses didn't take kindly to being run straight through a wall, and while she was not a common horse, Trell hated to push his luck. He couldn't image he had many chances left to redeem himself in Thalma's eyes.

"*Carian*..." Trell growled as the wall loomed.

"Hold on!" said the pirate with a toothsome grin, and—

—They were suddenly galloping through another courtyard surrounded by high stone walls. Trell pulled Gendaia to a halt.

"What are you *doing?*" Carian screamed at him, slapping Gendaia's flank desperately. "Don't stop! Ride for the other side! Go! Go!"

Trell had time to gaze with dismay at the many soldiers who were just then pouring into the yard, and then a dark-haired man in the livery of a noble house came rushing out of a door. He took one look at Carian and his eyes went wide. "It's that mad pirate!" he shouted in Veneisean, pointing heatedly. "Stop him! Stop him!"

Trell set heels to Gendaia, and she leapt into a canter, twisting around a soldier who made a grab for her reins and then darting across the wide yard toward an iron gate.

"We're going the wrong way!" Carian yelled as the Veneisean man led the pack of soldiers behind them, shouting all the while.

"Where is it then?" Trell snarled.

"The other gate. *Behind* us!"

Clenching his teeth, Trell dug in with his heels and reined Gendaia into a skidding turn that took out two men like toy soldiers, sending them sprawling. Trell heeled her forward again, back in the direction they'd just come. They passed hazardously close to the shouting Veneisean, and Trell got a good look at his face.

"*Mon dieu!*" the man exclaimed, his eyes going wide as saucers. "*Mon dieu!* It's zee brozaire!" He ran after Trell shouting in the common tongue, "Stop, sir! Stop! Your brozaire is looking for you!"

"Ha ha!" Carian exclaimed happily, for the gate and its hidden node were nigh. "And here...we...go!"

Gendaia crossed the node, and suddenly Trell and Carian were galloping on a grassy hillside beneath a solemn moon. Trell eased Gendaia, wherein he turned the pirate a black look over his shoulder.

Carian raised both hands. "Don't worry, I felt like walking anyway." He slid from Gendaia's haunches grinning from ear to ear.

Trell exhaled a measured breath and leaned forward to stroke Gendaia's neck. If anything, she seemed less disturbed than he was and began grazing happily in the meadow. Trell looked to the pirate, who was just then rolling himself a smoke, and inquired a might testily, "So how many more times must I save your life before we arrive at our destination?"

"You don't get any bonuses for that, you know," Carian muttered as he fumbled with his flint and dagger. He looked up with the fag hanging in the corner of his mouth, adding, "I'm not renegotiating our accord."

Trell gazed around into the night. "From Tregarion to where? And where are we now?"

"All of the Veneisean cities are connected with nodes," the pirate explained. "The stockades were built that way to ensure quick reinforcements and movement of troops throughout the kingdom. But the nodes are only accessed from within the stockades."

"That's why so many visits with the Tivaricum Guard?" Trell surmised. "To use their nodes to travel about the kingdom?"

"And here I thought you were just a pretty face."

Exhaling a tired sigh, Trell dismounted and looked around. "So where are we now?"

Carian exhaled a cloud of smoke. "In the Xanthian foothills, half a day or so north of Rethynnea. Hike that way a couple of miles," he added, pointing, "and you'll see the Bay in all its jeweled glory."

Trell pulled a flagon of water from his packs and took a long draught. As he wiped his mouth with the back of one hand, he gazed at the flagon wonderingly. It was amazing to think, with all the places he'd been and seen in the past three days, that this water might've come from the Akkadian side of the Assifiyahs. Capping the flagon again, he posed, "So what is this thing you seek that you'd brave Shi'ma, Veneisean soldiers and a homicidal housewife to claim it?"

Carian sat down in the long grass and extended his boots in front of him. He leaned back on one elbow and gazed at the starry heavens, blowing lazy rings of smoke toward the stars. "Remember Naiadithine's weld?" he asked in between circles.

Trell settled down beside him and rested elbows on knees. "If memory serves," he remarked with the shadow of a smile. "But I can't be certain—it was so long ago..."

"Yeah, you're funny. Do you want to hear this or not?"

"Indeed, Carian vran Lea."

Carian blew three rings of smoke in quick succession, his cheeks puffing and deflating with the motion. "Welds are a Nodefinder's greatest boon," he said, casting Trell a sideways glance. "Some—like the one we arrived on in Tregarion—are controlled by the Guild and can be traveled for an exorbitant fee—and people call *me* a pirate," he complained, shaking his head. "Anyway, outside of the ones controlled by the Guild, most of the welds are unknown in this day and age."

"Why?"

"Because there are only two weldmaps left in existence, and one of those is imprisoned with the Great Master in T'khendar."

Trell decided to come back to that curious nugget later, asking instead, "Somehow I got the idea that you could travel a series of nodes and leis and create something of a map yourself."

"Yeah," the pirate said, letting smoke filter up around his face, "but not with a weld. They don't work like that."

"And your omnipotent Guild doesn't have a map?"

Carian cast him an enigmatic look. "The Guild maps were housed in the Citadel archives. They were lost when Tiern'aval was ripped from the world."

Trell held his gaze. "I think I begin to see."

"You're a brighter lad than I gave you credit for," he complimented. "Usually the pretty ones haven't a pat of intelligence spread between them."

"Yes, it's a miracle I've made it this far in life. I'm sure to tumble into a ditch tomorrow and that will be the end of me."

Carian settled him a quizzical look, the fag hanging from the corner of his mouth emitting a thin plume of lazy smoke. "So what was all that back there at the stockade? Who do they think you are?"

This was the last subject Trell wanted to trivialize with conjecture or even speak about at all. "They didn't exactly expound on their theories, Carian."

"That's a fine stroke of ill luck for you, boyo." Then he gave Trell an odd look. "You...you could've opted out of our accord plenty of times back there, eh? But you didn't. Why?"

Trell shrugged.

"No, no," the pirate insisted, poking at him with his fag, "you deliberately stayed. Tell me why."

Trell turned him a level gaze. "You have your code, I have mine."

Carian shook his head. "I wouldn't have done the same for you, Trell of the Tides."

Trell smiled quietly to himself. "I know." He lay back in the grass and gazed at the stars, his attention drawn for some reason to search out Cephrael's Hand. He found the constellation floating just above the western horizon; strangely it looked as if it was rising instead of setting. "What do you know of Cephrael's Hand, Carian? Any Nodefinder legends surrounding it?"

"Tons," Carian said, turning to follow his eye to where the seven stars glowed. He flicked the dying butt of his fag off into the field. "But it's Cephrael who always interested me rather more than the stars attributed to him."

Trell tried to recall what he knew of Cephrael and found his education startlingly lacking considering how famous a personage he was. In fact, all he could remember about him came from the Rite for the Newly Departed. "'*Of gods in the known*," he quoted, "'*there remain only Cephrael and Epiphany, themselves immortal, the only true immortals, who were made in the Genesis to watch over this world...*'" He turned Carian a sheepish look. "That's all I remember."

"Yeah, there's a bit more to it," the pirate remarked blandly. "Cephrael and Epiphany are brother and sister by all accounts. The *Sobra I'ternin* names them as *angiel*, the Maker's blessed children."

"What's the *Sobra I'ternin?*"

"The manual for how to be an Adept. Everything we know about our race comes from it, but only the first part has been deciphered. It's written in patterns."

Trell arched brows. "I didn't realize patterns were a language unto themselves." He tried to imagine the concept. It was hard to envision.

"Yeah, they're not," Carian said, "or if they are, it's not any language known to mankind. So imagine trying to take a pattern and translate it into language. There are at least a hundred orders devoted to the work, most of them working out of the Sormitáge in Agasan, where the original manuscript is kept. Only Björn van Gelderan is rumored to have deciphered the work in full, but Epiphany only knows where *he* is now. Not that he's one to help," Carian added as an afterthought.

The Fifth Vestal… Trell frowned over a memory which nudged against his consciousness. But try as he might, the thought would not form. "Why do you say he's not one to help?" he asked absently.

"Well, with his betrayal during the Adept Wars and holding the Great Master prisoner and all," Carian muttered, "I'm thinking he's not exactly working in Alorin's best interests."

"So he's deciphered the *Sobra I'ternin*—"

"That's the rumor," Carian inserted.

"—but he doesn't share any of the knowledge with the Adept world? Why?"

"Got me. No one has ever understood why Björn van Gelderan does the things he does. Anyway, some say Cephrael is still among us."

"What, you mean…*among* us, like I might run into him on the road 'among us'?"

Carian grinned. "Some scholars think so. They say his hand is guiding the realm even now, that his merest touch can set events in motion to change the fate of entire kingdoms."

"How could he be guiding the entire realm if he's just walking around in Cair Thessalonia like anyone else?"

"He's still a god," Carian said, shrugging. "Isn't that the whole point of omniscience? If the guy can observe some Fire King schtupping his mistress in Avatar while at the same time listen to the petty whining of thousands, I don't guess it would matter much if he was also wandering around in Thessalonia looking to piss."

Trell frowned at him. "And what do they say of Epiphany, your Sormitáge scholars?"

His gaze turned uncharacteristically solemn. "They say she sees the future and the past with every waking moment, that in her gaze one might know his last twenty lifetimes or his ultimate end." He glanced at Trell and considered him for a moment. "There's an Adept legend which tells that in one sunrise, Epiphany saw the end of days. In her grief, she gouged out her own eyes that the vision might not prove true. Her tears formed the rivers of our world. Some say it's for her tears they named the Cry."

Trell had other ideas about the source of the Cry's fateful name, but he kept those to himself.

Sometime during the early morning hours, Trell drifted off. He woke from dreams of Fhionna to a dawn that broke the sky in striated bands of rose, violet and crimson-orange and sat up feeling stiff and cold and oddly missing the desert.

"Wakey, wakey," Carian said.

Trell turned to find the pirate walking up the hillside wearing his usual toothy grin. He held out a warm linen bundle, which Trell took curiously. Inside, he found hot sticky buns drenched in honey and meat pies stuffed with onions and spicy sausage.

At Trell's look of amazement, the pirate shrugged. "A Nodefinder need never go hungry. You ready, poppet? My Weldmap awaits."

They headed off soon thereafter, with Trell leading Gendaia on foot following a few paces behind the long-legged Nodefinder, who wandered happily through the meadow looking not unlike a tall, long-haired maiden in desperate need of a shave.

As they cleared the rim of the long hill they'd been climbing and gained a broad view of the Assifiyah range—seeming so close Trell thought surely he could touch the snow upon the spiny peaks—he said to Carian, "Hadn't you best tell me something of why you needed me along, my unscrupulous friend?"

Carian shot him a narrow look over his shoulder. Then he shrugged. "We approach the lair of my arch nemesis, Trell of the Tides, a particularly crafty Nadoriin who has perpetually eluded my attempts to steal the Weldmap. We finally struck a bargain, but I was…detained in carrying it out. This Nadoriin only speaks the desert tongue. I mean to make good on our bargain and get my map, but I needed another interpreter, as my last one vanished in the intervening months."

It seemed entirely too simple an explanation to have any part in the pirate's convoluted, completely crazed life. So of course, it had to be true.

"What will you do once you have your map?" Trell asked idly.

"I intend to rescue the Great Master from T'khendar," Carian answered.

"Oh," Trell said, only surprised by the things that no longer surprised him. "Well, good luck with that."

Carian shot him a toothy grin. "Thanks."

They made good time through the hill country, and it wasn't long after midday that the road they'd been following ended in a meadow. Carian ran ahead of Trell, rushing to the top of a hill. There, he turned with a triumphant look. "Ahoy the chase!" he exclaimed. Then he waved Trell to hurry, yelling, "Smartly now, laddie, before the villain escapes!"

Trell bounded onto Gendaia and cantered up the hill with her. Reaching the top, he reined in expectantly, but his face quickly fell into a puzzled frown.

Nested within the bosom of three hills was a tidy farmstead. A little farmhouse and a green-walled barn sat next to a paddock holding some goats and a chicken coop. On the south side of the cabin was a neat vegetable garden where sprawling winter squashes commingled with orange and gold pumpkins, a row of browned corn and mottled white gourds.

"Where is the villain?" Trell posed with mock seriousness. "Let him not attempt to bedevil us, or he shall come to know the sharp side of our steel."

Carian gave him a withering look. "Be on your guard," he murmured, casting a steely-eyed glare in every direction before drawing his cutlass and stalking long-legged down the hill with his wavy hair blowing in his wake. Trell trotted Gendaia after the pirate, trying not to read too little into the tranquil scene. Obviously the pirate had been duped by his nebulous 'arch-nemesis' before, and to this end the villain deserved Trell's due attention.

With goat-like stealth, Carian slowly nudged the cabin door open and peered inside. Then he spun and stalked across the yard toward the barn. Trell dismounted and looped Gendaia's reins over the paddock, nearing Carian just as he was reaching for the barn door latch.

Abruptly the doors catapulted open and a shrieking, grey-haired woman erupted through them brandishing a pitchfork. Carian swore an oath and ducked sideways, but she was close on his every turn, stabbing and slashing at him wildly. Trell caught one of her many phrases spoken in fast succession and realized she was swearing at the pirate in a Nadori dialect. He heard something about a camel and her daughter's honor amid the outpouring of curses.

Carian dodged and ducked and yelled vexedly back at the woman, but she was as spry as a spring chicken, and he just couldn't seem to shake her off. Trell finally intervened by pulling his sword and leveling it at the pirate, bringing startled looks from both and blessed silence.

The pirate glared accusingly at him. Trell shrugged with an at-least-I'm-not-a-crazy-madwoman look. Meanwhile the old woman in question held her pitchfork high and cast both of them a mistrustful glare. When it seemed no one was going to break the impasse, Trell turned to the woman and bowed his head.

"Goodwoman of the sands," he said in the desert tongue. "I am called Trell of the Tides. This man has brought me here to assist him in making good faith upon your accord."

"No, no bargain!" she declared, shaking her head. Then she said it again in the common tongue, though with a horrible and nearly incomprehensible accent, "No bhaargoon!" And she spat at Carian's feet.

Carian whipped his head to look at Trell. "Why did she do that? What does that mean?"

"Goodwoman of the sands," Trell said again in a soothing tone, "this man would make good on his promise and count the beans and the donkeys with you. He has gone to great trouble to make good on your accord."

She eyed him suspiciously, but she was listening. The pitchfork lowered just slightly, leveled now at Carian's throat. Trell kept his sword steady at the pirate's heart.

"Goodwoman of the sands," Trell said. "This man has braved Thalma's wrath and gained Naiadithine's favor to find you." Trell felt it was true in an indirect way. "I shall lower my sword, and we shall all drink the god-drink together. If it be Jai'Gar's will, we shall reach accord once more."

Her dark eyes flickered from him to Carian and back again. Abruptly she lowered her pitchfork and leaned on the end. "You speak knowledgeably of the gods," she replied, this time in a surprisingly cultured Nadori dialect, "but you are a Northman. Are you then Converted?"

"No goodwoman of the sands," Trell replied in the desert tongue. "I have spent the past five years in the shadow of the Pillars."

She arched brows. "You are not Converted, but you serve the Emir?"

"I did once."

"And now?"

Trell exhaled. "Now I am without kingdom."

"What's she saying?" Carian demanded. He gave Trell a hard look. "Did she say her daughter was pregnant? Because I had nothing to do with that!"

Thus did Trell enter into the role of interpreter and the true story came out. The woman began, rattling off her grievances while shooting incendiary glares at the pirate. Trell labored to keep up.

"She says you were supposed to return to her village in Kandori. She said you promised her a camel and five goats and that you promised to…marry her daughter?" He glared accusingly at the pirate.

"Now, that was never part of the bargain!" Carian growled, giving the woman an explosive look. "I've never even met her daughter," he insisted irritably, looking back to Trell. "And I tried to get her a damned camel, but the bloody Khurds wanted Belloth's bloody ransom for the creature and it didn't even look healthy. And not a one of them spoke a decent word of Common."

Trell relayed the pirate's response, to which the woman launched into another long tirade. When she was finished, Trell nodded and then told Carian, "She says when you didn't show up to fulfill your end of the bargain she got worried you would try to steal the map again and so moved her family away. She wants to know how you found her?"

Carian scowled at the old woman. "With difficulty," he grumbled.

Trell looked back to the woman, who laid out her demands. Trell took it all in and turned back to Carian. "She says doesn't want a camel anymore, because what would she do with a camel in Xanthe? Now she wants safe passage to Agasan and a chaperoned tour through Solvayre," and he looked back to the woman and added in the desert tongue, "You'll love it there, it's very nice."

"Agasan!" Carian veritably shrieked meanwhile. "A tour of *Solvayre?*"

"Yes. She wants to tour the Solvayre vineyards and sample their wines—she says she overheard a woman talking about just such a trip. She blames you for her daughter's capriciousness, since you never came back to marry her, and she moved them here and then the girl ran off with a—" Trell had to ask her to repeat some of her story. Then he continued translating, "a haberdasher's son. So now since she's already left her homeland and you've found her again to complete the bargain, she wants to do some traveling and see more of the world."

"This is preposterous!" Carian snapped exasperatedly.

"Oh, and she wants her wood pile restocked for the winter. About—" he looked back to her for clarification and then nodded. "Yes, about so high," and he held his hand to the level of Carian's head.

Carian glared in reproachful silence.

The woman tugged on Trell's sleeve. "Tell him I want the coin in Agasi silver—and I won't accept stolen gold from some poor captain's doomed ship. It has to be his own."

When Trell told him this, the pirate threw up his hands. "And how is she going to know if it's *my* money or not," he protested, shoving hands onto hips.

Trell gave him a shadowy grin. "I wouldn't bet against her, Carian."

Carian stalked off to swear by himself for a while.

The woman turned her dark eyes to Trell. "Come inside for tea, Trell of the Tides. Let that pirate blow off his steam at the goats."

Trell followed the old woman inside and watched as she stoked the fire in her stove and put on a kettle to boil. She bade him sit down at a scrubbed wooden table and then sat down across from him, pulling her knitted woolen sweater closer about her shoulders. "The old are always cold," she said in the desert tongue, giving him a sad smile. "I hear it is warmer in Solvayre. I am Yara, by the way."

"May the eye of Jai'Gar bless your table always, Yara," Trell replied, using the highest form of respect in his greeting.

She smiled approvingly. "The Emir taught you very good manners, Trell of the Tides. I would not have thought that of him, though I know little of the man, in truth. Only the angry tales told by my tribe."

"Doubtless both sides slander each other," Trell admitted. He held her dark gaze for a moment, and then he asked, "How did you come to possess a Weldmap, Yara? It seems a strange token for a woman of the sands."

She eyed him shrewdly. "Perhaps one day I will tell you," she said, "but today is not that day." She stood to tend to the kettle, which had begun whistling for attention, and poured boiling water into two ceramic cups, both painted in a mosaic pattern of blue, white and tan. It reminded Trell wistfully of Duan'Bai's elaborate minarets. "Do you miss the desert?" he asked Yara.

"Always," she said, giving him a smile. "Do you?"

"I think I do. More than I ever thought I would."

"We leave roots in any place we call home," she advised. "They tug at us to return." When Trell merely gazed thoughtfully at his mug, she asked, "How did you come to the land of sand and sun, Trell of the Tides? You don't seem the type to run from duty or disaster. What drove you south?"

"I was shipwrecked," Trell told her, certain of this truth for the first time in his life. "Naiadithine took pity on me and delivered me to a seaside village called The Tides. I don't remember much else until waking in the Emir's palace. That was five years ago."

"And you remember nothing of your former life?"

"I know none of my upbringing or my heritage," he admitted, "though I remember now that I had two brothers and was educated in a tower by the sea." He sipped his tea and was pleasantly surprised at its flavor, which reminded him of the *czai* tea they served everywhere in Duan'Bai. He added after another sip, "What memories I do have started coming back to me after I headed west."

The door opened, and Trell turned to find Carian standing in the portal. "Fine," he grumbled. "I'll do everything she asks. But tell her there's no more negotiating after this."

Trell translated, and Yara nodded, her dark eyes pinned inexorably on the pirate.

Carian turned and left.

Trell wandered over to the door and gazed after the pirate as he climbed the hill. If he knew Carian, it would be some time before they saw him again. The pirate wouldn't forsake an opportunity to play Trumps in order to win the money he meant to give to Yara.

The old woman came and stood beside Trell in the doorway. Her greying head barely reached his shoulder. They watched the pirate disappear over the hill together. "And that," she said then in the common tongue, "is the way to do business with a pirate."

At Trell's astonished look, Yara brushed her hands together definitively and returned to her chair. "Pirates can be trusted to keep to the Code, Trell of the Tides," she continued in the common tongue, speaking with the barest hint of a Nadori accent as she lowered herself into her seat, "but old women have a code of their own: Never let an impudent young scoundrel think he can get the better of you."

Utterly amazed, Trell leaned against the open doorway and gave her a look of admiration. "Count the wrinkles on a woman's face," he mused, "and that is the measure of her wisdom."

Yara arched a brow. "That is an old Kandori saying. Where did you hear it? Surely not in the Akkad?"

Trell smiled softly and shook his head. "I don't know where I first heard it," he admitted as he closed the door and returned to his chair. "There is much of my past that is lost to me."

"It seems that some of the best parts remain," she told him gently. She placed a hand on his as he sat down. "So," she said then, "which do you prefer? The desert language or the Common tongue?"

"The desert tongue," Trell said without hesitation.

"Then we shall speak thusly," she happily agreed, switching back to it. "So tell me, are you recently departed from the Emir's service? Know you anything of the war?"

Trell wrapped both hands around his tea cup, feeling its warmth taking off the day's chill. "The Emir employs a Mage now," he told her, "a very powerful magician. He recalled the Sundragons from isolation and set them to task patrolling the skies over Akkadian-held lands. The war has stalled as a result."

"Sundragons," Yara mused, arching a charcoal eyebrow. "My people know something of Sundragons. The Kandori fortune is said to have been amassed by a Sundragon. Some stories say the line of Kandori princes were sired by a Sundragon and they inherited the fortune when the creatures were banished; others say the princes fought the Sundragons and bested them, claiming the fortune as their plunder."

Trell couldn't imagine the drachwyr caring enough for worldly goods to bother amassing any amount of wealth. *Perhaps Rhakár*, but even he seemed above such things. Even less realistic was the idea that a Nadori prince bested a drachwyr in battle. Trell was willing to wage that even Mithaiya could defeat the strongest of Radov's Talien Knights.

Yara was considering him intently when he looked back to her. "Know you something of Sundragons, Trell of the Tides?"

"Perhaps a little," he admitted with a sheepish grin.

"There is an even older legend about the Kandori fortune," she offered then, eyeing him shrewdly. "It is said that a Sundragon once fell in love with a mortal girl, an Adept of the first strand. She was the most beautiful creature he had ever seen, but it was her compassion and intelligence that truly appended him to her. She in turn saw him for what he was, and she worked the Pattern of Life that they might live out an eternity together. The dragon showered her with gifts and riches, amassing a fortune greater than any the world had ever known, greater even than the Empress of Agasan or all of the Fire Kings of Avatar."

Trell sensed a certain truth in this story. For some reason, he thought of Náiir and his sad, dark eyes. "How did the story end?"

"They lived for hundreds of years together, the fair mortal girl and her dragon lover, but eventually the woman grew tired of life, though never tired of her dragon-prince. Yet he saw the sadness in her eyes, and how she yearned for a new life in the Returning. He saw that immortality was not meant for such frail creatures, for their minds were too fragile to endure the unending years. So he flew with her into the heavens, higher and higher, until she slept and would not reawaken. He used his dragon magic to pin her to the cosmos then, and there she remains, a bright star to light the way for other tired souls who would find their path to a new life in the Returning."

Trell considered the story with a thoughtful gaze. He wondered how much truth was in the legend and if he would ever have the chance to ask Náiir about it; but more than this, he was curious about mention of the Returning. "I didn't realize the Kandori believed in the Returning," he said.

She eyed him sagaciously. "Most truths are true whether you believe them or not, Trell of the Tides."

Trell conceded her point.

She sat back in her chair with a disagreeable frown. "But you are not completely wrong about us. The Kandori believe there could be gods above men, and we hold them in regard out of respect for our forebears, but we do not *know* it to be true, and we trust the empirical long before we trust to faith. The Nadori desert begets practicality in its children, for prayers don't bring rain when the aqueduct runs dry for lack of tending, and no amount of fervent chanting ever got crops planted or to harvest." She eyed him quizzically with her wrinkled dark eyes. "But you named the desert gods to me several times this day. Do you believe...or do you *know?*"

Trell considered her question. After a moment, he answered carefully, "I believe only what I have experienced."

"Ah ha!" she cried happily, clapping her hands. "We are not so different then. But come," she said, leaning across to pat his arm. "Let us ready a bed for you. No doubt that pirate will be long in returning."

"I can sleep in the barn," Trell offered.

"Nonsense. You can sleep in my daughter's bed. She won't be using it."

Trell rose to follow her, asking, "Where is your daughter now, Yara? Did she truly move away with her haberdasher's son?"

Yara turned him a look of quiet regret. "My Habivi has been thirteen years in the grave. She gave me six grandchildren before she passed. All of them are in Agasan with their families." She gave him a wry smile. "Do I look young enough to have a child of marrying age, Trell of the Tides? I thought you smarter than that."

Trell gazed curiously at her. "Why the lie, Yara?"

"That pirate trades in trickery and deceit," she said critically. "A taste of his own craft is good for him."

"He's not all bad," Trell said.

"No," she agreed, giving him a soft smile, "else why would I bother trying to teach him anything at all? Come now." She waved him to follow. "We'll make up a bed for you and then see what we can throw into the pot for dinner. If I'd known you were coming, I would've been better prepared."

"I'll try to give you fair warning next time," Trell said as he followed her from the room.

"You do that, *khortdad*. Surprise guests, like hemorrhoids, are rarely welcome visitors."

FORTY-NINE

'Do not be burdened with the morality of petty kings. My will shall be your guide.'

– The Prophet Bethamin

Ean dreamed.

In his dream, a voice called out to him from the darkness, calling his name. Ean felt fingers of menace reaching out for him; darkly twisted, gnarled things that once clenched would merely petrify. Ean turned and sprinted through the darkness, but no matter which way he ran, the voice grew closer, sharper. Suddenly a face appeared in front of him, and Ean drew back, cringing away from a man with boiling eyes...

The dream shifted, and Ean was back in camp. He looked around, seeing his companions sleeping beneath the silent night; even the zanthyr reclined quiet and still against a tree with his hood pulled low over his eyes. Ean got to his feet, pulling his cloak closer around him. He caught the flash of something in the distance, so he headed off into the trees.

There were hours yet until dawn, and the forest was drenched in fog. No stars were visible through the blanketing mist, and only a dim paling told of the moon. All was quiet, the air still, but Ean sensed that the night was alive.

He felt it in a hundred different places on his skin, in the way the fog rose and the near river rushed and the world continued living, moving and changing even while mankind slept. He sensed the patterns at large about the world, the many imprints working seamlessly in concert, hidden but active in propelling the realm forward through time. And he sensed an awareness, as if the night were its own entity that harbored the knowledge of everything happening within its ken.

Then, into this sense of calm, intruded chaos. Like rainfall pelting an otherwise still pond, a presence emitting waves of discord disturbed the quiet night. Ean felt him coming nearer, preceded by a dissonant symphony of frenzied energy, *elae* shrinking back from the touch of something foul, retreating as the tide from a treacherous shore.

Ean knew that he should do something to protect himself from the malevolent onslaught, as he'd done in other dreams, but the knowledge was frustratingly missing, trapped beneath a veil of black unconsciousness—though he knew on some level that once it had been second-nature to him.

And then the man appeared, the mist unfolding around him. Ean went cold; it was the same man who'd searched for him the night the zanthyr came, the face from the first part of his dream.

What is happening? Am I awake or dreaming still?

"Who are you?" Ean demanded. "What do you want?"

The stranger smiled, but his eyes were cold. "Your death," answered the man, "or your oath. Either will do."

Waves of malevolence charged the air between them. Ean couldn't imagine binding himself to any such man. "I would take my own life before I allowed it to be of use to you," he promised, though it took great effort to speak the words. It was as if the man already bound him with invisible waves of his chill power.

The stranger chuckled, a merciless sound. "Don't you know you are already my pawn?" he asked with unwholesome mirth, his eyes gleaming dangerously across the distance, the ground between them cloaked in fog. "You doomed creatures live out your existence only to benefit *our* aims. Were you to throw yourself from a cliff in this moment, it would be to our advantage as readily as if you put forth your talent of unworking to achieve those tasks I assigned you. You are but walking to your deaths—every moment you live is only taking you swiftly there. There is but one end for mankind," he finished, chuckling. "You cannot but seek it in your every breath!"

Ean railed against his words. "You're wrong," he argued, but his declaration lacked conviction. Tendrils of the man's power had him in their grasp, and he found it difficult to concentrate; strange, warped images kept impinging upon his thoughts, twisted images of terrible things. Fighting to stay focused, Ean clenched his teeth and gasped, "*You don't know us at all.*"

The stranger's grin was the face of Death. "You don't know yourselves. You live all your lives in denial of the inevitable. There is no future but death for mankind. What use to prolong it?" When Ean didn't immediately answer, the stranger gazed knowingly upon him. "So you begin to see, do you not? Is it not a kindness to unmake those who are but doomed already? Where is the mercy in perpetuating the torment, extending their suffering until they do, finally, expire?"

Ean shook his head. The man's words felt wrong—all wrong—yet he couldn't see any other truth through the power that clouded his mind. Twisted images of death and dying flashed painfully, and he felt his own will dying, a sputtering ember unable to catch the flame. *Does not everyone march toward death in the end?* he caught himself wondering. What was the purpose of this life if not to merely walk a long path toward a destination already known?

No. No!

"No," Ean declared, clenching his teeth, his gaze fixed defiantly upon the man. He tried to think of meaningful things, certain now that the stranger was intruding upon his mind, warping truths even as his dark power eroded *elae*. "No! There is purpose. There is greatness. There is love."

"Delusions all," whispered the stranger.

"There is virtue, there is goodness," Ean insisted desperately.

"Illusions devised to rationalize a pointless existence."

Ean felt the stranger's cold power reaching out for him again, and he shrank from it in horror. He began to feel that sense of unraveling from his dream. Looking down, he couldn't see his feet, lost as they were in the fog, but a sense of panic claimed him. He knew there was something he should do to defend himself; he knew he could battle this evil, but desperation shut him down, and fear gripped him in a dreadful embrace.

Ean spun away and ran headlong through the trees, through the fog, trying to escape the terrible power reaching out for him, trying to outrun the stranger's maniacal laughter. He tripped over a rock and barreled into the earth, scraping his chin, his palms, his knees. He cried out and leaped back on his feet, desperate to find his bearings, but he saw only dense fog in every direction. He was lost, and the power was close to claiming him. He could sense the tumultuous ripples that preceded its arrival, waves of deadly malice flying before the storm.

Ean made to run again.

"Ean..."

The familiar voice stopped him dead in his tracks, and he spun, reaching out toward the voice. "Creighton!"

In all his dreams since the night of their parting, he had not heard his blood-brother's voice. Hearing it now with such clarity brought a grief so sharp and powerful that he felt cleaved. He fell to his knees, reaching out again in the direction of the sound, tears streaming down his cheeks before he knew they had even formed. "*Creighton*..."

A figure approached through the fog, and Ean recognized the shape of his blood-brother's shoulders and the line of his body, even though his face remained hidden in the drifting mist. "Ean," he said again with sorrow and longing. "Don't do this. Don't let him defeat you before the battle is even begun."

Ean buried his face in his hands feeling a desperate sense of grief. "He twists *everything*. I can't see the truth. I can't see the beginning or the end of it—" Suddenly he looked up, and it was as though the world came back into focus.

"It is what they do," Creighton said simply. "It's why they're so toxic to us." He circled behind Ean and kneeled there, placing hands on the prince's shoulders.

With Creighton's reassuring presence, Ean felt the remaining vestiges of the stranger's power fading. He basked in the warmth of his friend's touch, feeling terribly weary, his eyelids fighting to stay open. He knew it was only a dream, but had he been given the chance, he would've lingered there to the end of his days. "How do I defeat him when he obscures the pattern from my sight, Cray?" he murmured. "How do I find where it begins and ends?"

Creighton gently guided Ean onto his side and brushed a cool hand across his eyes to close them. "You will learn. But not tonight."

"Don't go..." Ean whispered, but he was already tumbling back into dreamless slumber...

The Shade pulled free of Dagmar's hands and leaned his head back against the chair with a weary sigh. His mind ached, but not nearly as painfully as his heart. He lifted obsidian eyes to the Second Vestal, who gazed compassionately upon him.

"That was one of *them*, wasn't it," asked the Shade, "that man who was seeking Ean, trying to invade his mind?"

"It was," the Vestal confirmed.

The Shade shuddered. "My lord, how can a power feel so malicious in the hands of one man and so...neutral in my own?"

"His power radiates his intent," Dagmar advised, "and Malorin'athgul are naught but volatile creatures seeking the end of days."

The Shade exhaled heavily and closed his eyes. "I thought it would be wonderful seeing him again," he confessed. "Instead my heart feels...broken." He opened his dark eyes to meet the Vestal's pale green gaze. "I believed...when I took my oath, even then I believed...but now I see in a way that was unclear to me before. My lord," he entreated, furrowing his silver brow, "am I ready for this assignment? So much depends on what few moments are left."

"You have the First Lord's knowledge now within your ken," Dagmar advised. "Do not fear that it will elude you; when you have need of the understanding, it will present itself to you."

"But there is so little time and so much he must learn. The things you would have me teach him are dangerous workings even when crafted in their proper order, but I must instruct him with leaps and bounds, leaving much uncovered."

"Thus is the task before you," Dagmar agreed.

"A single misstep could kill him," the Shade whispered wretchedly. "I cannot bear the thought of his death upon my conscience."

"Yet he bears the thought of yours even now."

The Shade swallowed with the truth of this and bowed his head. This guilt was a torment he kept close to his heart, for it reminded him of the life he once knew and treasured. Composing himself, he met the Vestal's gaze. "I will guard his dreams, my lord, and I will reach out to him when the time is right."

Dagmar smiled. "Good." He held out his hands again, palms open. "Are you ready now to find her dreams?"

The Shade trembled at the thought, his own fears so palpable as to rest his weary head upon a pillow of them. But he was excited as well, for where there was life, there was hope. And that was something the Malorin'athgul could never understand.

"Yes, milord," he said as anxiety welled along with anticipation. He leaned to place his head within Dagmar's hands once more, providing the contact the Vestal needed for rapport.

Would she love him still?

The Shade rode a crest of hope back into the world of dreams.

"I've found him!" someone called. "He's here!"

Ean swam up from the depths of a dreamless sleep, becoming aware of voices near him. Finally he opened his eyes to find Alyneri hovering over him, her face pale and drawn. Immediately he sat up and took her by the shoulders. "What's wrong? What happened? Is someone hurt?"

She stared at him, horrified.

"Where?" Fynn called from far off, somewhere among the trees, and then the zanthyr emerged from the forest, a tall shadow moving with swift and powerful grace. "Here," he called to Fynn, and his deep voice filled the forest, a lion's roar.

Ean looked around and only then noticed that he wasn't in camp. "Where are we?" he asked. "What happened?"

"You tell us," Alyneri whispered. She tugged on his hand. "Come away from the edge—*please*, Ean. I cannot bear it."

Only then did Ean turn behind him and see the cliff. Had he but rolled onto his back during the night, he would've tumbled hundreds of feet to his death. Ean did move away from the edge then—and right quickly.

Fynn came running up, followed by Brody and Rhys. "Shade and darkness, you'll be the death of me!" he exclaimed with a heated glare. "What in Tiern'aval were you thinking wandering off in the middle of the bloody night? And how did you get past the watch?"

Ean suppressed a shudder as the chilling understanding hit him. "It was foggy," he murmured.

"It was clear as daylight all night long," Rhys said, sounding almost frightened.

Ean shifted his gaze to the captain. "In my dream, I mean." He tried to work some moisture back into his mouth, which had gone very dry at the prospect of how his night might've ended so differently.

"Let's get back to camp," the zanthyr said. He took Ean around the shoulder and encouraged him away.

Ean was dazed, as incredulous as he was disturbed. Had it been a dream, or had the man actually been there? And if *he* was real…what specter had appeared in Creighton's guise?

By Cephrael, I heard his voice!

The zanthyr turned him a look of bedevilment tinged with concern. "You must be able to protect yourself at least in your dreams, Ean val Lorian," he complained as they trudged through the forest together. "I cannot be everywhere at all times."

"I *thought* it was a dream," Ean commented, though he sounded uncertain. Shaking his head, he added, "It had to be a dream…"

The zanthyr considered him. "There are workings that blur the line between wakefulness and slumber," he advised after a moment. "They are dark workings and not attempted by the faint of heart."

"The man in my dream… it was the same man who came the other night," Ean confessed, still feeling intensely unsettled.

"That went without saying."

Ean pushed a hand through his cinnamon hair, his grey eyes troubled. "It was and it wasn't like the other dreams."

The zanthyr cast him a curious look. "What other dreams?"

Ean exhaled a measured breath. "I've been having dreams since I woke at Fersthaven. They almost always involve the same man and my unworking something…big…in the darkness beyond my sight. Sometimes I get to the end of the thread, and other times…" he shrugged.

"And last night?"

"Last night was similar in that I felt the same menace beyond my sight, this force that *hated* me and wanted me destroyed. The man spoke to me, but his words were… twisted. Treacherous. I couldn't see the pattern and couldn't find where to pull to begin to unravel it."

The zanthyr's gaze was penetrating. "How did you escape?"

Ean paused mid-step and stood still. The grief came welling back again tenfold. "My blood-brother," he managed, barely choking out the words. He pushed palms to forehead, feeling the ache of Creighton's loss as raw and anguished as the moment of its making, and then he shoved his hands through his hair and started walking again. "It was him."

The zanthyr arched a solitary raven brow.

Ean shook his head resolutely and hunched his shoulders as he stalked back to camp. "This cannot continue," he declared under his breath. "They'll keep *stalking* me until one of us is dead, and unless I do something about it, that is sure to be me." Abruptly Ean drew up short and looked to the zanthyr. "In my dream—or whatever it was—my blood-brother said I would learn to work my power. I cannot but imagine that I dreamed him, yet the message of the moment remains: I must learn to use my talent, and you…you can teach me." Ean was amazed that he hadn't thought of it before, for the solution was too simple. "You must teach me how to defeat him."

Phaedor's expression indicated he thought this unlikely. He headed back into camp and over to the fire where Tanis sat with Cayal, both of them looking immensely relieved to see their prince again.

"We'll stay here," Ean insisted, emphatic in his decision, "and you can teach me how to see through his spells and obfuscations."

Phaedor seated himself by the fire and rested one arm on bent knee, the other leg extended toward the flames. He pinned Ean with an assessing look. "There is a grave difference between unworking in a dream and doing it in life. The consequences are binding and irreversible."

"I've already done it three times," Ean pointed out. "I unworked the pattern binding the Marquiin to Bethamin's will."

"A stagnant pattern already in decay," the zanthyr returned. "This man will not be so easy a mark as that."

"Which is why I need your help," Ean insisted heatedly.

The others were filtering back into camp, but they kept their distance from where the prince stood glaring down at the zanthyr. Ean's countenance alone was enough to warn them off, but Tanis and Cayal also wore expressions that conveyed their desire to be elsewhere.

"If you pit yourself against those who seek your death," the zanthyr advised cautiously, "you will be entering the arena. Once inside those walls, the play is to the end. There is no opting back out of this game, my prince."

"He marked me as his enemy," Ean said hotly. "Björn marked me. I didn't ask to be tagged, but now they've done it, I intend to play as if my life depends upon it."

"It does," the zanthyr murmured with glittering emerald eyes.

Ean glared at him. "I'm tired of being bounced around from one near-death situation to the next, harassed and prodded and captured and freed like someone's bloody pawn."

The zanthyr's gaze was wolf-keen. "You want to enter this game as a player?"

"Yes."

"And do you understand the consequences of that choice?"

"I'm sure you'll delineate them for me," Ean muttered testily.

Phaedor pulled out his dagger and began toying with it, making it flip three times before catching it by the point. He glanced up at Ean under the spill of his raven hair, his eyes sparkling darkly in challenge. "Pawns move among the game without ever knowing a game exists," he told Ean, "never realizing they are being manipulated, only jumping at the Players' impetus like marionettes—flotsam on the sea of the game board, if you will." He paused to watch Ean sit down on a rock, his expression dark, and continued then, "Pawns are protected by their players, though they know it not. Yet their lives are carefully considered with every move, whether to keep them in play or sacrifice them for the greater good of the game."

Ean rested elbows on knees and hung his head, exhaling a tormented sigh. He felt the zanthyr's words—every one—like a dagger thrust to his gut. This had been his life since the moment he set foot upon the mainland; he'd been someone's pawn from the start—perhaps the pawn of multiple players—and he suspected the zanthyr knew this as well as he did. Lifting his gaze to the creature before him, Ean inquired tightly, "And players?"

The zanthyr leveled him an ominous stare. "Players make their moves at will, reassured only by their own resolve, facing dire consequences, protected by no one, and shielded by nothing but the force of their conviction."

Ean held the zanthyr's gaze. "How can I be a player if I don't know the game being played?"

"How can you be a pawn," Phaedor challenged in return, "when you know a game exists?"

Acknowledging the obvious truth of this, Ean straightened. He knew there was no going back, nor did he want to. He'd rather be a participant than a spectator, and certainly he'd rather play than be played. "So be it," he declared.

"Welcome to the game," Phaedor said, but there was something decidedly predatory about the gleam in his eyes. In an instant he was on his feet and gliding away from camp. "Coming, my prince?" he called without turning.

Feeling suddenly reluctant, Ean stood to follow, but as he trotted to catch up with Phaedor, the prince got the idea that somehow this had been the outcome the zanthyr was expecting all along.

Alyneri was grateful for the day spent in camp, for it gave her time to recover her composure, time to gather herself and her belongings back into order, time to reflect on what she'd witnessed and learned.

She spent a good part of the day walking the near woods gathering any medicinal plants she happened to pass, though mostly she just wandered, grateful for the opportunity to be alone with her thoughts. At one point she found herself out on the point where Ean had spent his night. She got down on hands and knees and inched to the edge, looking down to the frothing whitewater so far below. Then she lay there feeling dizzy and frayed, fighting off a latent sense of panic. It was a great force of effort to keep from fretting over what could've happened, for Ean had been *so* close to death that only divine grace must've saved him.

She said a prayer of thanks to Epiphany and then, out of respect, added a prayer of equal gratitude to Cephrael—for who knew if Ean wasn't somehow involved in some grand stroke of His hand. Certainly divinity was as logical an explanation for the many inexplicable things that had been happening to them as was any other source.

As she walked a circuitous route back to their campsite, Alyneri heard the zanthyr's deep voice drifting through the trees, and something compelled her to follow it back to its source. It was late afternoon when she came upon them amid a dense grove where towering redwood and spruce made a giant cavern of limbs overhead and barely a shaft of sunlight peeked through. She stopped at the edge of the dim grove and sat upon a thick, protruding root, which made a natural chair in shape, watching as Ean studied with the zanthyr.

The prince made no notice of her arrival, for his eyes were closed in concentration, his hands extended in front of him with palms out as if to stop an intruder, and though the zanthyr did not turn his disturbing gaze upon her, Alyneri was certain that he'd noticed her approaching long before she arrived.

As she watched the still scene, she became aware of *elae* being worked within, and the knowledge was unsettling. When an Adept worked their gift—whether it be Healing or truthreading or any other inherent Adept talent—the currents were rarely affected, though they carried with them a record of the working as they flowed. But when an Adept worked patterns outside of his talent, the currents were forced to shift and adapt. Sometimes these workings were so minor as to require little change in the currents to absorb them—such as a trace-seal. More detailed workings affected the currents like boulders in the path of a river; even then, the currents typically retained their course, merely shifting around or over the working but maintaining the same channel of motion.

The most dramatic workings of *elae* created such a disturbance in the currents that they were blasted from their natural course altogether, dispersing instead in waves radiating away from the point of contact. This type of working was incredibly dangerous, for it always then impacted the Balance—that most nebulous of Laws which was oft-interpreted and rarely understood—and could be detected by other Adepts who had the slightest sensitivity.

Alyneri's arms soon itched from the currents washing over her, which she felt as tingling upon her skin; waves scattering outward from the central disturbance that was Ean and the zanthyr. She couldn't conceive of what they were doing to require such a concentration of *elae*, but she didn't need to understand its nature to know that it terrified her.

Suddenly Ean cried out and doubled over, and instantly the itching ebbed and faded, the currents resuming their usual course. She resisted the urge to rush to him as he bent and pushed hands to knees, his head hung as if with exhaustion, for she knew that whatever working Ean was about, the zanthyr had it in hand.

"Shadow take me," Ean gasped, his breath coming ragged and his chest heaving. He looked up beneath his brows at the zanthyr, who stood as still as stone and seemed utterly unfazed, and managed, "How did you…*do* that?"

"It is a matter of how much force you can control. You were at your limit," he advised, and added with shadowy amusement, "I was not."

Ean straightened and wiped the sweat from his brow with one forearm. "That was better though," he said as he dropped his arm to his side, his shoulders slumped.

The zanthyr regarded him quietly. "It was."

"But not good enough. Not nearly good enough." Ean pushed palms to his temples and leaned his head back. Alyneri could tell he was completely exhausted and was only standing through sheer force of will.

"You must find your focus faster," the zanthyr agreed.

"I *know*," Ean said tightly. Alyneri wondered at the significance of this, though it was clear from Ean's tense expression that he understood too well what it meant. He swayed slightly in place, and Alyneri had seen enough.

"Ean," she said, calling his attention.

He dropped his hands and looked to her. "Oh," he said, giving her a smile. "Hi."

"You need to rest," she told him. She got to her feet and walked over to him, placing fingers to his temple, her palm cupping his face. It was so easy for her to find his pattern now—incredible it had been so hard that first time. She let some of her own lifeforce seep across into him through their contact. No need to draw upon *elae*; she had plenty to give to him.

He smiled and gazed into her eyes. "Thanks."

She frowned and dropped her hand. "Don't mention it." Looking to the zanthyr, who hadn't moved a hair, she said, "He needs rest or he will end up harming himself."

"I quite agree," Phaedor murmured.

Ean held up a hand in surrender. "Fine. I'll go find something to eat." He turned and left the grove, but Alyneri got the sense that it was a great effort for him just to place one foot in front of the other.

She turned to the zanthyr and frowned. "May I speak with you?"

"You've never needed my permission to speak your mind before, Duchess," Phaedor replied in his deep, resonant voice, akin to a purr but echoic of a growl. "Why start now?"

Alyneri drew in her breath and let it out in a sigh, furrowing her brow as she regarded him. "You do make it difficult, don't you?"

Phaedor cracked a shadowy grin and hooked thumbs in his sword belt. "What's on your mind, Duchess?"

"I was wrong before," she said, dropping her gaze.

"About?"

Her eyes flashed to his. "About you."

Phaedor arched a solitary brow. "Wrong in which way?"

"I can see that Ean needs you," she admitted, "and you must've known that he would, for you've come to help him and keep him safe."

"Have I?" Phaedor inquired, giving her a wry look. "What then of my 'impeccable timing' to quote the royal cousin?" He pulled his dagger and began tossing it idly. "You know of the conversation I reference: my arrival among your company just in time to protect you with my 'fell power' from a man who may or may not have been my own accomplice—a ploy merely to gain favor and earn a place of trust within your number. Were you not just discussing the matter with Fynnlar yesterday?"

Alyneri's expression darkened, but she was determined not to let the creature rouse her ire. She got the idea that he meant only to test her troth, and she intended to pass his damned test. "Ean's welfare isn't always Fynn's first concern," she answered.

"Nor is it yours," the zanthyr pointed out.

"But it is for me more often than it is for Fynn," she retorted irritably. Who was the infernal creature to so readily know her innermost thoughts, anyway?

"But that isn't why you've come to me. Is it?" His penetrating gaze swept her, and in that moment Alyneri thought he was perhaps the most handsome—and most frightening—man she'd ever met.

"I just…I—" but his manner had thrown her composure well out of reach.

"Let me," Phaedor offered. "You found yourself drawn to seek me out, but you're not certain why."

Alyneri huffed irritably and crossed her arms.

Phaedor chuckled. "Why not try the truth instead, your Grace. You have never been very good at dissembling." He tossed his dagger again, adding, "Which is one positive aspect of your nature."

Alyneri leveled him a smoldering look. The truth of it was he was right; she *didn't* know why she'd wanted to speak to him, but *his* knowing that didn't make it any easier to figure out. So she jumped to the other side of that creek and asked instead, "What is your connection with Tanis?"

Phaedor cast her a sage look. "Ah…so we turn to less difficult questions, do we? All right." He tossed raven locks from his eyes and regarded her coolly. "Why do you think I have any interest in the boy at all?"

"I know that you do," she asserted, arms still crossed. "Farshideh told me you were the one who brought him to Fersthaven as a boy, and I've seen the manner in which you look upon him."

He arched a raven brow. "And how is that?"

She held his gaze stubbornly. "Like a father."

The zanthyr flipped his dagger again. "I am no relation to the boy."

"I didn't say you were. But you have some interest in him, I know it is so."

"And you wish to assure yourself of my benign intentions, do you?"

"No." She approached him boldly. "I want to know *why*. I want to know how you knew when Farshideh was going to die, and why Tanis wasn't affected by Bethamin's Fire. I *know* you know these things." She stopped just a pace in front of him and forced herself to meet his gaze, but standing so close to him was even harder than she'd imagined. There was something about this creature that both thrilled and terrified her, and she felt entrapped by the mystery surrounding him, compelled to understand him. Frustratingly desirous of his trust.

The zanthyr calmly admired her with unrepentant candor until she blushed and stepped back and away, dropping her eyes. "Trust," he said then, "is a tricky, complicated bond, Duchess. Truth, however, is inherently simple and though often painful, is a much more remunerative pursuit."

With that, he turned and strode into the forest, disappearing among the dense darkness. She was only thankful that he hadn't vanished in front of her, and knew somehow that it was a parting grace, an acknowledgement that while he'd answered none of her questions, he had still granted her something in the exchange.

FIFTY

'There is no higher purpose to him than the playing of a game.'

– The Second Vestal Dagmar Ranneskjöld

The ferry harbor in the Free City of Cair Rethynnea was a series of long, wide stairs running all the way down into the azure waters of the Bay of Jewels. Rather than use a carved marble border wall like Cair Xerses, or the immense gilded gates of Cair Palea'andes, the city of Rethynnea welcomed its arriving guests with seventy hundred-foot columns situated atop the harbor stairs, each enameled in bands of garnet, silver and cobalt-blue. Beyond this impressive gateway, the massive temple-style structures, monuments and ornamental statues of Cair Rethynnea gleamed in their limestone casings, a glaring white centerpiece between the aqua sea and the azure sky.

Upon the ferry *Delia's Sprite,* Ean and his company watched as the city neared. They'd reached Cair Xerses that morning and from there had hired a ferry to transport them to the city of Rethynnea, which was known to all as the Jewel of the Cairs.

Ean stood at the ferry railing watching as they neared the harbor stairs, his expression darkly tormented, his thoughts conflicted. Somewhere in this city, Björn awaited. It was ill news he wished he'd never learned, nor was the manner of its gaining any more pleasant, though the dream had been almost blissful at first…

He'd raced with Creighton along a cold, windswept beach beneath rain-laden clouds. The wind whipped the deep charcoal waves into froth, and long lines of foam striated the dark sand, just waiting to be scattered by thundering hooves. They rode into the wind, their cloaks flying behind them, laughing with the thrill of the race. It was neck in neck, Creighton's black stallion inching his nose toward Caldar's, their flanks nearly touching. And then Caldar extended his neck, lengthened his leg, and fired forward, spattering Creighton in foam as he sped across the finish.

Laughing exuberantly, Ean eased back on his reins and trotted Caldar in a circle back to where his friend had slowed. It was strange to see him there, to hear his voice so clearly, and yet to find his face constantly shadowed and blurred. It troubled Ean. Did it mean he was already forgetting his blood-brother's features that he couldn't see him clearly even in his dreams?

"Congratulations, Highness," Creighton said as he dismounted. He led his stallion toward a bonfire protected in the lee of two high dunes.

Ean joined him there, settling into the fire's circle of welcoming warmth. Creighton tended the flames, and Ean watched him, glimpsing for one heart-breaking moment his blood-brother's familiar profile amidst the ever-shifting shadows that obscured his features.

After a long moment of silence, Creighton looked up from the flames and asked, "Are you ready now to try again, Ean?"

The prince sighed. It was a torment living in this half-world of dreams where

Creighton lived and yet did not, though a welcome torment compared to a waking world where all traces of him were lost. "Yes," he said. But then he frowned. "You know, the real Creighton knew nothing of these things." He toyed with a stick as he glanced up under his brows, scraping a deep, dark line in the sand. "Which begs the question how I am learning from someone who cannot exist? Are you my own memory from another life? Or someone sent by Dagmar in the guise of my friend—and if so, why the charade?"

Creighton looked sad—or at least the shifting shadows that concealed his face seemed somehow so. "I told you, Ean," he said, his words laden with regret. "In this place, I am who you want me to be."

Ean considered him. "I would have you be none other than you are."

"Truly?" Creighton lifted his head and stared at Ean, though the prince had only the impression of meeting his gaze. "Even should your dream of the friend and brother you loved be ended here and now? You are ready to say good-bye to Creighton Khelspath forever?"

I already have, Ean thought bitterly, but it was not the truth. He wasn't ready to let go of this apparition, however false it might one day prove to be. Even conversing with the specter of his friend was a joy beyond measure. "Let's try again," he said instead, and Creighton let the matter go as well, neither of them ready to face that moment.

Creighton stood. "Once again, I will work the layers of obscuring, and you must find the pattern in them—but quickly, for with each moment you delay my power grows stronger, the obscuring more solidly in place." He walked away from the fire to stand in the open where the wind whipped his ebony cloak and twisted his longish hair into dark flames.

Ean followed and came to stand before him.

Creighton lashed out.

The obscuring hit with powerful force—more power than any of their practices before. Ean threw up a mental shield against the cold power, as the zanthyr had taught him to do, though it gained him but a precious few moments in which to act. He used what reprieve he gained to cast his awareness toward Creighton, seeking the pattern inherent in his working.

Again and again he cast out in search of it, but always his awareness only skimmed the surface of the spell, never penetrating it. Creighton's obscuring appeared in Ean's mind-sight as sheets of blue-black ice, in places iridescent, and in others violet-pale. Ean's spear was a thin silver line, steel hard and needle sharp, but the ice of the obscuring was too thick, impenetrable, and his needle merely rebounded or skittered away harmlessly along the surface.

"Concentrate, Ean!" Creighton chastised.

Ean felt the obscuring begin to penetrate his mental wall, a dulling sensation along the fringes, like the first tingling of numb fingers. His concentration faltered, and that focus of awareness lost its structure; now a silver-thin thread wavered unsteadily beyond his grasp.

"No," Creighton growled. He banished his power, accentuated with a wave of his hand, and instantly Ean felt alert again. "It is too much for you still."

Ean uttered a groan as a painful pounding in his skull rushed in to fill the void left by the obscuring. He pushed his palm against the bridge of his nose and forced a measured breath. "No," he murmured then, dropping his hand and looking firmly back to his friend. "Do it again."

Creighton seemed hesitant. "We are safer here than practicing in the waking world, but you can still be harmed, Ean."

"No, I can do it," Ean assured him. He wanted to do it, too; partly for himself, and of course for the greater purpose of surviving his next confrontation with one of Björn's creatures; but mostly he wanted to do it for Creighton, because his friend had faith in him. Ean couldn't bear to let him down.

"Very well." Creighton lashed out again without warning, but Ean was quicker that time. He shielded his mind with the force of his intention—he was beginning to understand the concepts Phaedor had been trying to teach him, though he had to think of them in different terms. *A wielder is limited by what he can envision,* the zanthyr taught him, and Ean was coming to realize just how true that was. Every working might be worked differently by different wielders. The pattern was the same, but how a wielder envisioned its use varied greatly. The zanthyr had shown him how to layer his concentration, how to compartmentalize his thoughts even as one might analyze and compartment one's emotions, but the images which Ean envisioned for protecting himself were not the same images the zanthyr used. Ean conceived of his shield as a glowing golden ring surrounding his mind; he focused on the pattern and formed the ring, and was elated when he realized that within this ring, he felt secure.

Bolstered by his success, Ean formed the spear of his awareness and cast it forward, but he did not merely pitch it tentatively across the distance toward the glacial walls of Creighton's obscuring, he rocketed it.

Instantly he saw the pattern for which he searched, saw where it began and ended, knew how to deconstruct it. Instinct drove him, and he latched onto the end of the pattern and began to pull—

"Ean, no!" Creighton gasped.

Suddenly a flood of images and sound overtook the prince, shattering through his protective shield. He didn't understand what had happened, only that he couldn't stop the sudden deluge of perceptions that tumbled into his mind. Ean threw up his hand and staggered backwards, but it was no physical force that accosted him. Wave upon wave of images and sounds, memories and emotions, myriad perceptions and thoughts—they hit him unrelentingly until he fell to his knees, his mind reeling, a painful white light blurring his vision. "Make it stop!" he gasped.

Suddenly Creighton was there, placing a hand around the back of his neck, another pressing to his forehead…

And everything faded.

Silence slowly waned, and soon the sound of the waves crashing around his knees returned. Ean looked up with words of gratitude upon his tongue, but it wasn't Creighton who held him.

Shocked, he pulled free of the man and scrambled away, but as he gained his feet, reeling in confusion, it was only Creighton who stood before him.

"Who *are* you?" Ean gasped accusingly. "Who was *that?*"

Creighton held out a hand in entreaty, his features ever shifting, ever hidden. "Ean…"

Ean felt betrayed, his emotions so raw as to rend his soul in two. "That was…*him* wasn't it?" he only just choked out the words. "*You*…you're as false as the rest of them!"

"Ean, wait—" but Ean was already running, running…running for the grey haze that was the edge of dreams. He threw himself headlong into it—

—Yet it wasn't in blissful oblivion where he landed painfully on hands and knees, but a fire-lit library hosting another unwelcome visitor to his dreams that night.

Ean got to his feet, his entire body taut as a bowstring, his fury ready to erupt. He spied the man sitting in a shadowed armchair, and the glare he leveled the Second Vestal was piercing.

"Is all of this *your* doing?" he snarled. "Preying treacherously upon my deepest regrets—summoning the illusion of my slain blood-brother to make me into *his* pawn—a weapon for him to use against all that I hold dear! You—" he was so furious he could barely get the words out. "Raine spoke of you as a man of uncompromising honor! How can you be so…so *duplicitous*?"

Dagmar held his gaze regretfully. "Ean," he sighed, "you don't understand."

"Don't I?" The prince's tone was scathing. "Raine told me your loyalty was suspect, but I hoped…I gave you the benefit of the doubt. Now I see you're as corrupted by the Fifth Vestal's power—this *deyjiin*—" he spat the word like poison at his feet, "as Raine feared you would be. Tell me, my lord, did the Fifth Vestal seduce you or merely bind you to his cause? I have seen the Marquiin—I know what such workings do to a man."

Dagmar gazed sadly upon him. "The First Lord binds no man against his will."

"You went willingly into the dark then, did you?" Ean sneered, his tone thick with disdain. Suddenly the pent-up fury of months erupted out of him, aimed unerringly at the Vestal. "How can you support him?" he shouted, throwing out his hand to the nebulous ether. "All of you took a Vestal oath, did you not? Are you not sworn to *protect* this world?"

Dagmar pressed his lips together, his brow furrowed. There was no ire in him, only concern. "I have betrayed no Vestal oaths," he replied quietly, "…nor has my oath-brother betrayed his."

"No, of course not!" Ean scoffed. "Because murdering the Hundred Mages on Tiern'aval wasn't a break of faith. Or did history get that wrong, too?"

Dagmar's lips were set in a thin, hard line, his pale green eyes intent. Ean expected any moment that the words barely held in check would come tumbling out, but he only replied at last, and with regret, "That isn't my truth to tell."

"It doesn't matter," Ean growled. "Whatever he did or didn't do, of one thing I am certain: his creature slew my blood-brother in cold blood, and one day, I swear to you, I will make him atone for it."

"You have been wronged, Ean," Dagmar agreed, holding Ean's incendiary gaze with naught but compassion in return, "but not by us. Even now you are but a day's ride from the Cairs, and at whose behest?"

Ean knew Dagmar already had the answer he sought, but he gritted his teeth and replied anyway, "Raine's."

"Raine's," Dagmar repeated with slow precision, letting the name penetrate. "Raine D'Lacourte. Fourth Vestal of Alorin, infamous truthreader of legend, *raedan* beyond compare. Not an Adept working impinges upon the currents that Raine cannot decipher. You claim I have deceived you, Ean, but tis my oath-brother who sends you unwittingly into the very heart of danger." When Ean said nothing, only stared coldly at him, Dagmar continued, "For as long as you have been on the mainland, Ean, Björn has been in the Cairs. I assure you, Raine has known of the Fifth Vestal's location since he first set foot back in the realm." Dagmar held Ean's gaze so there was no avoiding the truth he spoke. "Raine purposefully sent you straight to Björn's doorstep."

Ean tasted the thick syrup of betrayal, and it nearly gagged him. "Why?" he croaked.

"Bait."

"*Bait.*" Ean felt a blood-rage welling and fought to control it, but the word still came out as a wolfish snarl. "Bait!"

"Above all else, Raine seeks Björn," Dagmar explained. "He believes you have a chance of drawing the Fifth Vestal from his hidden lair, since he obviously has an interest in you—"

"There's not a one of you that would hesitate to use me to serve your purposes!" Ean snapped. He took two steps forward and leaned in, his gaze so coldly angered that the face of the sun might solidify beneath it. "Well, I have news for you," he said with slow deliberation, "all of you, and your First Lord, too. Let it be known wide and far: *I am no man's pawn any longer*." And before Dagmar could respond, Ean cast himself from the dream.

Now he stood staring at the pristine city of Cair Rethynnea knowing everything—absolutely *everything*—had changed.

A shadow befell him, and Ean didn't need to turn to know who approached.

Well...almost everything.

"There is an unusual convergence of forces in Rethynnea," the zanthyr observed as he came to stand beside Ean. "The currents are riotous. Few maintain their usual channels."

"I'll pretend like I know what you're talking about," Ean muttered.

"It would be wise to contact the Fourth Vestal at once. We must know what he knows."

Ean clenched his teeth. "I told you, I don't want to see him."

"Yet you've given no reason why save to repeat yourself with uncharacteristic petulance."

Ean cast the zanthyr a dark look.

Gwynnleth approached then, coming to stand on Ean's right. She glared irritably toward the high hills. "Seth is here," she remarked.

"That would account for the discord I observed in the currents," Phaedor noted dryly.

She crossed arms and settled him an arch look. "One would think that after so many centuries the two of you would've learned to get along."

"One would think that through the centuries the mushroom might have evolved from a lowly fungus," Phaedor returned casually, "but time bears out that most life forms are simply too obtuse to elevate beyond their inherent limitations."

Gwynnleth glared suspiciously at him. "Which one of you is the mushroom in this example?"

"It doesn't matter," Ean said, speaking from a completely different train of thought. They both looked to him. "Seeing Raine, I mean," he said resolutely. "I need to tell him anyway."

"Tell him what?" Gwynnleth asked.

"That I will be his pawn no longer."

She frowned at him. "Well…that is one mark against you. And here you'd been doing so unexpectedly well."

"What?" he protested churlishly. "Why?"

"What's the point of telling anyone you'll not be their pawn? It's useless posturing, but very *Northern* of you."

"Posturing sometimes has its merits," Phaedor observed. "A viper's posturing has saved the lives of many a man ill-prepared to withstand its bite."

"My point exactly," she muttered.

Ean retreated to his thoughts while the conversation continued without him. On the one hand he felt despondent, wasted. His emotions were still raw and weeping wounds, his conscience angry and vindictive, desperate for vengeance, for atonement. But another side of him demanded answers and action. He wasn't simply going to bend over and take it, and he wasn't going out of the game without a drag-down all-out tooth and claw fight for the prize.

Whatever it was.

As the ferryman turned them toward a slip near the middle of the long dock, Ean gazed at the towering, multicolored columns at the top of Rethynnea's wide band of stairs and wondered what in Tiern'aval he was doing there. "So," he said cheerlessly, "what now?"

The zanthyr gave him a sideways look. "As a pawn," he offered, "you had no clear view of the game board. You couldn't know what other pieces are in play, what schemes devised; but there is one advantage you have now."

Ean frowned as he watched the ferry closing in on the dock. "Which is what?"

The zanthyr gave him knowing look. "The other players do not realize you are now one of them. Until you better understand the game, the smartest move you can make is to make no move at all. Wait, watch, observe what pieces are in play. Form your strategy, learn the rules."

"You're wrong," Ean said, turning grey eyes upon him. "There is another move I can make."

The zanthyr arched a raven brow. "Which is?"

"I can target the most valuable piece on the board and take it for my own."

The zanthyr eyed him with emerald eyes gleaming. "And do you know what piece that is?"

"Yeah," Ean said as the ferry bumped against the dock and men threw lines to secure it. He held the zanthyr's gaze. "Me."

High on the mountainside overlooking the Bay of Jewels, on the street running just below Rethynnea's famed Avenue of the Gods, a tavern stood in the shadow of the Pillars of Jai'Gar. At the furthest table in the darkest corner of this tavern, six men sat hunched over a game of Western Trumps. Four had been trumped out of the game, and the last two were down to five cards each. The stakes were high; in the pot was at least thirty Free Crown, a couple of rubies that looked as though they'd been pried out of a statue, and a silver medallion inscribed with a complex map of the seven seas.

The medallion belonged to the long-haired pirate with the five-day beard; the rubies belonged to the bald thief with the scar for a left eye. Neither of them intended to part with their belongings.

It was the one-eyed thief's turn. He kept glancing from his cards to those of the pirate as if trying to see through the ink to the telling pictures on the other side.

"It's your play, Smythe," Carian vran Lea reminded the thief.

Smythe scratched the stubble beneath his chin as he pondered his next move. The trick about Trumps was saving the best trump for last while not letting yourself get trumped out of the game, which meant frequently having to sacrifice a trump—the exact problem Smythe faced just then. His good eye flashed around the table in quick scrutiny of the other men, but they were staying noncommittal. They all knew Smythe's reputation, but they also knew what happened to people that crossed one of the pirates of Jamaii, such as the long-haired man sitting opposite Smythe.

Finally, the thief growled something uncomplimentary and threw down a Queen's Knave.

Carian remained stone-faced while he scanned his cards. There were lots of cards that trumped a Queen's Knave, but with just five cards left, he didn't have any to waste—and that was what Smythe was forcing him to do. *You're a sly bastard.*

Now the problem became which card to sacrifice? He could match the thief's Knave with another Knave—the smartest approach. Or he could trump him with a Priest and force him to play a decent card. Playing a Priest was always a tricky move, however. Sometimes it backfired on you.

He could also trump him with a Queen or her Lady, but such was risky if the thief had any Kings or—gods forbid—a hated Sorcerer. And neither of them could know which card the other was holding out for the final trump. A quarter of the deck was still on the table. Was the Ace there, or already in Smythe's hand?

Carian played it safe and matched him.

He could tell from Smythe's immediate indecision that he didn't have any more Knaves or anything to trump him with. That meant they would start a new play, each drawing one card. It could be the Ace.

They both drew.

Fynn and Brody were waiting at the pillars when Ean's company finished the long climb out of the harbor. The royal cousin had taken an earlier ferry in order to procure a villa for them, and he was in good spirits as Ean and the others joined him on the main boulevard in the city, called the Thoroughfare.

"Welcome to the Cairs, cousin!" Fynn said happily, opening hands to the massive city spanning the hills behind him. "Tis no fairer city in the realm than Rethynnea. Home to all races, friend to the friendless. Anything can be found here—for the right price, of course."

Ean had never been to the Free Cities, and he admitted the Jewel of the Cairs was impressive. Rethynnea's Thoroughfare, which ran the full five mile strip along the seashore, was jammed end to end with tents, wagons, stands, kiosks, and anything else man's imagination could use as a means to display his wares. As they rode, Ean passed merchants boasting pearls from the Northern Isles, colorful silks from the deserts of M'Nador, and emeralds, rubies and sapphires from the Bemoth mines. Everywhere he chose to look, his eyes were inundated with treasures—bolts of embroidered velvets and other pre-made finery, copper, silver and turquoise jewelry, stiletto daggers, the occasional sword of questionable history, and more food than anyone could imagine eating in a lifetime.

As could be expected from such a bustling sea port, Cair Rethynnea's shell-paved streets were jammed with people from every known land—if the variance of clothing was any indication of their point of origin—and the heartbeat of the city was a high-pitched hum of languages atop the accompanying clatter of carriage wheels, hooves, animal brays, and the regular commotion of commerce.

"Veneisean crystal is cheaper in the Cairs than in Venesia itself," Fynn was saying to any of them who cared to listen as they continued their slow progress down the wide boulevard, "and there's no Winery House that stocks more fine Veneisean reds than those found in the Cairs."

"As entertaining as this dissertation is, Fynnlar," the zanthyr interrupted, all business, "the prince hasn't come to the Cairs to sightsee and shop. What news of the Vestal?"

Fynn turned him a begrudging look, but it was unclear exactly what he found most objectionable—speaking of the Vestal, or speaking of the Vestal to Phaedor. "He awaits at our villa," the royal cousin grumbled, "and we've a stop to make on his behalf along the way."

Fynnlar was more subdued after that, his enthusiasm quashed by the zanthyr's lack of interest. As they rode through the loud, crowded streets, Ean took the opportunity to inquire, "What news from the city, Fynn?" He glanced to the zanthyr riding just behind them and added, "Phaedor says there's trouble on the currents."

"I daresay," Fynn remarked, still looking disappointed that no one wanted the rest of the tour. "A famous Healer vanished last week, the fifth Adept in a fortnight to have been taken. Many Adepts are considering leaving the city, and the governor—among others—is taking radical steps to keep them here. Adepts are already in short supply; as point of fact, I'll have to call in a debt in order to gain the services of an Espial for the Fourth Vestal. To top everything else, there's talk that the Karakurt's in town, which is really bad news for you. So, yes," Fynn finished, casting Ean a disagreeable look, "I'd say there's trouble all right."

At the next corner, which was demarked by a thick stone arch carved in the shape of two jumping dolphins, Fynn turned them off the Thoroughfare onto a winding boulevard that led through the gold district upwards toward the high hills. As they rode, Ean saw the silver-capped tips of two green pillars high upon the hillside.

"Is that…jade?" Cayal asked from somewhere behind, clearly espying the same towering columns.

"Those are the Pillars of Jai'Gar," Alyneri supplied. She rode just behind Ean, between the zanthyr and Tanis. "They must always be constructed of the purest green jade. That pair marks the entrance to Rethynnea's Avenue of the Gods."

"Jai'Gar," Cayal mused. "Is that one of the desert gods?"

"Their Supreme God," she replied, "from which all others are but faces of his aspects."

"I didn't know you were so knowledgeable about the desert gods, your Grace," Fynn remarked.

"There is much you don't know about me, Lord Fynnlar," she returned primly.

"A deplorable circumstance. Surely we must take action to correct it," and he gave her a suggestive grin.

"I'm quite comfortable with our relationship as it stands now, my lord."

"But we have no relationship, your Grace."

"Exactly."

Tanis had been staring at the pillars as they rode, watching them peeking in and out between trees and buildings. "Is that where the Temple of the Vestals is, my lord?" the lad asked Fynn. "On the Avenue of the Gods?"

"Yes, among other less savory temples," Fynn said without turning.

Tanis perked up. "Like what?"

Fynn cast him a long eye. "Let's just say there are some temples up there that people enter and never come out of."

Tanis's eyes went wide. "Really?"

"No, Tanis," Alyneri said, giving Fynn a hard look.

"Well, they don't come out the same anyways," the royal cousin grumbled.

"So what is this errand, Fynn?" Ean asked then.

"I told you already. The Fourth Vestal requires the services of an Espial."

"Doesn't he have one?" Alyneri asked. "What of that Franco Rohre fellow?"

"The Vestal goes through Espials like Fynnlar goes through wine," Gwynnleth noted.

"All I know is he needs the services of another one and I drew the short straw," Fynn complained.

"But you have someone in mind," Ean said.

"As luck would have it he's in town," Fynn replied, "and as I said, he owes me a favor."

"Who then would be this luckless fellow?" the zanthyr inquired.

Fynn cast him a sooty look. "A smarter man than me. He makes a point of *not* associating with the minions of enemy sorcerers."

"If that is your only criteria for establishing intelligence, my lord," Alyneri said, "it seems that much has been overlooked. Perhaps the man is merely a coward."

Ean gave her a surprised look. *Did I hear her rightly?* he marveled. *Did Alyneri just stand up for the zanthyr?* He caught Gwynnleth looking at her strangely also, which confirmed that he hadn't just imagined the exchange. Ean wondered what could've passed between Alyneri and the zanthyr that she had become his advocate? He glanced at Phaedor and caught the zanthyr watching him in return; and while

Phaedor's green-eyed gaze was ever impenetrable, the prince had the idea that the zanthyr knew exactly was he was thinking. Ean gave him a long look packed with meaning.

The zanthyr just grinned and flipped his dagger.

The long-haired pirate grabbed the one-eyed thief's hand before he could pull it back from the table. "Just a minute there, Smythe," Carian murmured. He locked eyes—or at least one eye—with the bald man in a viperous stare. "I do believe I've seen that card before."

Right then the four other men at the table scooted their chairs well out of arm's reach, making a great scraping noise that was known in gambler's slang as 'the exodus.'

Smythe snatched his hand free and let it come to rest on his dagger instead. "Are you calling me a cheat, Islander?"

The pirate leaned back in his chair and crossed muscled arms, a move that looked casual but actually put his hands closer to the long, curved knives he wore at each hip. "Maybe I am," he murmured.

Smythe jumped to his feet, sending his chair crashing to the floor in a move called 'the drop.' Somehow his dagger had appeared in his hand.

Half-way through Smythe's drop, Carian dropped too. Now they both stood glaring like predatory wolves, except the pirate held two daggers to the thief's one.

The four other men scrambled out of their chairs completely. There was no name for that, nor was there a special name for the general hush and shuffling that spread through the room as people paused in conversation or stood to watch the imminent fight—it was just called the hush and shuffle.

"You're a cheat and a thief, Smythe," Carian accused. "You forfeited the pot."

"Touch that gold, pirate, and you're one dead stinkin' pirate!"

Carian cast the man a feral grin. "Indeed. Think you so?"

Smythe's face darkened. He seemed to decide that he'd had enough of the audacious pirate and his overactive mouth, for in one swift move called 'the launch', Smythe was soaring across the table with his dagger aimed at the pirate's throat. The thief collided with Carian, and they crashed to the floor.

The crowd closed in around them to watch.

Ean's company parted ways outside the tavern where Fynn thought he'd find his Espial friend. Tanis and the ladies kept going, following Brody back to their new accommodations, while Ean, Fynn and the others went inside to meet Fynn's Espial contact. Fynn dismounted in front of the tavern and made to open the door—

Wherein his nose met immediately with someone's hurling fist. "*Ow!*"

It was inevitable that the brawl between the pirate and the thief would spread throughout the room before all was said and done.

Fynn swore in ill-humor and punched his assailant in the teeth. The man pitched backwards onto a table and then rolled off the other side.

While Ean and the others were scanning the room trying to get some feel for the melee, someone cried out above the noise, *"Damn you seven hells, vran Lea!"*

Fynn was nursing his nose, but he perked up at this and dove into the swarming sea of flailing arms, bodies, and the occasional chair. Ean and Rhys exchanged a pained look, and then they went in after him, with Rhys calling, "All right men, let's break it up!"

It took about five minutes, with the well-trained—and much practiced—King's Guard sparing no eyes, jaws or noses in their attempt to settle the brawl. When at last Fynn and Ean reached the core of the fight, they had to pull off many a man, and even beat a few in the back of the head with the flat of their blades, which resulted in no small number of indignant glares when all was said and done.

At last they got to the bottom of the pile. Rhys pulled off one man by grabbing his scraggly hair and yanking as hard as he could—to which the man protested as shrilly as a wench—and Fynn pummeled another atop his balding head with the hilt of his sword, wherein the man collapsed without further ceremony.

The one man who remained standing had a long, curved dagger clenched between his pearly white teeth and another in his hand. A tall pirate, he had wavy black hair that hung long to his waist and the scruff of a five-day beard shading his lean jaw. It was impossible to know how long he had been standing atop the chest of the bald thief with a scar instead of a left eye, but the latter might've made some protest beyond his muted groans had the pirate not had one of his shiny black boots pried into the thief's open mouth.

As a reluctant hush settled through the tavern, Carian smiled around his dagger and proclaimed with good cheer, if a mite slurred, "Oh hullo, Fynnlar. Come to pay me at last, have you?"

"It's the other way around, Carian vran Lea," Fynn remarked with a steely gaze, "and yes, I've come to call in your debt."

"*This* is your Espial?" Ean protested.

Carian turned to the prince for the first time, and Ean thought he saw recognition flash in his brown-eyed gaze before he looked back to Fynn. In an uncharacteristic display of magnanimity then, the islander stepped down off the thief, kicked him hard in the ribs and scolded, "I hold this matter settled, Smythe, you bilge-sucking blaggard. Dare cheat me again and your life won't be worth your weight in salt." He kicked the moaning man again in the gut and then sheathed his blades with a flourish of crossed arms. Then he grinned. "So. What did you want to talk to me about, Fynnlar?"

Fynn looked around at the wrecked tavern and its many begrudging onlookers and offered a mite thinly, "Shall we share a drink to everyone's health and call it a day?"

It seemed a grand idea.

The thief crawled off, Carian claimed his loot and medallion from the floor, and not too much later, the tables had been righted, those who could sit were sitting again, those who couldn't had been carried or dragged away, and Ean, Fynn and Carian had righted the table where it all began and were seated around it sharing a drink. Rhys and the men settled into smaller tables surrounding the three, forming a protective buffer for conversation.

After thirstily downing his first goblet of wine and calling for another, Fynn settled elbows on the tabletop and peered at Carian. "What are you doing in town, anyway, vran Lea? I heard you'd vanished for the better part of a year."

"Business trip," Carian murmured. His dark eyes were fixed for some reason quite candidly on Ean. "So what do you want, Fynn?"

"An acquaintance of mine needs to procure your more honest services."

"Oh, those services, eh?" The pirate pulled out a leather pouch and set to rolling the leaf into a fag. He used a nearby oil lamp to light it, then exhaled a cloud of blue smoke and leaned back against the wall. All the while, his eyes never left Ean. "So you're the man's cousin," he observed to Ean then. "That would make you a…rather important man, wouldn't it?"

Ean found the pirate's manner uncommonly strange. "Some would say so," he admitted.

The islander raised brows. "But not you?"

Ean shrugged. "I've never pondered such things."

"Indeed?" The islander gave him an appreciative look. He took another drag off the fag and let the smoke filter up around his nostrils while he watched Ean in silence.

Fynn frowned at him. "Look, do we have an accord or not, vran Lea?"

Carian seemed to have all but forgotten Fynn, for the pirate leaned over the table and pinned the prince with an assessing look. "Tell me…might you have a brother?"

Ean blinked at him.

"What's the matter with you tonight, Islander?" Fynn complained. "That thief get in a lucky blow? You're loopier than ever."

Ean felt unnerved by the man, but not for any reason he could explain. He took a long draft of his ale to quell the feeling and confessed as he lowered the glass, "I had three brothers…once. They're all dead."

The islander leaned back and draped an elbow across the back of his chair, his dark-eyed gaze penetrating. "Sure about that, are you?"

"Carian, you go too far," Fynn criticized.

The islander's gaze shifted to Fynn. He began blowing smoke rings at him.

Suddenly a shadow befell their table, and Ean spun to find the dark form of the zanthyr towering over him. "Shade and darkness, Phaedor," the prince hissed as he settled back against his chair. "*Must* you do that?"

"Look Fynn," Carian observed, motioning with his fag while gazing indolently at the zanthyr, "it's the Demon Lord come to claim your debt at last."

"Don't be ridiculous, Islander," Fynn grumbled. "Even Belloth knows better than to trust a zanthyr with his handiwork."

Phaedor's emerald eyes fixed on the pirate, and he did not seem well-disposed toward him. "Well, Carian vran Lea," he remarked, "I didn't expect to see you again so soon."

Ean choked into his ale.

"There now," Carian leaned forward and clapped Ean on the back, casting him a frown of concern. "All right then?" the islander asked.

Ean wiped his mouth with the back of his hand and lifted incredulous eyes to Phaedor. "You know this man?"

The zanthyr gave him a withering look—clearly Ean should have known better than to ask the obvious. Phaedor turned back to Carian and observed in a deprecating tone, "I hope you've learned the value of patience by now, Islander. I already have my hands full protecting one man who can't keep himself out of trouble. I do not need another."

"I can well protect myself," the islander retorted. Then he grumbled darkly, "What are *you* doing here anyway? I thought you only lurked beneath rocks in T'khendar."

"Where I might've left you to your eternity if not for my inherent good nature," the zanthyr remarked. He looked back to an astonished Ean and motioned to him to make room at the table. While Ean moved closer to Fynn, Phaedor eyeballed a nearby chair, wherein it scraped across the floor of its own accord, spinning in the last so the zanthyr could sit down. Which he did.

"Show-off," Carian muttered.

Phaedor ignored him. Being a zanthyr, he was expert at selectively ignoring anyone he chose. He settled his wolf-keen gaze on Fynnlar then. "Have you bothered to ask what you were bidden, Fynnlar val Lorian? Or do you so easily forget why we've come here?"

Fynn glared at him sullenly. It seemed most everyone felt the child in the zanthyr's company. "I didn't forget."

"The Fourth Vestal has need of your skills, Carian vran Lea. Take you exception to his need?"

Carian stared petulantly at him. Abruptly he leaned forward and demanded in a skeptical hiss, "Why are two val Lorian princes running errands for the Fourth Vestal?"

"Come and find out for yourself, Islander," Fynn muttered disagreeably. "The more the merrier the road to hell."

Ean gave him a withering look.

"Carian?" Phaedor pressed, ever unshakable. "What say you?"

The pirate sat back again, and his gaze swept the faces assembled before him. He seemed to consider for a moment while his expression remained thoughtful. Then he shrugged. "Why not?"

"Excellent. Then let us go, gentlemen," and the zanthyr was out of his chair and heading for the door before the others even managed to stand up.

Outside of the tavern, night was falling, and by the time they acquired a horse for Carian, the sky had darkened to a cobalt blue, paling only slightly where it sloped to the western horizon.

"Just for the record," the pirate grumbled to the zanthyr as the company turned north, heading into the hills, "I was well on my way to escaping that dungeon before you showed up."

"Escaping to where?" Phaedor challenged, sounding irritated. It was clear that he and the pirate had some history, and it seemed the zanthyr did not recall it fondly.

"What did that matter?" Carian protested.

The zanthyr glared at him. "It mattered if you wound up in another cell, or the

Valley of the Suns, or in the middle of the table during a meeting of the Council of Nine. You well know how the nodes of T'khendar are twisted."

"I would've found the Great Master," the islander insisted. "I *would have*, and we'd be one Vestal closer to restoring Alorin's Five."

Phaedor turned and leveled him a reproving look. "That was no time to be gallivanting around Björn's dungeon in search of his favorite prisoner."

"No time like the present," Carian argued. "I'd be back there already if I had my map."

"You've already proven yourself a fool many times over to the world at large," Phaedor returned, gazing at the pirate through the spill of his dark hair. "Who else are you trying to convince?"

Carian apparently couldn't find an adequate retort, for he said nothing, only turned to Ean looking deflated. "Is it true?" he asked the prince. "This creature travels among your company?"

Ean nodded.

The pirate shook his head, incredulous. "You do you realize who he is, don't you?" he asked under his breath.

"I don't see that it matters," Ean answered absently, his mind occupied with a host of more important mysteries for which there were equally no answers. "He has offered me his services, and I've accepted them for as long as he desires."

Carian grunted derisively and muttered, "And I thought *I* took chances."

FIFTY-ONE

'As a forest fire sparks from the smallest ember, so shall a single man effect the end of days.'

– The wielder Malachai ap'Kalien to the Council of Nine

Alyneri d'Giverny was ushered into the room where Raine awaited by one of the villa staff. As the man was closing the doors behind her, Alyneri scanned the elegantly furnished room and its three sets of mullioned double-doors, all of which opened onto an expansive patio. She found the Vestal there, standing before an iron railing covered in flowering jasmine, gazing out over the expanse of city and azure sea beyond.

"*Oh*," Alyneri exclaimed as she joined him outside, steepling fingers before her lips, "it's so beautiful!"

Raine turned to greet her with a quiet smile. The Fourth Vestal was ever composed, ever controlled, but Alyneri sensed a great unease within him. "Thank you for meeting with me on such short notice, your Grace," the Vestal said, his diamondine eyes seeming unearthly and out of place accompanied by such an unprepossessing manner. "I deeply apologize for the haste, for I know you've only just arrived after a very long journey. I will try to keep this brief."

Alyneri just nodded.

Raine motioned her toward a marble table where refreshments had been set, a plate of fruit and cheeses and a decanter of white wine, the pitcher sweating in the early evening heat. As they sat, Raine poured her some wine and inquired, "Has Ean confided at all in you? What can you tell me of his Adept progress since leaving Calgaryn?"

Alyneri accepted the wine with trepidation, for his question stirred uncomfortable memories.

As they'd boarded the ferry that morning, Ean had been in particularly foul humor. When she'd asked him of his troubles, he'd growled that Raine had betrayed him but offered no further explanation. Alyneri couldn't fathom the remark—Raine was one of the most respected of the realm's Vestals, and hadn't he been the one to send Gwynnleth to their aid? If only Ean hadn't been so unpredictable since Chalons-en-Les Trois. Alyneri didn't know what to believe.

So she took a sip of the wine, found it a welcome relief to the day's stress, and relaxed a little in the Vestal's company. "I know some," she admitted then, drinking more of the wine, which was quite good. "He's worked the lifeforce a few times—but you've no doubt seen these effects on the currents—and he's been having strange dreams. He won't speak of them to me, but on the days after such dreams, he is distant and... unapproachable." She dropped her eyes to the goblet in her hands, watching the golden liquid swirl and still.

"What else?"

Alyneri glanced up again. "There is a dragon hunting him," she confessed, suspecting Raine had seen it already in her thoughts, "and a strange man—a *malevolent* man—who came into our camp one night in search of him. T'was only the zanthyr's skill that kept us hidden and safe from harm."

Raine drew back slightly. "The zanthyr?"

"Phaedor," she said, meeting his gaze. "He joined us three days south of Chalons-en-Les Trois. The day after the dragon appeared."

Raine peered wondrously at her. "Did you all see this dragon? Are you certain of its nature?"

"Several saw it fly past. I did not personally. It attacked Ean's mind…somehow. He thought it was because the creature knew his pattern."

She drank her wine then, only noting the glass was empty when she felt that warmth in her stomach and a lightness come to her head. Raine was watching her intently, waiting for the rest, and Alyneri pressed her lips together as she considered him. Regardless of Ean's fears, surely there was no harm in telling the Vestal what everyone in the company already knew.

She set down her empty goblet, and Raine refilled it for her as she continued, "In the last few days, Ean's started practicing with the zanthyr. I came upon them once; whatever they practiced, it created huge changes in the currents."

"Yes, I've seen evidence of their practice," the Vestal admitted. "But there was something else I was hoping you might know about. Something that happened earlier, perhaps while still in Chalons-en-Les Trois."

Alyneri shook her head. "I know of no working there." She dropped her eyes, adding quietly, "We've really only spoken once since then. He doesn't confide in me much. Perhaps the avieth would know more."

"Gwynnleth?"

"I've seen them talking in depth, though since the zanthyr joined us, Ean spends most of his time with Phaedor."

Raine regarded her pensively, his expression troubled. "I confess it disturbs me to hear that this zanthyr now travels among your company. The man called Phaedor is an elusive creature with questionable motives."

"I do not doubt your knowledge of him, my lord," Alyneri admitted, her eyes lifting to meet his. She added hesitantly, "…but if there is anything I am certain of, it is that Phaedor would let no harm come to the prince even should it mean his own end."

Raine arched brows. "That is quite the avowal. I do not think it glibly spoken… nor do I receive it offhandedly."

Alyneri nodded, feeling weary and suddenly weak of heart, her fortitude drained dry. What a strange twist of events to find that she trusted the zanthyr more than the Fourth Vestal; it was terribly depressing.

Raine clasped hands in his lap and leaned back in his chair considering her quietly. "I *have* wronged him, you know."

Alyneri's eyes flew to his and her breath caught as her heart did a little jump. It was so difficult dampening her thoughts, and the Fourth Vestal was so very perceptive… "My lord, I—"

Raine held up one hand. "Ean is right. I used him, and unapologetically so. I used him to lure out my oath-brother, to force his hand." He leaned forward then. "But it's almost over," he told her with hope lightening his tone. "None of it has been for naught. My oath-brother has finally made a mistake—it seemed an impossibility, and yet I am certain that we now hold the upper hand. We have people in place. There is but one last scene to this play, and when Björn van Gelderan appears in the denouement, we will be in position to take him."

Alyneri stared at the Vestal. It seemed too incredible to be believed—that this might all be over when no end had seemed in sight... "What will you do then?" she whispered.

Raine exhaled a measured breath and sat back in his chair. "Bring him to Illume Belliel," he announced. "Let him stand trial for his crimes. There must be atonement."

She pressed fingers to her lips. "Is...will Ean still be in danger?"

"Unfortunately, yes. The net is cast too far to draw in all of the players with one haul, but we shall prevail, your Grace. Fear not. Recent events lead me to believe that Balance is finally on our side."

Alyneri knew truthreaders couldn't lie, and she suspected he truly believed what he said, yet something in Raine's words seemed...thin. "Is there anything else, my lord?"

Raine considered her quietly with his hands clasped in his lap. He wore one of those looks that many truthreaders claimed, the kind that made you feel they knew everything you were thinking before you thought it. "No, your Grace. Thank you for your time."

Alyneri pressed hands upon the table as she rose to leave, but then she reconsidered, wrestling with her conscience. Finally, she turned back to him, rested fingertips upon the smooth marble top, and cautioned, "Have a care when you speak with Ean, my lord. He is not the same man you knew in Calgaryn."

Then she departed.

Tanis had just finished his third piece of pie and was finally feeling full when the prince arrived back at the villa. The lad rushed to greet everyone as the prince and the others were entering the grand hall. The zanthyr was the first inside, and he glided across the marble floor as if knowing exactly where to go, though Tanis didn't think Phaedor had ever been there before. Ean and Fynnlar followed inside trailing a tall man dressed all in black, with long, wild hair and two curved blades at each hip. Upon closer inspection, Tanis saw the man wore four silver hoops pierced through each ear and a tiny gold loop in his right nostril, and he determined with a thrill of excitement that the man must be a pirate.

No doubt one of Lord Fynnlar's contacts from Jamaii!

Raine D'Lacourte emerged from a side passage almost at the same moment that the zanthyr was disappearing down a different one. "Ah, Ean," said the Vestal, coming forward to greet the prince. "It is such a relief to see you safely here. I would speak with you as soon as you are settled." He looked to Fynn and then to the pirate leering behind him. "And you must be my new Espial."

"My services are for hire," Carian corrected, "but I'm no man's Espial, be him mortal, Vestal or god."

"Of course," Raine said accommodatingly. "I will pay you Guild wages for your services to begin at once."

Carian eyed him shrewdly. "I'll need one day's wage in advance and tonight to conclude my own affairs, but I can return ere noon tomorrow."

"That should be satisfactory. There is much to be done."

Still the pirate watched Raine with narrowed gaze. "So just to clarify, that would be *daily* wages then, for as long as I'm in your employ?"

"Indeed."

Carian grinned. "Then we have an accord."

Gwynnleth entered then, coming in from a long row of open doors leading out to a patio and the gardens beyond. She attracted Carian's eye at once, and the pirate broke into a leering grin. "Now there's a pretty chase. And who might you be, poppet?"

Gwynnleth turned her tawny gaze on Ean in accusation. "You're claiming friendship with pirates now, Northerner?" she remarked. "That will be two."

Ean shook his head and indicated Raine. "The Vestal hired him," he returned, "not me, but I'm pleased to do the introductions. Gwynnleth, may I present Carian vran Lea of Jamaii. Carian is a Nodefinder."

"Of the *highest* degree," Carian said with a wink and a less-than courtly bow. Because Gwynnleth only stared openly at him with one wispy brow arched in dubious regard, Carian grinned broadly back at her and inquired, "See something you like, birdie?"

The avieth rested a hand on her short sword at her hip. "I was merely thinking how like my niece you seem with hair so long and pretty like a girl's. I used to braid my niece's hair with jasmine flowers and ribbon." Her tawny eyes swept him from head to toe, wherein she added tartly, "Mayhap the same treatment would improve your likeness somewhat."

Carian grinned. "You can braid my hair any way you like, birdie, so long as you're sitting on my cock while you're doing it."

"I fear I would have trouble finding it," she remarked flatly.

"I fear I'm obliged to prove you wrong."

"Carian," Raine cut in, "I would that you might make a brief stop on your way to conclude your own affairs." He took the pirate by the shoulder and walked him toward the door, passing near to Tanis as he said in a low voice, "There is a node I need you to investigate. Be careful to merely look upon it—dare not travel its pathway. It is likely being watched. But I would know where this portal leads. It is of *vital* importance." He leaned and whispered something into Carian's ear, wherein the pirate nodded.

Carian lifted his gaze over Raine's shoulder to fix on Gwynnleth then. "Don't fret, birdie. I'll be back to your side tomorrow."

"I shall lament the hour."

Carian spun and headed for the door, nearly colliding with a man just then coming in, a stout man with shoulders twice his breadth and biceps like boulders. His red hair had the same auburn fire as Gwynnleth's, but his nose was aquiline and fierce. And Tanis knew him at once.

Seth Silverbow!

Seth shoved the pirate off with an indignant oath and headed on inside, tawny eyes glaring at everything and everyone. "The perimeter is secure," he reported to Raine as he stalked across the marble floor, his silver-fletched arrows catching the light. He espied Ean and gave him the once-over. "You must be the prince that caused all this trouble then."

"Seth," Raine murmured.

"I would gladly abdicate my role in it, my lord," Ean returned, his gaze hard.

Seth frowned at him. "No doubt."

Ean looked to Raine, but his gaze did not soften. "A moment to freshen up, my lord, if you will allow it?"

"Of course. I will call upon you later."

"Ean..." Fynn said, but the prince waved him off as he headed down the hall after the zanthyr.

Fynn gazed after him and then growled suddenly, "Is there anything to drink in this god-forsaken place?"

"A meal is set for us on the patio," Gwynnleth told him, and so they all headed out into the soft night to take the meal that Tanis had already enjoyed. To his delight, he found that his place had been cleared and new flatware set, and even better, he realized his stomach easily had room for more. So it was that he sat and ate with two Vestals, an avieth and a royal prince beneath the twilight skies of Xanthe, and while the meal lasted, life was very good.

The prince did not return during the meal, nor did her Grace appear, and eventually Raine excused himself ostensibly to check on the former. When Seth was finished, he leaned back in his chair and looked around, and his amber eyes caught at Tanis's belt, wherein he rumbled, "Merdanti?" Hard amber eyes settled on Tanis. "What's a boy doing with a zanthyr's dagger?"

Not expecting such direct address, Tanis started with a little squeak. Instinct made him reach for the dagger in question, and his eyes were wide as he managed, "Phaedor...uh, gave it to me, your Excellence. A—gift to remember him by, he said."

"On a cold day in M'Nador," Fynn remarked.

Tanis shot him a frustrated look.

Seth seemed baffled by his explanation. "That creature never ceases to confuse me," he muttered.

"How is that, my lord?" Tanis braved to inquire.

"Zanthyrs are impervious to enchantment of any nature," Seth replied, still glaring at the muted blade at Tanis' belt as if expecting it to strike him. Then he added under his breath, "which is what makes them such infernal nuisances."

"And human weapons leave not even a scratch," Gwynnleth added.

"But a weapon that *can* hurt them is one of their own enchanted blades," Seth continued. "Merdanti, they are called, named for the rare element used for their forging. Merdanti weapons are the only weapons that can mark a zanthyr. As you might expect, they guard such weapons with their lives—carry every one of their blades on them all the time, in fact."

"Safest place, I suspect," Fynn muttered.

"Yet here the boy wears a zanthyr's Merdanti dagger," the Third Vestal finished in a tone of utter befuddlement, pointing at said blade.

In that moment, it became frighteningly clear to Tanis just how important the weapon he carried at his belt. *He gives me something I could use to harm him?* The boy felt the blood draining from his face. *Why?*

Seth cast him a keen look. "Aye, you see it now, lad. You could kill the creature with that blade—ironically a blade of his own making." He settled Tanis a pointed stare and added, "You're the only one here who could."

When the servant announced Raine's arrival at Ean's rooms, the prince was standing on his patio staring out over the bay. He felt a strange prickling sensation in the back of his neck. It had started just before they arrived at the villa, and it only grew stronger and stranger as the night deepened.

He sensed more than heard Raine's arrival on the patio behind him.

"Hello, Ean."

Ean made no reply. He felt there was no love lost between them. What had Raine ever done for him but turn him against possible allies and set him upon a course toward the Vestal's own ends?

"You have a right to be wroth with me, Ean," the truthreader said, coming forward, "but I would have you understand that it has been to the good of all." His tone became hopeful as he continued, "We've made inroads into the Karakurt's organization, a course that could never have been accomplished without you. We may even soon apprehend...but it's too early to speak of that," he corrected himself. "Still, you must understand, Ean, none of this could've happened without you. I regret not telling you of my plans, but I felt it was necessary."

Ean turned him a scathing look. "Yes, it's easier to control your pawns when they don't know they're in a game."

Raine looked hurt by his words. "I have wronged you Ean," he admitted. "I confess it to you most humbly, and I ask you humbly to forgive me."

Ean turned away clenching his fists at his sides. He knew the Vestal's apology was heartfelt, yet he also suspected that Raine would make the same choices again if given the chance, that he wouldn't hesitate to use Ean or any other pawn when opportunity presented.

"You know, it's ironic really," the prince said bitterly as he gazed out over Rethynnea and its long stripes of twinkling lights that were the main boulevards, the pulse of the city day and night.

"What is?"

Ean glanced at him over his shoulder. "Ironic that the only one of my advisors I can trust is the one who warned me *not* to trust him."

Raine regarded him with concern marring his fair brow. "Ean," he murmured, coming closer, "that zanthyr is Björn's creature through and through. You must know that."

Ean turned him a furious glare. "The only reason I'm speaking with you at all is at 'that creature's' behest!"

"Indeed," Raine murmured, sounding less than pleased. "The Healer mentioned that you've become quite appended to Phaedor. She seems somewhat taken within him herself. Ean..." he took another step toward the prince. "The zanthyr is adept at influencing the emotions of others, securing loyalties which otherwise would hold him suspect. It is what they *do*, how they manipulate others into their diverse and destructive games."

Ean had really had enough. "All you ever do is warn me against those who might help me," he snapped. Then he grunted and looked away again, shaking his head. "You know, for all your vehemence against him, the Fifth Vestal is the only one of you whose every action has been to *remove* me from danger. He is the only one who hasn't put me in harm's way just to achieve his own ends."

"Perhaps not yet," Raine noted soberly.

But Ean was beyond listening to him. "And if Phaedor is Björn's creature," he continued, "it only affirms this truth, for the zanthyr has done nothing but help and protect me since ever he came into my life."

That you're aware of, a little voice amended, but Ean wasn't listening to his conscience either.

Raine regarded the prince with stoic forbearance. "I would not see you come to harm, Ean. At every turn I have tried to protect you, given you companions who would help you—"

"No longer," Ean declared, turning him a defiant look. "I am your pawn in this game no longer."

"Phaedor fills your head with Björn's philosophies," Raine said exasperatedly, his composure momentarily shaken, "but you have no idea what it means to be a player in the Fifth Vestal's game!"

"And who's going to teach me?" Ean demanded with a heated glare. "You? What will you tell me of my abilities? I'm certain you know much of them that you're not saying."

"I would ask first how you came to work a petrification pattern?" Raine retorted.

Ean laughed mirthlessly. "See. You *take* only, offering nothing in return." Abruptly he spun to face the Vestal and growled, "I don't know the first thing about crafting a petrification pattern, but I know how to unwork one, and did, in Chalons-en-Les Trois." Stilling himself, he settled Raine a look of cold indifference. "And that, my lord, is the last explanation you will ever get from me for free."

He turned and walked swiftly toward a spiraling staircase that led down into the gardens.

"Ean, please don't do this!" Raine called after him. "You're not ready to face your enemies unprotected!"

But Ean barely heard him, for the tingling in the back of his neck had spread to his skull and was now a buzzing hive inside his head.

As soon as he could slip away, Tanis went in search of the zanthyr. He found him at last in the gardens sitting on a boulder facing the bay. So still and dark, Tanis almost had to know he was there to be able to see him; the lad was quite surprised to have found him at all.

"You should be asleep, Tanis," Phaedor murmured without turning, somehow knowing it was the boy that approached from behind. In the still of the night, Phaedor's manner seemed ever more distant and impenetrable. Tanis so admired this dark, mysterious creature, and he wished more than anything that he understood him better.

The lad sat down on the rock next to the zanthyr and pulled out his dagger. He ran his fingers absently over the smooth stone blade that was yet sharp enough to slice his flesh at the merest pressure. Tanis found something calming about the feel of the dagger in his hand, and fondling it had become a habit of late.

Phaedor eyed the boy out of the corner of his eye, taking note of the weapon in his hands. "Wondering why I gave you my dagger?" he asked softly.

Tanis glanced up to find the zanthyr's emerald eyes pinned compellingly upon him. He forced a careless shrug, though he didn't feel the least bit careless about it. "You said it was a gift," he answered uneasily. "Something to remember you by."

The zanthyr smiled. "You remember our conversations well," he observed. "I'm flattered."

Tanis broke into nervous laughter; the idea that the zanthyr could feel flattered by anything was hard to accept.

Phaedor regarded the boy crookedly for a moment. "Tell me, Tanis," he said as he returned to scanning the moonlit bay, "what do you think about the prince's decision to have me travel as part of his company?"

"I…I was—am glad for it, my lord," Tanis admitted, because it was the truth.

Phaedor cast him a suspicious look and said in his ominous purr-growl, "Tell me why."

It was one of those times when the zanthyr seemed truly frightening, a chilling reminder of just who and what he was. Tanis swallowed and tried to keep his voice from shaking. "You—you must know why, my lord," he managed, glancing from his twitching fingers to the zanthyr and back again.

Phaedor cocked a brow at him and murmured in an ominous tone, "Think you so?"

Tanis felt flustered, and he stared hard at his hands. "Why did you give me the dagger then?"

Phaedor waved offhandedly. "A gift. Nothing more."

Frustrated by his elliptical manner, Tanis asked, "Are *you* glad the prince has you travel with us?"

Phaedor chuckled and cast him a curious eye. "Tanis, you are indeed odd," he remarked. "Care you really about the feelings of a zanthyr?"

Tanis was shocked by his question. "Of course I do!" he declared rather indignantly. "You've feelings just like the rest of us."

Phaedor really laughed at him then. "Oh, lad," he sighed with obvious amusement, "I've told you before: you've imagined me attributes I don't possess. Zanthyrs have little use for human emotion."

But Tanis wasn't convinced. "You cannot lie to me, my lord," he said, only hoping it was true.

The faintest glimmer of surprise shown in Phaedor's eyes, and he asked again, "Think you so, truthreader?"

Tanis nodded. "Your actions prove the falsehood of such words," he declared. Then something else occurred to him, something far closer to the truth than he could ever know. "I think, my lord," Tanis began carefully, "that you have loved greater than any of us. You would have us believe your heart is of stone, when really it burns with a passion that mankind cannot even imagine."

Phaedor turned profile to the boy. He stared straight ahead for a long moment of silence, sitting threateningly still. At last, he murmured in a tone of aching regret, "Tanis…I am *not* human. You cannot wish me so."

Tanis shook his head. "My lord, with Epiphany as my witness I do not wish you so. But I…I think you're mistaken."

Phaedor glanced to him. "How so?"

Tanis squeezed the hem of his cloak, which had become twined between fingers and blade, and braved, "I…I do not claim to understand your problems, my lord, but in my opinion, human is as human does. There are lots of men who seem no more human than…than the Marquiin!" and shuddering, the boy added, "and they are the furthest from human of any man I've ever seen!"

Phaedor seemed to relax a little. He gave Tanis a gentle smile only slightly tinged with sorrow. "You are indeed an innocent, Tanis. It is little wonder so many among this company confide in you."

Embarrassed enough to look away lest the zanthyr see him blushing, Tanis gazed at the star-studded horizon and asked quietly, "Is that why you gave me your dagger, my lord? Because you knew you could trust me?"

"No, Tanis."

Tanis turned to him with sudden overwhelming curiosity. "Then why?" it was almost a plea.

Phaedor looked to him, and his gaze fell velvet soft upon the boy. "I gave you my dagger, lad," he answered in a tone underscored by a lifetime of haunting sorrow, "because I knew you trusted me."

Alyneri woke to a tapping upon her window. It confused her at first, but when the tapping persisted, she sat up in bed and then got up, slipping into her dressing robe as she went quickly to the glass doors leading to her patio.

To her surprise as she pulled back the curtains, it was Ean that stood upon the landing. She quickly unlatched the door and let him enter, her mind a jumble of reasons for why he might've come, the most desired, of course, being the least likely.

"Alyneri," Ean breathed as she closed the door again behind him. He fell to his knees and took her hands in his, pressing them against his skull. "I am invaded," he whispered miserably. "Please…"

Concerned, Alyneri knelt before him and buried her fingers within his soft cinnamon hair. She closed her eyes and sank quickly into rapport, but she found nothing—no torn strands, nothing untoward, and yet…*his pattern does seem different.* There was the faintest disturbance within it, the outermost ripple of a tiny pebble dropped into a still pond.

She withdrew from rapport, but her hands lingered in his hair. "The good news is there's nothing really wrong with you," she told him. Dropping her hands, she sat back on her heels and frowned. "The bad news is something is definitely disturbing your aura; your pattern reflects it." She searched his face with her eyes. "What are you experiencing?"

"It feels like a hive of bees in my head," he snarled, squeezing shut his eyes. "It won't…*stop*."

"How long has this been happening?"

"It started a few hours ago."

"Have you…have you spoken to the zanthyr about it?"

"No."

She reached out a hand and cupped his cheek, her gaze compassionate. "Perhaps you could try to get some sleep."

Ean turned his face into her hand and kissed her palm. "Alyneri," he whispered, his eyes closed, "I am so sorry that I've hurt you. I never meant to."

Alyneri felt tears come unbidden, and for once she didn't try to stop them. "I know that, Ean."

"Everything is different now," he confessed, opening his eyes to gaze tragically upon her, "so different from when we left Calgaryn. Remember joking about Morin's rumors? Once I could still see the light in our journey. Now…" He lowered his lids to look at his hands and shook his head slowly from side to side. "Now I see nothing but darkness, even in my dreams."

"I have seen you after waking from such dreams," she confessed. "What plagues you there?"

"More than dreams," he said without looking at her. "The man who came to our camp—or someone very like him—haunts me endlessly in them, but it's more…it's—" He glanced up, looking tormented. "You'll think me more the fool if I tell you."

"Impossible," she said, winking.

He gave her a grateful smile that didn't quite touch his eyes. "Fair enough. I have met Dagmar in my dreams," he confessed then, "and Creighton too, or at least his… ghost."

Alyneri stared at him.

"See," he said, exhaling heavily, "I knew you would think me a fool."

But Alyneri was stunned for a different reason. "*Ean…*" she said, marveling that he didn't also see what he'd done.

He turned and gazed off into the room, unable to look at her. "Whatever scolding you have for me for foolishly believing in dreams, I'm sure it's deserved."

She grabbed his face and turned his eyes to meet hers. "Ean," she repeated, staring hard at him, "you just named the dead. You just *named* Creighton."

Ean did see it then, and his face drained of color.

"What does that mean?" she whispered, her breath suddenly coming faster. "What does it mean that you named him?"

Ean held her gaze looking thunderstruck. For a long time he simply stared at her. Then he shook his head, whispering, "...It means—*oh*, Epiphany spare me from this wretched buzzing in my skull!" He pushed palms to temples and sank forward to rest elbows on his knees. Clenching his teeth, he finally growled, "I think I should find the zanthyr."

Alyneri rose at once. "I will send for him."

"No," Ean said, releasing his arms to his sides. He stood as well. "I will find him. I'm sorry I bothered you. Goodnight, your Grace." He took her hands and kissed both palms, but then he hesitated, her fingers still in his. Looking into her eyes then, he professed, "You have always been the truest of friends to me, Alyneri. Would that I might've been as fair a friend to you."

And before she could form a reply, he was gone, slipping back out through her patio door into the night.

Ean never made it to the zanthyr's quarters.

He'd barely made it off Alyneri's patio before his head was zinging with such fervor that he had to stop every few staggering steps to get his bearings again. Long minutes would pass where he was simply focused on placing one foot before the other with no attention to where he was heading. There was little room for thought among the insects swarming in his head, so it was Fortune's eye alone that graced him with a vision.

He'd stopped to lean upon a statue while the swarming in his head subsided enough to press on, when a shadow fell across the lawn before him. It might've been but a trick of the light, but sudden lucidity snapped on like dry brush catching a spark, and Ean spun toward the familiar shadow even yet knowing that Creighton couldn't be standing there in the flesh.

No one was behind him, in fact, but the shadow had served its purpose, for Ean realized that if nothing was physically wrong with him, then the noise and vertigo accosting his mind and body must be the result of some spell; and if it was the result of a spell, Ean should be able to block it.

It hadn't occurred to him until that very moment, until a vision of Creighton reminded him of the pattern he'd worked so many times in his friend's company.

Ean began to envision the pattern of protection, the pattern the zanthyr had taught him. He focused on it and nothing else, pushing aside all of the noise, ignoring his body's confused signals. He concentrated on the pattern until he saw it clearly in mind, until it glowed. He felt *elae* surge into him, into the pattern he held in close control; maintaining this focus then, he used the power of the pattern to build a wall around his mind, his glowing golden ring. From the smallest, innermost point, he extended his ring of protection, pushing all else outward, clearing from the center. Relief flooded him as he began to feel the buzzing dissipate, and it strengthened his certainty of action. Outward, Ean pressed the ring, pushing all else before it, until he once again felt his conscious awareness within the space of that glowing sphere. Safe, secure, controlled.

Ean looked around then as if for the first time. He found himself on a long expanse of lawn that ended in a cliff and the villa's wide-open view. That's when Ean heard the thumping. At first distant, the sound slowly gained in intensity. Ean lifted his gaze to the night sky, and there, low to the far horizon, he saw the creature approaching.

Yes, come, he thought, his gaze steely. *Your enchantment has failed. I am ready to fight you.*

Long moments grew into longer minutes as the creature made its distant approach, but Ean did not remove his eyes from his enemy. It flew through the night as a spectral shadow, reflecting neither moonlight nor starlight nor lights from the near city, and as it neared, Ean saw clearly two fiery golden orbs peering out from the utter darkness of its elongated head.

Wings whipped and buffeted the night as the creature settled on the lawn near the cliff, blocking a huge swath of both starry sky and city lights. And then, suddenly, the darkness simply vanished, and a man walked up the hill toward Ean.

Ean opened himself to the flow of *elae* and drew a long draft of it into the image of his pattern until the pattern was sated and full and he could hold no more without bursting. He was ready.

"I do not like looking the fool," said the man as he approached, "but ego is the province of cowards and ignorant men. I would teach my brothers there are uses for your kind, but you are proving me sadly flawed in that assessment."

It was a strange *déjà vu* to face the man in the flesh—though he realized the man before him was not the one in his earlier dreams—but Ean would not be distracted by his presence, nor by the ill portents that charged his memories. "Because I would not be turned to your twisted doctrines?" he challenged.

"Because you refuse to see truth," the man returned as he continued his steady advance. "Any creature that lives in such denial does not deserve what grace is given to it, for what life is it living then but a fiction—a fantasy? The only purpose for your kind's living at all is to know your end and embrace it—and to help others embrace their ends."

"To live for death alone seems like no kind of life to me," Ean retorted.

"Because you refuse to understand that there *is* nothing else for you," the stranger finished angrily. "All else is but illusion, a fiction invented by craven, mortal creatures terrified of facing the beyond."

Ean kept firm hold of his pattern in mind as the man stopped five paces away from him, close enough to see the yellow in his eyes. He refused to fall prey to his twisted truths this time. "If that were so," the prince challenged, "what point of birth at all?"

"Yes, you see the futility," the stranger agreed, eyeing the prince with that terrible, malevolent gaze.

Ean had the feeling that he'd stood upon this crossroads before, and the words that followed seemed foreign upon his tongue. "We will prevail in the end. We are many, and you are few."

The man laughed. "We are *legion,*" he hissed. "You cannot hope to defeat us! We hold sway in every corner of your existence. We weave our webs over every exit, for there is no exit but one. Death awaits you. Unless…" His gaze was electrifying as he offered, "Join us. Join our crusade to bring the truth to those who wallow in the darkness, blinded by lies invented to obscure them from their true purpose."

The prince felt power rolling over him, the same as he'd felt the night the man came to their camp, the same as his dream—a net of obscuring casting for the tender flesh of his thoughts.

And Ean lashed out, shooting his spear as he had practiced with Creighton, holding nothing back. The stranger reeled backwards, but his mind remained as impenetrable as granite. Ean's awareness shattered against it, gaining no hint of his pattern.

In retribution, the stranger threw out his hand, and a wave of power hit Ean in the chest, thunder without sound. He flew backwards through the air and landed with whiplash force, leaving a long scar of bare dirt as he was sent skidding through the grass. Pain lashed all along his backside, and Ean knew with the first pangs of fear that his spine had broken.

He held desperately onto his pattern, however, protecting his mind. But it was not his mind that his enemy cared about anymore.

Before Ean could move from the trench his body had dug in the grass, the stranger was looming above him, his face a mask of indignant fury. "I am RINOKH!" he snarled, his voice booming through the night, a reverberant thunder that rattled Ean's insides. "You dare to challenge me with parlor tricks!"

A crushing force slammed Ean back into the earth, flattening a great sphere of earth around him. He gasped and strained beneath it, but there was no escaping this force. He heard his rib bones crack. Pain shot in waves down his arms and legs, and still, Rinokh waged that terrible power upon him, pressing him further into the earth. Ean knew pain and terror as a lover with a single face as he both felt and heard the fragile bones of his feet snap and pop. With every second the force pinned him, his bones grew weaker beneath the onslaught, he was a ship pulled beneath the crushing sea, the ribs of his hull splintering one by one. His breath came in painful, ragged gasps as his collarbone shattered, nearly sending him over the edge. His hands shattered in a wave of agony, the bones of his arms following, and all the while Rinokh watched with cold satisfaction as Ean was inexorably crushed alive.

Nothing could have prepared Ean for this pain, yet he could not even draw breath to scream, to call for help, to beg.

Rinokh leaned over him, his gaze as ominous and fierce as a hurricane sea. "You will know my power now," he advised.

And Ean did.

The cold settled in first, a searing cold that soon had the prince's broken body trembling, but that was only the beginning. He felt every inch of his skin and bone being devoured, muscles quivering and snapping in death. Ean roared with the pain, but still no sound escaped him—perhaps the cruelest torment of all.

Finally, as Ean's vision began to blacken at the edges and he managed only the barest hiccupping of breath into shredded lungs, Rinokh knelt beside him, licked his thumb and pressed it to Ean's forehead.

The prince thought he'd known pain before this moment, but he hadn't. Not by a mile.

"Give my regards to your Maker," Rinokh sneered.

And Ean plummeted into the depths of inhuman agony.

FIFTY-TWO

'Never try to out-stubborn a cat.'

– A well-known Xanthian proverb

As **Trell** expected, Carian was long in returning. When he did finally arrive, he came rolling over the hill riding a wagon loaded with firewood and whistling a jaunty tune.

Yara set down a bowl she'd been drying from dinner and joined Trell at the door, watching as the pirate slowed the team of two draft horses to a halt between the house and barn. "Ahh…self-interest," remarked Yara with her twinkling dark eyes fastened on the pirate, "tis the greatest productive force known to man."

Carian jumped from the wagon and skipped to the door. "Ready, poppet?" he asked Trell eagerly.

"For?"

"Traveling. Tell her my part is done and to hand over my map."

"Our accord isn't closed until you stack that wood, Islander," Yara said in the Common tongue.

Carian drew up short, his mouth agape. "*You*—!" he shouted, stabbing his finger repeatedly toward her. "You speak Common, you batty old wench!"

"A far cry better than you," she agreed, giving him a disapproving once-over with her dark, crinkled eyes. "And if you want to lay hands on that map tonight, you'd best hope that wood reaches my roofline, Carian vran Lea, else you'll be hauling and chopping ere morning."

For a startling moment, Carian was speechless. Then he burst out laughing. He spun a fast circle on his heel and rushed forward, grabbing Yara in an embrace that had her feet dangling off the ground. "I submit!" he laughed, bobbing her like toddler in his arms as she beat at his head and yelled for him to set her down. Finally doing so, he fell abruptly to one knee and pulled out a bag that clinked alluringly. "You take the king, mistress," he submitted, bowing his head as he held out his coin.

Yara eyed him shrewdly and then snatched the bag from his offering hand. "And don't you forget it," she snipped.

"No," he solemnly promised, regaining his feet. "I shall never forget."

"And think twice before trying to steal from an old woman," she scolded with a shaking finger.

"Indeed, indeed," he admitted. "I have been appropriately schooled." He brushed past Trell on into the room and pulled a folded parchment from inside his vest. "Papers for travel," he told her, laying them upon the table. "Everything you'll need to see Solvayre—all above board. The wagon and horses are yours, too. Keep them, sell them," he shrugged, "whatever you wish."

Yara broke the seal on the parchment, and as she read it over, she broke into a slow grin. For an old farm woman, she still had a lovely smile. When she was done reading, she folded the papers carefully again and looked to Carian. "Hadn't you best be about that wood pile, vran Lea? It's not getting any taller while you're standing there grinning."

Carian saluted her, nodded to Trell and headed outside.

Trell followed him out. "That was a good thing you did, Carian," he murmured as they walked toward the wagon of wood.

"We had an accord," the pirate said. "I came through on my end. She'd best come through on hers."

"No doubt she will," Trell assured him.

Trell helped him stack the wood then, and when the better part of an hour had passed, they were finished. Carian stood in the wagon to toss the last few logs on top of the pile, and the very last one just brushed Yara's roof. "See," he said triumphantly. "Never let it be said I fall through on my word."

"So it would seem you're a man of honor," Trell agreed, smiling. "Against all odds and the Code no less."

The Nodefinder jumped down from the wagon and clapped Trell on the arm. "Thanks for the help. Hadn't you best be about your horse, poppet? I've got pressing business in the Cairs. A new client, as it happens."

"Already?" Trell said, fascinated by the pirate's ever-adventurous lifestyle.

"Hey, I'm a man in great demand," he said, puffing out his chest. "So…" he waved Trell off toward the barn. "Get your mount, my handsome. I've got a surprise for you when we get to Rethynnea, one you are sure to enjoy." Then he scratched his head and added on second thought, "Well, I think you'll enjoy it."

But Trell shook his head and smiled. "I'm going to stay for a while."

"What?" Carian took him by the shoulders and peered at him intently. Looking him up and down with a frown of concern, he glanced back at the farmhouse and then cautioned, "Boyo, she's too old for you. I know she's a spritely minx of a wench when she's got her gander up, but wouldn't you really rather a spring chicken than a withered old hen?"

"It's Gendaia," Trell explained, suppressing a smile.

It had happened that morning. Trell had been out to the pasture to see about a sheep that one of Yara's neighbors had reported missing. On his return, while crossing a shallow ford in the near river, Gendaia had stumbled. Trell thought nothing of it at the time, but by the time he reached the farm, she was lame. He could see nothing visibly wrong with her leg, but he wouldn't risk her.

Carian sobered upon realizing that Trell truly meant to stay behind. "You're seriously not coming with me?"

Trell shook his head. "I daren't press Gendaia until she heals. I can make my way south at any time."

Carian looked uncharacteristically stricken. "But our accord…"

"We'll call it a debt owed," Trell told him, placing a hand on his shoulder. "You can take me to the paradise of my choosing some day."

Abruptly the Nodefinder's gaze turned shrewd. "One free trip to paradise—that doesn't include a return, you know. You'll have to negotiate extra for that."

"Agreed, islander. One debt. One trip across the node of my choosing."

Carian shoved out his hand. "Then we have a new accord."

Trell clasped wrists with him, and the pirate grabbed him in a rough embrace.

As he pulled away, Carian's brown eyes seemed uncommonly kind. "You are a good man, Trell of the Tides. No," he decided, frowning, "a great man. It has been my honor knowing you."

"Until we meet again," Trell said with a quiet smile, ever uncomfortable with praise.

Carian nodded. Then he went inside.

Yara was waiting for him at her scrubbed wooden table. She'd taken off her sweater, and now the garment lay in front of her where she was carefully clipping the threads that secured the woolen lining.

"Well?" Carian said as he sauntered inside. "Where's my map?"

"I'm not about to tear the lining of my warmest sweater just because you're in a rush to make your escape, Carian vran Lea," Yara said without diverting her concentration from her careful work. "Have a seat," and she motioned with her head toward a chair across the table.

Trell entered and closed the farmhouse door as Carian was sitting down. He smiled as he watched the chair-bound Nodefinder bobbing like a school boy itching for the sunshine, his impatience making a jumping bean out of him.

Finally, Yara had worked her way all along the bottom and side of the hem and peeled back the heavy wool. Beneath it, carefully preserved, was an ancient looking piece of canvas worked all over with spheres and dark, jagged lines. Elaborate writing and scrollwork illumined all four sides, but the writing was in a language Trell didn't recognize. He felt certain that Krystos would've been able to read it, however, and made a decent guess when he said, "Is it Old Cyrenaic?"

Carian was grinning from ear to ear, but as he reached to take the canvas in his hands, it was with the utmost reverence. "Old Alaeic, actually," he murmured as he looked rapturously upon the map. "The language of the *angiel*, the Maker's blessed children."

"*Ma dieul tan cyr im'avec*," Trell said quietly.

The islander spun to stare at him. "Where did you hear that?"

"A zanthyr spoke it to me at the Mage's sa'reyth." He shrugged. "That's all I know of the saying, but I got the feeling there was much more to it."

Carian grunted and shook his head admiringly. "You really do get around, don't you?"

"I've had my share of adventures even before meeting you, Carian vran Lea, though none quite so…flamboyant, I'll admit."

Carian rolled up the map and slid it inside his vest. He stood. "You really won't come?"

Trell shook his head, smiled.

Carian turned to Yara. "Tell your daughter hello for me, old woman."

"I'll do that when next we meet, Islander," she murmured, her dark eyes inscrutable.

Trell followed Carian outside, where the islander turned and clasped wrists with him again, but he didn't let go when Trell did, holding the latter fast. "Trell," he said, suddenly serious, "if you ever tire of your journey and are ready to know the truth that awaits at the end, if that day comes…" and he held Trell's grey-eyed gaze with his own dark one, "*when* that day comes, go to the Guild Hall in Cair Rethynnea. Tell them Carian sent you. They'll know what to do."

Trell gazed into the pirate's eyes. "I see," he murmured. The truth was clear: somehow since they parted, the Nodefinder had discovered Trell's identity—or at least thought that he had. How easily the answer seemed to come to others while yet managing to elude him. There were four people in the realm thus far who were sure they knew this truth; Trell wondered if he would ever be one of them.

For a moment as he held Carian's intent gaze, the thought of knowing the truth seemed an irresistible temptation; he felt its pull painfully within his chest, so palpable was his desire, so urgent was his need. Yet he owed more to those who had counseled him so wisely: to Istalar, whose advice to learn to see with his three eyes meant taking nothing at face value; to Loghain, who reminded him that what is directly in front of him may yet be untrue; and to Ramu, most of all, who taught him that all things must be learned in their time. In the intervening weeks, these ideas had become more than mere advice. They had inserted themselves into the woof and warp of his honor and were nigh inextricable. Trell knew there would be a time to learn this truth, and he also knew somehow that this was not that time.

He gripped the pirate's wrist in farewell. "Thank you, Carian. I will remember."

Carian flashed one last grin and turned away, sauntering up the hill with that telltale swagger, his wild hair blowing behind him. Trell watched him until he disappeared over the ridge, and then he returned to Yara's cabin and quietly shut the door.

Ever the adventurer in search of fine wine, Fynnlar val Lorian left their villa shortly after dinner to take in his favorite past-time at his favorite establishment in Rethynnea. That the Villa D'Antoinette was also the gathering place of the best courtesans in the city was merely a boon; Fynn went there mainly to gather news of the type that must be conveyed with the utmost secrecy, for lives were lost should it fall into the wrong hands.

The Villa D'Antoinette was such a place, and secrets divulged there were exchanged in a no-man's-land, a neutral sanctuary where the only crime was indiscretion, but its penalty was death. Accordingly, the Villa D'Antoinette played host to spies from every espionage agency in the realm—from Fynn's Fellowship to Agasan's Order of the Glass Sword and all of those in between. It was also the home of the infamous courtesan Ghislain D'Launier, who had never lost a game of Kings—be her opponent a sheik, a prince, a scholar or the Empress herself.

Fynn was greeted at the door by a gorgeous brunette in a golden gown so lavish it would've rivaled the court of the richest Avatar Fire King. "Welcome, my lord," said she, curtsying low to bless Fynn with a view of her ample cleavage. "What is your pleasure tonight?"

"Just good wine and good company, my dear," he replied, though his eyes were already searching the crowd for a particular head of hair.

Leaving the courtesan at the door, Fynn made his way through the mansion at an idle pace, partaking long enough of the delights in each room to satisfy his desire, lingering no longer than was required. He of course paid homage to Ghislain, who he found in one of her many game rooms lounging idly on a settee in a striking gown of emerald velvet. She was sipping from a golden chalice while hosting six consecutive games with six different opponents, each of the latter looking serious and dark. She nodded a hello to Fynn, her dark eyes sparkling with invitation, but Fynn was far to savvy to involve himself with Ghislain D'Launier in any capacity.

He continued making his slow progress through the manse until he finally reached the third floor and one of several of Ghislain's extensive libraries. There, he found his quarry.

Fynn grabbed a book and settled into a leather armchair next to a dark-haired woman of middle years. Her masses of ebony hair were piled in cascading waves upon her head, and if there was a grey hair among them, Fynn would be hard-pressed to discern it among the glossy curls. She wore a sanguine silk gown slashed with violet and a five-stranded necklace of ancient gold coins; and in the place of rings, every finger was tattooed with a different ornate symbol.

"Good evening, my lady," Fynn said.

She looked up from her book, settling dark-brown eyes on Fynn. Her lips spread in a slow smile. "Fynnlar val Lorian," she murmured in a voice that was deep and sultry and tinged with hints of her desert roots. "Have you come to pay me the money you owe me?"

Hearing the expected question, which was only asked if the venue was safe for repartee, Fynn quickly replied in kind, "If I did, what would we have left to talk about?"

"Oh…family, I suppose," she remarked. "One can always talk of family, can one not?"

"Especially the crazy ones," Fynn agreed neutrally.

She settled her book in her lap and shifted to better face him. Hence followed a deeply encoded conversation that none but those well versed in their double language could understand. "I was thinking recently of my brother," she observed idly. "He was an adventurer, you know. Spent quite a lot of time at sea exploring new kingdoms, always searching for Thalma's fabled homeland where rivers ran with gold and the sweet water gives eternal life. The gods favored him in this quest, I feel certain, for he should've died many times over; yet while he never found Thalma's legendary island, he always returned with some new trinket as a memento of his travels."

Fynn swallowed as he stared at her, for the hidden meaning behind her words was crazy—no, not crazy, nigh on *impossible*. "He sounds a fair fellow, your brother," Fynn managed. "Mayhap I could meet him some day."

"Alas, a pirate stole his favorite sword and he went in search of him. I haven't seen him since."

"How long ago was that?"

"Five years to the day."

"Indeed," Fynn whispered, feeling clammy under his shirt. "How very unfortunate. Have none of your relatives heard from him either?"

"My mother claims she saw him once in the market, and my cousin says he thought he saw him in the service of a count, but these are only stories."

Fynn's heart was racing. "Well, I hope he may turn up one day." He looked to his empty goblet. "Excuse me, Livinia," he murmured. "I fear the wine has gone to my head."

"Perhaps some air, my lord," she advised sagely, nodding toward two glass-paned doors leading to a balcony.

Fynn stood and bowed politely. "As always, your company is a pleasure."

"Likewise."

"Friends and fellows, Livinia."

"Friends and fellows," she murmured. She returned to her book and the royal cousin took his leave.

Outside on the balcony, Fynn gripped the railing and took several deep, measured breaths. The practice was supposed to be calming, but all it seemed to accomplish was to make his head spin faster. The things she'd told him…it was almost impossible to believe, but Livinia had assured him that her source was beyond question.

By Cephrael's Great book! Fynn wiped a hand across his sweaty brow and gaped into the night. *Trell is alive!*

Alyneri gave up on sleep shortly after Ean left her room. She'd tried lying in bed for a while, but it was too lonesome and depressing, so she got up again, donned her robe, and headed out onto her patio. Her rooms overlooked the gardens, and she imagined she could hear the waves breaking along the coastline, though it was quite impossible from such a distance.

Still, it was pleasant sitting outside in the night listening to the creatures that thrived while humanity slept. Nights in the north were always cold, even in the heat of summer, and by now Calgaryn would be buried under several feet of snow. How amazing it was to sit outside in the deep of the night and enjoy the air, so soft upon her skin. The sound of the crickets was lulling, and she was almost ready to drift off again when the thump of something landing on her patio woke her with a start.

Alarmed, Alyneri jumped out of her chair and spun, grabbing the table for support. She relaxed when she saw it was only Phaedor. "Shadow take me," she exclaimed in a bare whisper, deflating. "It's you."

But the zanthyr advanced toward her with formidable intent, and his black gaze did not lighten. Instead, he swooped in and swept her off her feet. She let out a little squeal as he cradled her body against his chest and ran, but she really screamed as he leapt for her balcony railing, caught it with one booted foot and launched the both of them over the side.

Too startled to wonder at this strange behavior, Alyneri squeezed her eyes shut against the dizzying rush of wind as they fell three stories to the earth. She was certain the zanthyr had lost his mind, that they would be crushed to death at any moment, but he landed with barely a jerk, already running.

That's when she understood.

"*No!* Oh, no!" she gasped, a sick feeling clenching in her stomach. "What's happened? Where is he?" She struggled in the zanthyr's strong grasp, tears coming to her eyes with sudden desperation. She beat her fists upon the stone that was his chest and shouted as he ran with her, "Tell me, damn you!"

But the zanthyr carried her as if upon the wind, trees flying past faster than the eye could follow, the rhythm of his running feet a barely discernable thumping in the night. Only moments later they emerged onto a broad lawn. She saw a dark form half-submerged in a raw trench in the earth, and her heart leapt to her throat.

The zanthyr released her as they reached Ean's side, and he threw himself to his knees beside the prince. For a moment, Alyneri stood back in shock. To see him thusly, his eyes staring and cold…she felt faint…

The zanthyr was on his feet again and had her roughly beneath the arms at once. "He lives," he declared. "He *lives*," he said again, shaking her somewhat ungently, "but not for long without our help. Pull yourself together, Healer!"

Letting out a whimper, Alyneri nodded weakly.

The zanthyr returned to Ean's side and laid hands upon his head. When Alyneri made to do the same, however, Phaedor hissed, "Don't! Not yet!"

She pulled her hands back quickly, but not before she'd felt the chill rising off of Ean. It was the most horrible thing she had ever experienced. While the zanthyr worked his craft, Alyneri covered her face with her hands and tried to stop shaking. She didn't need rapport with Ean to know his body was broken. To see him lying with his limbs at such wrong angles…his flesh misshapen and black with bruising… She drew in a shuddering gasp and stifled a sob, trying to find the courage to face what was to come.

The zanthyr remained still as stone for longer than Alyneri liked to recall, every single moment of waiting spent taut with fear. Finally, Phaedor said, "Now."

Alyneri lifted her face out of her hands and pressed palms to her eyes. Taking her bottom lip between her teeth, she nodded.

It took immense bravery and every ounce of discipline she could muster for her to lay her hands upon Ean's broken body knowing what she would face. She wasn't wrong in her expectations.

"*Oh, Cephrael, no!*" Alyneri stifled a shuddering cry. Nearly every bone in his body was broken—his pattern was so frayed she could barely find it. The jagged, bitter truth scoured her raw. There wasn't enough of Ean's pattern left to weave back together. To save him, it would have to be recreated in its entirety. Feeling anguish welling in concert with despair, Alyneri looked in desperation to the zanthyr.

"It can be done," he assured her in his deep voice so alike in resonance to the crashing roar of the sea. "It must be done."

She drew in a shuddering breath. "But I don't know it!" she wept, so wracked by grief she could barely focus through her tears. "I cannot repair so many threads of an unknown pattern. If just a little more had been left—"

"*I* know it," the zanthyr said, his voice a calm presence amidst the raging storm of fear. "I will guide you." He placed a warm hand over her own and captured her gaze, lending her strength. "You and I will weave him back together again."

Alyneri bit her lip, her breath coming in shuddering sobs, but the zanthyr's gaze was unwavering. It *would* be done, she realized, the thought lending her strength to face the task ahead. If the zanthyr willed it so, no force within the realm could prevent it.

So did they begin.

Alyneri gathered what strands of Ean's pattern she could find and began smoothing the ends, and the zanthyr guided her in their re-weaving. His presence in rapport was a powerful force, a brilliant light shining too brightly to look directly upon. It occurred to her at some point as they worked together that the zanthyr was darkness and mystery without, but within, his aura shone with divine purity…a power so potent…like the very spark of the cosmos itself.

I have drawn out of Ean the power that sought to leech his life, the zanthyr told her at one point much later in their working, their minds so closely connected in rapport that she wasn't sure if he'd said the words aloud or simply placed the thought into her head. *But we must work quickly now, for he was drained to a single ember.*

Alyneri had known that much just from looking at Ean's pattern—what parts of it had remained, that is; what was usually so bright and shining had become as dull as ash. But the strands she and the zanthyr had rewoven were golden threads leading back to the burned and frayed remains of his lifeforce, and ever so slowly their brilliance was overtaking the ashen roots. Heartened, Alyneri worked tirelessly, always aware of the zanthyr's near presence, always grateful to know he was there.

Dawn came, and daylight drew the others. Fynn, Tanis, Rhys, Dorin, Bastian, Cayal, Raine and Seth…they all came with expressions of shock and dismay, outrage and regret, but neither Alyneri nor the zanthyr made accommodation for them, nor stopped in their administrations to explain the tragedy that had occurred during the night.

The sun grew higher, warming the day, and people came and went. Guards rushed to and fro, servants spoke in whispers; food was brought and went uneaten, until finally all had come, some lingering to provide quiet comfort or support unclaimed, and taken their leave once more.

Only Tanis stayed the course, sitting at Alyneri's side with dutiful patience, saying nothing, asking for no attention, merely a quiet, calming presence. Finally, when the sun shone low in the clear blue heavens and their shadows fell long upon the grass, Alyneri inhaled with a resounding shudder, released Ean's head as she withdrew from rapport, and tipped over into Tanis's lap.

The others rushed forward from the fringes then, their faces drawn, red-rimmed eyes pinned expectantly on the zanthyr. With the utmost care, he lifted Ean from the wreckage of the yard and cradled his limp form against his chest. "What can be done has been done," he told them, offering no more hope than the truth. Then he turned and carried the prince to the villa.

Rhys carried Alyneri in his arms following after the zanthyr. She fell asleep along the way, but she woke again as someone was putting her into her bed. She managed to open her eyes just enough to see Tanis helping her under the covers. "Your Grace…" the boy murmured miserably, but she was too tired for explanations…

When she woke again, it was to find the zanthyr standing at her bedside. Night had fallen, and a meal sat untouched on her table. She thought to push up but was too weak even to lift her arm. Phaedor placed a cool hand across her forehead, and she wondered in her deliria of exhaustion how his hands always managed to be just the right temperature. "Ean…" she whispered.

"Improves," the zanthyr replied.

She inhaled a whimpered cry, for the ache she felt was a palpable thing.

"Sleep, your Grace," the zanthyr admonished gently. His hand brushed across her eyes, and she slid back into darkness...

The third time she woke, it was to again find the zanthyr standing over her. She gazed up at him for a long time, feeling admiration so deeply for the man that it was nearly overpowering. "You're healing me, aren't you?" she whispered, looking up at him. "Renewing my strength while I've been sleeping?"

"I am no healer," he said with a shadowy smile.

"I beg to differ." With great care, he helped her to sit up in bed, wherein she noted her table again set with a meal. "Lunch?"

"Breakfast. Are you hungry?"

"Famished." She held out her hand to him, and he helped her to the table. She felt weak but stronger than she might've imagined after what they'd done.

What they'd done was the impossible.

She was still reeling from the shock of Ean's near death and the success of his revival as part of the same endless moment, loss and relief inextricably but confusingly entwined. Sitting carefully, for she felt immensely dizzy if she moved her head too quickly, Alyneri took up a piece of toast and managed to chew it, though just holding the bread exhausted her.

We rebuilt him from the smallest ember of his soul!

No one would believe such a thing could be done, but now that Alyneri knew it was possible, she promised never to let a man die if even a single strand of his pattern could be found.

The zanthyr sat with her while she ate regarding her in silence. She was acutely aware of his presence but in a way that made her heart jump happily every so often. The zanthyr had claimed an inexplicable part of her heart as they'd worked so tirelessly to save Ean, and she found herself thinking of him wistfully that morning, wishing he would linger much longer than the shared time of a single meal. It was more than a bond of duty they shared now, more than concern for the same man; during those long hours of rapport, Alyneri saw something in the zanthyr that few had ever been allowed to witness, and she felt sealed to him now in a way that quite confused her.

When she'd eaten all she could, she lifted her gaze to meet his. He'd been watching her steadily all the while, his face so perfect in its construction, his eyes disconcertingly compelling. She found herself blushing beneath his stare, but she didn't care that he saw her blush. He'd seen her naked soul, and she'd seen his. "I know what you are," she observed after a moment.

He broke into a crooked half-smile, his eyes glittering with amusement. "Indeed, your Grace?"

Immediately her face flushed from the bold declaration, but she held his gaze. "Yes. You're a mirror."

He arched a brow, intrigued. "Do explain."

"All of your charades," she said, "your banter and impudence...it's all in mimic of others. You mirror back to people the same emotions they radiate toward you—mistrust, contempt, ill regard...tempered of course by your own disposition, but mirrored all the same."

"A fascinating observation, your Grace," the zanthyr noted, and she was relieved to realize there was no sarcasm in his tone, only interest. "Yet if this assessment be true, then must needs I have no identity of my own? Who am *I* then, really, if I am but a mirror?"

"You're not *only* a mirror," she corrected, looking bashfully away. "Just a mirror to those who…who need you to be."

"You haven't answered the question," he noted.

She lifted her gaze and forced herself to consider him then—not that looking upon his beauty was the least bit objectionable, but holding his intense gaze for any amount of time was as difficult as staring into the sun. She remembered the brilliant light that was his aura as they worked through the night to save Ean, and she braved, "Who are you really? I must submit that your nature is closest to Tanis's own."

Phaedor really arched brows then.

Seeing not the man before her now so much as the image of him as they'd shared rapport, Alyneri continued thoughtfully, "There is compassion in you that isn't quantifiable in words." Then she chided with a gentle smile, "Don't bother trying to deny it, Phaedor, for I have seen your truest aura with my own soul's eye."

Phaedor cast her an enigmatic look. He stood and helped her to rise also, taking her hand in his. "And what will you do with this information, now that you have so decided?"

"I suppose…I suppose I shall love you for it," she admitted suddenly, surprised by her own brave candor. "What else can I do?" she added with a tragic smile as they walked toward her bed. "I am doomed to love men who do not love me."

At this the zanthyr paused and took her chin in hand. He gazed down into her eyes and told her in his deeply resonant voice, "The man to whom you have given your troth will love you more deeply, more completely, than you will ever comprehend."

Alyneri caught her breath, and gooseflesh sprouted on her arms. She knew prophecy when she heard it.

Suddenly tears flooded her eyes in an unexpected release of emotion that was as baffling as it was unavoidable. Before she could think what she was about, she stood on tiptoes and planted a kiss upon the zanthyr's mouth. It was meant as a token of her gratitude, yet a zanthyr's kiss was like no other. The moment her lips met his, she felt electrified and heady; and though it was the briefest of exchanges, she still felt her knees go weak and was grateful that he maintained a strong hand upon her elbow.

"Perhaps a little more rest, your Grace," the zanthyr suggested as she pulled away, gazing down at her with a shadowy smile.

Wide-eyed and dizzy, Alyneri didn't trust herself to speak. She nodded.

Phaedor helped her back to her beside, and Alyneri climbed beneath the covers still tingling from head to toe. He left her then, but it was a long time before she stopped remembering the feel of his kiss and drifted back into slumber.

FIFTY-THREE

'The angiel and their earthly brethren are inextricably tied to the realm; thus is their gravest mission to ensure its posterity.'

– *Sobra I'ternin*, Eleventh Translation, 1499aF, *Genesis, Book 2, Verse 74*

T**anis thought** Faring East was possibly the most crowded street he'd ever seen. Carriages, wagons, carts, and coaches packed the wide boulevard, which was divided down the middle by islands of orange trees groomed into perfect spheres, while men and women of every race and even more varied attire maneuvered the shell-paved streets.

Prince Ean had made no change in the five days he'd been unconscious, and everyone was out of their heads with worry for him. To make matters worse, Fynn and Brody had gone missing the day after his Highness was attacked, but the Fourth Vestal assured him that the royal cousin was merely looking into something and would return soon.

The others seemed to occupy themselves well enough, but her Grace couldn't take it—she couldn't handle watching the prince lying there with the shadow of death upon him, barely breathing, his face pale and drawn and his eyes bruised. She knew, and so Tanis knew, that the bruises were everywhere on his body, and the constant reminder of what had been done to him made her physically ill. So she'd asked the captain that morning if he would accompany her into town, and Rhys, having also had enough of staring impotently at his dying prince, had agreed.

Thus the three of them headed off to the Market District to do some shopping, an activity which her Grace had always declared to be 'soup for the feminine soul.' Of course, in contrast to other ladies of the peerage, her Grace's shopping list called for such items as Brushroot, Kingsfoil, and that most rare of commodities, Black Krinling Oil; and her list of places to visit included apothecaries, gypsy Healers, and alchemists.

As Rhys, Alyneri and Tanis walked the Thoroughfare—called Faring East, Faring North, or Faring West by the locals, depending on what stretch of the five-mile boulevard one was traveling—Tanis saw representatives from every imaginable race: golden skinned Bemothi in their colorful, flowing silks, women and men both with long, ebony hair gathered into jewel-studded combs or held at the nape of their necks with metal bands; Khurds in turbans and loose desert robes, scarves across their faces so only their deep, dark eyes could be seen; and pale and powdered Veneisean high-born dressed in elaborate lace and embroidered satin, the men wearing ornate half-capes and carrying silver-worked canes, the women tittering beneath scallop-edged parasols trimmed in long, beaded fringe.

There were others too, of a darker variety: Xanthian Foresters dressed in hunting garb, with arm-guards for archery sewn into their paneled suede jackets, longbows slung over their shoulders. Jamaiian sailors walked along with their jaunty swagger, long hair tossing on the sea breeze, ears and noses full of silver hoops, some of them dangling charms or jewels; and of course there were plenty of sellswords, too. Tanis may have only been fourteen, but he could spot their type, and whenever he turned his truthreader perception their way, a feather-light brush with their mind, he came away again feeling…oily.

But all the joy of encountering these myriad races was lost when they reached the Piazza del la Mer. Across the wide paved plaza on the far side of its central fountain, a large group of people were mingling in front of a stone wall, and her Grace walked closer to investigate it. Tanis saw that the wall was plastered with pictures, some drawn skillfully, others hastily penned. Many had the perfection of an Illuminator's hand—those artists who used the fourth strand to pin the exact image of a man upon parchment, canvas or even stone. These latter illuminata seemed uncannily lifelike, staring with eyes that might truly have been looking out from the other side of the paper.

Men, women and children gathered before the wall, the base of which was stacked with mounds of wilting flowers, prayer beads, melted candles and spattered wax, and a host of miniature idols representative of various faiths.

Her Grace stopped to gaze sadly upon the display. "A mourning wall," she murmured.

Rhys turned her a disagreeable look.

Tanis had never seen anything like it. "What's a mourning wall?"

"A shrine for the missing and the lost," she answered. She walked closer, passing between the line of mourners and the stacks of offerings to gaze intently at the many pictures. Tanis saw men and women depicted there and some children as well. A good number of the pictures had a tiny symbol somewhere upon the canvas—a circle crossed with three lines that formed a jagged letter A. He counted easily twenty faces marked with the symbol just within easy sight. Tanis knew that symbol, called the *iederal'a*. It was the symbol of the Adept race. He forced a dry swallow.

"Look how many are missing," Alyneri exclaimed in dismay, though her voice was a bare whisper. She pressed fingers across her mouth and shook her head, her brown eyes wide.

"Someone is waging war against us," said an old man who had been staring at the illuminata of an older woman with lustrous white hair, her blue eyes the azure hue of the Bay, which even then dominated the distance, viewed between a sculptured archway across the square. He turned to look at Alyneri with tormented dark eyes. "Tis not enough, the insidious wasting that threatens our race," he said, glowering from beneath bushy white eyebrows, "but now they systematically exterminate us, one by one. At least Malachai's damnable war was one we could see, with enemies we could fight. How do you fight against Balance? What chance have we when the Maker has determined our race to die?"

Upon hearing the man's words, the image of the stranger who'd invaded their camp sprang to Tanis's mind. He remembered the cold malevolence of the man, how his very presence felt antipathetic to their world, and he wondered if the old man was wrong. What if *someone* was behind all of the terrible things happening?

Alyneri walked over to the old man and looked at the image of the woman. "She was your wife?"

He nodded. "A Healer. She had the biggest, kindest heart of anyone I've ever known. And now…"

"Epiphany willing you shall meet again in the Returning," Alyneri murmured.

His gaze hardened in bitterness. "That's enough for you, is it? The idea of meeting again in the next life?"

"I find encouragement in it, yes."

He looked back to the image of his wife. "Then you haven't known true love." He leaned and kissed the illuminata and then turned his back on them and walked away.

Alyneri glanced sadly to Rhys, and they moved on as well.

When they finally reached the tailor recommended to her Grace by the villa's Seneschal, Rhys offered to let Tanis accompany him while he ran his own errands. Her Grace had turned morose since leaving the mourning wall, so the lad jumped at the chance to escape the miasma of her mood, for it reminded him unceasingly of Prince Ean's dire state.

The city streets were jammed with traffic as Tanis followed the captain down the sidewalk, dodging merchants and squirming around stands and kiosks as he tried to keep up. Rhys walked with his back rod-straight, towering above most everyone they met on the street, and with his massive shoulders and Kingdom greatsword across his back, the crowd parted to let him pass, leaving Tanis to maneuver through the flotsam in his wake.

Rhys first stop was the city's premier armorer where the Captain placed an order for his men. Tanis spent the time browsing in the shop, and he came across an arm-sheath that he suspected would fit his dagger from Phaedor perfectly. Grabbing up the sheath with excitement, he turned and asked the craftsman, "Sir, how much for this?"

Rhys cast him an ill-humored look over his shoulder, but Tanis had his own money and didn't care what the captain thought.

The armorer, who was white-haired if still robust, gave him a fatherly sort of smile. "Seven shillings, lad," he replied.

Grinning with excitement, Tanis approached the counter. He laid down the sheath while he retrieved his money, counted out the correct change, and handed it over. As the merchant was depositing the coin into his lockbox, Tanis withdrew the dagger Phaedor had given him. He laid that on the counter too, alongside the sheath. "Will this fit, do you think, sir?"

The armorer's eyes widened upon sight of the weapon. "What in Tiern'aval…?" He picked up the dagger and looked it over. "Merdanti?" He lifted a bewildered gaze to Tanis. "How did such a fair youth come by a *zanthyr's* dagger?"

"It was a gift, sir—Raine's truth," Tanis told him while Rhys glared and the armorer gazed in wonder. Then he propped elbows on the high counter and confided, "but my lady, you see, she doesn't like my wearing the dagger on my belt. She says I might as well attach a target to my back for all that carrying a Merdanti dagger is inviting for trouble, but I'm fourteen now, and there's no reason I shouldn't wear it, and—"

"A gift?" the merchant repeated as if he'd heard nothing else. He looked utterly mystified. "From whom?"

Tanis gave him a curious look. "From the zanthyr that made it, sir. How else could one come by a zanthyr's dagger?"

At that, Rhys snatched Tanis's dagger out of the merchant's hand, swiped his new sheath off the counter, and marched him outside. Back on the street, he shoved both items into Tanis's hands and growled, "Mind you don't tell our business to anyone else!"

Then he took off in his brisk walk, forcing Tanis to run after him while trying to secure the dagger into its new sheath and the new sheath to his forearm while keeping his sleeve lodged above his elbow and one eye on where Rhys was headed.

Their next destination was to see about a new horse for Cayal, whose mount had fallen lame soon after their arrival. After arguing with the merchant for at least ten minutes, Rhys finally agreed to a price that was half of what the man had first asked for the horse. For a few extra shillings, the man agreed to have his boy deliver the new steed to the villa where they were staying, and then they were off again.

As he trailed along after the captain, Tanis began to wonder about the business transaction he'd just witnessed. So he asked Rhys, "My Lord Captain?"

Rhys gave him a sideways glance full of immediate annoyance. "What?"

"Was that horse really worth ten crown?"

"He was worth what I paid for him and not one shilling more," Rhys said.

"Did the owner know that?"

"Of course."

That confused Tanis. "But if the horse is only worth the five crown that you paid for him, and the owner knew that, then why did he ask for ten crown?"

"Because it's customary," Rhys said. "You never ask for what something is worth because you'll end up getting less than it's worth."

"But that doesn't make sense," the boy protested. "Why ask for more than what something is worth if you know what it's really worth? If it's really worth what you're asking for it, people should pay it. Right?"

Rhys gritted his teeth. "No. If he only asked for five crown people would think that the horse was only worth two and a half, and then he wouldn't get the price that the horse was fairly worth."

"But you knew the horse was worth five crown, right?"

He nodded.

"Was that just because the man asked for ten?"

Rhys gave him an aggravated look. "I knew the horse was worth five crown because I knew the horse was worth five crown."

Just then they crossed a street where they narrowly avoided being hit by a covered wagon full of gypsies, veered around a mother scolding her mud-smeared child, and wove their way through a display of vegetable-laden carts blocking the sidewalk while their owner chatted with a friend. Those immediate dangers then past, Tanis returned to the conversation.

"So you knew the horse was worth five crown," he repeated to the captain. "So that means that if the man asked for five crown, you'd have paid him five crown without an argument?"

Rhys scowled at him. "Do you always ask so many questions?"

"I'm just trying to understand," Tanis replied. "If no one ever teaches me anything, then you can't expect me to get any smarter. What if I have to buy something one day for you, my Lord Captain? Wouldn't you like to know I'd do it right?"

Rhys gave him a sooty look.

"So would you have paid him the five crown?" the boy persisted.

"No, I'd have paid him three."

"Three!" Tanis exclaimed. "But you said the horse was worth five! Three hardly seems an honorable fee, my lord. Why wouldn't you have paid him five?"

"*Because,*" said Rhys with an affronted glare, "if the owner was stupid enough to only ask five crown for that horse, then he deserved to get three for it. The horse would be better off with a smarter owner anyway."

As Tanis was pondering that logic, they ducked under a wooden scaffolding, barged through the middle of a brawl of rumpled-looking children, and turned up a side street toward a sword maker's workshop, the craftsman coming highly recommended by a man named Ewan Favre, who was somehow connected to Fynn and whose name Tanis had heard mentioned with enough frequency to cause him to remember it. Just outside the sword maker's, Rhys turned and gave Tanis a penetrating look. "Now keep quiet while we're inside. That means keep your wagging mouth shut."

"I know what it means," Tanis grumbled.

In and out and they were back on the street.

"You know, my lord," Tanis remarked as they headed through a square of upscale taverns whose patrons sat at café tables shaded by orange trees, "I'll never learn a thing if I don't ask when I don't understand something."

"Children should be seen and not heard," Rhys muttered.

"I'm hardly a child," Tanis protested. "I'm—"

"I know, I know," he cut in testily, "you're *fourteen* now."

"And besides," Tanis pointed out, "Prince Ean asks just as many questions as I do when he's trying to understand something."

"So?"

"So..." Tanis paused, frowned at him. "So, I mean, I don't talk any more than he does."

"And your point?"

Tanis thought about that for a moment. Then he gave the captain a suspicious look. "Are you saying Prince Ean talks too much?"

Rhys halted, turned, and glared at the boy. "I'm saying *you* talk too much," he grumbled. Then he spun on his heel and strode on.

When Tanis caught up with him, the lad said, "Don't you think it's important to ask questions, my lord?"

Rhys assumed a pained expression. "What do I look like to you, Tanis? The Book of Cosmic Answers?"

Tanis frowned.

"Who am I to say yes or no?" Rhys went on. "I'm a soldier. I do what I'm told. I'm supposed to follow orders, not question them."

"But I'm not a soldier."

"You don't say."

At this juncture, Tanis concluded that it wasn't easy to carry on a conversation with someone who didn't want to converse with you.

They stopped to look around a saddler's shop whose window display had caught Rhys' eye, and that reminded Tanis of the horse and the fact that he was still confused about it. As Rhys was admiring a cantled saddle tooled with inlaid silver, Tanis ventured to ask, "My lord? About that horse. If you didn't know that the horse was worth five crown, might you have paid the man what he asked?"

Rhys gave him a tormented look.

Tanis persisted, saying, "I just don't understand why someone would ask a higher price for something than he knew it was worth."

At that, the saddler looked up from the stirrup he was piercing and grinned at Rhys. The captain flushed, grabbed Tanis by the ear and dragged him from the shop.

"Look, Tanis," he growled as the boy stumbled along after him batting at the captain's fingers, which felt like steel pincers on his fragile ear, "you don't need to know the logic behind every single thing that happens in the entire realm."

"I was only asking!" Tanis yowled as he tried to pry his ear free of the captain's hold.

Rhys released him, and Tanis darted out of reach with a glare like an affronted barn cat. "If someone picks a fight with you," Rhys went on, "you don't stop to ask him why. You just hit him back, right?"

"Unless he's bigger than you are," Tanis pointed out, "in which case you run."

Rhys shook his head and grumbled something about boys raised without a father's hand.

"But about the horse, my lord," the lad said after ensuring he was well out of fingers' reach. "It seems to me that if the man knew that he could only get half of what he asked for, and he wanted ten crown for the horse, then he should have asked for twenty crown."

"Twenty crown!" Rhys exclaimed. "Why that's absurd! No one would pay that price."

"But they're not expected to," Tanis pointed out. "By custom rule, he'd have gotten half of what he asked—that is, ten crown—which is still twice as much as the horse is worth but half what he asked for, and since he was already making a profit on the horse when selling at five crown, then he could have come away twice the richer."

"It wouldn't work that way, Tanis," Rhys said.

"Why not?"

"Because his competitor would undersell him at ten crown and no one would buy from him at all."

"That doesn't make any sense," the boy muttered.

Rhys looked over at his bewildered face and fought to suppress a smile.

"So, my lord?" Tanis asked a little later as they were walking across another square whose stones were damp from the spray of a cascading fountain in its center.

Rhys clenched his teeth. "What?"

"Would Prince Ean have paid the man five crown?"

Rhys scowled. "His highness would have paid him *twelve*."

"But the man was only asking for ten!"

The captain harrumphed irritably. "My point exactly."

Leaving the square, they turned a corner and headed back through the garment district toward the tailor's, walking beside window after window packed with bolts of colorful cloth, elaborate gowns, velvet cloaks and courtly attire, or frilly hats with lots of feathers that Tanis marveled anyone would wear. Who'd want to go to court looking like a rooster?

The captain had gotten ahead of him while Tanis was gawking at the strange hats. When the lad caught up with him again, he inquired in earnest, "My lord, do you really think it wrong of me to ask so many questions?"

In front of them, a glassmaker stood on his front stoop shaking the remains of a broken vase and scolding a pair of young boys who looked ready to bolt at any second. "Who am I to judge, Tanis?" Rhys replied, eyeing the demonstrative merchant with mild annoyance as they passed. "I'm just a soldier; it's all I've ever been trained to do. Your life is destined to be far different from mine, you being a truthreader and all. I mean, by the time I was your age, I was already a squire for the King. By seventeen I'd entered my formal training, and I was knighted at twenty."

Tanis gazed at him rather wistfully as he thought about such a life. "I've always wanted to be a knight," the lad confided. "Do you think I might ever have the chance, my Lord Captain?"

Rhys' look softened. "You know the right people, Tanis," he replied, "Prince Ean trusting you the way he does, and you're sure to be given your own place at court when we return to Calgaryn." Then he frowned. "You'd need a title though."

Tanis certainly didn't have one of those. He gave the captain a meager smile instead. "That's all right, my lord," he responded. "I don't really need to be a knight."

At the next corner, they got stuck on the wrong side of a wagon loaded with sacks of flour. The driver was trying to maneuver his team backwards up across the sidewalk in order to line up the rear of his wagon with the baker's unloading platform and making a real mess of things. Rhys regarded Tanis the entire time they waited, with the shrill voice of the irate glassmaker still resounding in the distance. "You're a good lad, Tanis," the captain said as they began walking once more. "Your heart is pure."

A thought occurred to Tanis then, and after thanking Rhys for the complement, he said, "You must really care about Prince Ean, don't you, my lord?"

"What makes you say that?"

"Assumption?" Tanis replied.

Rhys shrugged. "The prince is destined for greater things than I," he admitted, neither one of them willing to speculate if their prince would in fact recover, finding the hope of full recovery as the only acceptable truth. "Never in my life would I have imagined such a quest as his, but his Highness is so intelligent—half the time he's predicting the day after tomorrow while I'm still pondering over yesterday's failings."

"He is smart," Tanis agreed.

"And he's so quick on his feet," Rhys continued, his voice colored with a certain measure of pride, "he thinks fast and reacts faster—which traits make a good soldier. Plus, he's always following right along with things. You can't put one past Prince Ean."

"I think he's very lucky to have you protecting him," Tanis told him.

The captain shrugged. "He's got that zanthyr now. I just don't trust the damnable creature. His Highness doesn't realize his own importance to his father and his kingdom, else he wouldn't either."

"Phaedor cares very deeply for Prince Ean."

"Does he now?" Rhys eyed him skeptically. "I suppose he told you that?"

"No," Tanis admitted, "but that doesn't mean it's not the truth. You've never told me that you care about Prince Ean, but I know that you do."

Rhys gave him a sour look...grunted.

After that, they darted across the street, slipping between a covered wagon with two red-cheeked girls peeking out the back and a violet coach pulled by a quad of matched greys. On the sidewalk again, they turned a corner around a jeweler and came in view of her Grace's chosen tailor at the far end of the lane. Tanis was relieved to see the shop; he might not have volunteered to go along with the captain if he'd known so much walking would be involved. Moreover, they'd long missed lunch, and his stomach was protesting mightily.

As they side-stepped around a tinker mending a copper pot in the middle of the sidewalk while a mother-hen of a woman stood waiting impatiently above him, Tanis pointed out to Rhys, "You know, my lord, admitting that you care for someone doesn't mean you're admitting to weakness."

Rhys came to a dead halt and spun to glare at the boy. He looked half-furious and half-mortified. "Stay. Out. Of. My. Head," he growled, emphasizing each word with a stone-hard finger jabbed in Tanis's chest.

"I'm not *in* your head," the lad insisted, shrugging away.

Rhys turned and strode off again. When Tanis caught up with him, he said, "But even if I was, that doesn't make what I said any less true."

"You have an annoying habit of talking out of place, boy," Rhys grumbled.

"I can't help what I know," Tanis argued. "It's not my fault if your feelings are obvious to me. And anyway," he blustered on, "you shouldn't be thinking that you're not important to Prince Ean—"

Rhys stiffened and looked like he was about to say something, but he hunched his shoulders and pushed on instead.

"—because you are. You've got the most important job of any of us. Prince Ean may not always be able to depend on the zanthyr, but he knows he can always depend on you, my Lord Captain. The King gave you the honored position of guarding the life of his only remaining son. What could possibly be more important than that?"

Rhys halted to yield way to a Krothian noblewoman, her ladies-in-waiting, and her stewards coming out of a shop. The veiled ladies had their heads together talking in whispers, while the two liveried young men looked haggard beneath their bundles of packages, hat boxes, and long bolts of silken cloth.

"Fine," Rhys muttered as the youths labored past.

His acknowledgment caught Tanis off guard. "I beg pardon?"

"I said *fine*," Rhys repeated. "Perhaps all of your questions are doing you some good. You might show a bit of intelligence—*sometimes*." He started off again.

"Does that mean you don't mind my asking questions, my lord?" Tanis inquired with a bright smile as he rushed to catch up.

"I guess not," Rhys reluctantly conceded. Then he added hastily, "As long as you don't ask *me*."

Alyneri was seated at a little table in the back room of the tailor's shop when Tanis and Rhys returned. Her Grace looked to have enjoyed a meal—the remains of which Tanis eyed wistfully—and was sipping on a cup of hot tea. "Ah, how good of you to return, my Lord Captain," she observed as Rhys barged in ever the bull in the china shop, "and so promptly at the stroke of midday as we discussed."

Tanis had noticed that sarcasm was generally wasted on Rhys.

"Are you ready?" the captain barked.

Alyneri sighed. "Yes, Captain." She set down her teacup on its delicate saucer and stood with graceful precision, as if dining at the King's table instead of the back corner of a dressmaker's workroom. Nodding a farewell to the tailor's wife, a mousy little woman who was mostly concealed behind the wire-framed torso she was laboring to attire in an organza gown, her Grace handed a large rectangular package to the captain and preceded him from the store. As he followed, Tanis thought of showing her Grace his new arm sheath, but he reconsidered at the last minute, guessing rightly that the information might not be so well received.

As the unlikely trio of healer, truthreader and solider walked—with Alyneri in the lead lest Rhys set the pace and push them all into a sweat—her Grace put a hand on the much taller Captain's arm and said, "If you don't mind, my lord, I'd like to continue east to an apothecary which is said to boast a supply of Black Krinling oil from Dheanainn. It is all but impossible to find this particular oil in Dannym."

Rhys sighed and shrugged. Perhaps all the walking had gentled him toward her, or else he really was just too tired to argue about it.

As they continued along Faring East, Tanis passed store upon store whose tall front windows displayed an array of eye-pleasing artifacts—fine hardwood tables and gilded chairs upholstered in velvet or striped satin, jewel-hilted daggers and gold-worked swords, a sea of stained-glass lamps hanging from elaborate chains, perfumed soaps and scented oils in colored glass bottles, fine lace linens and heavy down-filled quilts; countless stands displaying beads, statues, gems or bangles; vases and carpets from the Akkad; Agasi porcelain; ivory, jade and ebony artifacts from Avatar…the vista was endless.

"Just how far is this place, your Grace?" Rhys muttered as they were passing a store displaying leather goods of varying design.

"I was just told it was on Faring East, my lord," she answered.

"And who told you this again?"

"The alchemist of Z'hin—you remember…the store with all the bat wings?"

"Oh," he said, frowning. "Him."

"He said if I wanted Black Krinling Oil, there was only one place to go for it, and that was the apothecary on Faring East."

"Faring East is a long road, your Grace," Rhys grumbled.

Tanis didn't begrudge the captain his complaint; he was the one carrying all of her Grace's packages.

"At some point it becomes Faring North, so it can't go on forever," Alyneri reminded him sweetly.

For some reason, the captain didn't seem heartened by this news.

They soon passed a prosperous inn called the Heart of the Lion, which was entered by way of two gold-wrought doors shaded by a luxuriant crimson awning trimmed in gold fringe. Just beyond the awning, a *taverna* opened upon the street by way of a wall of tall double doors—all of them thrown wide to let in the day—so that as Tanis walked by, he had a clear view of the inn's guests as they refreshed themselves at little round tables draped in white linen or at the wide bar along the back wall. At present, the *taverna* sported a healthy congregation of patrons, all of whom looked as prosperous as the inn itself, if told from their lavish garments and the way the inn's wait staff bent, bowed, blanched and bolted.

Just beyond the *taverna*, they came upon the apothecary.

Alyneri stopped before a simple wooden door set with a stained glass window in the image of a gryphon. The orifice looked rough and provincial next to the Heart of the Lion's ornate, gilded entrance. Her Grace straightened the bodice of her gown, though it needed no tending on her trim figure, then nodded to Rhys to open the door, which he did.

Tanis was quick to ask her before she entered, "Your Grace, may I wait outside?"

Alyneri looked surprised, but she replied, "I suppose, Tanis, but mind you don't wander off." She turned and went in, and Rhys followed, not quite slamming the door behind them.

Tanis slipped back to the inn and sat down in an unobtrusive chair at the outermost table of the café, which was growing more crowded by the minute. It seemed a large wedding party had just arrived, for the flower-strewn bride was still perched on one shoulder of her groom in the Bemothi style while he labored to find a place to sit and the rest of the boisterous guests converged on two hapless waiters. At a table closer to Tanis, a sallow-complexioned Veneisean lord dressed in garish violet-red satin was courting a rather corpulent lady in a mustard yellow tulle gown, whose torrid color clashed violently with the man's attire. Just looking at the pair of them made Tanis's eyes hurt.

As he was rubbing them, a serving girl broke through the crowd of wedding guests and rushed up to Tanis with her tray held high. She set down a glass mug filled with a pale amber liquid in which floated a drowned looking mint leaf and rushed off again without a word. Tanis leaned over and sniffed the drink. Unsurprisingly, it smelled of mint.

As Tanis was sitting back again, his eye caught on a man on the far side of the café. His long black hair was slicked back from a noble's peak, and his almond-shaped eyes tilted slightly up at the corners. He wore a jacket of amber velvet with thread-of-gold cloth pulled through the slashed sleeves, the collar open to reveal a crimson silk shirt beneath.

Tanis couldn't say why the man captured his eye, only that there was something about him, something…fascinating. He had a dangerous sort of look to him though, a certain feral quality, as if he would as easily gut you as offer to buy you a drink. Like the wedding guests, the stranger had that amber-eyed, caramel-colored skin of a Bemothi, and yet Tanis felt sure the man was from somewhere far more remote. There was something vaguely familiar about him, too, although Tanis was hard-pressed to say what it was.

As if feeling the lad's gaze upon him, the man turned his head and looked directly at Tanis. Two odd sets of eyes regarded one another then; one pair colorless, the other strangely golden—yea, even from that distance, Tanis could see the way the man's irises danced around a black pupil. Tanis resisted the urge to flinch, though his pulse quickened at once.

Beware! instinct shouted—no, it screamed.

Immediately on the heels of this warning sense, Tanis felt a sharp, stabbing pain behind his eyes, and suddenly terrible visions flashed to mind: images of mangled flesh and torture and rivers of blood—*so much blood!* Tanis saw the stranger drawing the razor edge of a blade through the flesh of his victim's back, blood pouring from the wounds, drenching bare fingers that steamed as they touched…

Tanis tore his eyes away from the man and stared at the table top while his heart raced and his eyed burned with threatened tears. He trembled as strongly as if he stood naked in the wind-ravaged northern wastes. That fiery gaze and the images behind it had unnerved him immeasurably, and he felt a dry-throated panic and a sudden sense of being trapped. Both sensations urged him to stand and flee, yet Tanis was scared to try lest he discover that he somehow couldn't move.

Abruptly, the serving girl appeared in front of him, blocking all view of the stranger. Tanis looked up at her with such a surge of relief that he might have kissed her had he not been so afraid his knees would buckle if he tried to stand.

"Oh!" she exclaimed when their eyes met. She darted a guilty look around the café, as if expecting to see the city guard coming after her. "Are you…" she whispered, leaning closer to him, "are you here to question me, milord?"

"Uh, no," he replied, barely croaking out the words from a throat as suddenly parched as the desert sands. "No, I'm…" he worked a little moisture back into his mouth. "I'm just waiting on my lady, if it's all right. She's next door," and he thumbed over his shoulder toward the apothecary's shop, glad to note that his hand, at least, wasn't shaking.

"Oh," said the girl, looking relieved. Then she frowned. "Is the tea not to your liking, milord? May I bring you something else?"

Tanis had forgotten about the drink. He cast it a mistrustful look. "It's tea, is it? Cold tea?"

"To cleanse your palate," she offered helpfully.

Tanis blinked at her. "My what?"

She seemed to see him then as if for the first time. A young lad in a tailored blue-grey tunic detailed in silver thread, the fine garments of a nobleman's son, with shoulders too broad for his slender frame, sandy hair falling across a slightly pointed nose, and colorless eyes like the deep waters of a clear running stream. "Oh," she said for a third time, "you're just a youngling, aren't you?" Smiling then, she reached out and cupped his cheek. Tanis thought she had a pretty smile, even if her front teeth were crooked. "Cider then," she decided. "We've some just up this morning—not too long in the barrel, if you get my drift," and she winked as she left, taking the untouched tea away with her.

Cold tea, Tanis marveled. He wondered if her Grace had ever heard of such a thing.

That's when he noticed the stranger stand up in a swirl of amber cloak and leave the tavern without so much as a glance his way. Still feeling jittery, Tanis followed the man with his eyes, frowning. After such a terrible shock as the stranger had leveled him, Tanis thought he would've cast him a parting glance at least, but the man seemed to have forgotten Tanis entirely. The lad pondered this with furrowed brow. Could it be that the stranger hadn't intentionally caused the interchange of gruesome images? If so, the man didn't know that Tanis was aware of his crimes…

The strangest feeling beset the lad upon this realization. He felt compelled to know what dark business this stranger was about; he felt it was somehow his duty, as if he owed it to the Vestals, to Prince Ean, and to Phaedor…as if stopping the man from committing more crimes was entirely his responsibility now.

Moving so slowly and deliberately that he might've been entranced, Tanis stood and followed the stranger out onto the street.

Alyneri started as Rhys slammed the apothecary door, and she spun her head with an accusatory glare.

"Sorry," he muttered.

The front room of the shop was lined with shelves sporting a myriad of jars, some containing herbs and other hosting samples of a less appealing character, but even with Rhys' bold announcement of their arrival, no one came to greet them.

After waiting for longer than seemed appropriate, Alyneri offered, "I'll just go and see if someone's in the back. I shouldn't be but a moment."

Rhys grunted something unintelligible and found a chair, though the tiny thing was much too small for his bulk; he looked not unlike a bear attempting to sit upon a child's seat.

Alyneri headed through a partition and into the next room. It was also empty of a living soul, though some of the specimens that eyed her through their large glass jars seemed entirely too lifelike for comfort. "Hello?" she called, looking around. That's when she noticed that a heavy door inset with bubbled glass was ajar. She pushed her head through the parting and called down the long hallway, "Is anyone here?"

She thought she heard voices from a room at the far end, so she slipped through the opening and followed the sound, not noticing that the heavy door slid closed behind her. Sounds of clinking china and feminine voices became clear as she reached the end of the hall. Rounding the arched opening, Alyneri drew in her breath sharply.

Two sets of eyes lifted to behold her, one unknown, and one entirely unwelcome.

"Why Alyneri," said Sandrine du Préc, "what an unexpected surprise!" She stood from the table where she was having tea and came around to embrace the Duchess. Alyneri smelled the woman's familiar fragrance as she returned her embrace—albeit uneasily—and the scent brought an uncomfortable fluttering to her stomach.

Pulling away, Sandrine took Alyneri's hand and turned to the dark-eyed woman sitting at the table. "Maegrid, may I present the Lady Alyneri d'Giverny, Duchess of Aracine."

The woman Maegrid nodded her head respectfully with lowered eyes. "An honor, your Grace. Please, won't you join us?"

"Truly, you have impeccable timing," Sandrine said as she released Alyneri's hand and returned to the table. "Maegrid was just about to pour the tea."

Maegrid set out another cup and saucer for her, and Alyneri realized the matter had already been decided. "You are the Apothecary?" she asked politely as she sat down, though her heart was racing and she felt a sense of *wrongness* about the entire scene. What was Sandrine doing here?

The woman nodded with downcast eyes, her attention upon the dark tea flowing out of the pot.

"The Duchess is here on pilgrimage," Sandrine noted to Maegrid. She looked to Alyneri and told her, "I paid visit to the temple yesterday, myself. To stand within Alshiba's compassionate hands…there is absolution in it, I vow."

"I have not yet visited the temple," Alyneri murmured.

"Mayhap we should go together," Sandrine suggested with a smile. "I am eager to return."

Alyneri met her gaze and suppressed a shudder. The way Sandrine looked at her… it was as though the woman saw her as a thing to possess, and her smiles were always reptilian.

With downcast eyes, Maegrid handed Alyneri her tea, and she sipped it politely. It was redolent with anise, cinnamon and clove and sweetened with licorice root. Alyneri drank more deeply of it and set down the cup in its saucer to find Sandrine watching her hungrily.

She felt her heart flutter. "I confess my—my surprise, Sandrine," Alyneri managed. "Such a…coincidence."

"Coincidence, or providence," Sandrine replied with that coldly calculating smile. "Have you not come for Black Krinling Oil?"

Alyneri took another drink from her tea to hide her dismay. As she set down the cup, she noticed her hand was trembling. "How did you know that?" she managed.

"Any Healer worth her craft has a stock of Black Krinling Oil, and Maegrid has the only supply in all of Rethynnea."

Alyneri gazed fretfully at her and wondered what she wasn't saying. "I think, perhaps, I should be going," she said as she stood. Abruptly the room spun, and the next thing she knew she was lying on the floor.

Sandrine's face hovered above hers. She pulled back Alyneri's eyelids and gazed into each eye. "Good," she pronounced, looking up at someone out of Alyneri's view. "Take her."

Hands lifted Alyneri from the floor. "You…what…?" she managed, but her heart felt weak and her breath wouldn't come. She realized only then that she hadn't seen either woman drinking of the tea.

They carried her outside into an alley, her faceless kidnappers, and laid her on the seat inside a carriage. Alyneri managed to drape a clammy, trembling hand across her forehead but knew that sitting up would be out of the question.

Dizziness, slow heartbeat, cold skin, and she checked my eyes for dilation… Alyneri reviewed her symptoms and knew what drug she'd been dosed with.

Sandrine climbed in the coach and sat on the seat across from her. "Wait there," she said to someone beyond Alyneri's line of sight. She watched the woman write something with parchment and quill and then hand it to whoever awaited outside. "When we are gone, take that to the man waiting in front of the shop—but do not be hasty to deliver it."

"Yes, milady," came the answer.

"And tell your mother I hold her obligation fulfilled."

Sandrine shut the door and sat back on her seat as the coach headed off. She looked inordinately smug.

Alyneri shut her eyes and focused on her breath; Laudanum was a dangerous drug, and they'd clearly dosed her heavily. She knew the slightest miscalculation of the dose would have her in convulsions, or could even stop her heart. But she doubted Sandrine du Préc would have miscalculated.

"There now, dear," murmured Sandrine. Alyneri felt the woman's hand caressing her cheek and would've shuddered had she only been able to move. "You'll sleep soon," Sandrine told her, "and when you wake…" but Alyneri had already slipped away into darkness.

FIFTY-FOUR

'Treason is a matter of perspective.'

– The Espial Franco Rohre

The pirate Carian vran Lea stood in the shadow of Raine's statue in Rethynnea's Temple of the Vestals wearing a ponderous frown. He fancied himself one of the most talented Nodefinders of his day, but the node before him defied even his skill.

What have they done?

It was instinct alone that told him the node had been tampered with, for surely he could find no trace of villainy upon it—leastwise not from where he stood. Now, if he *traveled* it…but Raine had forbidden that course to him.

This was his fifth visit to the node, for the Vestal had him inspecting it daily. This was highly annoying to Carian, who had pointed out that he wasn't likely to find something on day five that he didn't find on day one, but the man was paying him by the day just for standing around, so Carian went. Besides, he was sick of watching so many people moping about acting as if the man they served was already dead.

The islander wasn't alone in the temple that afternoon. The usual late-day traffic came and went, various Adepts upon their business, pilgrims seeking healing beneath the cup of Alshiba's hands, others merely tourists coming to gawk and stare. What seemed a constant stream of young women came to place flowers at the feet of the Great Master's statue—by the end of the day there would be a veritable pile of flowers waiting to be carted away by the temple caretakers. Carian eyed the ladies with a crooked grin. *And what will you do when the Great Master is freed from his prison and stands there in person to receive your praise and prayers?*

Carian wanted to be there to witness that moment. He wanted to see the Second Vestal restored to his place of honor among all of the peoples of Alorin, and it wasn't lost on him that he might already be upon that most vital of quests if not for the Fourth Vestal. Yet in truth, Raine's need wasn't what drew Carian to commit to his service; it was Fynn, Ean, and Trell, and the strange confluence of events that led him to cross paths with three val Lorian princes within a span of days. Carian wasn't a religious man, but he'd seen Cephrael's Hand glowing in the heavens too often of late. Something was afoot in the realm; history was in the making, and he meant to be a part of it this time.

He'd told no one about meeting Trell—he felt he owed him that much—but Ean's accident had made it much harder to hold his tongue, especially around Raine. Now, five days later, the youngest val Lorian prince looked even closer to death than he had on the night of his attack; Carian worried he'd soon be forced to tell what he knew of Trell.

"Do you come to honor the Vestal?" a voice asked from behind, interrupting Carian's thoughts.

The pirate turned to find a man standing in a fall of sunlight streaming down from the temple's crystal dome. Tall and on the slim side of muscular, his tousled brown hair fell across soulful brown eyes. Carian immediately thought he looked familiar, and then he realized why: the man looked not unlike Raine D'Lacourte, if a slightly broader version.

"I was just wondering, as you've been standing in front of the Great Master's statue for a while now," the man offered by way of explanation.

Carian peered narrowly at him. "What's it to you?"

The man shrugged, smiled in a way that didn't quite touch his eyes. "Or perhaps you were interested in the node?"

Carian stiffened, suddenly alert. A blade appeared in his hand. "What do you know about it?"

The man raised palms in surrender. "Would you strike down a brother in the Guild, my pirate friend?"

Carian eyed him suspiciously, noting that he wore no obvious weapon. Then he spun his blade and sheathed it with a flourish. He nodded toward the node. "What do you know of it?"

"There seems something strange about it," the man observed. Then he shook his head and murmured, "More a feeling than anything else." Absently, he reached into his coat and withdrew a flask. First taking a sip, he then offered the flask to Carian. "Shall we share a drink and ponder the matter?"

The pirate swiped the flagon, sniffed it, and then shot back a long draft. A fiery spirit flamed his throat, more heat than taste, though there was something of mint and vanilla in it. "Absinthe," he growled as he handed it back to the other man.

The man smiled wanly as he pocketed the flask. "Not your stuff of choice?"

"*Blaargh*," Carian shook his head. "Tis naught but suited for artists and poets," he muttered, eyeing the man narrowly. "You fancy yourself one of them?"

"I traveled as a minstrel for a while," the stranger admitted.

"And now?"

"Now?" He drew in a deep breath and let it out again. "Now I am in service to another."

Carian harrumphed disagreeably by way of offering condolence. Being in service as a Nodefinder meant being chained to another man's whims, and while he was admittedly in service himself at the moment, Carian had no intention of making it a permanent arrangement.

He went back to peering at the node. He walked around it to view it from all sides, and the other man followed silently in his footsteps. To Carian's skilled eye, the portal opened upon a buttressed hallway. Tapestries hung in the distance, and long shafts of sunlight played across the wide passage. It might've been a corridor in any castle in the known realm—or in any unknown realm, for that matter. Without traveling it, there was no way to be certain where the node led.

No one seemed to be watching from the other side of the portal, as Raine had warned, but Carian wasn't keen to test the Vestal's premonition; Raine D'Lacourte was rumored to be attuned to the realm in ways that most couldn't understand.

Besides, he had an uncomfortable feeling that he was missing something.

"Were you thinking to travel upon it?" asked the stranger.

Abruptly Carian rounded on him, pushing his face within inches of the other man's. "Why're you so interested in my business? What's it to you?"

The man backed off looking instantly contrite. "I beg your pardon. I just saw you here alone..." He looked over his shoulder, adding softly, "My patron is...occupied, and I thought only to share a drink with a fellow Guildsman and maybe a story to pass the time..."

Carian followed the stranger's gaze and saw a man in a sky blue coat kneeling beneath the hands of Alshiba's statue. He looked back to the stranger, decided to trust him, and dropped his voice to mutter, "There's something about this node that I mislike, but I can't put my finger on it. I would know more of its nature, but I've reason not to travel it."

The man considered him quietly. "Shall I travel it in your stead, my friend? I vow there is something odd about it, but until one travels a node, one cannot really know."

"Too true," Carian agreed.

"I rather think someone has tampered with it. A *raedan* could tell us, no doubt. Alas," he said with a smile, "I see none nearby."

Carian didn't divulge that, indeed, it was the realm's foremost reader of the currents who set him upon this miserable task. Instead he grabbed the man's arm and cautioned, "I daresay it could be dangerous for you, boyo."

The man gave him a rueful smile. "Isn't it always?"

Carian swept him with his eyes. "I gave my word that I would stay on this side of it, otherwise..."

"But of course," remarked the stranger with an offhanded wave. He withdrew his flask and handed it to Carian. "Have another drink while I'm away," and off he went across the node. Carian watched him walk down the hallway on the other side until the haze of passage obscured him from view. After about five minutes he was back again and looking none the worse for the endeavor.

"I confess nothing seemed amiss," he told Carian as the pirate handed his flask back to him, minus several swigs. "The passage goes on for some time, but I saw no one about."

Carian gave him an approving look. "You've done me a service. Mayhap I shall be able to repay it someday. What's your name, friend?"

"Franco," he said, holding out his hand.

Carian did a double-take—how many Francos were members of the Guild? The familiar name gave him pause. He'd never met Franco Rohre, but he didn't doubt that this *could* be him—what with the many bizarre coincidences happening at present, it almost had to be. He clasped wrists with the man nonetheless, though he eyed him inquisitively now. "Carian vran Lea."

"Well met, Carian," Franco murmured.

"Aye," he announced then, still eyeing him speculatively, "I must away. Fair skies on your travels, my friend."

"And yours," said Franco, gazing solemnly after Carian as he departed.

Fynnlar val Lorian barged through the double doors into the study Raine was using for his office and announced, "It's him!"

Raine turned from the window. "You're certain?"

"Undoubtedly."

The Vestal crossed the room to a desk he'd claimed for his use. "Tell me everything," he ordered as he took his chair.

Fynn walked to the sideboard. "It happened in Tregarion," he began as he chose a libation from the ample supply. He poured a goblet of wine and turned to lean back against the cabinet while he swirled the dark liquid, watching as it clung heavily to the glass. "The Lord Commander of her Majesty's Tivaricum was the first to notice him..." Fynn explained. He went on to tell the tale of Trell's discovery as the Lord Commander himself had relayed it to him.

Raine's eyes grew wide with the telling. When Fynn was finished, the Vestal leaned back in his chair and steepled fingers before his lips. His diamondine eyes were as hard and intense as their namesake stone as he inquired in a low voice made all the more fearful for its restraint, "If Indora's Magisteré recognized Trell val Lorian as a prince of Dannym, why *in Cephrael's name* did they not detain him?"

Fynn belched and motioned with his goblet as he answered, "He made a miraculous escape. It seems the Lord Commander originally crossed paths with my illustrious cousin while in pursuit of an infamous pirate. Apparently they were traveling together."

Raine arched brows. "A prince of Dannym in league with a pirate? Why does that sound so familiar?"

Fynn belched. "Well, you guessed right," he muttered. "The pirate was none other than our own Carian vran Lea."

Raine regarded Fynn as if held immobile by force.

Fynn downed the last of his wine and poured himself another glass. It had been that kind of week—not that he needed a reason to drown himself in drink. Staring into the liquid a second time, he said, "It seemed clear to the Lord Commander that Trell doesn't know his heritage."

"*C'est incroyable,*" Raine announced in his native Veneisean, all composure lost to disbelief. "Trell lives!" He shook his head and stared hard at Fynn. "Where has he been all this time?"

"The Lord Commander said Trell gave a name in the desert tongue—not his own name, mind. 'Amahkayaleel' or some such."

After a moment, Raine placed both hands on the desk before him and leveled Fynn a telling look. "Who else knows of Trell's survival?"

"That we can be certain of?" Fynn shrugged. "A few in Veneisea. The Lord Commander, the Magisteré, one of Indora's Voices. But there's no telling who else has come into contact with my cousin and recognized him. Come to think of it..." Fynn suddenly remembered Carian's strange questions when first the pirate had laid eyes on Ean. He looked around. "Where is vran Lea, anyway?"

"Late," replied the Vestal with no small measure of discontent. Then he added in a steely tone, "Rest assured, I will have questions for him upon his return."

"You and me both." Fynn tossed back the dregs of his second glass of wine and poured a third. He was finally starting to feel human. He grabbed the wine bottle and walked to the Vestal's desk, taking a seat in chair across from him. "What news of Ean?"

Raine pursed lips and shook his head, his expression falling into worry. "Phaedor and the Healer have tried repeatedly to reach him, but to no success. His body has healed, yet still…"

Fynn felt the bottom drop out of his heart. "He's…dying?"

Lips tight, Raine nodded.

Fynn dared not even think of what it would mean to lose Ean—to him personally, to their family, to the kingdom… "Is…is there nothing we can do?" he asked, wishing he didn't sound quite so desperate.

The Vestal pushed to his feet and wandered back over to the window. He clasped hands behind his back. "Ean should have died. His body was crushed. The Healer described his pattern as so frayed there wasn't enough of it lingering to repair."

This was information Fynn hadn't heard before, and it wasn't the least bit heartening. "Then…how?"

Raine turned over his shoulder with one arched brow. "The zanthyr wove his pattern back together—from memory."

Fynn gaped. "*Balls of Belloth*," he hissed. "He can *do* that?"

"Apparently."

Fynn scrubbed at his beard as he gazed at the Vestal in disbelief. "Say he succeeded, as he claims," he posed, somewhat wide-eyed—because truly, no one knew what a zanthyr could or couldn't do, "then why hasn't Ean awoken?"

Raine looked back out the window. After a moment, he admitted, "It is my fear that when Phaedor and Alyneri pulled Ean back from the grave, a vital part of him did not return."

The words left Fynn feeling threadbare. "So you're saying…he may never wake?"

Raine turned from the window. "I fear it is a possibility we must be willing to face." When Fynn said nothing, only stared forlornly into his wine, Raine walked over to him. "Come," he said, placing a hand on Fynn's shoulder. "You should see what has been afoot during your absence."

Fynn brought his bottle and followed the Vestal from the room and through the mansion until they emerged onto a high balcony bathed in the light of sunset. Men were amassing in the yard below, heavily armed and well armored. Among them stood two men in black robes that Fynn had never seen before but misliked immediately, which meant they were probably wielders. He also saw the two avieths walking among the troops assessing weaponry and general readiness. Of Carian vran Lea, there was no sign.

"Do you go to war, my lord?" Fynn posed as he poured the last of his wine into his goblet and frowned at the deadly assembly.

Raine placed his hands on the railing and looked out over the yard below. "Of a fashion," he murmured. He was quiet for a moment, and Fynn used the time to drink his wine. Finally, the truthreader offered, "The Fifth Vestal's hand is wide in this realm, Fynnlar, and his fingers are long. How deeply he is embroiled in recent turmoil I am still uncovering, but there are some things I do know." He glanced in Fynn's direction and declared, "First, Björn van Gelderan pretends himself a Mage in the Emir's employ."

"I *knew* it!" Fynn hissed.

"Aye." Raine cast him a grim look. "Your instincts guide you well. Björn summoned the drachwyr—those beings you know as Sundragons—from the nether-reaches of the realm to do his bidding, and he gathers to him those of the Fifty Companions who would foreswear their allegiances to this realm and serve his cause. Franco Rohre followed upon this path, I am certain, and I fear…" his hands tightened upon the railing, and he gave Fynn a sideways look as he finished, "I fear the Fifth Vestal means to claim your cousin as well."

"*Ean?*" Fynn sputtered.

"Indeed, should he live. By force or by persuasion, I fear he will soon be lost to us."

"We can't just let the bastard take him!"

Raine's gaze was flinty. "I assure you, I have no intention of it."

"Is that what all of this is about?" Fynn motioned with his goblet toward the men, who were forming into four lines.

Rather than answering him, Raine looked out over the assembly. After a moment, he said without turning, "I mean to take Ean to Illume Belliel, Fynnlar."

Fynn choked into his wine.

"In the Cityworld," Raine went on, eyeing him dubiously, "Ean will be safe from all machinations—safe from my oath-brother and his creatures; safe from the Karakurt and the many other factions seeking his life. Safe until…well, until we can restore order to your uncle's kingdom, for one, and Ean can take his rightful place in line for the throne."

Fynn had stopped listening after the Vestal said 'cityworld.' "Illume Belliel…" he gasped, his throat still burning. The famed cityworld was deemed a utopia unlike anyplace in the known realms, the veritable center of the universe. "I've never heard of anyone traveling to Illume Belliel besides the Vestals."

"There is precedent for it," Raine assured him.

They retreated to silence after this discussion, for there was much to ponder; but as Fynn remained with the Vestal, he couldn't shake the sense that Raine was telling him only part of the truth.

He had that uneasy feeling again—the prescient one that warned of bad things to come—and it only intensified as the night deepened. Once again, however, he found himself unable to flee the scene, no matter how ill his stomach. *Fool! Fool man!* he scolded himself, gritting his teeth as he watched the warriors in the yard begin a group exercise, moving slowly through the sword forms in an exacting display of skill. *You should leave now. It may be your last chance!*

But Fynn knew he could not.

Still, he lamented his choice with every breath. It was a prudent man who gave a wide girth to a Vestal's activities, and *especially* when forewarned of them; for in Fynn's experience, often enough it was the Vestal's *other* plans—the ones he wasn't telling you about—that bit the deepest and bled the longest.

Fynn cursed silently. *Cousin, if you live, I'm going to throttle you!*

Ean walked across misty moors through palls of drifting fog, seeing only the spectral shadows of others who walked the same interminable path. Beneath the sparse grass was barren earth, and each step stirred a fine grey talc that clung to his bare skin. He felt neither breath nor heartbeat in his own chest, and there was no sound anywhere in the realm, only a suffocating veil of sorrow.

On he walked, bereft of hope, only knowing in the half-awareness of dreams that someone grieved for him—grieving himself, though for what he was unsure. Memory was a haze into which his mind couldn't travel, his life before a jumble of disjointed images too faint to be seen through the melancholy. Lost of time and self, Ean wandered among the endless plains certain of nothing save that this was his eternity.

Until, suddenly, he came upon a bridge.

It was incongruous. Its railings were opalescent, silver-pale and sparkling, and upon the bridge stood a man whose face remained in shadow.

Ean halted before him. This man had substance, he didn't belong there.

"Will you cross this bridge with me, my friend?" asked the man.

Ean gazed indifferently at the bridge. "Why should I?"

"To regain your future and your past."

A spark ignited at these words, a spark so faint it was but a pinprick of light in a vast darkness. Immediately a torrent of despair descended to attack the feeble light, and a spear of sorrow pushed Ean to continue on, to leave the bridge and the unwelcome stranger. Why should his future or his past matter here?

But the spark merely fluttered beneath the onslaught of despair. It was the tiniest of flames, but it would not be ignored.

Hope, Ean realized. *This man brings hope.*

He looked back to him. "Where does the bridge lead?"

"To pain," he answered with honest regret.

Ean dropped his head, and deep within, his consciousness shuddered. "I do not seek to know pain," he whispered, sensing somehow that he had known it too intimately already.

"And yet without pain, we cannot know joy," the stranger advised.

Joy. The word seemed so foreign, so unwelcome there among the grey mist of mourning, yet the spark that was hope grew brighter at the idea that joy could exist. Ean lifted his eyes to look upon the faceless stranger. "I am…afraid."

"That is good. Out of fear sprout the roots of courage."

Hope. Joy. Courage.

The spark grew brighter, stronger. Ean began to see colors in the bridge, rainbow hues licking the delicate filigree of its railings.

He swallowed and took a step closer to the bridge. The stair to reach its path was not high, yet Ean trembled before it. As he looked up again, he saw that the man's face was now visible, an ageless, handsome face with eyes of vibrant blue. "What will I find on the other side?" he whispered.

The blue-eyed man smiled. "Yourself."

Ean closed his eyes and dropped his head. *Yes*, whispered the tiny spark, *we must cross. We are not supposed to be here.*

But the mist enveloped him, gathered and embraced him. *Stay*, it seemed to coax. *What is there for you across the bridge but pain? Here there is no pain.*

Yes, there is no pain here, Ean knew, but there was no feeling of any sort save melancholy and sorrow. The stranger had awakened hope, joy and courage, and lost though he was, Ean had a sense that these things were worth enduring pain to regain.

Ean looked up at the stranger, and taking a deep breath, he stepped upon the bridge. Slowly he lowered his hands to the pearlescent railings. They were smooth and cool. He knew his path now led across the bridge, but still he trembled in the knowing. "Can we...walk together?" Ean asked the blue-eyed man.

"If you would have me at your side."

"Yes," Ean whispered. "Please."

The blue-eyed man stood next to Ean, and though he did not offer his arm, and Ean did not ask to hold it, he felt strength just in knowing the other was there. Still, every step was a force of will; not merely the will to face what awaited, but the will to tear himself free of the clinging pall of hopelessness and regret that held him so firmly in its grasp. Step by step he moved further from the misty moors; step by step the blue-eyed stranger walked at his side, ever faithful, until at last they reached the end.

And there, Creighton awaited.

Ean drew up short, stricken immobile. The shock of seeing Creighton's face with such clarity—his soulful brown eyes and his smile so full of eager life—brought memory crashing back. Wave upon wave unfolded over him, great billowing folds of the unending timeline of his life and all of his losses, mistakes and regrets.

Ean collapsed to his knees, covered his face with both hands, and wept. He wept for his grievous mistakes. He wept for his lost brothers. He wept for his parents' sacrifices and his friends' unfailing support and ill-founded trust. He wept for betraying their hopes, for the life he had squandered, for the future that was lost.

He wept until tears would come no longer.

"Courage," Creighton advised solemnly once Ean had quieted, "comes in fully knowing the threat one faces and deciding to stand against it nonetheless. Until that moment of understanding, there is no courage, there is only haste. No bravery, merely brazen recklessness."

"I have failed you," Ean whispered, unable to look upon his friend's countenance though it was so dear to him. "My recklessness was my undoing, and now I cannot avenge your death."

Creighton knelt to meet Ean eye to eye. "Ean," he said, capturing the prince's gaze with his own, "you are not dead."

Ean lifted his head and looked forlornly upon him. "I *am* dead, and so are you. I see your face clearly now at last, but there is no justice in it, no atonement, only grief."

"Ean," Creighton entreated with a tinge of frustration, "you see my face because *you* stand upon the path of the dead. Step down from the bridge and reclaim your life."

Ean looked behind him to where the bridge disappeared into the mist. "I don't understand," he whispered, turning back to Creighton. "I would rather stay here with you."

"Ean, you cannot stay here," Creighton returned, his expression tense and worried now. "Your body withers without the force of your will. It has healed in the days since your encounter, but it needs you to restore it life."

Ean pushed palms to his eyes. "No, this is but a dream," he insisted.

"Step off the bridge, and I will prove it is not."

Ean dropped his hands and looked at him in wonder. "How?"

Creighton stood and held out his hand. "Do you trust me, Ean?"

"I trust my blood-brother with all that I am," the prince replied miserably, "but...I am not sure that you are him."

Creighton dropped his hand and frowned at his friend. "I have been afraid," he confessed after a long, tense silence. "Afraid that if you knew me for what I am now, you would love me no more. But if flesh is what will prove my troth, then let it be thusly that we meet."

The words were a raw wound. "Tell me of what chance you speak," Ean whispered, fear and hope warring for purchase in his heart.

Creighton gave him a tragic smile and shook his head. "First, you must step down from the bridge."

Holding Creighton's gaze, Ean slowly got to his feet. He suspected that the pain the blue-eyed stranger spoke of was still awaiting him, that he'd only had the barest taste of it in his tears, and he knew suddenly why Creighton spoke to him of courage. He must find the courage to face life again, knowing its pain, knowing its heartache, knowing its dangers and losses and terrible cost.

With a swallow, Ean stepped off the bridge—

—And woke with a shuddering inhale, gasping the breath of a drowning man pitched suddenly to shore. Then followed the pain, pouncing with ferocity upon every muscle from eyelid to littlest toe. Ean moaned, and even that was painful.

A shadow befell him, and Ean focused to see the zanthyr approaching from a near corner. The intensity of concern in Phaedor's emerald eyes brought waves of gratitude, and for a moment Ean was silenced by the devastating emotions that overcame him. All the tears he'd shed in his dream paled next to what he felt upon seeing the zanthyr again. However could he repay such a debt? However could Phaedor forgive him for such utter disregard for his own life?

And yet, as Phaedor approached, Ean knew that he *had* forgiven him, that nothing mattered to the creature save that Ean lived, the incident left behind them upon a long and shadowed road.

Phaedor placed a hand on the prince's shoulder, and Ean felt a cooling calm settle through him. The pain in his body gradually faded, and his breath came more easily. "I thought you said you were no healer," Ean whispered hoarsely, feeling a gratitude so powerful toward the man it was nearly overwhelming.

The zanthyr cracked a shadowy smile. "I also warned you not to trust me," he murmured.

Ean drew in a deep, shuddering breath and exhaled slowly, feeling his body tingling with new life...life that had come within an inch of being lost—*again*. Among the knowledge he'd regained while crossing that ethereal bridge back from the beyond was the certainty that he'd fought this same fearsome power *twice* before.

I am RINOKH!

Ean shuddered at the memory, drawing a curious eye from the zanthyr. "How long?" Ean whispered, dreading the answer.

"Five days."

The knowledge was a blow. After what had been done to his body—which even now was too unbearable to dwell upon—how could he possibly be alive after that? What had they done to save him? He remembered nothing of the healing, but he knew unquestionably that Alyneri and the zanthyr were to thank for it.

"How is Alyneri?" he asked then, curious suddenly that she wasn't also there to see him wake. "Is she…?"

"She endures," the zanthyr said, and Ean realized he was trying to spare him the pain of more guilt. "She will no doubt return tonight to sleep in her chair," and he nodded toward an armchair by the hearth, "as she has done every night while you slept." He considered the prince for a moment then. "What do you remember?"

Ean grimaced. "Everything."

Abruptly the zanthyr turned from his bedside. "And see that you do," he growled, his manner suddenly gruff, "for the next time you pit yourself against a Malorin'athgul—untrained, untested!—you won't have Fortune's grace upon you."

Ean swallowed. "I know." He cast a troubled look at the creature. "How…how bad was I…really?"

The zanthyr arched a warning brow. "It would only scare you to know."

Ean believed him.

He was becoming aware of his body again now, feeling toes and thighs and shoulders stiff and sore, but it was a sweet pain, the kind that comes from healing. He watched the zanthyr as he walked to the window to gaze out through the glass-paned doors, a tall, statuesque figure backlit by the glow of sunset. "You said a name," Ean whispered then. "Malorin'athgul. This is the creature Rinokh? Björn's creature?"

"Björn van Gelderan does not command the Malorin'athgul," Phaedor replied without looking at him. "They are your enemy, not the Vestal."

How can you be so certain? Ean bit back the question, though he was aching to know the truth of it; but he knew such a thing would only go unanswered. That Phaedor spoke it, so it must be true. But this was a truth Ean could not accept.

Even though a part of him truly wanted to.

For some reason he thought of the blue-eyed man who'd braved the Bridge of the Dead to find him, who spoke so honestly and candidly about the trials he would face. What kind of man was Björn van Gelderan really? Ean desperately wanted to know, but there was justice to be claimed in his blood-brother's honor, and Ean would not forsake Creighton this retribution, no matter his own desires.

Creighton… Oh, Creighton! To have seen his blood-brother's face so clearly in his dream at last…knowing now it was only a dream. It was agony anew. Ean clenched his teeth, protest welling, tightening his chest. "No," he growled, his voice at last regaining its timbre. "The Vestal's Shade slew Creighton. He must answer for the crime."

Phaedor regarded him coolly for a long moment, during which time Ean slowly came to feel the fool. There was nothing quite like being stared down by the zanthyr to put a man in his place. "Raine will want to know of your recovery," Phaedor said finally, and then he left.

Ean stared after him, chagrined. Without warning, the unexpected vision of Rinokh pressing his thumb toward Ean's forehead and the utter black agony that followed beset him. The memory brought a latent shudder and flashes of agonizing pain which twinged still-healing muscles. Ean quickly quashed the vision, walled it away behind webs of unwillingness, imprisoned in a corner which he planned to never again peer. But the memory alone had done its work, for Ean felt shaken anew, his healed muscles tense and trembling with anger.

Rinokh, he thought with a swallow. Just the word seemed sharp against his mind.

Malorin'athgul.

The two names seemed to have an intimate connection, as if formed from the same dark matter. *But who or what are they?*

"Ean…" Ean spun his head with a startled intake of breath, but that same breath abandoned him as his mind fought to understand the vision before his eyes.

It cannot be!

The silhouette of the man who stood across the room was unmistakable, even if his face was masked by shadows, for Ean had seen him many times in his recent dreams. Gaping at the figure, Ean pushed up in bed, his face stricken with bewilderment and shock.

"Your eyes do not lie," said Creighton, his voice as unmistakable as the regret that infused it.

"*No*," Ean gasped hoarsely. "You were slain!"

"I promised you I would come," Creighton murmured.

Ean stared for one brief moment, then he scrambled out of bed and lunged for his sword on a near dresser. His muscles shook violently as he ripped the weapon from its scabbard and leveled it at the intruder across the room. "I *know* my blood-brother died that night," he insisted hoarsely. "I won't be twice a fool!"

The figure held up a black-gloved hand in entreaty. "Please, Ean," he whispered, the ache in his voice palpable. "Permit me a token as proof of my troth." When Ean made no motion, the man glided across the room to lay something small in the center of Ean's bed. All the while his head was bowed, his face unseen, yet Ean did not deny that everything about him, from the manner of his movement to the set of his shoulders, was exactly like that of his lost friend and brother.

Once the man had retreated to his shadowed corner, Ean moved closer to the bed. Keeping his sword upraised, though his arm trembled beneath its weight after so many days abed, he lowered his eyes to espy what lay upon the covers.

His breath caught in his throat.

A woman's ring, a single ruby set in silver filigree carved in the shape of a rose.

It was as if the ring pierced an arrow into his heart. Ean dropped his sword and fell to his knees, drawing in a shuddering breath. He stared at the ring, his vision blurring as he recalled Creighton's sheepish grin as he proudly displayed the engagement ring he meant to give to Katerine. The ring, like his blood-brother's body, had vanished that fateful night.

Tears flowed freely across his cheeks as Ean slowly picked up the delicate ring and studied it. After a moment, he gripped it tightly against his palm, pressed fist to his heart, and lifted a tormented gaze to the man standing across the room. "I'm listening," he whispered.

"You are correct, Ean," Creighton confessed, sounding infinitely apologetic, as if this moment felt as dreadful to him as it did to Ean. "I died that night, but it was not the Shade who claimed my life. There was another."

With startling clarity Ean recalled the exchange that had preceded the battle upon the cliff, and the knowledge was a blow that left him gasping.

I am Prince Ean! Creighton had claimed, a claim that had confused their enemies and provided the chance for escape. But the Geshaiwyn assassin would've left nothing to chance; the man would've found and killed both of them just to be certain he'd found the right mark. Ean was amazed he hadn't realized this truth before. The Shade had arrived in time to save the real prince from a lunatic's blade named Jeshuelle, but the false prince had not been so lucky.

Sickened by the sudden understanding, Ean whispered wretchedly, "It was the Geshaiwyn…wasn't it? He found you…first."

"Yes," Creighton confirmed, and Ean felt the pain of his death all over again. "As I lay dying," Creighton confessed then, "the Shade called me to him. Even drenched in my own blood, while there was life within me, I could not but comply with his command."

"I remember," Ean whispered. He closed his eyes and forced a swallow. "I remember you walked strangely. It was…horrible…"

"Ean," his blood-brother's voice drew his gaze. "Ean, the Shade saved my life that night, though the means by which it occurred was…unimaginable."

It was not meant to be this way with you…

The Shade's words took on a terrifying new meaning.

Afraid now to look away lest Creighton's specter vanish, Ean cast him an anguished look. "Are you truth…or illusion?"

"I live," Creighton whispered out of the shadows of his hood, his own voice charged with his emotion, "but I am…not as you remember me."

Weakened to his very core, Ean slowly got to his feet, his thoughts and heart a riot of confused feelings for which there could be no expression. Pressing hands upon the mattress, he pinned the other man with a heated gaze. "Are you yet my brother, bound of oath and blood?"

"Yes, but—"

"Were you not raised at my side, my confidant, my closest friend? Did you not make yourself a target that I might live?" He clenched his teeth and declared tightly, *"Did you not give your life for mine?"*

Creighton bowed his head. "Yes, Ean, but—"

Ean straightened. "Then you are exactly as I remember."

Creighton lifted his bowed head, and the prince caught a flash of his friend's eyes beneath the shifting shadows that obscured his face. "Do you mean that?" he whispered.

Ean's chest was tight, his throat ached and his eyes burned, but he meant it wholly when he replied, "With all that I am."

Crayon took a deep breath and squared his shoulders. Then he approached, letting the shadows that obscured his features fade with each step until once again Ean looked upon the undiminished face of his blood-brother.

Ean's heart was racing, his breath coming too fast. In the last few moments he guessed, somehow, what Creighton had become, but it was still a shock to see him thusly. He held Creighton's obsidian gaze as long as he could, and then he slumped, sitting sideways on the mattress. His head spun, and he dropped chin to chest and tried to get a hold of himself. What could not be...*was*.

"How?" he managed, a bare whisper.

"The First Lord," Creighton said quietly. He stopped with his hands at his sides, his silver features caught in an expression of grave indecision. Creighton still looked himself beneath the silver mask, which was an exact impression of his features as ever they had once been. "He saved my life, even—"

"As he saved mine," Ean finished in a tormented voice. He spun the Shade, his brother, a heated look. What wretched irony was this...so many brash mistakes, so much anger and vengefulness, and all of it misfounded!

"Everything that's happened," Ean gasped, despairing of guilt, "all that has come since that night—all the trials we've endured, the danger I've put the others in... we're all *here* at this moment in this place because of *your* death."

"You're here, Ean," Creighton corrected regretfully, "because there was no other way to save your life."

Taken aback, Ean asked, "What are you saying?"

"There is too much you need to understand for me to explain it all here, now, but you are deserving of answers, and I can promise them to you."

Ean could do no more than accept that the Shade standing before him was indeed his friend, for to ruminate on the circumstances was too dire, too ironic...too dreadful. But he was wary of immortals that promised much and delivered little, who took and gave nothing in return. So he held Creighton's gaze and challenged, "If not here, where? When?"

"Ean..." Creighton frowned down at the black leather gloves that covered his silver hands. Glancing back up beneath his brows, he posed, "Have you never asked yourself why Raine D'Lacourte is so interested in you? Why he chose to become involved in your affairs?"

Ean stiffened. "How can you know such things?"

"Have you never wondered why Raine so vehemently implored you *not* to seek out the Fifth Vestal?"

Now Ean gaped. "How do you know about that?" he hissed.

Creighton bent and retrieved Ean's sword from the floor. He laid it upon the bed as he came closer. "That night in the pit," he began, standing now within arm's length of the prince, "when you stopped the Geshaiwyn's blade from killing you... that night, you worked the fifth strand."

Ean went cold. He held Creighton's gaze, but his blood was ice in his veins.

"Raine D'Lacourte knows that Adepts born with the gift of unworking are closely appended to the fifth strand," Creighton said. "While they are not necessarily fifth-strand Adepts in the strictest sense, they have within them the dormant trait that could blossom into the full gift of the fifth."

Abruptly Ean couldn't hear any more. He pushed the Shade roughly out of his path and made for the doors, staggering outside onto his patio. The night was calm and balmy, redolent with honeysuckle and the scent of the sea, but the air felt thick in his lungs and clung damply to his skin.

Chest heaving, Ean gripped the patio railing and fought to clear the buzzing in his head—quite a different sort from the night of Rinokh's attack.

After a long moment of silence, as he stared somewhat desperately toward the distant glimmering Bay, Ean whispered, "The *fifth*..." and the statement held within it fear and hope that were both of them terrible to think upon.

Creighton came to stand in the doorway, his silver features gleaming in the moonlight. "Beyond the great Markal Morrelaine, there are but few wielders alive today who can compel the fifth," he offered. "What minor workings they manage may seem impressive, and certainly they require enormous skill, yet they do little to disturb the currents. But to work the fifth as an *Adept*, Ean...it would make you immensely dangerous."

Unable to look at Creighton, Ean worked the muscles of his jaw, his throat clenched by betrayal and fury. "What does Raine want with me then?" he managed.

"He would seek to keep you from your gift. The First Lord believes the Fourth Vestal will take you to Illume Belliel as soon as possible."

Ean shot him a tormented look. "And what would be so wrong in that? I know nothing of these gifts."

Creighton crossed the balcony to stand at his side, so close they might've been as the boon companions of old; only now there was a vast divide between them. "If you mean to ever defeat the Malorin'athgul," Creighton advised by way of answering, "you must become everything you can be—trained, tested, beaten and bested in trails aplenty until you have certainty with your talent."

Ean turned to face him fully, anger and anguish both vying for purchase upon his features. "And who would teach me these things?" he asked hoarsely, immensely weary of contesting the same point with a revolving wheel of personages. "The zanthyr? Yourself? More midnight lessons in my dreams?"

Creighton gazed quietly upon him. "I think you know."

The knowledge was a terrible blow. Agonized, Ean spun away, hunching his shoulders against the truth as much as the supernatural creature his blood-brother had become. "Then it's as I feared," he whispered wretchedly. "He would make me his weapon."

"He would give you *knowledge*, Ean," Creighton returned. "How you use it is up to you."

FIFTY-FIVE

'Oh, his warped sense of justice can be quite convincing.'

– The Fourth Vestal Raine D'Lacourte

F**ynn was** ruminating on the ill hand of Fate when Carian vran Lea finally showed up. The pirate came swaggering out onto the balcony with his usual nonchalance, his black hair long and wild about his shoulders.

"Well, it's about time," Fynn complained, shooting the pirate an annoyed look. He wasn't sure if he was more irritated by the pirate's lateness or the fact that he'd been forced to keep company with the Vestal in Carian's stead.

Raine turned from the railing and settled the islander a hard gaze. "Ah, Carian," he murmured with undertones of discontent. "You have much to answer for. But first, what did you discover of the node?"

The pirate leaned back against the outside wall and pulled out his pouch of tabac. "Nothing I didn't already know," he muttered, unconcerned by the Vestal's veiled threat as he rolled the leaf. Lighting the fag in a lamp hanging from the wall, he exhaled a cloud of blue smoke and eyed Fynnlar as he noted, "Like I said before, without traveling the node, I can't learn much else about it." He took another drag and then offered, "But something's going on. There's a shady fellow hanging around the temple."

"What sort of fellow?" Fynn inquired.

Carian frowned at him. "The *shady* sort. Calls himself Franco."

To which Raine and Fynn replied with uniform surprise, "Franco *Rohre?*"

Carian eyed Raine up and down. "Tall fellow, looked not unlike yourself."

"Carian," Raine declared heatedly, "Franco Rohre is the reason you were sent to investigate that node, for I saw traces of his working of the second strand upon the currents. You *must* learn what he's done, for I assure you something *has* been altered."

"Undoubtedly," the pirate agreed, "but expertly so. I wager the Great Master himself couldn't have done a nicer job of hiding his work. I'll tell you this much: Franco traveled the node while I looked on, and I saw nothing untoward in the passage beyond it, but I repeat myself in saying that without *traveling the node myself,* I can't tell what's been done to it."

"Traveling it is out of the question," Raine declared with a definitive wave of his hand. He shook his head, crossed arms and pressed his lips together tightly, looking aggravated. After a moment, his gaze flashed to Carian. "I have no evidence beyond instinct," he told him then, "but I am reasonably certain that Franco Rohre is in the service of the Fifth Vestal."

Fynn let out a slow hiss.

"Indeed?" Carian arched brows. "That then must've been the man I saw."

Raine pinned him with a piercing look. "What man?"

Carian blew three smoke rings and offered, "I saw a man across the temple whom

Franco claimed was his patron."

Raine grabbed his arm. "You *saw* the Fifth Vestal?"

Carian eyed Raine's fingers gripping his arm until the truthreader released him. He took a long draw on his fag then and remarked, "Whether the man I met was the infamous Franco Rohre and his patron the Fifth Vestal....well," and here he looked the two of them up and down quizzically, "that's your concern."

"That the Fifth Vestal walks Alorin at all is everyone's concern, Carian vran Lea," Raine returned critically. "He—"

But he got no further, for just then the zanthyr appeared amongst them.

Fynn started so fiercely he nearly fell over the railing—but even more frightening, he only just managed to retain his wine—and Carian snarled an oath under his breath, but Raine merely gazed upon the zanthyr with reluctance, an expression of concern blended with annoyance revealing more of his feelings than was his usual wont. "What news then, Phaedor?" he inquired.

"The prince wakes."

The Vestal roused immediately, straightening with interest. "Is he himself? Does he recall—"

"He remembers all," Phaedor assured him, and his tone was black as the deep ocean on a starless winter night. He swept the Vestal with his emerald gaze. "The prince spoke the name of his attacker."

"Indeed? And who does he claim it was?"

"Rinokh."

The name sounded as the crack of lightening; Fynn felt the word rumble in his chest and even fancied he saw ripples stirred in his wine. Raine leveled the zanthyr a heated stare. After a strained silence during which time Fynn grew highly uncomfortable, worrying a confrontation was imminent, the Vestal finally grunted and looked away. "It must be a trick," he declared under his breath. "Björn works *deyjiin,* as do his Shades. There is no other explanation."

The zanthyr's gaze was unyielding. Fynn was very glad he wasn't on the receiving end of it. "There is one," he remarked.

"*Fantasy,*" Raine hissed with sudden heat, uncharacteristically flustered. He leveled the zanthyr a look of censure. "Malorin'athgul are but the stuff of legends, Phaedor."

"The Adept Wars are the stuff of legends in this age," the zanthyr returned evenly. "Dare you claim them a fiction?"

Raine looked frustrated as he considered the creature. "I have peered into their dark corner," he admitted, his expression grim. "Tis nothing attributed to them that cannot also be attributed to Björn. I know your loyalty to him, Phaedor, but the pieces fit."

"The pieces fit *both* puzzles," Phaedor warned in a low growl, "and one fits better than the other. Put your pieces together dispassionately, Vestal, and then look upon the picture you've made—if you dare. One will provide clarity while the other becomes more muddled still, motive buried in obscurity because *no motive exists.*"

"You are hardly an impartial voice!" Raine protested. Abruptly he shook his head and looked away again, dropping his head resolutely as he braced both hands against the railing. "Logic dictates but one villain in this matter."

Phaedor pinned the Vestal with a compelling stare. "This answer is not a question of logic but one of courage. You did not display it three centuries ago, but perhaps you will find it now."

Carian let out a low whistle.

Raine's expression darkened. "Yes," he admitted begrudgingly, turning to level a diamond-hard gaze upon the zanthyr, "we were cowards in those times. We couldn't bring ourselves to believe what Björn had become. We trusted to his sense of duty, we chose to think the best of a man so admired. But three centuries have proven how falsely placed our hopes," he added in a defiant hiss. "I am willing to call him a traitor now and put no more faith in his goodness. T'khendar has poisoned him even as it poisoned Malachai—dare you deny it!"

Phaedor's look of disgust was unbearable even to Fynn. "I never made you out to be a fool until tonight," the zanthyr remarked, his tone redolent with contempt. Then he vanished.

Fynn started with a hissed intake of breath and turned a fast look around, but the creature had fully disappeared. "I *hate* it when he does that," he snarled under his breath.

Carian flicked the butt end of his fag over the railing and muttered something about insufferable immortals before disappearing back inside the villa.

Raine stared at the place the zanthyr last stood, his expression fiercely tormented.

Seeing the opportunity to make his escape, Fynn downed his wine and left the Vestal to square off against his own demons. He didn't know what Malorin'athgul were, and he was pretty sure he didn't want to know. All he cared about just then was that his cousin was awake.

Fynn hurried through the villa toward Ean's rooms with thoughts of how to tell him that Trell lived running through his head, but all the while a sense of urgency was building until he was veritably running up the stairs by twos and threes. He finally burst into Ean's suite and sprinted across Ean's sitting room, throwing open the bedroom door, and—

"*Shade and darkness!*" Fynn staggered back, drawing his blade. With a cry of outrage, he rushed headlong into the room brandishing the weapon.

"Fynn, wait!" Ean shouted, but the Shade who stood beside him merely raised his hand, and Fynn was ripped off his feet. He flew ten paces through the air and crashed into the corner, collapsing upon the floor with an undignified thud and clatter of steel.

Ean turned Creighton a glare of reproach, but the Shade was unrepentant. "We've little time now, Ean," he advised. "Hurry."

Dazed and bewildered, Fynn struggled to rise. His head was throbbing painfully, and when he pressed fingers to his skull they came away wet with blood. He lifted val Lorian grey eyes to view his cousin, who was hurriedly shoving clothing into a bag, and then looked to the Shade who stood behind him.

Then he looked harder.

His eyes widened in horror. "*Creighton?*"

"I'm sorry, Fynnlar," Creighton murmured, sounding contrite even if his silver features revealed none of the emotion. "There is no time for explanations."

Fynn's skin crawled just looking at the freakish doppelganger of Ean's blood-brother. That's when he realized he couldn't move. "*You—bastard*," he snarled.

Ean spun a look from Fynn, who paused awkwardly, halfway to standing, to the Shade, who shrugged helplessly. Looking displeased, Ean closed his pack and slung it over his shoulder, but as he approached, Fynn saw that the prince was frightfully unsteady on his feet. The Shade walked just behind him, and his silver face was unmistakably that of Creighton's. The entire scene was so incomprehensible that Fynn worried he'd finally crossed the line from inebriation into hallucination.

"I'm so sorry, Fynn," Ean echoed the Shade, and his agonized expression seemed to convey the canyon of betrayal that now must lie between them. "I know you can't possibly understand." He grunted ruefully and added under his breath, "I barely understand, myself."

Fynn glared at him in brittle accusation.

"Ean..." the Shade urged from the doorway.

With one last look of regret, Ean turned away from Fynn and followed the Shade outside.

Fynnlar remained in his guise of an ill-conceived statue—immobile save for the unending stream of invective he muttered to occupy the time—until a chambermaid finally came to tend Ean's hearth and found him standing there. She ran off in a rush of screaming, which drew Brody and the soldiers, who fetched Raine and Seth, who finally tracked down the zanthyr, who to his utter disgust released him as easily as the Shade had bound him.

Then Fynn told them what he'd been trying to tell them all along—though no one had been listening amid the surprise and commotion of trying to free him. The instant he could move, however, Fynn grabbed Raine roughly by the shoulders. "Listen to me, you deaf-eared lout! He *took* Ean!"

Raine stiffened, and the room went silent. "Who took Ean?"

Fynn rubbed the fingers of one hand with the other, trying to work some blood back into them. He aimed an ill-humored glare at Phaedor. Somehow he was sure this was the zanthyr's fault. "A Shade."

Raine's eyes widened. "A *Shade?*" he hissed, grabbing Fynn's arm. "Where did they go?"

"They didn't exactly delineate their plans to me!" Fynn snarled. He jerked free of the man.

Raine looked ready to explode. "Fortune curse us all, it's happening tonight!" He turned to Seth. "Ready the men—and find Carian vran Lea!"

Abruptly the room cleared. Only the zanthyr remained, watching Fynnlar with arms crossed.

"What?" Fynn remarked churlishly. He walked over to pour himself a glass of wine from a decanter mulling on Ean's mantle.

"A Shade *took* Ean," the zanthyr repeated dubiously, clearly questioning Fynn's recounting of events. "It begs the question, *what* Shade?"

"Yes, and he gave me his name right after we exchanged the usual pleasantries," Fynn snapped, "which first involved slamming me against the bloody wall." He took a long draft of the wine, but it had mulled too long and was bitter, like his humor.

As he lowered the goblet, he found the zanthyr still leveling him an unrelenting stare. "Oh, all right!" he growled, hating the abominable creature with every waking breath. "I thought..." He dropped chin to chest, stared at his boots, and grumbled, "I thought I might've...recognized him."

"As?"

Fynn shot him a frustrated glare and answered through gritted teeth, "Creighton."

"Ah...so." Abruptly the zanthyr spun in a swirl of his dark cloak and headed outside onto the balcony.

"Where are you going?" Fynn shouted, rushing after him.

Phaedor turned a look over his shoulder, green eyes alight. "To avert disaster." Then he launched himself over the railing.

Alyneri woke.

She swam up through a drugged fog and finally opened her eyes to find that the coach had stilled. The pattering of rain upon the roof helped bring her back to full consciousness. She tried to sit up on the seat, but her head started pounding so violently that she worried she'd be sick. So she lay there weakly instead trying to find her breath.

Outside she heard male voices talking in urgent, hushed tones

"...t'were better we waited for the rain to clear, like the Healer's coachman said as they departed. This way becomes treacherous—"

"We will press on," another man snapped. "You have lanterns to light your path. Do so."

"Yes, milord," the first returned, but Alyneri heard the anxiety in his tone. A moment later the carriage door opened and a man ducked inside. He pushed back the hood of his drenched cloak and looked upon her with piercing dark eyes. His pointed black beard and moustache were also dripping.

Alyneri's head was swimming. "You won't get away with this," she managed, though she feared that indeed they would—whoever they were.

"Oh, I've planned more completely than you give me credit for, my dear girl," replied the man. "What do you think your prince will say when he sees Sandrine's note, written in a feminine hand, telling him that you need freedom to follow your Healer's calling, begging him not to follow? Think he'll question such a note, do you?"

"He'll never believe it," she gasped, but in truth she feared that Ean would. "And Tanis will...know it's...not from me."

"Really?" The dark-eyed man settled Alyneri a smug smile. "Even should your dutiful pup truthread the boy who brings the note, what will he see in his memory? That the child saw a blonde woman sitting in a coach write a note in her own hand and beg him give it to the captain, but not until her coach was far away."

Feeling the truth of this as a terrible clenching pain in her stomach, Alyneri closed her eyes and willed the world to stop spinning. She listened to the pelting rain and tried to soothe herself with measured breaths. Outside, the storm was a constant, and a cool, damp breeze coming in through the cracked window was soothing. "Where are we?" she asked as the pattering rain made waves before her vision.

"In the mountains north of Rethynnea."

"Where..." she had to fight off a feeling of imminent nausea. "Where are you... taking me?"

Just then the heavens opened up and the rain became a downpour. "My master would have your company at his side as he rides victoriously into Calgaryn palace as its new king."

"...What?" Alyneri thought she must've mistaken his words. "Your master?"

"Lord Stefan val Tryst," replied the man with a wicked smile. "Duke of Morwyk." He rapped upon the wall for the driver. "Move on!"

The coach lurched into motion, and Alyneri swallowed back the roiling contents of her stomach. "They'll be looking for me by now," she whispered.

The man sat back in his seat and eyed her skeptically. "Think you so? I am not so certain."

"Then why such haste?" Alyneri managed.

"Our master is not a patient man, and it has taken me some time to find you on his behalf."

Alyneri closed her eyes and tried to swallow back the bile in her throat. To find herself in the clutches of a man sworn to the Duke of Morwyk, knowing as she did the Duke's penchant for all things Bethamin...it did not bode well for her future. *Why* Morwyk had taken this deadly interest in her was quite beside the point.

They rode on in silence for the better part of an hour, wherein Alyneri almost drifted into sleep several times. As the rain battered their coach, the wind picked up, whipping and whining through the canvas. Suddenly, the coach lurched sideways, and the man shouted a curse at the driver. He was reaching for the door to ostensibly upbraid him more, when the coach lurched again, and Morwyk's henchman was pitched to the floor. He grabbed for his seat as the coach slid sideways on a precarious angle. "What's happening?" Alyneri cried, and then, suddenly, the world turned upside down.

Alyneri fell from seat to floor and then crashed into the man as they both came up hard against the roof of the coach. Alyneri heard a crack, and the man screamed. She clawed for a handhold as the coach started sliding again. All around her she heard wood tearing in protest and the terrified cries of horses gone mad. Her captor had fallen strangely silent, and still the coach slid beneath them upside-down through the mud. Abruptly something caught, and the coach spun around, flipping a limp Alyneri across to the other side of the compartment.

The door above them caught on something and ripped open. Rain and mud swarmed inside, burying her captor, who lay unmoving at the far end. Dazed and sick, Alyneri pushed up against the door. Just then the coach rammed into something immovable and flipped up, spitting Alyneri through a hole in the canvas. Her head collided with something immobile and blunt as she flew past, and then she pummeled chest-first into the mud. Slime filled her mouth, choking and blinding her as she went sliding in a downward plunge.

The cliff edge came up abruptly, and then Alyneri was falling.

Lucidity came as a parting gift.

It was an oddly peaceful last few moments tumbling through the darkness in concert with the rain, knowing she was going to die but so numbed by the laudanum that she couldn't find the emotion to care. Only as she heard the roar of the river, swollen with the rains, did she think of Ean with love and regret.

And then she hit.

FIFTY-SIX

'I am Rinokh. Hear my roar.'

– An Avataren saying, origin unknown

Ean hung on by a hair.

His body had been barely healed—barely restored of life—before he wrested it from his sheets and headed off with his blood-brother's Shade—for surely this iteration of his closest friend was but a shadow of the man who was—and his mind…his mind was even less prepared for the journey. One would think, with all of the myriad events Ean had witnessed since his return from Edenmar, that most any happening would now fall beyond question; but there was something so disturbing about traveling with Creighton's Shade, that Ean's tortured mind just could not wrap itself around the idea of it. So he pressed on by force of will alone, determined to claim his fate rather than be claimed by it.

Yet he was tormented by questions—both those unknown and answered, for Creighton had already told him more than he could process in the short time they'd been together. The vast web upon which he was caught was too intricate, its secrets based on history too obscure, for him to comprehend much of what Creighton had said. His friend was a wealth of knowledge and seemed willing to divulge further secrets if the telling of them would ease Ean's mind, but Ean couldn't bring himself to ask for more. Already he felt overloaded, weighted down by each strange new truth.

How could Creighton know so much? How could he have grown this depth of understanding in the relatively short time they'd been apart? Had death been such a revelation? Every time Creighton told him something, it opened a whole new line of disturbing questions such that Ean was soon reeling beneath them all. And while he'd trusted his friend unquestionably, he wasn't certain he could entirely trust his friend's Shade—too many betrayals from recent 'advisors' had left him disheartened and wary of those who would don the mantle of this role.

There was a distance between them now, as if the barrier between life and death still separated them. Creighton had crossed over this barrier while the prince was held behind; and though through some trick of magic Creighton stood beside him again now—the same man in every way that should matter—the prince still felt his absence.

"Ean," Creighton said as they rushed down a dark passageway, the last leg of an already distressing journey, "you don't have to do this."

Ean trailed a hand against the wall for support as he followed the Shade. "I know," he said. He was feeling lightheaded and weak and knew he should probably still be abed, but the idea of staying behind—of waiting to see what the Fourth Vestal had in store for him—set his temper to simmering. Even so, as they came to the end of the tunnel and faced a long flight of stairs, Ean looked upon the climb with a sinking feeling of dismay.

Creighton paused at the stair, his silver features set with concern. "Perhaps a moment to catch our breaths?"

Ean gratefully bent and pushed hands on knees. He bowed his head while Creighton stood over him, a dark shadow not unlike Phaedor but all too reminiscent of the creature named Reyd, the man Ean had watched drive a blade through Creighton's neck; the Shade who'd ultimately slain—and somehow resurrected—his best friend.

The myriad associations made him shudder.

Creighton put a black-gloved hand on Ean's shoulder, and there was naught but care in his voice as he asked, "Are you all right?"

Ean just nodded, swallowed. While he let his racing heart ease and his breathing settle, he looked up into Creighton's obsidian eyes. It was so unnerving to see his friend's familiar features encased in chrome…to know the power he now possessed.

Creighton's dark gaze swept Ean in turn, and he stressed again, "It is not too late to change your mind. This battle tonight need not be yours."

"And who will then be Rinokh's bait?" Ean challenged dourly.

"It is not so difficult to attract the notice of the Malorin'athgul," Creighton answered. "You need only work the lifeforce once to draw his eye to us here, and then…" but he broke off, biting his tongue, and looked away.

Ean knew the truth: his presence was vital if their plan was to see fruition, yet he also knew that his blood-brother feared for his life. So did he. The prince managed a grim smile. "It's too late to turn back down this path, isn't it? I chose to play in the game, and now…" he pushed a hand roughly through his hair and shook his head, "…and now there's only one way out, I fear." The words came with surprising ease for the gravity of their truth. It frightened him, this commitment he'd made in glib fury that fateful morning, giving his oath to the zanthyr and the Maker alone knew who else on the far receiving end of Fate's ear. And now…? Knowing merely the essence of what lay in store was enough to make his bones ache.

Creighton held his gaze. "The First Lord says the path out is always through the deepest dark of the core. One cannot skirt the edges to find a way across this battle, for the edges never touch." He gave Ean a smile that was meant to be encouraging, yet it was frightful to see. "Through the darkness then, and the First Lord awaits on the other side. But I wonder…" He considered Ean with careful regard. "Are you ready for that meeting?"

Ean looked up beneath his brows, still trying to find breath that he couldn't seem to catch. "The truth is…" he admitted then, feeling strangely absolved in the confession, like a sharp pain had finally lessened in his chest, "your death and the need to avenge it was all that held me back from seeking him sooner. And now…" he shrugged.

Creighton regarded him cautiously. "You've truly thought this through? Your friends, your family, all whom you cherish—they will believe you've betrayed them."

Ean pushed up, letting out a heavy sigh as he straightened. "I have, haven't I?" When Creighton merely gazed upon him, Ean murmured tightly, "Lead on, my brother." And he motioned to the stairs leading up to his destiny.

Wordlessly, the Shade turned and began the arduous climb. Ean was panting long before they reached the top the heavy iron door that opened onto a vast marble-sheathed temple. Across the long gallery—which easily spanned four-hundred paces and was deserted at that late hour—four enormous statues stood on pedestals, their forms illuminated by shafts of arcane light angled down from a wide dome high above. A fifth pedestal stood empty, but the light remained upon it, illuminating dust motes like fireflies in its stead.

"The Temple of the Vestals," Ean panted wondrously.

A figure moved out from behind the statue of Dagmar Ranneskjöld, and the Shade led Ean across the distance to meet him halfway. It wasn't until they were close that Ean realized he knew the man. "Franco?"

Franco Rohre came to a halt in front of him. He looked very much the same as when last they'd parted—somewhat disheveled and wearing a smile that didn't quite lighten the brooding shadows behind his brown eyes. "My prince," Franco greeted with a humble bow. "It's a pleasure to see you again."

Ean sort of stared at him while memory of Raine's words flashed to mind…*I believe his loyalties to me were preceded by those to another…* "And you, Franco," he murmured. As they looked at each other, Ean saw something in Franco's eyes that perhaps had always been there but whose meaning had eluded him before. He asked quietly, "Have you always served the Fifth Vestal?"

Franco held his gaze, but it was a moment before he admitted the painful truth. "I have been sworn to him for three-hundred years."

"I see." And he did—it made sense of many things. Suddenly feeling lightheaded, Ean pressed a hand to his temple and swayed unsteadily.

Franco swung a heated look to Creighton. "What happened to him?"

"Malorin'athgul," the Shade returned grimly.

Franco's eyes flew wide. "When?"

"Five days ago. I thought—"

"It doesn't matter," Franco waved off the question and looked instead to the prince. "Do you know what we are at this night, Ean?"

"Without question," Creighton returned on his behalf. "The First Lord would have it no other way."

"Then let us be about it—"

"I'm afraid I can't allow that," a man's *elae*-enhanced voice carried to them from far across the temple.

Ean cringed, knowing Raine's voice all too well.

Franco exchanged a look with Creighton and slowly turned to face the entering Vestal. "My lord," he said, affording Raine a respectful bow across the distance. "What a pleasant surprise. I hope my abrupt departure from Calgaryn did not leave you too long without means."

Ean saw a long line of armed men fanning out behind the Vestal. Among them walked both avieths, and he suspected the pirate must be somewhere within their ranks as well—so many of his friends come to witness his betrayal. It was a bitter tonic to his resolve.

"It's not too late for you, Franco," Raine said, his voice carrying easily to them on the currents of *elae*, his expression regretful, if resolute.

Franco barked a bitter laugh. "My lord, it has been too late for me since before Tiern'aval fell."

"I'm sorry you feel that way."

Still the soldiers continued filing in. There might've been three-hundred if there were fifty. Ean felt weak-hearted just looking at them.

Franco hissed heatedly to the Shade, "Can't you bind them?"

Creighton cast him a level look. "If I could, Espial, I would already have done so. They have some kind of—"

"Pattern?" Raine offered from across the distance, arching brows. It was eerie the way he so easily conversed with them; could he hear their thoughts just as readily? "Yes, I learned some things about Shades in my time," Raine said. "One was a certain pattern that protects from many of your powers. It has limits, of course," he added as he lifted his gaze to the dome. "It cannot protect from the hounds, but I hear you need moonlight to raise them. A pity it is overcast tonight."

"Yes," Creighton murmured, obsidian eyes pinned on the Vestal. "A pity."

"I'm sure he had nothing to do with *that* either," Franco muttered inhospitably.

Raine looked to the prince then. "Ean," he said, calling his gaze, "I'm afraid you must come with me."

Ean felt the first vestiges of hatred forming for the man. "How do you justify it?" he returned, his tone derisive, his eyes condemning. "You knew everything I needed to know and told me nothing. You sent me south beneath the auspices of safety knowing I would draw every assassin and all manner of fell craft to relentlessly harrow myself and my companions. You would make me your pawn and keep me ignorant and helpless while deadly forces hunt to kill. *Tell me*," he demanded, "how do you justify your betrayal?"

"Everything I have done has been for your own good, Ean," Raine replied simply, opening palms skyward as if it was a foregone conclusion. "I must make choices for you which I know you would make if only you better understood the threat."

"If only *I* better understood—?" Ean stared at him. Then he barked a contemptuous laugh. "I think you're the one who doesn't understand—or doesn't *believe*."

"Belief is irrelevant to truth, Ean," Raine replied. He glanced to his small army and saw that all were in place. "And now, I think, we should get this over with. Surrender your weapons."

Ean merely stared hatefully at him.

"You're outnumbered," Raine pressed. "Surely you don't mean to resist?"

"My lord," Franco replied, stepping forward as if to close the hundreds of feet between them with a simple step, his words crossing that same distance in peaceful entreaty, "I have been commissioned to speak for the Fifth Vestal in negotiating a resolution. He would see no blood shed this night and offers you a chance to avoid the needless sacrifice of your men."

"My men?" Raine looked incredulous. "You three stand against three-hundred!"

"Looks can be deceiving," the Shade was heard to murmur.

"Even were it so," Franco returned with a sideways glance at Creighton, "the First Lord offers his hand in treaty. If you would know his mind, his purpose, leave this place tonight as a measure of your troth. In so doing, he will unto you all knowledge of his intent."

Ean knew it was a heady boon Franco offered. More than anything, Raine D'Lacourte wanted to know Björn van Gelderan's purpose for returning to Alorin.

For a moment the Vestal seemed to be considering the offer, and Ean's hopes lifted; their task that night would be easier without the burden of more lives lost. But then Raine shook his head. "No," he growled. "It is too late for treaties. My oath-brother has many crimes to answer for. There can be no clemency, only restitution."

Franco's expression fell, and Ean's hopes went with it.

"Ean val Lorian," Raine warned, "if you would avoid the needless death of your friends, surrender yourself into my care. You *know* I mean to see no harm come to you. If you resist..." and here he opened palms to the sky, finishing resolutely, "their blood is on your hands."

"No my lord," Franco corrected, "it is on yours." He turned an inquiring look to Creighton.

The Shade shrugged. "What must be must be."

Franco looked bleak. "Do it then."

Creighton closed silver eyelids and called upon his brethren, upon the mental link that bound them all. Soon his body blurred and became two, then ten, each form separating out from a single center. Creighton had told Ean about the mind-bond, that a dozen Shades would stand with them this night, but Ean hadn't known what he meant until that moment.

A great grumbling and shouting arose from the ranks of Raine's men, who seemed less enthusiastic about battling twelve Shades than they had about facing one. Ean suppressed a shudder at the sight and tried to remind himself that the eerie specters were on his side.

Grimfaced, Raine ordered, "Take them."

The avieth shouted a battle cry and himself led the charge. In response, the waiting Shades drew their dark blades with a swirl that rippled down the line. They rushed as one to meet the advancing men.

"Raine's wielders must be near," Franco told Creighton as he also drew his blade, adding hurriedly, "They would have to concentrate on the pattern to keep it strong."

"I have already found them," the Shade replied, his obsidian gaze penetrating the ranks of approaching soldiers. "You know what to do," he added, and then he faded.

Franco placed himself in front of Ean. "Fear not, Ean. We won't let them take you."

"That's reassuring," Ean muttered, knowing this battle was but an appetizer for the main course of their activities that night. As he drew his own sword and felt his arm tremble beneath its weight, he knew with grim certainty that he was in no condition to fight. Yet, as he readied to face the oncoming men both physically and mentally, a deep memory surfaced, floating to mind as if from the deepest depths of the sea. Ean pushed a palm to his aching head and—

He had it.

Just in time, for soldiers broke through the line of Shades and surged around them in a flood, coming to claim him in Raine's name. Acting with the instinct, Ean poured his energy into the strange pattern imposing itself on his consciousness and pushed it outward, casting it beyond himself and Franco toward the approaching soldiers—the same pattern he'd unknowingly used to insert the barrier between his shoulder and a stabbing Jeshuelle.

The nearest man rammed into the field of solidified air and was repelled five paces backwards, taking several others down with him.

Franco shot him a tense look. "That's a nice trick. How long can you hold it?"

"Not…long," Ean grunted. It was costing him greatly to hold the pattern in place in his weakened condition.

"Don't waste your strength then. We press for the node." He looked to the gathering men and his gaze hardened. "Let them come."

In part reluctant and part relieved, Ean released the pattern, letting its energy dissipate on its own. It was immediately evident when the last of the pattern's energy faded, for a man standing close to them who'd been pressing on the invisible wall suddenly pitched forward onto his knees. The others swarmed in, and Franco and Ean raised their blades to meet them, the clash of their swords joining in dissonant harmony with the ongoing battle.

With Franco close at his side, Ean deflected blade after blade, only praying that Fortune's grace would be upon them. His head was pounding, his breath coming raggedly into tormented lungs, but he held onto his weapon and stayed close to Franco as they pressed through the sea of men toward the node.

At least the first part of his task was done. That working would certainly draw the Malorin'athgul to them now. But where was Creighton?

Cloaked in night, Creighton swept among the advancing ranks of swordsmen with nary a whisper to mark his passing. Raine might have found a pattern that protected against a Shade's ability to bind men to his will, but a Shade had other tricks, lesser known, and Creighton had all of the First Lord's knowledge at his disposal. Thus, as he passed as a shadow among the soldiers, his hand unerringly found each sword, each dagger, with a single caress, the slightest kiss of *deyjiin* upon the blades. T'was not enough to destroy the weapons—*no*, only to weaken their integrity, dull their edge. While he couldn't touch all, enough would suffer a malady of blade to hopefully keep his companions from harm.

Creighton felt reasonably sure that his tiny working of power would be enough to shift the balance in the battle without disturbing the Balance of the game itself, but it was a dangerous wager. He understood now that it was always a dance; Balance was a capricious sprite that wooed one moment and bit the next. To skirt that line was a wielder's greatest—and deadliest—challenge, for Balance governed all. Even a Shade was not immune to Its laws.

Having done all he could to aid Ean and Franco for the moment, Creighton reached the end of the advancing ranks and flicked as a shadow across the distance toward the two wielders who stood apart from the others. They would be casting the spell that worked against his power. Doubtless Raine would be protecting his wielders as they wove their pattern of protection over his army, but Creighton knew that no spell could be so complete as to fully insulate a man from a Shade's craft. This was something the Vestal didn't understand—much to his peril. Creighton acted then to instruct the truthreader by taking away that which he most treasured, for this was the First Lord's will.

The sounds of battle were fierce behind him as Creighton neared the two black-robed wielders. They were foreign-looking men with pale hair and cold eyes, their gazes focused just then on the distant battle. With his particular enhanced vision, the Shade could see the outline of the pattern they worked among their auras, but their pattern didn't concern him; it was the warped space around *them*—the *Vestal's* spell of protection—that required his attention.

Creighton suspected the Vestal would be thorough in his working, and after a moment's inspection of the pattern he determined that indeed Raine had been—the dome of warped space was in fact a sphere fully enclosing the two wielders. It would be impenetrable for a man, but for a Shade…

Creighton disapparated.

His consciousness spread to encircle the dome, surrounding and enfolding it even as it surrounded the wielders. Perceiving the sphere in its fullness then, the Shade could sense both the pattern of its creation and the pattern being worked by the wielders within; he saw the intricacies of both patterns, and understood their intent.

But one was his singular focus. Looking to Raine's sphere of protection, Creighton sought the finite division between shadow and light, those fractions of spaces between particles too small for the human eye to see.

There.

He poured his consciousness through the minute spaces then, seeping between the particles to slowly gather again inside the protection of Raine's sphere. How simple it would be to claim both wielders in the First Lord's name, to smite them unto death. But Creighton knew that every wielder would be needed, in the end.

As Creighton readied his consciousness for the moment of congregation, he understood that the Vestal's pattern was not a working Raine could banish with an off-handed wave. It had taken time to craft the pattern into existence, and its energy must be fully expended, the pattern left to dissolve of its own. Even after Raine stopped concentrating *elae* into his pattern—which he would do instantly once he saw Creighton appear within his protective dome—the pattern's accumulated energy would have to disperse before Raine would be able to reach those inside the sphere.

With great satisfaction then, Creighton contracted the molecules of his being in a swarming inward rush, a surge of invisible particles instantly imploding into one predesignated form.

He congregated.

In one moment there was nothing. In the next, a silver-faced Shade stood behind the two wielders, who were so focused on their own spellcraft that they perceived none of his arrival. Raine saw his appearance at once, of course, but there was nothing the Vestal could do. He watched in helpless fury as Creighton searched again for that finite division of shadow and light and then channeled *deyjiin* into the parting, tearing the very fabric of the realm. In the span of a single breath, a silver-violet line speared down from on high and broadened to reveal a glossy black emptiness. The fabled dimension of Shadow.

The two wielders did notice him then, and they spun with shouts of alarm, but Creighton had the both of them in hand. His strength was that of fifty men when required; he merely channeled all of his force into those parts of his amorphous body which most needed the power. With a man in each hand, he spun and slung one and then the other through the parting, instantly releasing the portal, sealing off their screams.

Raine's spell was fading, and Creighton made himself thin as he walked through the mottled dome, its power diminished now, its integrity lost. He turned and locked gazes with the Vestal, their eyes alone closing the distance between them.

Can you read my mind? Creighton wondered with his obsidian eyes fastened on the man. *I hope that you can.*

Raine's gaze shifted and widened, and in the same moment Creighton heard a voice say accusingly behind him, "What manner of creature might *you* be?"

At last!

Creighton shifted the arrangement of his features from forward-facing to back, reassociating the necessary components in the opposite direction to see what was once behind. The man who faced him now was not unlike the First Lord's *drachwyr* in coloring, though his cold eyes held nothing but malice.

Creighton knew him, but the knowing was not without fear. Yet for all his apprehensions—and they had been aplenty when receiving the assignment—in this the moment of their first meeting, Creighton knew all. The information was simply accessible, like a window opened in his mind. He knew how to fight this man. He knew how to do what must be done. "I might ask the same of you," he replied, readying himself.

"I am Rinokh," announced the man as if his name alone should bespeak his nature. And in fact it did, to those who knew it. Rinokh's gaze swept the room, noting the battle with disinterest…until his gaze fell upon Ean.

Creighton saw Ean as Rinokh did: a single dark ember amid a glowing golden aura, a veritable beacon among an undulating sea of black-clad soldiers.

"*You*…" hissed Rinokh, his face becoming a mask of malevolence. "You should *not be*." Then his rage exploded.

Ean knew the moment Rinokh neared. The sense of malice that preceded his actual presence was strong enough to elicit a visceral response, for his body recalled too strongly the malignant feel of the man's power upon it.

Raine's untimely arrival was a complication that Ean feared would prove fatal. He didn't stand a chance against Rinokh without Creighton to protect him, and the Shade was nowhere in sight. As the sense of Rinokh grew stronger, all of Ean's focus became on just reaching the node. In the end, that's all that mattered; whether he lived or died, he had to reach that node.

Drenched in sweat and sick with fatigue, Ean channeled every ounce of will into keeping hold of his sword and repelling the attacks that came at him from every angle. Franco was clearing the way for them, but his efforts had not been without cost, and his tunic was bloody along his left side. Ean's strength was being taxed so greatly that he was barely staying on his feet, and his breath came in painful gasps. Each time he swung he feared this time he would lose his balance, his footing, or his life; every blow of his sword reverberated into his bones. Had he been stronger, had his head been clearer—had he not just been resurrected from the dead several hours ago—it might've been a very different scene.

Just then a wedge of men drove between Ean and Franco, separating them and sending Ean stumbling. Three split off to attack the Espial while two others turned their swords against the prince. And now Rinokh had arrived—the prince saw him two-hundred feet across the room as clearly as if he stood right before him—and Ean knew he was doomed.

Three bone-shattering blows from the man leading the assault against him demanded Ean's attention in full, and two more blows sent him staggering. His vision went black and he stumbled into one of the fallen, so dizzy that he nearly fell. Someone caught him around the chest, and he struggled against powerful arms until he heard a deep voice murmur, "Be calm, my prince."

Relief flooded Ean with the unmistakable voice, but there was no time for thanks, for Raine's men were upon them. Phaedor released Ean onto his feet and spun to face the swordsmen, taking both down with two quick figure-eights of his Merdanti blade. "Come, Ean," he said then, looking to the prince. "Your destiny awaits."

Phaedor set his own course through the battle with Ean following in his wake. The zanthyr was a formidable force, and in the time it had taken Franco to forge ten feet Phaedor had crossed five times that distance. A press of six men fell beneath the zanthyr's blade as Ean finally reached the tall marble block that was the Fifth Vestal's pedestal, and another five saw their end while Ean braced himself against the cool stone trying to clear his head. After that, no one risked coming near the zanthyr's blade.

Trying to will the world to stop spinning, Ean looked to Phaedor. "You shouldn't be here," he gasped.

The zanthyr cast him a dubious look that spoke volumes.

"I mean…" Ean corrected with a grim glance across the room, "Rinokh is here, and Creighton told me—"

"It doesn't matter what the Shade told you."

"But Raine will think—"

Phaedor leveled him an implacable stare. "Let me worry about Raine."

Overruled, Ean turned to lean back against the pedestal. He felt nauseated and weak, and his muscles shook at strange times.

"You have overtaxed yourself," the zanthyr noted in disapproval. "Again."

Ean shot him a vexed look.

Suddenly there was a flash, and Ean spun with his sword ready.

But it was only the avieth materializing out of the form. "Easy, Northerner," she cautioned, eying his blade dubiously.

Letting out his breath as Ean lowered his weapon, his attention went to the battling Shades, who were once again holding the line against Raine's forces. Stunned by the needless loss, he gave the avieth a hard look. "Gwynnleth…I saw you with the Vestal. Are you not on his side?"

Gwynnleth arched a ginger brow. "Is there a clear side in this?" She eyed the battle beyond them with her tawny eyes narrow and fierce. "The pirate brings men by the wagonload across a node to fight Shades who are dead already. I ask you: to what purpose serves this fight? It could go on forever, Shades slashing, men dying."

"No," murmured the zanthyr with his emerald eyes pinned intently across the sea of men. "Not forever. Rinokh—"

Abruptly he threw himself across Gwynnleth and Ean nary a second before the concussion hit. Soldiers toppled like matchsticks beneath the blast, thunder without sound as it washed across them. The force of the eruption slammed Ean against the pedestal, knocking the wind from his lungs even behind the zanthyr's protective shield. Ean watched men being flattened to the stones and knew he and Gwynnleth would've been tossed like ragdolls to break against the far wall if not for the zanthyr's protection.

As the gale faded, Ean slowly pushed away from the marble to find an ocean of unconscious men, and on the far side of the human sea…Rinokh coming for him.

"Get the islander and attend the Vestal," Phaedor hissed to Gwynnleth, who rushed to the task surprisingly without query.

"He comes," Ean whispered, trying to control his rising panic.

Phaedor turned him a telling look, the air heavy with his unspoken censure. "You play a dangerous game tonight, my prince."

Ean swallowed. "I know."

Men were starting to recover from the blast, the floor now a mass of undulating bodies as what soldiers still lived pushed to hands and knees, but Rinokh came unhindered. Waves of hatred preceded him, abrasive against Ean's fragile mind, and he recoiled from the feel of the man's power, his tortured body trembling with its touch. What courage it took to remain there locked in the Malorin'athgul's sights! For he knew the man came with perilous intent, having felt the effects of his power already to his mortal end.

But Ean remained.

A thousand hopes and fears flashed through his head in that short span of time, but none of them jeopardized his commitment. Creighton had died for him once, and now it was Ean's turn to show his color. Beneath this troth, what fear could weaken him? What end could possibly threaten his resolve?

The Malorin'athgul halted fifteen paces from Ean, his face a glaring, vicious display of his fury. The men regaining their feet between Ean and the man scrambled away, sensing even as mortals that his was a power beyond their reckoning. So did a circle spread in an ever-growing distance as men crawled with desperate will to free themselves from Rinokh's seething anger.

But Ean remained.

The cold waves of *deyjiin* washed over him, but Rinokh had given no will to their purpose and so the power's touch merely chilled Ean, drawing gooseflesh and shudders from his already stressed system.

The zanthyr had vanished, though Ean barely noticed. He was glad of it, though, for he wanted no other lives upon his conscience.

"*You*," hissed Rinokh, the word sounding a curse upon his tongue, "should have died."

Ean felt his malice, the waves of *deyjiin* shifting—altering—to reflect subtle changes in his will. The prince sensed that the only reason the man had not yet attacked him again was the mystery of his survival.

Somehow he found the courage to reply, but where the words came from, he didn't know. "I told you once," he said, surprised by the strength in his voice, "Balance is with me."

"*Balance*," the man spat. "You know nothing of it."

"And yet here I stand," Ean pointed out, and then, as Creighton had instructed him, he added, "If not Balance, what answer then beyond divine will?"

The Malorin'athgul's eyes widened, and his lips drew back in a snarl. He pointed a hand at Ean and the prince felt his power electrify, readying to be channeled. He braced himself, and—

Creighton materialized between them just as Rinokh released *deyjiin*. The power flowed into the Shade, who stood with an expression of grave regret. Ean felt only its fringes harmlessly washing over him.

In that moment, he did as Creighton had instructed. Though he'd feared he wouldn't muster the resolve to once again attack Rinokh, Ean found it surprisingly easy to pierce his awareness toward the Malorin'athgul. Once again, his spear glanced off the man's hardened mind, but this time it left a chink, a handhold, the tiniest unraveling thread. Ean latched onto it.

Rinokh meanwhile roared in fury at being balked. He tried to strike the Shade out of his way, but his arm passed right through him. Startled, he clawed for the Shade with both hands, but though Creighton stood clearly before him, Rinokh could not find purchase upon his person.

Momentarily distracted from Ean by this new mystery, the Malorin'athgul stalked Creighton with predatory fascination. "*You* should not exist," he declaimed, palms raised before him. Power leapt from his hands into the Shade, who seemed to simply devour it within his raven-clad chest, his expression never wavering.

"It's time, Ean," came a sudden voice from behind, and Ean knew Franco had finally made it there. The man looked hardly steadier on his feet than the prince was—and certainly he was a good deal bloodier—but he slipped a looped rope around Ean's wrist and tugged it tight. "Are you ready?"

Ean only half saw him, for he was concentrating on the one thread extending from Rinokh's mental shield. He finally had a firm hold upon it. "I'm ready," he said.

He closed his eyes to better hold the thread, and he pulled.

To Raine, everything seemed to happen at once. The Shade somehow slipping *inside* his spell, the sudden infuriating loss of his wielders, and then the man—the strange, malevolent man…

At first, from so far away, Raine thought the man to be the Sundragon Şrivas'rhakárakek, who he'd battled so long ago, but where Rhakár exuded arrogance, this man seethed with enmity. Instinctually he opened himself to *elae*—

What he saw sent him staggering.

The currents of *elae* were rippling away from the intruder in gigantic waves—not from any working of his design, but as if in abhorrence to his very being. Raine had never seen anything like it—not even when Shades worked *deyjiin* did such a disturbance occur. The significance was beyond imagining.

It cannot be!

His blood turned to ice in his veins.

And then the stranger erupted.

Only because Raine was already patterning to protect himself from the battle was he spared the brunt of the blast. Still the shockwave hit him with incomprehensible force, pitching him off his feet to fly several paces through the air. His men were flattened beneath the onslaught, dominoes falling as the blast exploded outward. The walls of the very temple shook, and dust showered down from the ceiling.

The Shades who'd been strung out in a line against his men simply dimmed and faded, ostensibly returning into the one form from which they'd come. The stranger stalked across the room then, but Raine hardly noticed him in that moment, for the currents held him captive, his mind struggling to comprehend what his eyes observed.

Where the man had been standing remained a mottled grey circle, and it took precious seconds for Raine to understand what it meant. But then he knew.

The land itself had been consumed of life.

He devours the fifth, Raine realized, growing colder still as the terrifying understanding hit him.

For a heartbeat he stared, stunned to inaction by the formidable implications of this man's existence. Then he noticed the virulent man stalking across the room and realized who he was heading for.

Ah, Cephrael, no!

Raine jumped out of his stupor and rushed among the fallen, rousing the men nearest him, some of who were just beginning to stir. "Get up! Get up!" he roared. "He's getting away!" So intent upon his purpose he was that he nearly ran into Gwynnleth, who rushed up with Carian at her side.

The avieth took Raine boldly by the shoulders. "You must stop this senselessness, my lord! You must let Ean go."

Raine swept her aside. "If you would help Ean, *help me!* Rouse the others!"

Gwynnleth leveled him a look of indecision, but then she moved to the task, and the islander followed her lead. Soon the zanthyr and Seth were also moving among the men, and in short order easily a hundred had been restored to their feet.

Raine wasn't sure how he was going to do it, but he knew he had to stop the stranger. As he looked urgently across the distance, he was stunned yet again by the scene: the man was pressing an advance upon the Shade, channeling power into him in a never-ending stream. The currents were wild around them, a hurricane-tossed sea of choppy peaks and sharp-edged waves.

"Epiphany protect us," Raine murmured, momentarily awed, his shock complete. His gaze darted to the zanthyr, who stood now with Seth, and he knew then that Phaedor had spoken the truth about the stranger's dark nature. By Cephrael's Great Book, how was he ever going to convince Alshiba when he himself would never have believed had he not seen it with his own eyes?

His men were restored and ready. "Stop that man!" he ordered, and to their credit, they rushed to capture the fell creature who was stalking the Shade across the hall.

Time stretched before Raine, lengthening as it seemed to slow. Desperately he watched his men running to attack the man who was pressing the Shade on the retreat, his power ravaging the currents with wild abandon, and then Raine's gaze found Ean, saw the course upon which the...*Malorin'athgul*—even in his thoughts Raine stumbled over the word—was in vicious pursuit.

Raine blanched.

He could predict the certain end. He knew his men would not make it there in time, but with *elae* to fuel his strength, he could. He sprinted toward the advancing line; and seeing him go, a puzzled Gwynnleth and Carian followed.

"*Ean!*" Raine shouted as he pushed through the ranks of his men, scattering them before him in his haste. He finally broke through the front line and was within ten steps of the prince when the world went white.

The last thing Raine remembered was the ghastly look on Rinokh's face.

Ean heard someone call his name over the sound of running men, but he dared not shift his attention off that one fragile thread. He didn't know what pattern the thread was part of, but Creighton had told him enough to understand that whatever it was, it was crucial that Ean didn't let go. So he held on, putting all of his mental energy behind it. His face reddened with the effort, his breath came in ragged gasps when it came at all, but he kept tension upon the line until...

Rinokh suddenly spun with a hiss, his face contorted with fury, and Ean felt a mental jolt as the man lashed back at him. He jumped toward Ean with lethal intent, crossing the distance in mere seconds, his hands extended, and the prince saw power erupt—

Creighton launched into Rinokh, ripping him off his feet, and they tumbled past just inches from Ean's chest. Rinokh snarled in a language that sounded as foreign as it was dreadful as he and the Shade slid across the floor, his power revolting against the Shade's affront, battering Ean with angry ridges. Creighton had Rinokh clenched in a vice-like embrace, and he dragged him inexorably toward the point where Franco had vanished.

Ean dared not even hope. All of his effort was on holding that thread. His entire body trembled beneath the onslaught of *deyjiin*, which emitted from Rinokh riotously, the power every bit as antipathetic toward life and *elae* as it would've been had Rinokh put will behind its intent.

And then something changed. The Shade reached the point where Franco had vanished, and Rinokh's face became a mask of horror.

Power erupted.

Ean was thrown backwards, his head hitting the floor with a sharp flash, but still he held onto the thread. He felt something heavy on top of him and tried to get his breath, tried to push whatever it was off, but it might've been part of a statue for all he could make it budge.

And at the other end of the thread, he felt something shift, like the tensile string had finally snapped. Suddenly the thread was unraveling, tumbling back upon him in huge waves, forming piles of ethereal silver all but burying his awareness.

Undone.

Whatever it had been, it was no more. Perhaps Ean hadn't actually unworked Rinokh, but he had succeeded in holding onto the thread of his being as Creighton pulled him across the node; and the distance, if not the force of traveling unprotected along the very pattern of the realm, had unraveled the entire pattern, woof and warp.

As the ringing in his ears began to fade, a terrible rumbling took its place, and Ean realized what he'd thought was his own body shaking was actually the floor beneath him.

Finally the pressure upon his chest lessened, and Ean blinked to focus upon the zanthyr's emerald eyes looking into his own. "We have to stop meeting this way," he managed, casting Phaedor a rueful grin.

Frowning in disapproval, the zanthyr got to his feet and hauled Ean up beside him with one arm. Ean swooned. He gave the zanthyr a look of wondrous gratitude, overwhelmed by his unrelenting, if inexplicable, protection.

But there was no time for thanks. Even as Ean was trying to wrap his mind around what had happened, Raine's statue began crumbling. A grey miasma was spreading across the stones devouring everything it touched, turning rock to sand, wood to ash, and any man unlucky enough to be caught within its embrace into dust. The prince looked through the temple and saw to his horror that the entire building was disintegrating.

Raine's men, those who survived the second blast, were already running. Ean spotted the Vestal himself rousing not far away, and Carian was helping Gwynnleth to stand just beyond Raine.

Ean looked back to the zanthyr too choked with emotion even to form words.

Phaedor gazed solemnly back. "Farewell, my prince."

"Come with me," Ean choked out, a sudden desperate need to stay with the zanthyr overwhelming him.

"Who would then stop this destruction? *Deyjiin* will continue its consumption until there is nothing left of our realm." He shook his head and placed a hand on the prince's shoulder. "Take care, my prince. May Fortune's eye remain upon you," and with one last look entreating caution, he turned and swept across the crumbling temple toward Raine.

"Ean!"

The prince turned. Franco stepped out of the node looking singed and holding tight enough to his end of the rope attached to Ean's wrist that his knuckles were white. Ean could only imagine the forces Franco had endured to hold the node open long enough for the Shade to pull Rinokh across, and he didn't want to imagine what must've occurred on the other side of Rinokh's wrath.

Franco grabbed the prince into his arms in a relieved embrace. In that moment, the Fourth Vestal's statue toppled and fell in a thunderous roar to shatter upon the stones behind them, huge clouds of dust erupting in its wake. The Espial stared through the haze and locked gazes across the distance with Raine himself.

"Dare not follow us, my lord!" he shouted in warning. He pulled Ean roughly against him as he stepped back across the node.

Raine regained consciousness with a gasp. Slowly sitting up, he saw that he'd broken his fall on a man who himself had been impaled on the sword of a third, the blade narrowly missing Raine's shoulder. As he climbed off the dead man, Raine realized similar ends had found many of his men, who'd been tossed and pitched like flotsam on a storm-ravaged sea. A groan behind him drew the Vestal's eye to where Carian was helping Gwynnleth to rise, and all across the gallery, men regained their feet, but no sooner had they done so than they broke into a run.

Rinokh's fell power had shaken the very foundations of the temple, and now it was crumbling down upon them. To the accompaniment of a deep and threatening rumble, stone dust fell in waterfalls from the dome as the marble disintegrated beneath *deyjiin's* consumptive wrath. Pillars crumbled, broke and tumbled, and the floor turned a mottled grey and fell away into sand, opening huge pits of darkness into the levels below.

Raine looked around desperately until he saw across the distance that the zanthyr had Ean in hand. He shook his head in amazed wonder, but just as quickly his expression turned to dismay, for Franco Rohre appeared behind Ean.

Just then Raine's own statue crumbled and fell with resounding thunder. Raine threw an arm across his eyes, and when the dust cleared, Franco had Ean in his arms.

"Dare not follow us, my lord!" the Espial shouted, and even as Raine lunged toward him, Franco and the prince were gone.

"Don't!" The zanthyr was suddenly beside him. He grabbed Raine's arm, holding him back.

Raine shoved him off. "What will Björn do with another fifth-strand Adept?" he hissed. His fury at losing Ean far overshadowed the devastation around him; it threatened to overwhelm all reason. Four quick steps and Raine grabbed up the pirate by the coat, dragging him forward. "We've got to follow them!"

Gwynnleth shot the zanthyr a telling look, so much encapsulated in that brief, fervent glance, and then she rushed after the retreating Nodefinder.

"No—*Gwynnleth!*" shouted Seth from across the hall. He surged into the form and flew toward her through the showering marble sands, but he was too late.

Carian reached for Gwynnleth's hand even as he grabbed Raine's arm, and then they were all three leaping across the node, vanishing a second before Seth dove down, capturing only empty air in his gilded talons.

Across the way, Raine landed on his hands and knees in sand, momentarily dazed. He took one look around, however, and swore furiously. "How could you bring us *here?*" he hissed. "Are you *mad?*"

Carian's eyes widened as he realized where they were. "*No*," he declared in his own defense, slamming a fist into the garnet sands, "this isn't right! The node opened onto a passage—with tapestries! I'm telling you this *isn't* where it leads!"

"*This is where it led*," Raine growled through gritted teeth.

Carian sat back on his heels and pushed a hand through his tangled hair. "*No*," he insisted, looking around in dismay. "I *saw* him travel…it…" Abruptly his words trailed off and Raine saw understanding come into his gaze.

"What?" asked the Vestal, catching only glimpses of his strongest thoughts. "What do you know?"

"It doesn't matter," the pirate returned. "We're here now, and here we'll stay."

Raine's expression was grim as he locked gazes with Carian. "T'khendar," he murmured even as Gwynnleth began to scream.

The zanthyr watched Seth swoop low, and then, with a raucous, angry cry, fly upwards, soaring through the shattered dome and out into the night.

Waterfalls of shimmering marble sand poured down around him, forming great piles upon what parts of the floor remained, the temple itself crumbling now at an alarming rate, but still he remained. His ancient eyes watched the currents, seeing how they shifted and changed, noting patterns that were beyond even Raine D'Lacourte's skill. So it was that he saw the subtle glint come into the second strand and lifted his eyes just as the man stepped across the node.

He wore a jacket the color of sky, and his glossy dark curls had not changed in all the centuries they had known one another.

Their eyes locked.

The temple instantly became so charged with *elae* that the slightest misthought could have ended their existence. With two fifth-strand adepts working *elae* in such close proximity, the very air was alive and just barely containing its own power. An odd sort of elation could be sensed between them—a harmonic of serenity and regret. For seconds—seconds that could have been hours—neither moved nor spoke, yet so very much was communicated though that interlocking of equally depthless eyes… through the bond that bound them still.

It was a rare moment.

"It's been a long time," Björn murmured, finally breaking the silence.

Phaedor just watched him in his quiet, intense way. Theirs was a bond of centuries of trust, but also a bond of the strongest magic, and both were bonds even death could not sever.

"We should hurry," the zanthyr said.

Björn nodded. He opened his hands, palms up, and the zanthyr did the same, so that they stood as mirrors of one another perhaps twenty paces apart. Closing their eyes, their minds perfectly synchronous, they reached out with the power only an Adept of the fifth might master and began the laborious process of recalling Rinokh's devouring *deyjiin*.

They worked through the night.

The moon watched in solemn silence, the stars gleaming their fascination, as the two men painstakingly reined back Rinokh's sprawling power, drawing it forth from stone and wood, earth and iron, tearing its sharp claws out of rock, out of walls, even out of the rising wind.

As the sun rose over the Assifiyahs, bringing golden light into the world and setting the heavens to flame, Phaedor drew the last tendril of *deyjiin* from the realm and exhaled a long, shuddering breath, a cool wind across the marble sand. Around him, the Temple of the Vestals was a crumbling relic, its marble walls half-devoured, the dome destroyed and roof open to the sky, but the realm had been cleansed of Rinokh's destructive power. Already the currents were resuming their natural path.

Phaedor released *elae* and lifted his gaze to his master.

Björn smiled.

And Phaedor spoke to him for the last time. "Be careful, *ma dieul*," he whispered. It was a fervent plea, a desperate entreaty, a haunting warning all in one.

Björn gave him a long look, conveying more with his deep blue eyes than any words might express. Then, with one last glance of farewell, he turned and crossed the node, vanishing as if he had never been.

EPILOGUE

T*rell of the Tides.*

Trell woke to the echo of Naiadithine's whisper and the lingering feel of Fhionna's kiss upon his mouth. Sitting up in his bed, he glanced over to see Yara still asleep. The storm had been fierce last night, but the grey dawn light beyond the room's single window hinted at a clear morning to come.

Feeling strangely unsettled, Trell climbed from bed and pulled on his britches, shoving them absently into his boots. He grabbed his heavy cloak and threw it around his bare shoulders before wandering out into the misty dawn. The sun hadn't yet cleared the high hills, but patches of sky could be seen through the drifting morning mist.

He checked on the animals as he headed across the farmstead, but all was well with Yara's tidy holding. And then he turned in the direction of the distant river.

Yes, it was there he was meant to go.

It was a ten minute walk, long enough for his boots to become soaked and to wish he'd donned more than a cloak against the cold. He wasn't sure what drew him to the river, perhaps some essence of a dream he could no longer recall, remembering only Naiadithine's parting whisper.

As he walked, his hand found its way to Lily's engraved silver vial, its sides etched so prettily with floral designs that oddly reminded him of Fhionna. As he clenched the little vial in his hand, he thought of Carian and the others who claimed to know his identity, and he wondered if they were correct this time. Friends and strangers had been telling him who they thought he might be for years, but Trell wasn't interested in who they *thought* he might be. And he knew too well that simply because someone *felt* certain of his origins, that didn't make the information true.

No, he had to discover the information for himself. The end does not justify the means. His honor—to himself and to his friends—kept him on his path, wherever it may lead.

At the moment, however, it seemed to be leading to the river.

The water was high after the night's rains, swollen beyond its bounds. As Trell watched, an uprooted tree bobbed past, testimony to the river's strength. Something was caught within its branches, a dark canvas upon a mangled frame that might've belonged to a coach or a covered wagon.

A protruding boulder downstream caught his eye, the fast-moving water churning and frothing around it. He walked over and climbed upon its slick face, finding a seat at its furthest edge. He hugged his knees and drew his cloak around his legs…and listened.

Beneath him, muddy water surged, the rushing music in his ears sounding no different from the song of the Cry, though they were very different rivers.

All rivers sing the same song, each in harmony to the other.

Had Fhionna told him that? Or had the knowledge come with a dream, one of so many of late? He couldn't remember now, but he knew it to be true.

Since saying farewell to Carian, Trell had spent more than a few hours sitting at the river's edge honing his ear to the riversong. While it never sang to him as clearly as it sang to one of its own daughters, Trell fancied he could now sometimes hear its melody as cleanly as if the pirate hummed it right next to him.

That morning, however, as Trell cleared his mind to let the riversong in, he realized the water sounded angry, troubled, anxious. It rushed in haste, not because it was laden with heavy rains, but in order to...*what?*

Trell shifted on the rock and concentrated again. Opening his mind to listen, he finally found purpose to his sense of anxiety. Something was very wrong, and the riversong brought news of it. He tried to understand the cacophony of voices that was the river's music, but even had he the skill, his own unease now inhibited the quietude necessary for understanding.

Frustrated, Trell lifted grey eyes to frown upstream. Another uprooted tree was coming toward him, carried upon the rushing waters, one end a tangle of gnarled roots draped in debris. But as the tree bobbed and spun, a flash of something within the mass caught his eye.

Suddenly tense, Trell stared at the tree, willing the waters to shift and turn it that he might better see what had snared his attention so completely.

Just as the tree floated past, Naiadithine complied, for the massive tree snagged upon something buried deeply and caught, swinging around to bring the root system close.

And there, tangled within the roots, was a woman.

Trell was out of his cloak and diving into the river before he had a chance to think. The muddy water was bracingly cold, and as he surfaced, Naiadithine swept him directly to the tree, slamming him against its thick trunk. With the water sweeping over his shoulders, Trell inched his way along the slippery wood until he could grab the roots. He hauled himself up into the root thicket and wedged his knees in place. Only then did he reach for the woman's head. She was covered in mud, but her face was free of the water and he hoped—he prayed—that she might still be alive. He felt for a pulse at her neck, holding his breath until...*there*.

She was alive, but barely so, a pulse so faint he might've missed it without his gift of patience.

Trell lifted his head and looked around for anything to aid him, and in that moment the tree dislodged from the deep water and floated once again on the current. He watched with growing hope as the river carried him ever closer to a curve in the bank. Could it be that Naiadithine *wanted* him to save this woman? It certainly seemed so, for with one great thrust, the river shoved the tree into the far bank, wedging it momentarily into the earth.

Trell knew he had only seconds. As the far end of the tree began swinging around with the current, he scrambled into the shallows and gathered the woman into his arms, disentangling her only an instant before the massive tree was ripped away again.

Trell fell backwards onto a grassy bank with the unconscious woman on top of him. He lay there panting for a few heartbeats, allowing his heart to settle, and said a prayer of thanks to Naiadithine for her help. Then he rolled the woman gently onto the grass beside him.

With tender care, he cleaned the mud from her face, noting with concern the deep bruises around her eyes and the swollen gash in her head. He looked her over carefully then, and found that her arm was also broken. He couldn't know what damage she'd retained deeper within, but the bruising around her eyes did not bode well for her condition. He'd seen many a man who fell from on high display bruises of this nature, and most of them died in a few short hours though nothing had seemed outwardly wrong. To his knowledge, no Healers lived nearby, so he knew it was up to him and Yara to help this woman.

First making a splint for her broken arm using sticks and cloth torn from her skirt, Trell then gently lifted her in his arms. As he headed back toward the farm beneath a bright morning sky, he thought he heard Naiadithine's approving whisper.

Follow the water, Trell of the Tides.

Errodan Renwyr n'Owain val Lorian, Queen of Dannym and the Shoring Isles, stood upon the icy, snow-crusted pier as dawn colored the wintry morning clouds in pale rose-gold. She stood with straight shoulders though grief ravaged her, voices of the unknown taunting of the terrible future in store.

There was no news of Ean save that he lived, but somehow she no longer feared for her youngest son. He was upon his path with boon companions to aid and protect him, and she had faith that Destiny had need of his life still. No, it was her own fate, and that of her king, that terrified her now.

Her green eyes lingered on the ship sailing out of the harbor with the tide. Soon it would be around the point and out of view, but so long as she could see its sails, she meant to remain there.

She could just make out Gydryn's tall form on the poop deck, his silver-edged cloak taut in the wind. From such distance, he seemed a young man—broad-shouldered and lean, virile, emboldened by the vigor of youth and ready to stare death in the face with an impudent grin. No doubt he felt a measure of those things still, for he was such a man yet in many ways, even with fifty years beneath his name. But for Errodan, watching her husband sail away even as both of her sons had before was almost too much to bear.

"He will return to you," Ysolde said quietly. She slipped an arm around Errodan's waist and let her take comfort in their closeness, though there was little reassurance in it. Her husband sailed into the face of treachery while she remained to face a different demon, a man by the name of Stefan val Tryst, Duke of Morwyk. Should either of them survive the next few months would be by Epiphany's will alone, for gods knew the odds were against them.

Errodan feared the dark times ahead; she knew it would take all of her strength to weather them.

Wrapping an arm about her Companion in turn, Errodan pulled Ysolde closer, lamenting that her Companion's slim waist was such a poor substitute for her husband's solid form. "Epiphany willing," she breathed in reply, barely voicing the statement lest Fortune take offense.

The ship was rounding the point now. In only moments it would be gone from her sight. Errodan caught her bottom lip between her teeth lest it tremble and betray her feelings to those who watched. She wished in that last moment of parting that she might reach out to her husband and pull him back to her to never again let go.

Then the ship was gone.

"Fair winds," Ysolde said.

Keeping her expression neutral by raw strength of will, Errodan pressed a hand to her belly and tried to breathe deeply through the nausea. Though she had every reason and right, it wasn't fear that made her sick that morning.

She turned to Ysolde.

"He will come back to you," the Fire Princess reassured again.

Swallowing her resolve, Errodan looked back to the deep sea, which was golden now beneath the rising sun. "Yes," she murmured with her hand cupped protectively across her belly that was still flat though she measured two months into the pregnancy, "he must." *For his fourth child awaits his blessing.*

CPSIA information can be obtained at www.ICGtesting.com
Printed in the USA
LVOW080644160812

294399LV00002B/3/P